LIGHTS

AN ONI PRESS PUBLICATION

For Mom and Dad

LIGHTS

Brenna Thummler

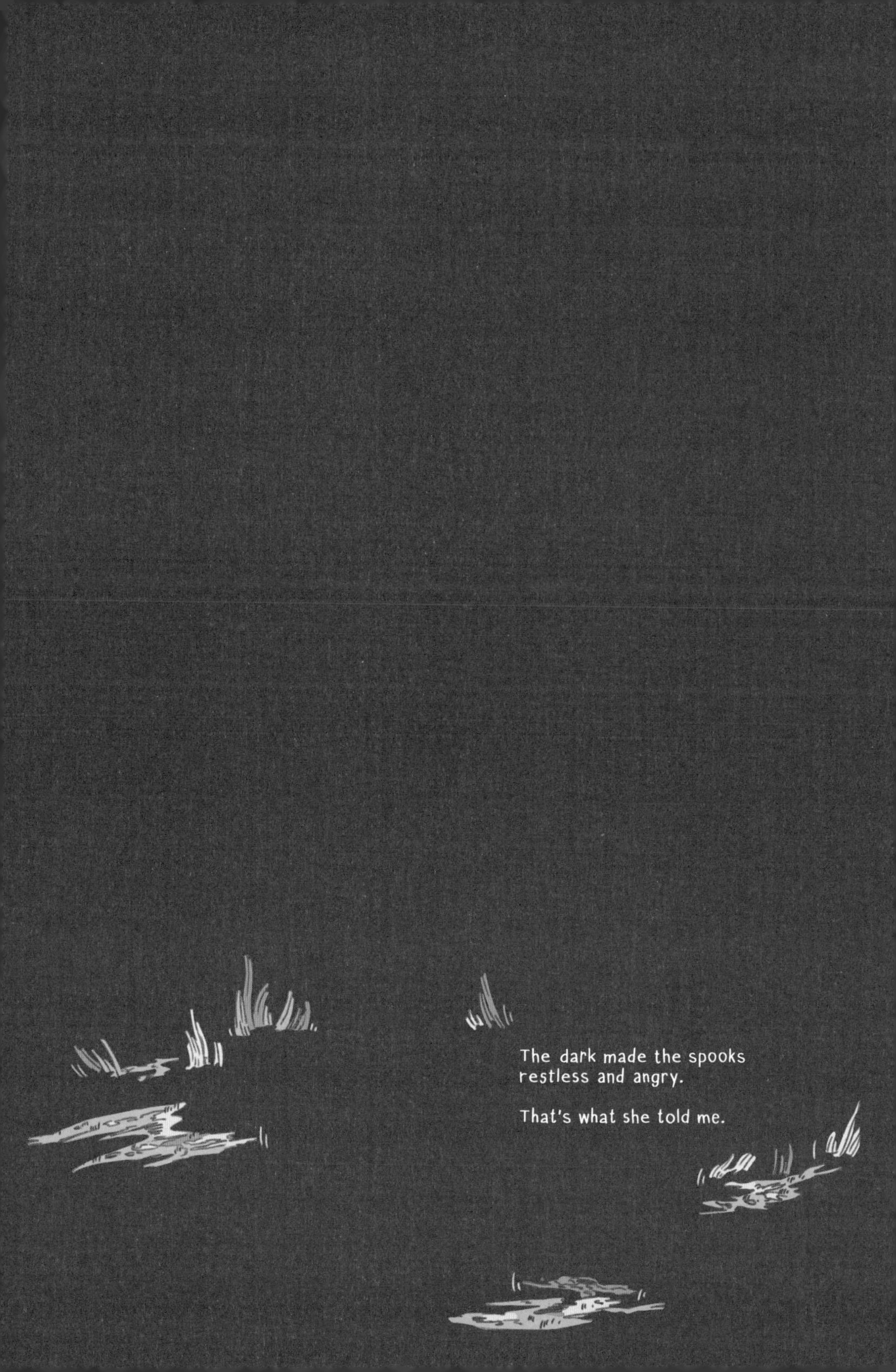
The dark made the spooks restless and angry.
That's what she told me.

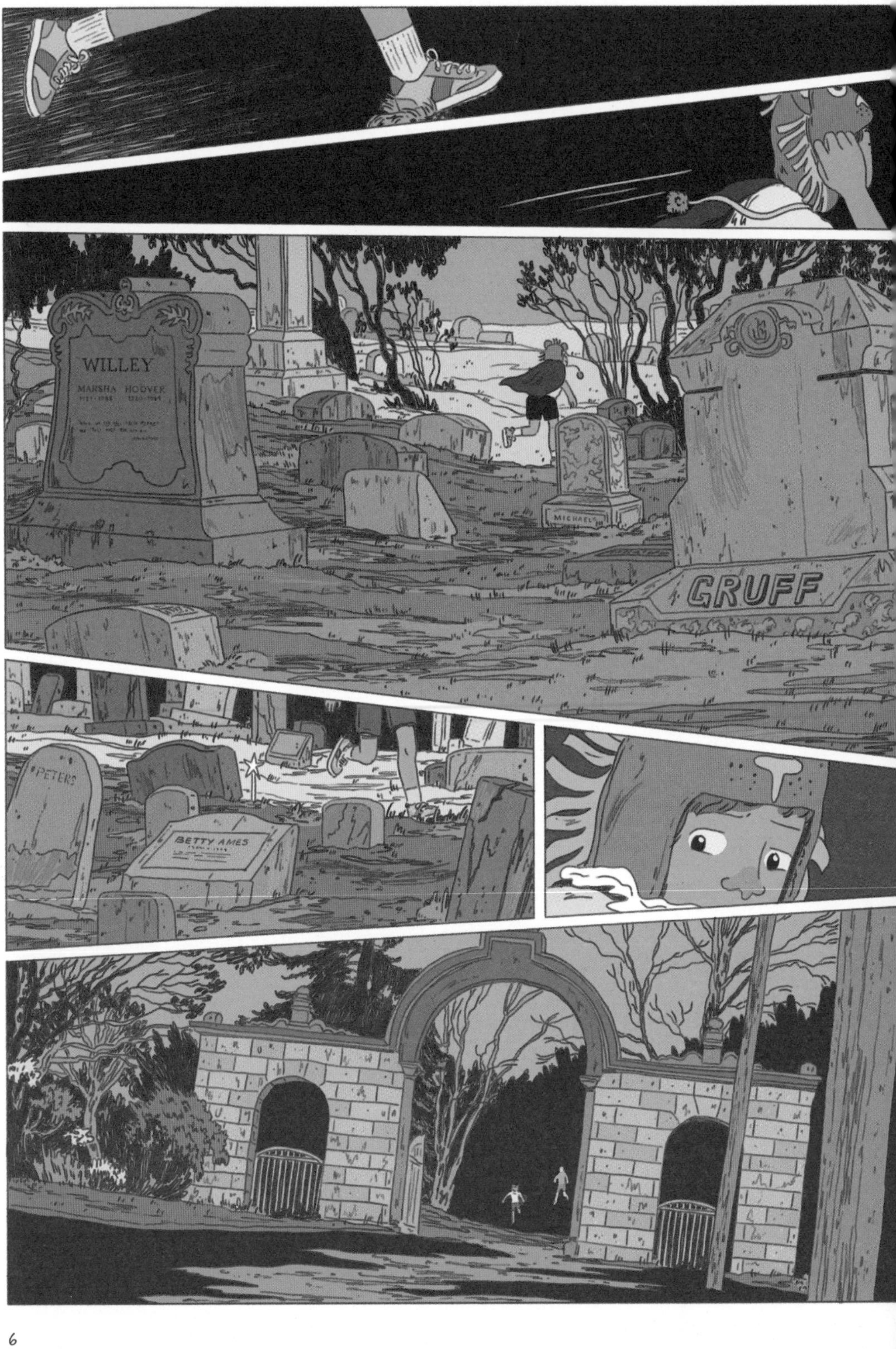
WILLEY
MARSHA HOOVER
MICHAELS
GRUFF
PETERS
BETTY AMES

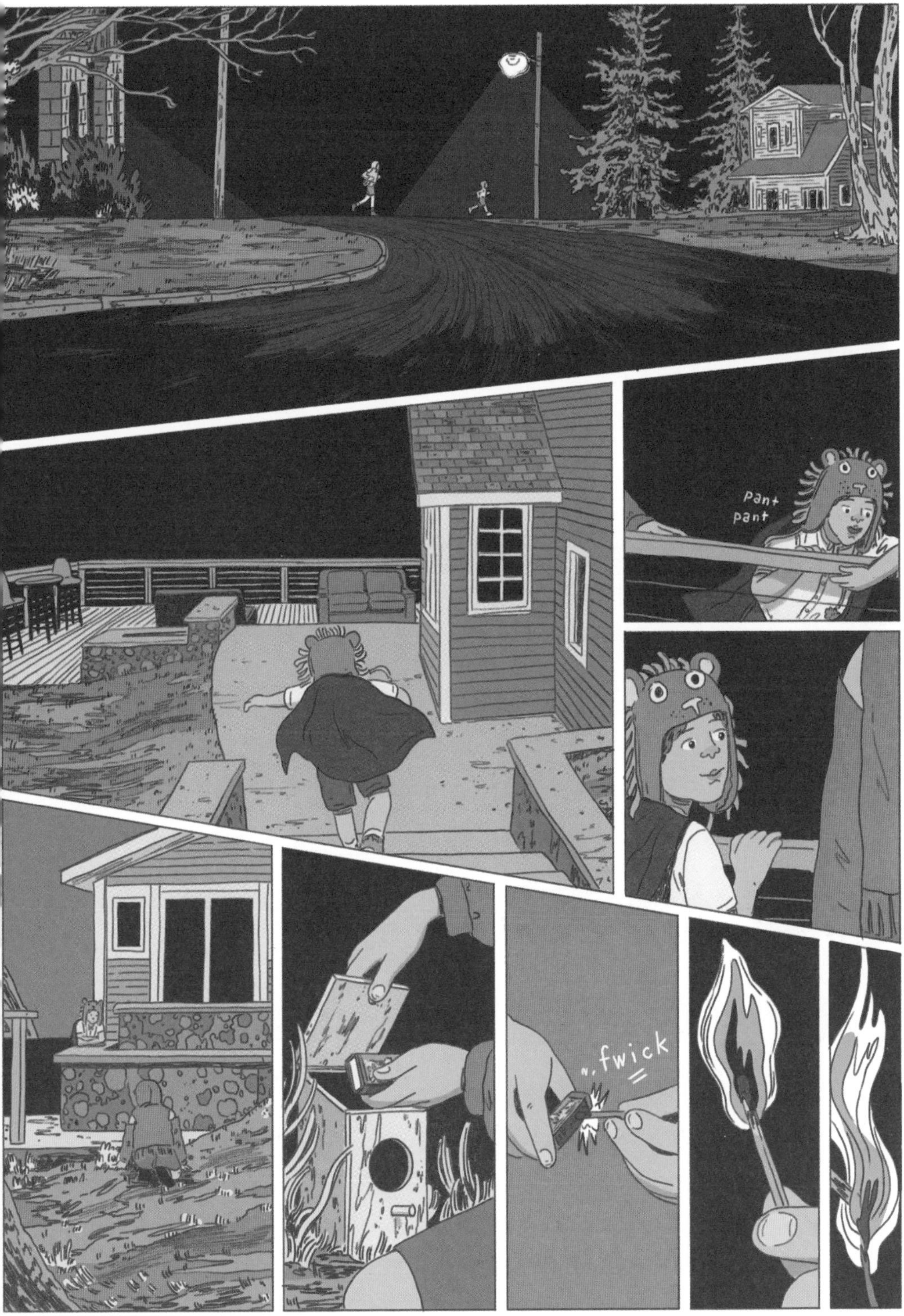
pant
pant
fwick

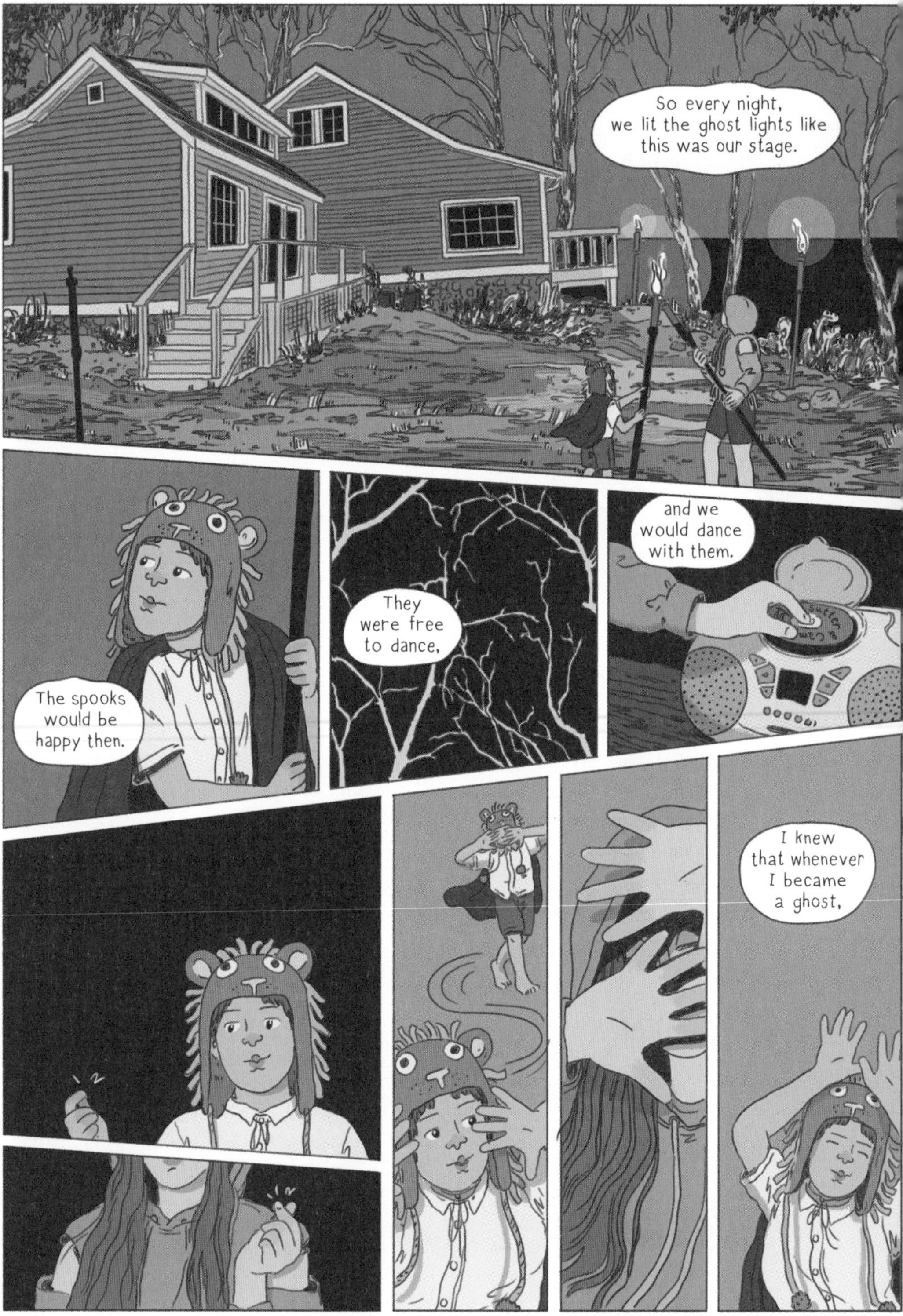
So every night, we lit the ghost lights like this was our stage.
The spooks would be happy then.
They were free to dance,
and we would dance with them.
I knew that whenever I became a ghost,

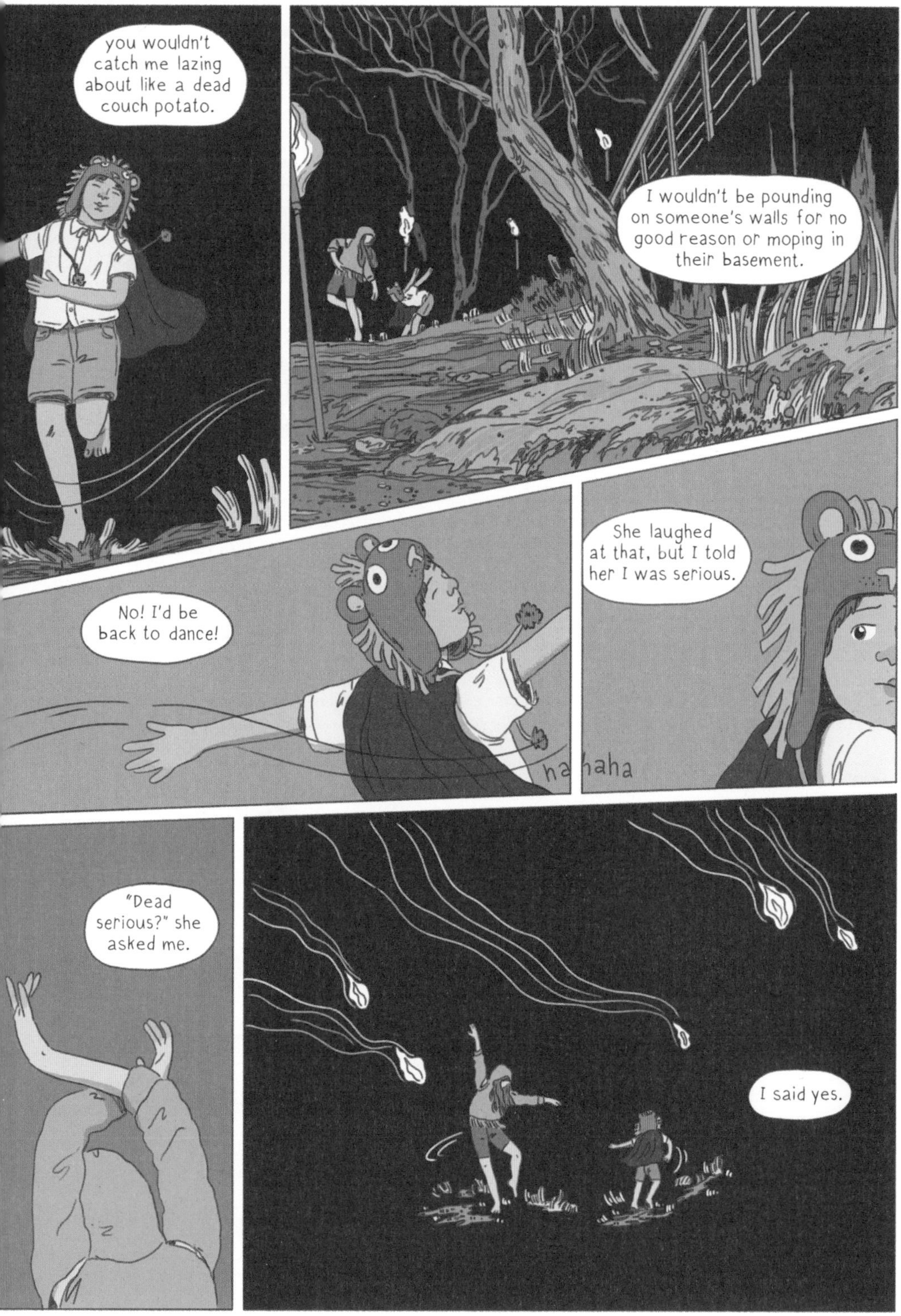
you wouldn't catch me lazing about like a dead couch potato.
I wouldn't be pounding on someone's walls for no good reason or moping in their basement.
No! I'd be back to dance!
hahaha
She laughed at that, but I told her I was serious.
"Dead serious?" she asked me.
I said yes.

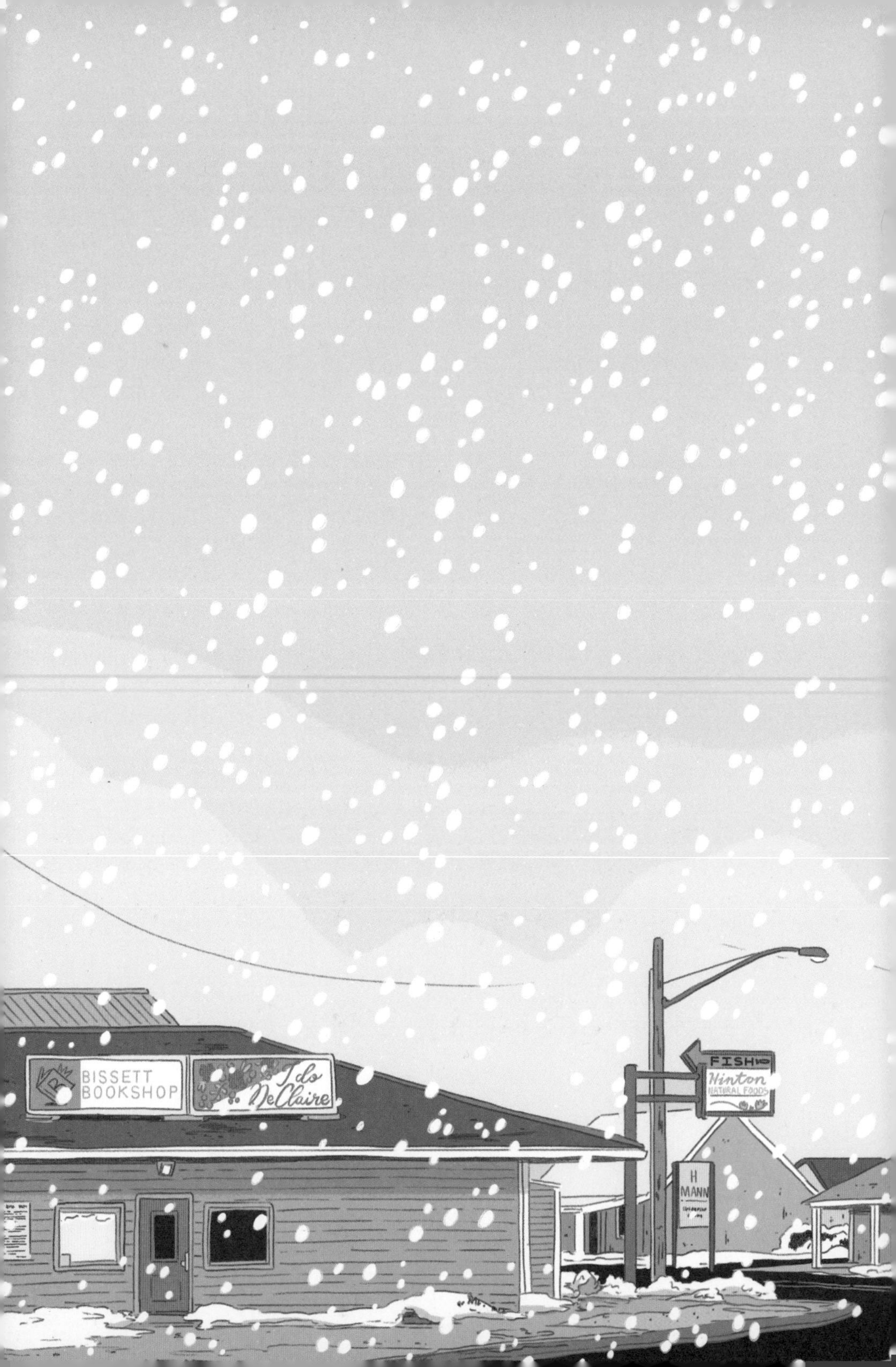
BISSETT BOOKSHOP
I do DeClaire
FISH
Hinton
NATURAL FOODS
H MANN

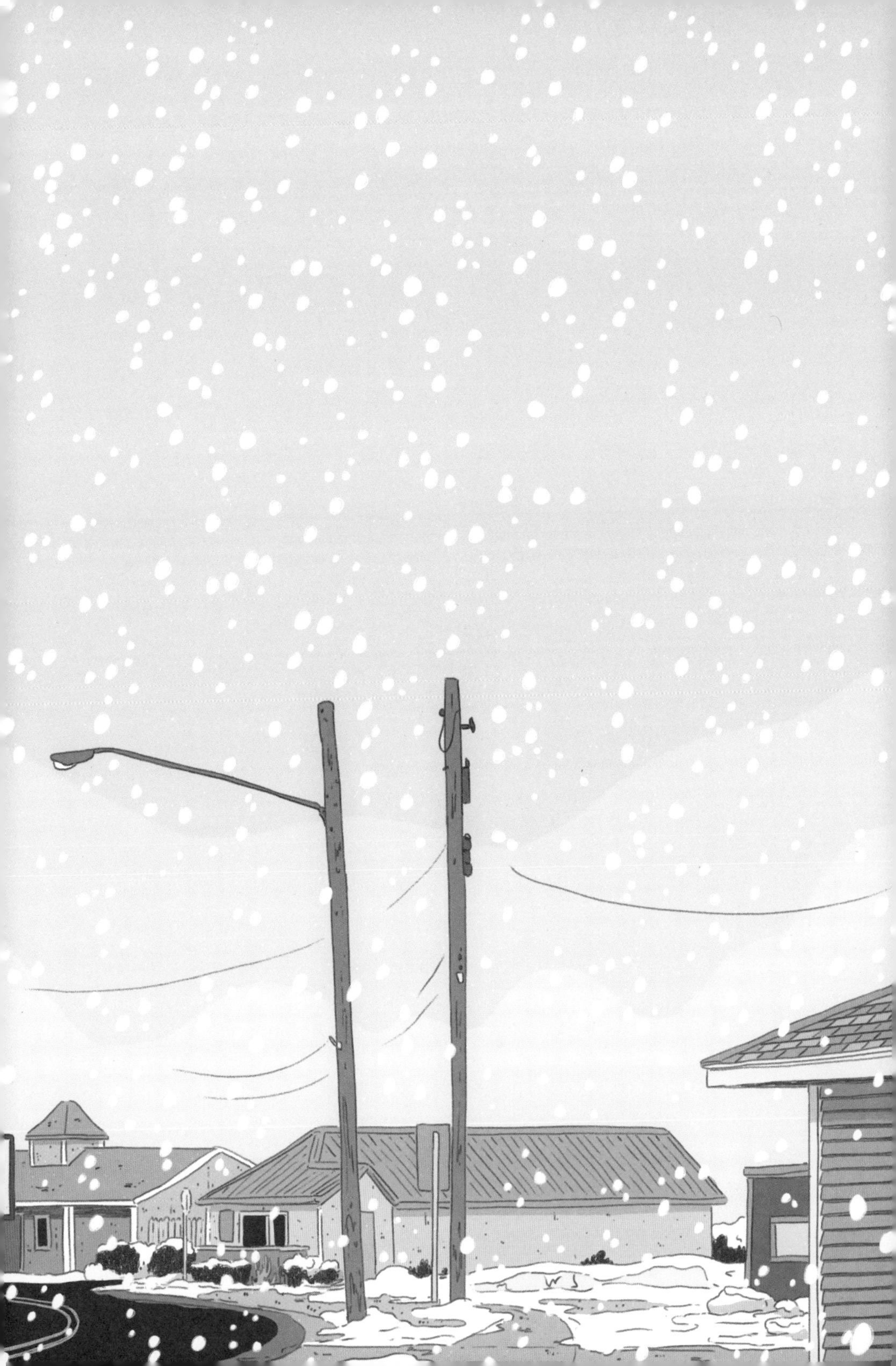

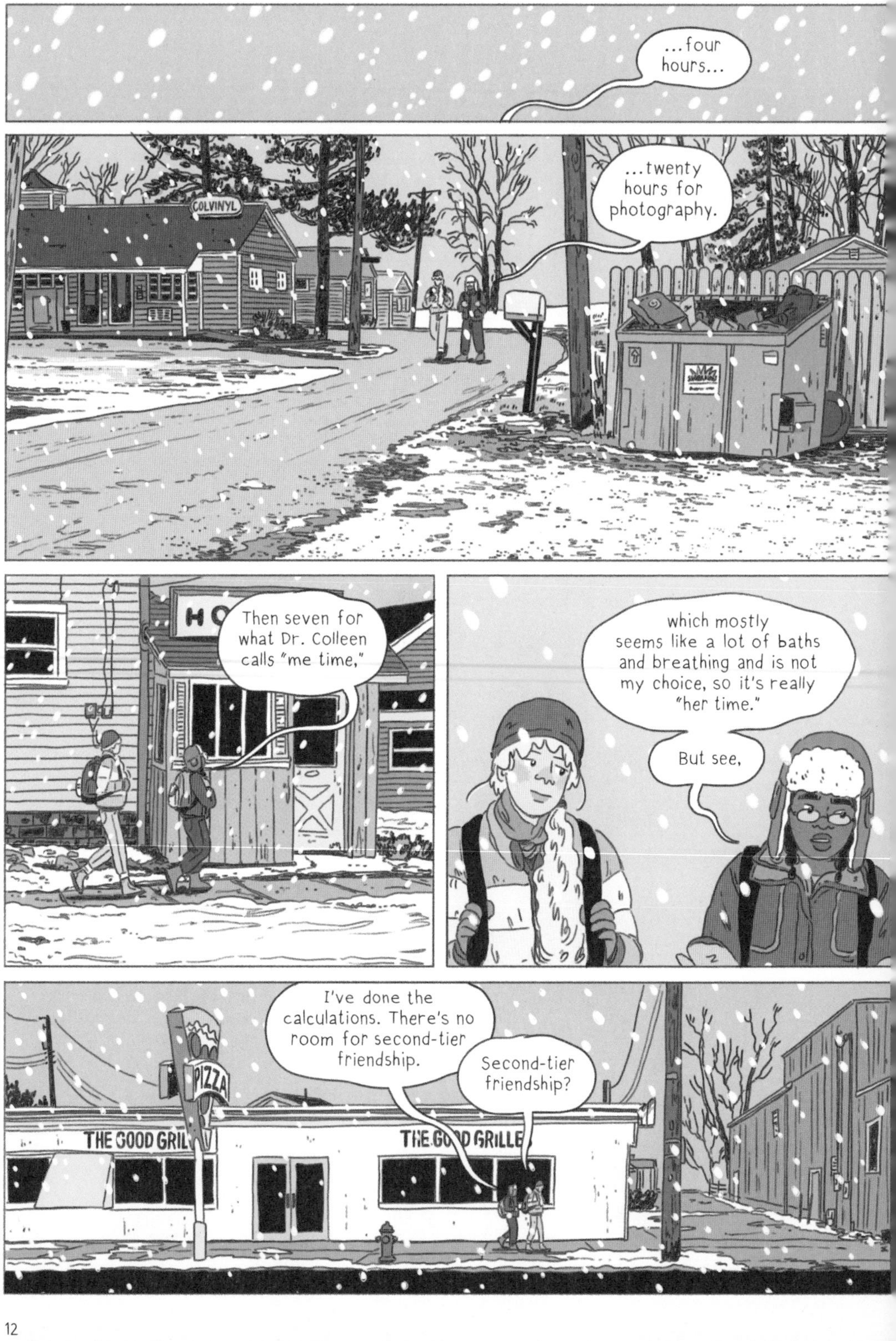

...four hours...
COLVINYL
...twenty hours for photography.
Then seven for what Dr. Colleen calls "me time,"
which mostly seems like a lot of baths and breathing and is not my choice, so it's really "her time."
But see,
PIZZA
THE GOOD GRILLE
THE GOOD GRILLE
I've done the calculations. There's no room for second-tier friendship.
Second-tier friendship?

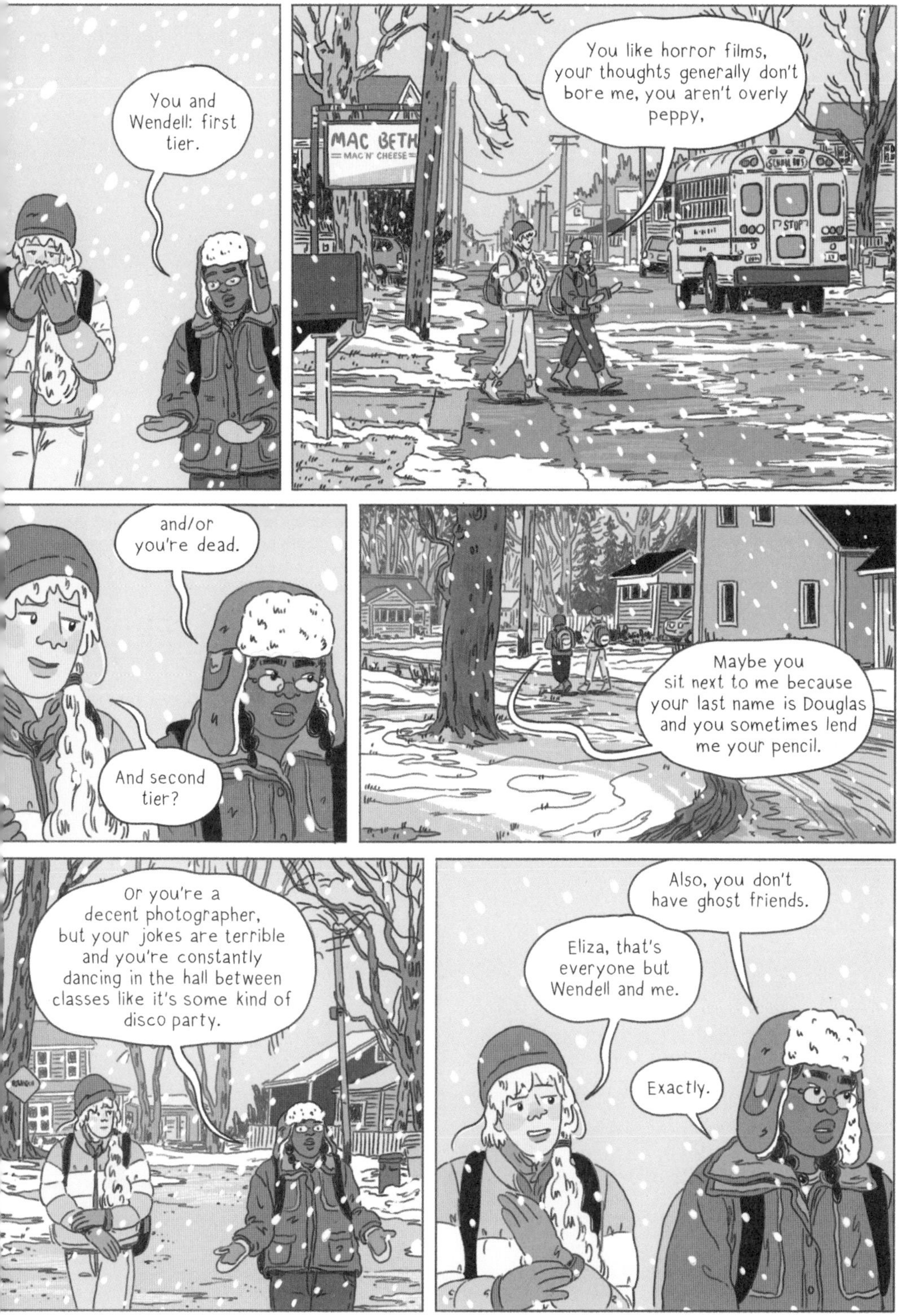
You and Wendell: first tier.
MAC BETH MAC 'N' CHEESE
You like horror films, your thoughts generally don't bore me, you aren't overly peppy,
STOP
and/or you're dead.
And second tier?
Maybe you sit next to me because your last name is Douglas and you sometimes lend me your pencil.
Or you're a decent photographer, but your jokes are terrible and you're constantly dancing in the hall between classes like it's some kind of disco party.
Also, you don't have ghost friends.
Eliza, that's everyone but Wendell and me.
Exactly.

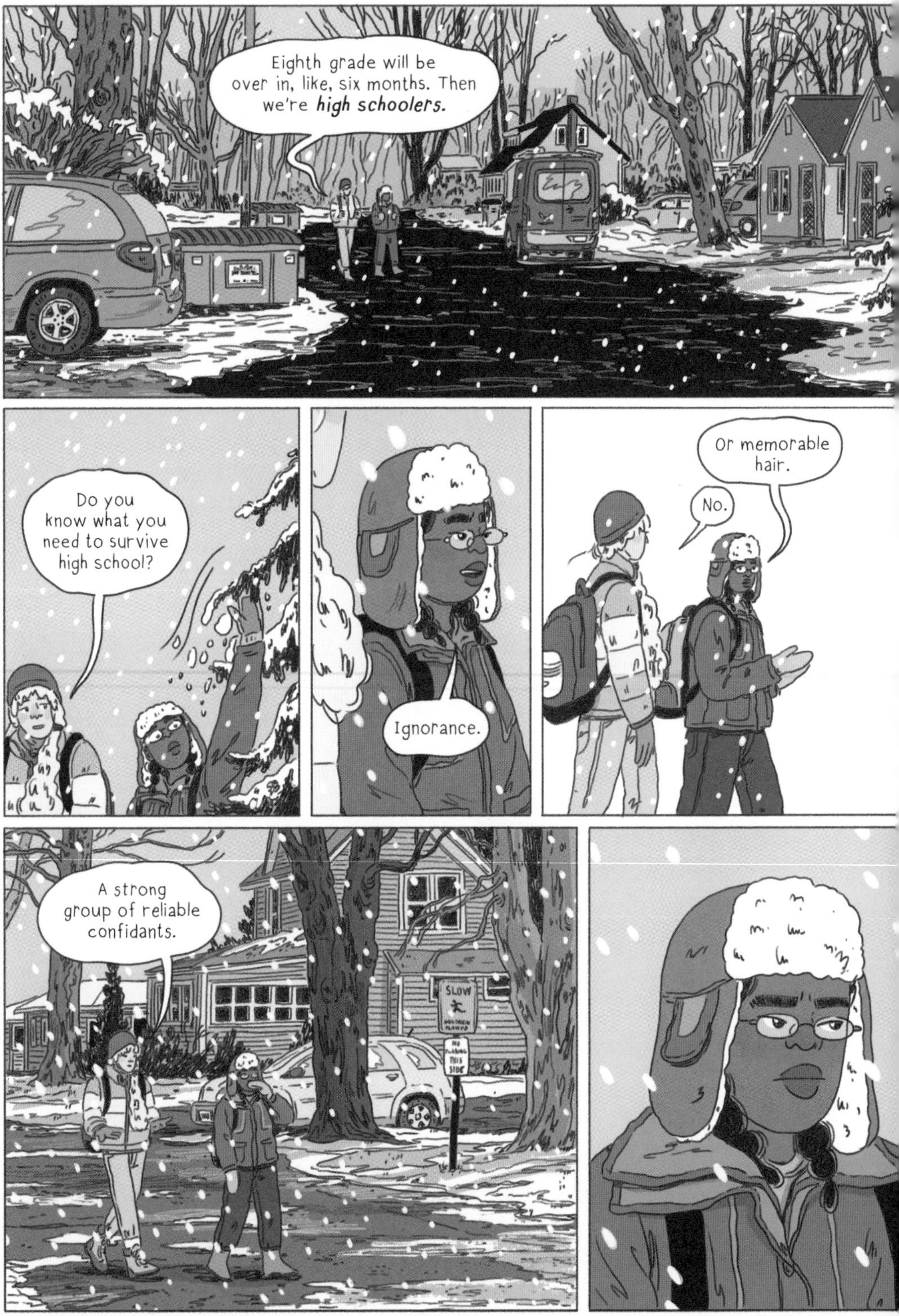
Eighth grade will be over in, like, six months. Then we're ***high schoolers.***
Do you know what you need to survive high school?
Ignorance.
No.
Or memorable hair.
A strong group of reliable confidants.
SLOW
NO PARKING THIS SIDE

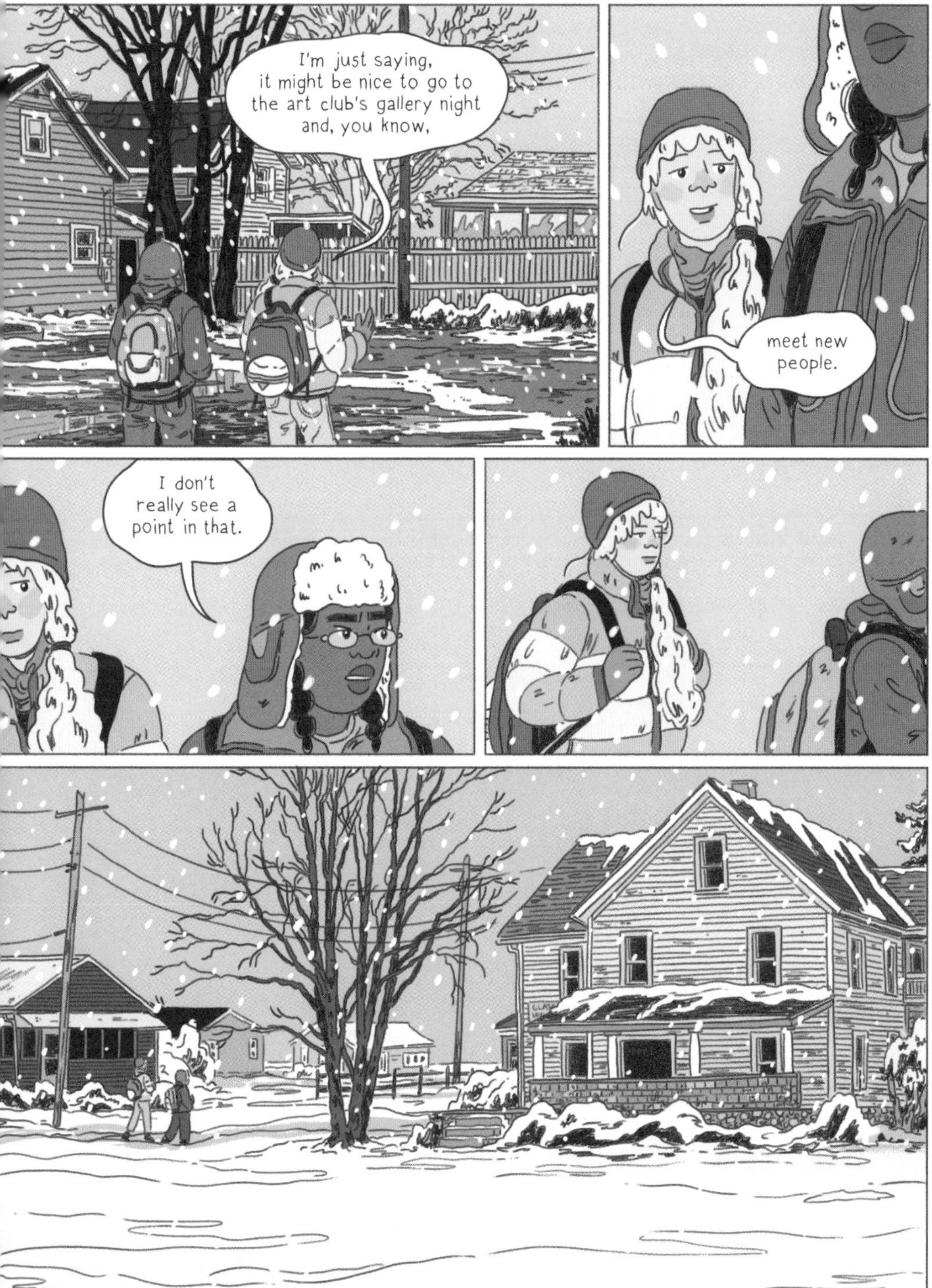
I'm just saying, it might be nice to go to the art club's gallery night and, you know,
meet new people.
I don't really see a point in that.

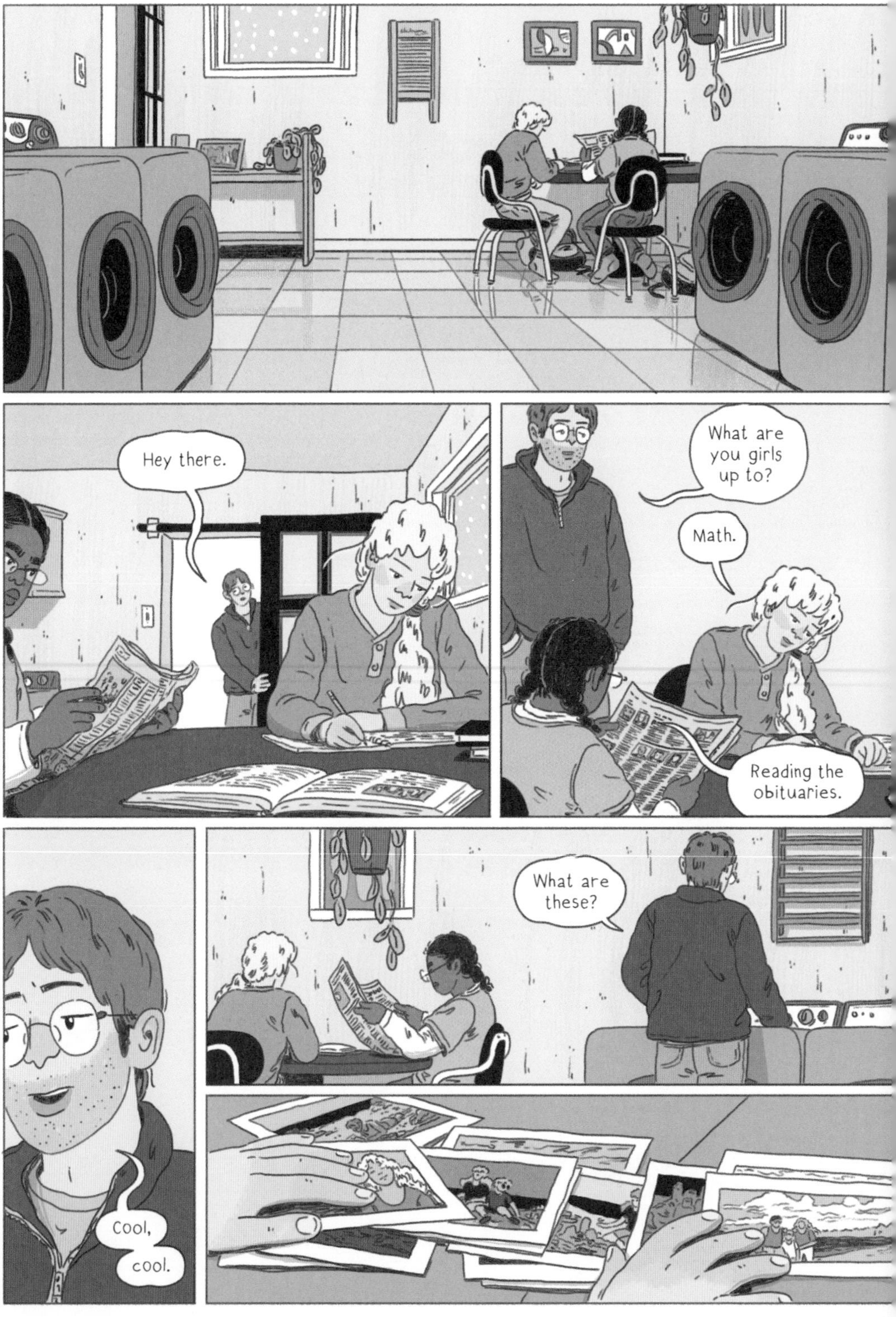
Hey there.
What are you girls up to?
Math.
Reading the obituaries.
Cool,
cool.
What are these?

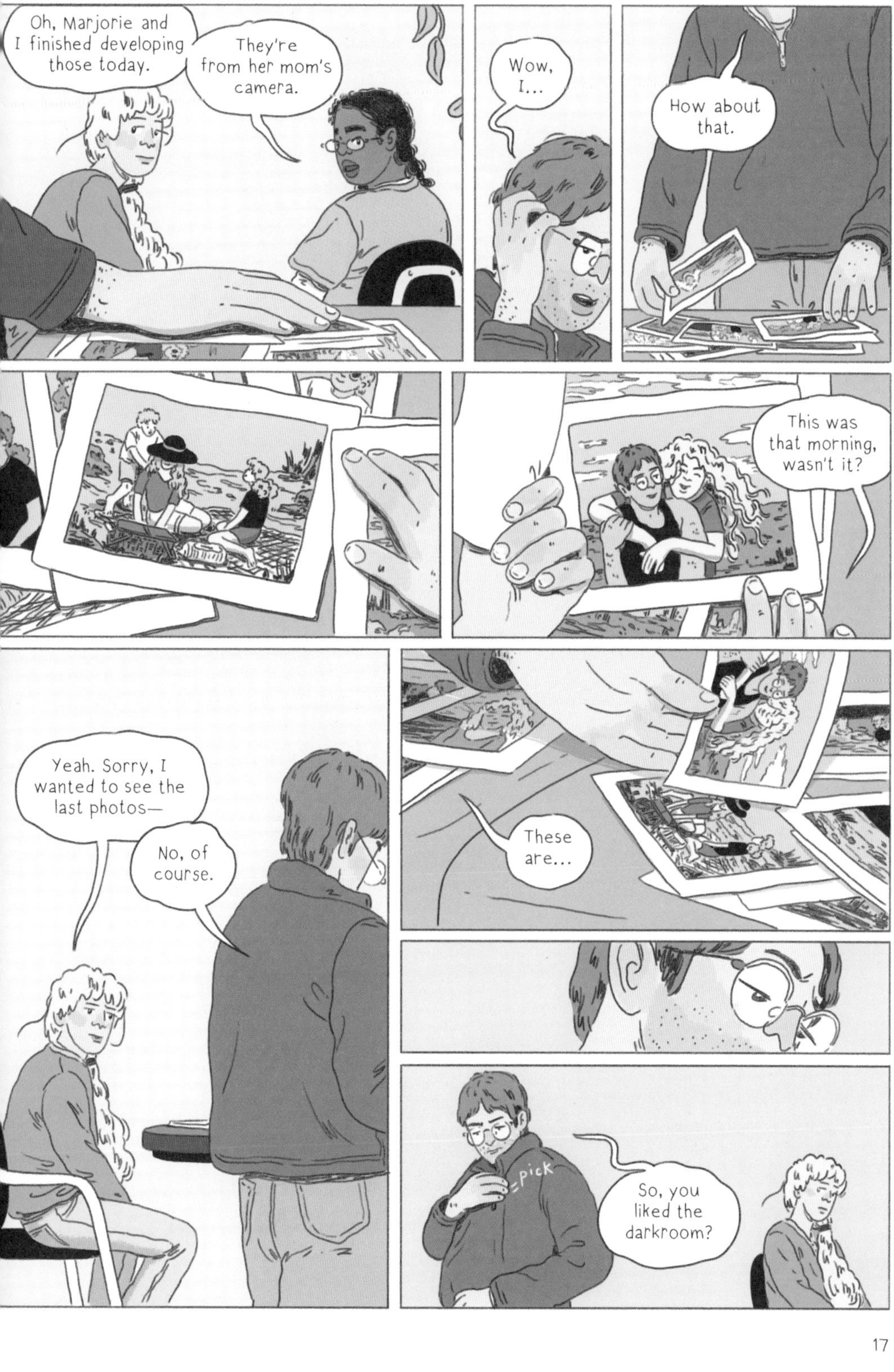
Oh, Marjorie and I finished developing those today.
They're from her mom's camera.
Wow, I...
How about that.
This was that morning, wasn't it?
Yeah. Sorry, I wanted to see the last photos—
No, of course.
These are...
pick
So, you liked the darkroom?

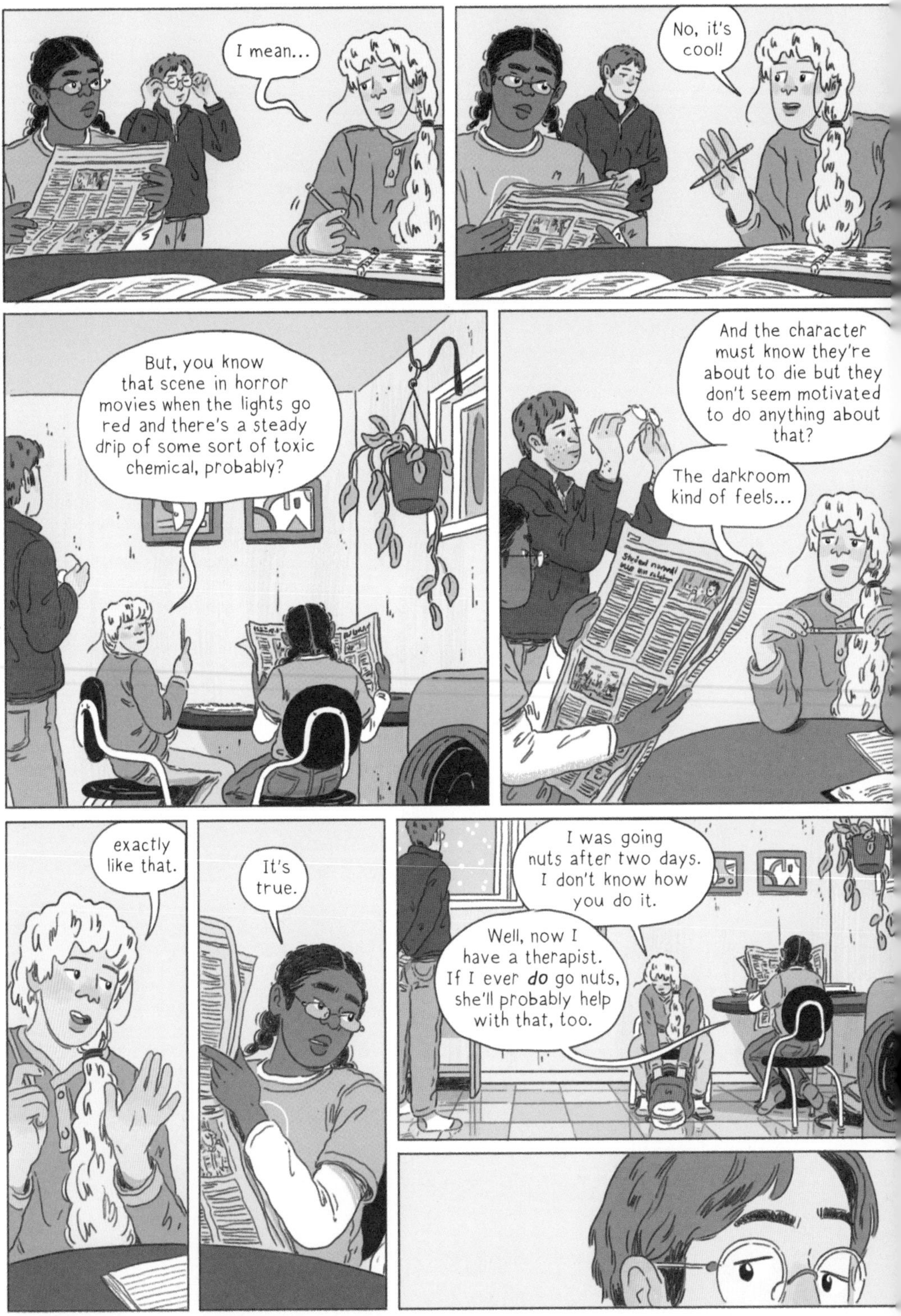
I mean...
No, it's cool!
But, you know that scene in horror movies when the lights go red and there's a steady drip of some sort of toxic chemical, probably?
And the character must know they're about to die but they don't seem motivated to do anything about that?
The darkroom kind of feels...
exactly like that.
It's true.
I was going nuts after two days. I don't know how you do it.
Well, now I have a therapist. If I ever **do** go nuts, she'll probably help with that, too.

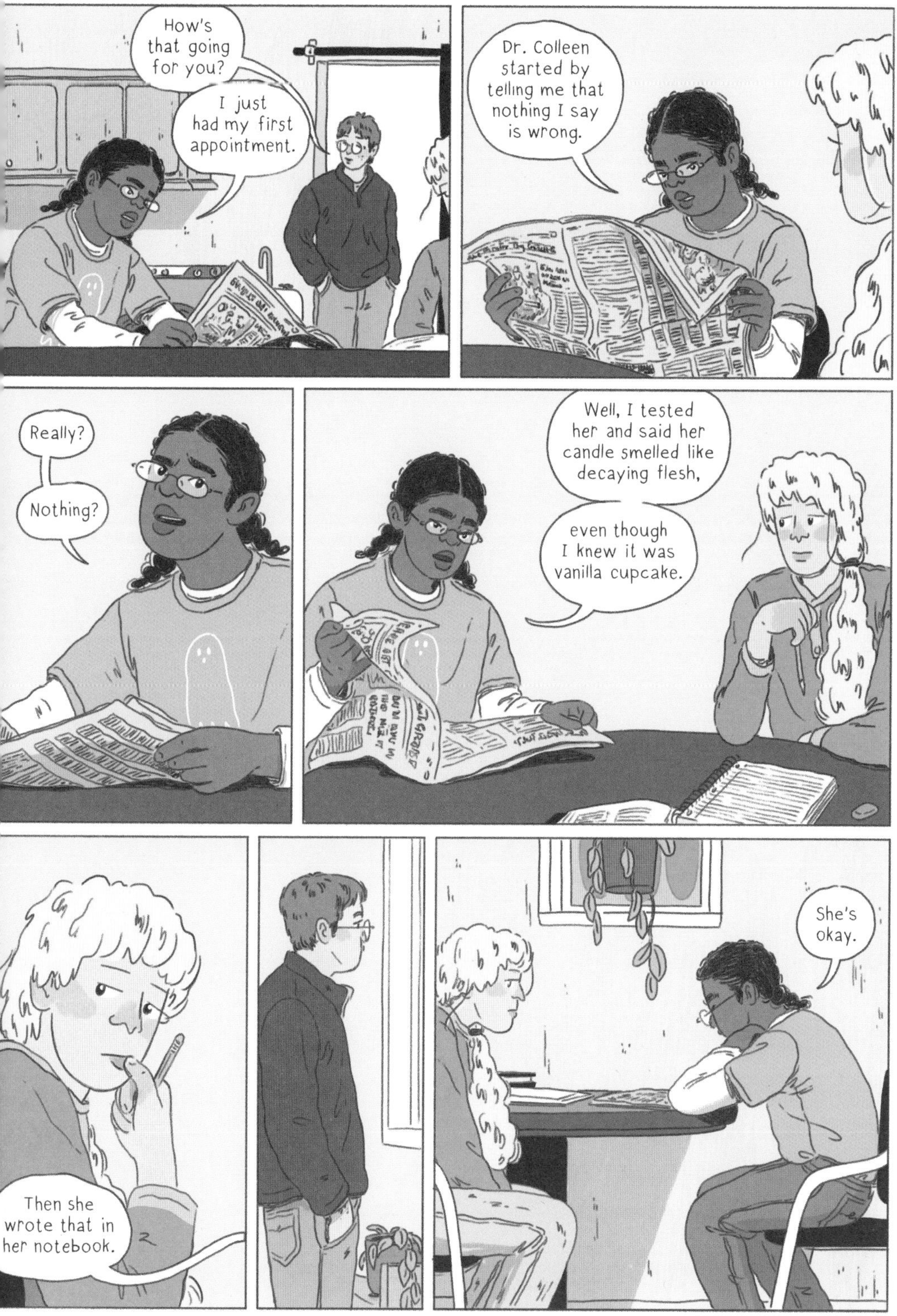
How's that going for you?
I just had my first appointment.
Dr. Colleen started by telling me that nothing I say is wrong.
Really?
Nothing?
Well, I tested her and said her candle smelled like decaying flesh,
even though I knew it was vanilla cupcake.
Then she wrote that in her notebook.
She's okay.

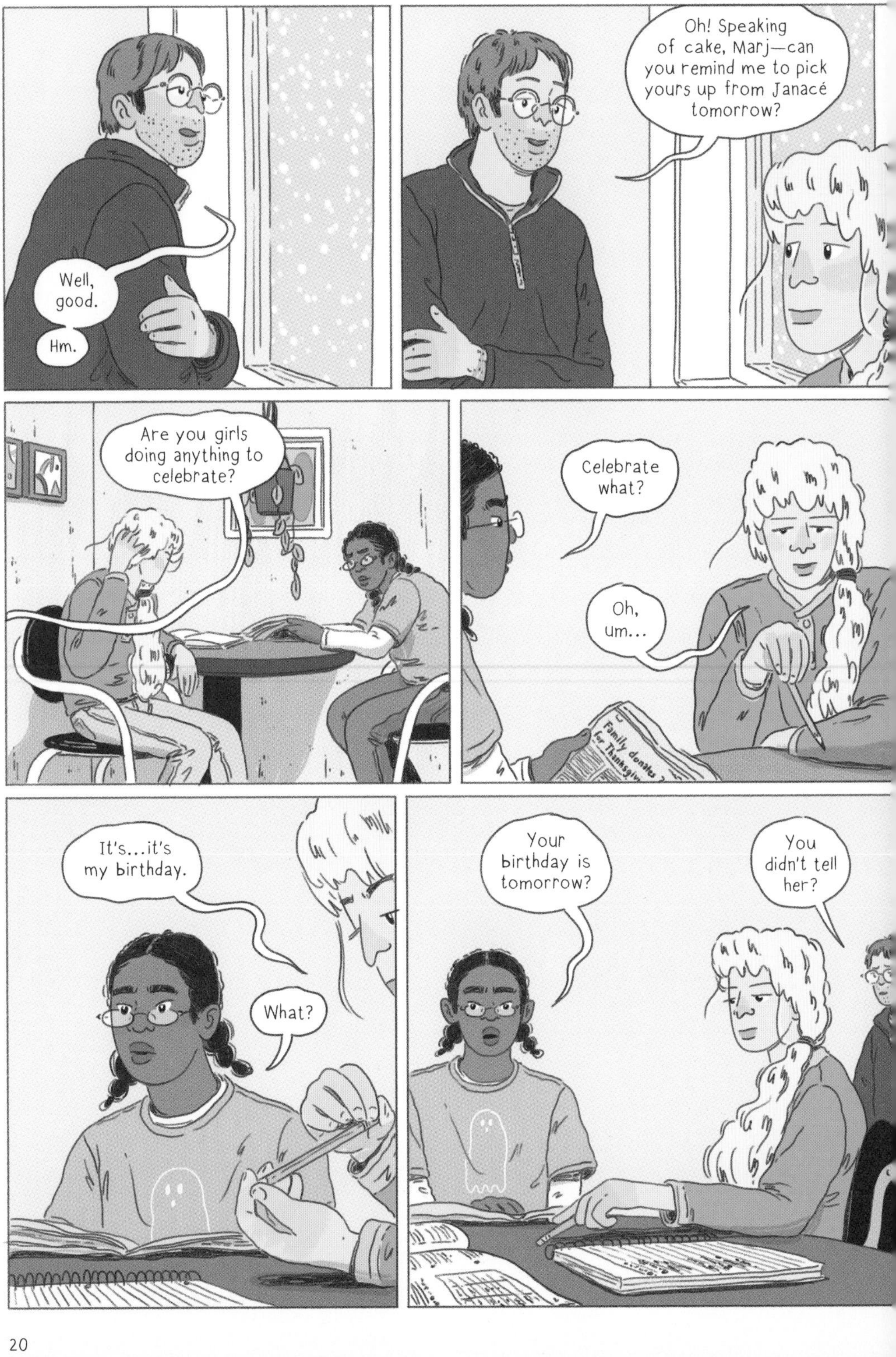
Well, good.
Hm.
Oh! Speaking of cake, Marj—can you remind me to pick yours up from Janacé tomorrow?
Are you girls doing anything to celebrate?
Celebrate what?
Oh, um...
It's...it's my birthday.
What?
Your birthday is tomorrow?
You didn't tell her?

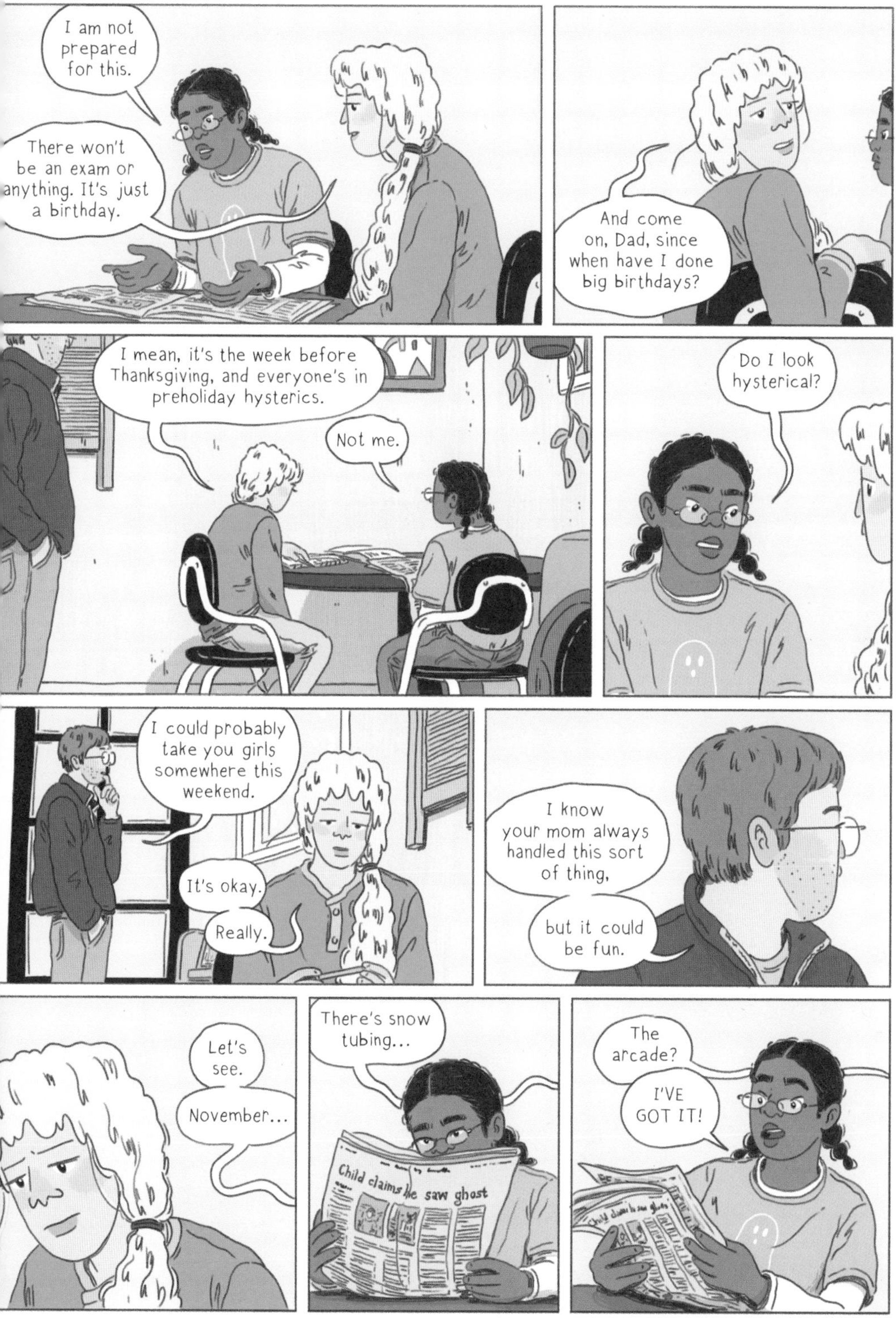
I am not prepared for this.
There won't be an exam or anything. It's just a birthday.
And come on, Dad, since when have I done big birthdays?
I mean, it's the week before Thanksgiving, and everyone's in preholiday hysterics.
Not me.
Do I look hysterical?
I could probably take you girls somewhere this weekend.
It's okay.
Really.
I know your mom always handled this sort of thing,
but it could be fun.
Let's see.
November...
There's snow tubing...
Child claims he saw ghost
The arcade?
I'VE GOT IT!

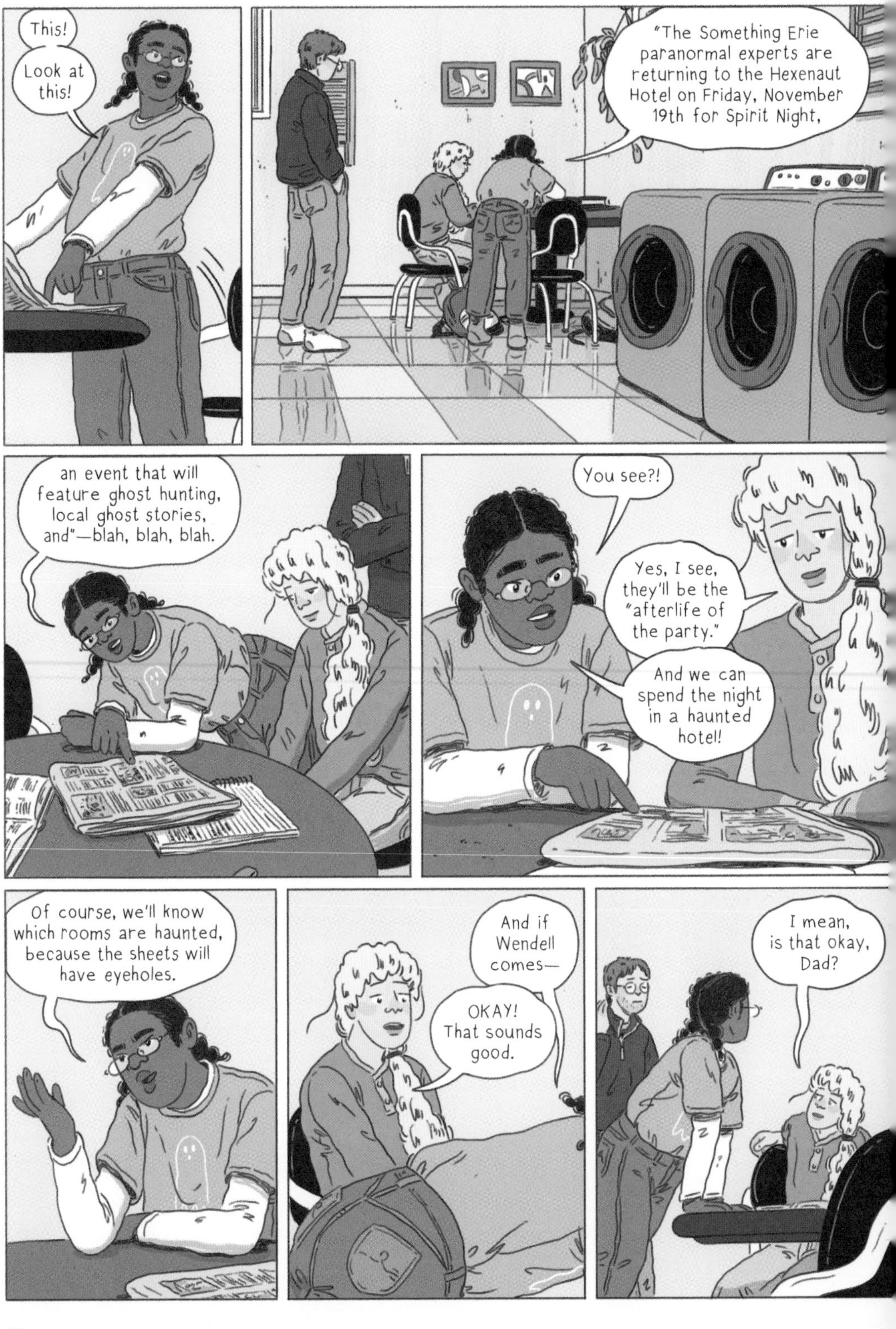
This!
Look at this!
"The Something Erie paranormal experts are returning to the Hexenaut Hotel on Friday, November 19th for Spirit Night,
an event that will feature ghost hunting, local ghost stories, and"—blah, blah, blah.
You see?!
Yes, I see, they'll be the "afterlife of the party."
And we can spend the night in a haunted hotel!
Of course, we'll know which rooms are haunted, because the sheets will have eyeholes.
And if Wendell comes—
OKAY! That sounds good.
I mean, is that okay, Dad?

If that's what you want to do...

It's a definite "no" to snow tubing?

That's where you basically fall down a hill over and over, right?

I'll call the hotel and find out more.

Who's Wendell?

Marjorie's cousin.

November Play

The Finster Bay Gazette

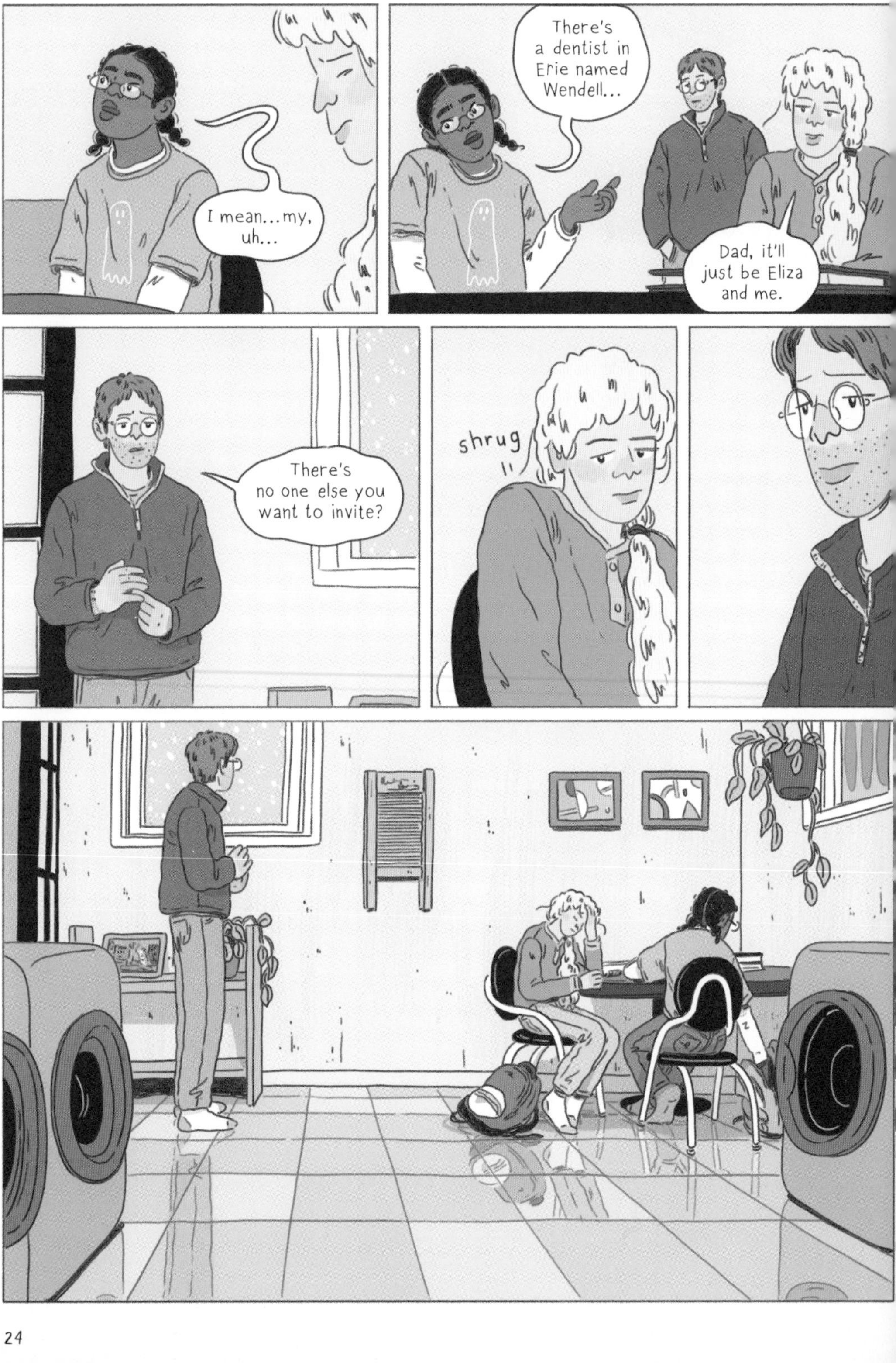
I mean...my, uh...
There's a dentist in Erie named Wendell...
Dad, it'll just be Eliza and me.
There's no one else you want to invite?
shrug

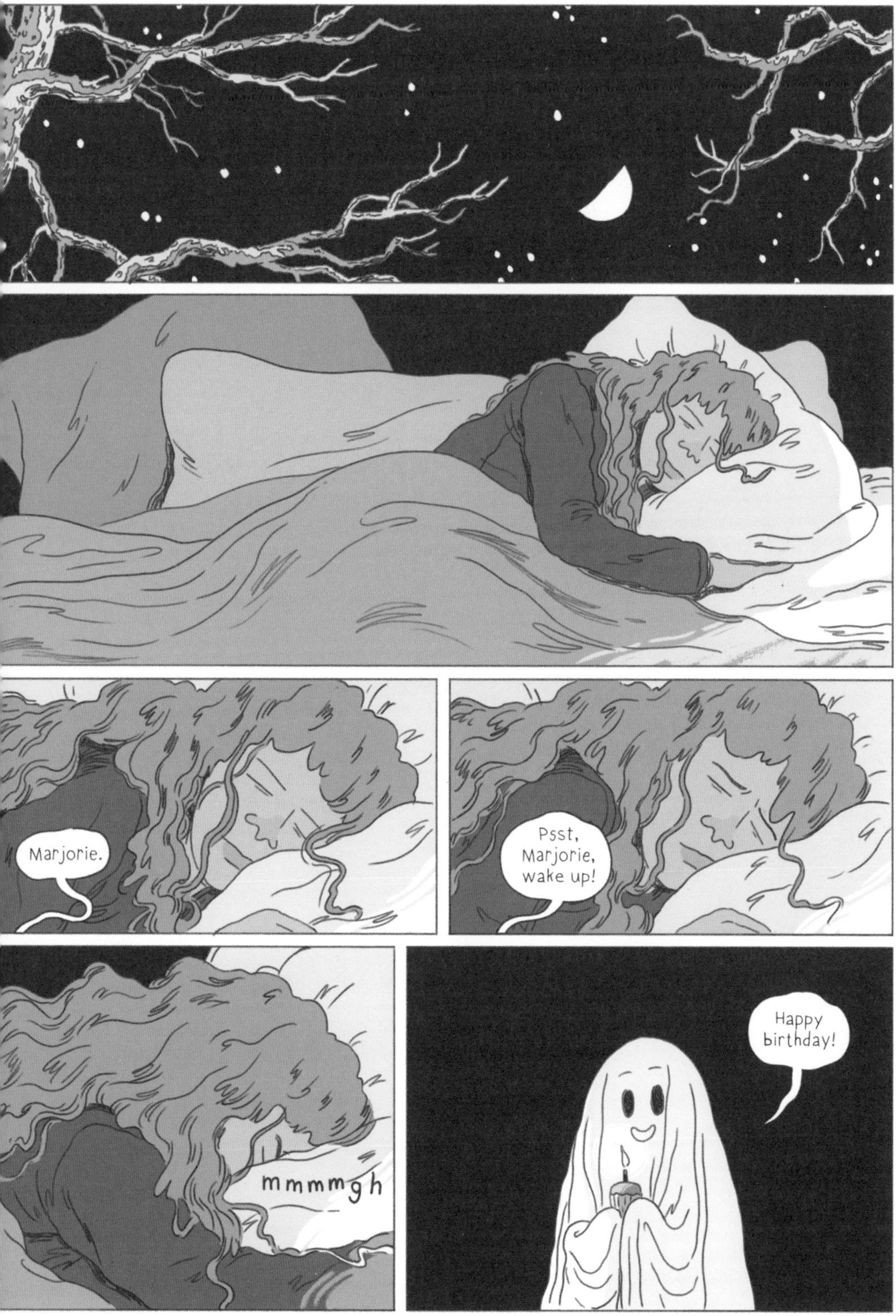
Marjorie.
Psst, Marjorie, wake up!
mmmmgh
Happy birthday!

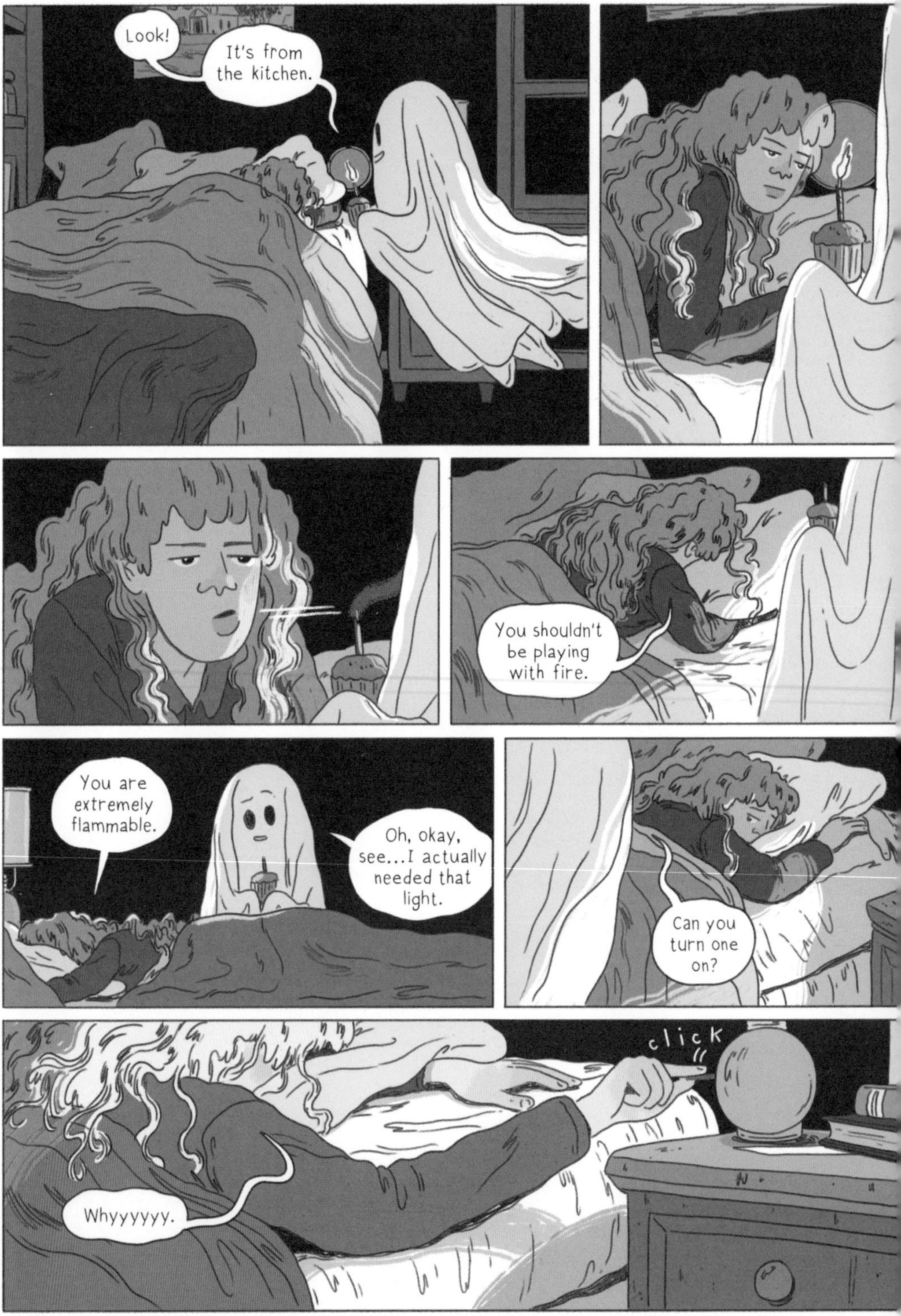
Look!
It's from the kitchen.
You shouldn't be playing with fire.
You are extremely flammable.
Oh, okay, see...I actually needed that light.
Can you turn one on?
click
Whyyyyyy.

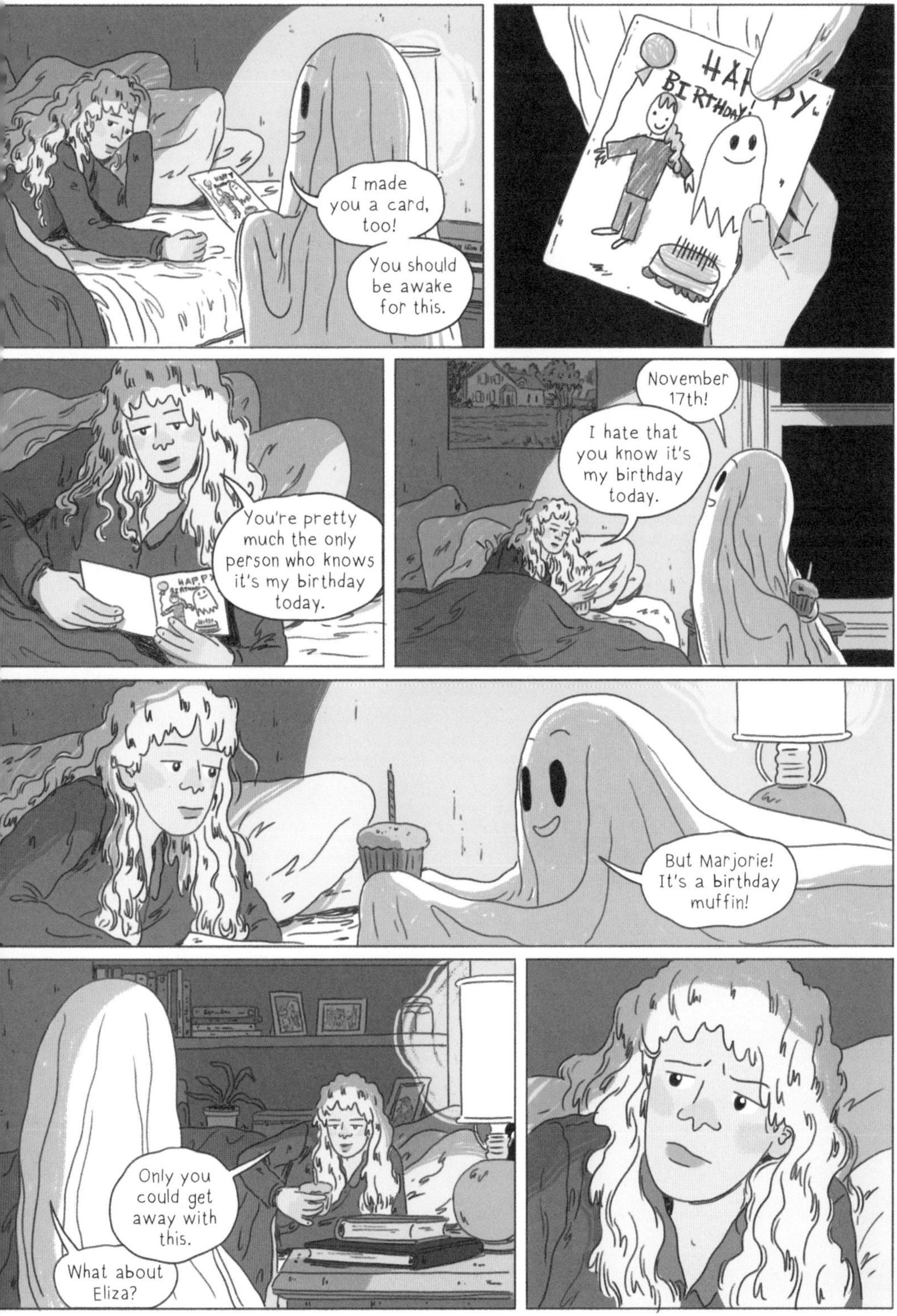
I made you a card, too!
You should be awake for this.
HAPPY BIRTHDAY!
You're pretty much the only person who knows it's my birthday today.
November 17th!
I hate that you know it's my birthday today.
But Marjorie! It's a birthday muffin!
Only you could get away with this.
What about Eliza?

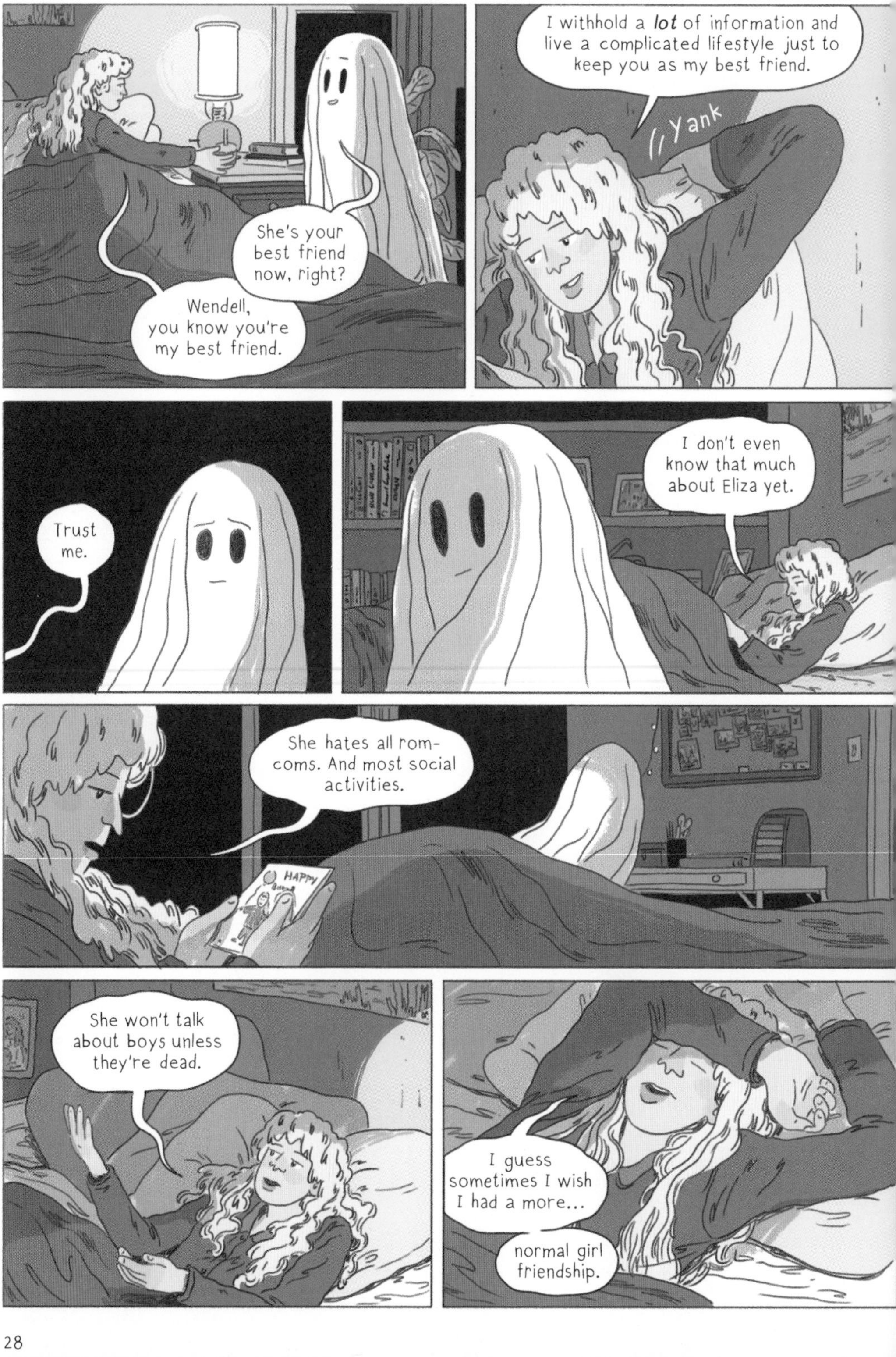

She's your best friend now, right?
Wendell, you know you're my best friend.
I withhold a *lot* of information and live a complicated lifestyle just to keep you as my best friend.
Yank
Trust me.
I don't even know that much about Eliza yet.
She hates all rom-coms. And most social activities.
HAPPY
She won't talk about boys unless they're dead.
I guess sometimes I wish I had a more...
normal girl friendship.

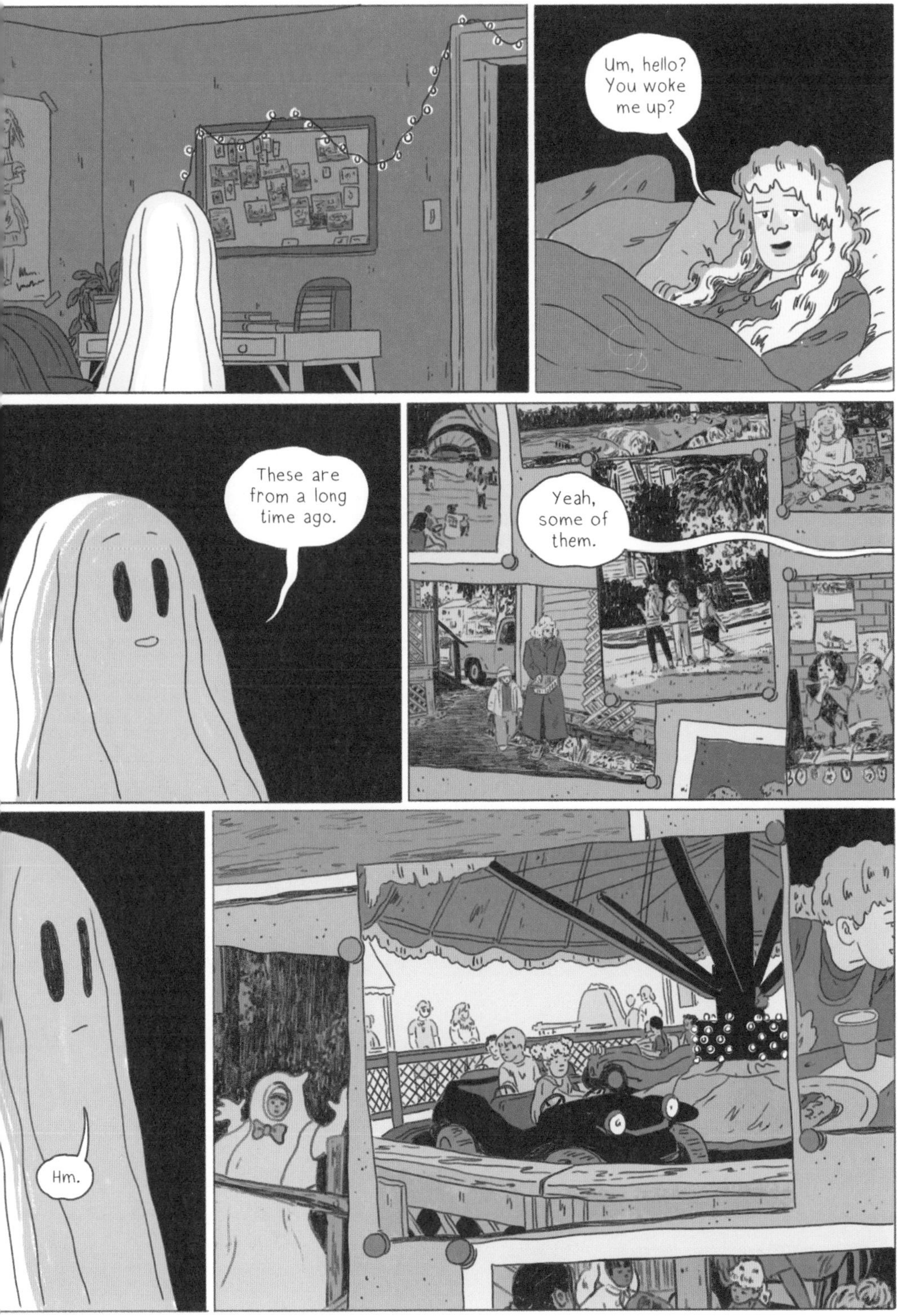
Um, hello?
You woke
me up?
These are
from a long
time ago.
Yeah,
some of
them.
Hm.

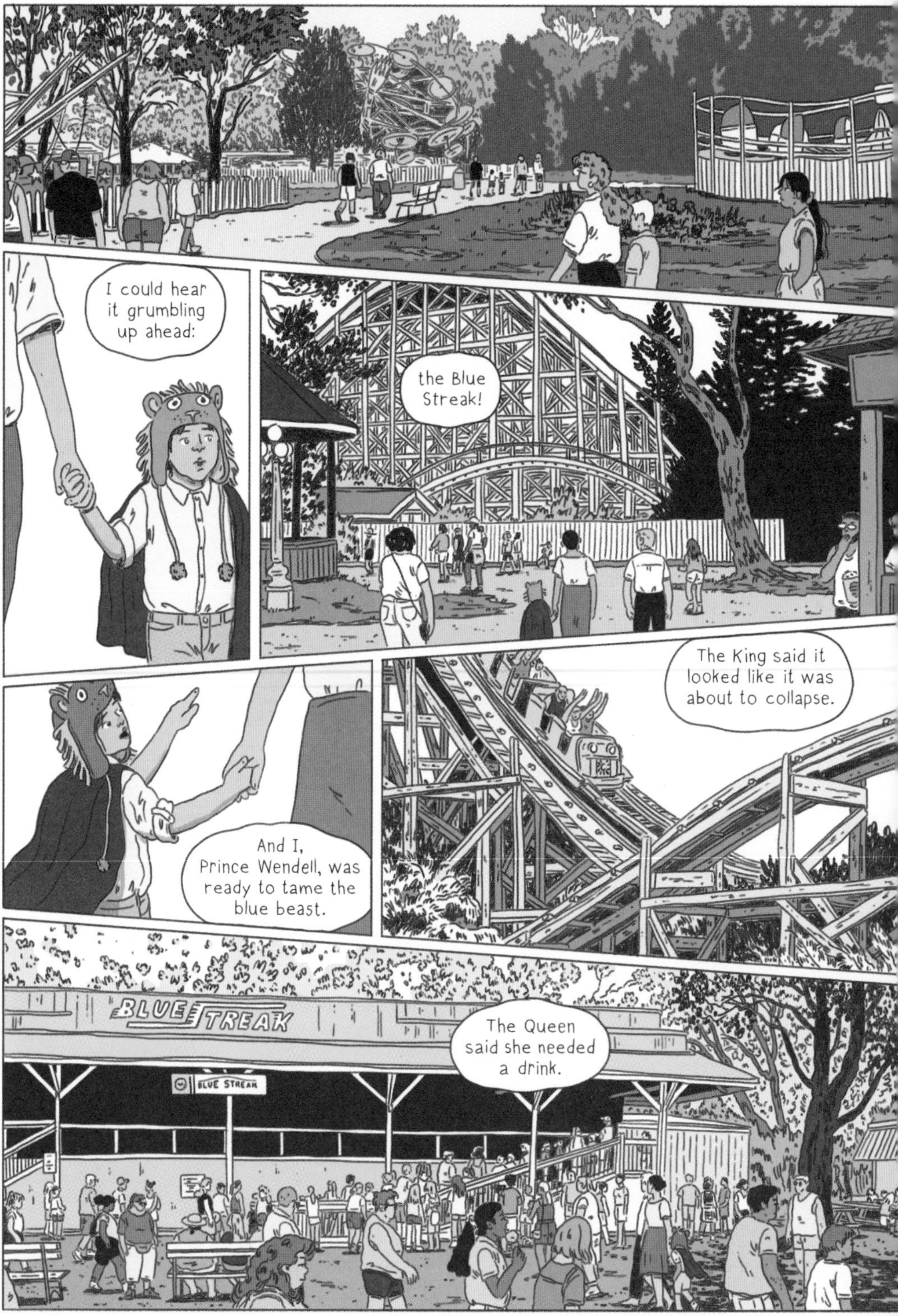
I could hear it grumbling up ahead:
the Blue Streak!
The King said it looked like it was about to collapse.
And I, Prince Wendell, was ready to tame the blue beast.
BLUE STREAK
BLUE STREAK
The Queen said she needed a drink.

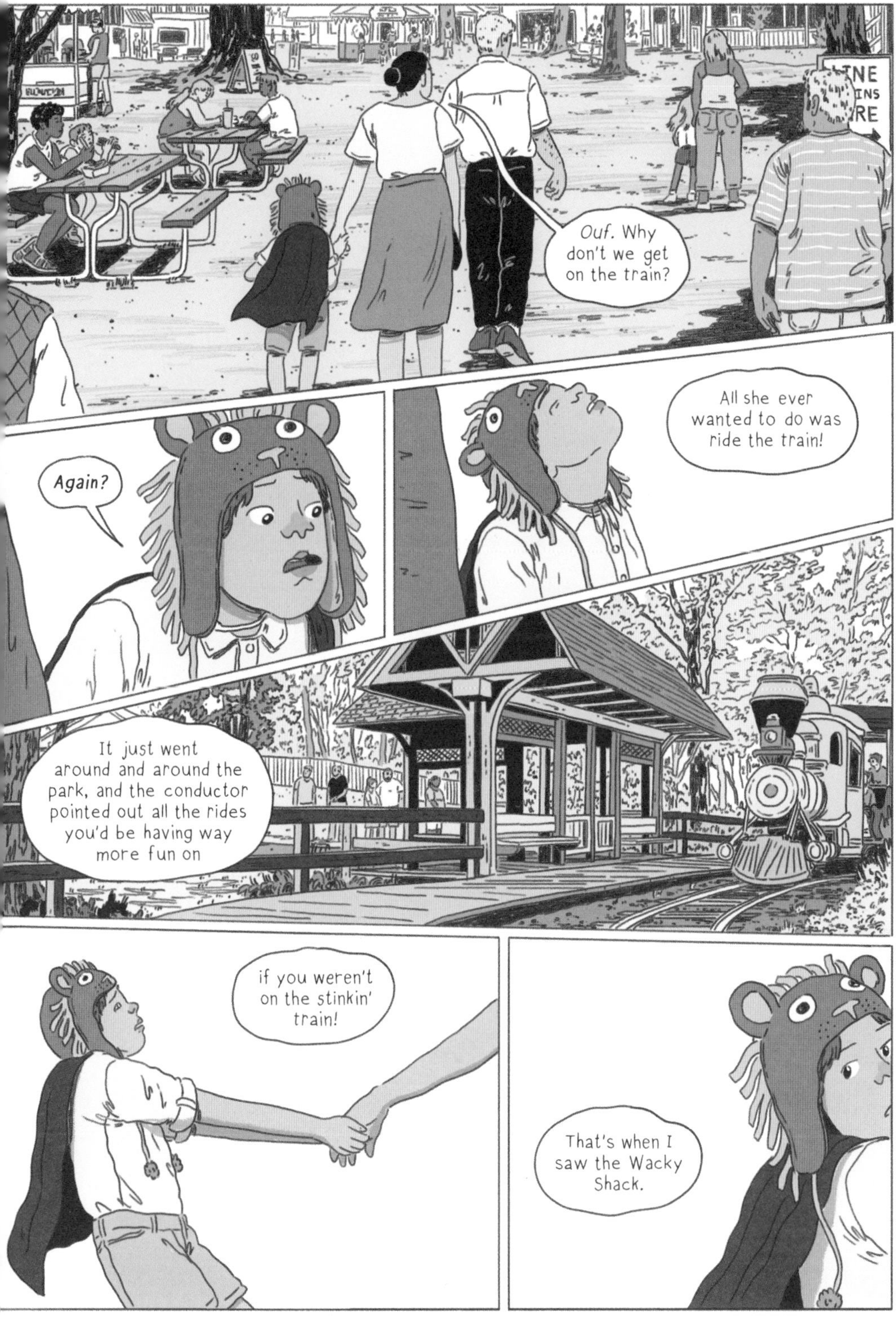
Ouf. Why don't we get on the train?
Again?
All she ever wanted to do was ride the train!
It just went around and around the park, and the conductor pointed out all the rides you'd be having way more fun on
if you weren't on the stinkin' train!
That's when I saw the Wacky Shack.

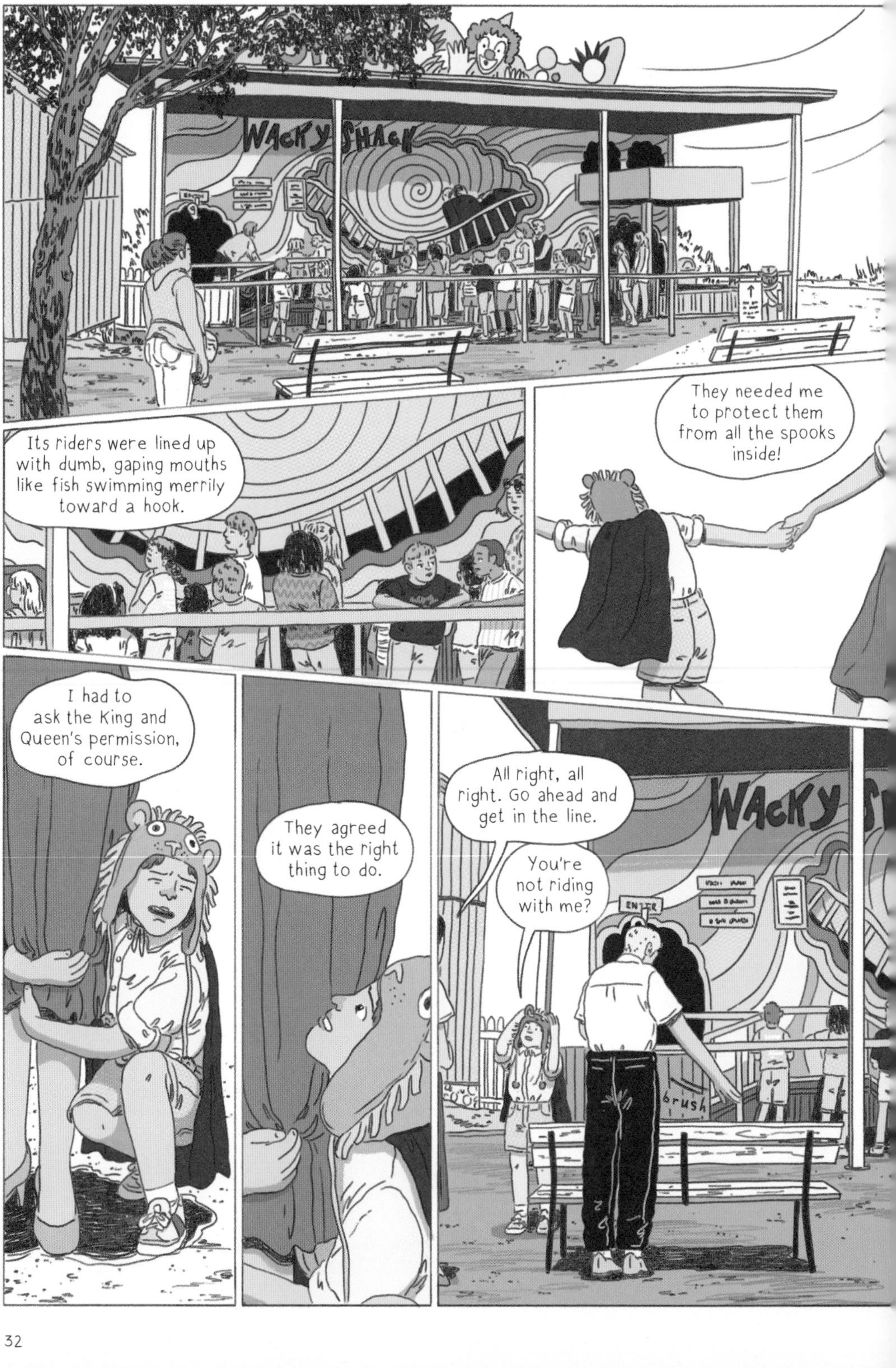
WACKY SHACK
Its riders were lined up with dumb, gaping mouths like fish swimming merrily toward a hook.
They needed me to protect them from all the spooks inside!
I had to ask the King and Queen's permission, of course.
They agreed it was the right thing to do.
All right, all right. Go ahead and get in the line.
You're not riding with me?
WACKY
ENTER
brush

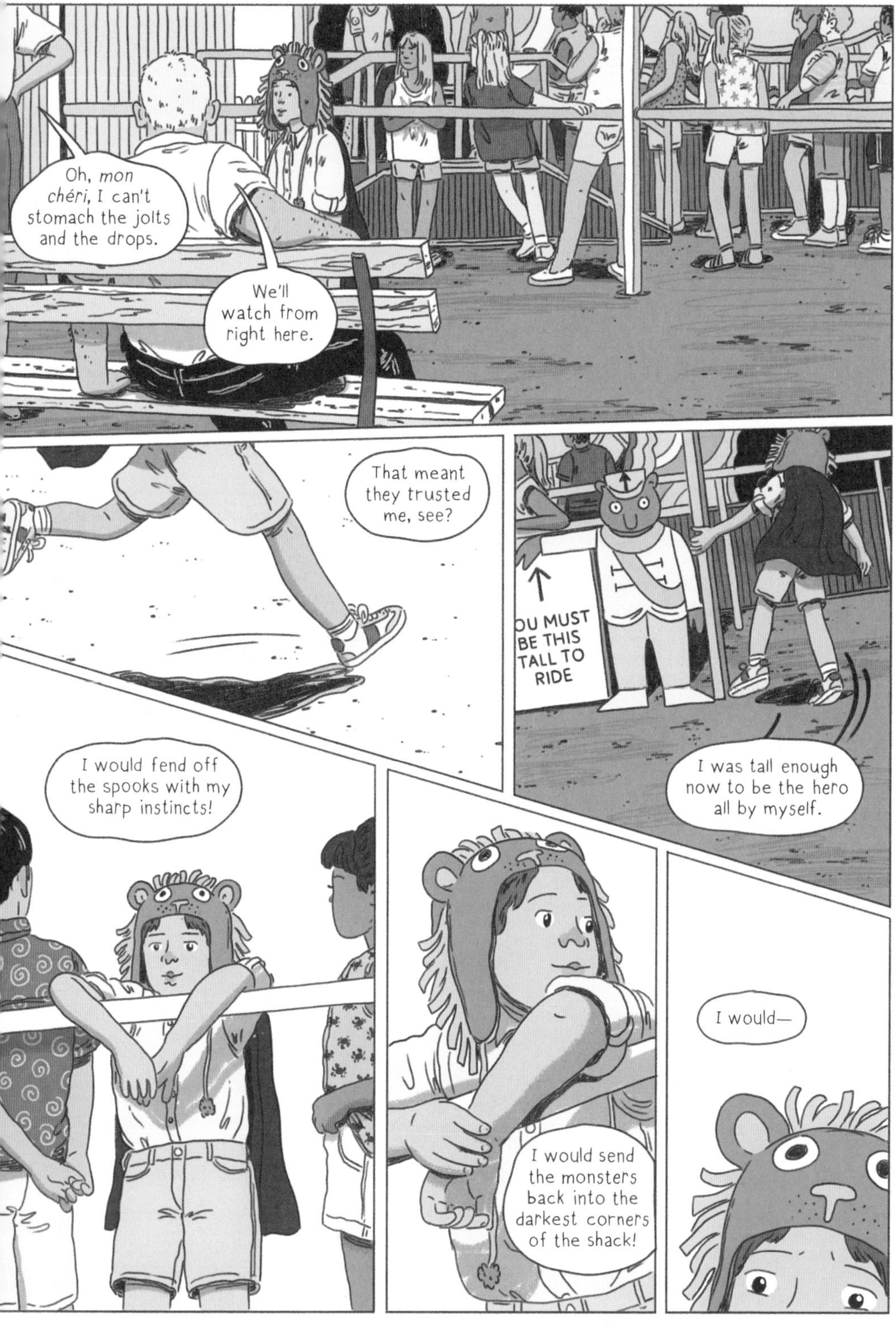
Oh, *mon chéri,* I can't stomach the jolts and the drops.
We'll watch from right here.
That meant they trusted me, see?
OU MUST BE THIS TALL TO RIDE
I was tall enough now to be the hero all by myself.
I would fend off the spooks with my sharp instincts!
I would send the monsters back into the darkest corners of the shack!
I would—

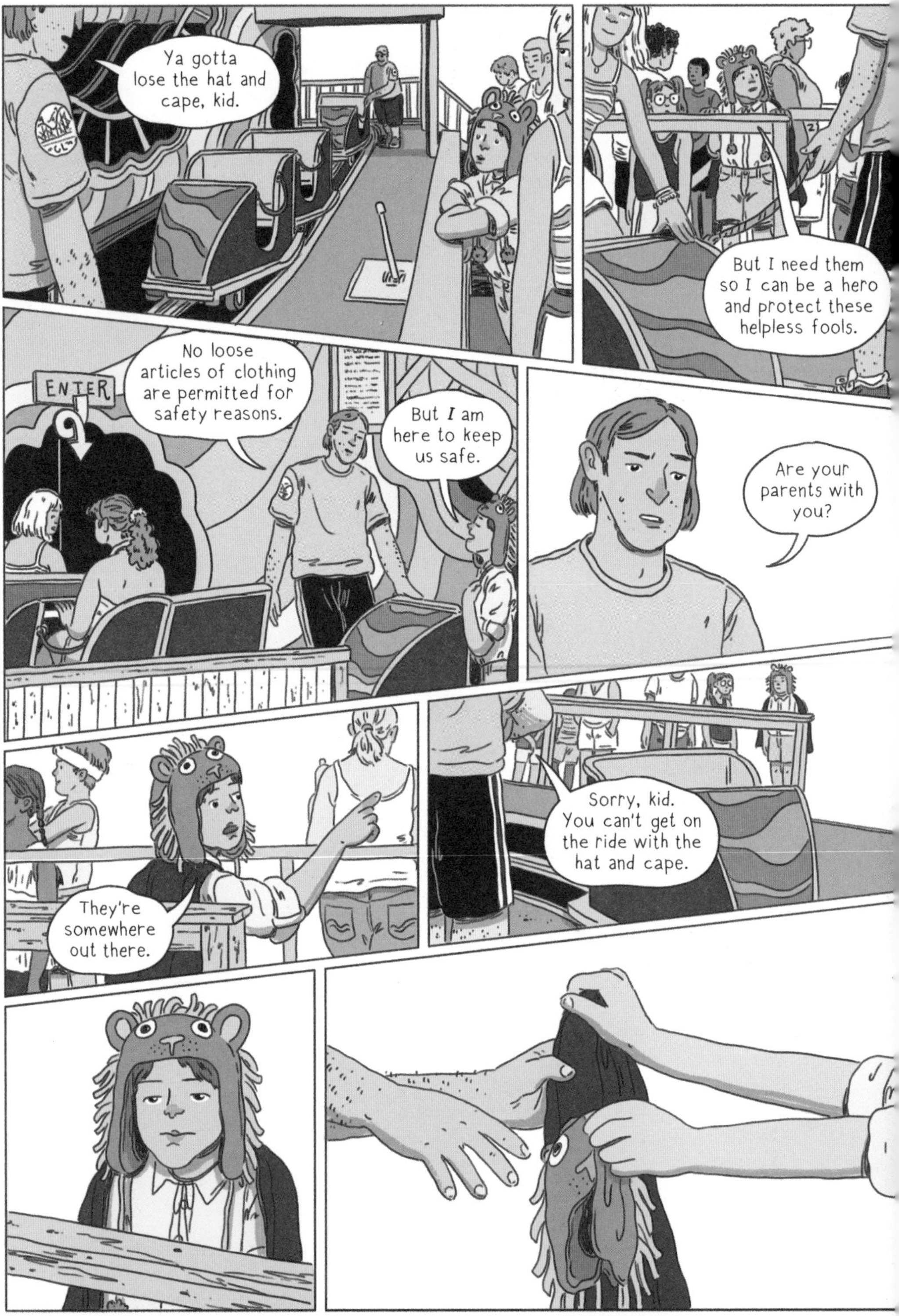

Ya gotta lose the hat and cape, kid.
But I need them so I can be a hero and protect these helpless fools.
ENTER
No loose articles of clothing are permitted for safety reasons.
But *I* am here to keep us safe.
Are your parents with you?
They're somewhere out there.
Sorry, kid. You can't get on the ride with the hat and cape.

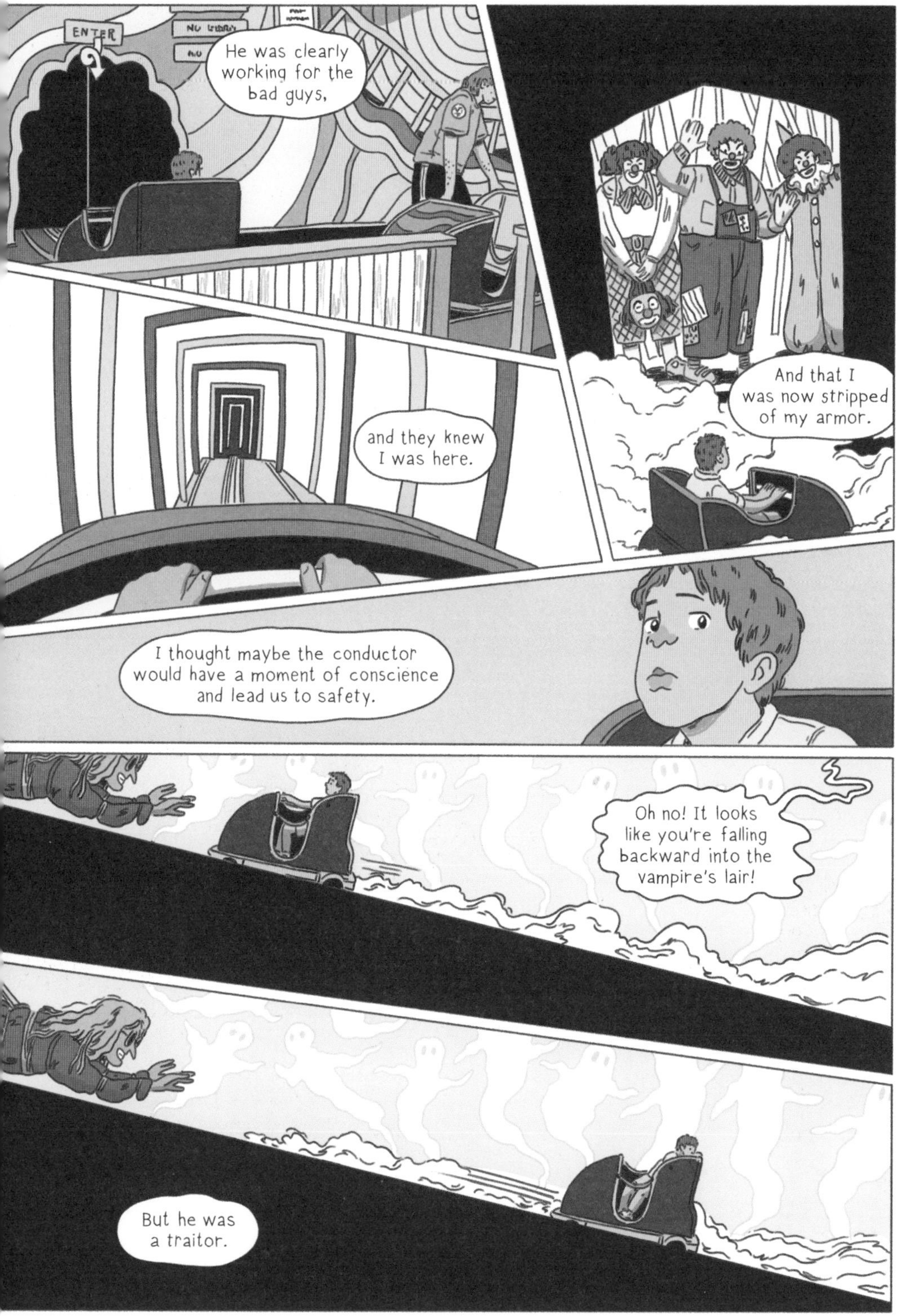
ENTER
He was clearly working for the bad guys,
and they knew I was here.
And that I was now stripped of my armor.
I thought maybe the conductor would have a moment of conscience and lead us to safety.
Oh no! It looks like you're falling backward into the vampire's lair!
But he was a traitor.

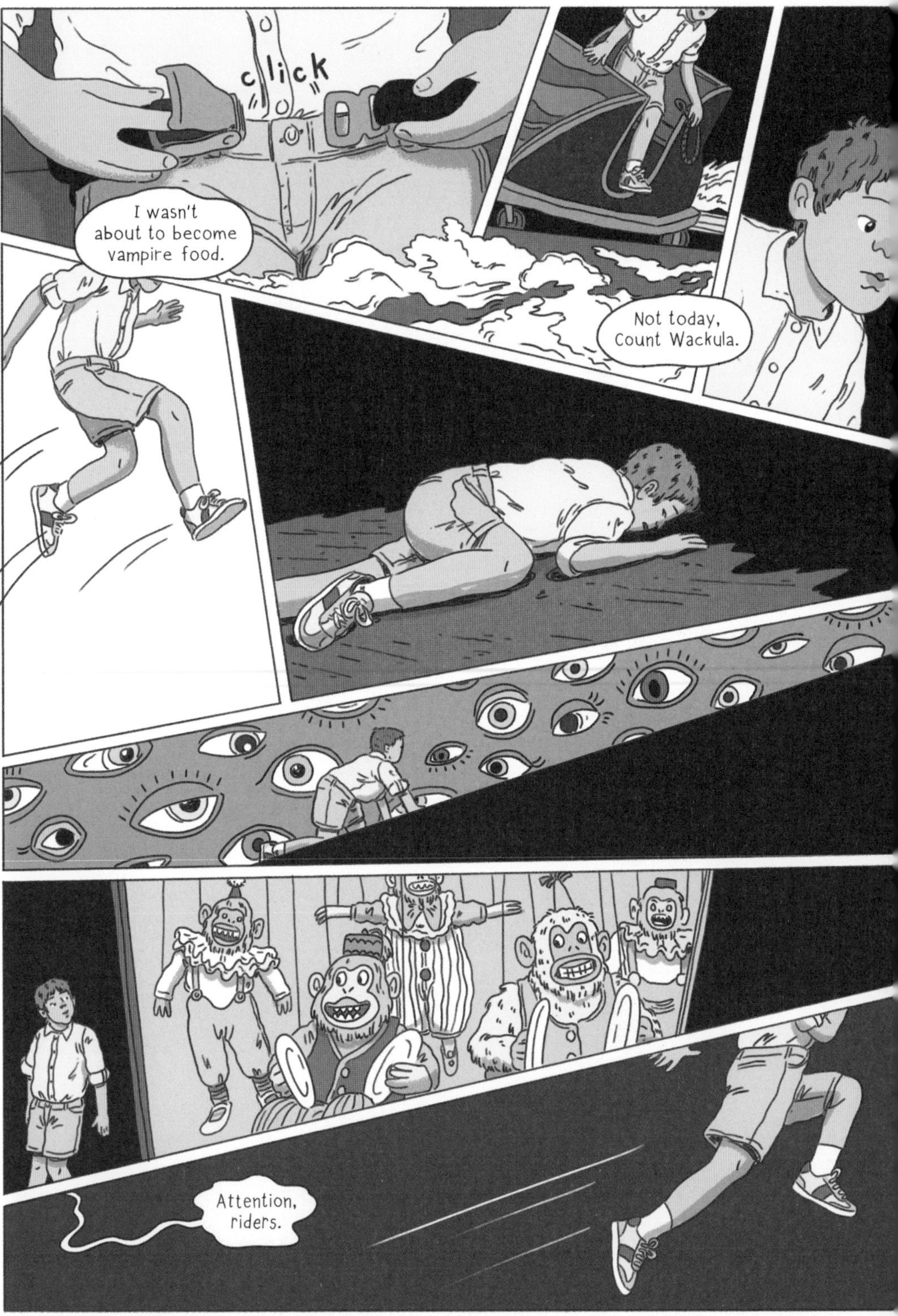

click
I wasn't about to become vampire food.
Not today, Count Wackula.
Attention, riders.

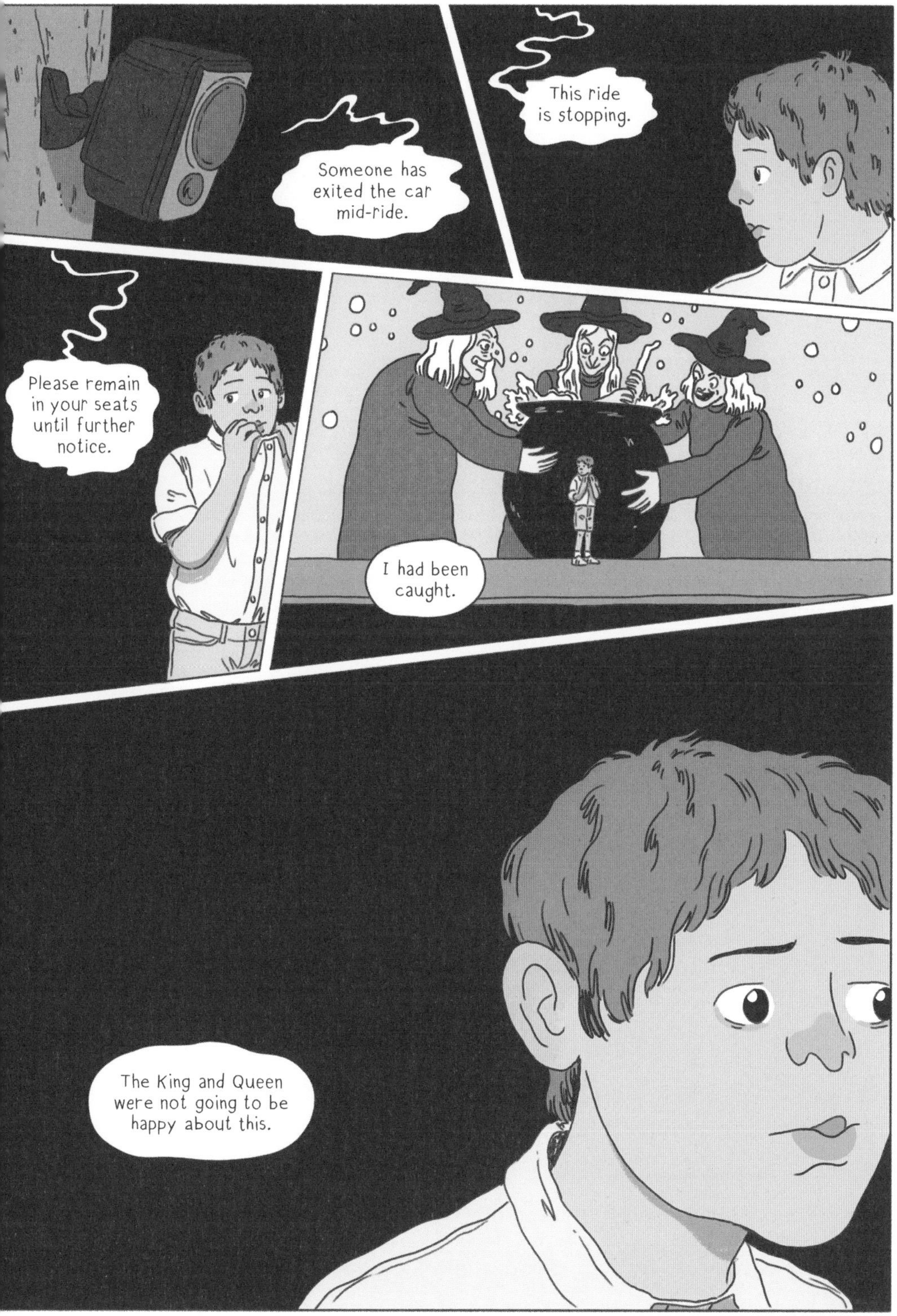
Someone has exited the car mid-ride.
This ride is stopping.
Please remain in your seats until further notice.
I had been caught.
The King and Queen were not going to be happy about this.

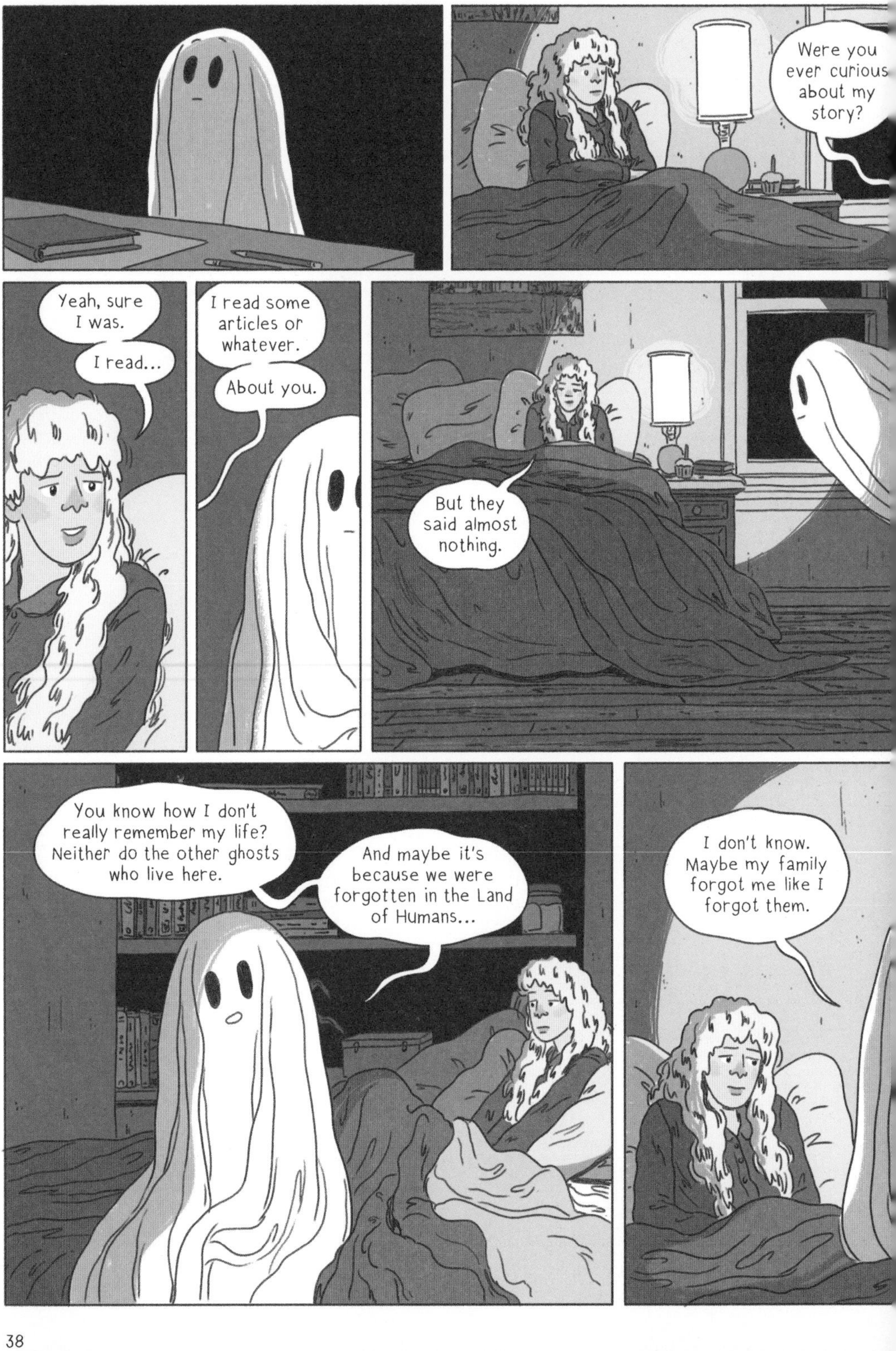

Were you ever curious about my story?
Yeah, sure I was.
I read...
I read some articles or whatever.
About you.
But they said almost nothing.
You know how I don't really remember my life? Neither do the other ghosts who live here.
And maybe it's because we were forgotten in the Land of Humans...
I don't know. Maybe my family forgot me like I forgot them.

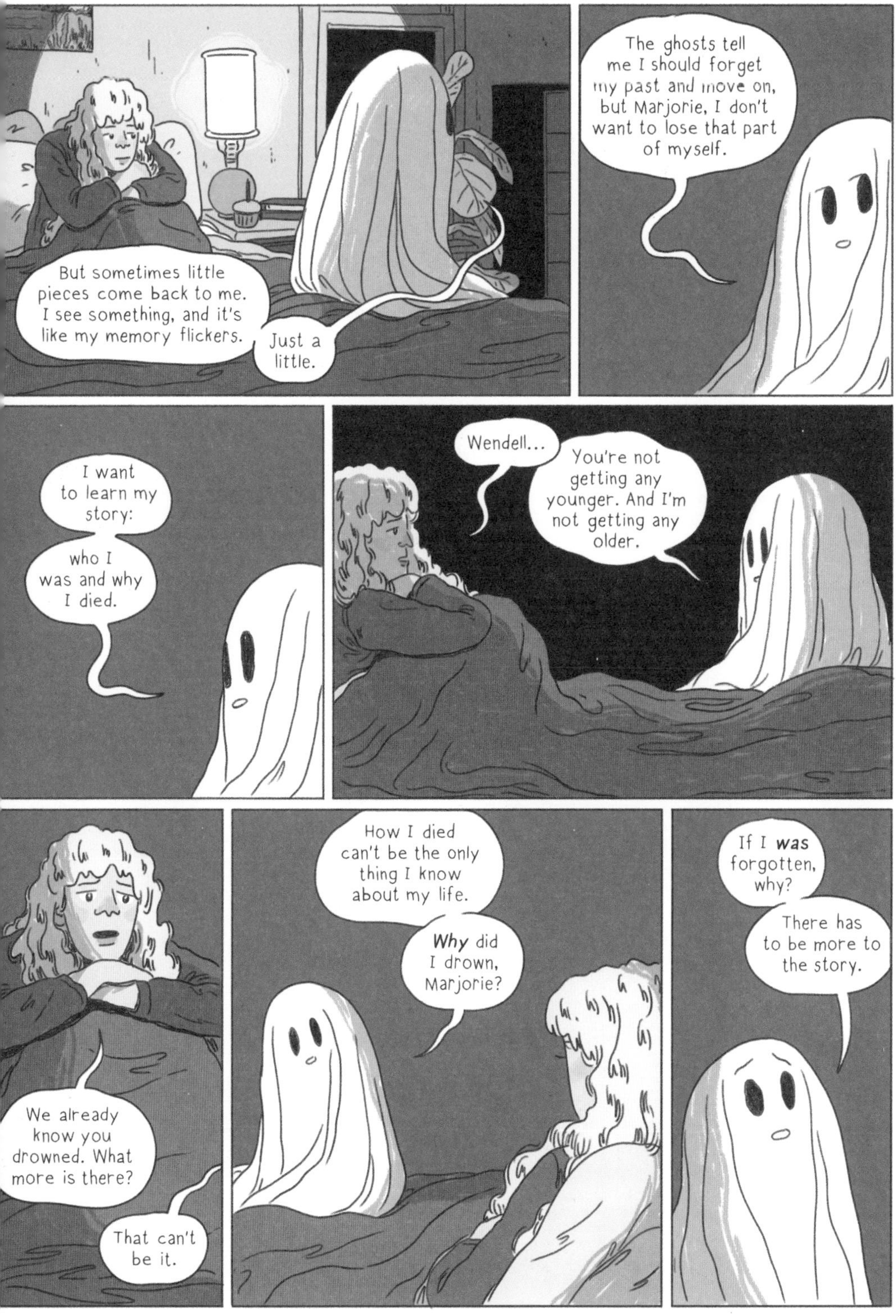
But sometimes little pieces come back to me. I see something, and it's like my memory flickers.
Just a little.
The ghosts tell me I should forget my past and move on, but Marjorie, I don't want to lose that part of myself.
I want to learn my story:
who I was and why I died.
Wendell...
You're not getting any younger. And I'm not getting any older.
We already know you drowned. What more is there?
That can't be it.
How I died can't be the only thing I know about my life.
Why did I drown, Marjorie?
If I **was** forgotten, why?
There has to be more to the story.

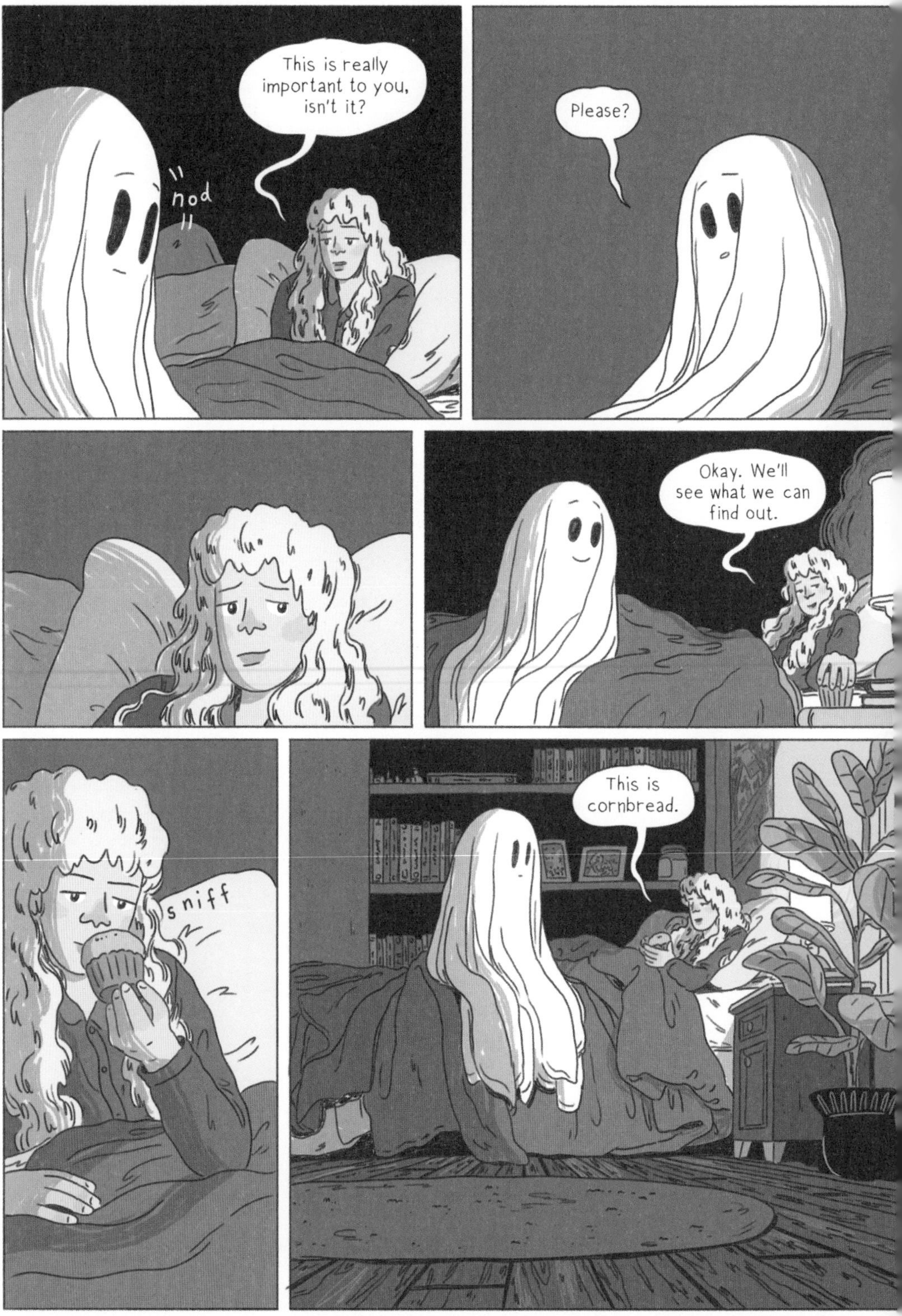
This is really important to you, isn't it?
nod
Please?
Okay. We'll see what we can find out.
sniff
This is cornbread.

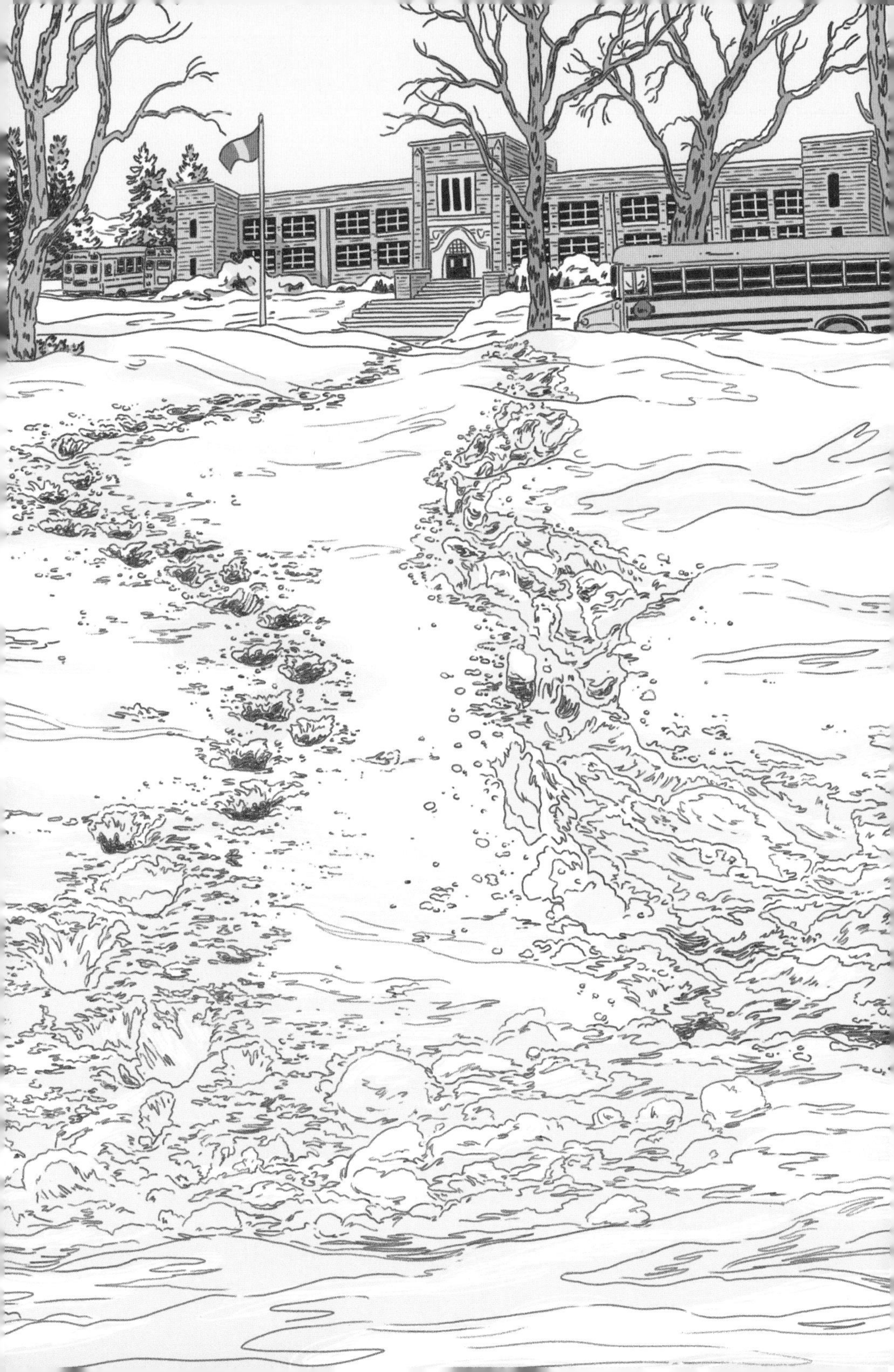

hehehe

Fins

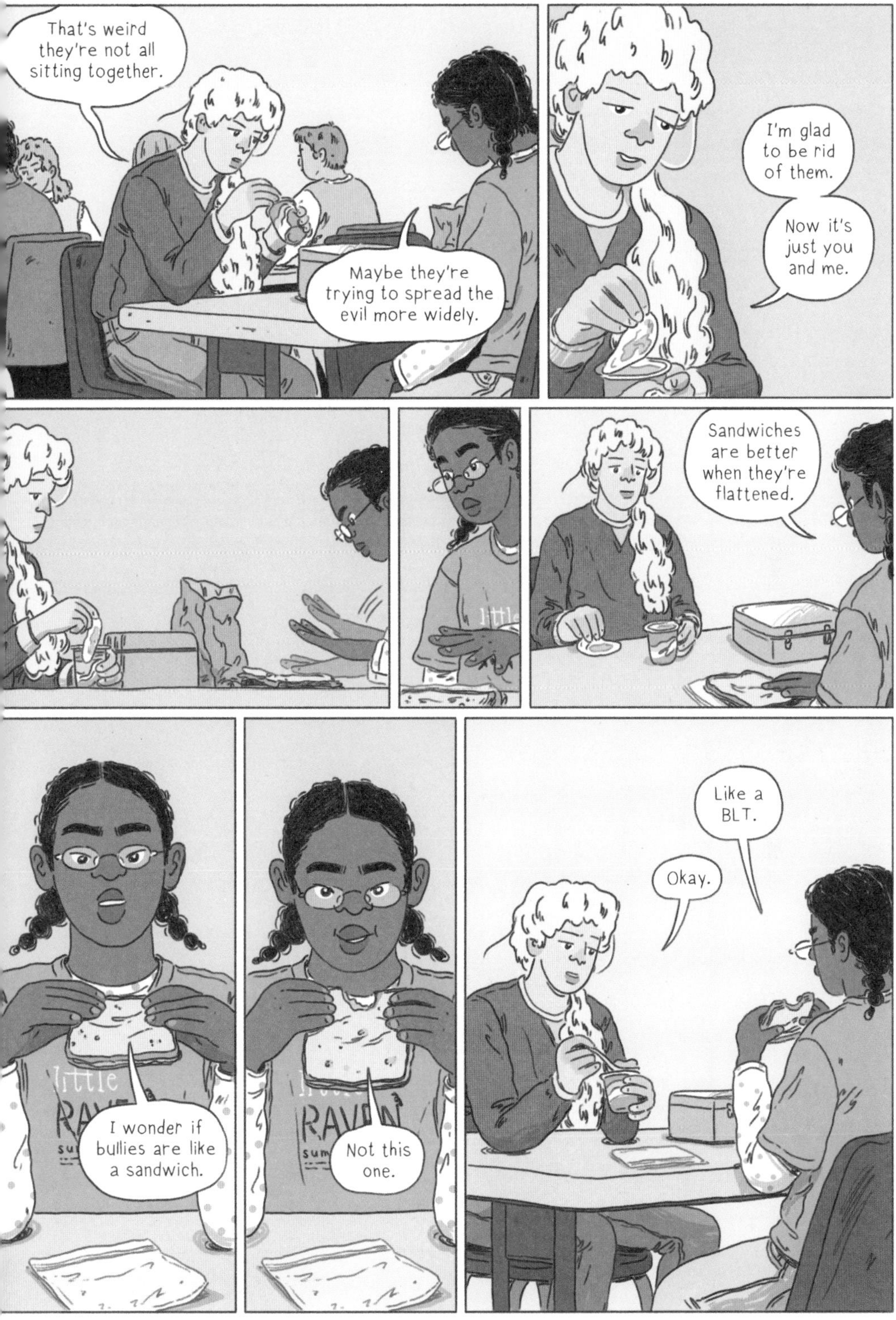
That's weird they're not all sitting together.
Maybe they're trying to spread the evil more widely.
I'm glad to be rid of them.
Now it's just you and me.
little
Sandwiches are better when they're flattened.
little RAVEN sum
I wonder if bullies are like a sandwich.
RAVEN sum
Not this one.
Okay.
Like a BLT.

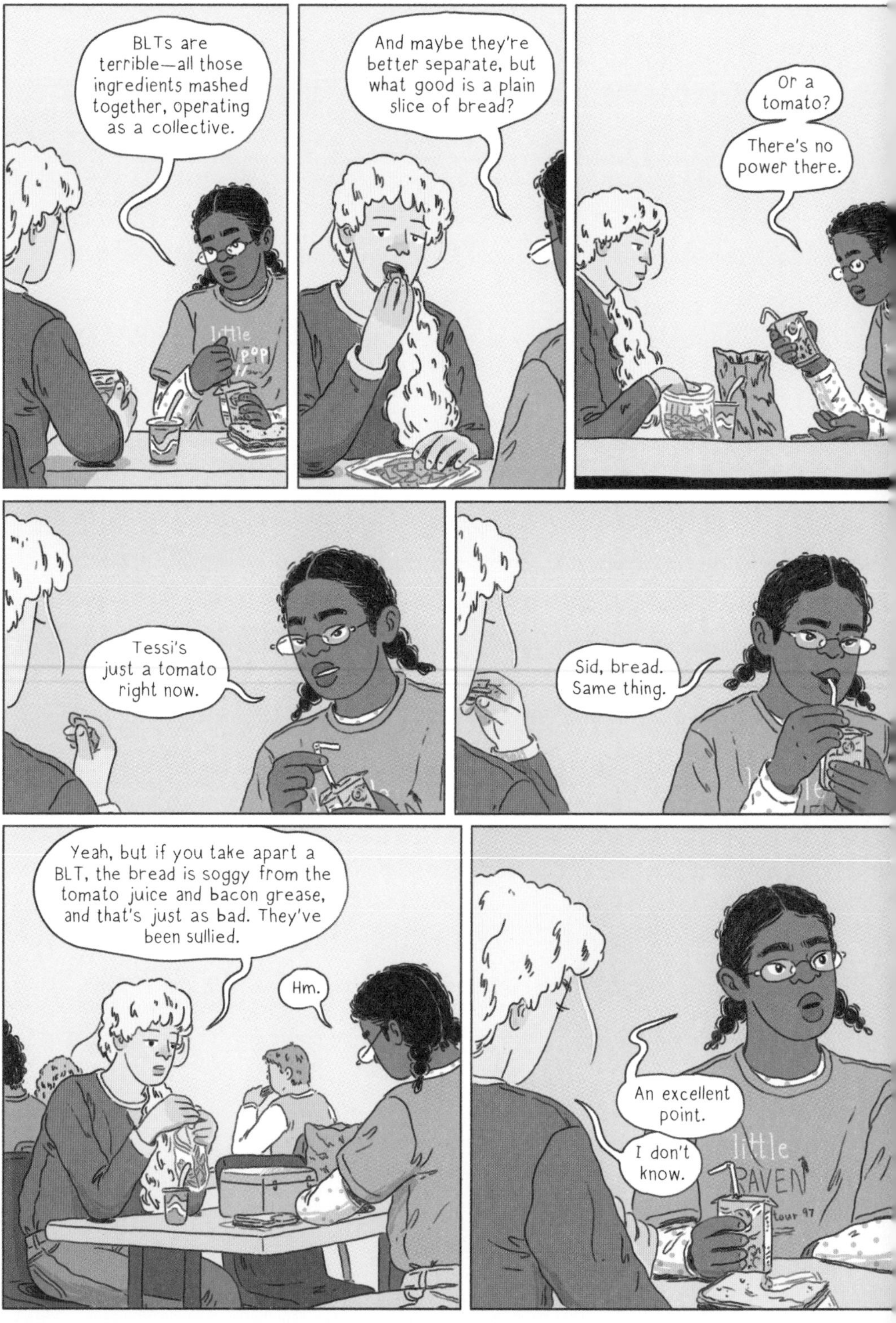
BLTs are terrible—all those ingredients mashed together, operating as a collective.
And maybe they're better separate, but what good is a plain slice of bread?
Or a tomato?
There's no power there.
Tessi's just a tomato right now.
Sid, bread. Same thing.
Yeah, but if you take apart a BLT, the bread is soggy from the tomato juice and bacon grease, and that's just as bad. They've been sullied.
Hm.
An excellent point.
I don't know.
little RAVEN tour 97

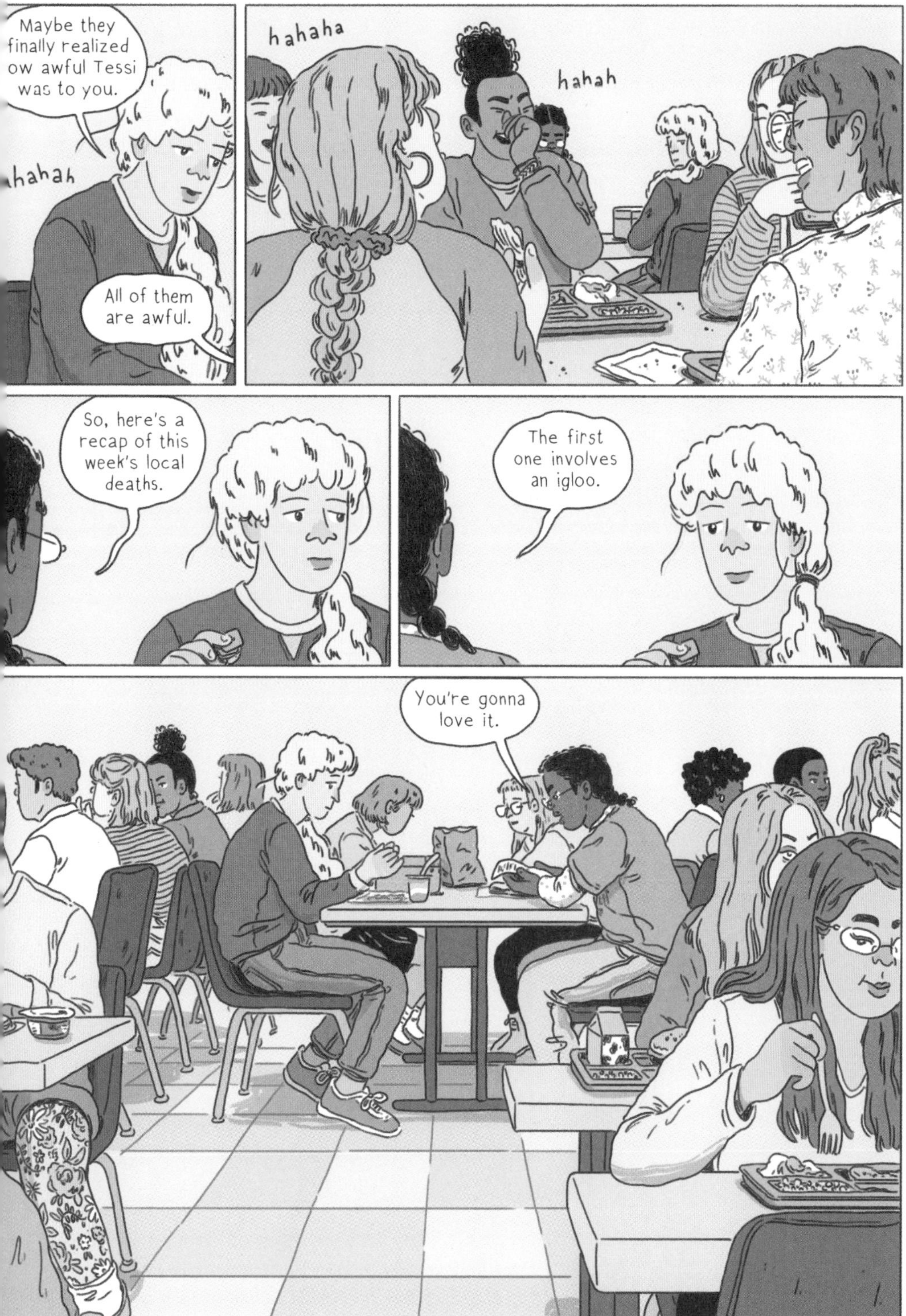
Maybe they finally realized ow awful Tessi was to you.
hahah
All of them are awful.
hahaha
hahah
So, here's a recap of this week's local deaths.
The first one involves an igloo.
You're gonna love it.

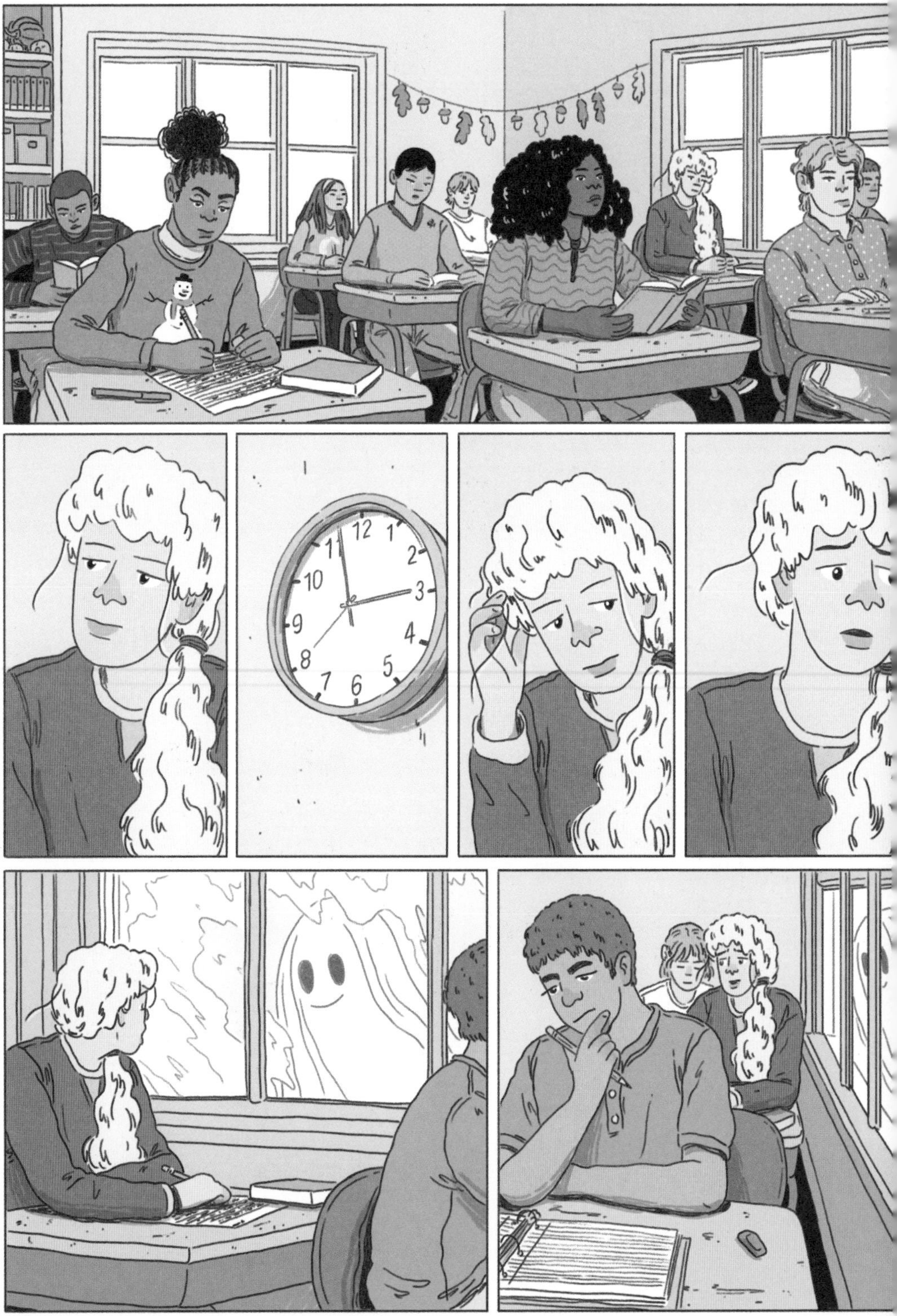

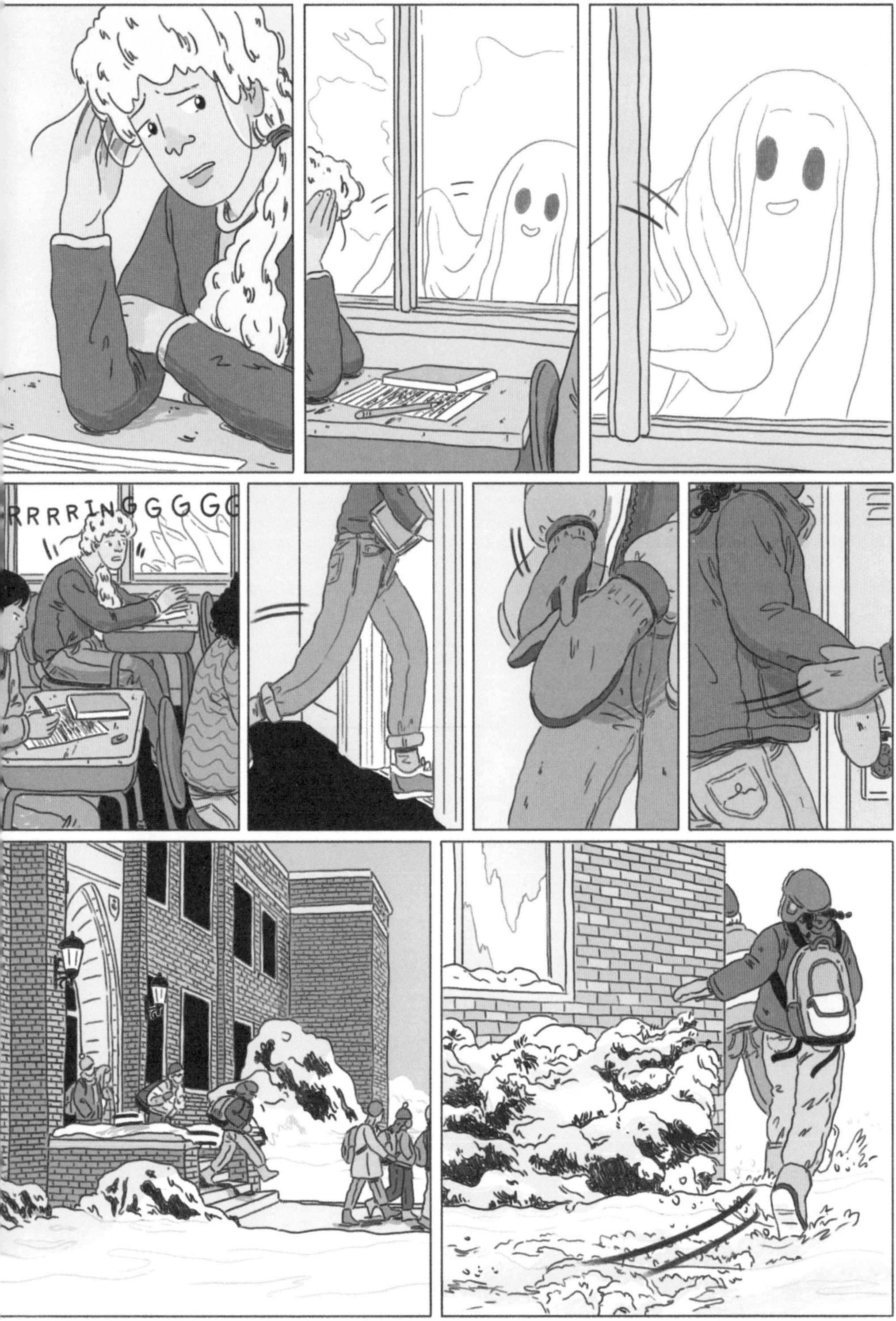
RRRRINGGGGG

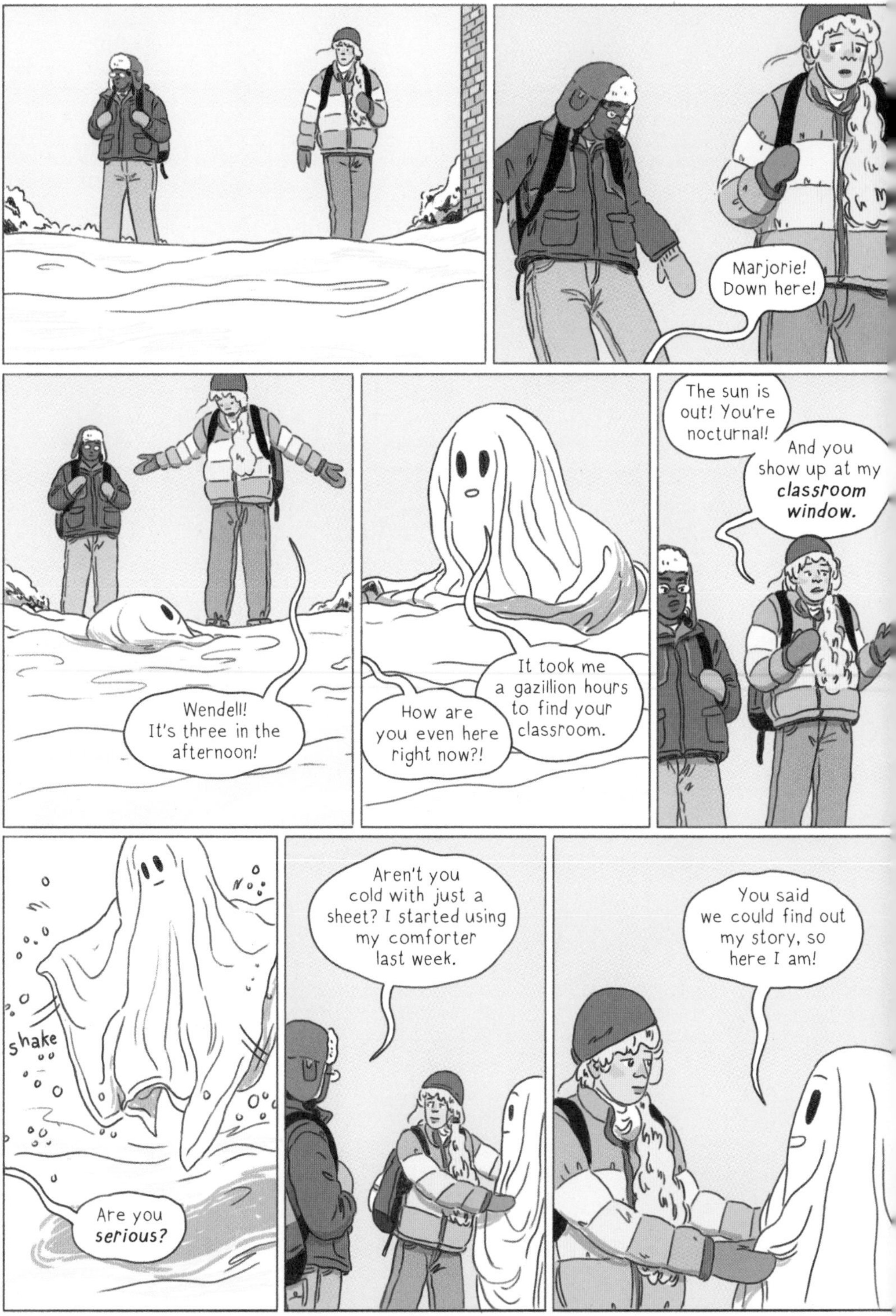
Marjorie!
Down here!
Wendell!
It's three in the
afternoon!
How are
you even here
right now?!
It took me
a gazillion hours
to find your
classroom.
The sun is
out! You're
nocturnal!
And you
show up at my
**classroom
window.**
shake
Are you
serious?
Aren't you
cold with just a
sheet? I started using
my comforter
last week.
You said
we could find out
my story, so
here I am!

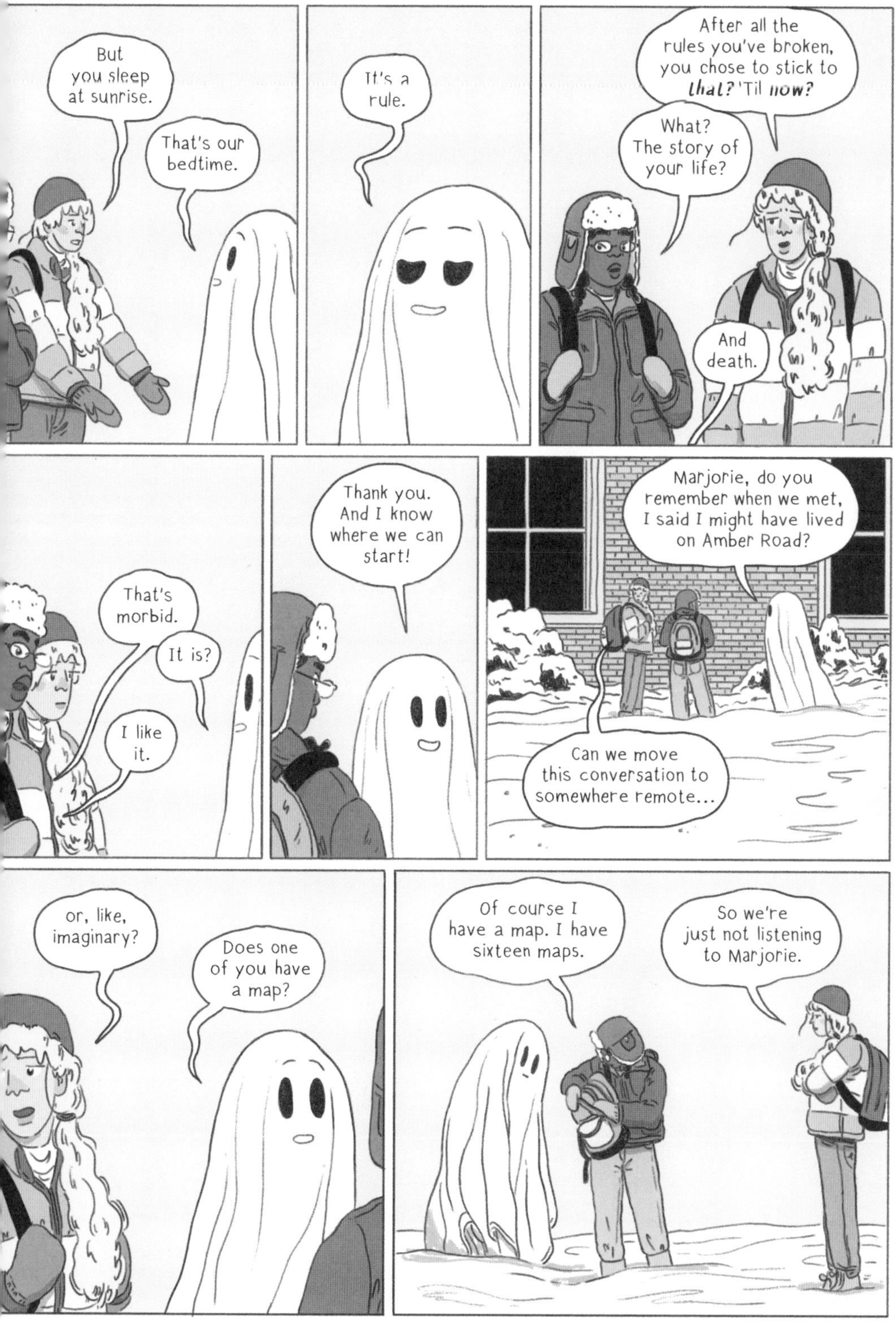

But you sleep at sunrise.
That's our bedtime.
It's a rule.
After all the rules you've broken, you chose to stick to *that?* 'Til *now?*
What? The story of your life?
And death.
That's morbid.
It is?
I like it.
Thank you. And I know where we can start!
Marjorie, do you remember when we met, I said I might have lived on Amber Road?
Can we move this conversation to somewhere remote...
or, like, imaginary?
Does one of you have a map?
Of course I have a map. I have sixteen maps.
So we're just not listening to Marjorie.

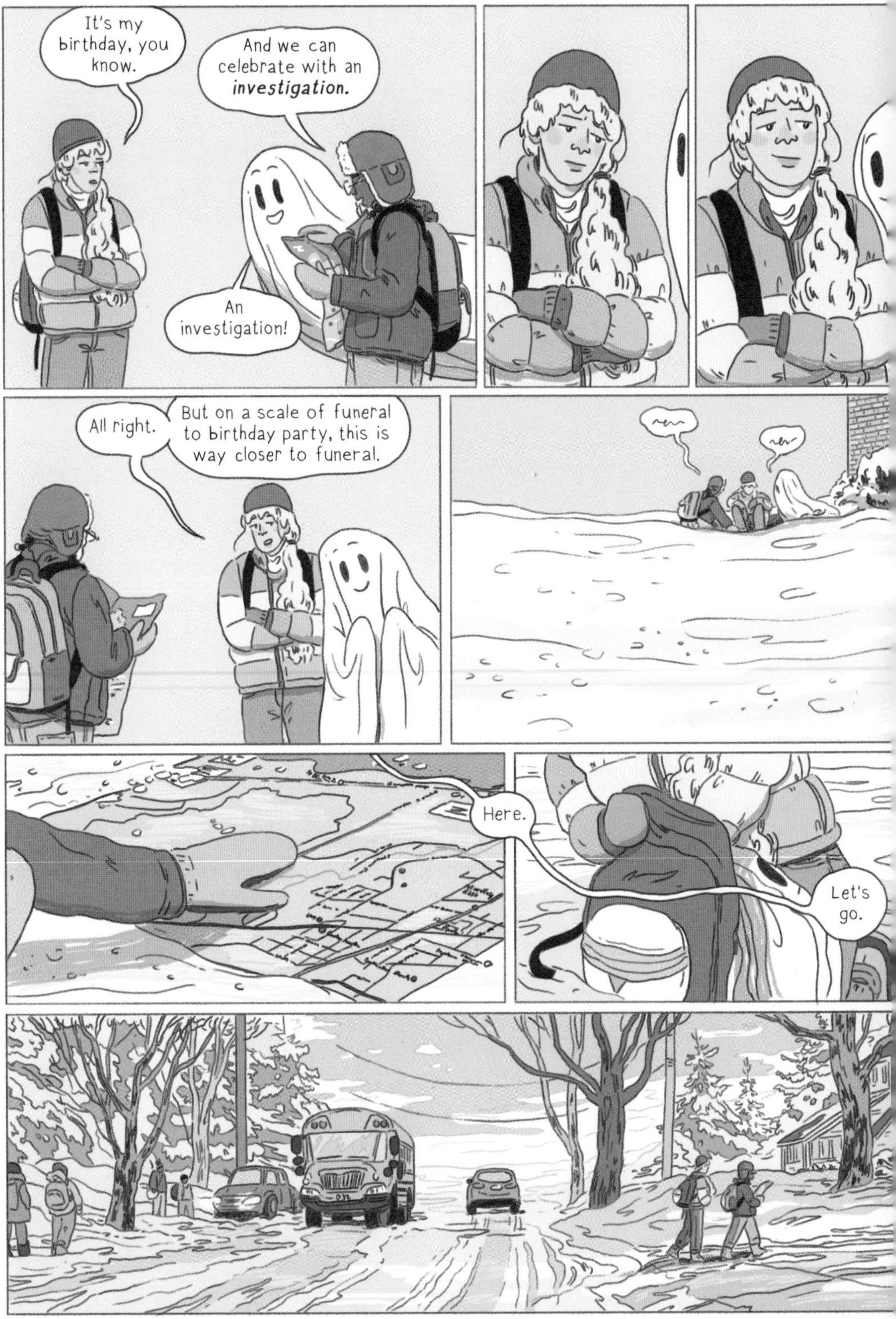
It's my birthday, you know.
And we can celebrate with an ***investigation.***
An investigation!
All right.
But on a scale of funeral to birthday party, this is way closer to funeral.
Here.
Let's go.

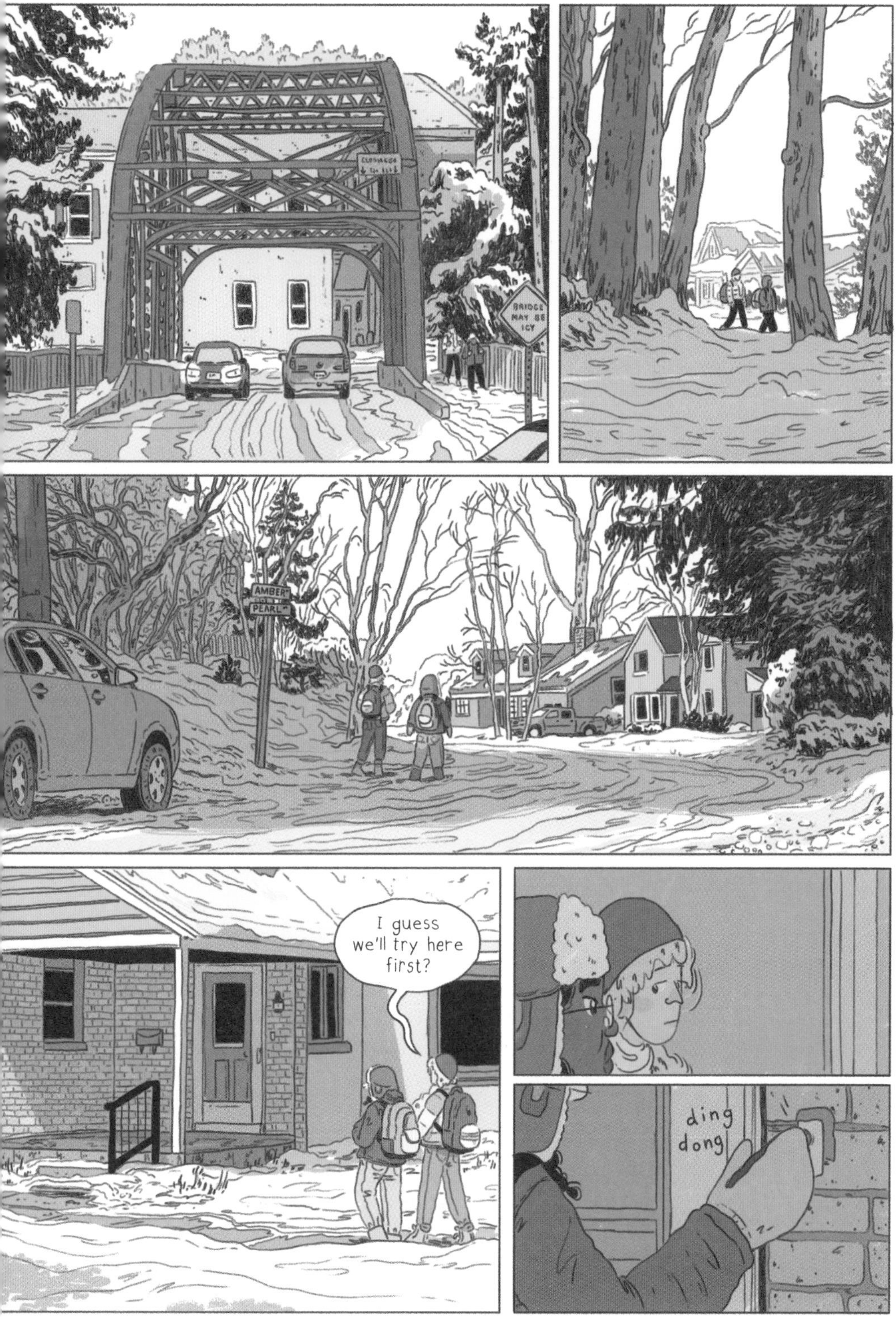
BRIDGE MAY BE ICY
AMBER
PEARL
I guess we'll try here first?
ding dong

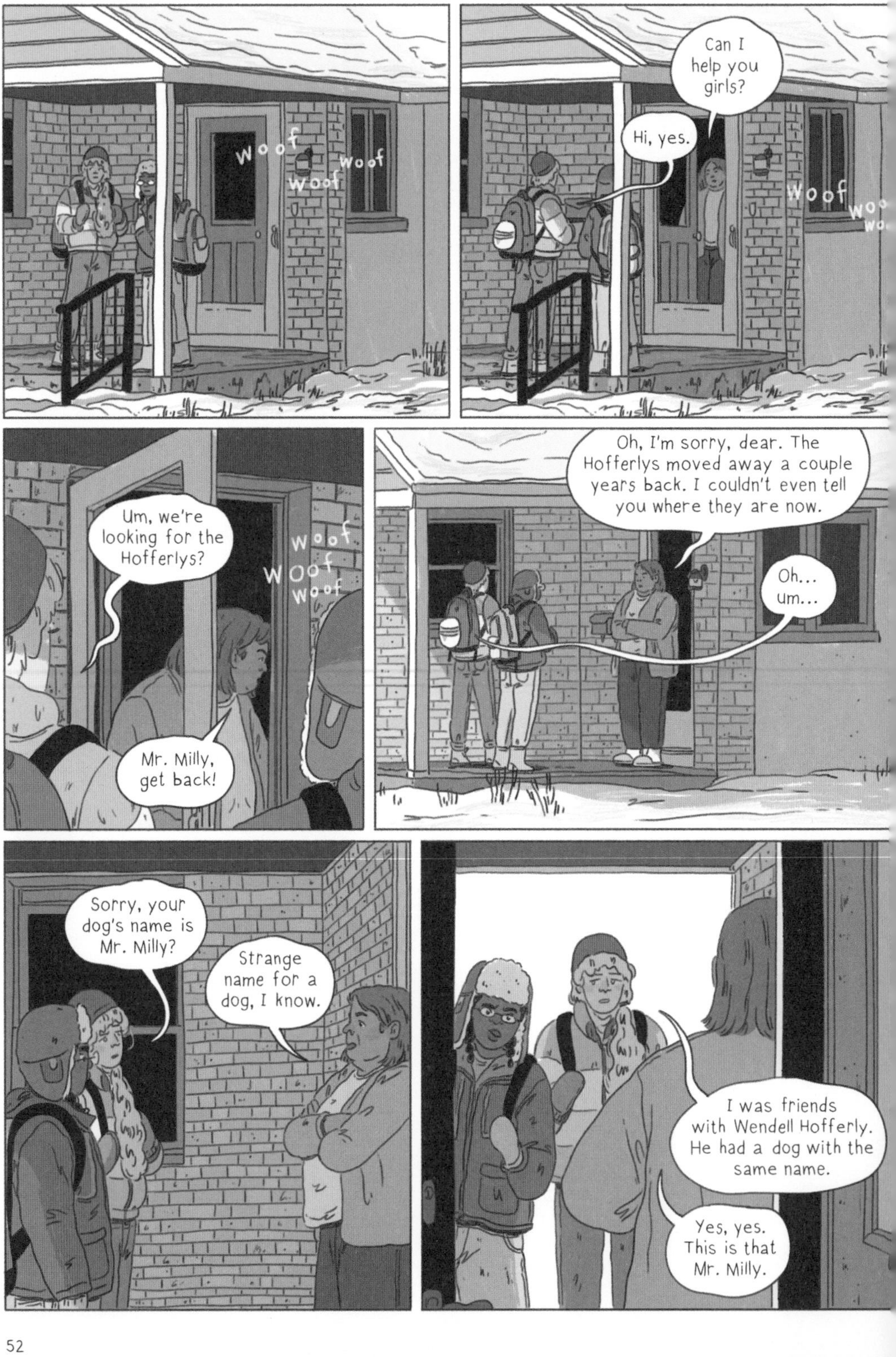
woof
woof
woof
Can I help you girls?
Hi, yes.
Woof
Um, we're looking for the Hofferlys?
woof
woof
woof
Mr. Milly, get back!
Oh, I'm sorry, dear. The Hofferlys moved away a couple years back. I couldn't even tell you where they are now.
Oh... um...
Sorry, your dog's name is Mr. Milly?
Strange name for a dog, I know.
I was friends with Wendell Hofferly. He had a dog with the same name.
Yes, yes. This is that Mr. Milly.

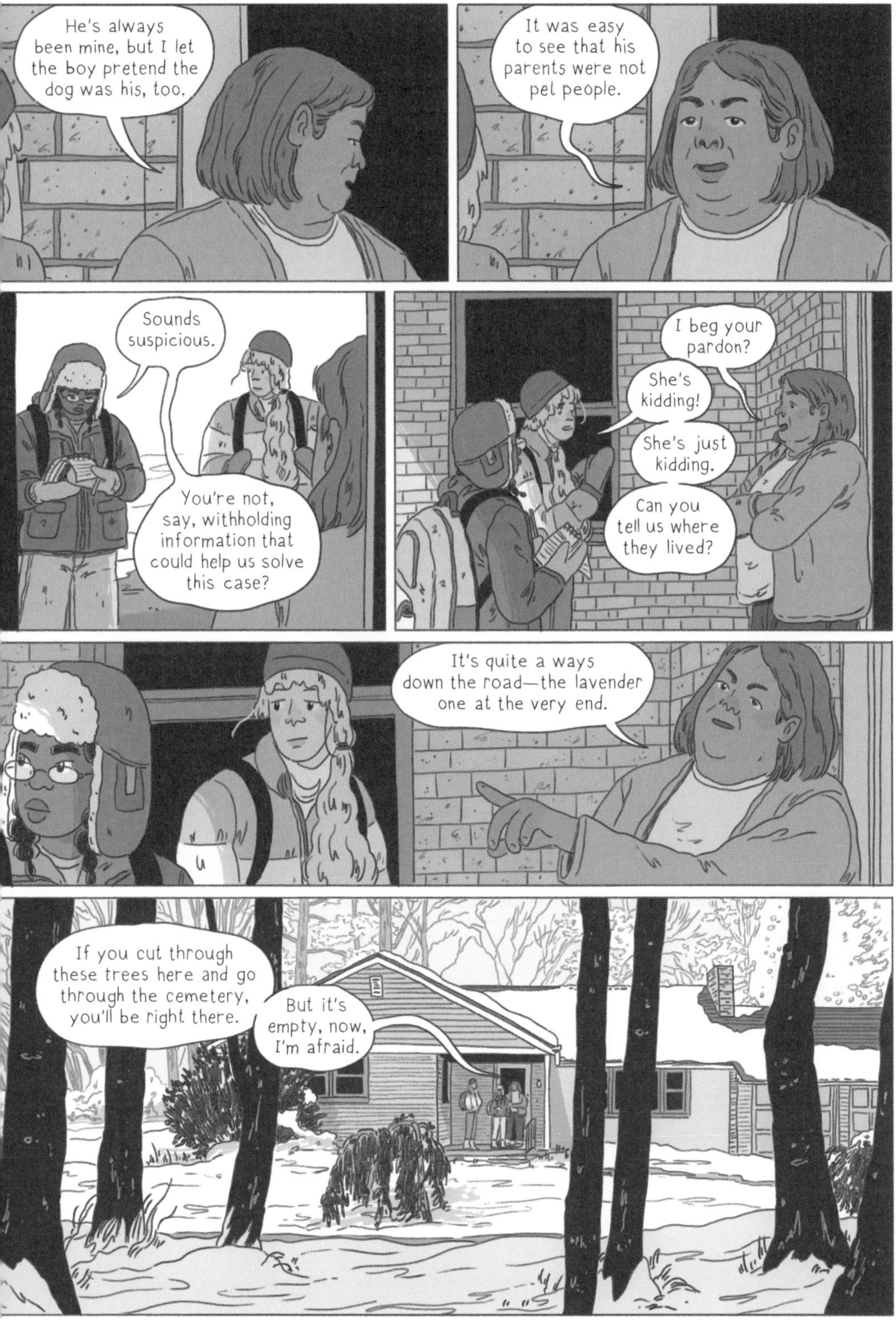
He's always been mine, but I let the boy pretend the dog was his, too.
It was easy to see that his parents were not pet people.
Sounds suspicious.
You're not, say, withholding information that could help us solve this case?
I beg your pardon?
She's kidding!
She's just kidding.
Can you tell us where they lived?
It's quite a ways down the road—the lavender one at the very end.
If you cut through these trees here and go through the cemetery, you'll be right there.
But it's empty, now, I'm afraid.

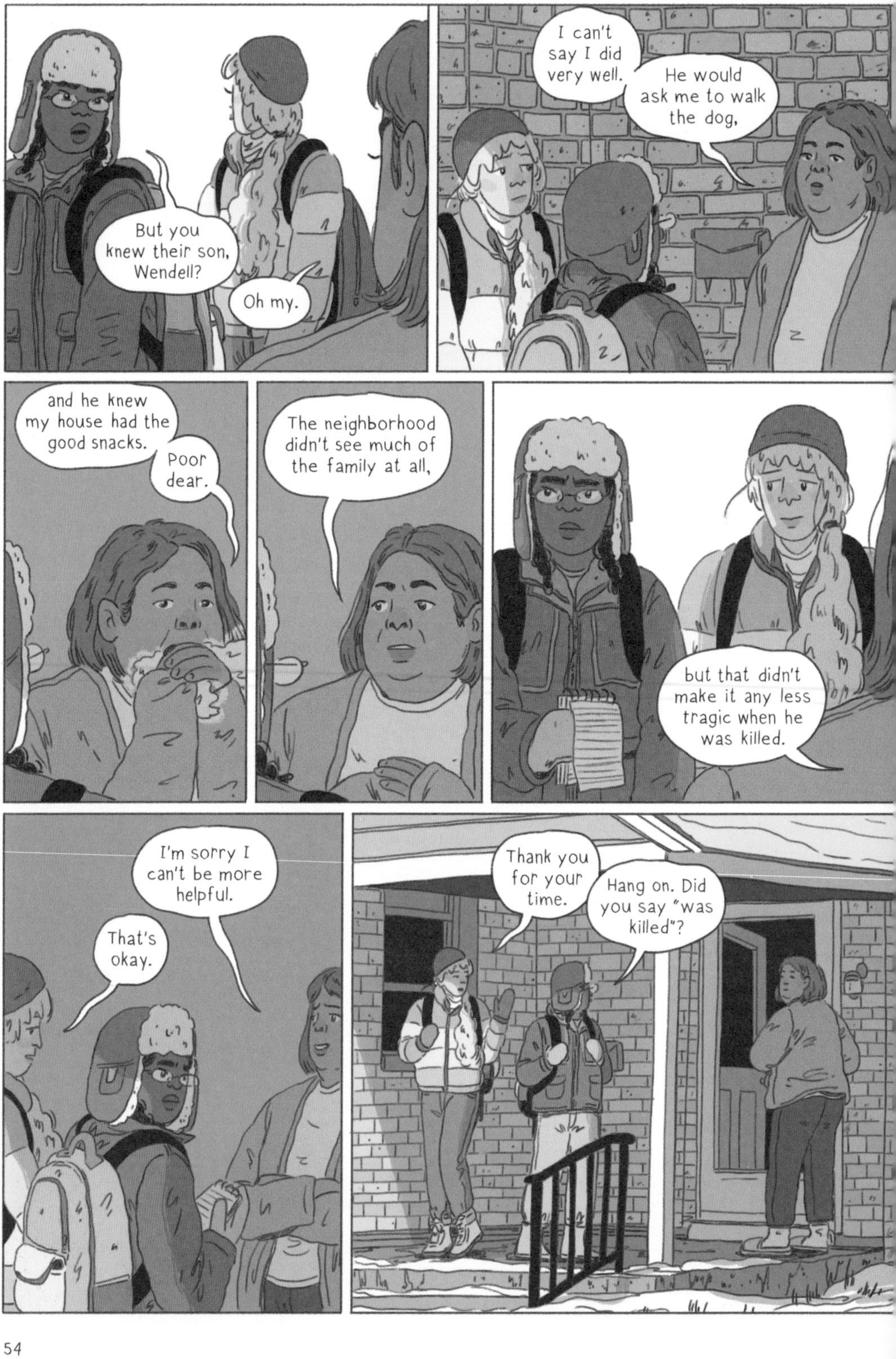
But you knew their son, Wendell?
Oh my.
I can't say I did very well.
He would ask me to walk the dog,
and he knew my house had the good snacks.
Poor dear.
The neighborhood didn't see much of the family at all,
but that didn't make it any less tragic when he was killed.
I'm sorry I can't be more helpful.
That's okay.
Thank you for your time.
Hang on. Did you say "was killed"?

I probably shouldn't say anything.

I don't like to get caught up in all the scuttlebutt—could be a bunch of phooey.

There were rumors, though, that it wasn't an accident.

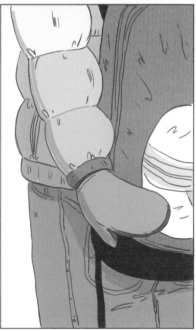

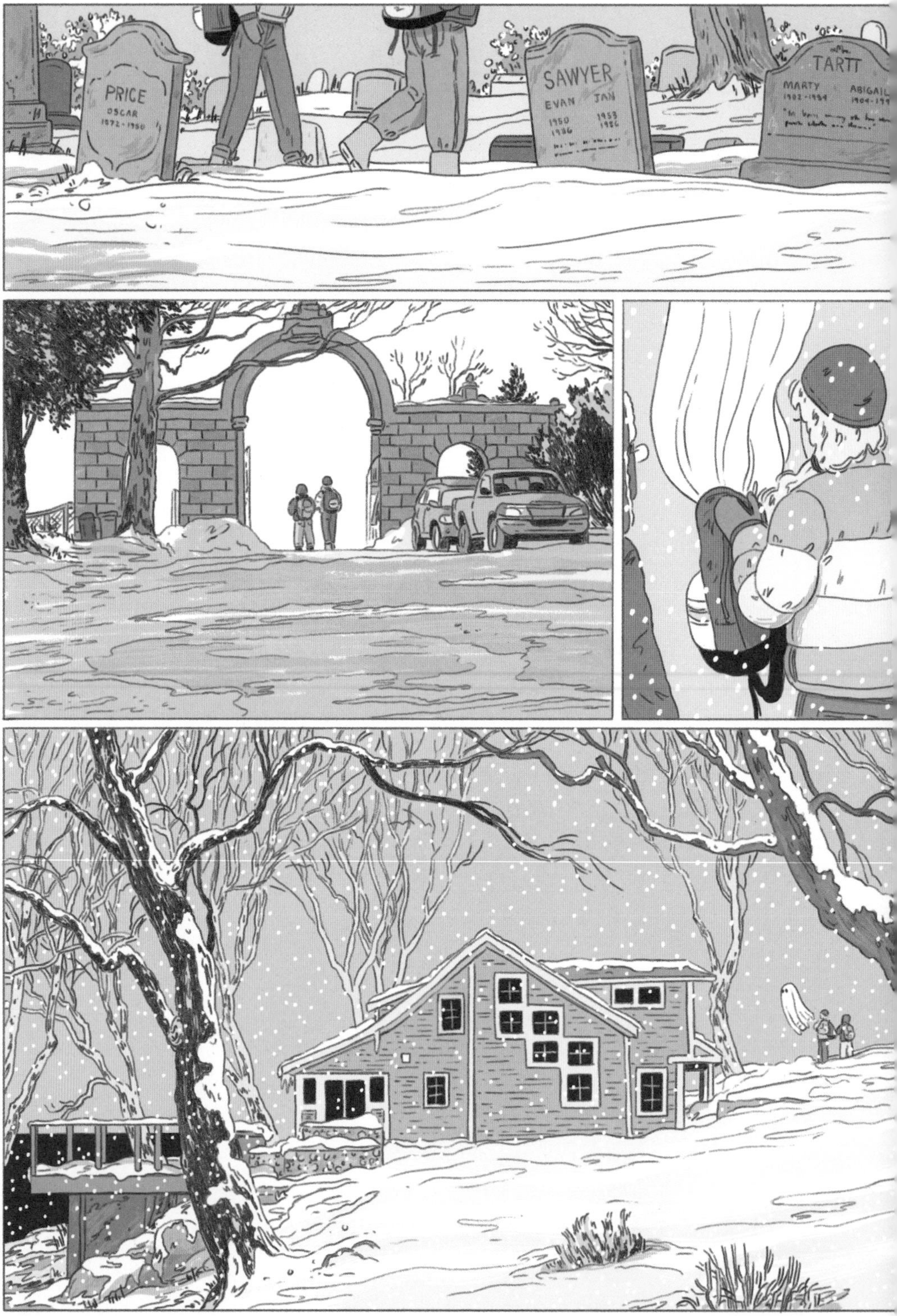
PRICE
OSCAR
SAWYER
EVAN
JAN
TARTT
MARTY

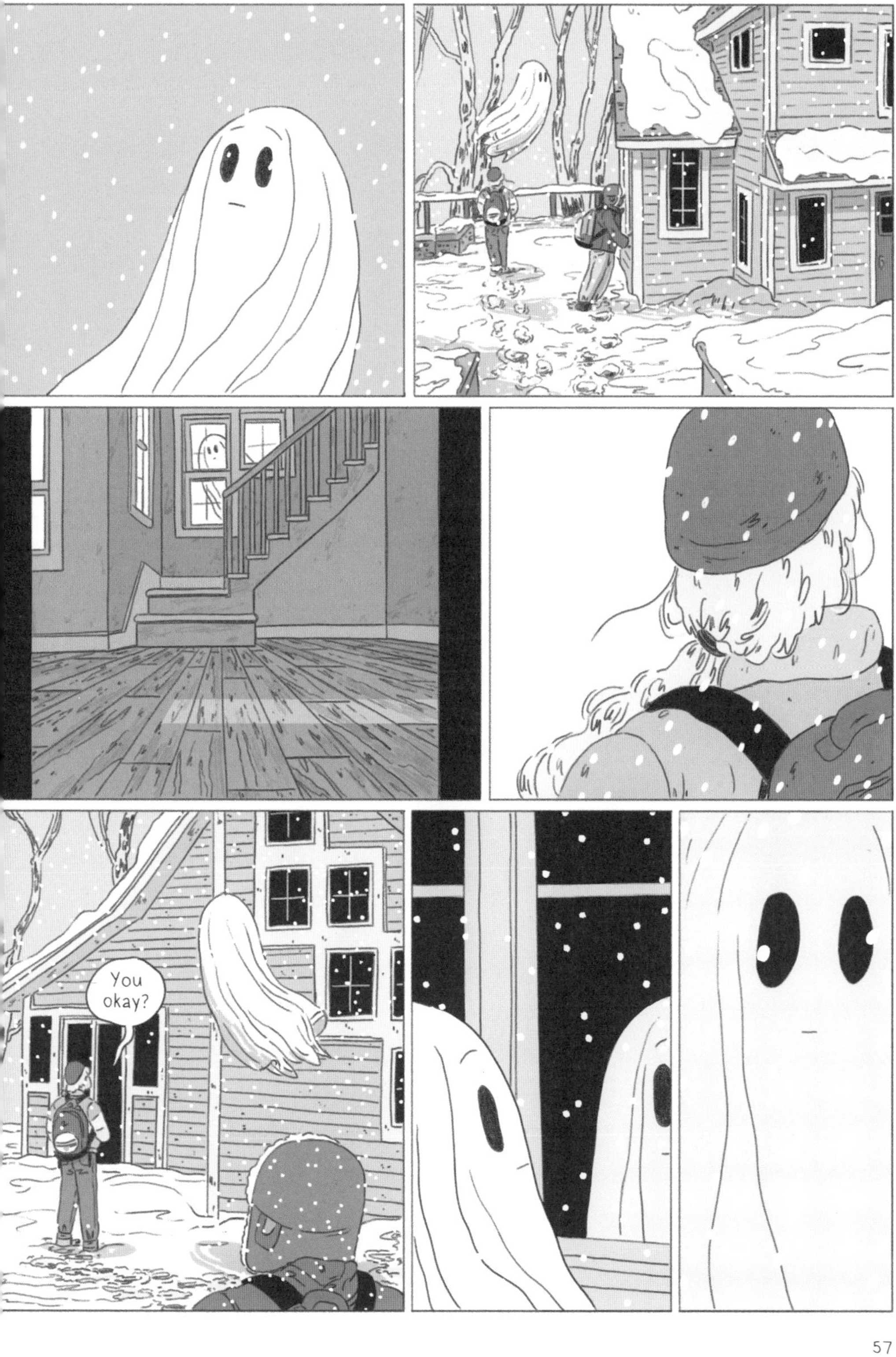
You okay?

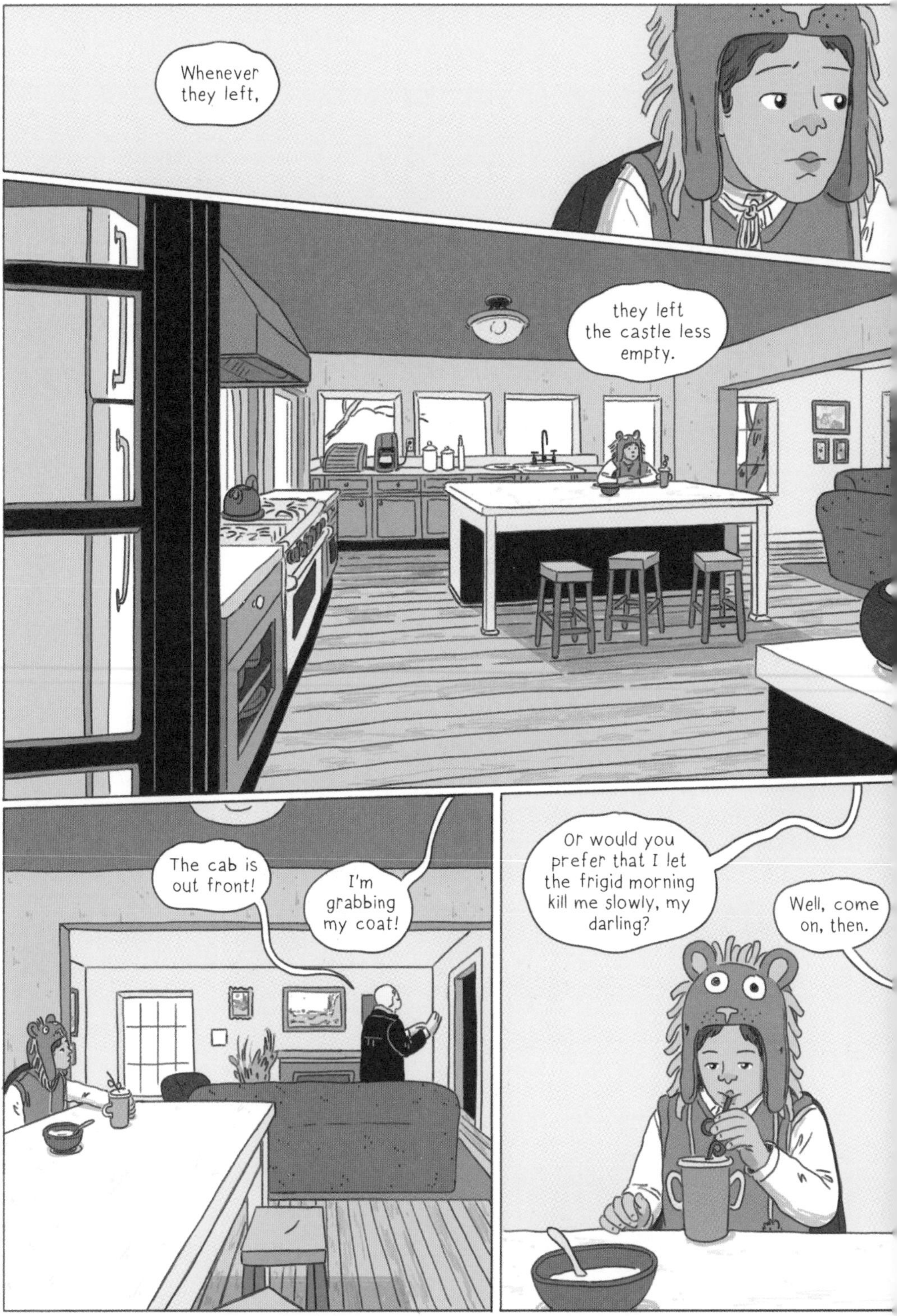

Whenever they left,
they left the castle less empty.
The cab is out front!
I'm grabbing my coat!
Or would you prefer that I let the frigid morning kill me slowly, my darling?
Well, come on, then.

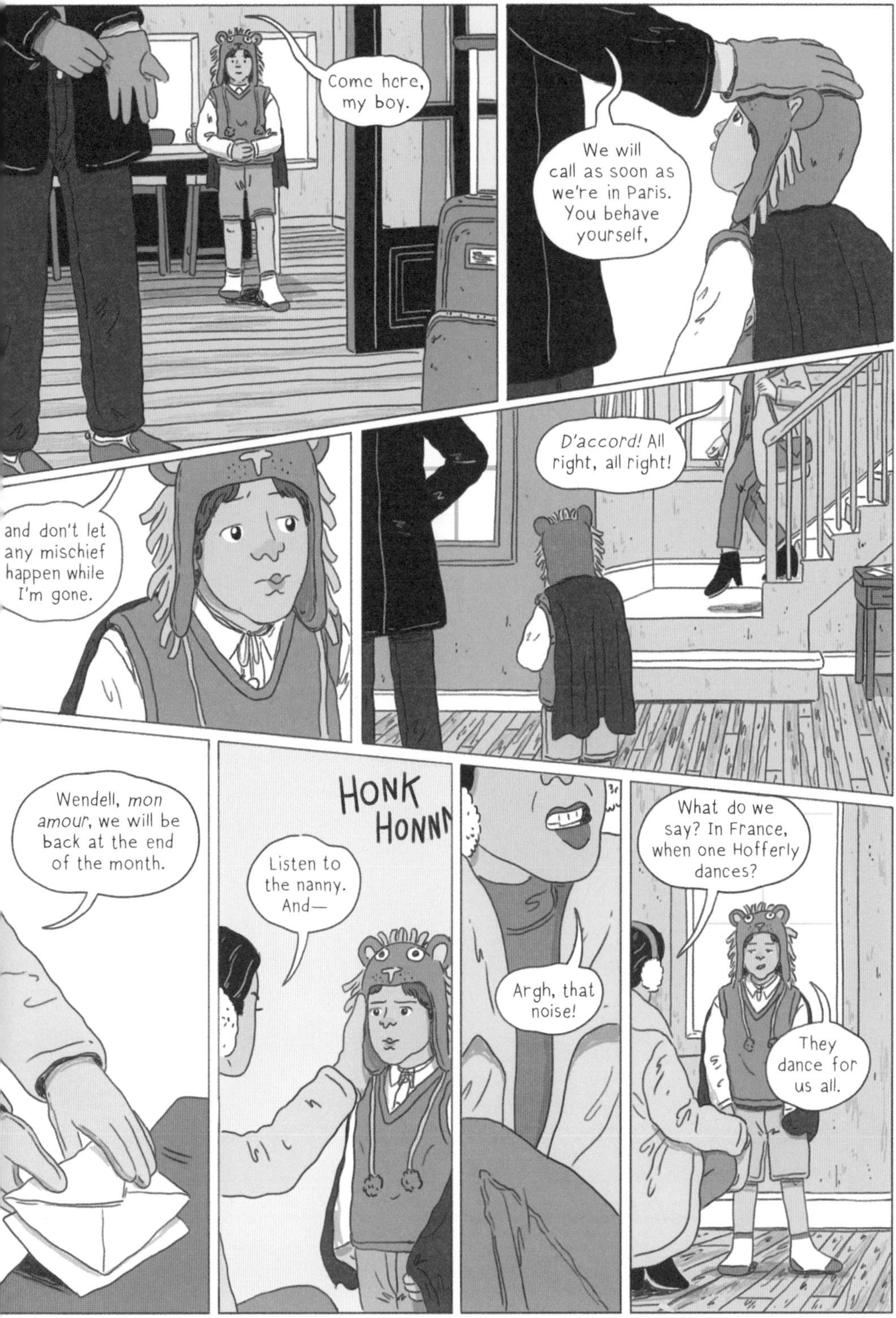
Come here, my boy.
We will call as soon as we're in Paris. You behave yourself,
and don't let any mischief happen while I'm gone.
D'accord! All right, all right!
Wendell, *mon amour*, we will be back at the end of the month.
HONK
HONNN
Listen to the nanny. And—
Argh, that noise!
What do we say? In France, when one Hofferly dances?
They dance for us all.

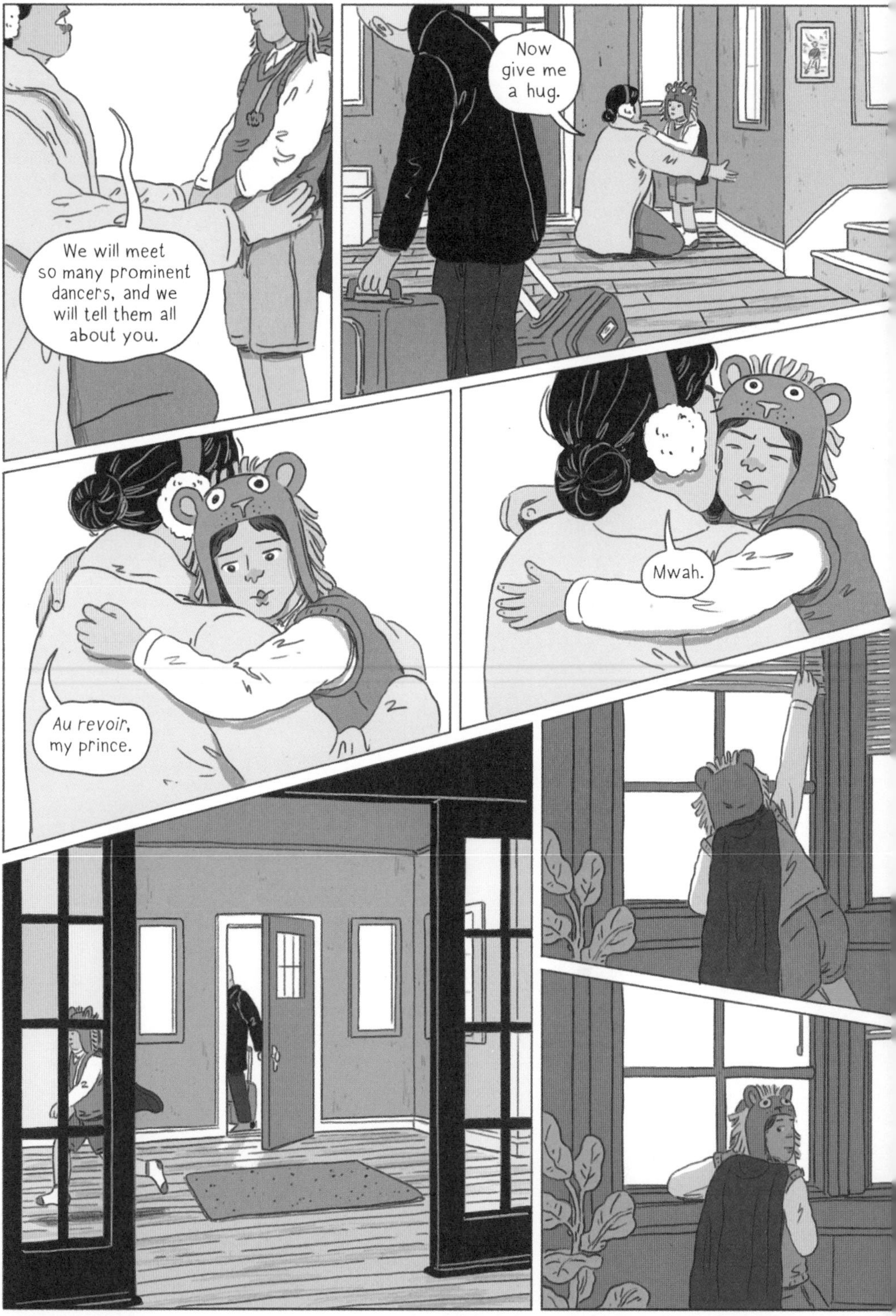
We will meet so many prominent dancers, and we will tell them all about you.
Now give me a hug.
Au revoir, my prince.
Mwah.

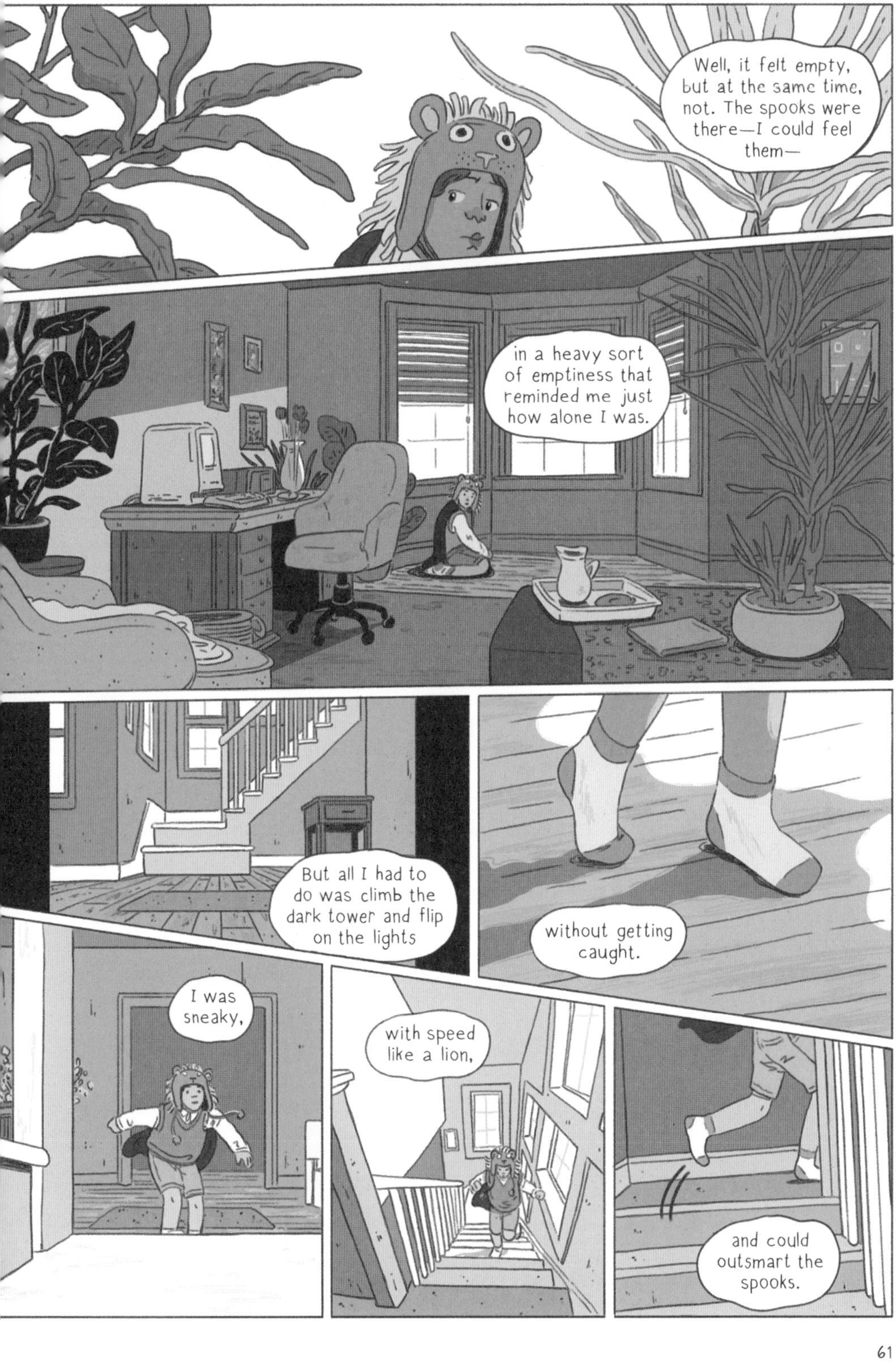
Well, it felt empty, but at the same time, not. The spooks were there—I could feel them—
in a heavy sort of emptiness that reminded me just how alone I was.
But all I had to do was climb the dark tower and flip on the lights
without getting caught.
I was sneaky,
with speed like a lion,
and could outsmart the spooks.

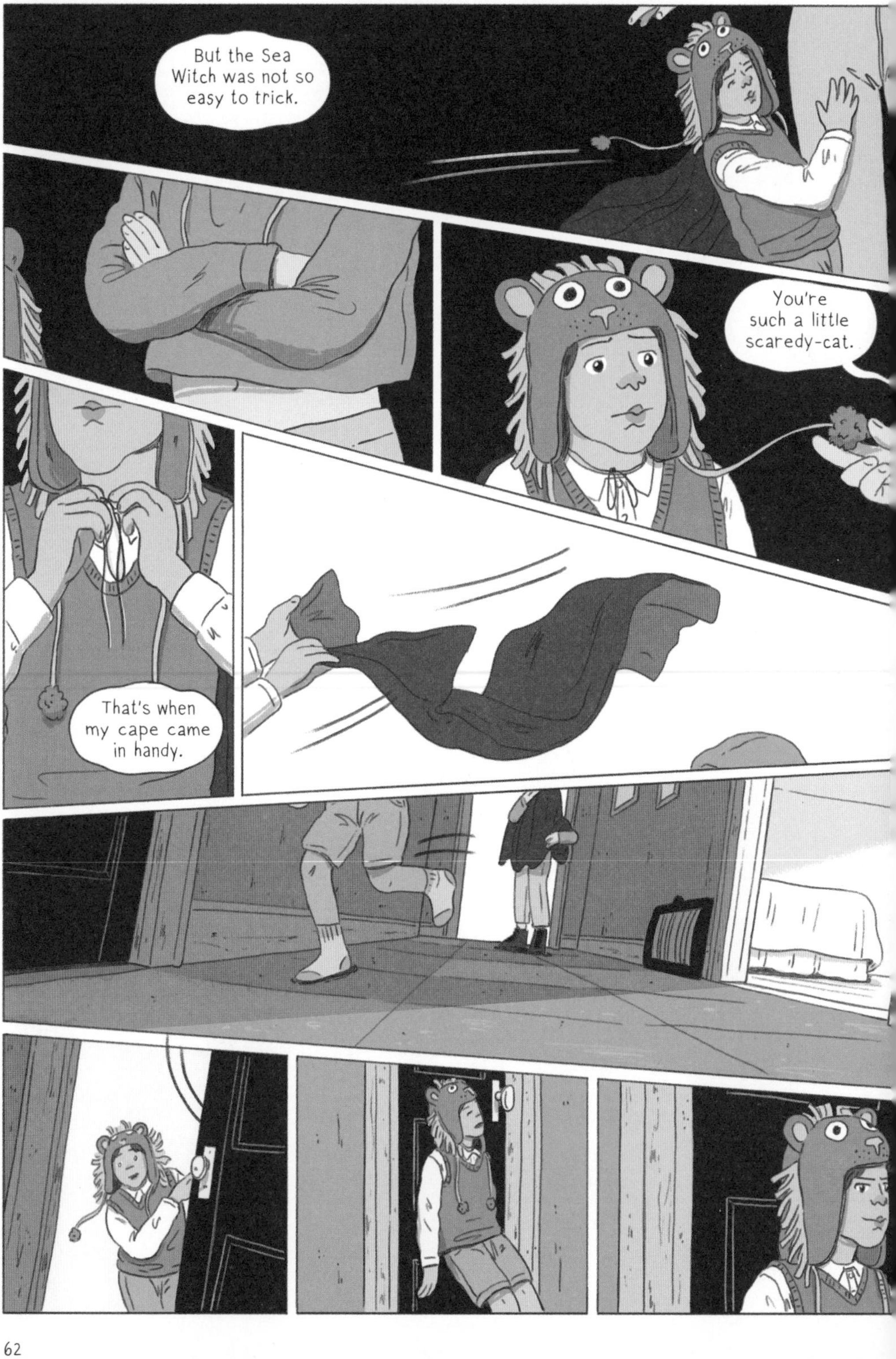
But the Sea Witch was not so easy to trick.
You're such a little scaredy-cat.
That's when my cape came in handy.

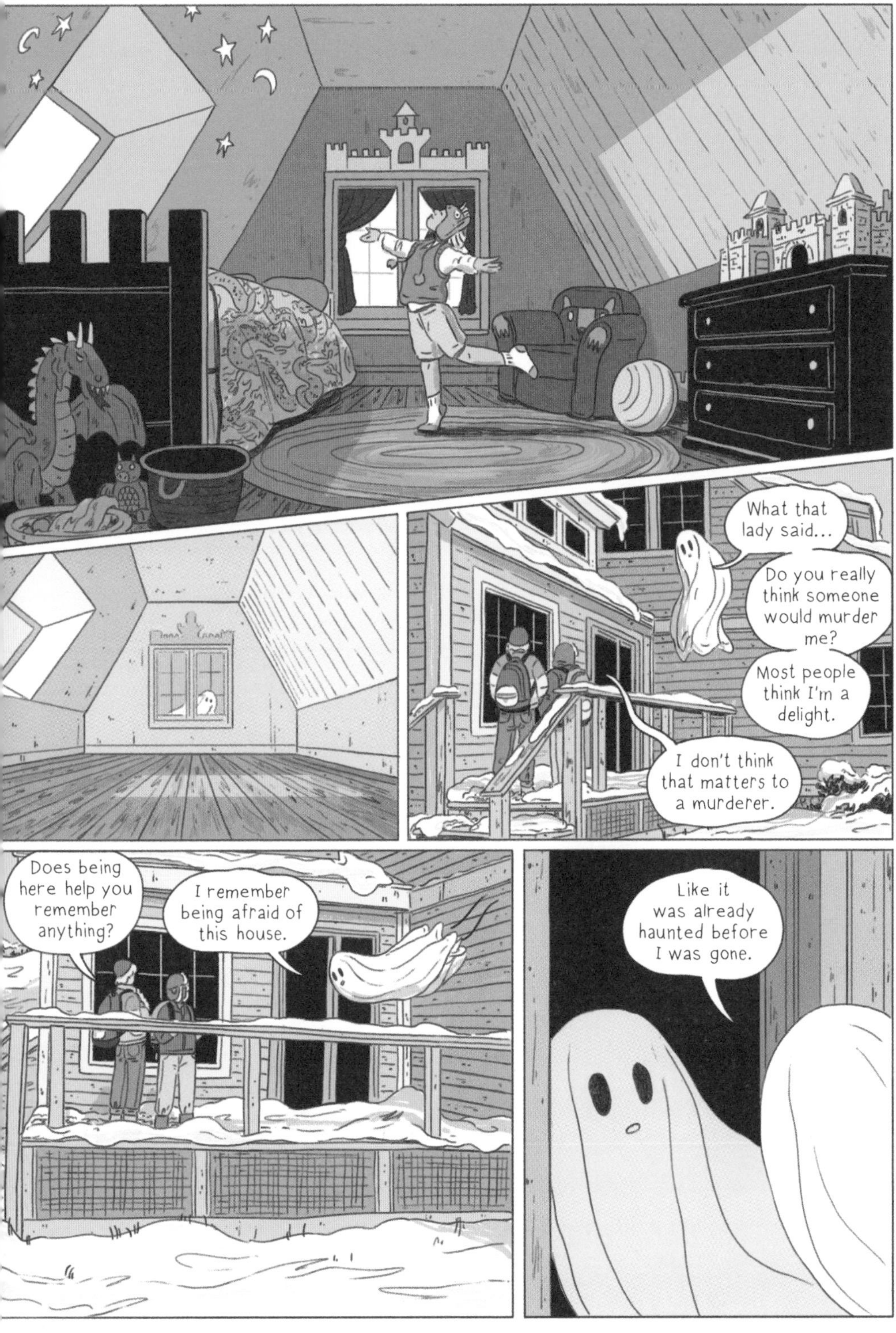
What that lady said...
Do you really think someone would murder me?
Most people think I'm a delight.
I don't think that matters to a murderer.
Does being here help you remember anything?
I remember being afraid of this house.
Like it was already haunted before I was gone.

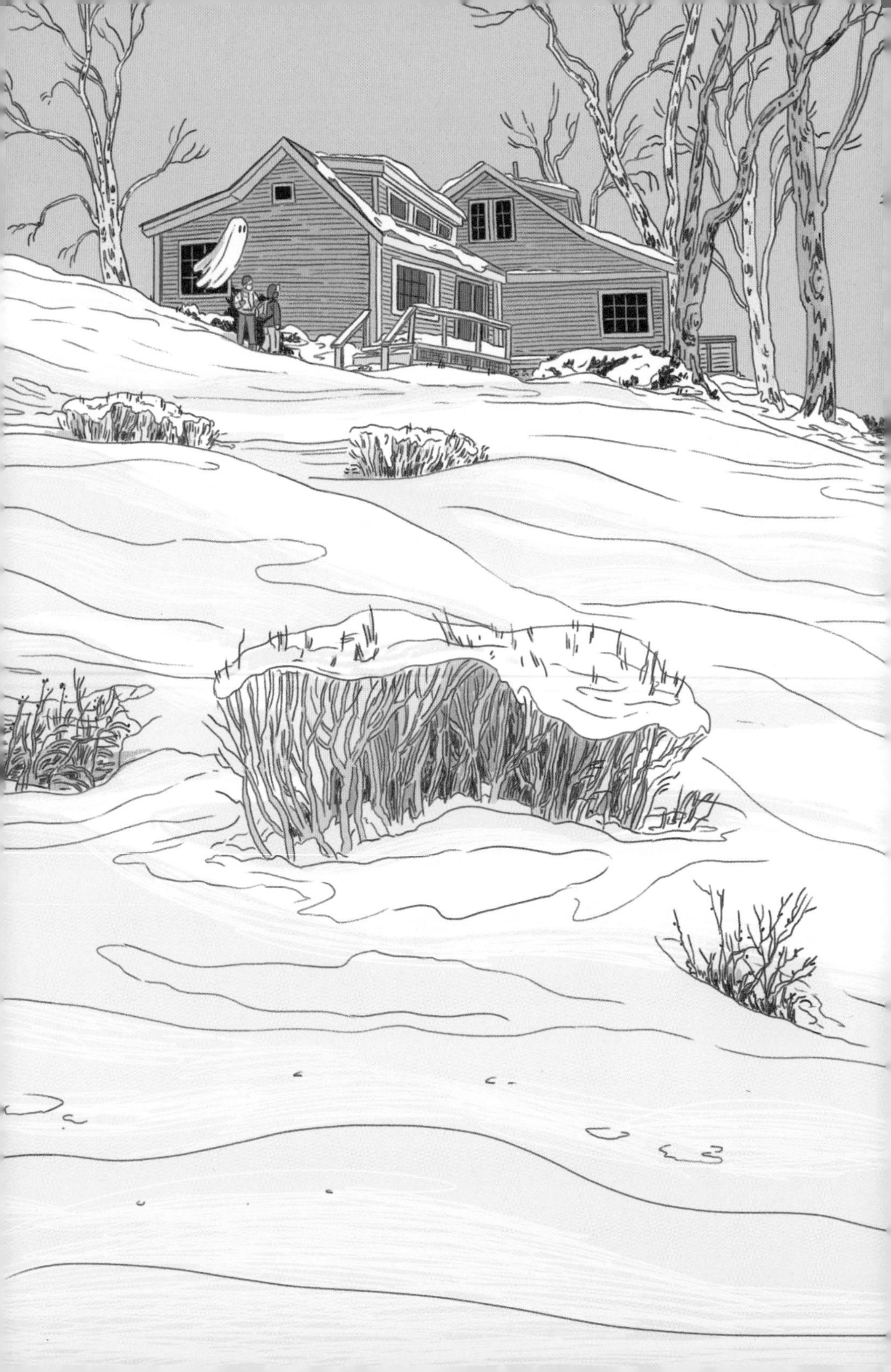

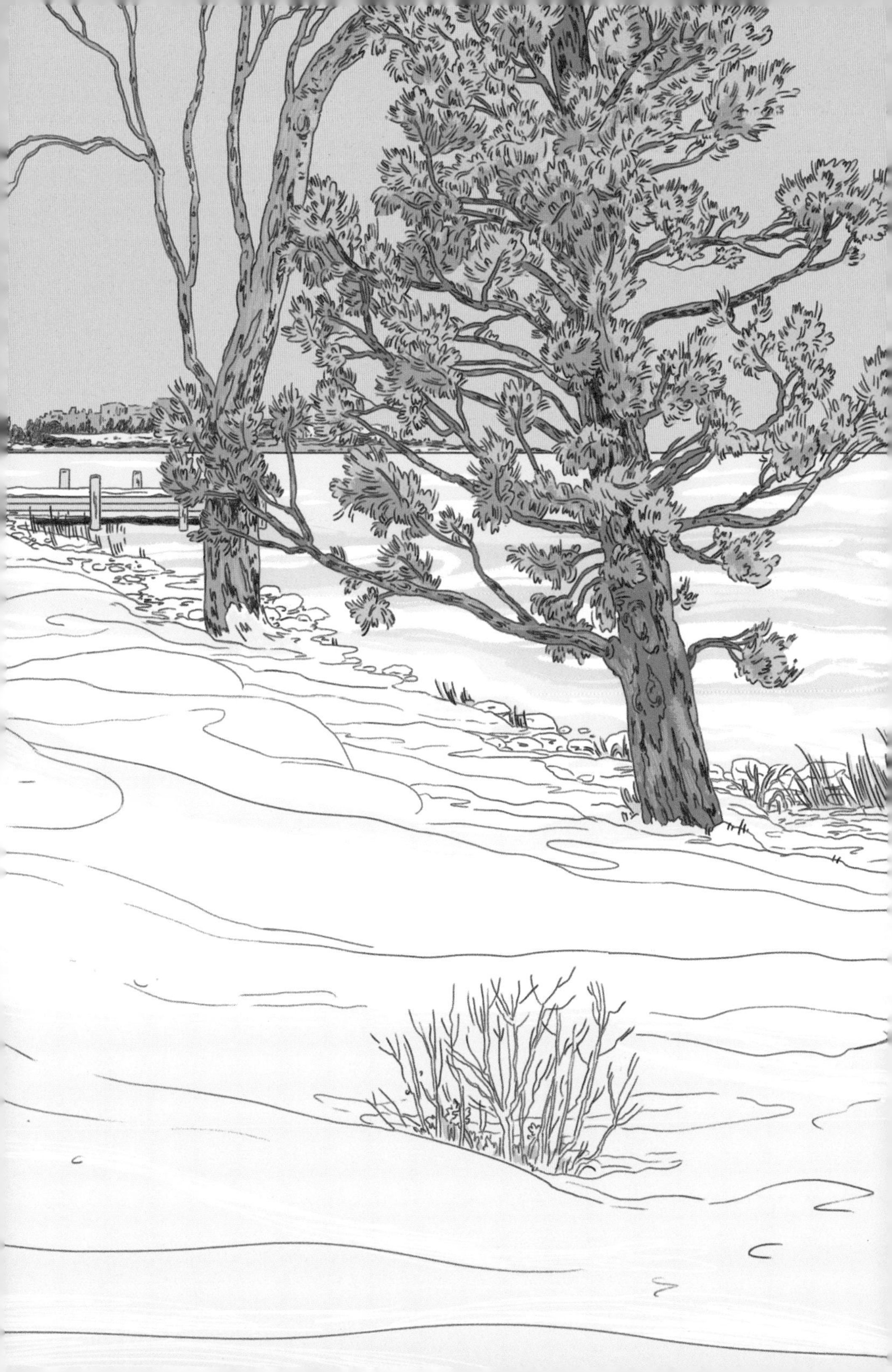

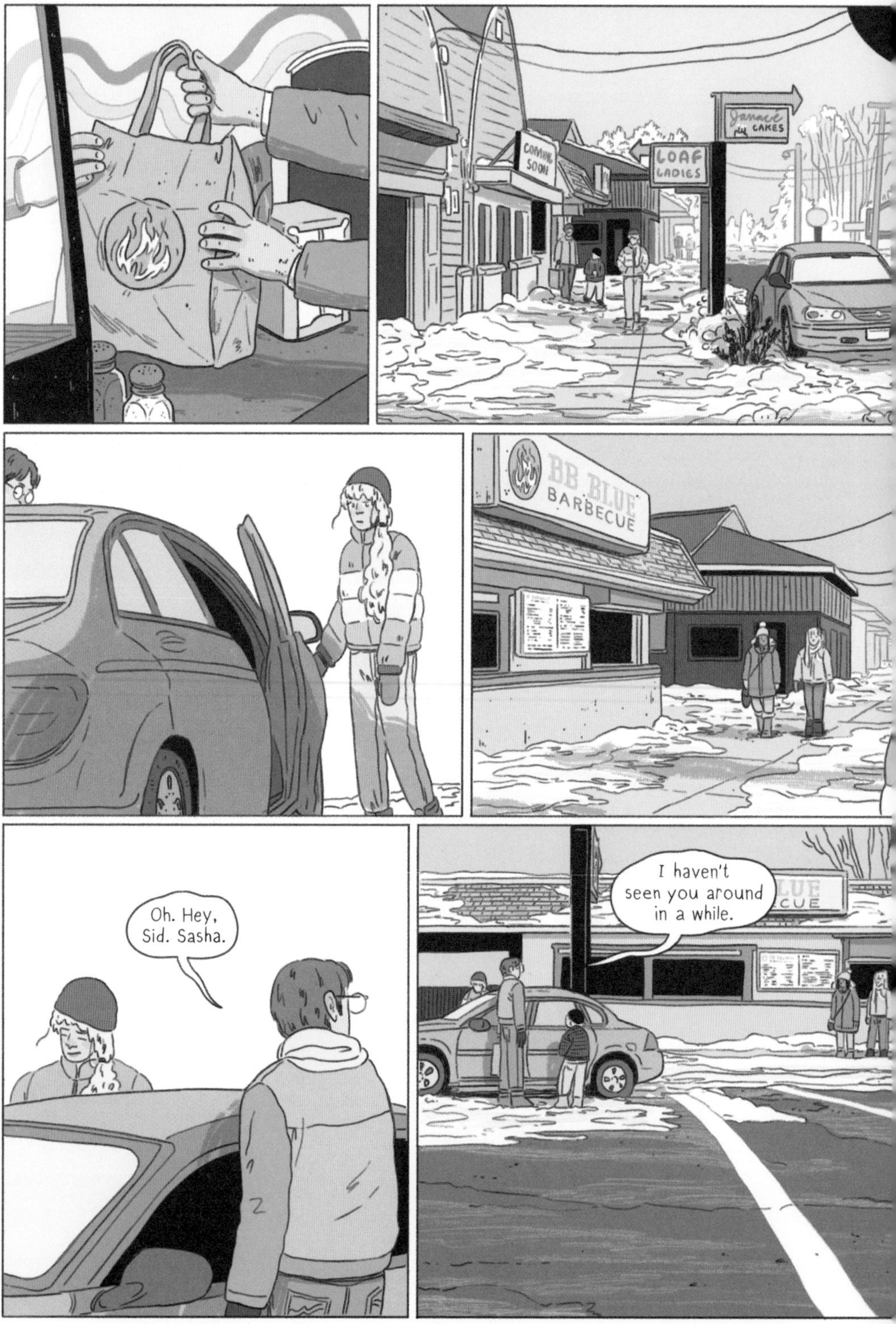
COMING SOON
LOAF LADIES
CAKES
BB BLUE BARBECUE
Oh. Hey, Sid. Sasha.
I haven't seen you around in a while.

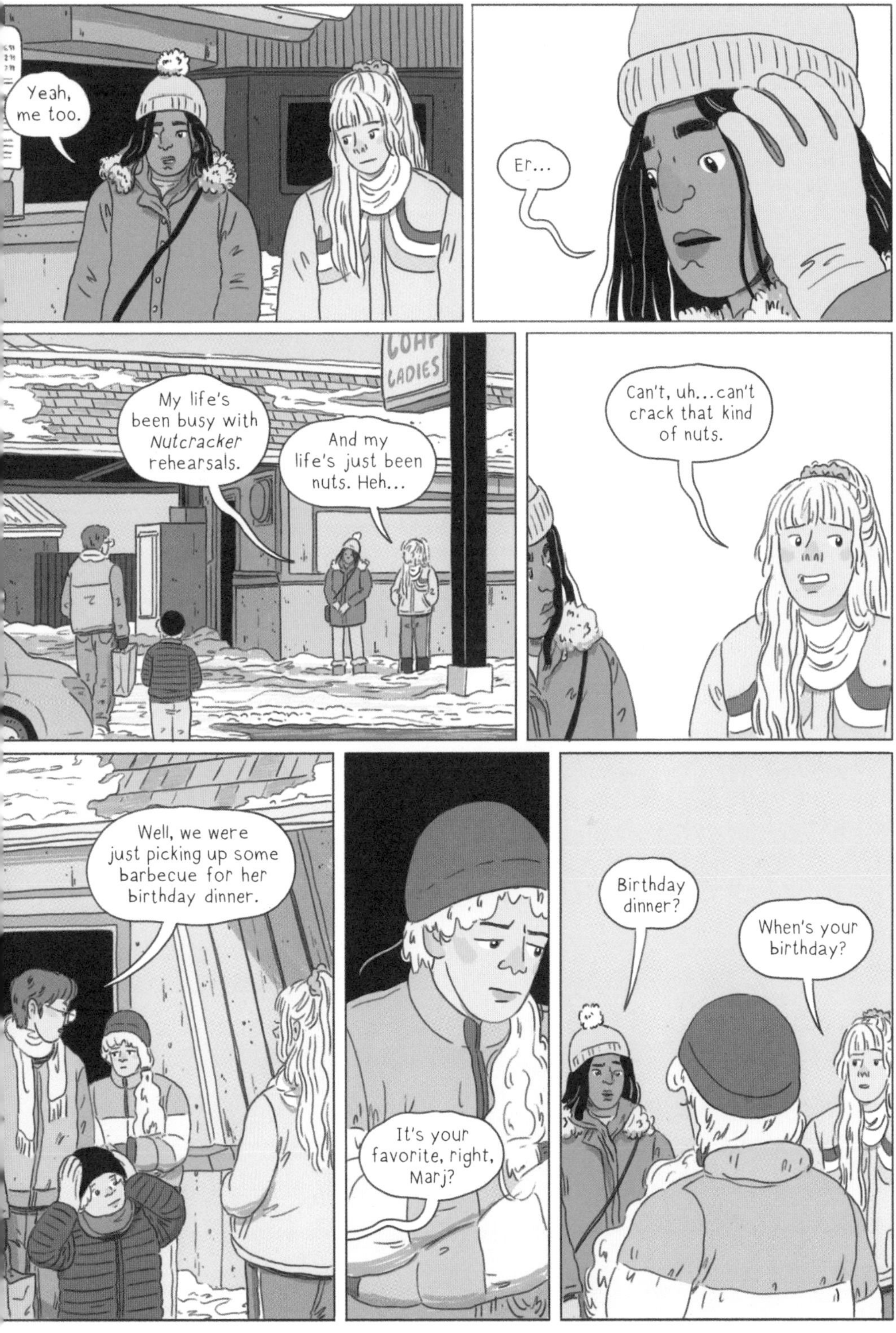
Yeah, me too.
Er...
COAP
LADIES
My life's been busy with *Nutcracker* rehearsals.
And my life's just been nuts. Heh...
Can't, uh...can't crack that kind of nuts.
Well, we were just picking up some barbecue for her birthday dinner.
It's your favorite, right, Marj?
Birthday dinner?
When's your birthday?

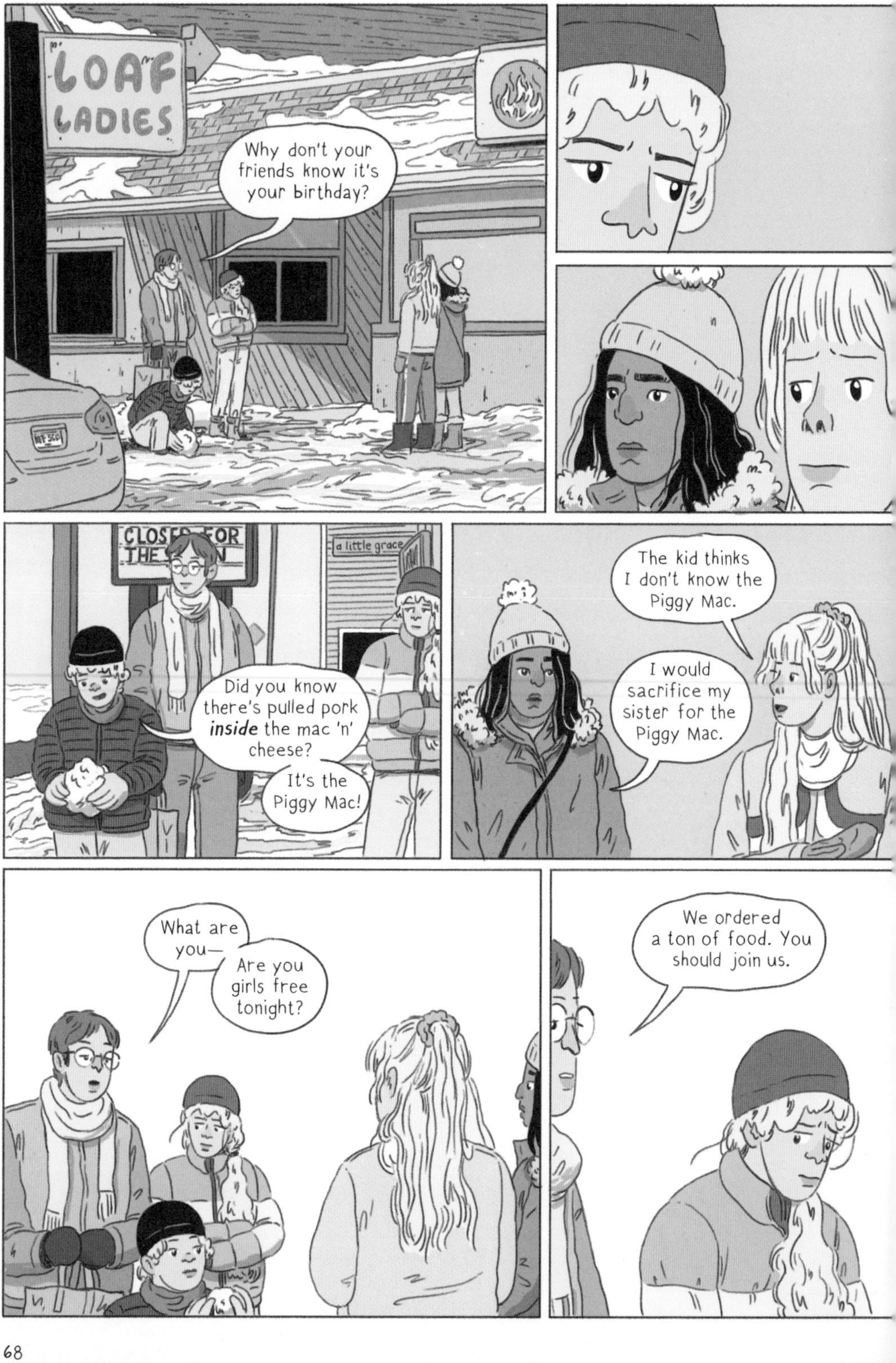
LOAF LADIES
Why don't your friends know it's your birthday?
CLOSED FOR THE
a little grace
Did you know there's pulled pork *inside* the mac 'n' cheese?
It's the Piggy Mac!
The kid thinks I don't know the Piggy Mac.
I would sacrifice my sister for the Piggy Mac.
What are you—
Are you girls free tonight?
We ordered a ton of food. You should join us.

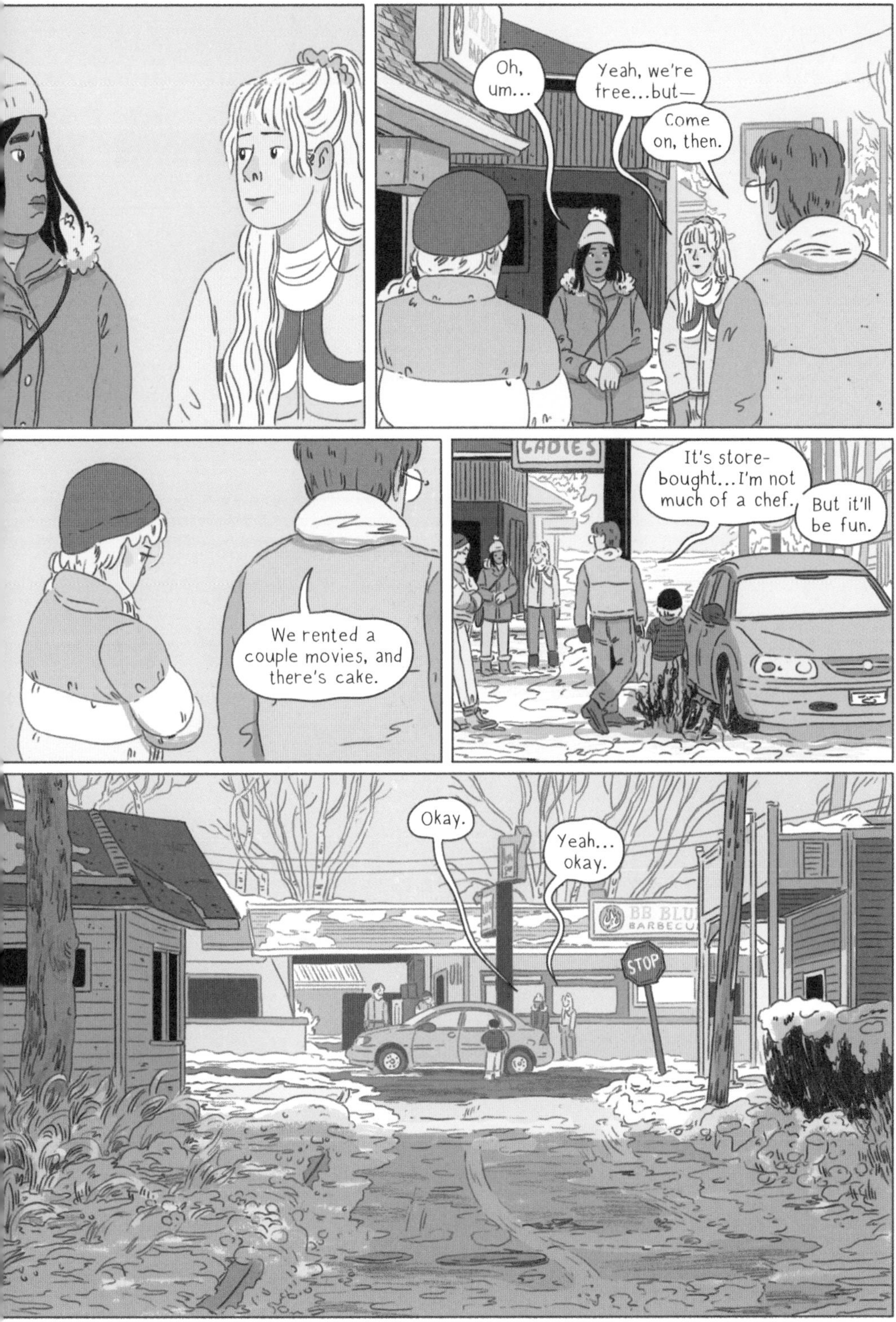
Oh, um...
Yeah, we're free...but—
Come on, then.
We rented a couple movies, and there's cake.
It's store-bought...I'm not much of a chef.
But it'll be fun.
Okay.
Yeah... okay.
BB BLU
BARBECU
STOP

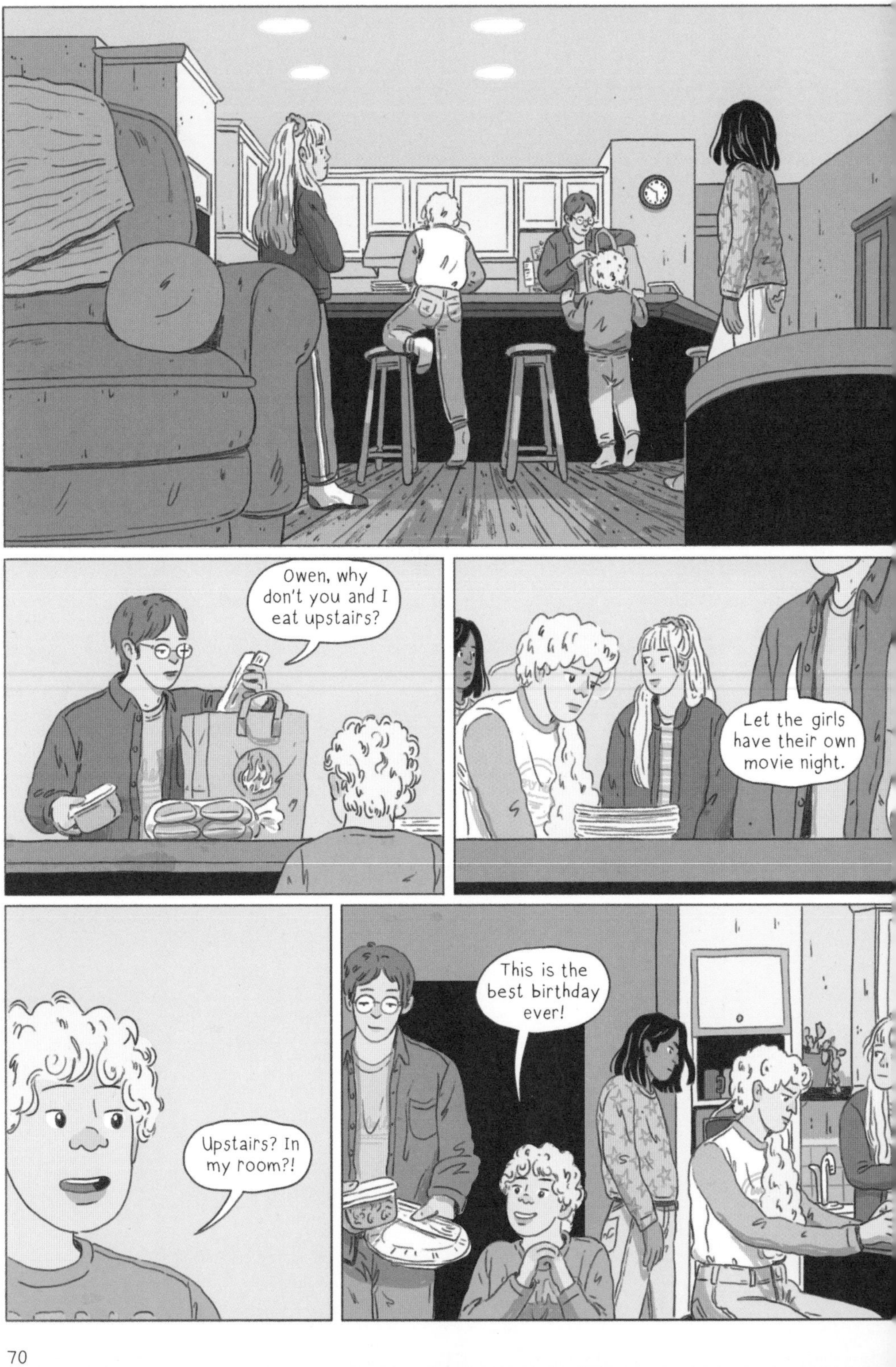
Owen, why don't you and I eat upstairs?
Let the girls have their own movie night.
Upstairs? In my room?!
This is the best birthday ever!

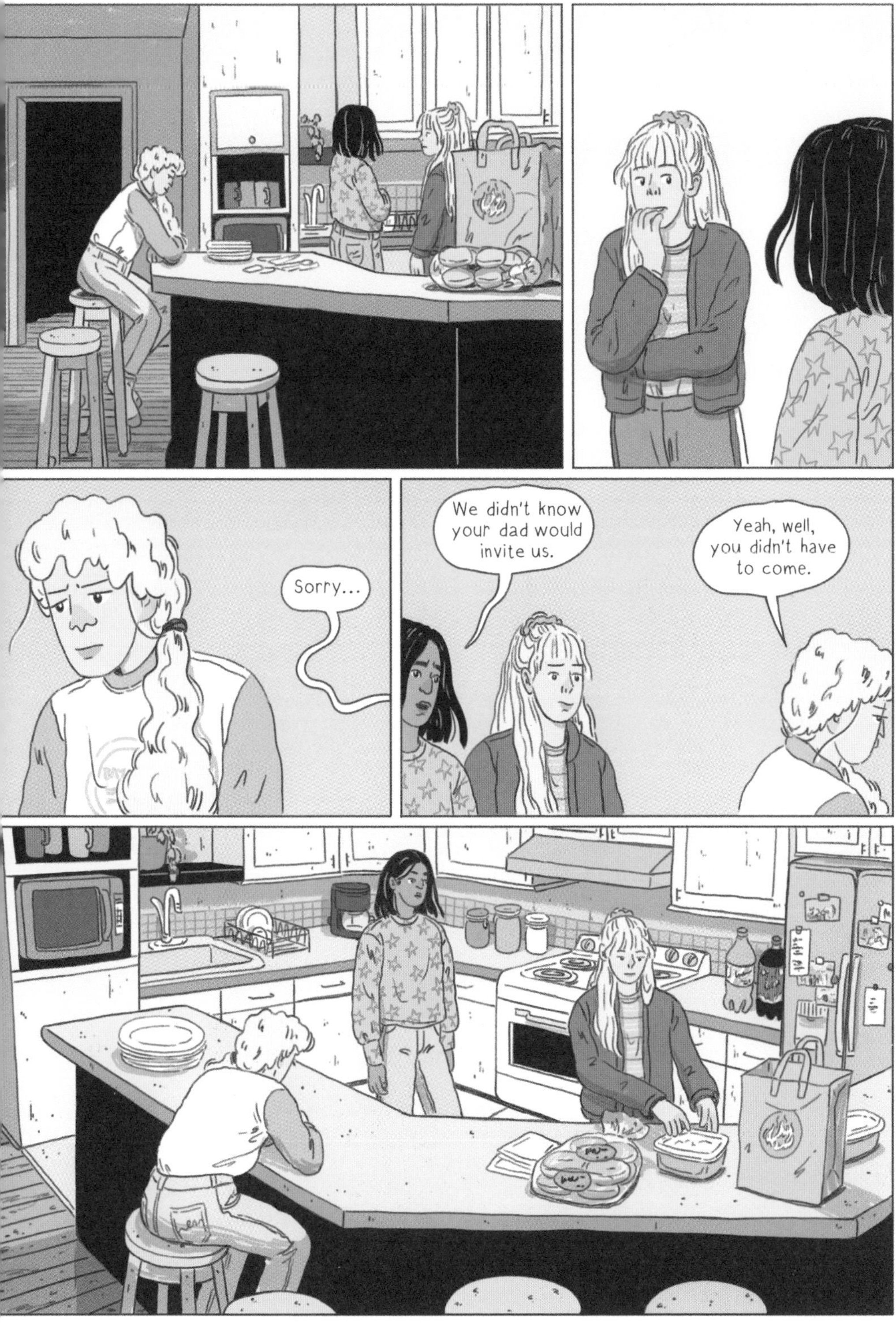
Sorry...
We didn't know your dad would invite us.
Yeah, well, you didn't have to come.

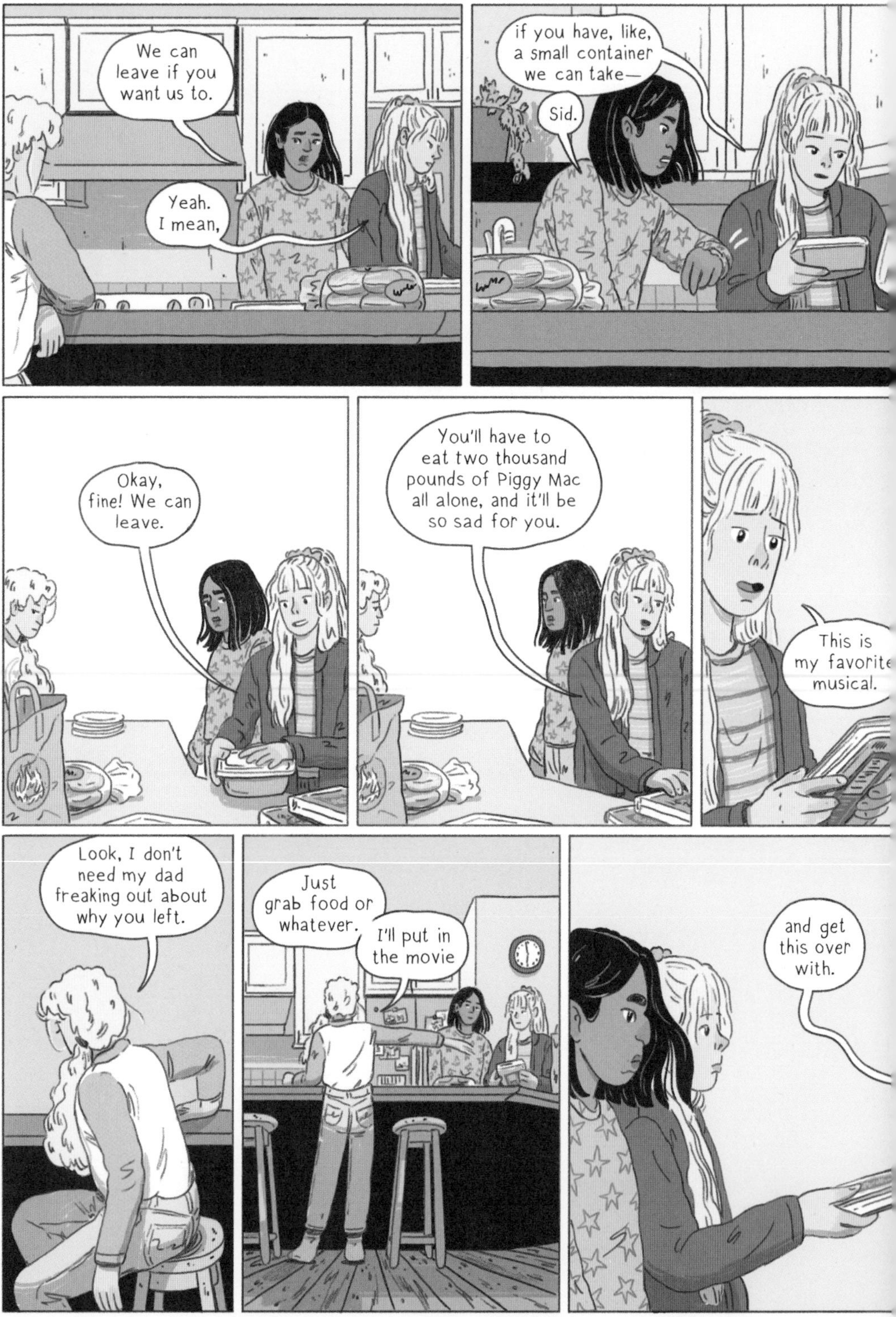
We can leave if you want us to.
Yeah. I mean,
if you have, like, a small container we can take—
Sid.
Okay, fine! We can leave.
You'll have to eat two thousand pounds of Piggy Mac all alone, and it'll be so sad for you.
This is my favorite musical.
Look, I don't need my dad freaking out about why you left.
Just grab food or whatever.
I'll put in the movie
and get this over with.

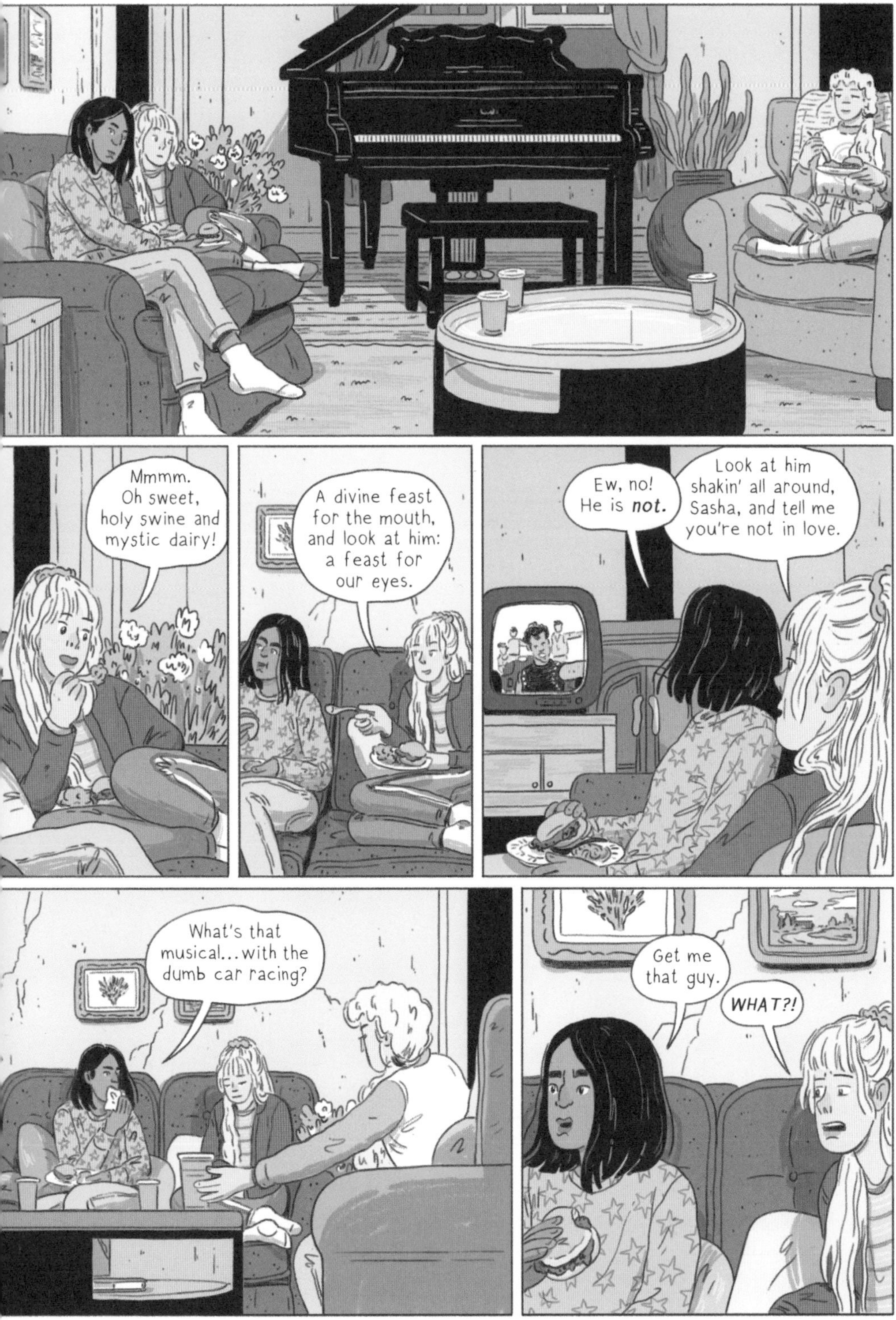

Mmmm. Oh sweet, holy swine and mystic dairy!
A divine feast for the mouth, and look at him: a feast for our eyes.
Look at him shakin' all around, Sasha, and tell me you're not in love.
Ew, no! He is **not.**
What's that musical... with the dumb car racing?
Get me that guy.
WHAT?!

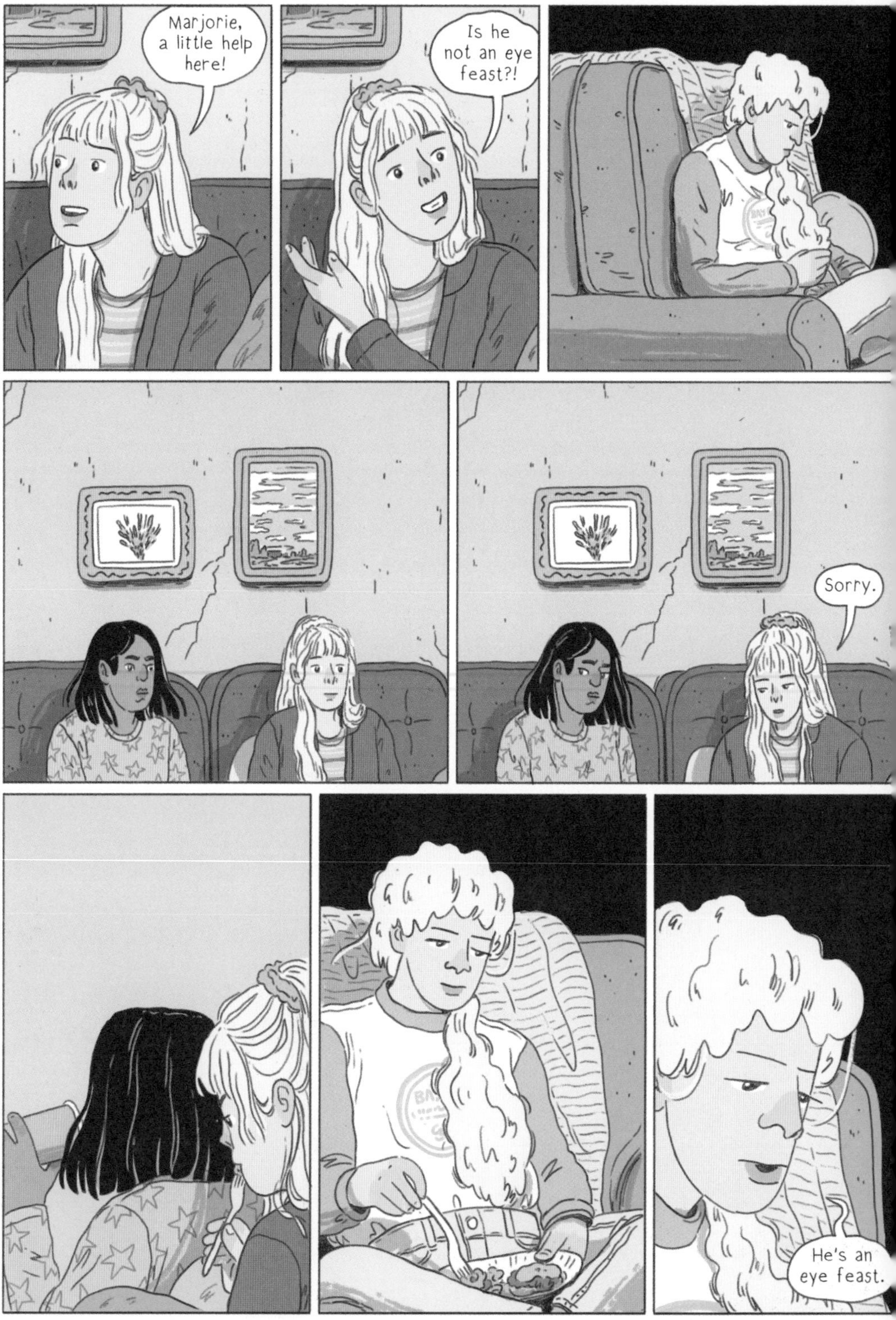
Marjorie, a little help here!
Is he not an eye feast?!
Sorry.
He's an eye feast.

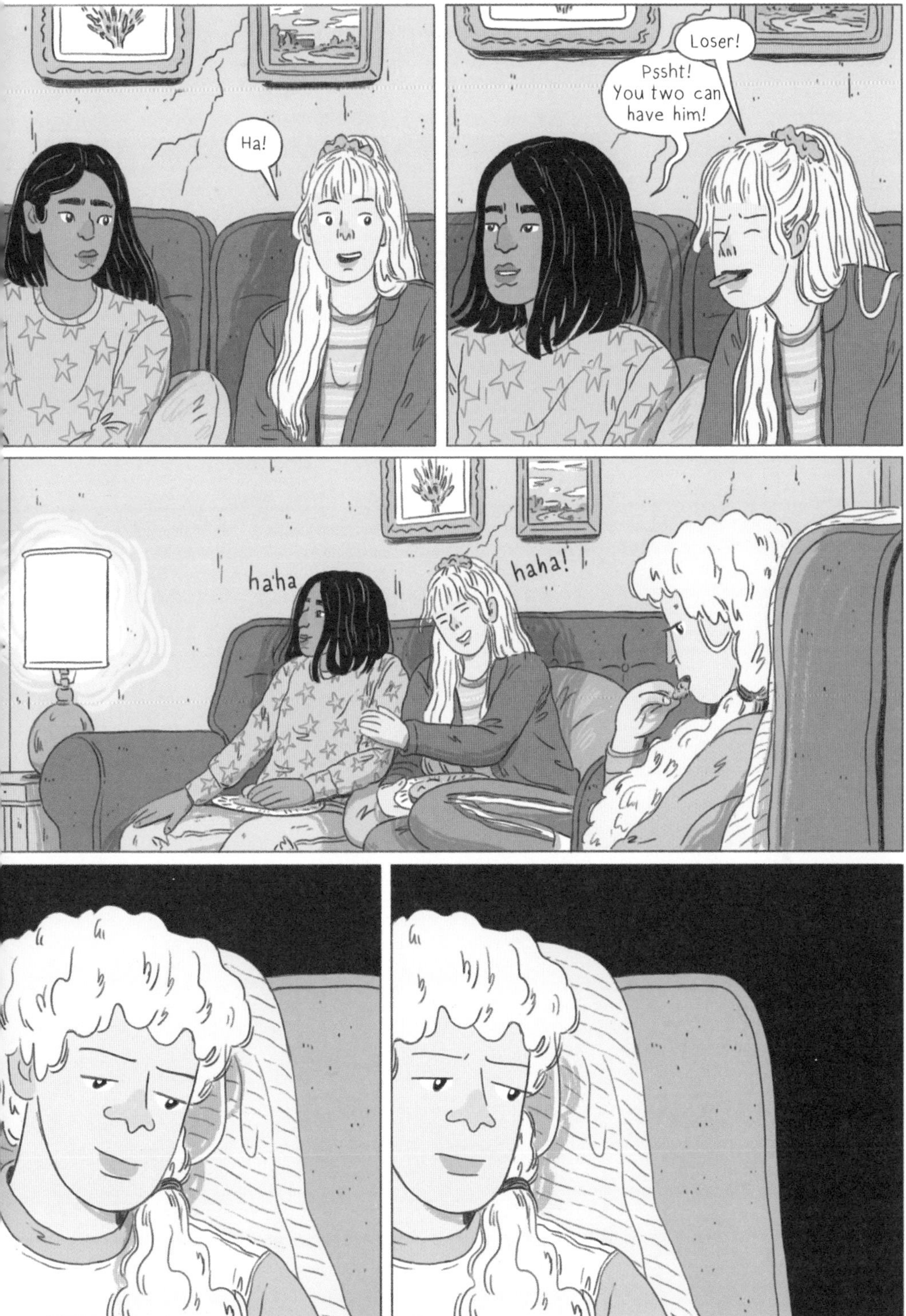
Ha!
Loser!
Pssht! You two can have him!
haha
haha!

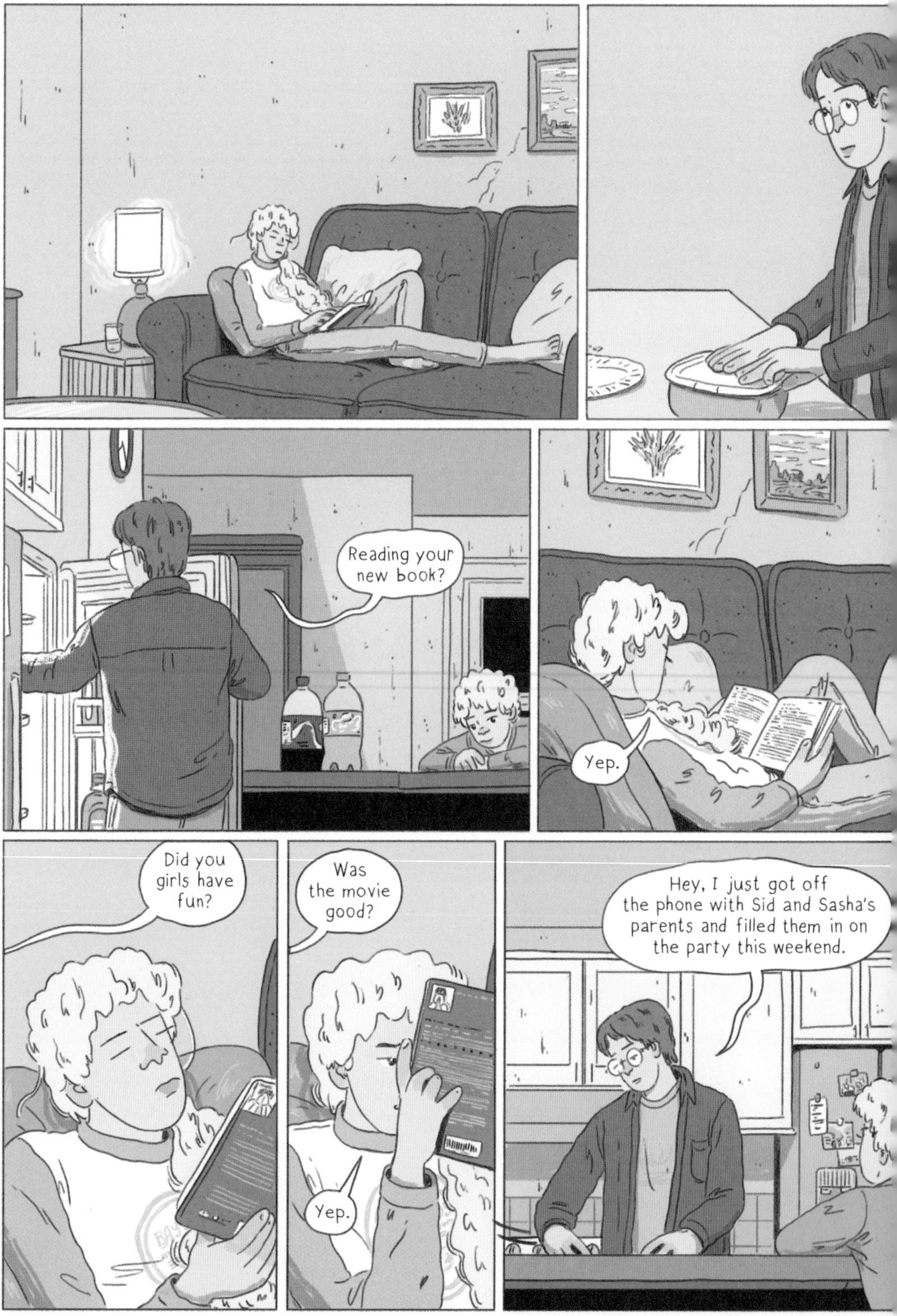

Reading your new book?
Yep.
Did you girls have fun?
Was the movie good?
Yep.
Hey, I just got off the phone with Sid and Sasha's parents and filled them in on the party this weekend.

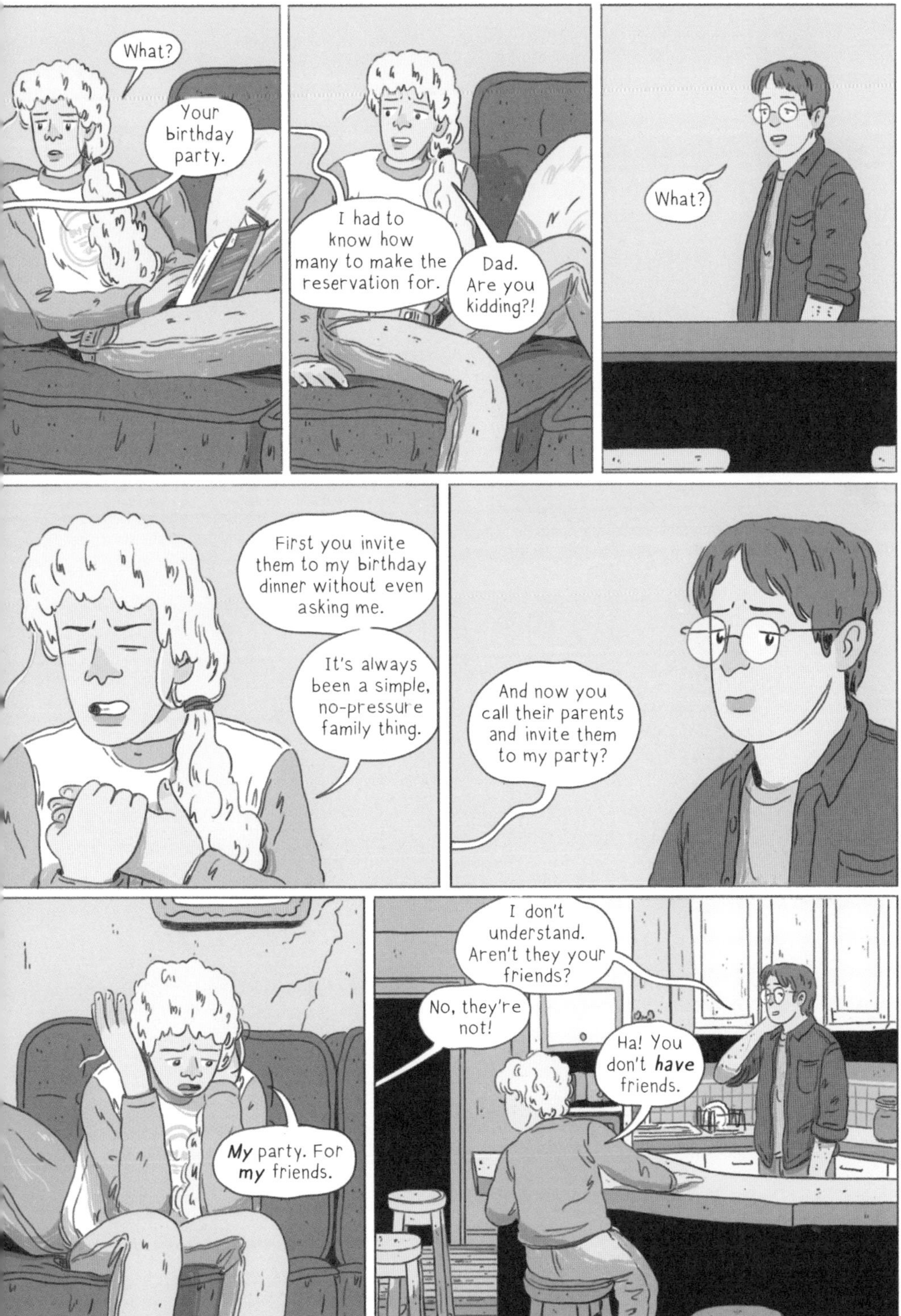
What?
Your birthday party.
I had to know how many to make the reservation for.
Dad. Are you kidding?!
What?
First you invite them to my birthday dinner without even asking me.
It's always been a simple, no-pressure family thing.
And now you call their parents and invite them to my party?
My party. For my friends.
I don't understand. Aren't they your friends?
No, they're not!
Ha! You don't have friends.

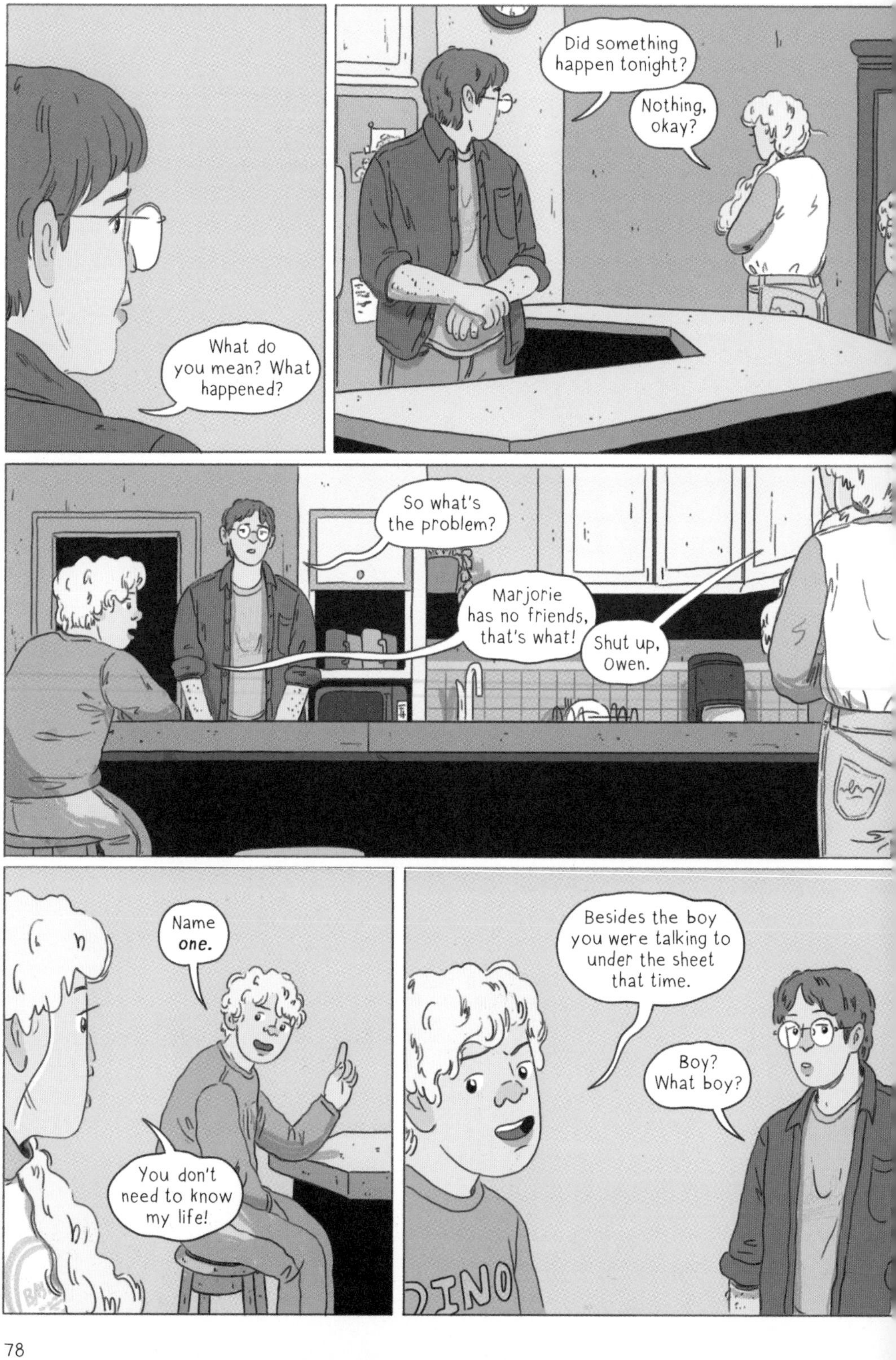
What do you mean? What happened?
Did something happen tonight?
Nothing, okay?
So what's the problem?
Marjorie has no friends, that's what!
Shut up, Owen.
Name **one.**
You don't need to know my life!
Besides the boy you were talking to under the sheet that time.
Boy? What boy?
DINO

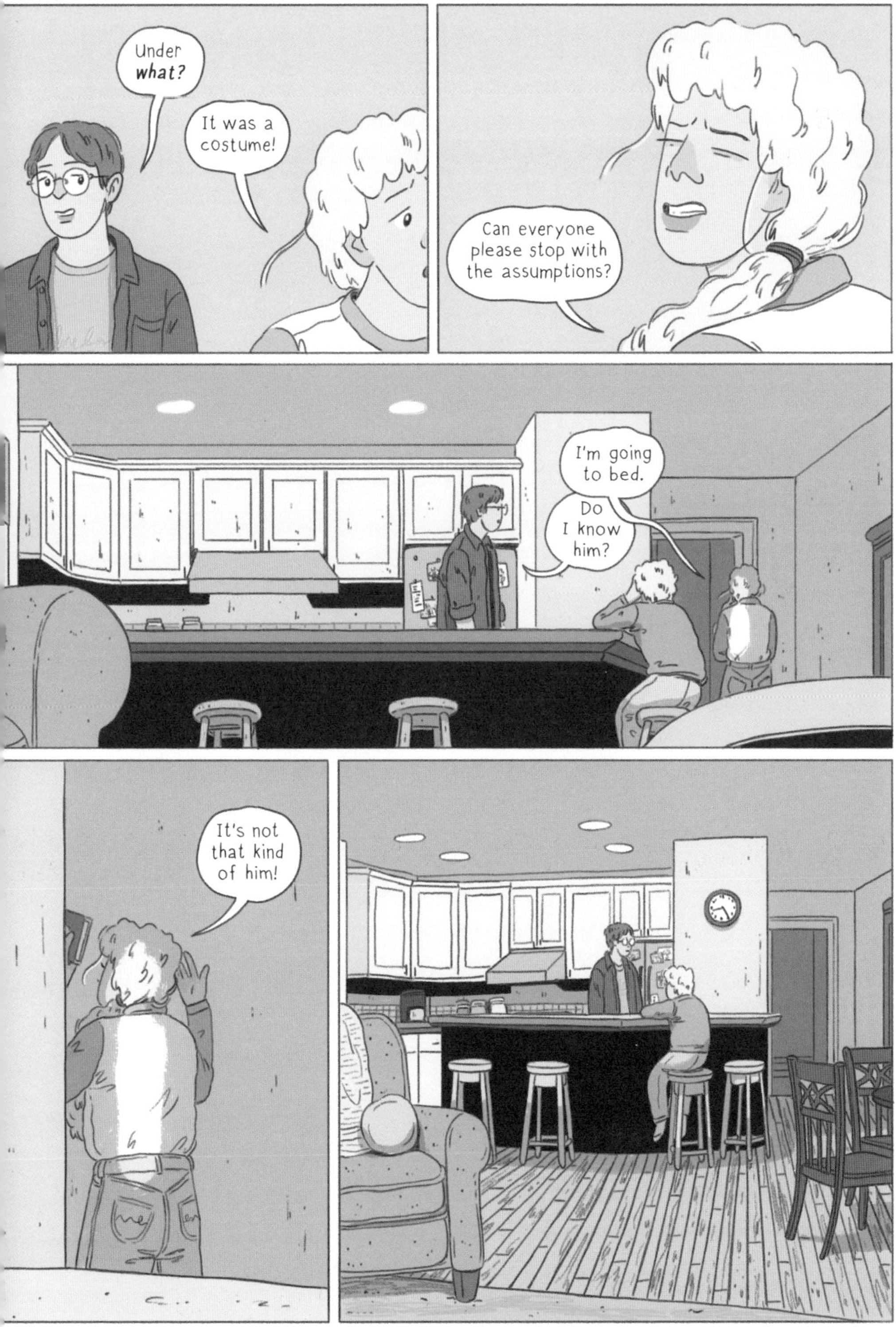

Under **what?**
It was a costume!
Can everyone please stop with the assumptions?
I'm going to bed.
Do I know him?
It's not that kind of him!

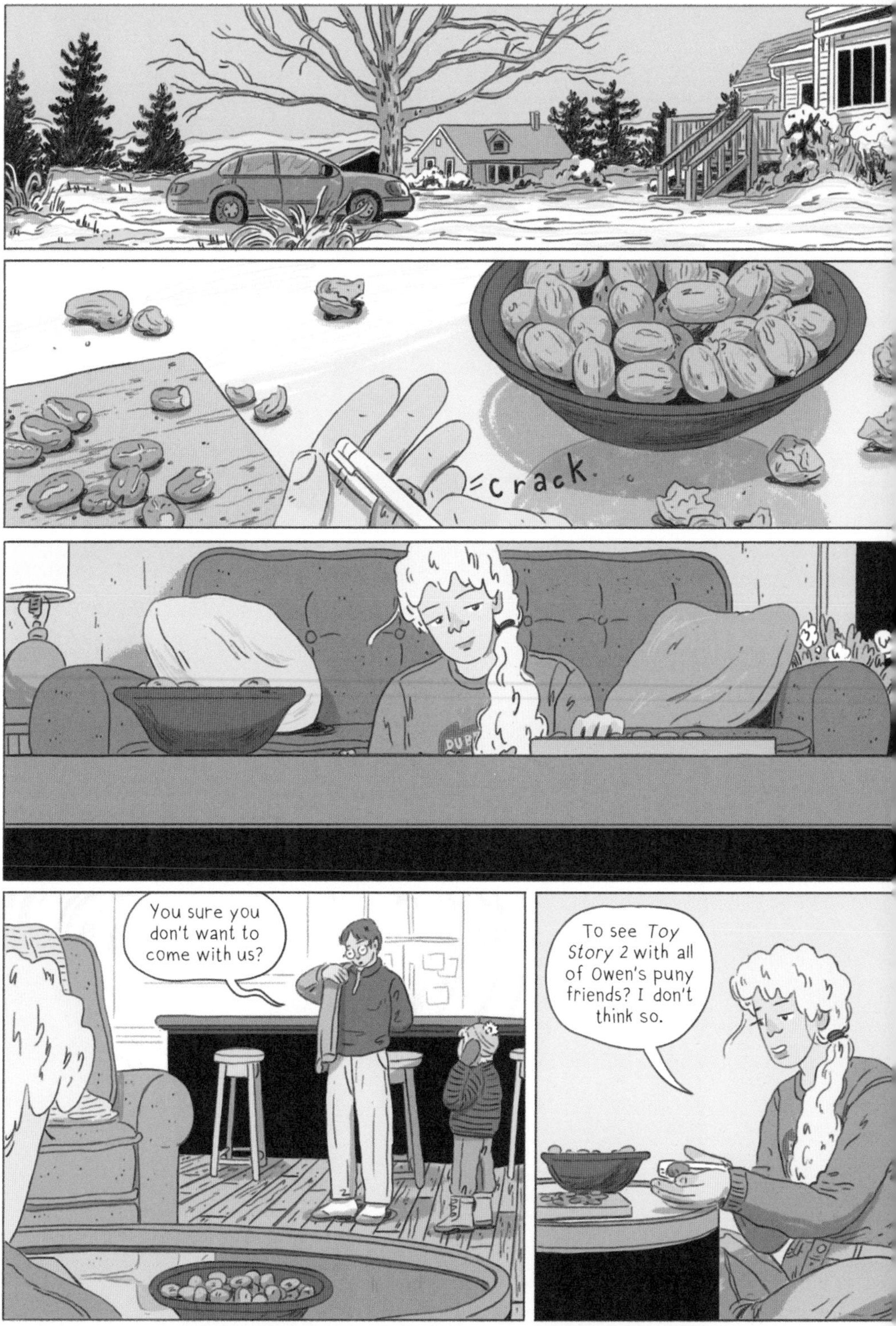
crack
DUP
You sure you don't want to come with us?
To see *Toy Story 2* with all of Owen's puny friends? I don't think so.

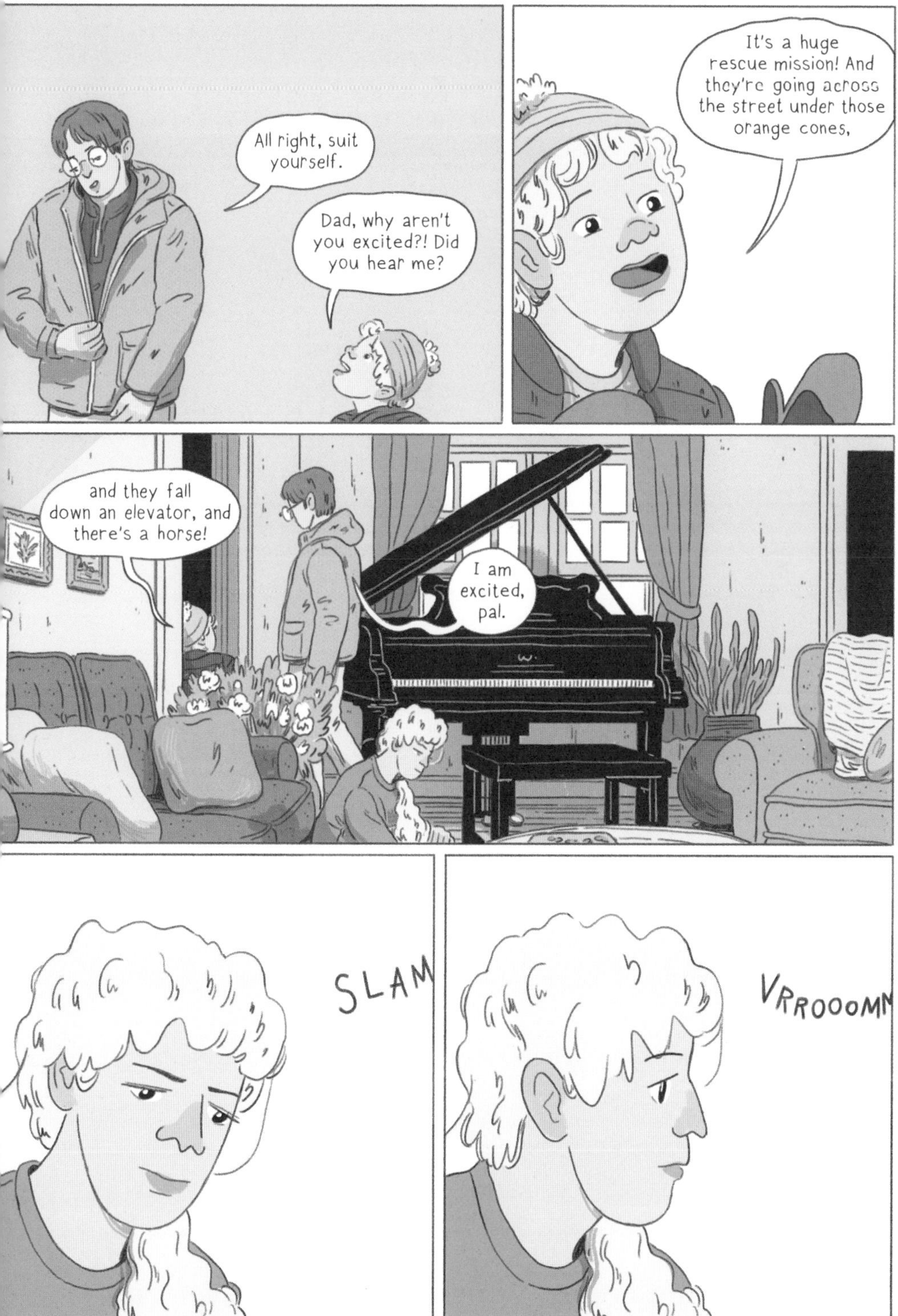
All right, suit yourself.
Dad, why aren't you excited?! Did you hear me?
It's a huge rescue mission! And they're going across the street under those orange cones,
and they fall down an elevator, and there's a horse!
I am excited, pal.
SLAM
VRROOOMM

Hey, Wendell! You can come out now!

What's that?

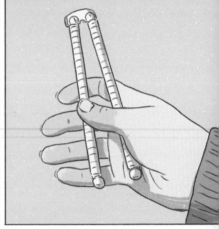

A nutcracker. We do this every Thanksgiving for Mom's pecan pie.

That doesn't look like a nutcracker.

What do you think a nutcracker looks like?

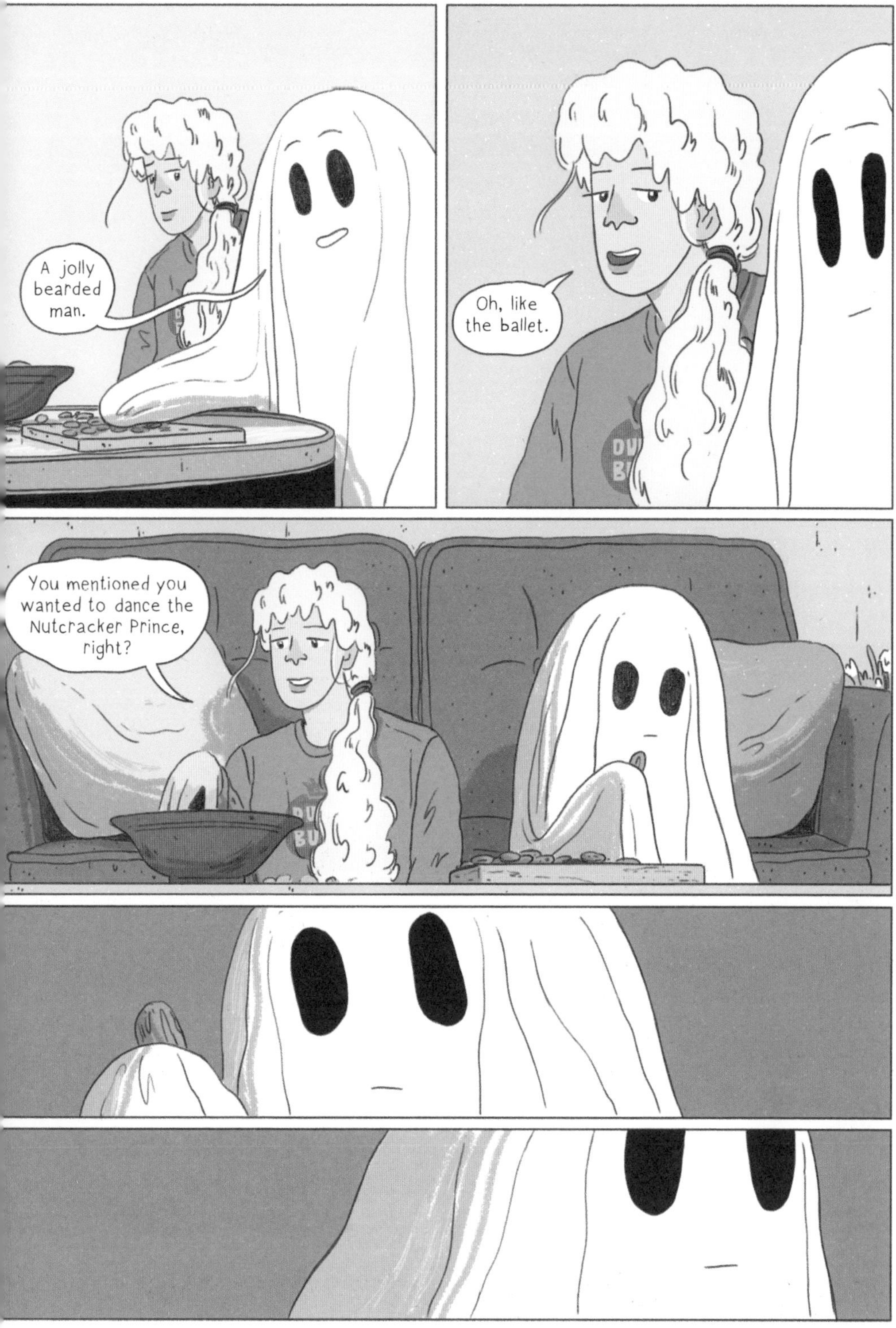
A jolly bearded man.
Oh, like the ballet.
You mentioned you wanted to dance the Nutcracker Prince, right?

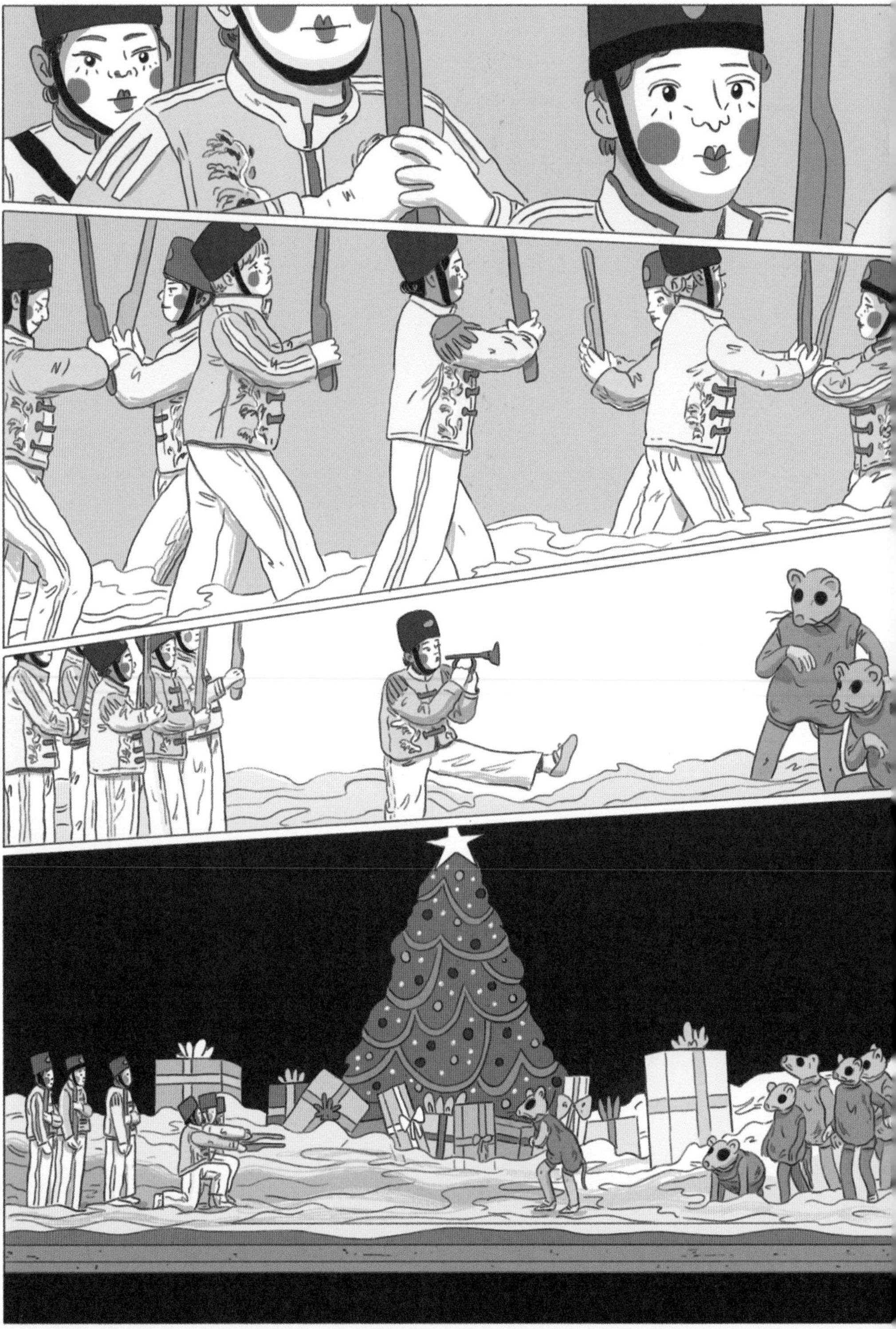

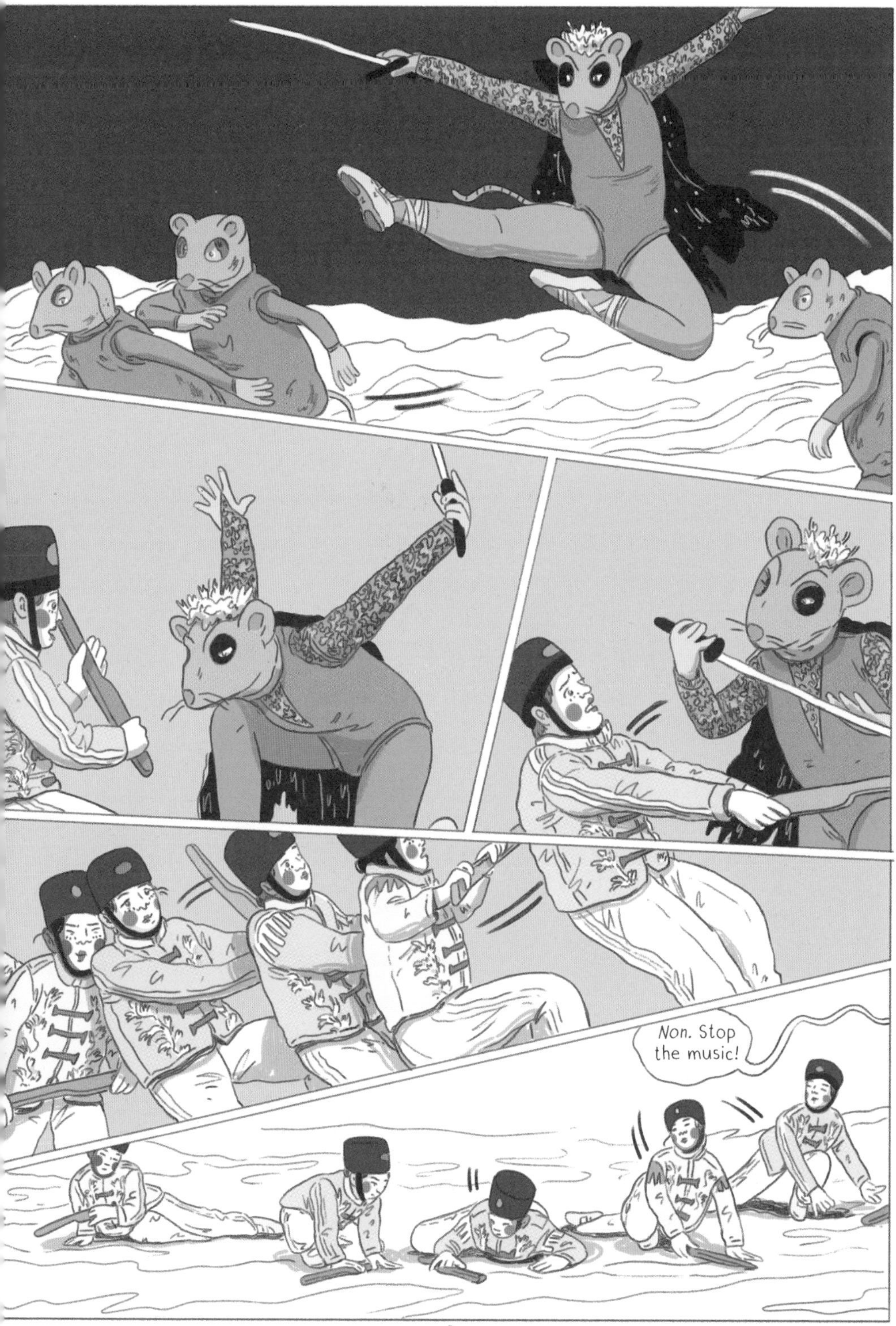
Non. Stop the music!

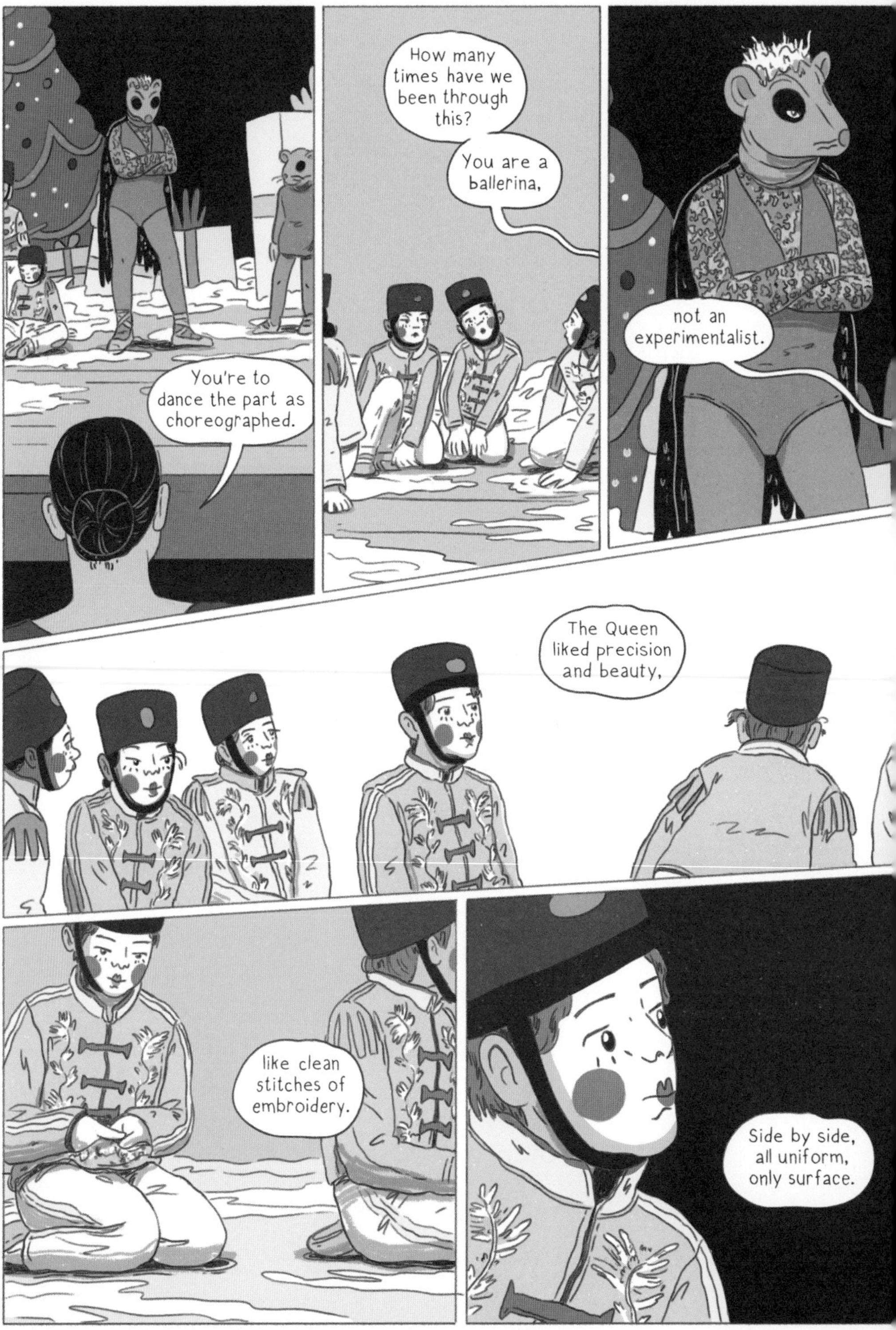

You're to dance the part as choreographed.
How many times have we been through this?
You are a ballerina,
not an experimentalist.
The Queen liked precision and beauty,
like clean stitches of embroidery.
Side by side, all uniform, only surface.

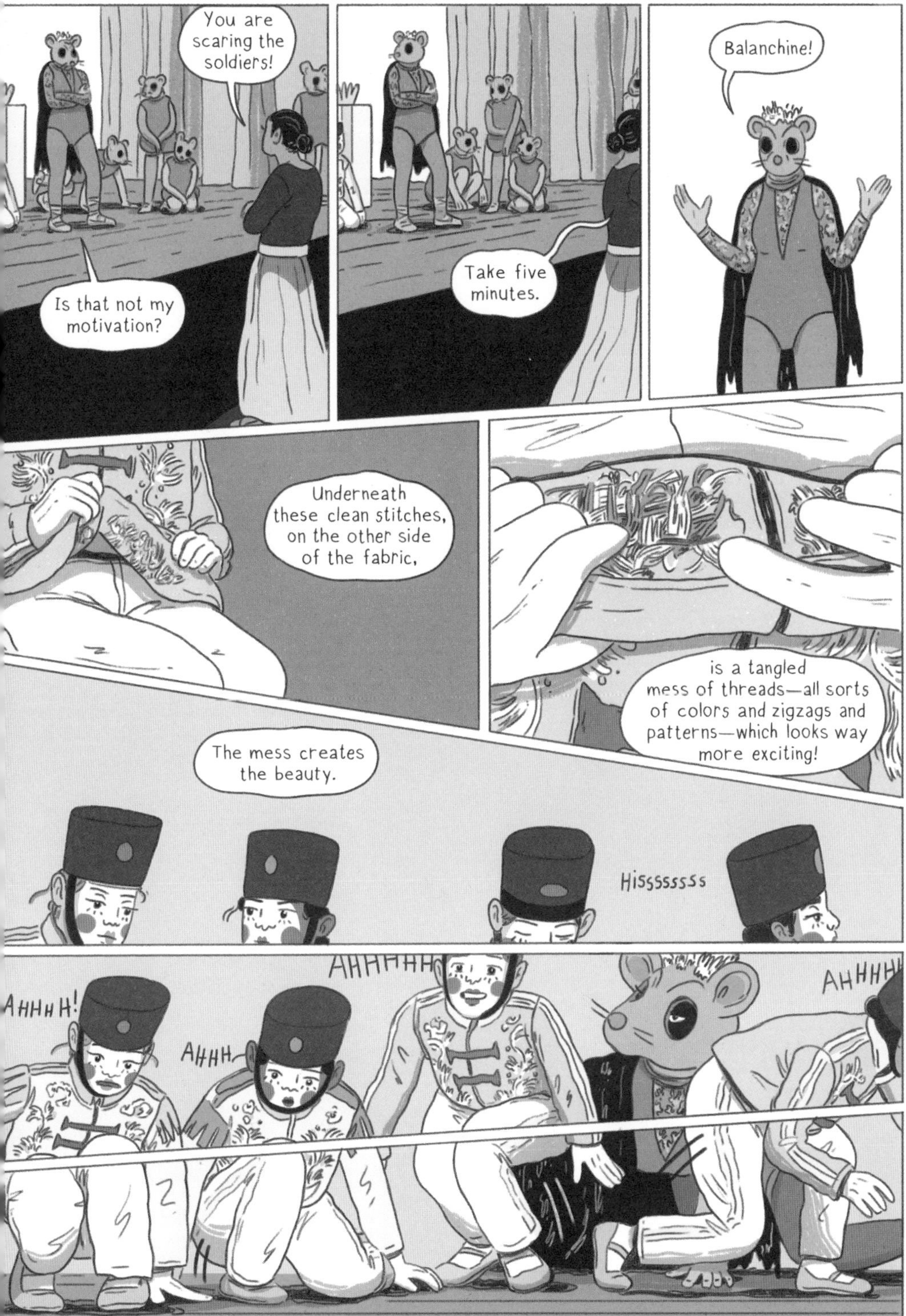
You are scaring the soldiers!
Is that not my motivation?
Take five minutes.
Balanchine!
Underneath these clean stitches, on the other side of the fabric,
is a tangled mess of threads—all sorts of colors and zigzags and patterns—which looks way more exciting!
The mess creates the beauty.
Hissssssss
AHHHH!
AHHH
AHHHHH
AHHHH

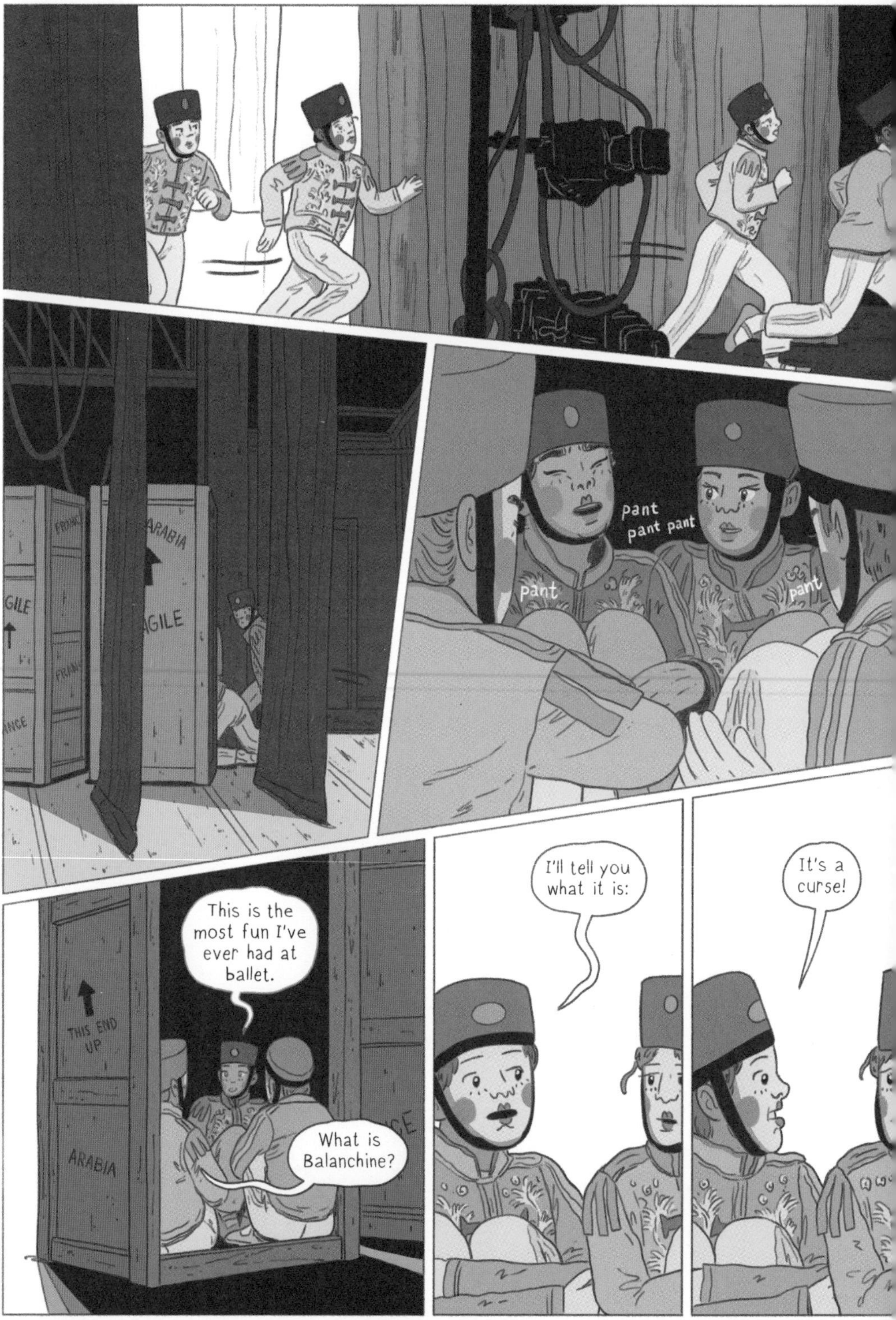

FRAGILE
ARABIA
FRAGILE
FRANCE
pant
pant pant
pant
pant
THIS END UP
ARABIA
This is the most fun I've ever had at ballet.
What is Balanchine?
I'll tell you what it is:
It's a curse!

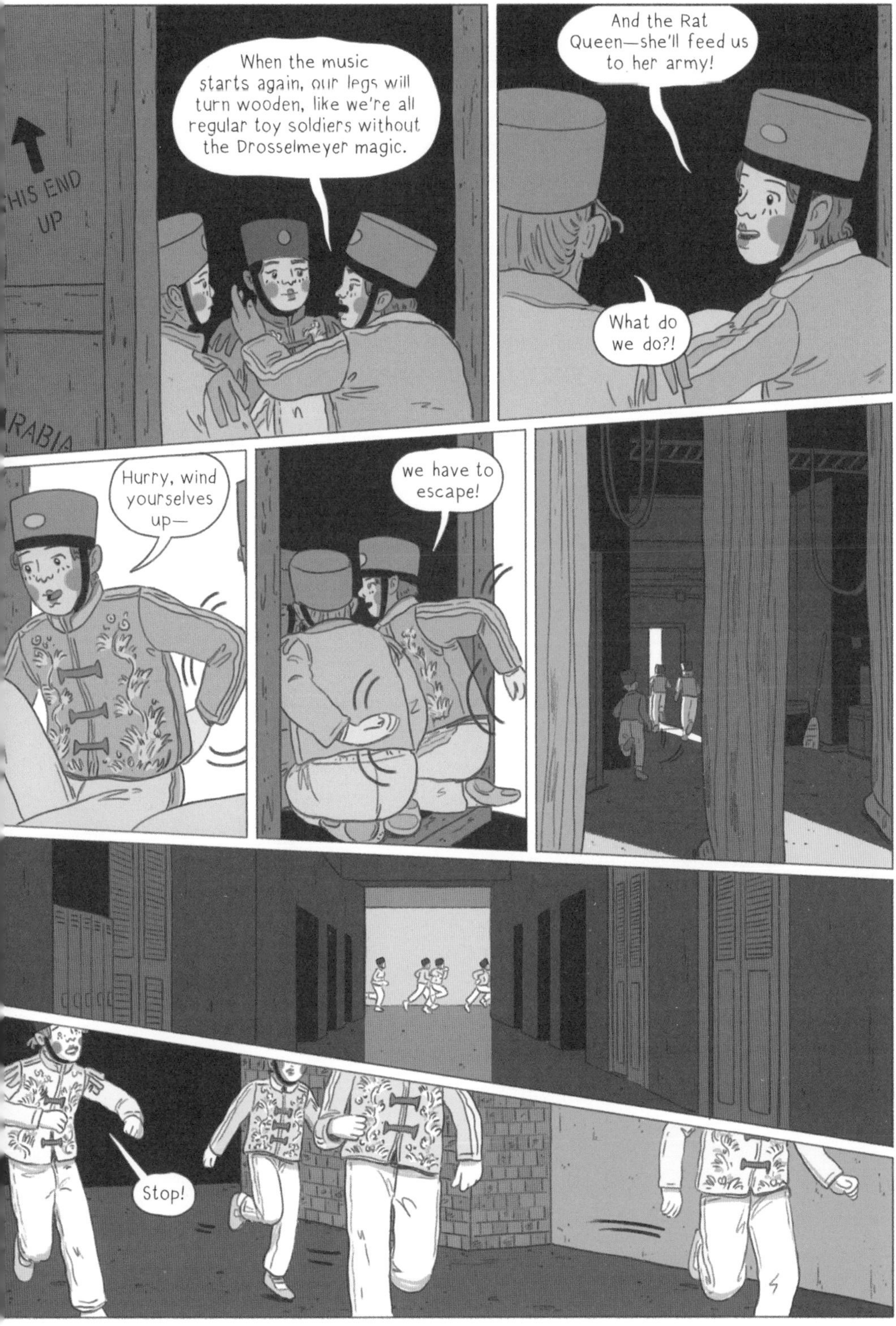
THIS END UP
RABIA
When the music starts again, our legs will turn wooden, like we're all regular toy soldiers without the Drosselmeyer magic.
And the Rat Queen—she'll feed us to her army!
What do we do?!
Hurry, wind yourselves up—
we have to escape!
Stop!

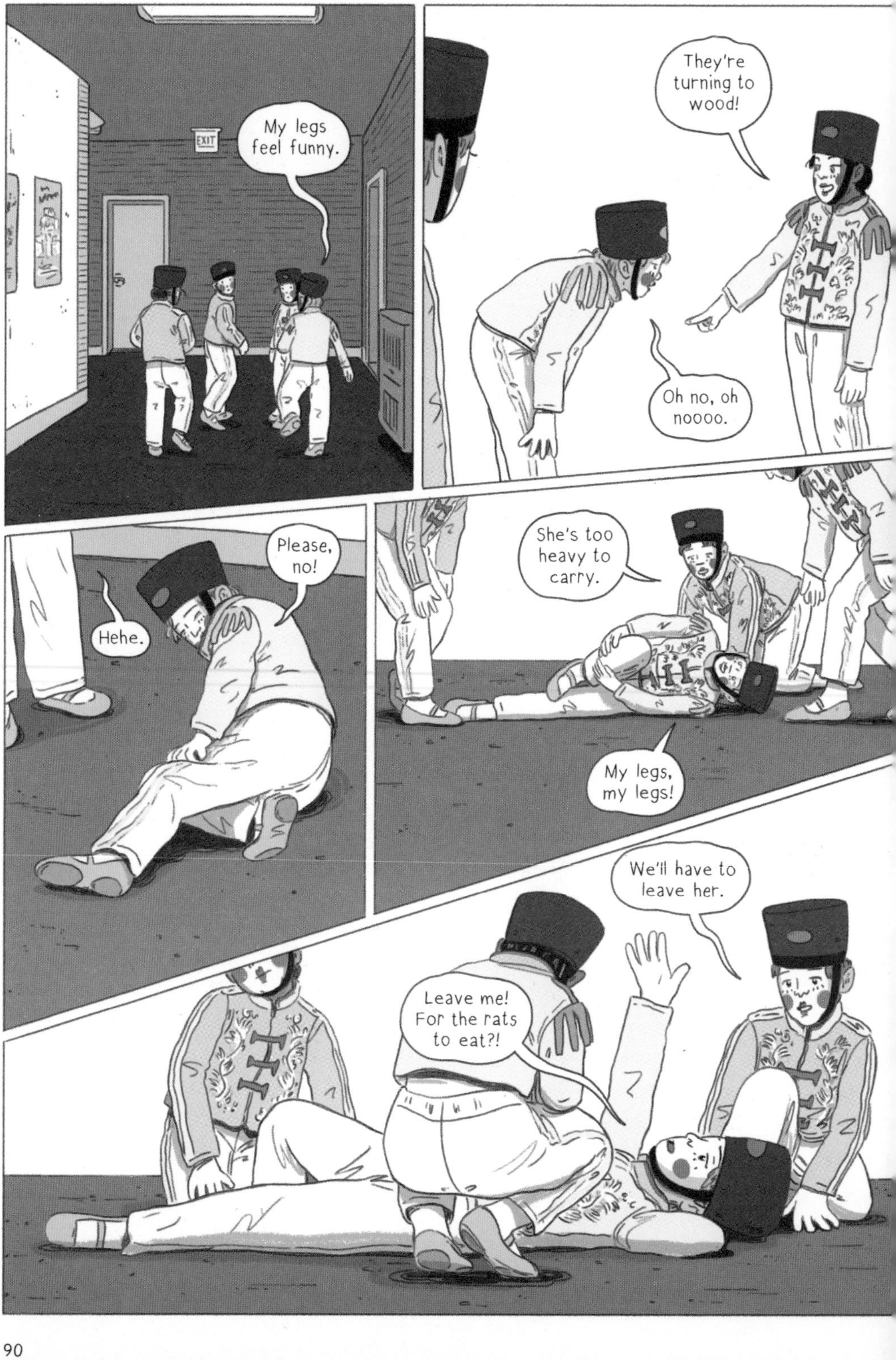
EXIT
My legs feel funny.
They're turning to wood!
Oh no, oh noooo.
Please, no!
Hehe.
She's too heavy to carry.
My legs, my legs!
We'll have to leave her.
Leave me! For the rats to eat?!

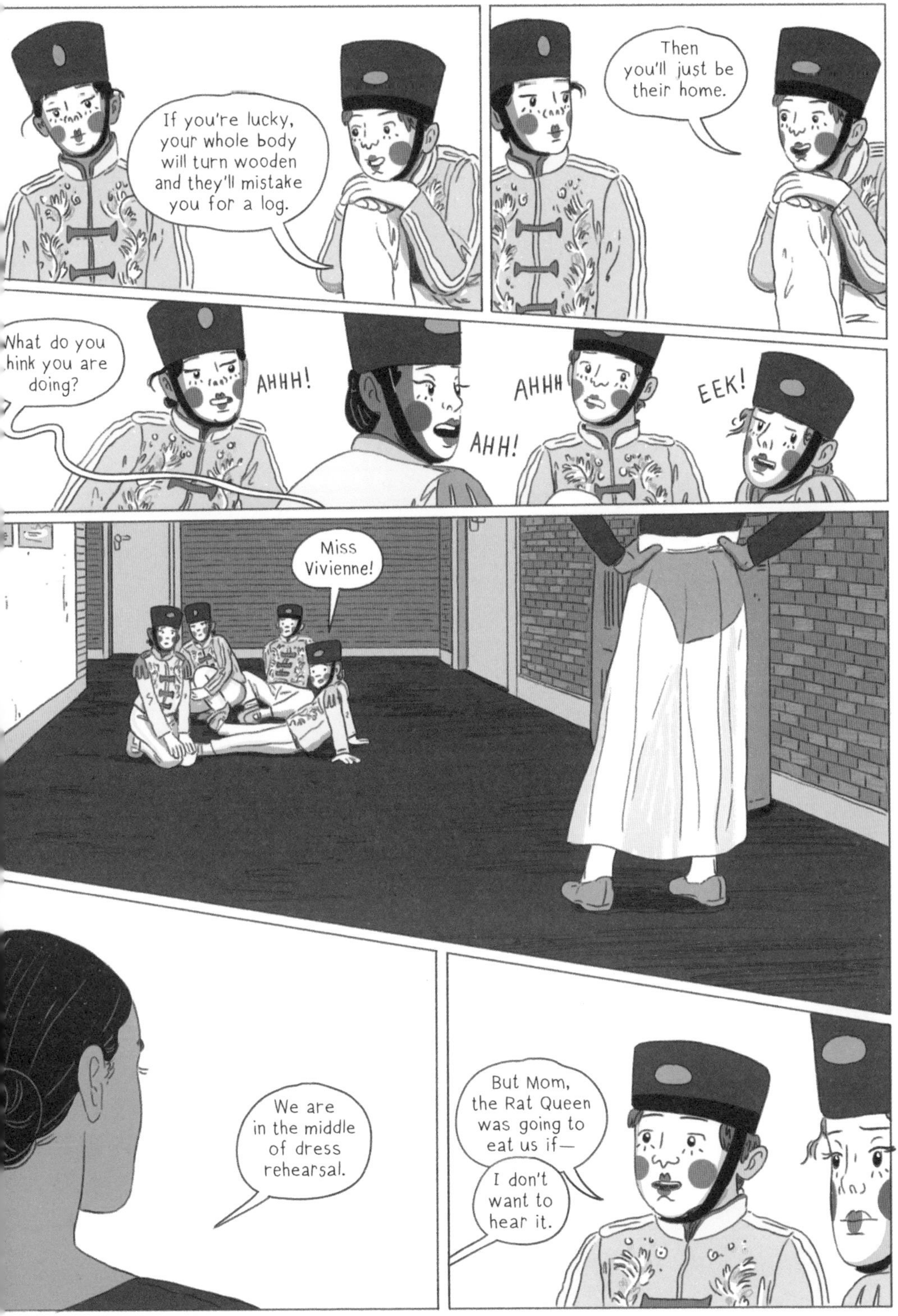
If you're lucky, your whole body will turn wooden and they'll mistake you for a log.
Then you'll just be their home.
What do you hink you are doing?
AHHH!
AHH!
AHHH
EEK!
Miss Vivienne!
We are in the middle of dress rehearsal.
But Mom, the Rat Queen was going to eat us if—
I don't want to hear it.

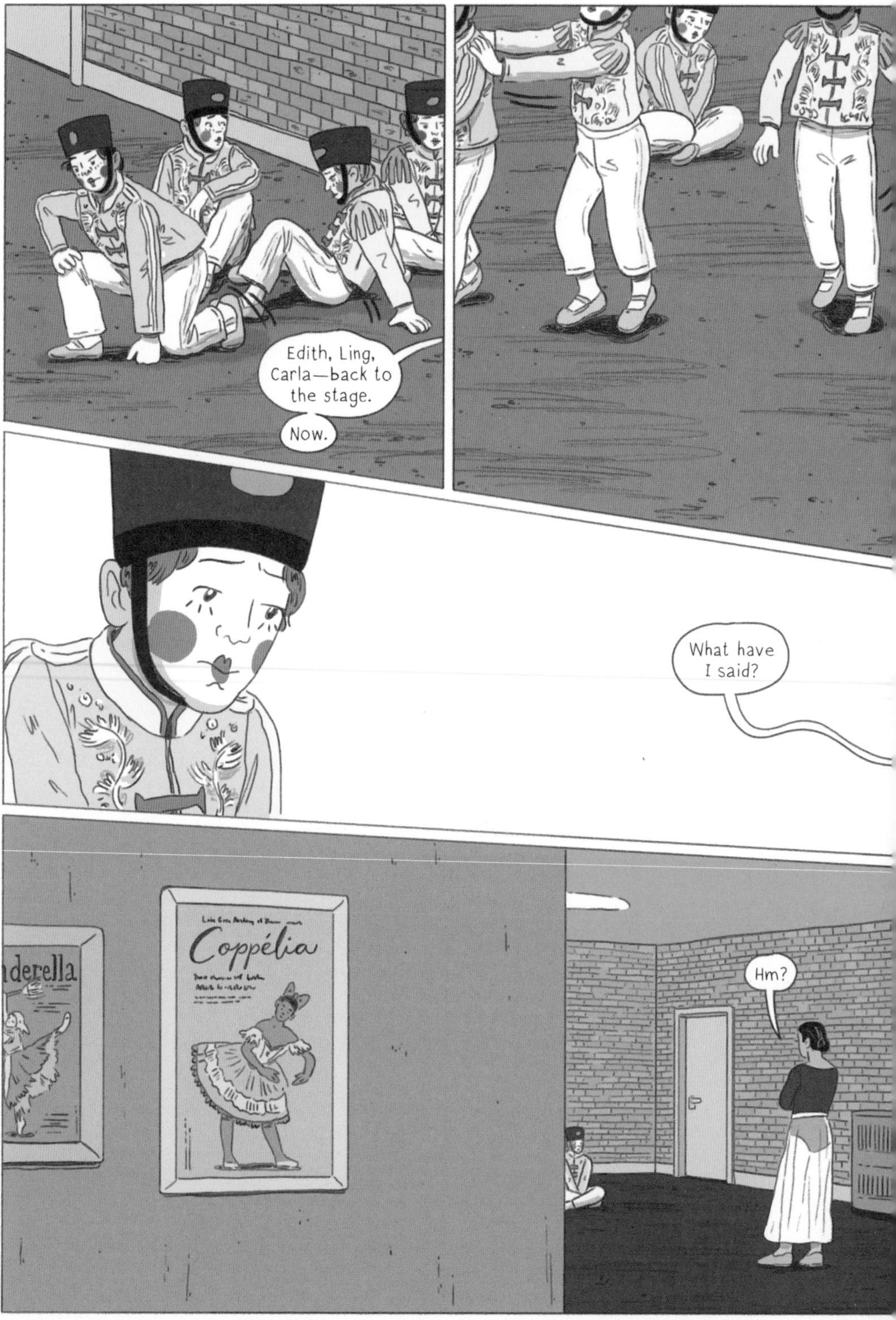
Edith, Ling, Carla—back to the stage.
Now.
What have I said?
Coppélia
Hm?

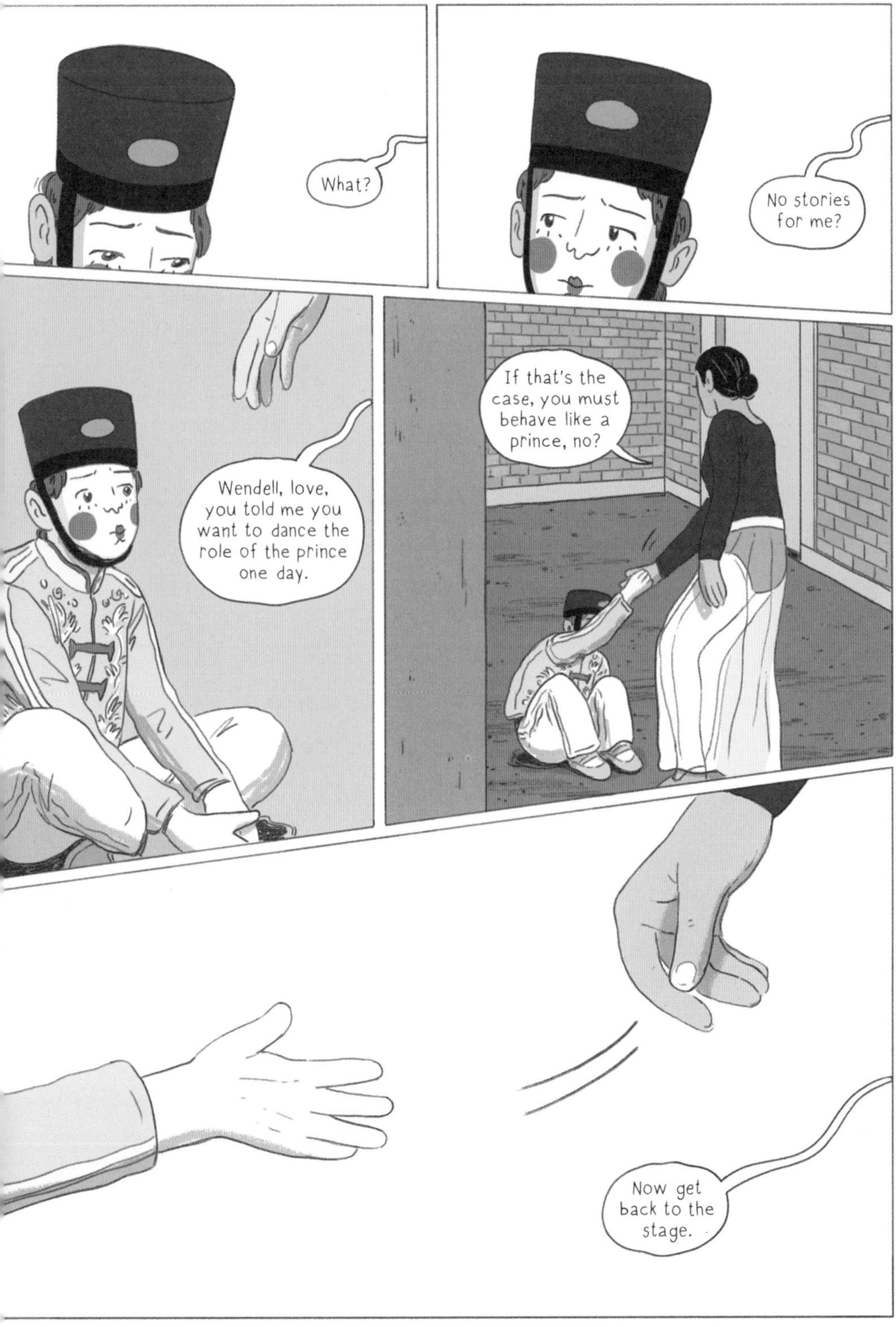
What?
No stories for me?
Wendell, love, you told me you want to dance the role of the prince one day.
If that's the case, you must behave like a prince, no?
Now get back to the stage.

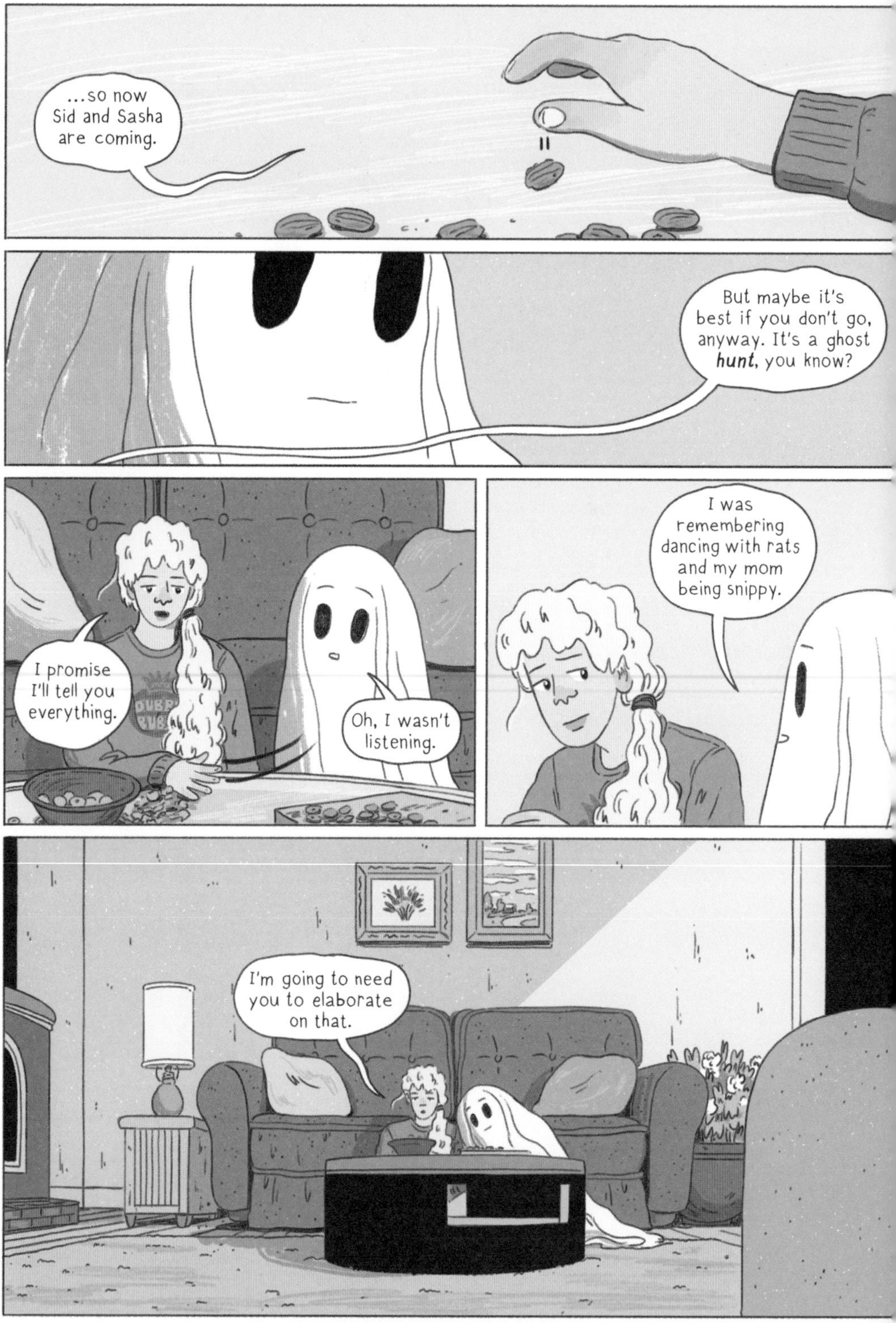
...so now Sid and Sasha are coming.
But maybe it's best if you don't go, anyway. It's a ghost *hunt*, you know?
I promise I'll tell you everything.
Oh, I wasn't listening.
I was remembering dancing with rats and my mom being snippy.
I'm going to need you to elaborate on that.

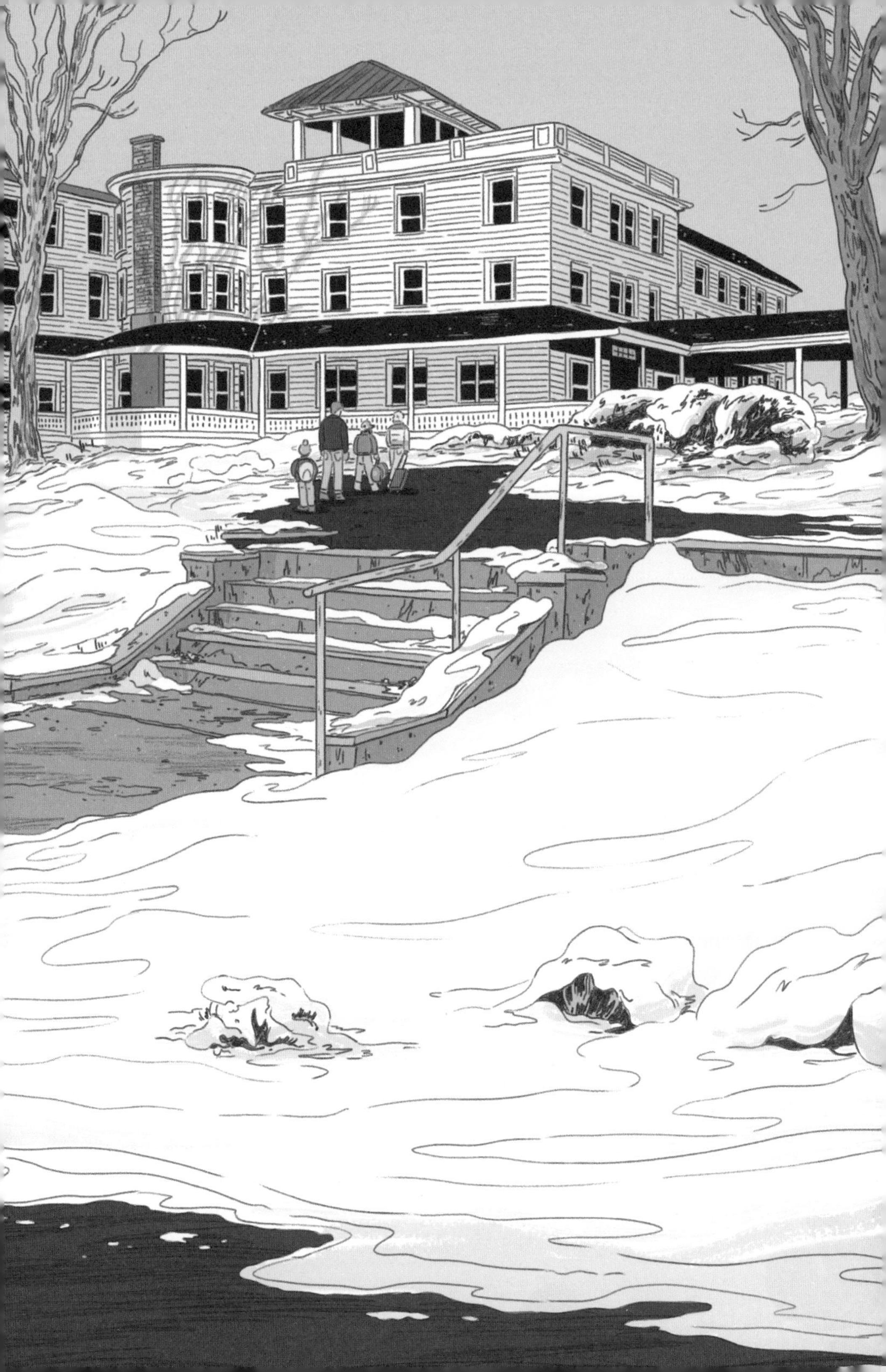

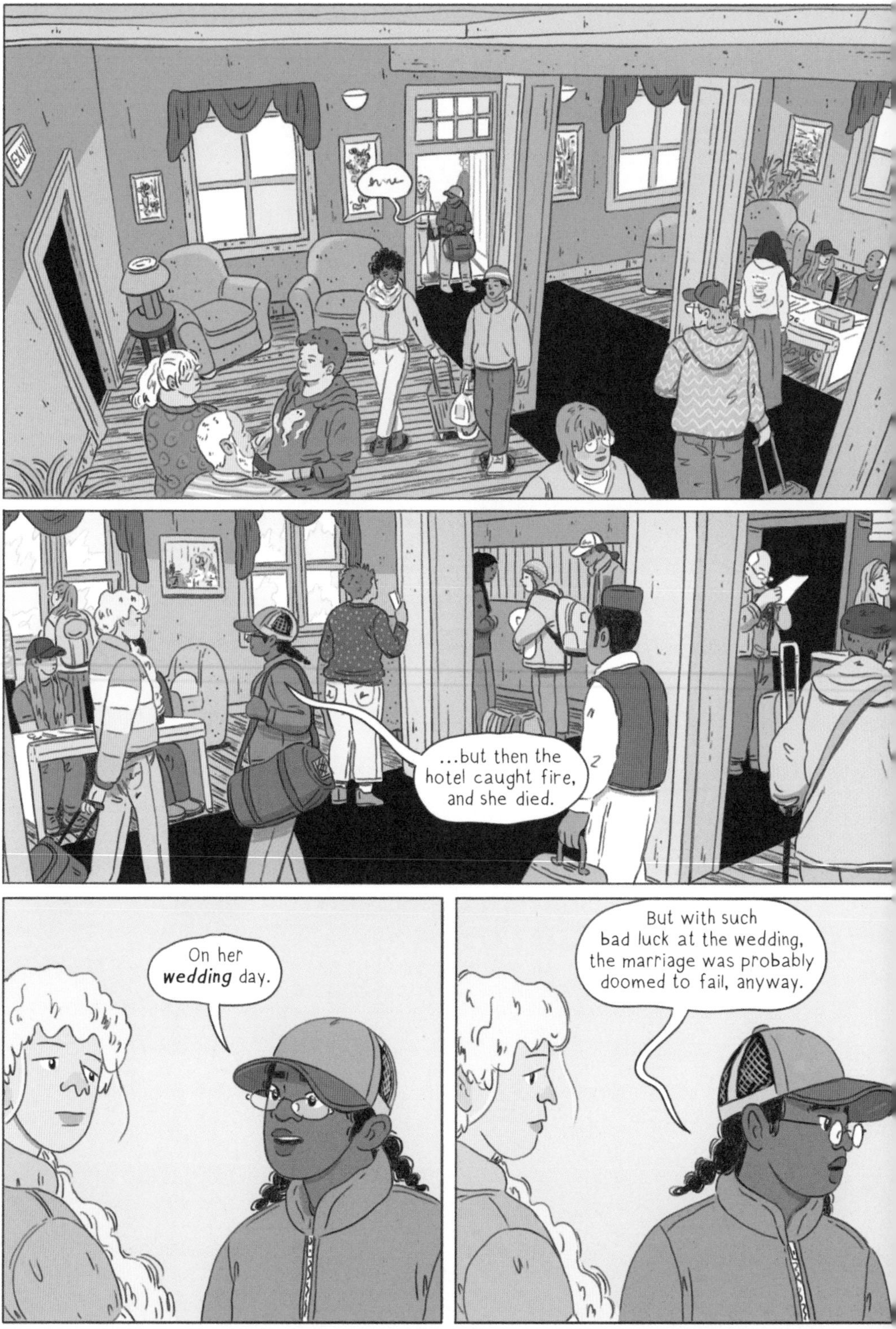
...but then the hotel caught fire, and she died.
On her **wedding** day.
But with such bad luck at the wedding, the marriage was probably doomed to fail, anyway.

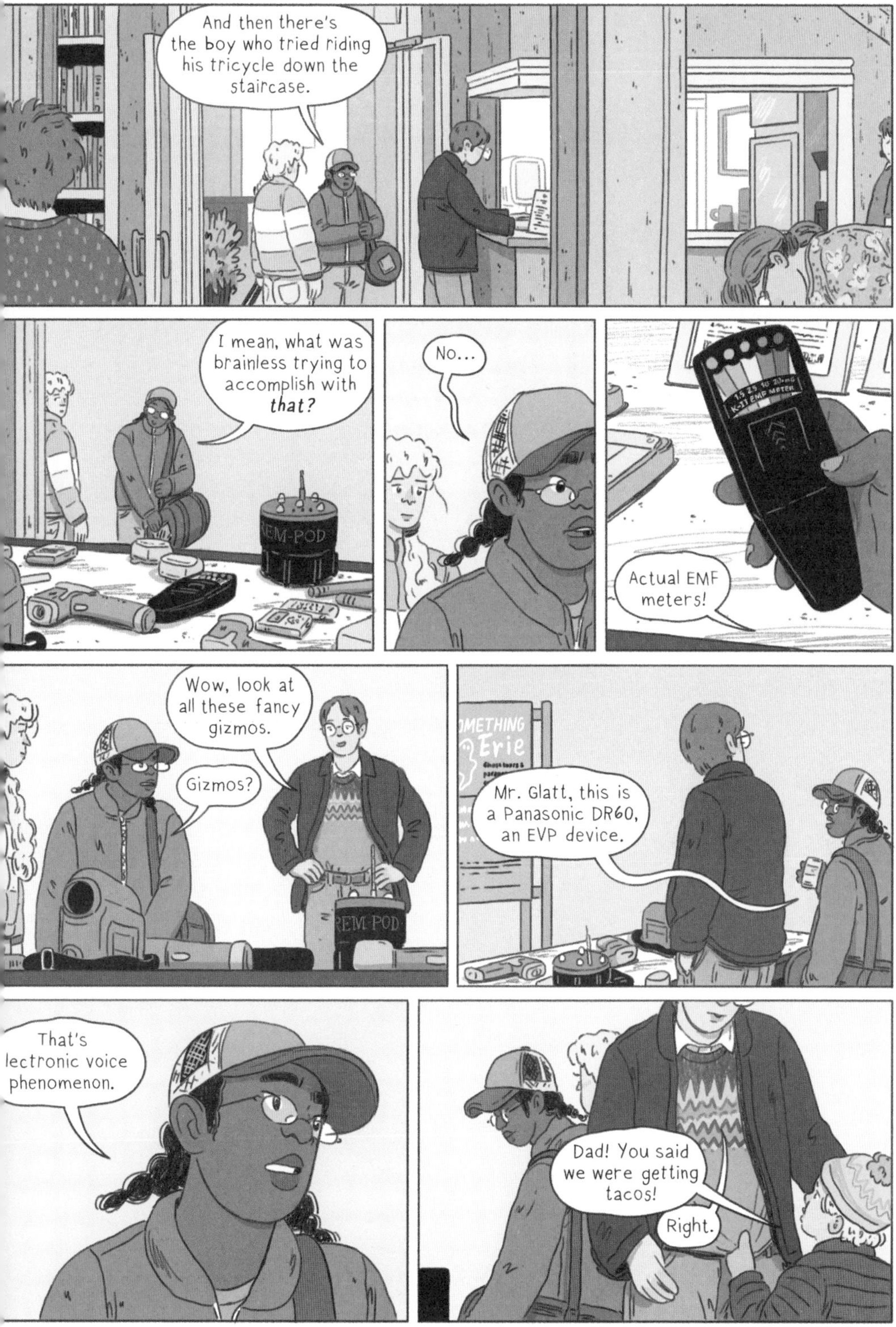
And then there's the boy who tried riding his tricycle down the staircase.
I mean, what was brainless trying to accomplish with *that?*
REM-POD
No...
Actual EMF meters!
Wow, look at all these fancy gizmos.
Gizmos?
REM-POD
Mr. Glatt, this is a Panasonic DR60, an EVP device.
That's lectronic voice phenomenon.
Dad! You said we were getting tacos!
Right.

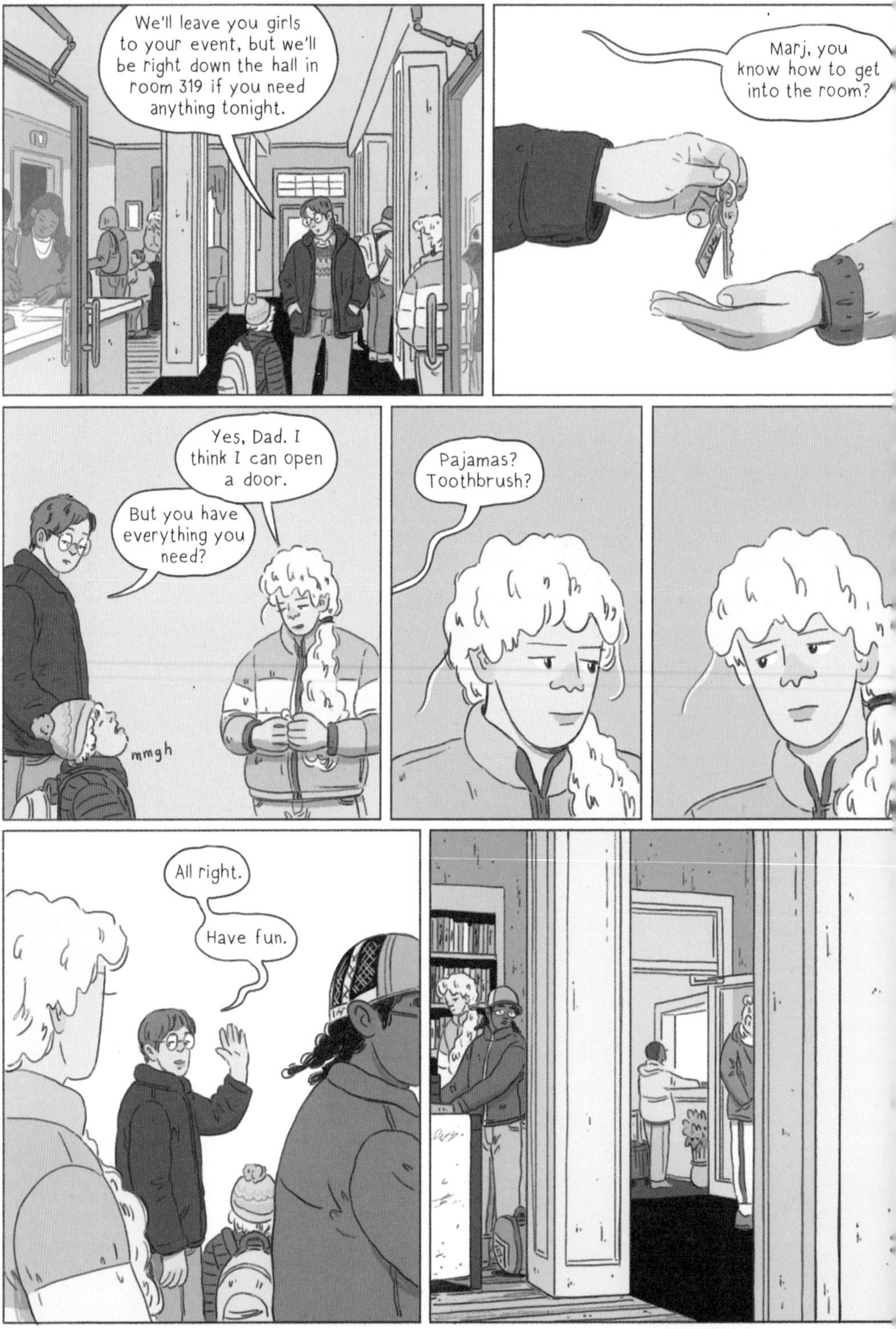
We'll leave you girls to your event, but we'll be right down the hall in room 319 if you need anything tonight.
Marj, you know how to get into the room?
Yes, Dad. I think I can open a door.
But you have everything you need?
mmgh
Pajamas? Toothbrush?
All right.
Have fun.

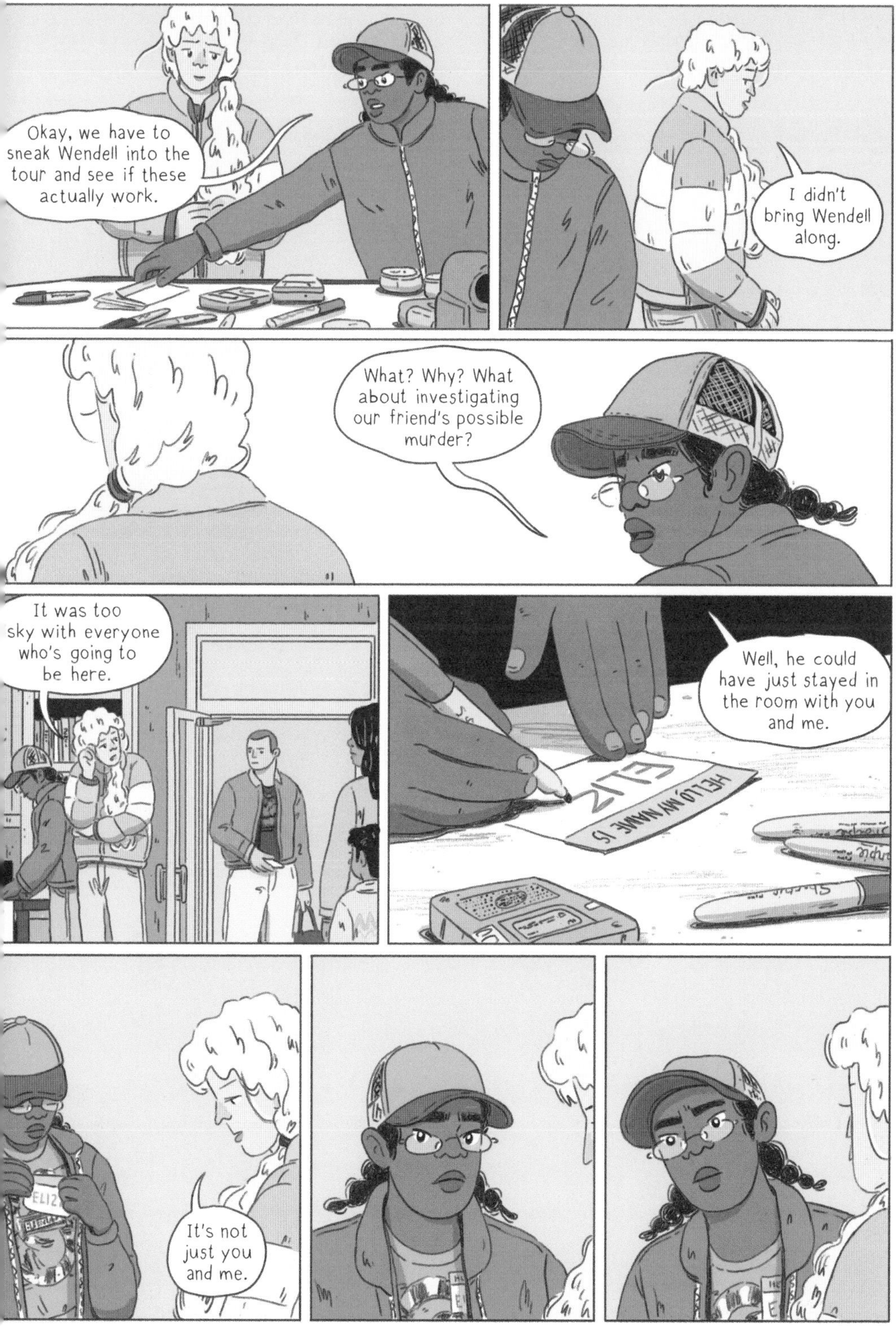
Okay, we have to sneak Wendell into the tour and see if these actually work.
I didn't bring Wendell along.
What? Why? What about investigating our friend's possible murder?
It was too sky with everyone who's going to be here.
Well, he could have just stayed in the room with you and me.
HELLO, MY NAME IS
ELIZ
It's not just you and me.

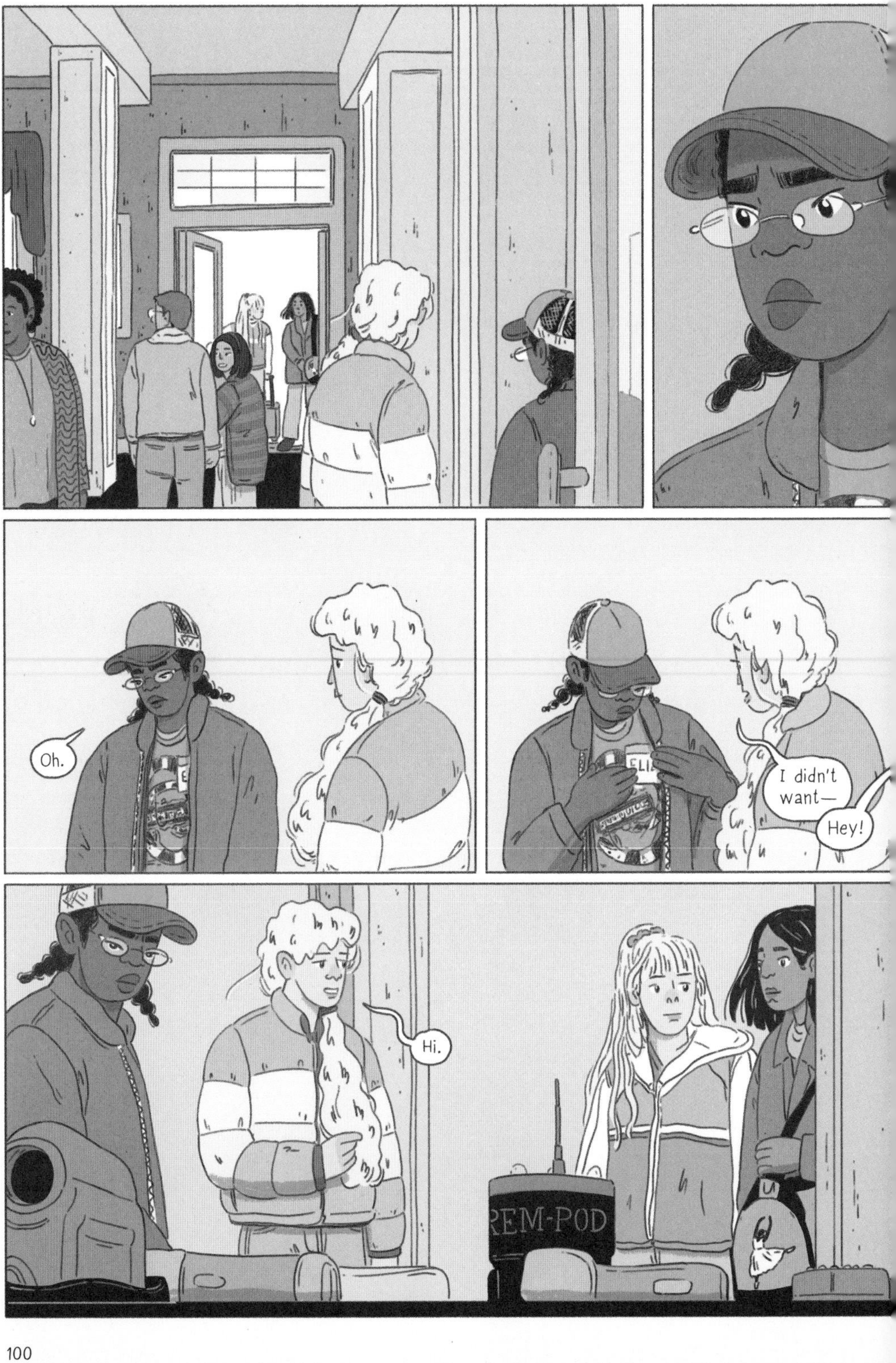
Oh.
I didn't want—
Hey!
Hi.
REM-POD

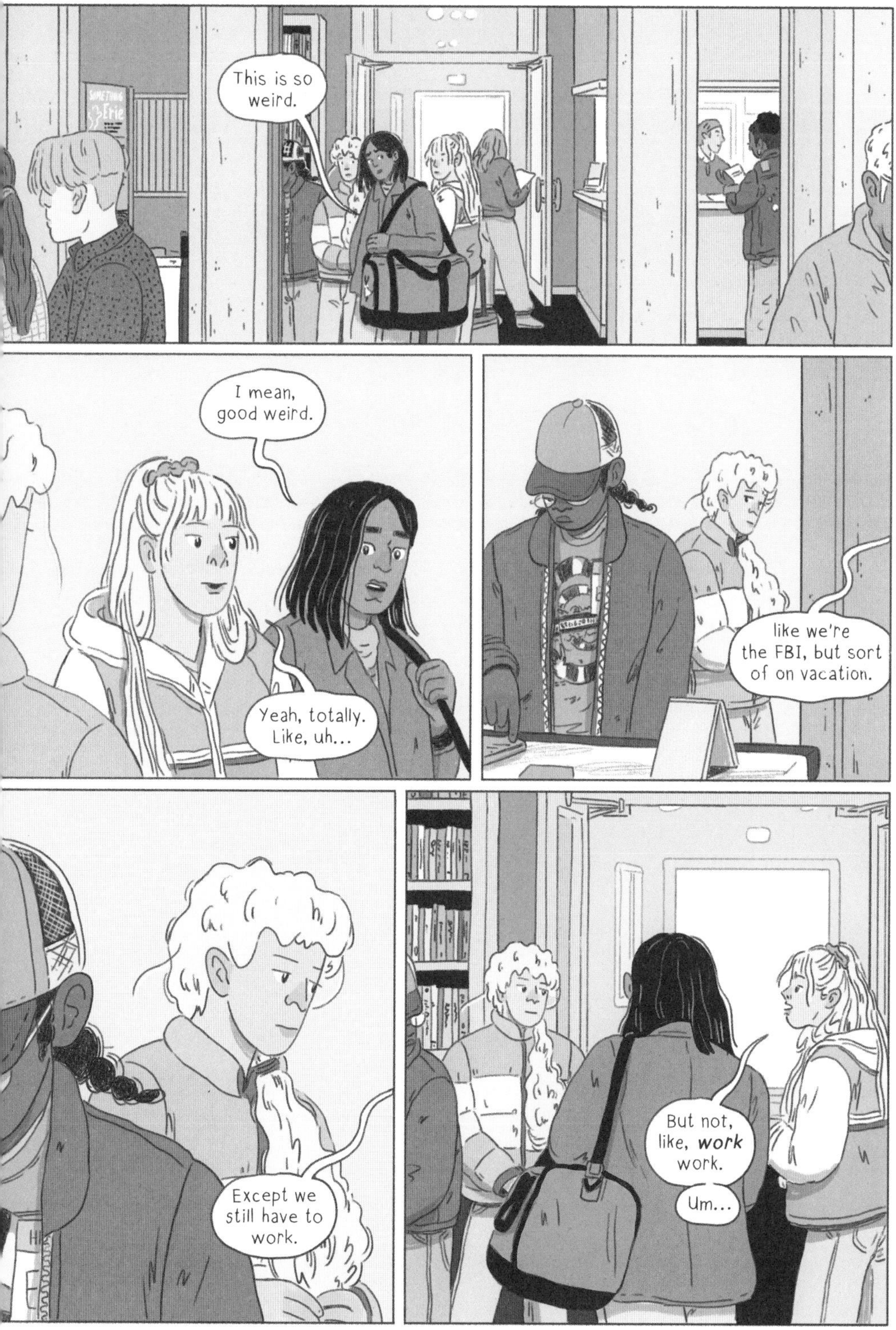
This is so weird.
I mean, good weird.
Yeah, totally. Like, uh...
like we're the FBI, but sort of on vacation.
Except we still have to work.
But not, like, **work** work.
Um...

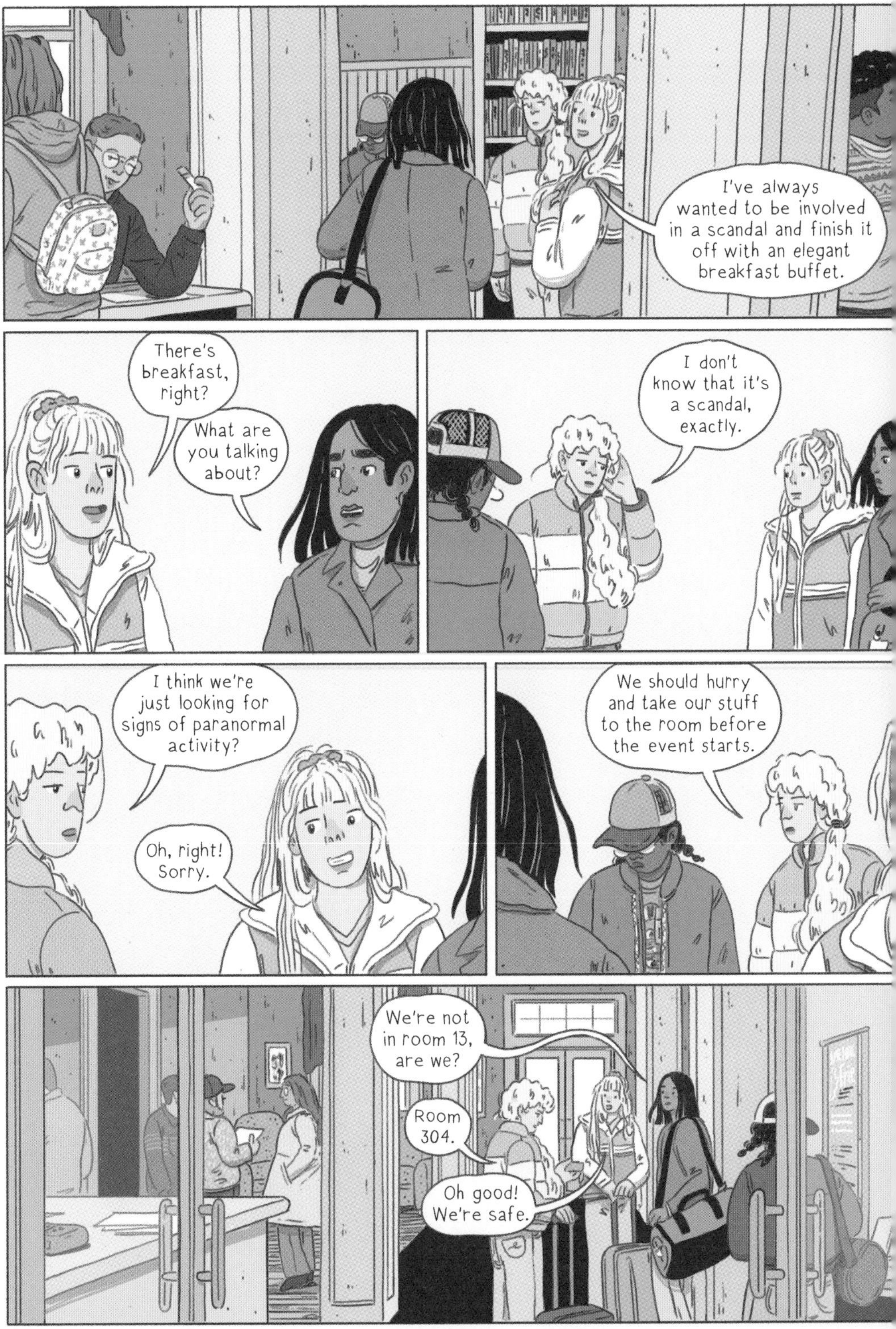
I've always wanted to be involved in a scandal and finish it off with an elegant breakfast buffet.
There's breakfast, right?
What are you talking about?
I don't know that it's a scandal, exactly.
I think we're just looking for signs of paranormal activity?
Oh, right! Sorry.
We should hurry and take our stuff to the room before the event starts.
We're not in room 13, are we?
Room 304.
Oh good! We're safe.

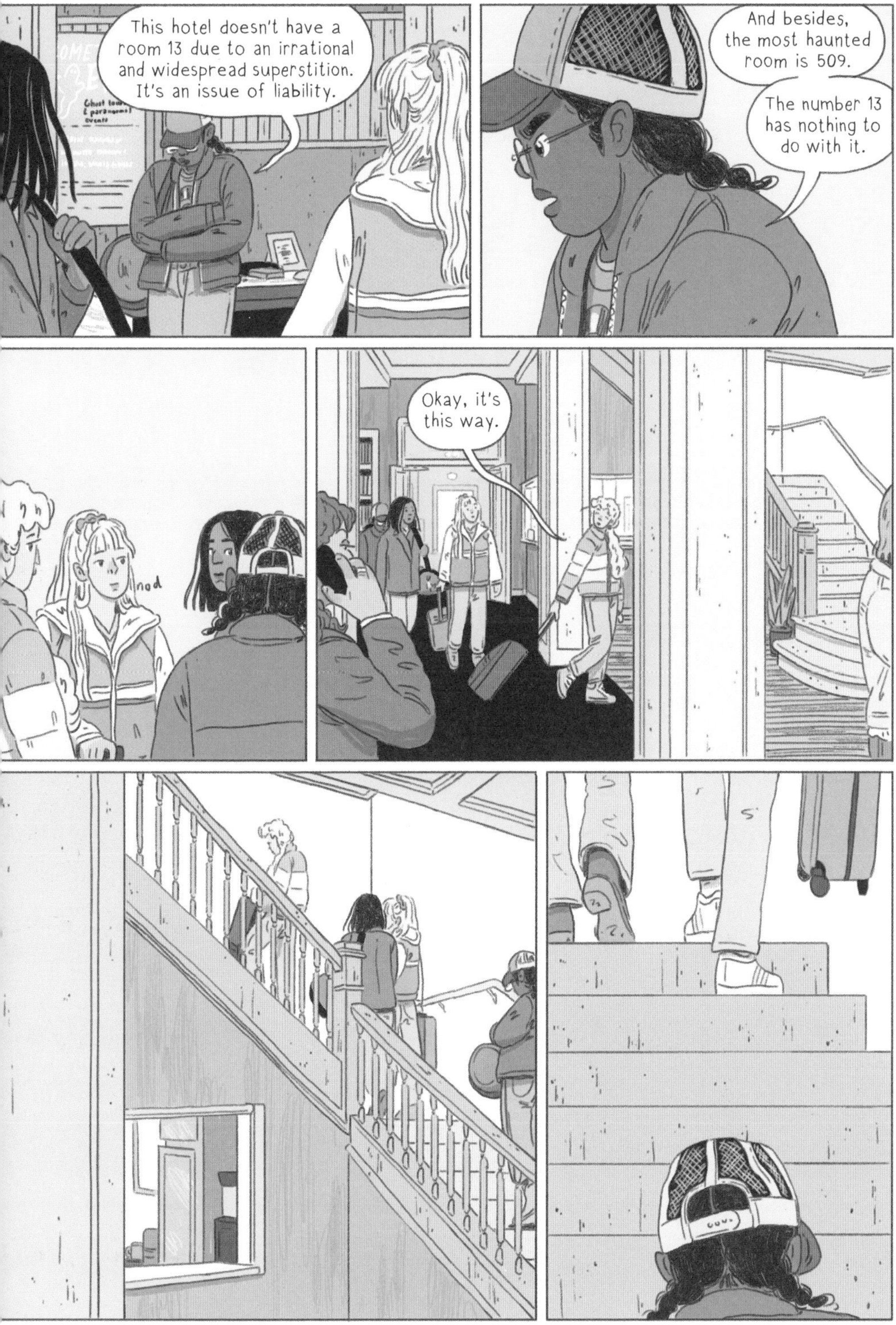
This hotel doesn't have a room 13 due to an irrational and widespread superstition. It's an issue of liability.
And besides, the most haunted room is 509.
The number 13 has nothing to do with it.
nod
Okay, it's this way.

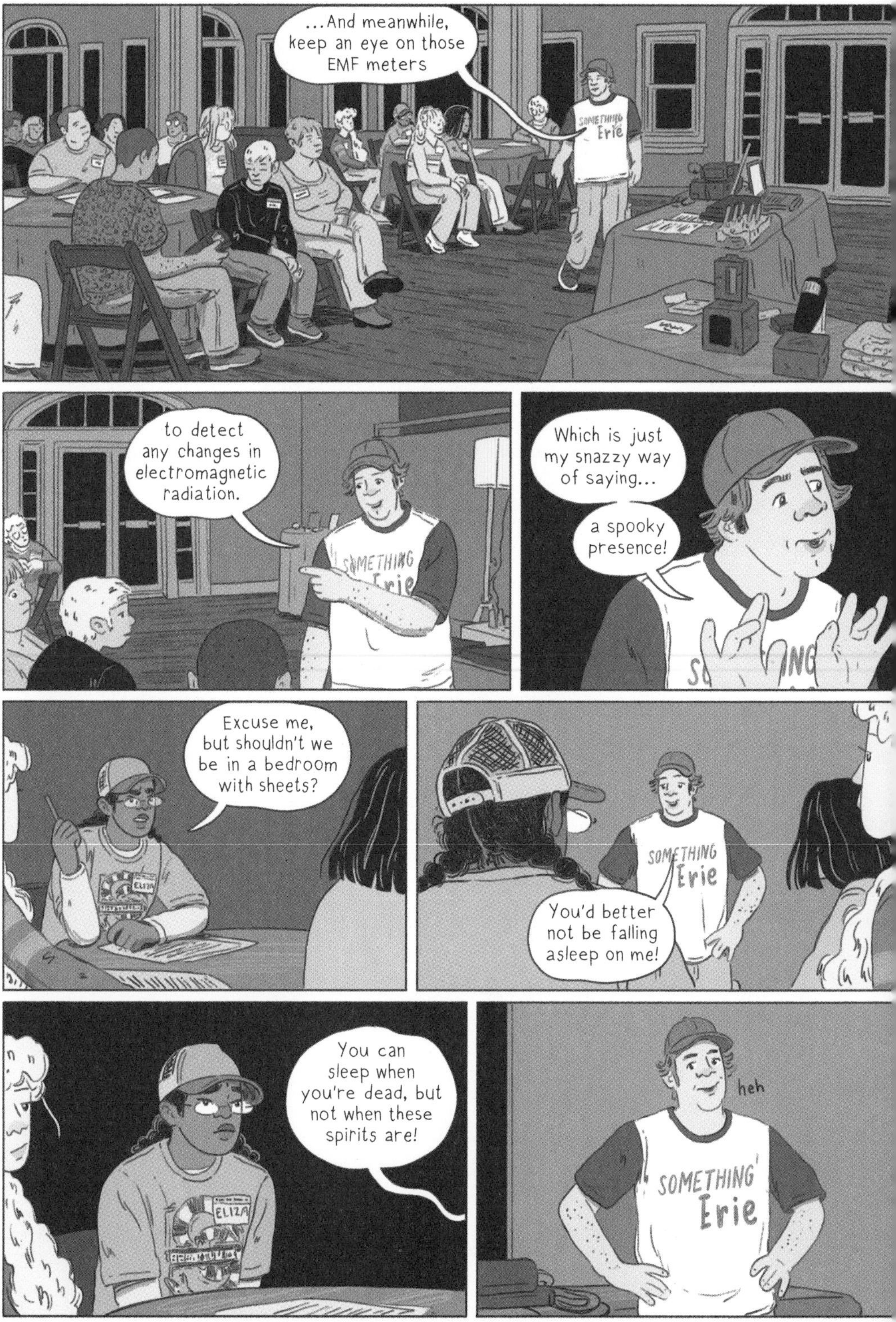
...And meanwhile, keep an eye on those EMF meters
to detect any changes in electromagnetic radiation.
Which is just my snazzy way of saying...
a spooky presence!
Excuse me, but shouldn't we be in a bedroom with sheets?
You'd better not be falling asleep on me!
You can sleep when you're dead, but not when these spirits are!
heh

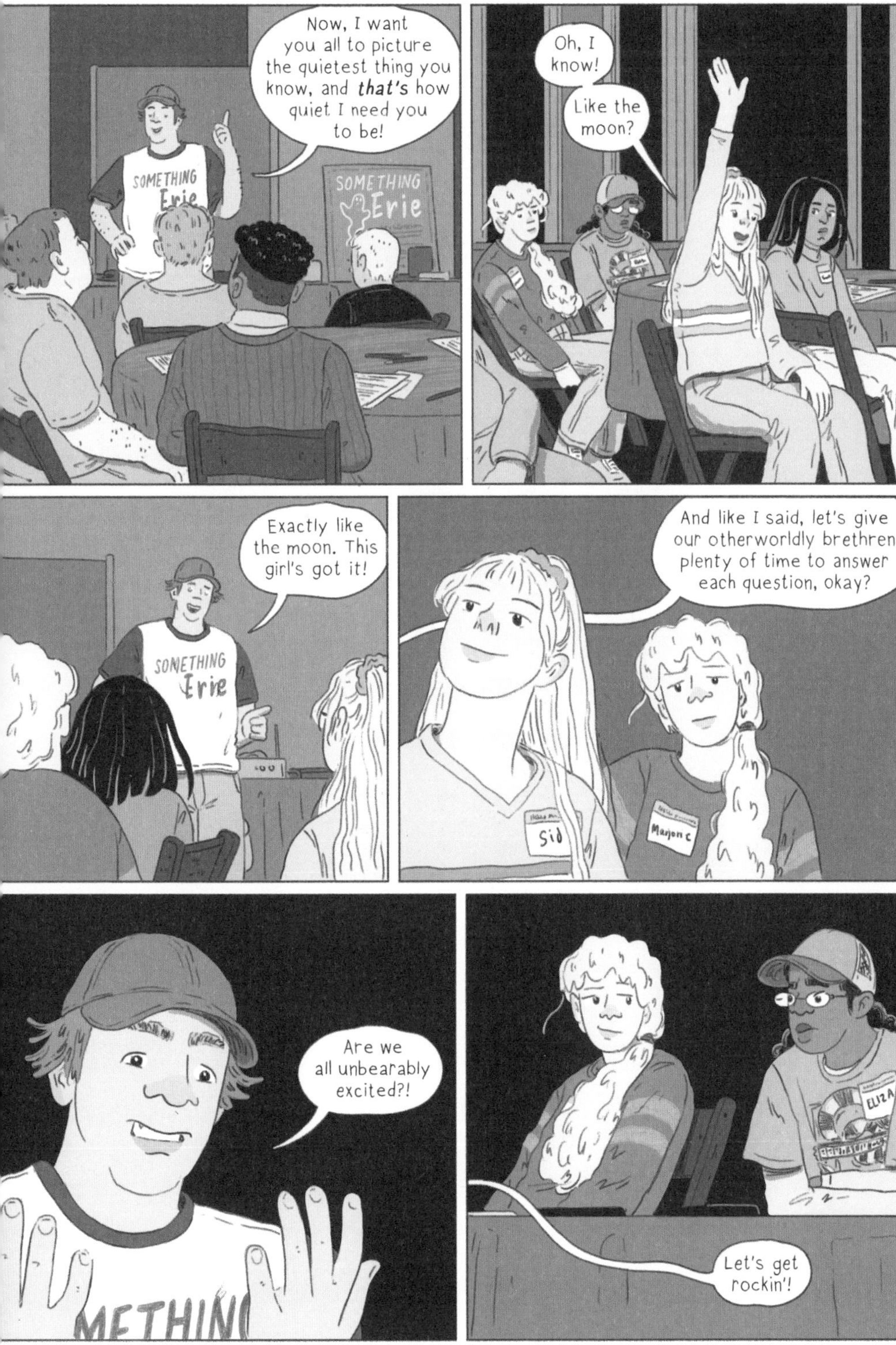
Now, I want you all to picture the quietest thing you know, and **that's** how quiet I need you to be!
SOMETHING Erie
SOMETHING Erie
Oh, I know!
Like the moon?
Exactly like the moon. This girl's got it!
SOMETHING Erie
And like I said, let's give our otherworldly brethren plenty of time to answer each question, okay?
Sid
Marjorie
Are we all unbearably excited?!
METHIN
ELIZA
Let's get rockin'!

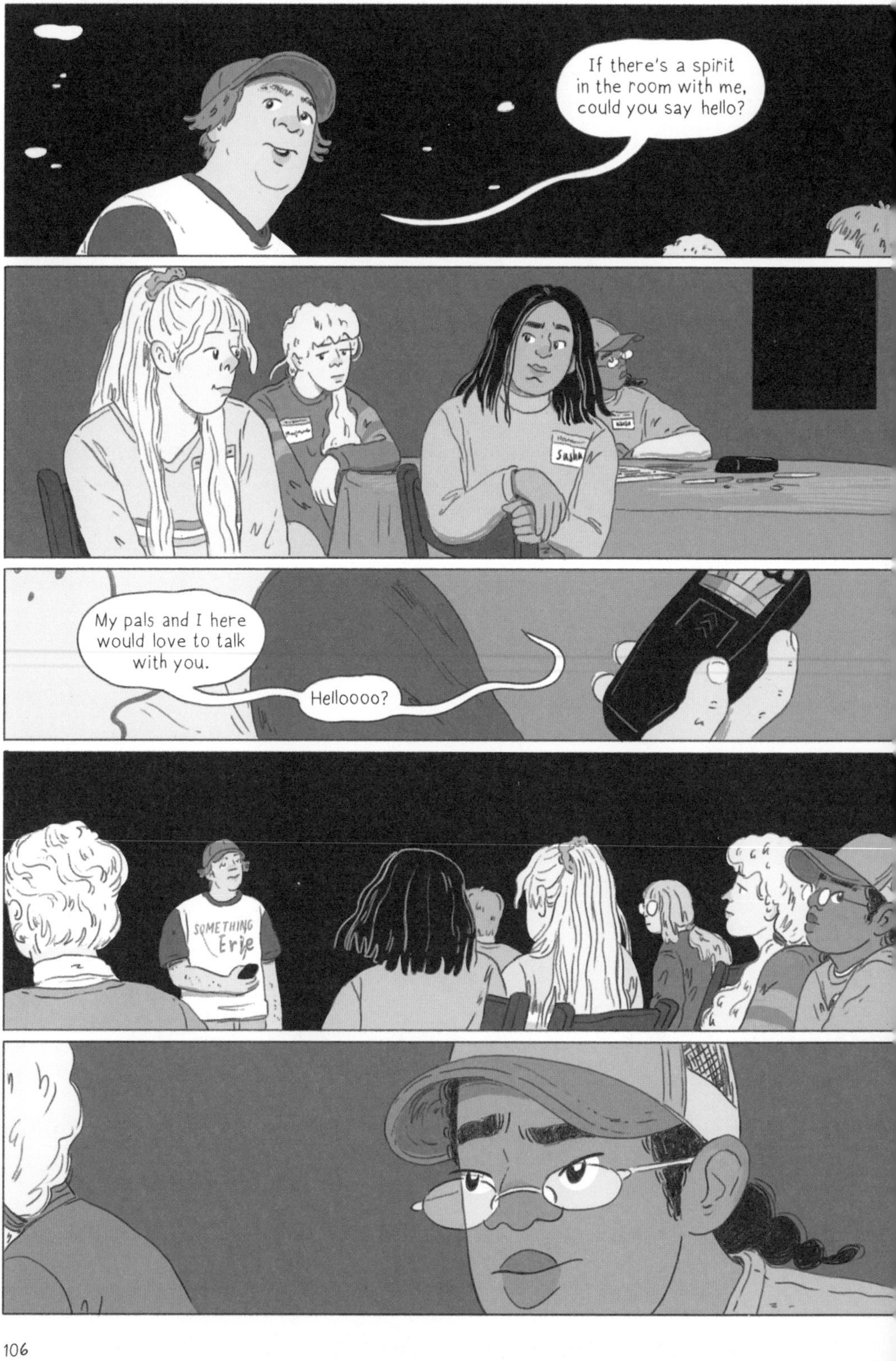
If there's a spirit in the room with me, could you say hello?
Sasha
My pals and I here would love to talk with you.
Helloooo?
SOMETHING Erie

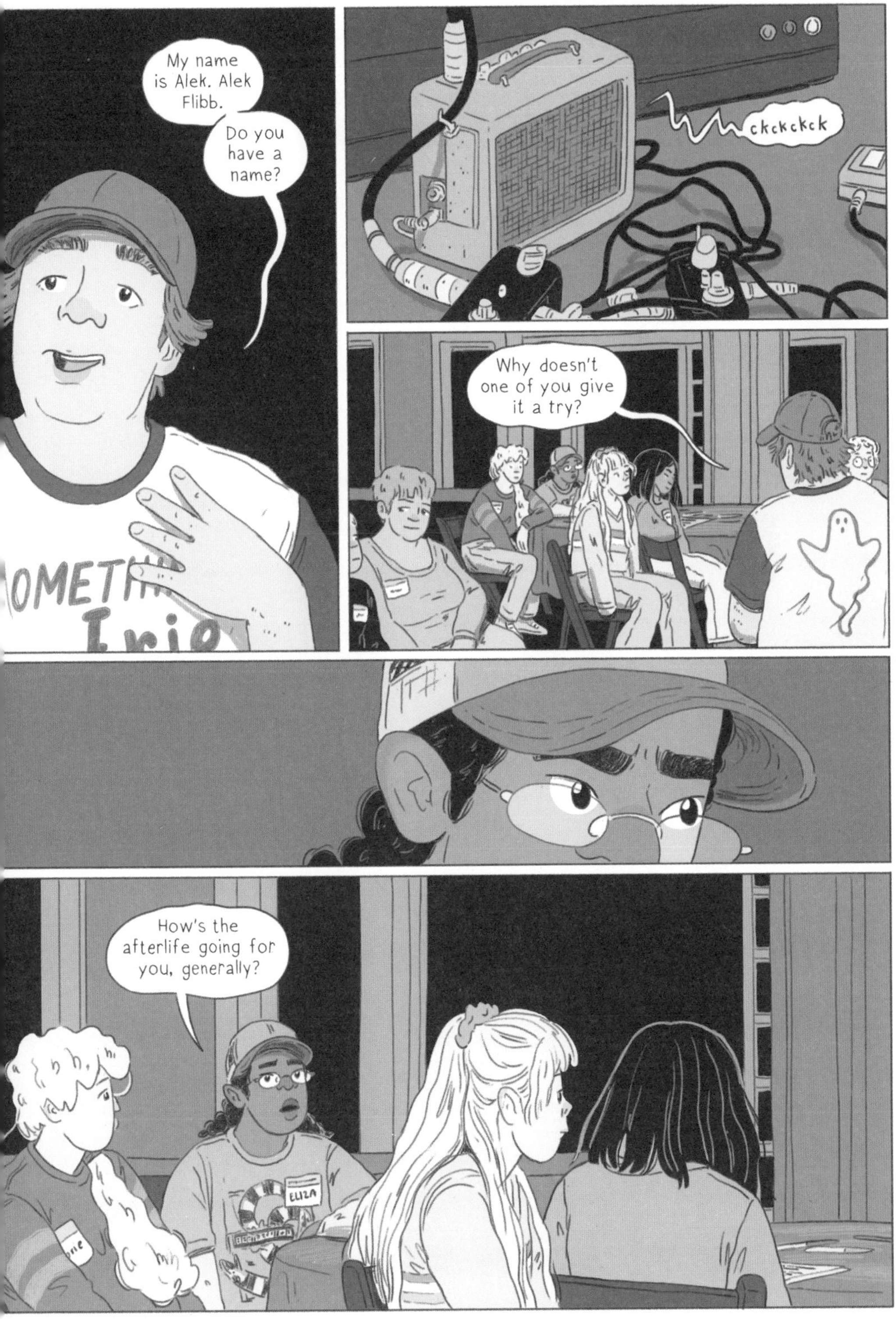
My name is Alek. Alek Flibb.
Do you have a name?
ckckckck
Why doesn't one of you give it a try?
How's the afterlife going for you, generally?

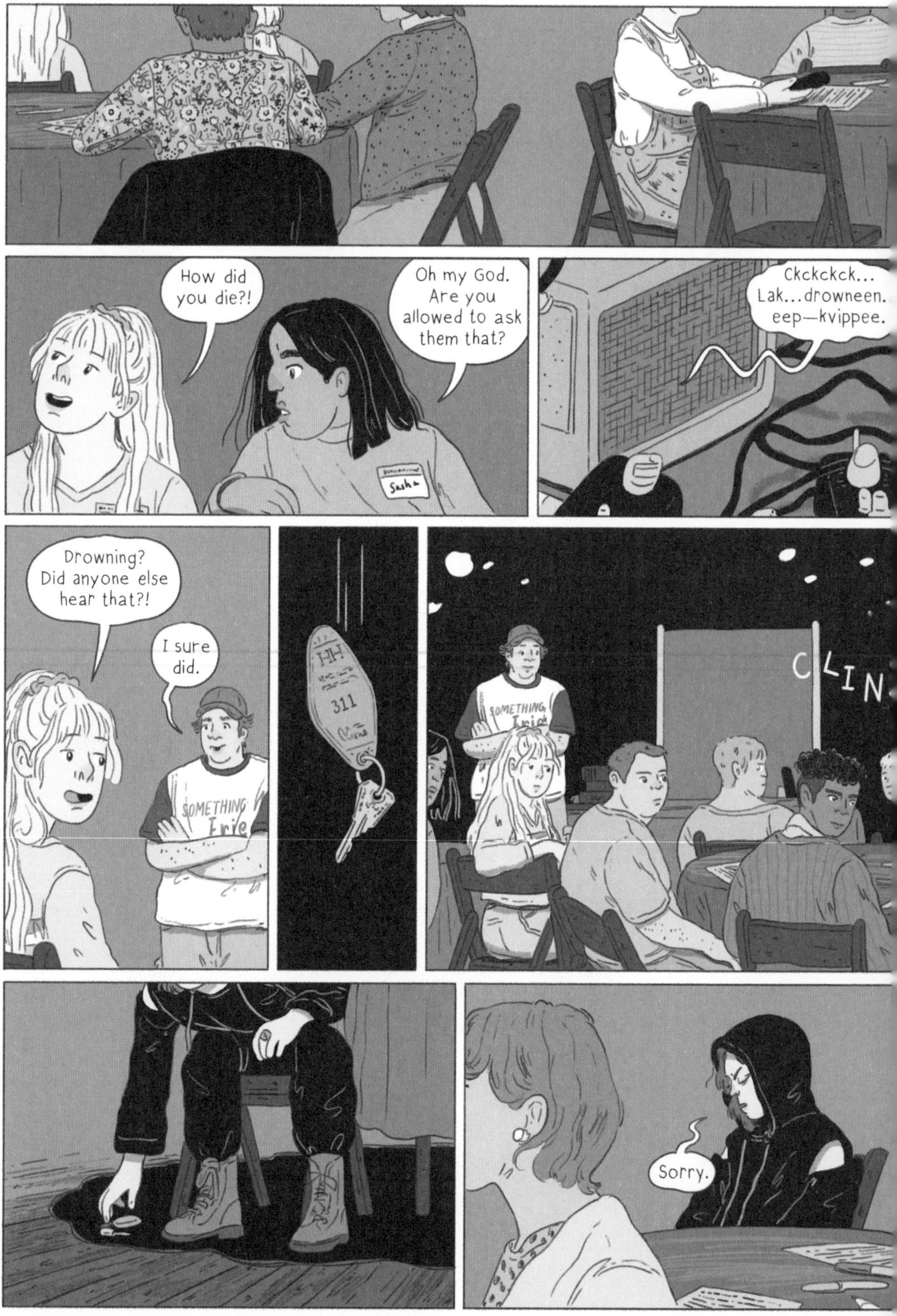
How did you die?!
Oh my God. Are you allowed to ask them that?
Sasha
Ckckckck... Lak...drowneen. eep—kvippee.
Drowning? Did anyone else hear that?!
I sure did.
SOMETHING Eerie
HH
311
Sorry.

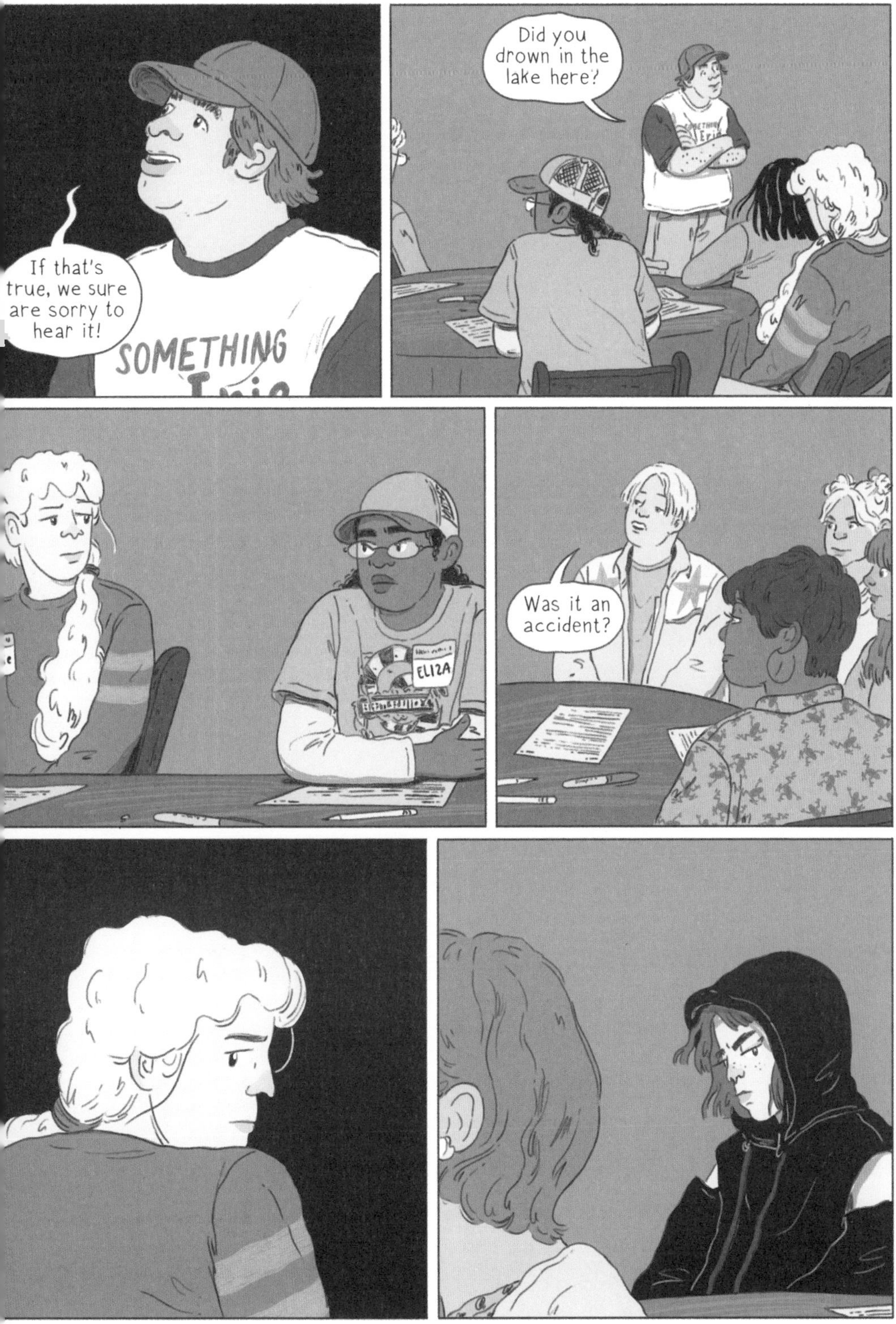
If that's true, we sure are sorry to hear it!
SOMETHING
Did you drown in the lake here?
ELIZA
Was it an accident?

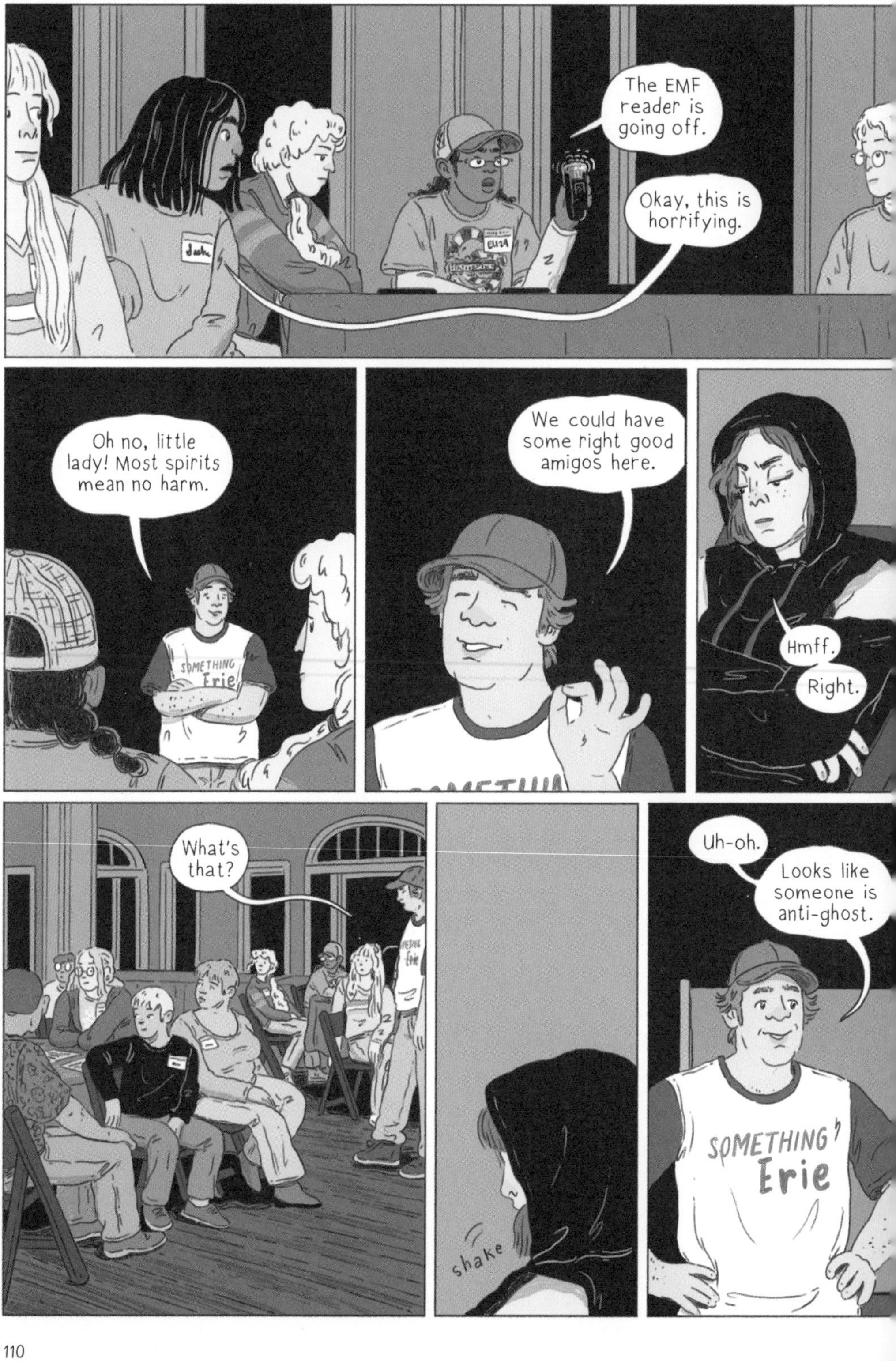
The EMF reader is going off.
Okay, this is horrifying.
Oh no, little lady! Most spirits mean no harm.
SOMETHING Erie
We could have some right good amigos here.
Hmff.
Right.
What's that?
shake
Uh-oh.
Looks like someone is anti-ghost.
SOMETHING Erie

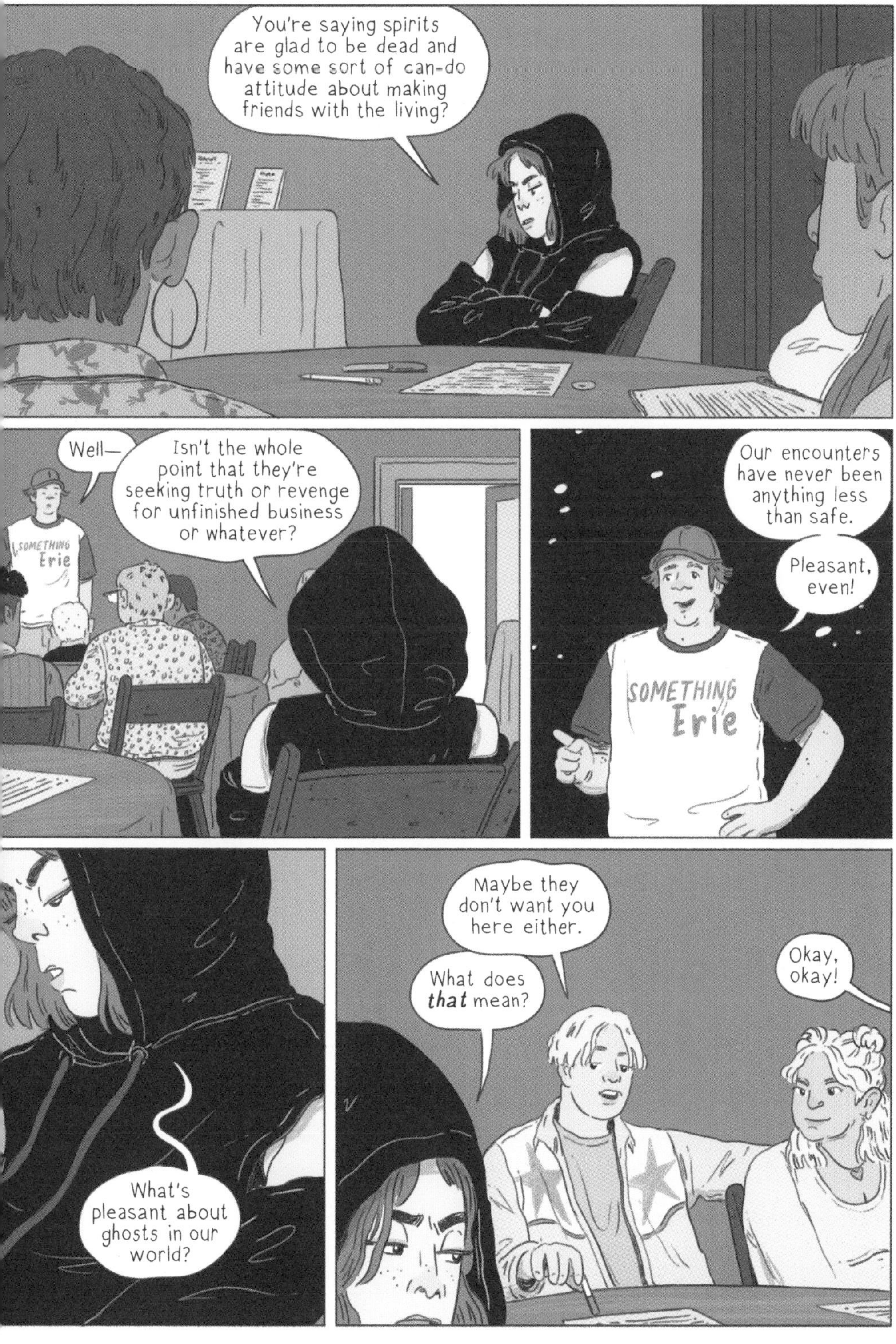
You're saying spirits are glad to be dead and have some sort of can-do attitude about making friends with the living?
Well—
Isn't the whole point that they're seeking truth or revenge for unfinished business or whatever?
SOMETHING Erie
Our encounters have never been anything less than safe.
Pleasant, even!
SOMETHING Erie
What's pleasant about ghosts in our world?
Maybe they don't want you here either.
What does ***that*** mean?
Okay, okay!

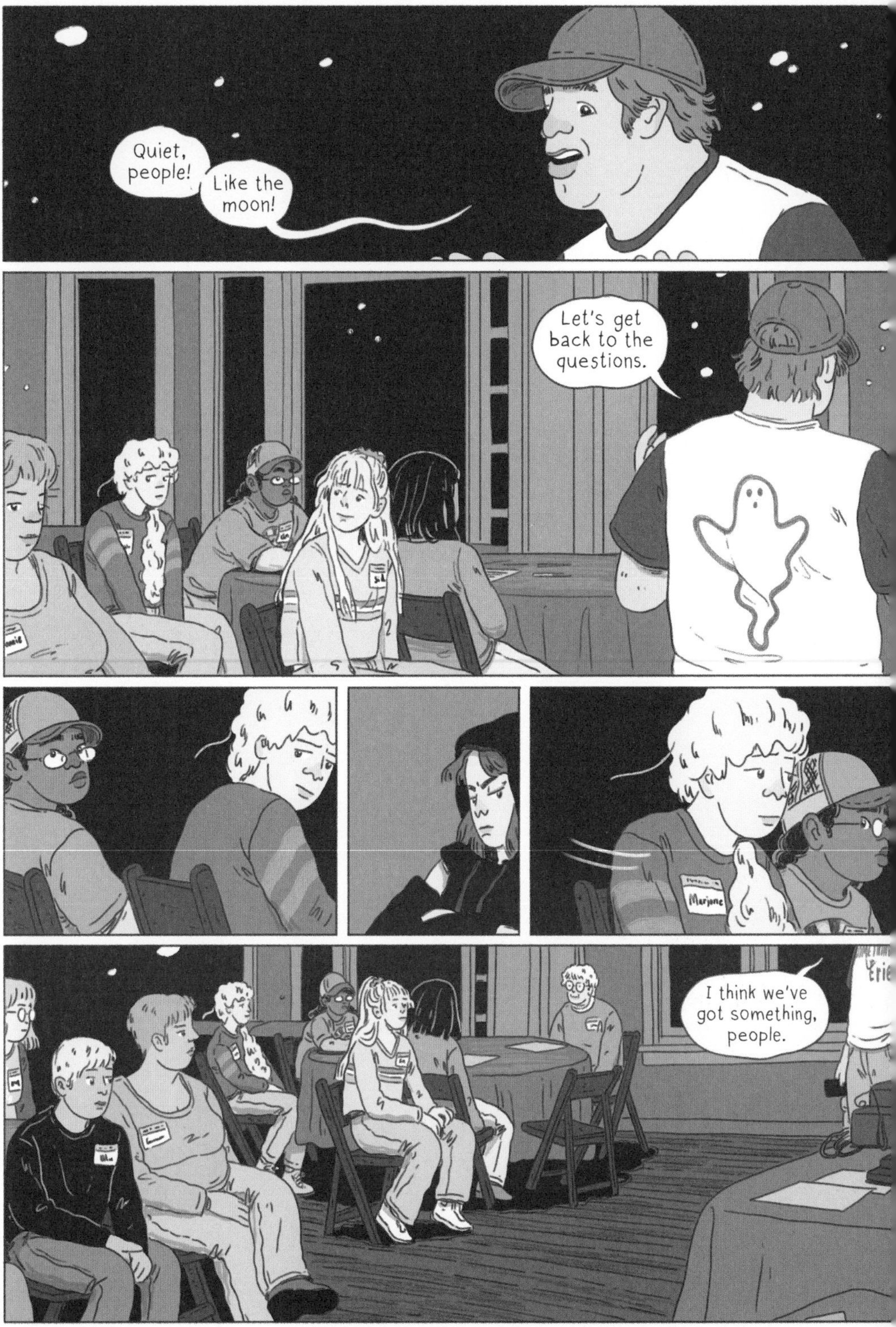
Quiet, people!
Like the moon!
Let's get back to the questions.
I think we've got something, people.

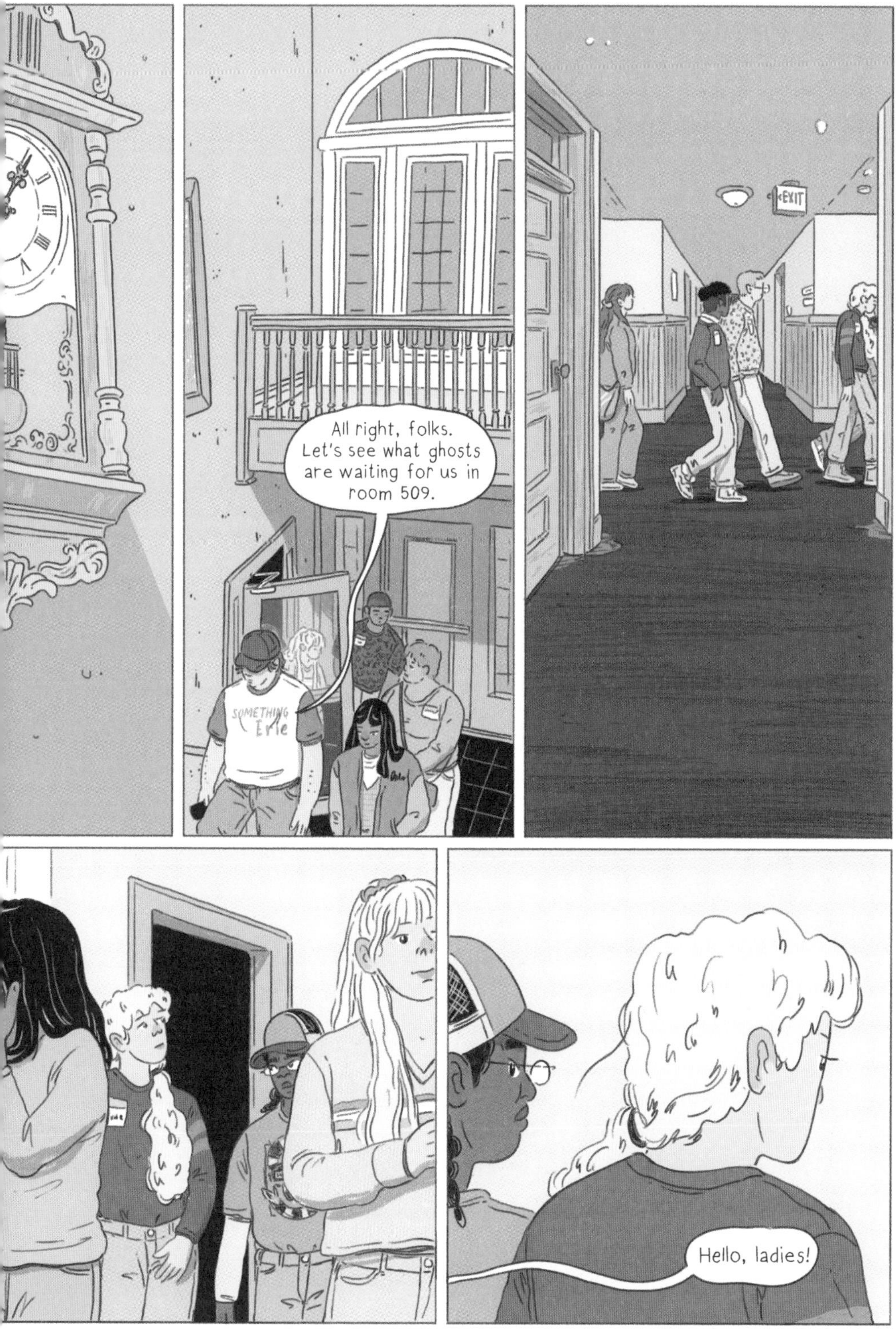
All right, folks. Let's see what ghosts are waiting for us in room 509.
SOMETHING Erie
EXIT
Hello, ladies!

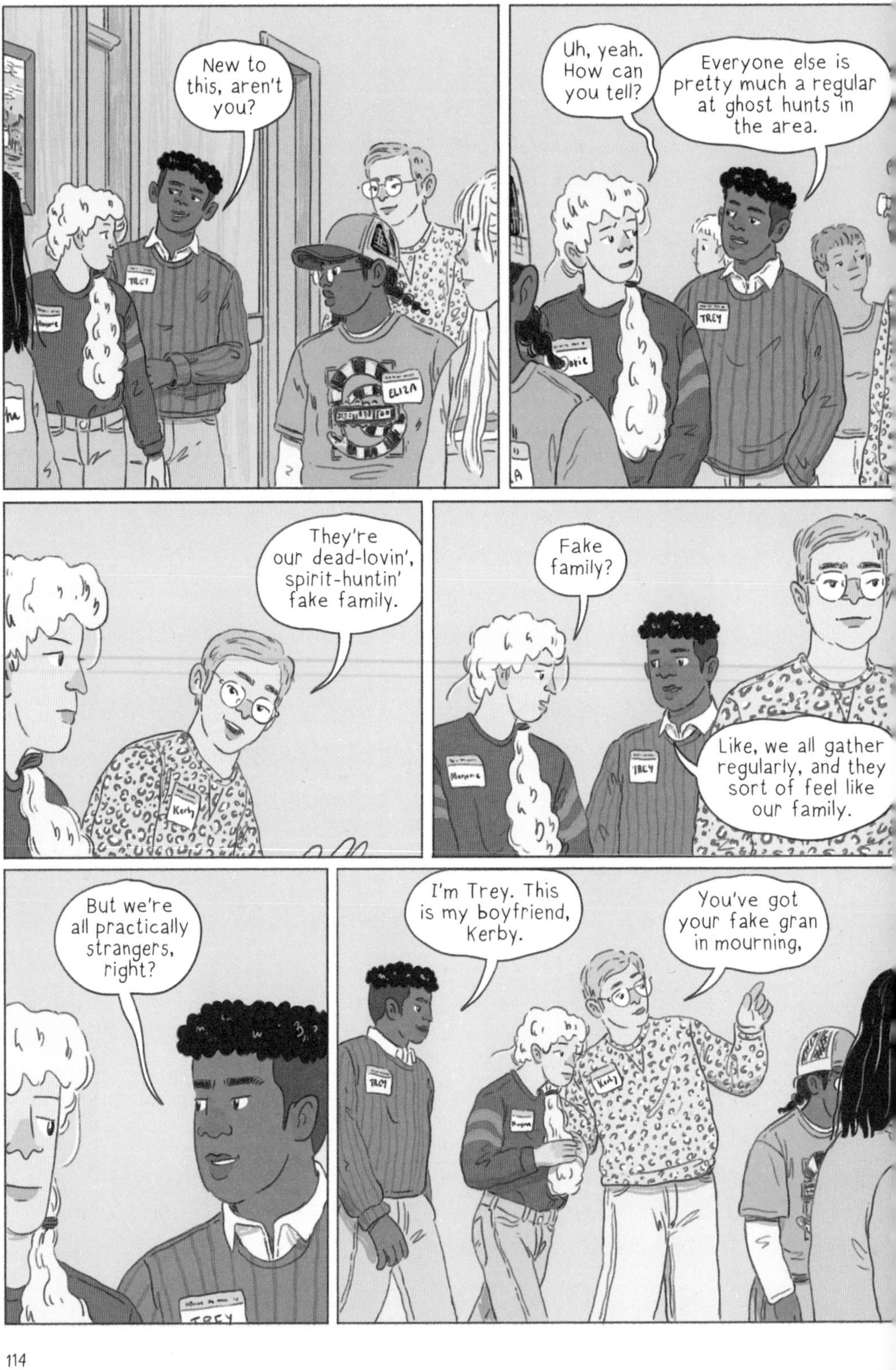
New to this, aren't you?
TREY
ELIZA
Uh, yeah. How can you tell?
Everyone else is pretty much a regular at ghost hunts in the area.
TREY
They're our dead-lovin', spirit-huntin' fake family.
Kerby
Fake family?
TREY
Like, we all gather regularly, and they sort of feel like our family.
But we're all practically strangers, right?
I'm Trey. This is my boyfriend, Kerby.
You've got your fake gran in mourning,
TREY

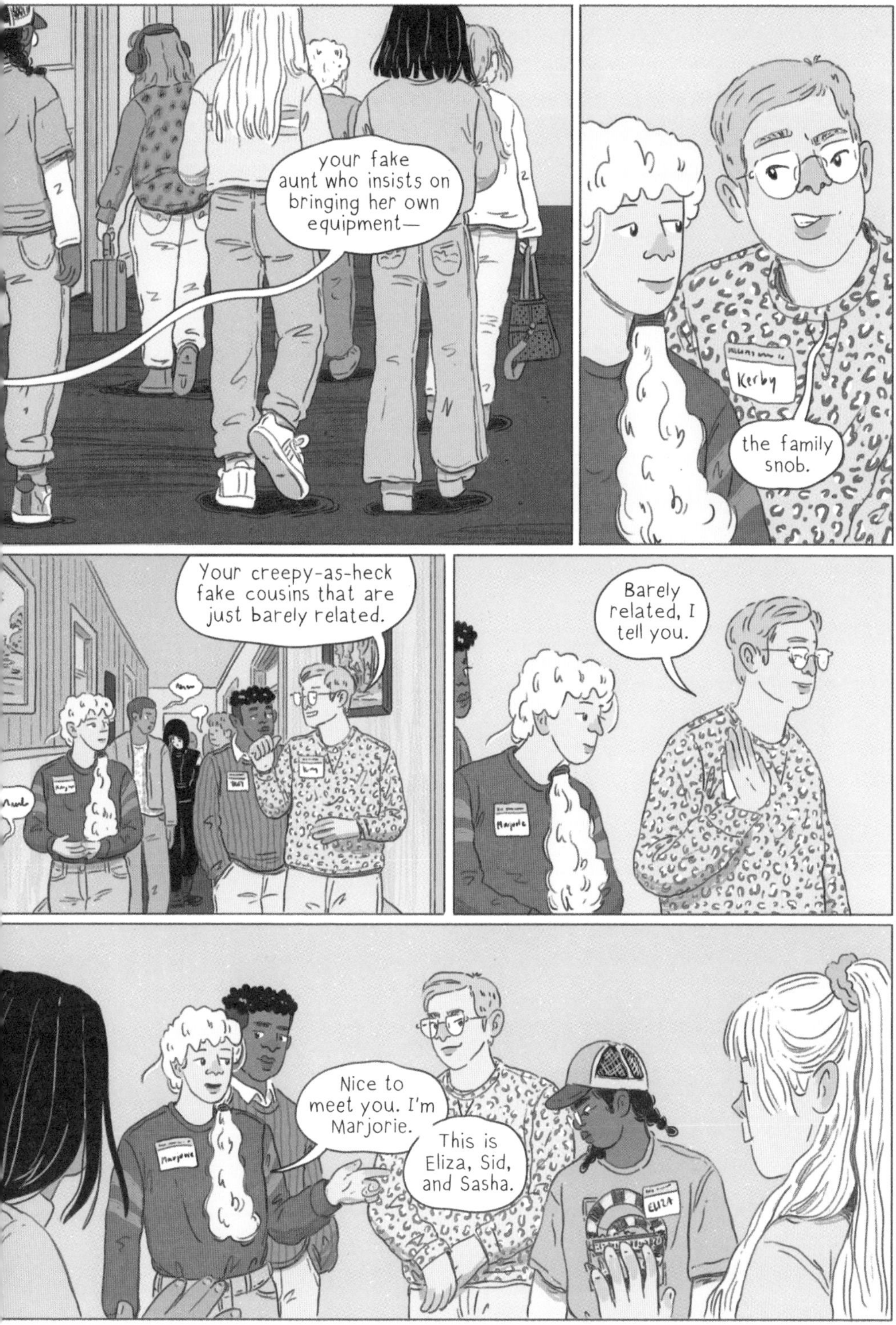
your fake aunt who insists on bringing her own equipment—
Kerby
the family snob.
Your creepy-as-heck fake cousins that are just barely related.
Barely related, I tell you.
Nice to meet you. I'm Marjorie.
This is Eliza, Sid, and Sasha.
ELIZA

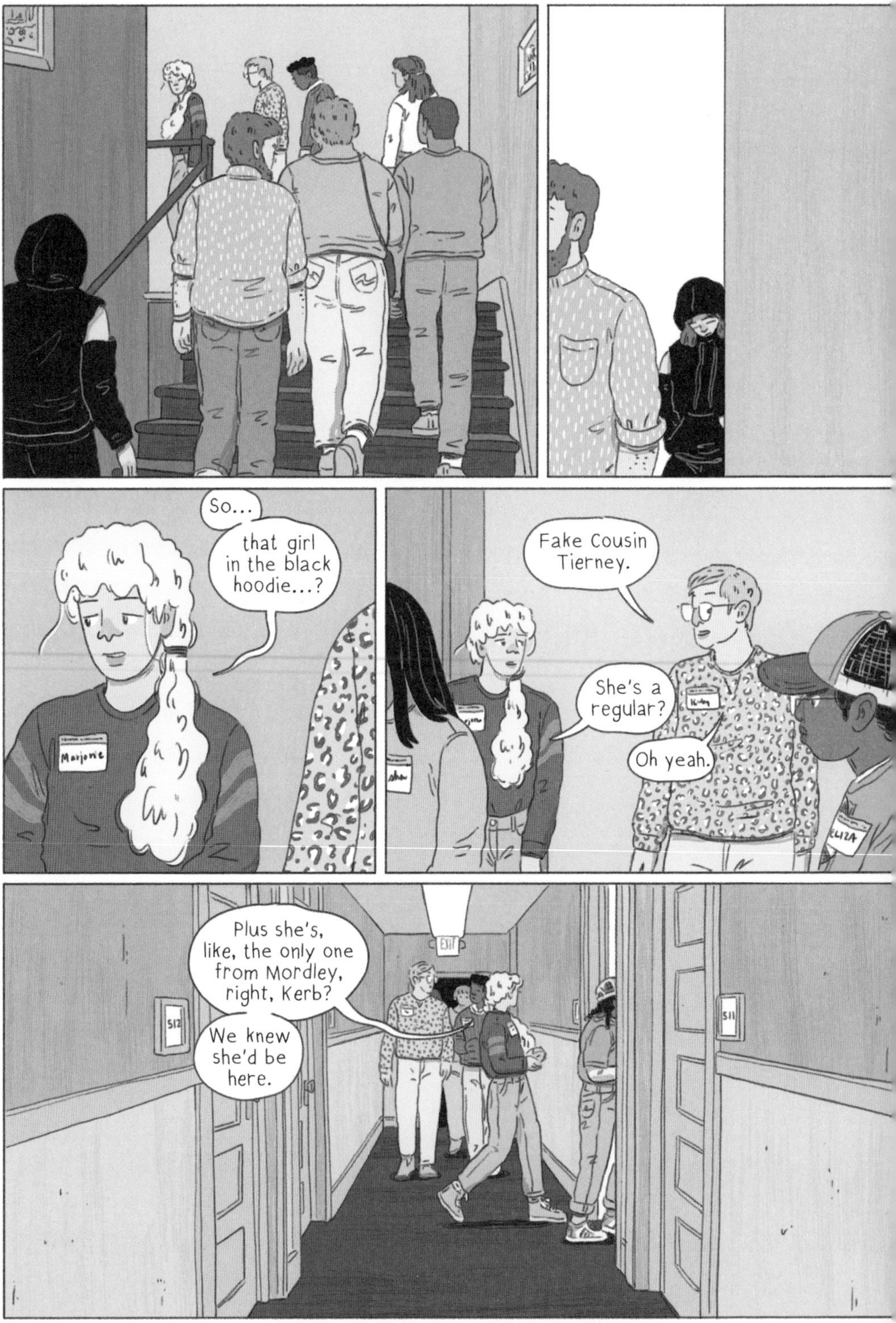
So...
that girl in the black hoodie...?
Fake Cousin Tierney.
She's a regular?
Oh yeah.
Plus she's, like, the only one from Mordley, right, Kerb?
We knew she'd be here.

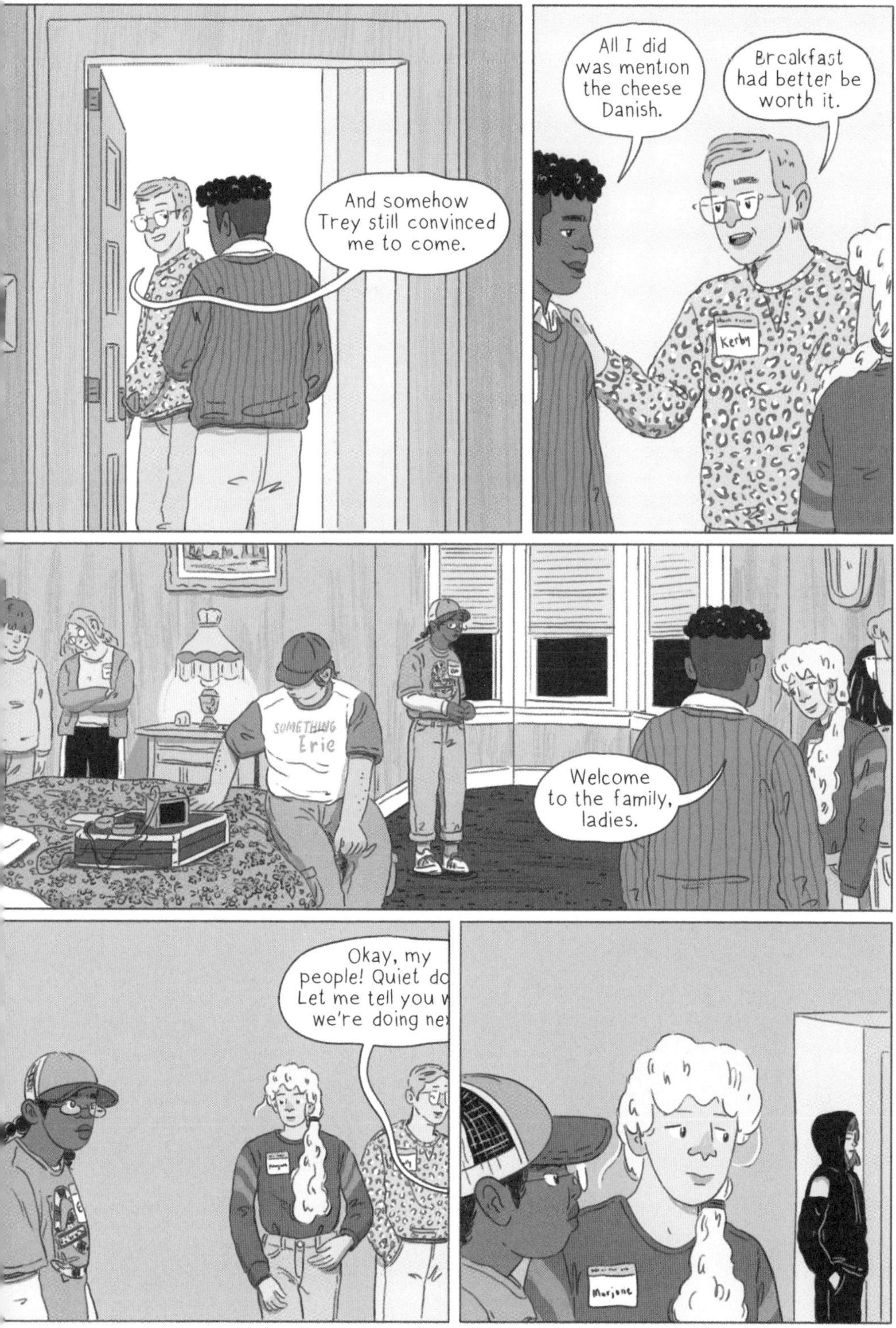
And somehow Trey still convinced me to come.
All I did was mention the cheese Danish.
Breakfast had better be worth it.
Kerby
SOMETHING Erie
Welcome to the family, ladies.
Okay, my people! Quiet do
Let me tell you w
we're doing ne
Marjorie

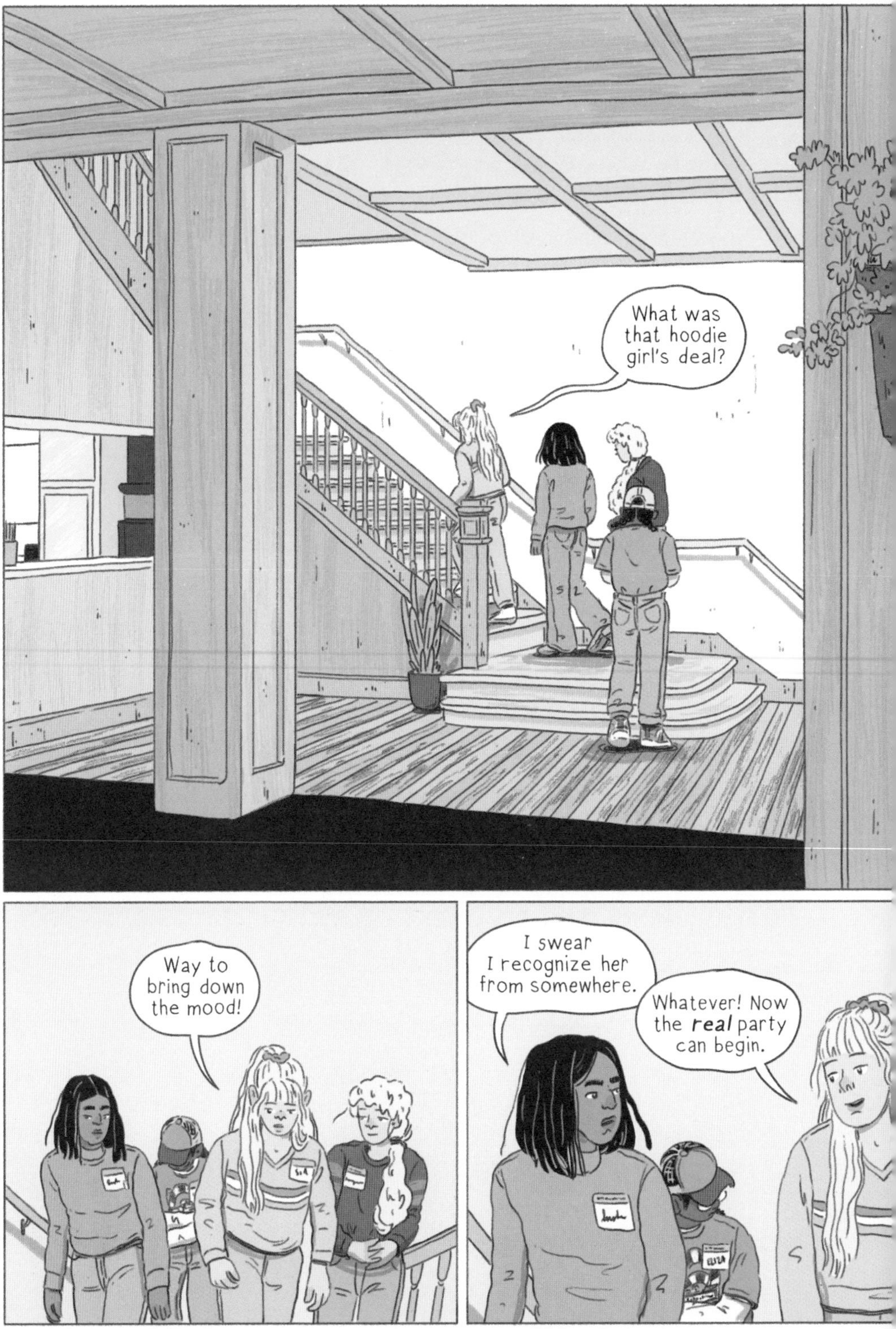
What was that hoodie girl's deal?
Way to bring down the mood!
I swear I recognize her from somewhere.
Whatever! Now the *real* party can begin.

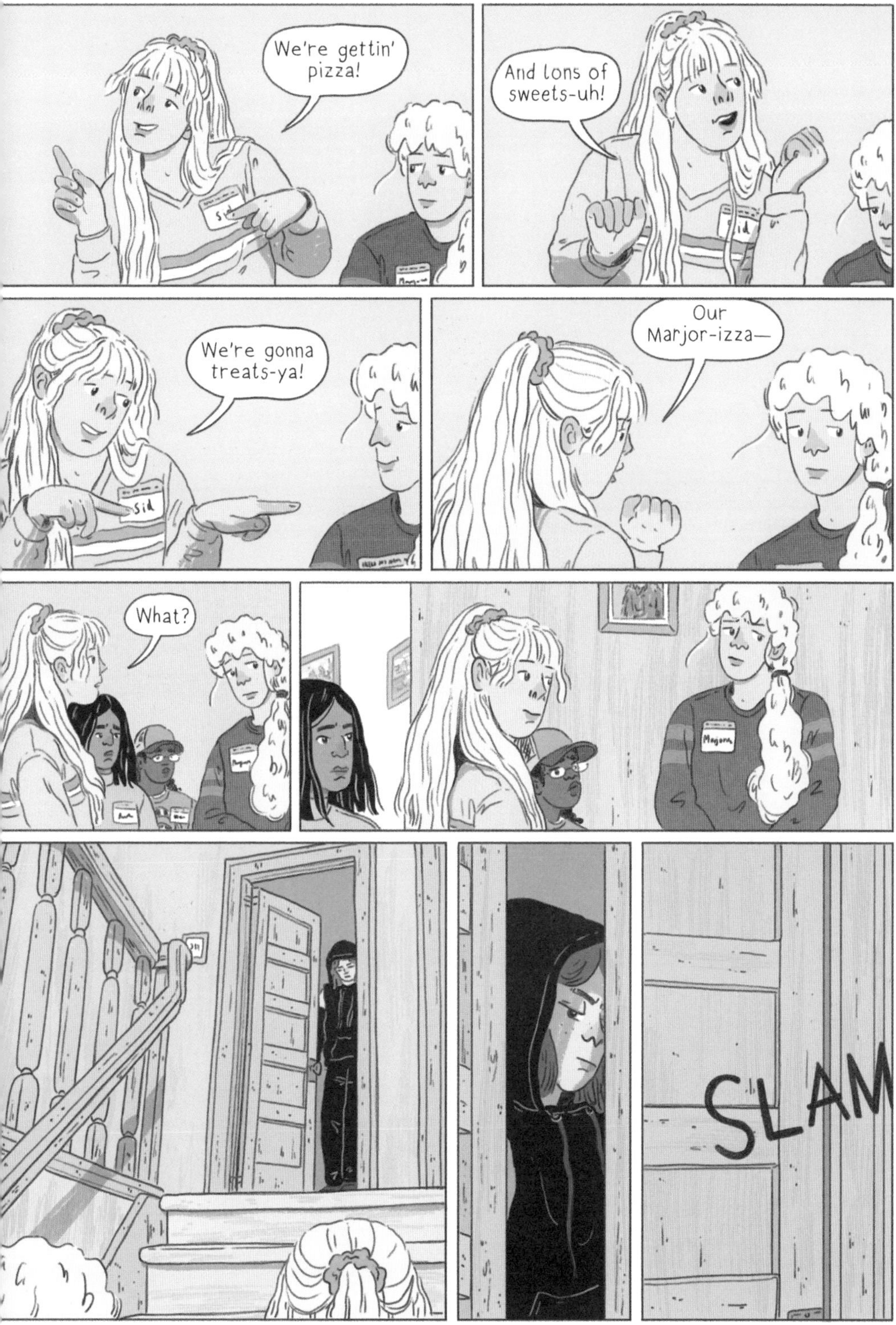
We're gettin' pizza!
And lons of sweets-uh!
We're gonna treats-ya!
Our Marjor-izza—
What?
SLAM

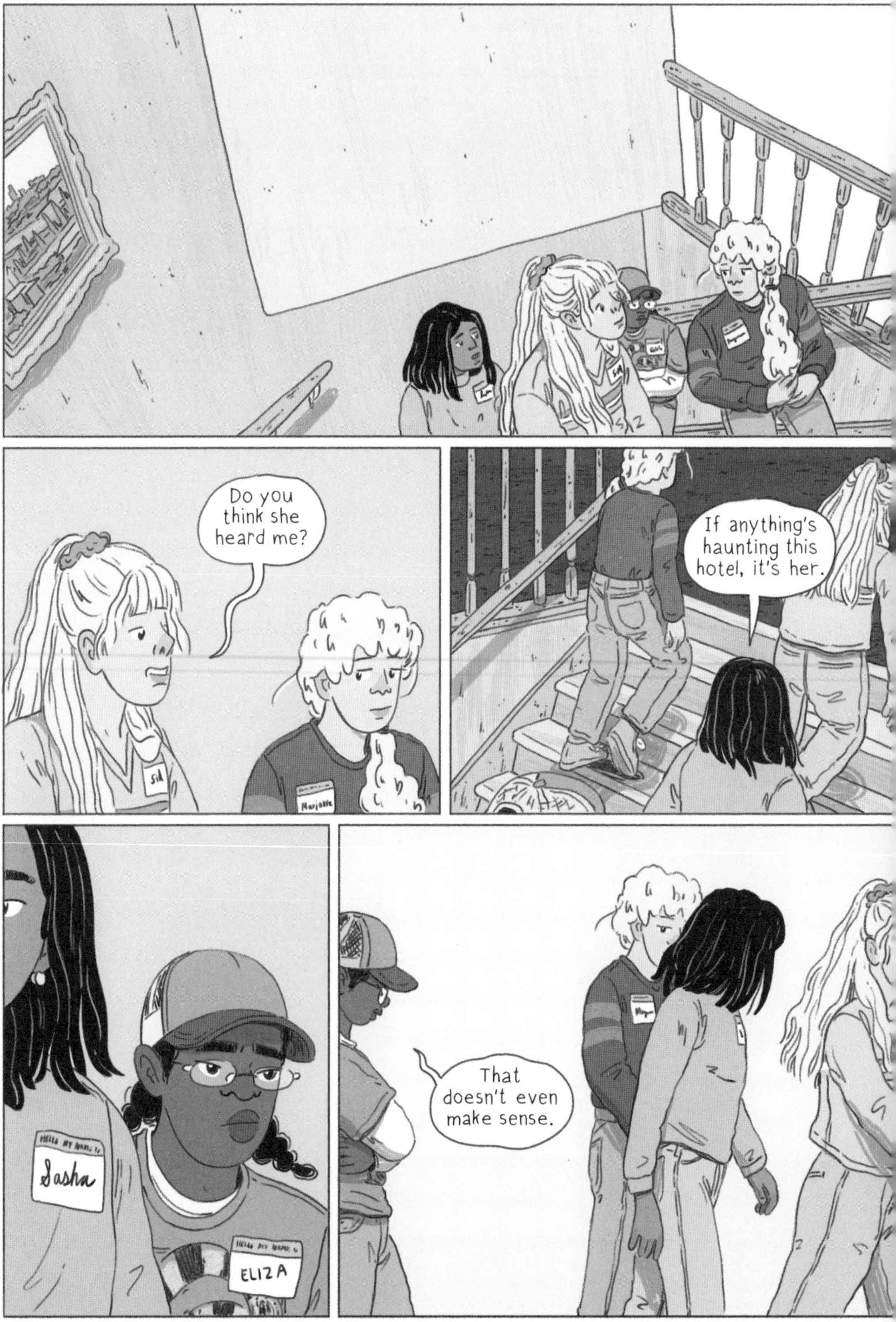
Do you think she heard me?
If anything's haunting this hotel, it's her.
Sasha
ELIZA
That doesn't even make sense.

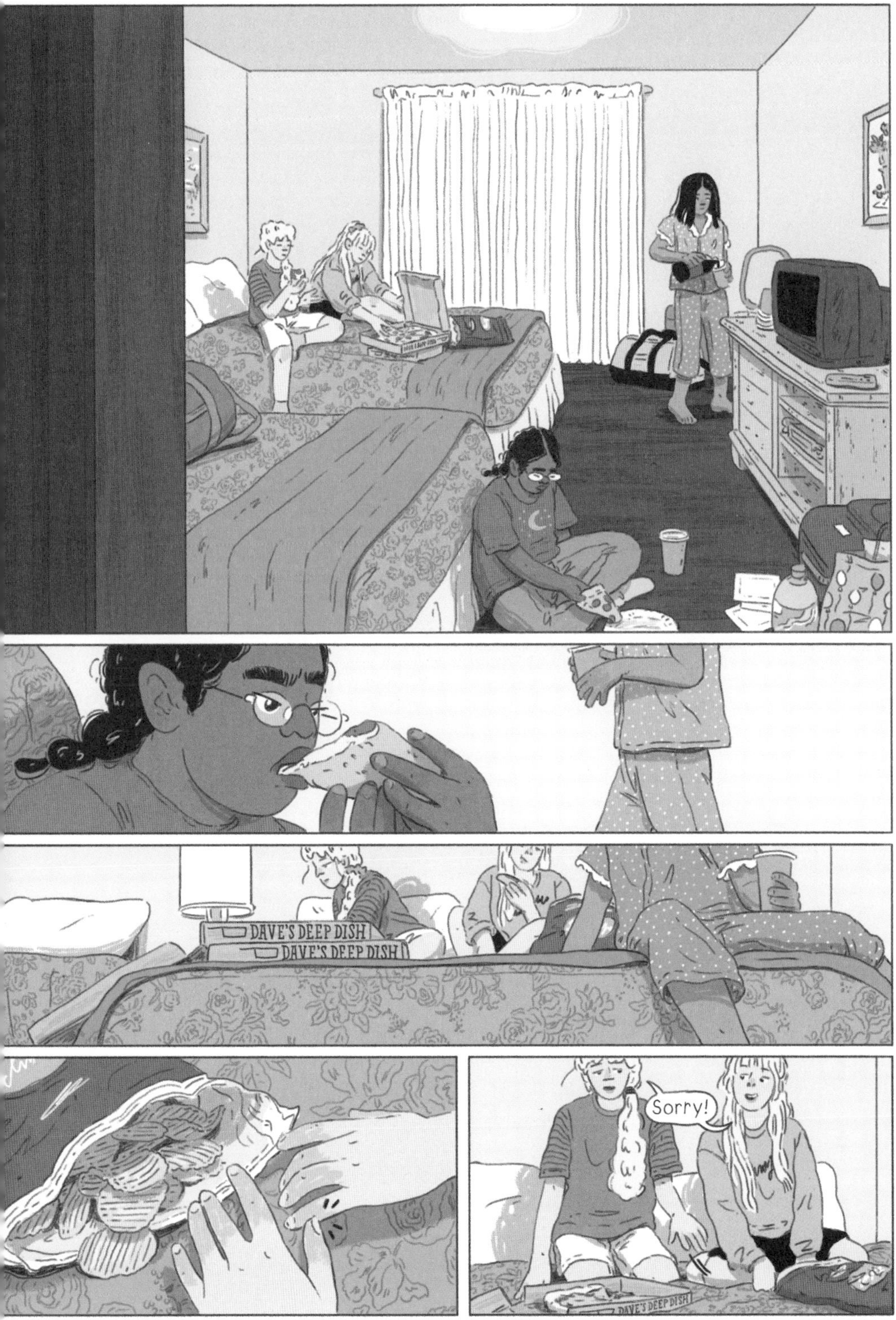
DAVE'S DEEP DISH
DAVE'S DEEP DISH
Sorry!
DAVE'S DEEP DISH

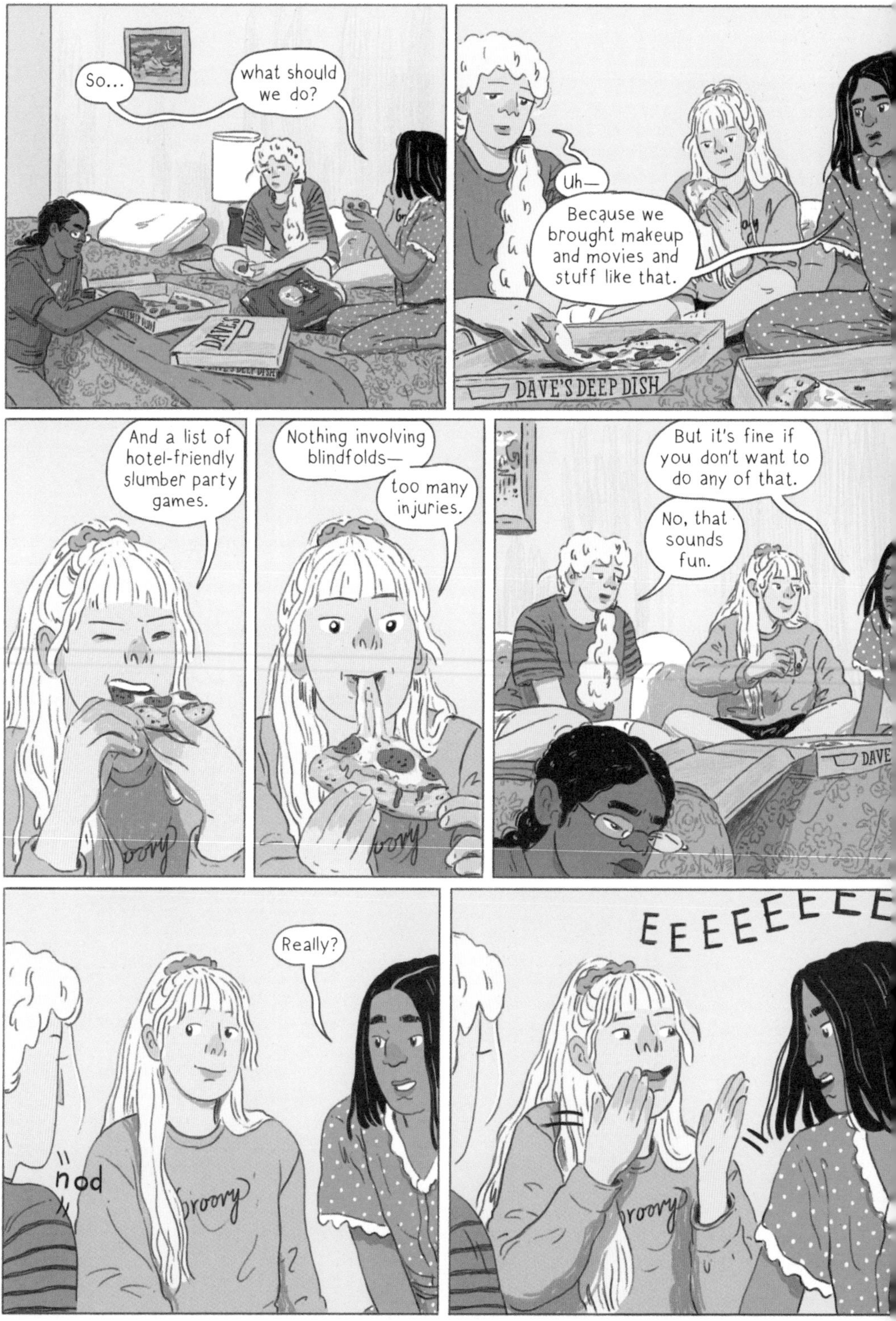
So...
what should we do?
Uh—
Because we brought makeup and movies and stuff like that.
DAVE'S DEEP DISH
And a list of hotel-friendly slumber party games.
Nothing involving blindfolds—
too many injuries.
But it's fine if you don't want to do any of that.
No, that sounds fun.
Really?
nod
EEEEEEEE

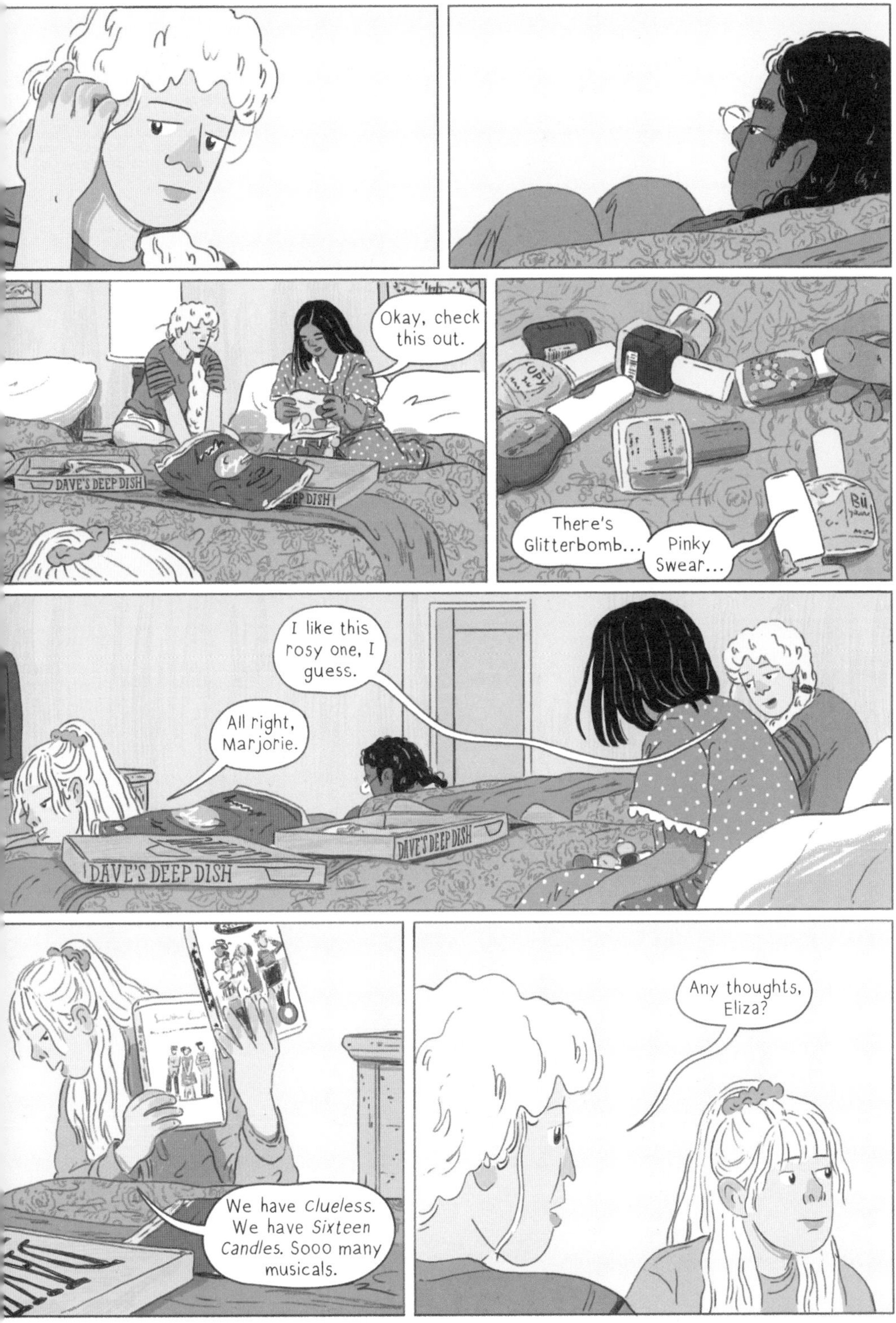
Okay, check this out.
DAVE'S DEEP DISH
DEEP DISH!
There's Glitterbomb...
Pinky Swear...
I like this rosy one, I guess.
All right, Marjorie.
DAVE'S DEEP DISH
DAVE'S DEEP DISH
We have *Clueless.* We have *Sixteen Candles.* Sooo many musicals.
Any thoughts, Eliza?

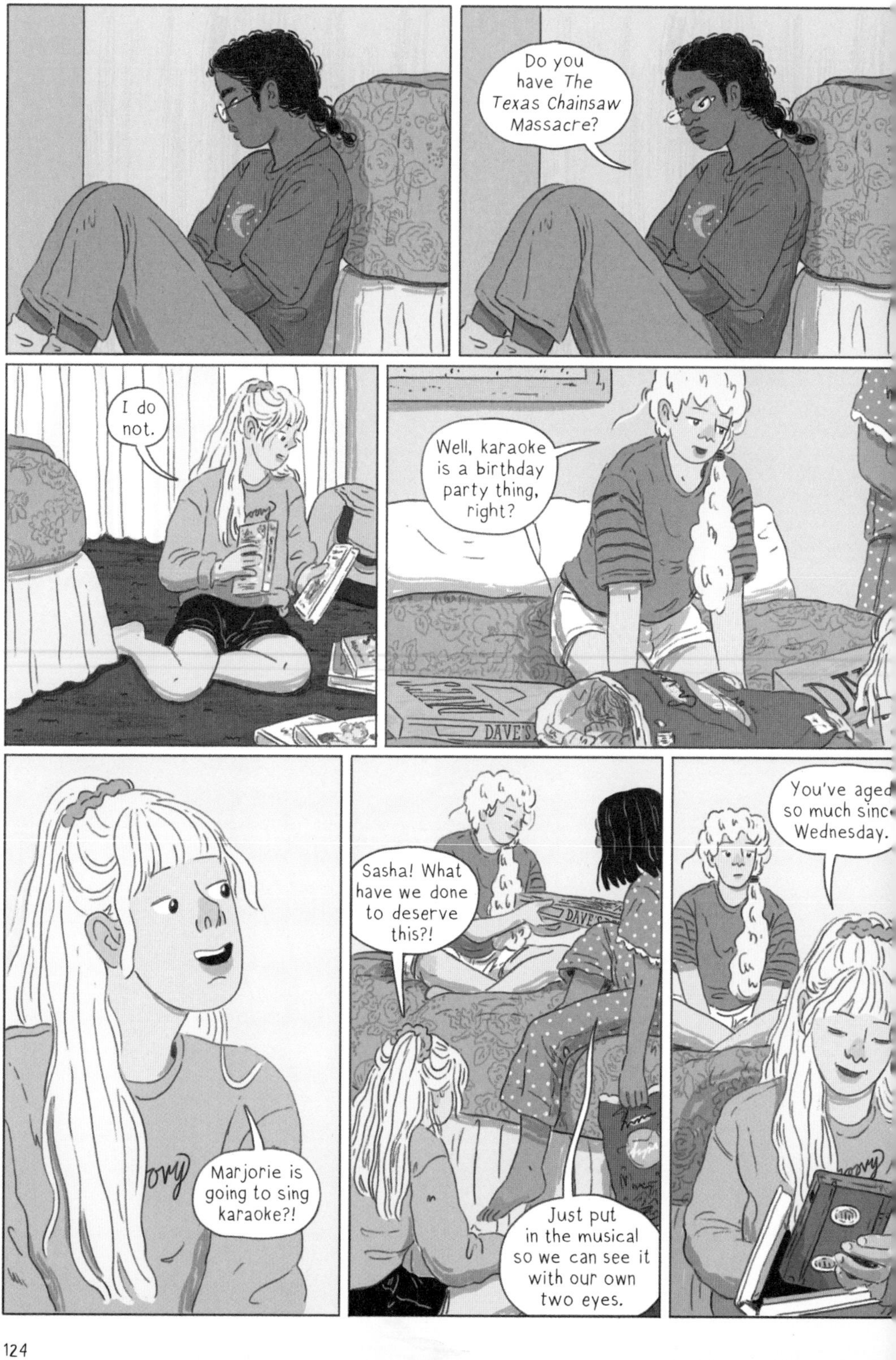

Do you have *The Texas Chainsaw Massacre?*
I do not.
Well, karaoke is a birthday party thing, right?
DAVE'S
Marjorie is going to sing karaoke?!
Sasha! What have we done to deserve this?!
Just put in the musical so we can see it with our own two eyes.
You've aged so much since Wednesday.

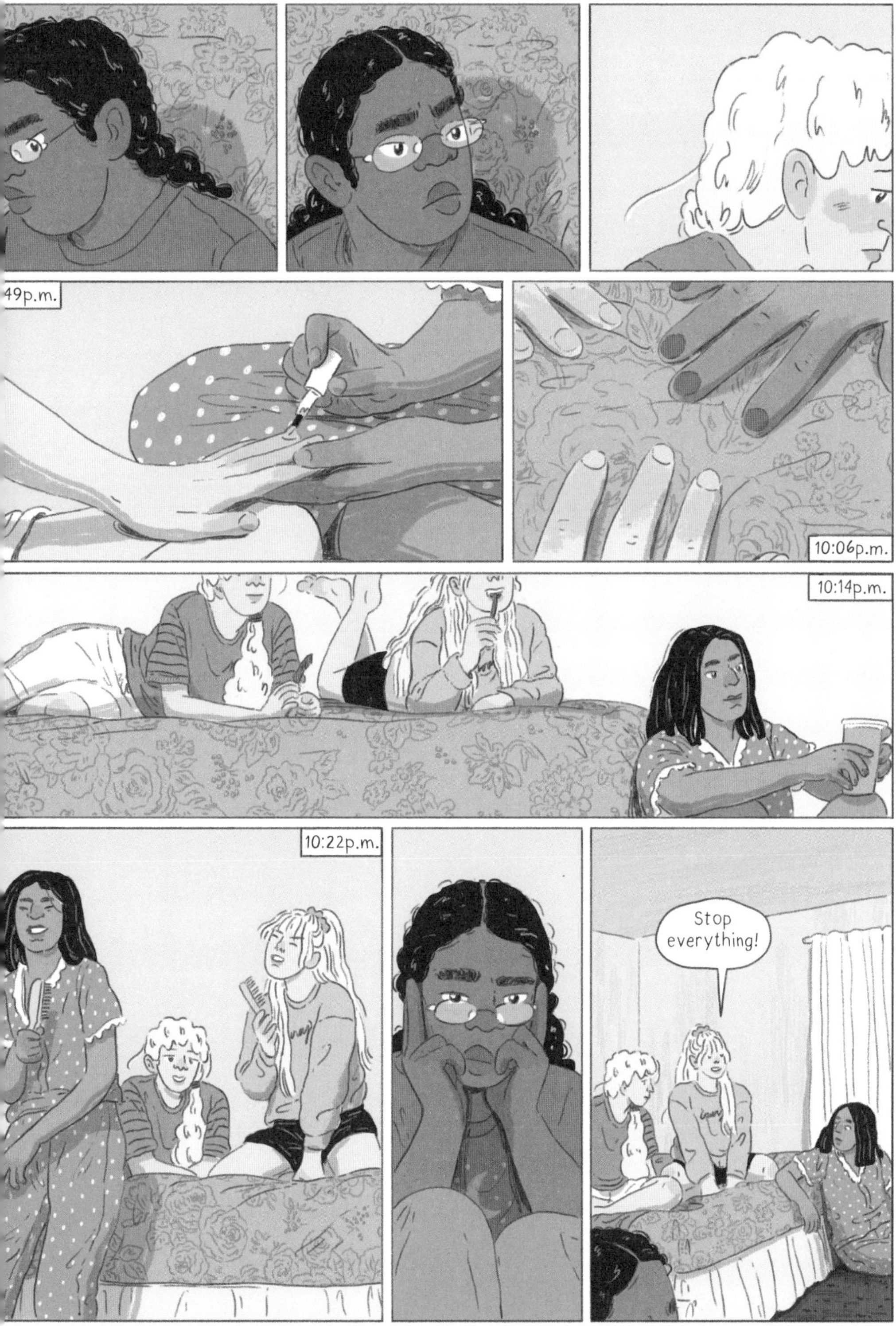
49p.m.
10:06p.m.
10:14p.m.
10:22p.m.
Stop everything!

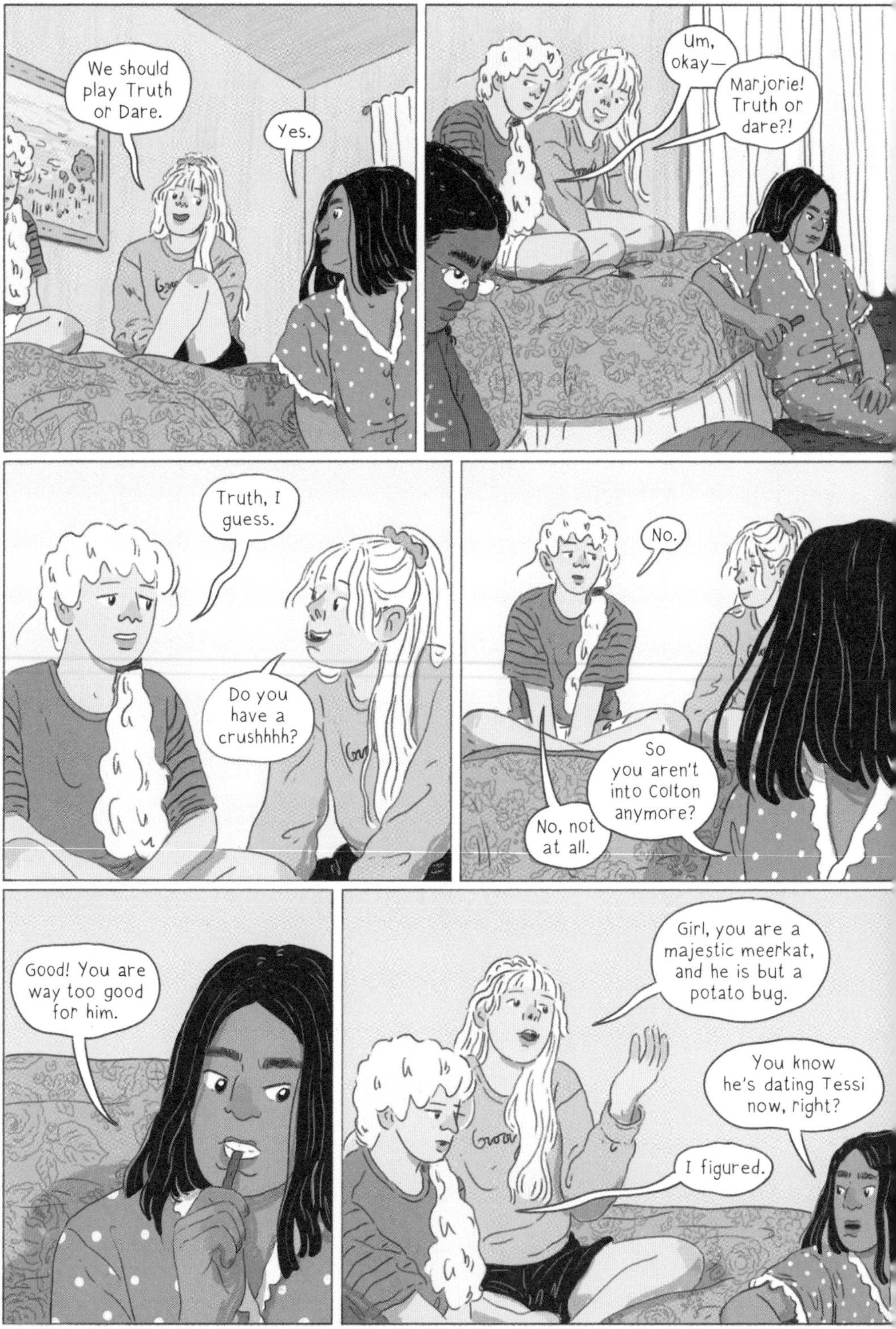

We should play Truth or Dare.
Yes.
Um, okay—
Marjorie! Truth or dare?!
Truth, I guess.
Do you have a crushhhh?
No.
So you aren't into Colton anymore?
No, not at all.
Good! You are way too good for him.
Girl, you are a majestic meerkat, and he is but a potato bug.
You know he's dating Tessi now, right?
I figured.

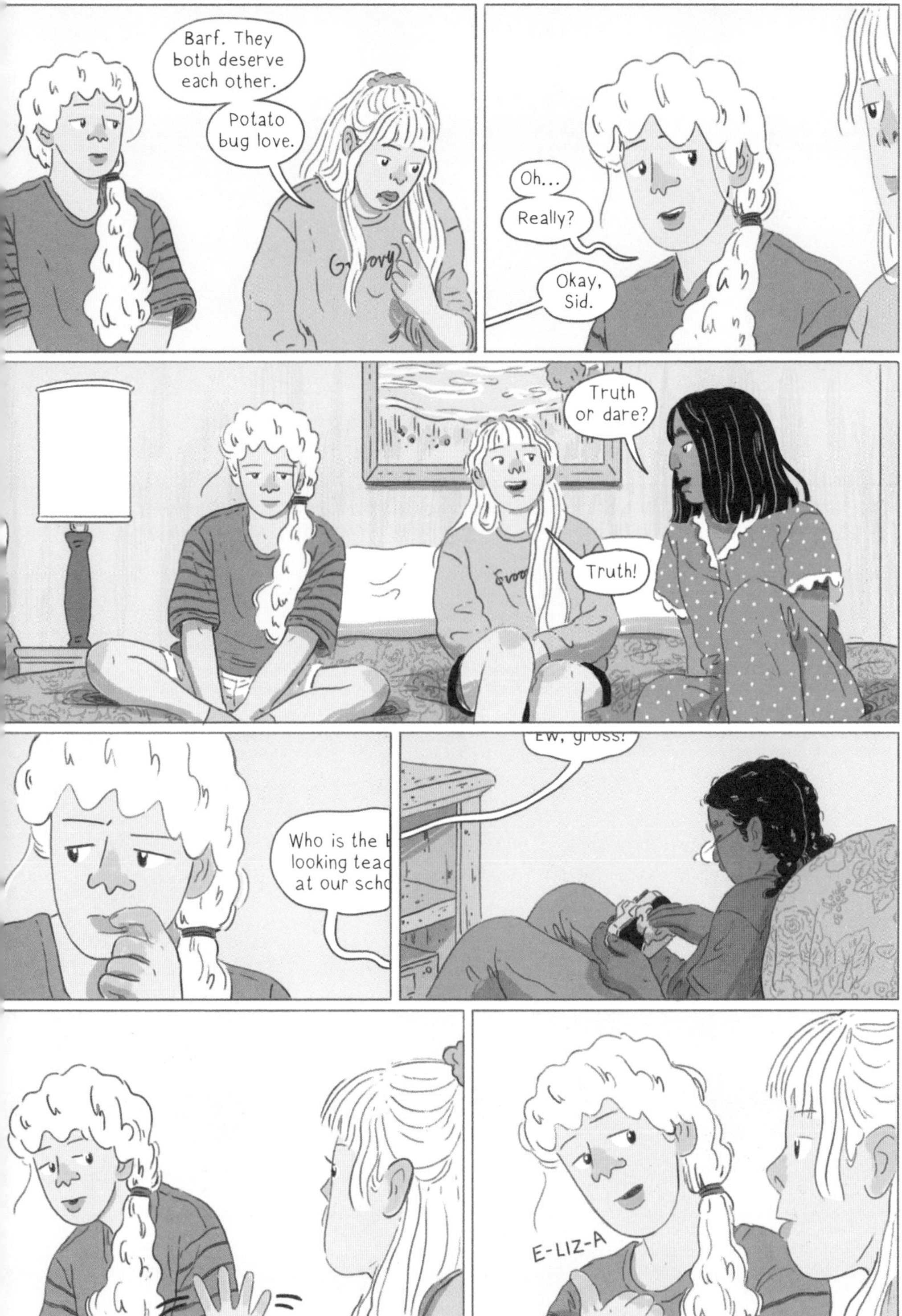

Barf. They both deserve each other.
Potato bug love.
Oh...
Really?
Okay, Sid.
Truth or dare?
Truth!
Who is the
looking tea
at our sch
E-LIZ-A

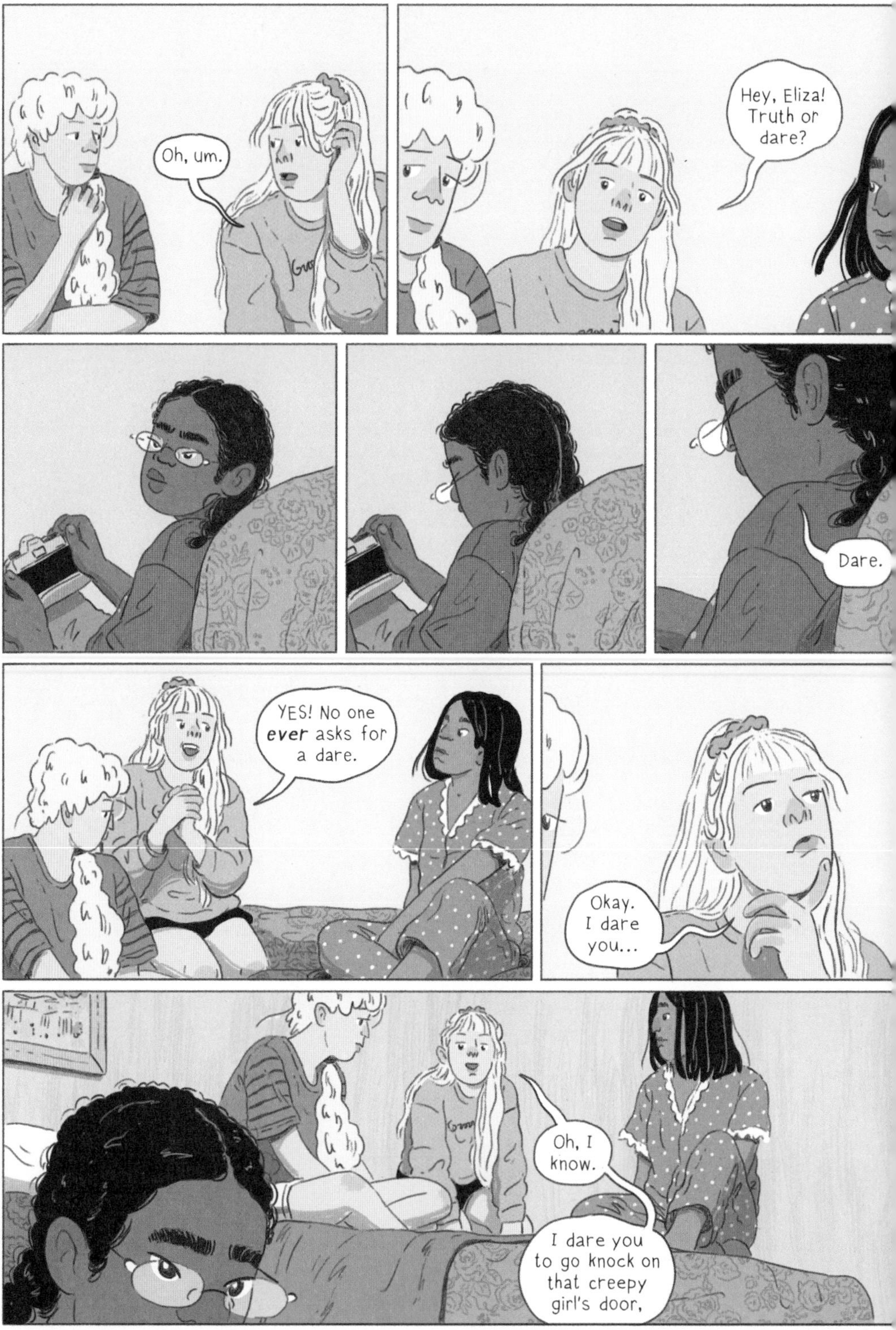
Oh, um.
Hey, Eliza! Truth or dare?
Dare.
YES! No one **ever** asks for a dare.
Okay. I dare you...
Oh, I know.
I dare you to go knock on that creepy girl's door,

and when she answers it, take her photo to prove you did it.

Wait, I'm not sure if that's—

Eliza!

Oh my God! She's doing it!

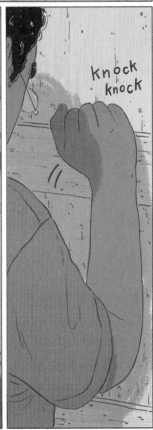

knock knock

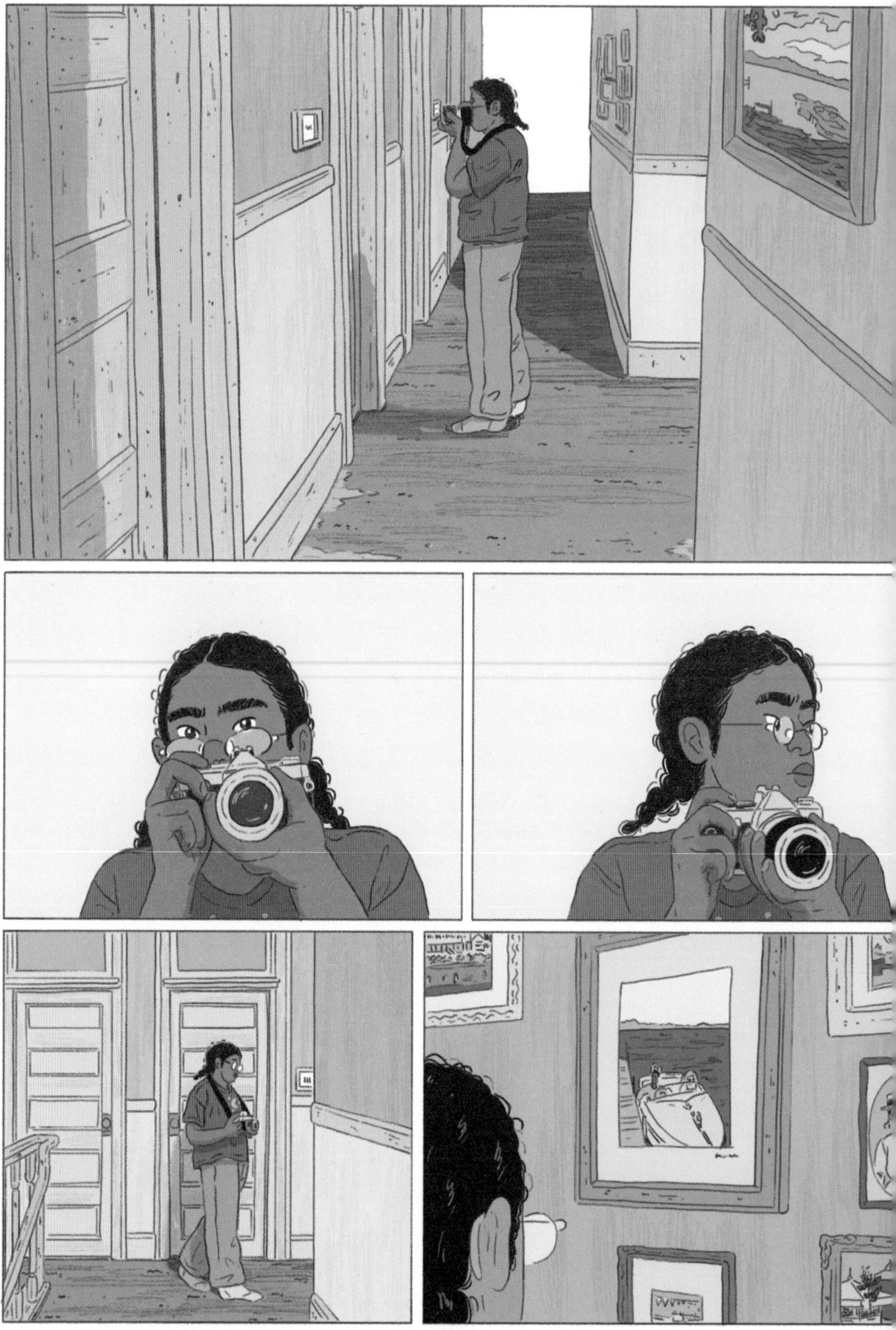

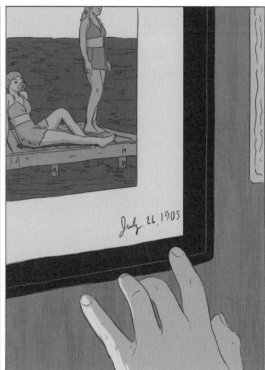

July 26, 1905

CLINK

rustle

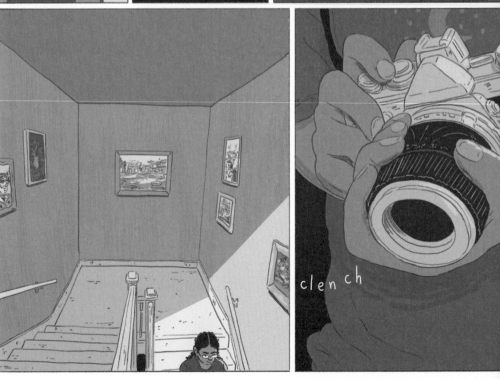

clench

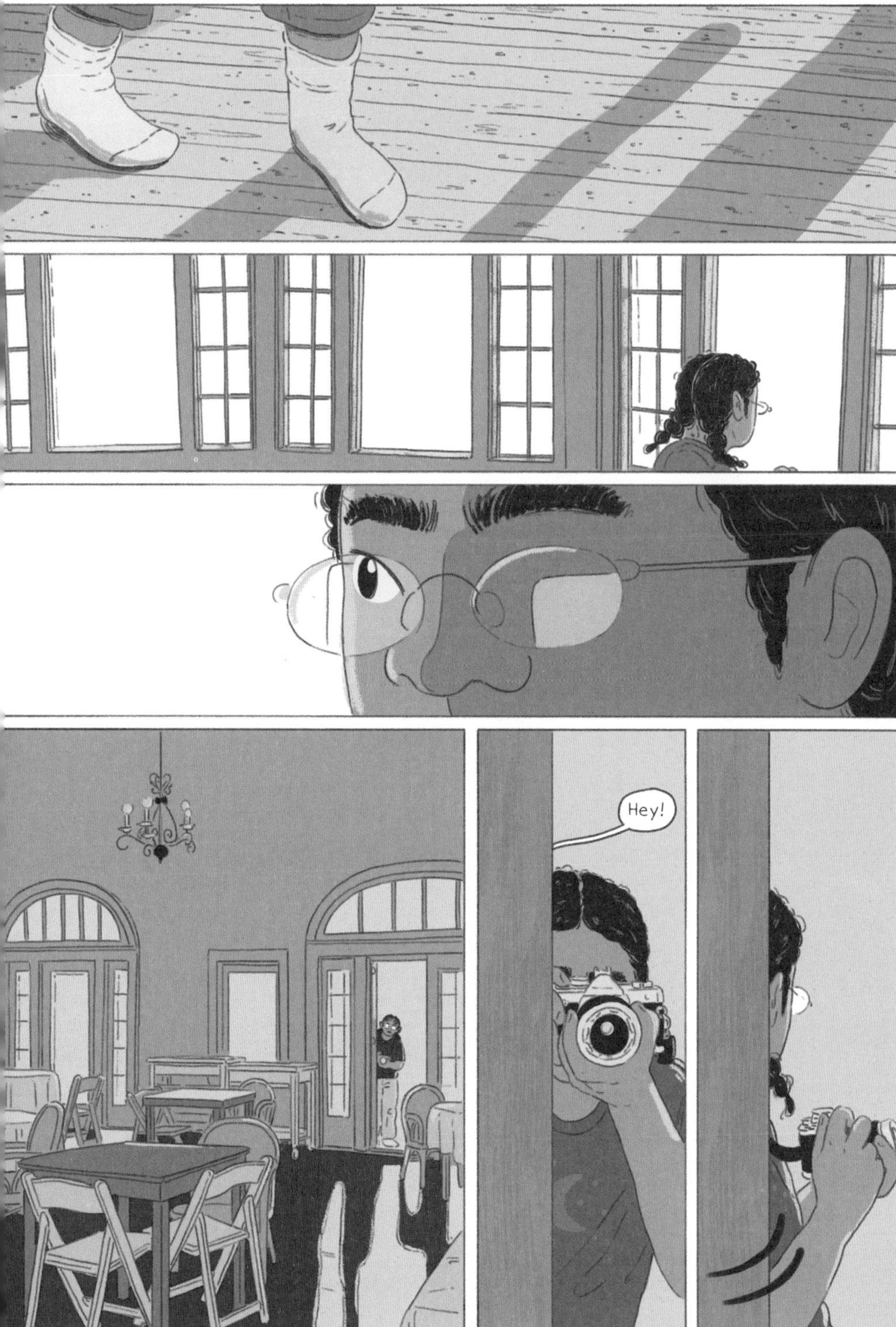
Hey!

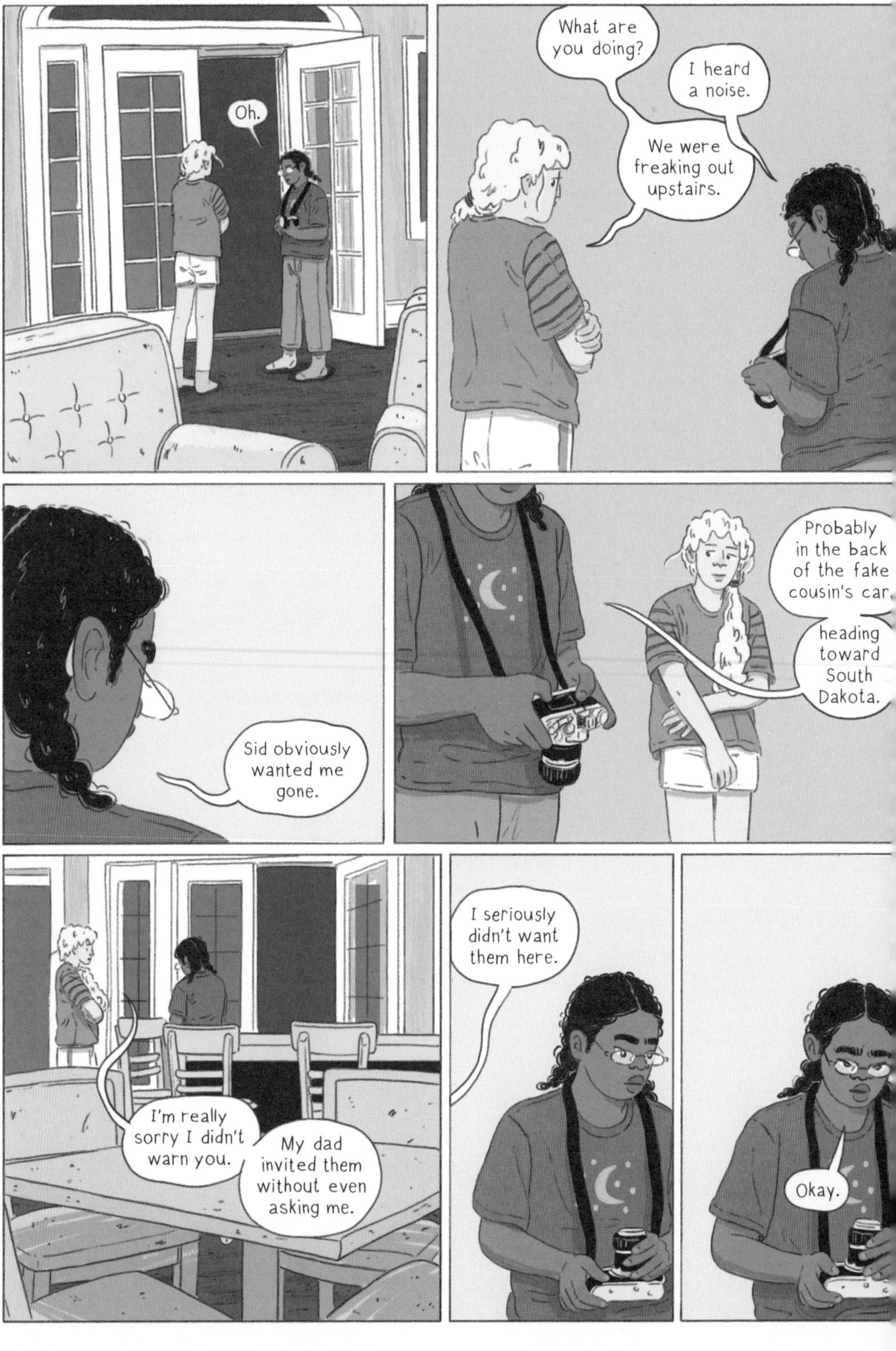
Oh.
What are you doing?
I heard a noise.
We were freaking out upstairs.
Sid obviously wanted me gone.
Probably in the back of the fake cousin's car,
heading toward South Dakota.
I'm really sorry I didn't warn you.
My dad invited them without even asking me.
I seriously didn't want them here.
Okay.

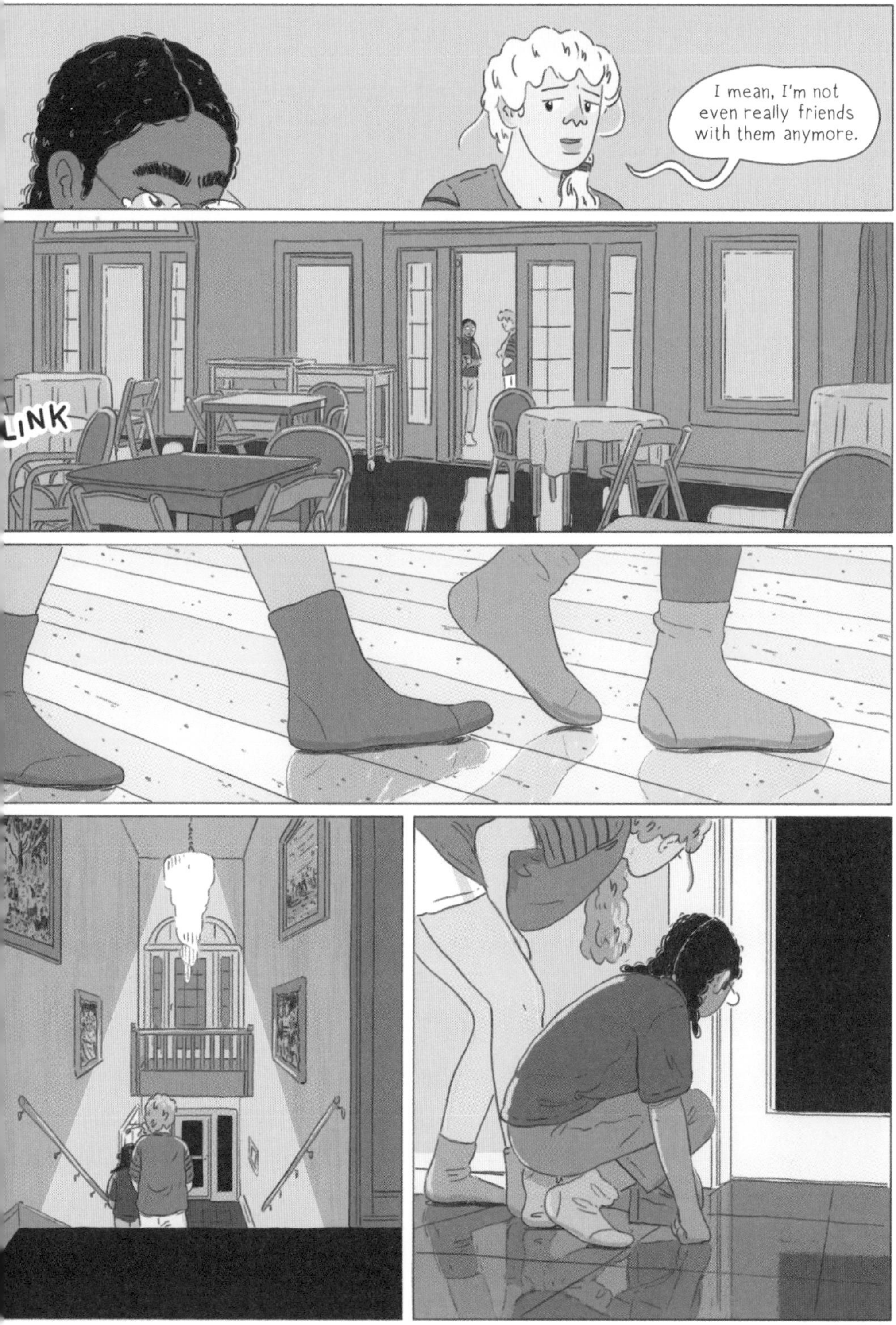
I mean, I'm not even really friends with them anymore.
LINK

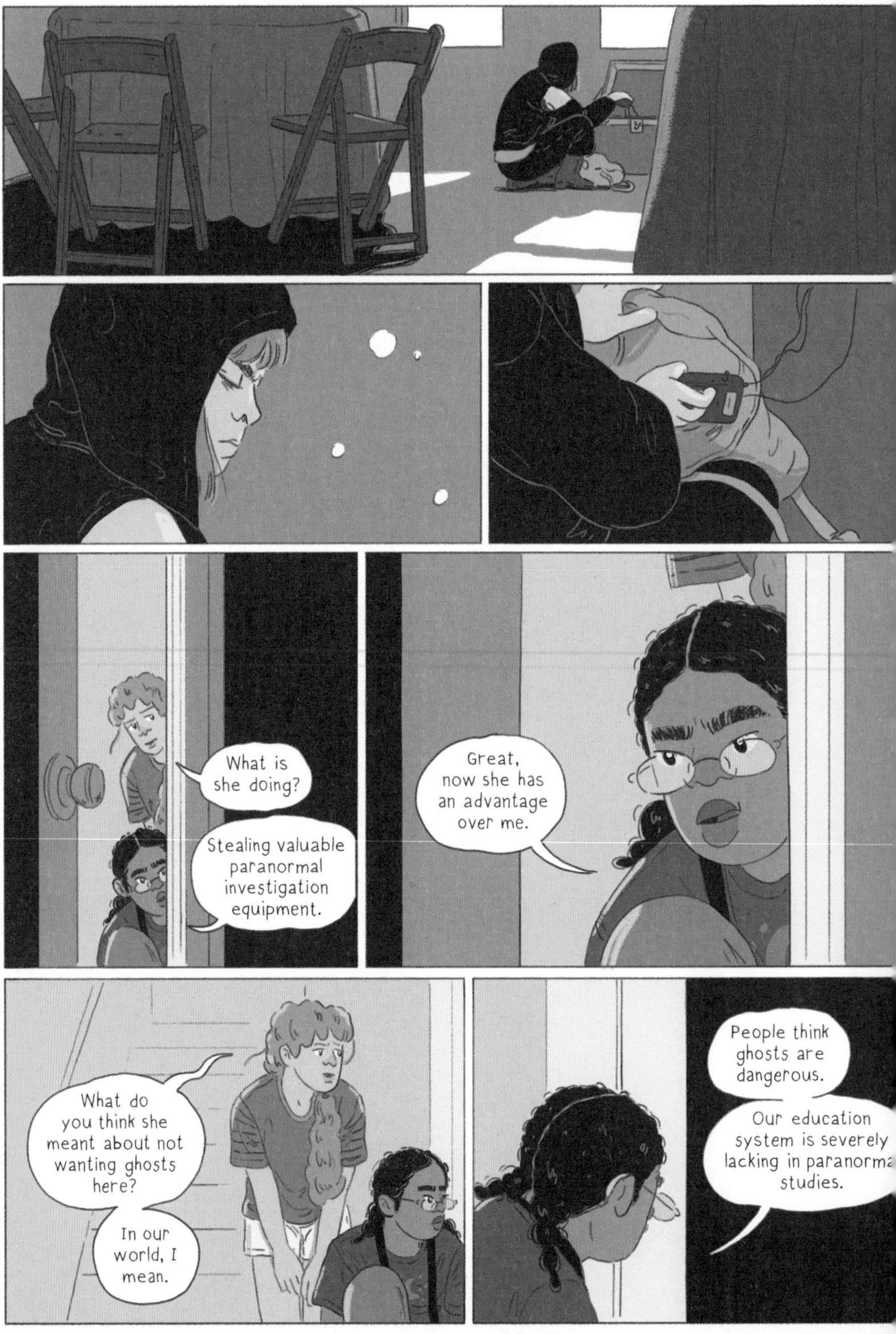
What is she doing?
Stealing valuable paranormal investigation equipment.
Great, now she has an advantage over me.
What do you think she meant about not wanting ghosts here?
In our world, I mean.
People think ghosts are dangerous.
Our education system is severely lacking in paranorma studies.

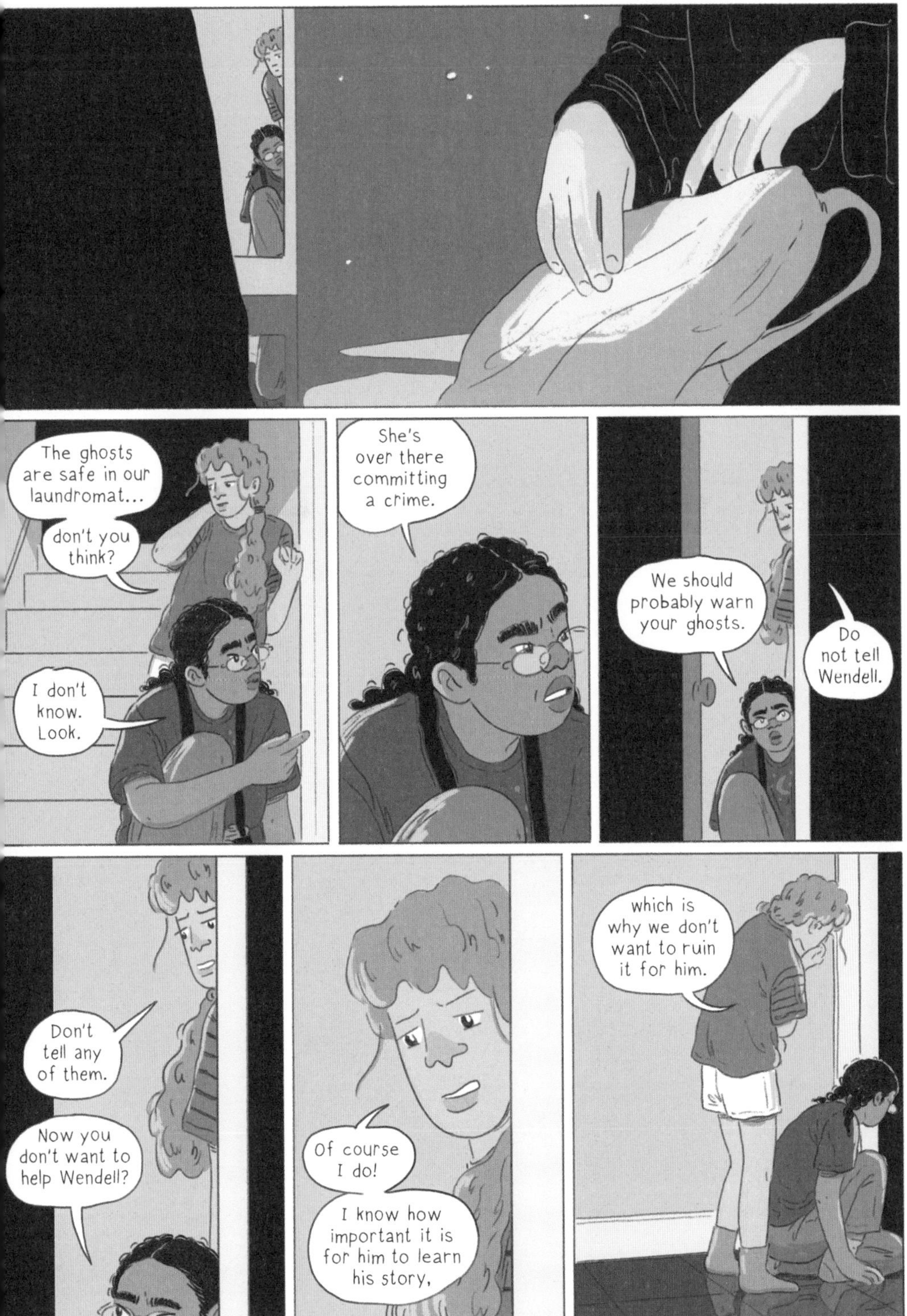
The ghosts are safe in our laundromat...
don't you think?
I don't know. Look.
She's over there committing a crime.
We should probably warn your ghosts.
Do not tell Wendell.
Don't tell any of them.
Now you don't want to help Wendell?
Of course I do!
I know how important it is for him to learn his story,
which is why we don't want to ruin it for him.

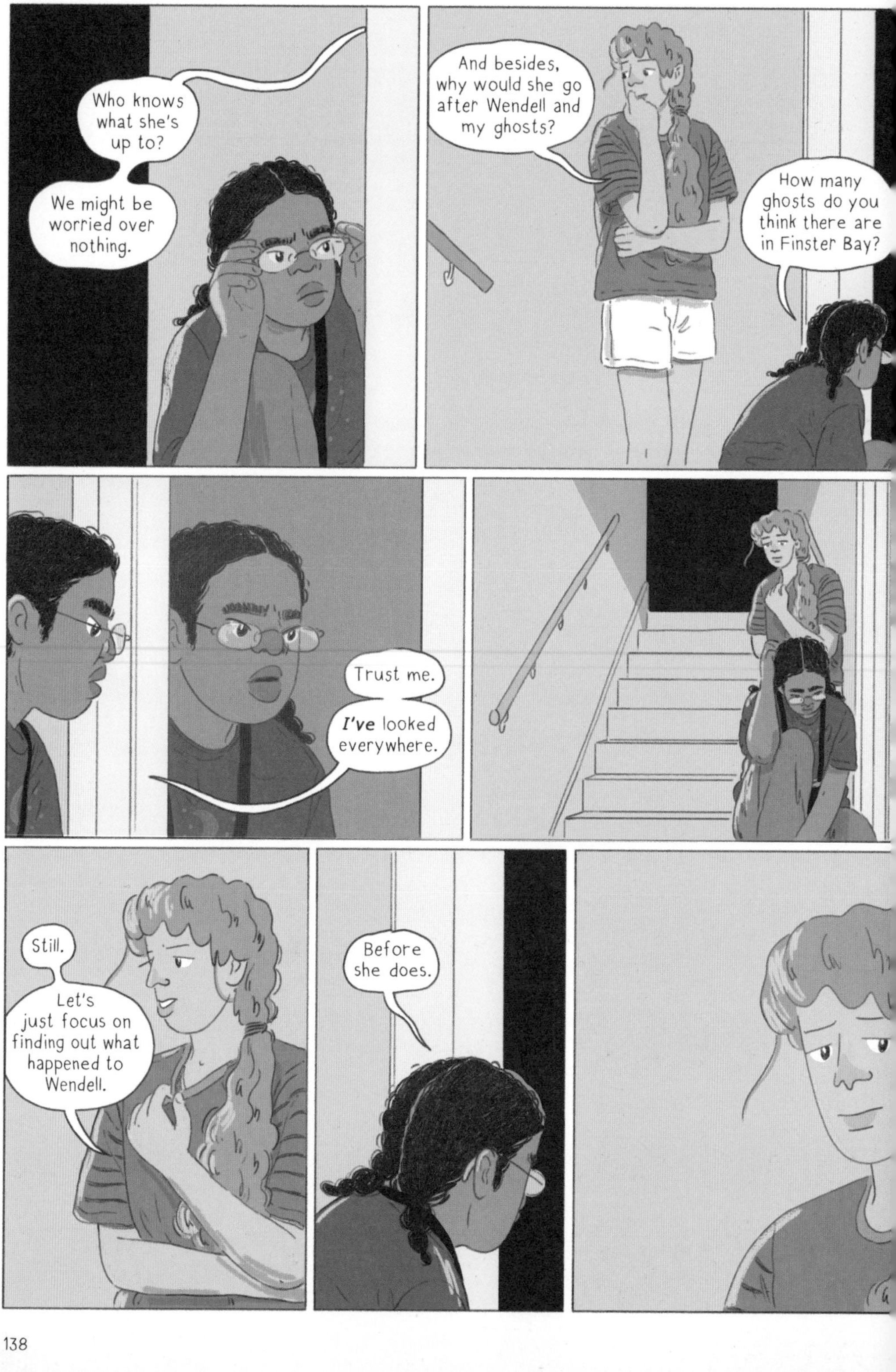
Who knows what she's up to?
We might be worried over nothing.
And besides, why would she go after Wendell and my ghosts?
How many ghosts do you think there are in Finster Bay?
Trust me.
I've looked everywhere.
Still.
Let's just focus on finding out what happened to Wendell.
Before she does.

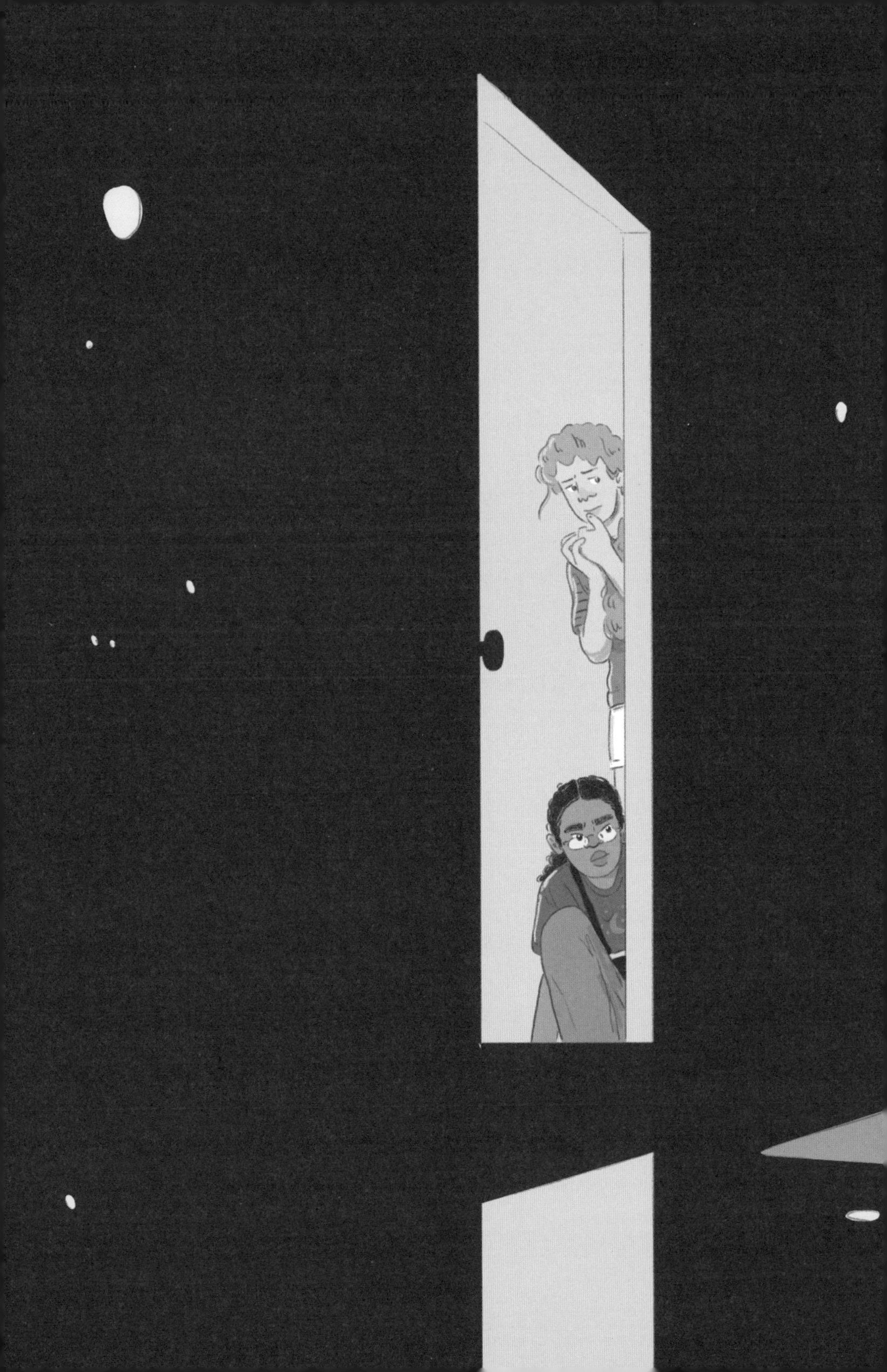

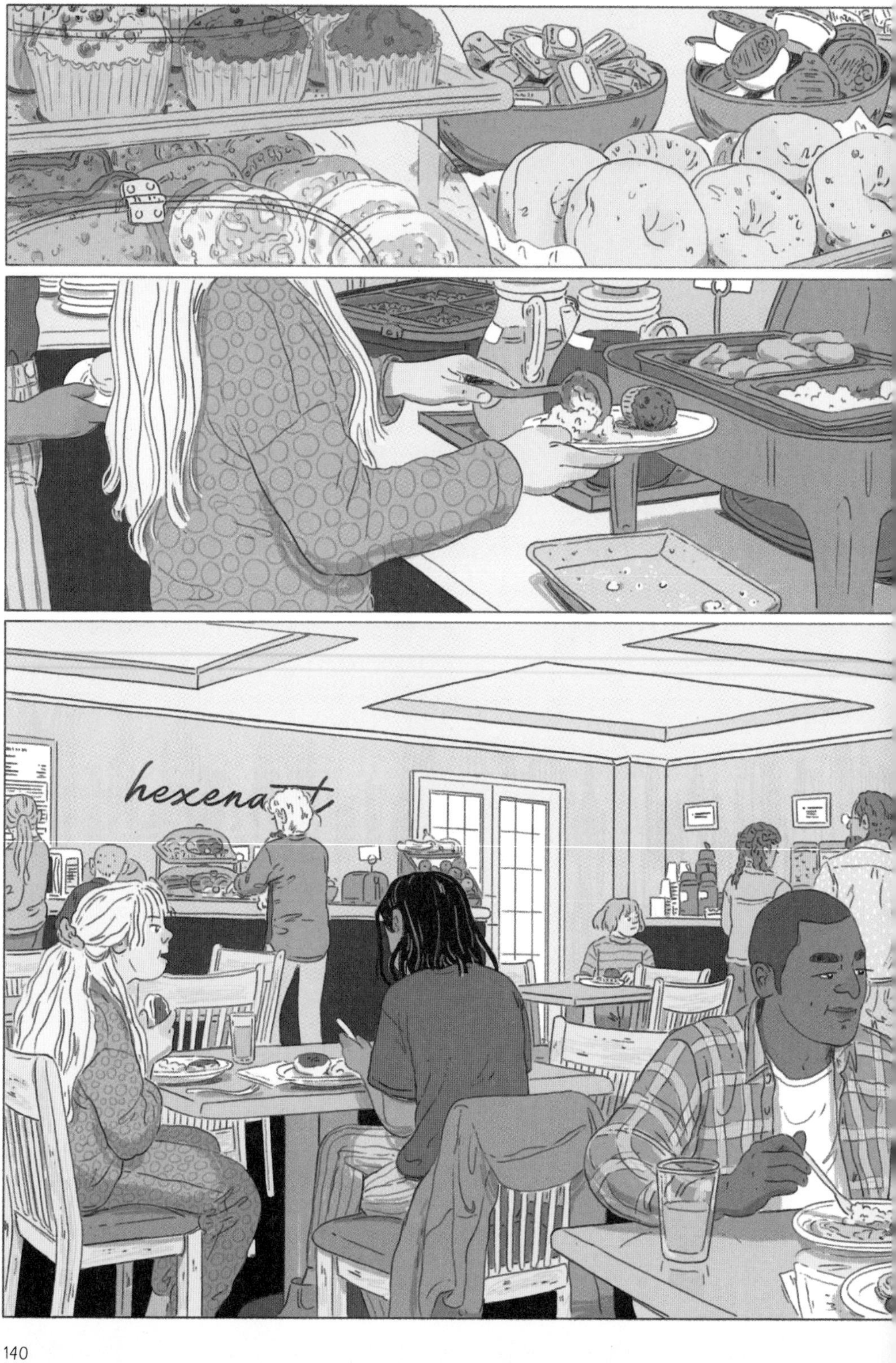

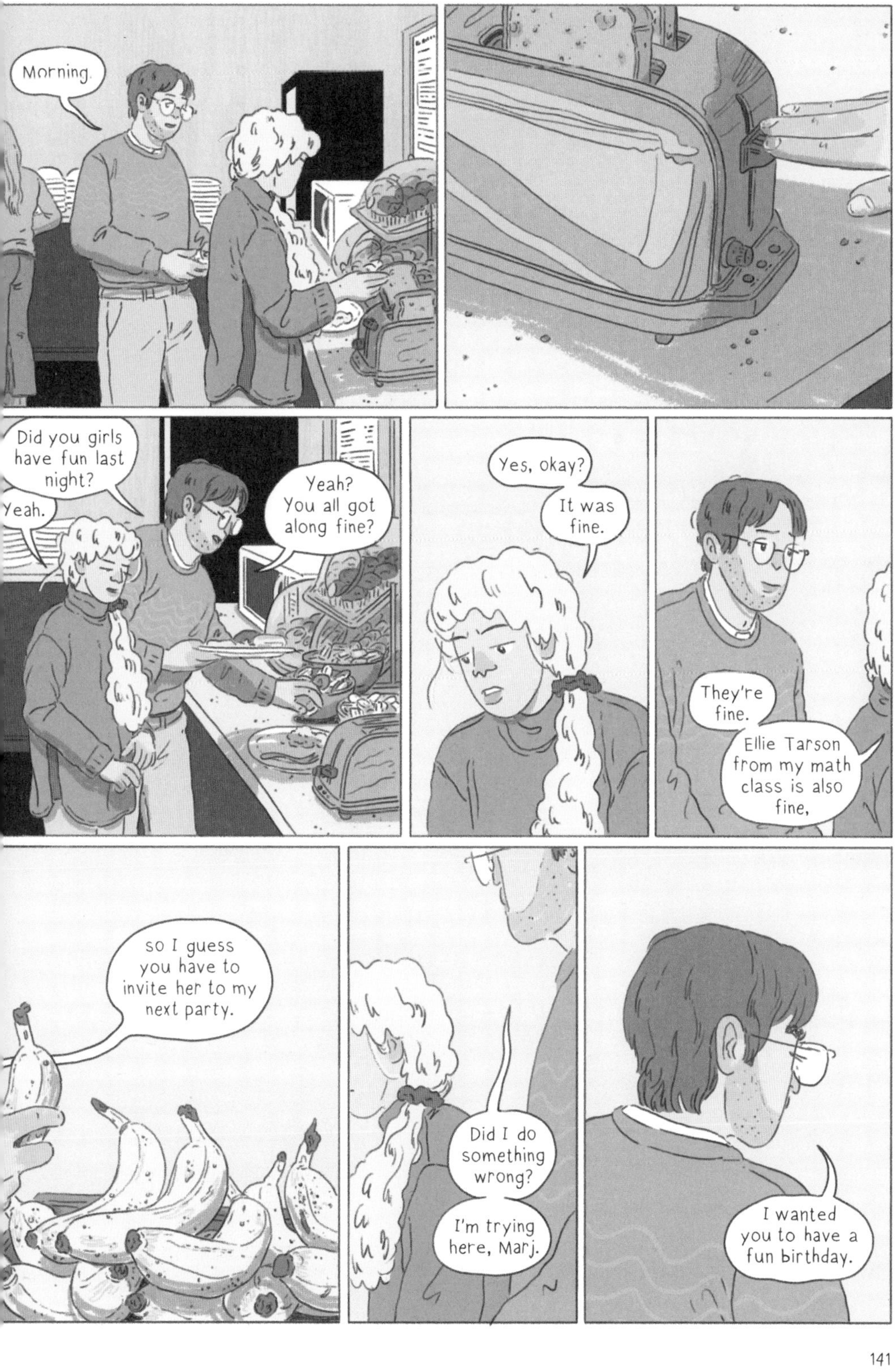

Morning.
Did you girls have fun last night?
Yeah.
Yeah? You all got along fine?
Yes, okay?
It was fine.
They're fine.
Ellie Tarson from my math class is also fine,
so I guess you have to invite her to my next party.
Did I do something wrong?
I'm trying here, Marj.
I wanted you to have a fun birthday.

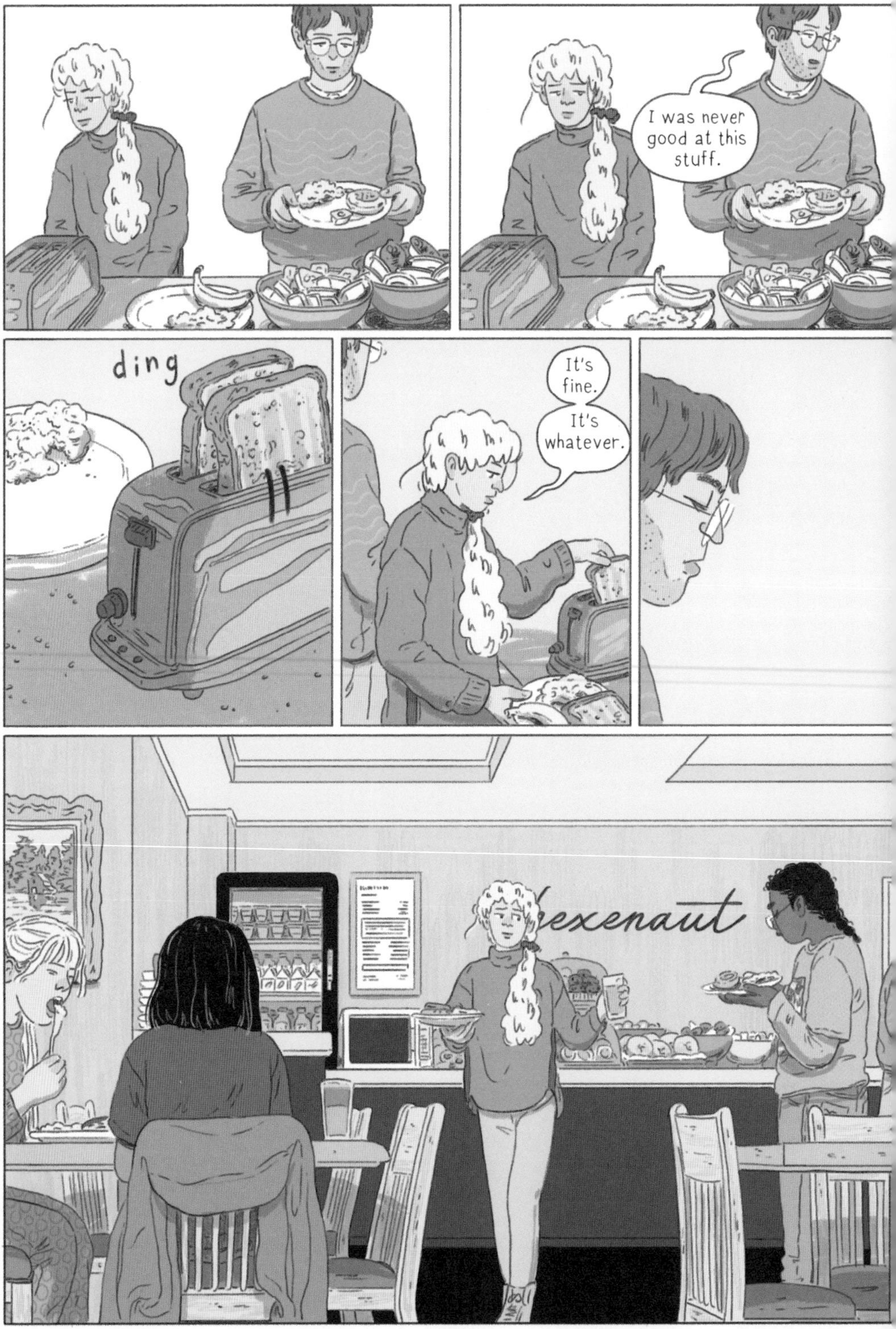
I was never good at this stuff.
ding
It's fine.
It's whatever.
exenaut

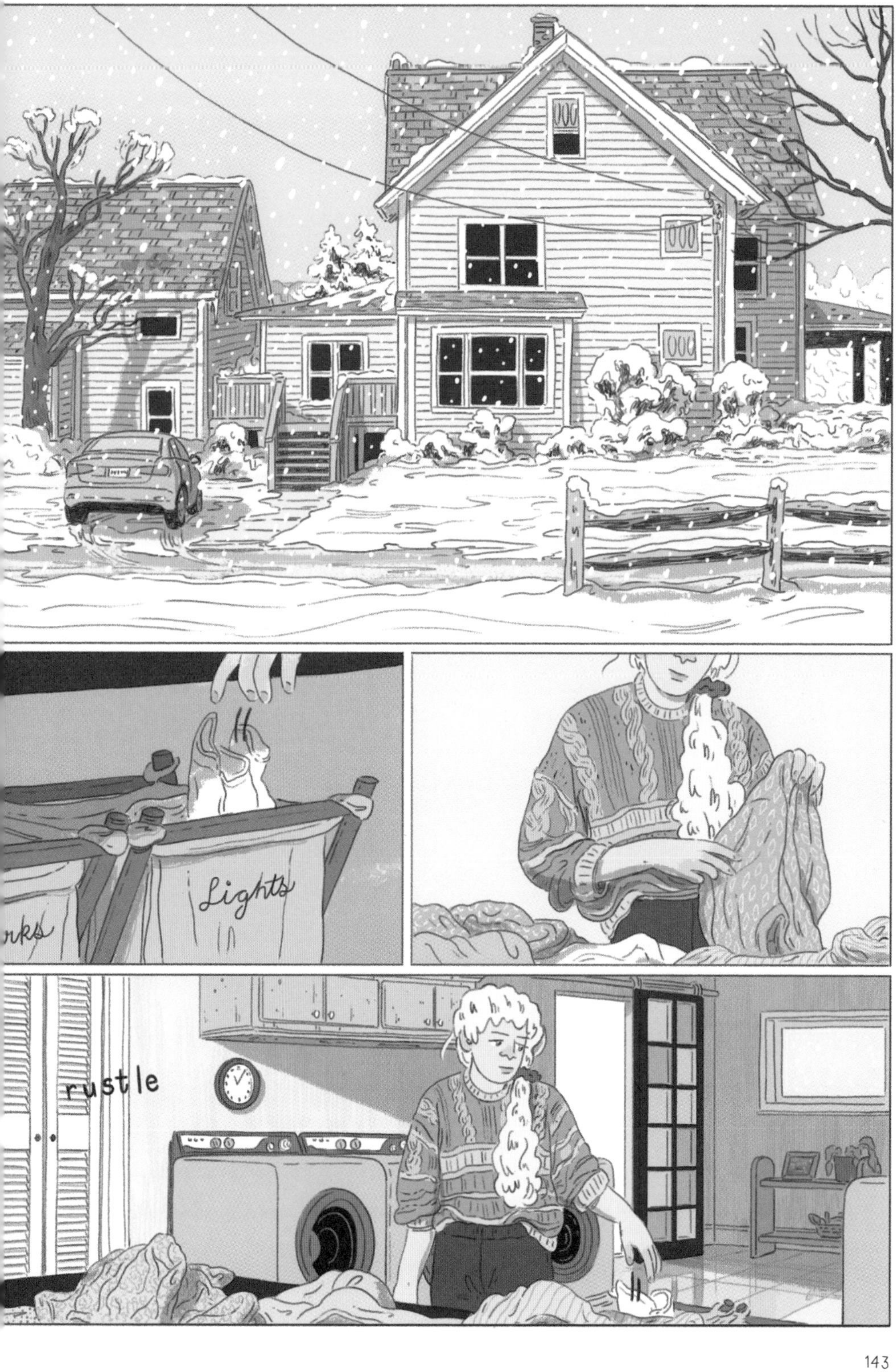

rks
Lights
rustle

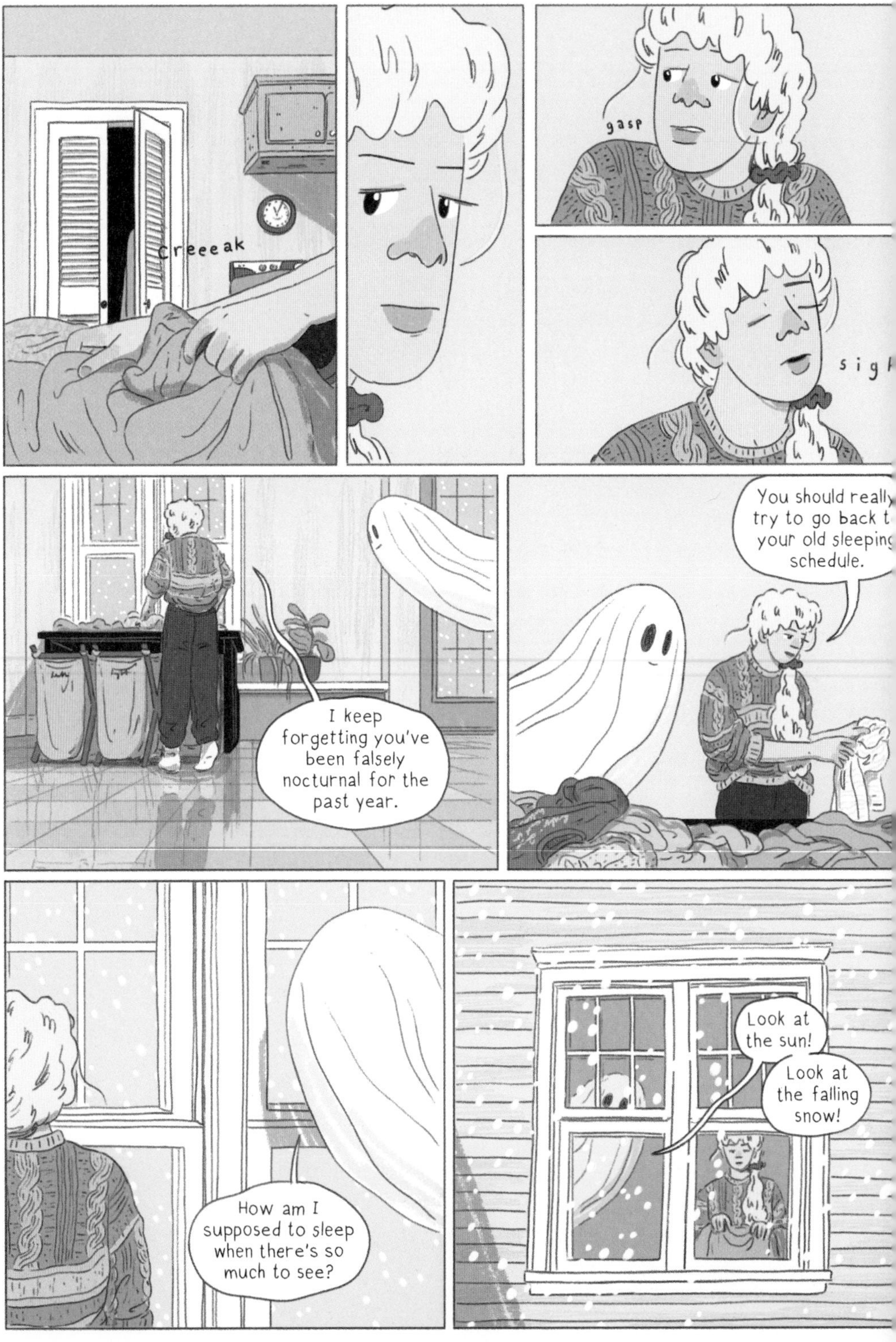
creeeak
gasp
sigh
I keep forgetting you've been falsely nocturnal for the past year.
You should really try to go back to your old sleeping schedule.
How am I supposed to sleep when there's so much to see?
Look at the sun!
Look at the falling snow!

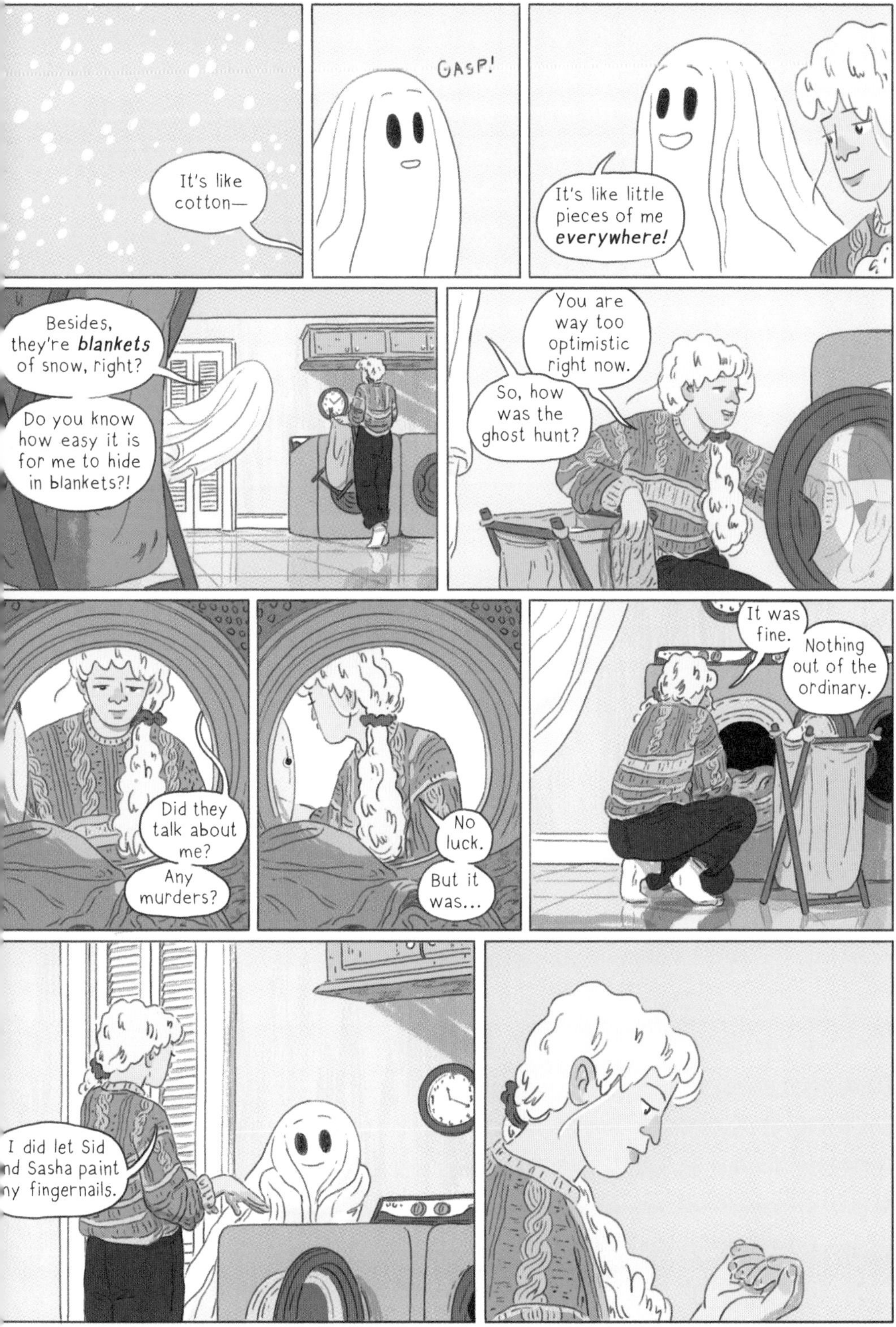
It's like cotton—
GASP!
It's like little pieces of me *everywhere!*
Besides, they're **blankets** of snow, right?
Do you know how easy it is for me to hide in blankets?!
So, how was the ghost hunt?
You are way too optimistic right now.
Did they talk about me?
Any murders?
No luck.
But it was...
It was fine.
Nothing out of the ordinary.
I did let Sid
nd Sasha paint
ny fingernails.

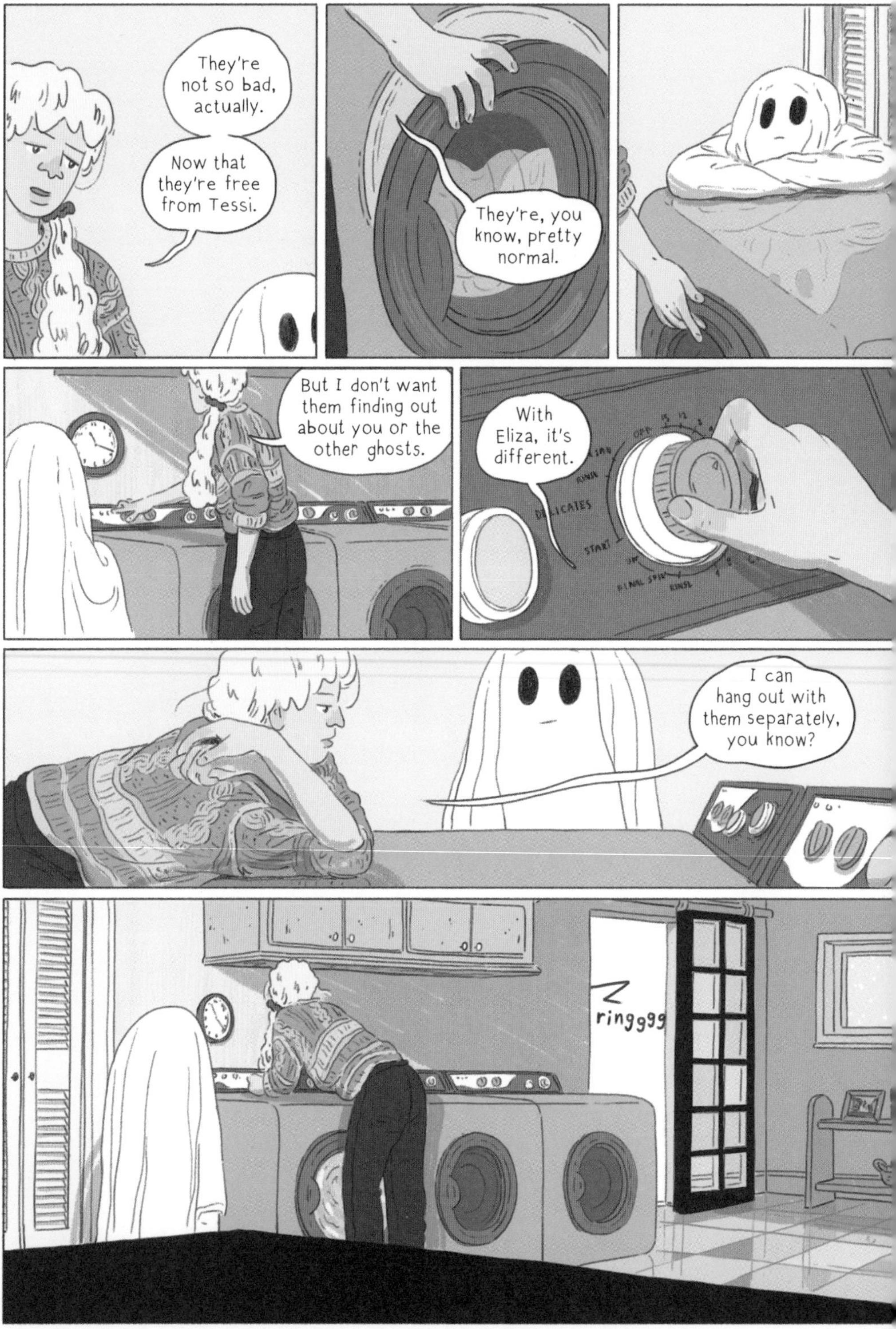
They're not so bad, actually.
Now that they're free from Tessi.
They're, you know, pretty normal.
But I don't want them finding out about you or the other ghosts.
With Eliza, it's different.
I can hang out with them separately, you know?
ringggg

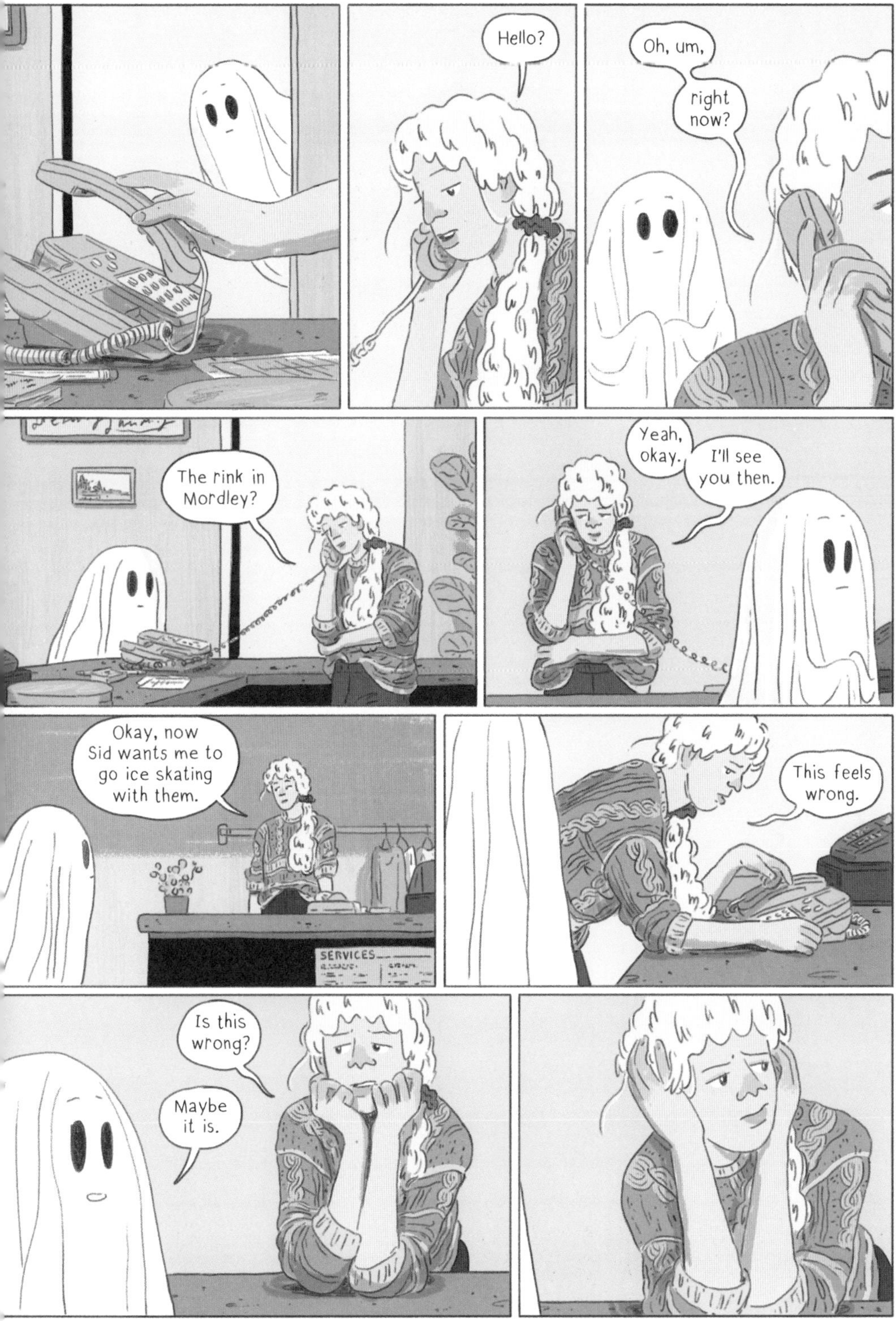
Hello?
Oh, um,
right now?
The rink in Mordley?
Yeah, okay.
I'll see you then.
Okay, now Sid wants me to go ice skating with them.
This feels wrong.
Is this wrong?
Maybe it is.
SERVICES

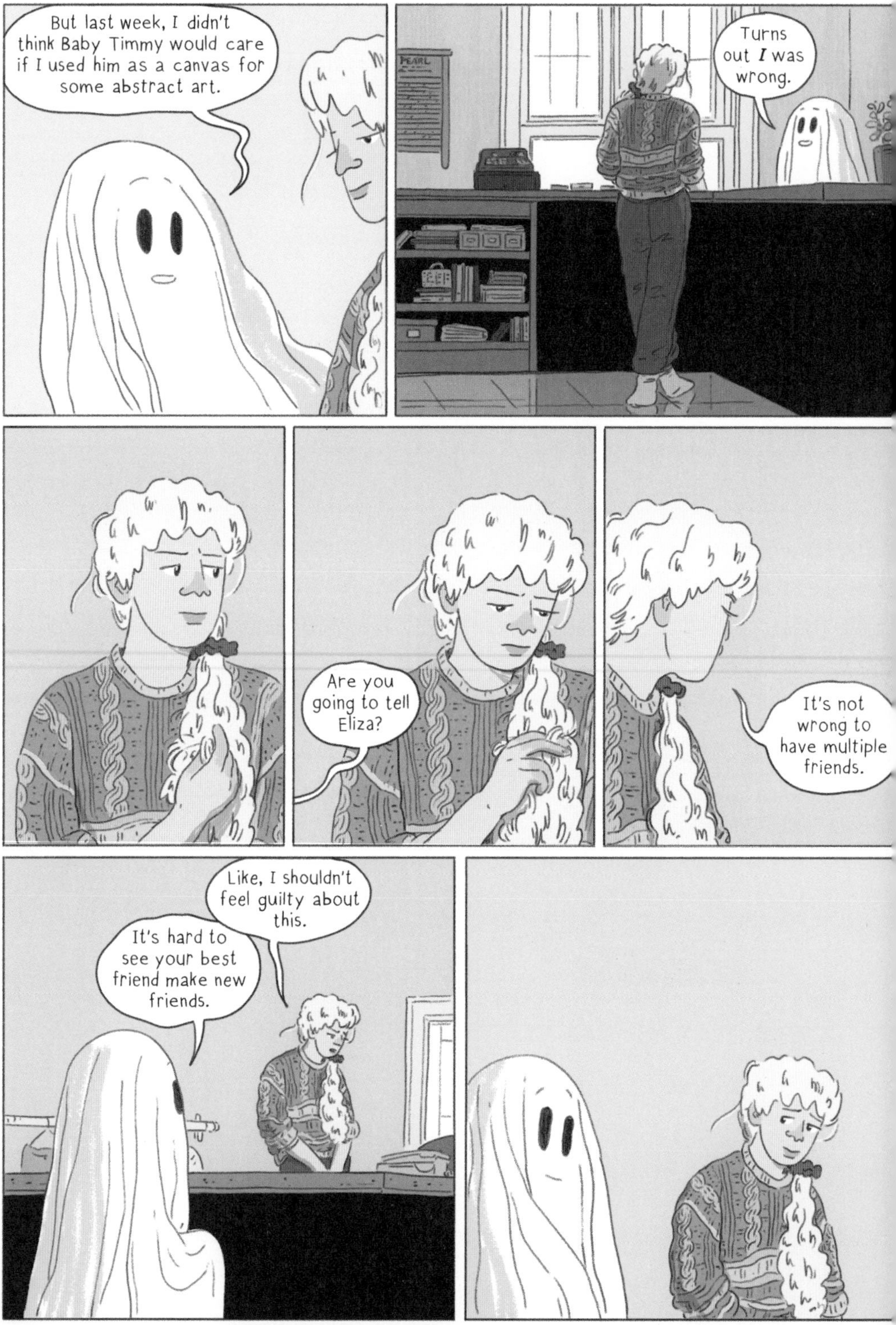
But last week, I didn't think Baby Timmy would care if I used him as a canvas for some abstract art.
PEARL
Turns out *I* was wrong.
Are you going to tell Eliza?
It's not wrong to have multiple friends.
It's hard to see your best friend make new friends.
Like, I shouldn't feel guilty about this.

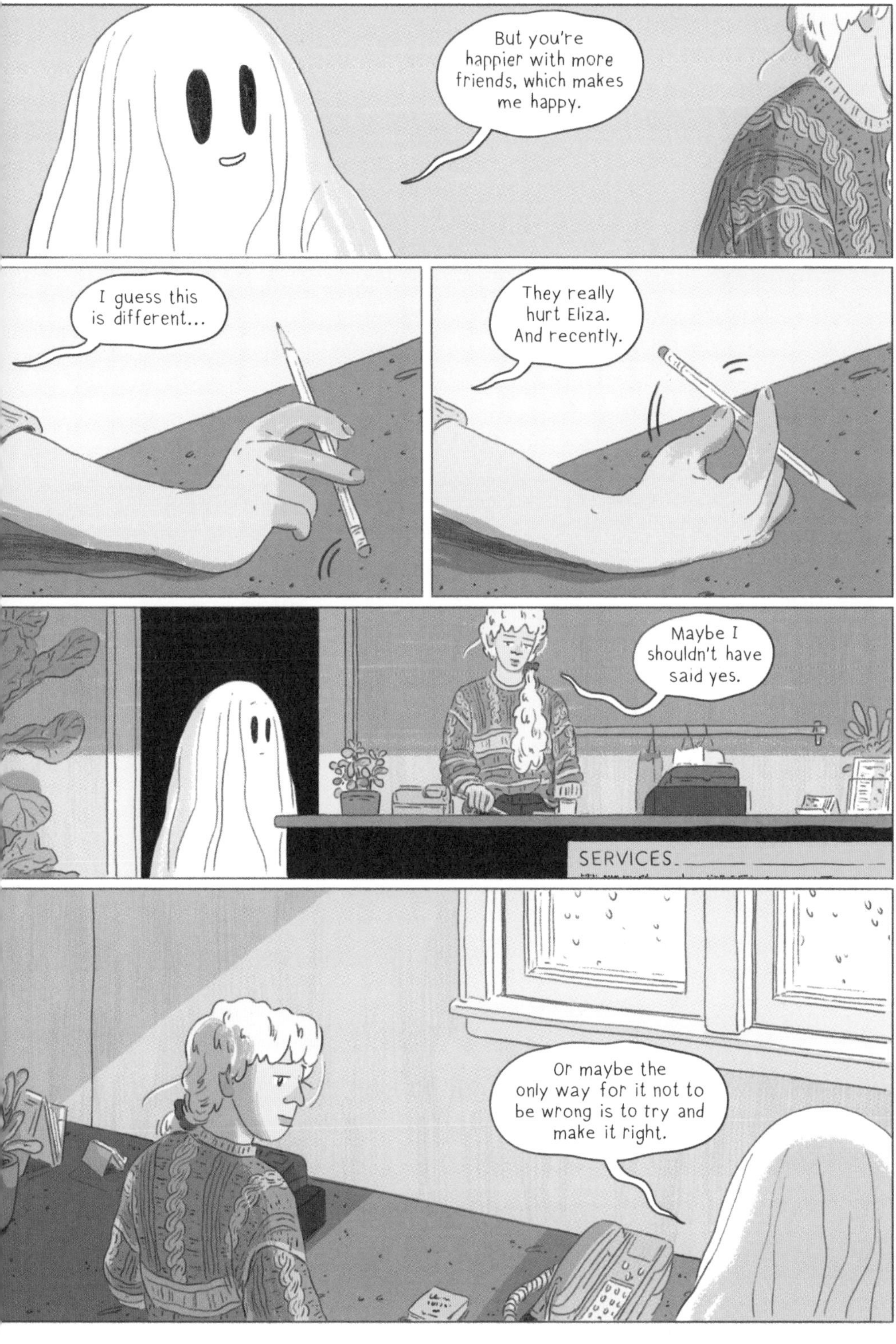
But you're happier with more friends, which makes me happy.
I guess this is different...
They really hurt Eliza. And recently.
Maybe I shouldn't have said yes.
SERVICES
Or maybe the only way for it not to be wrong is to try and make it right.

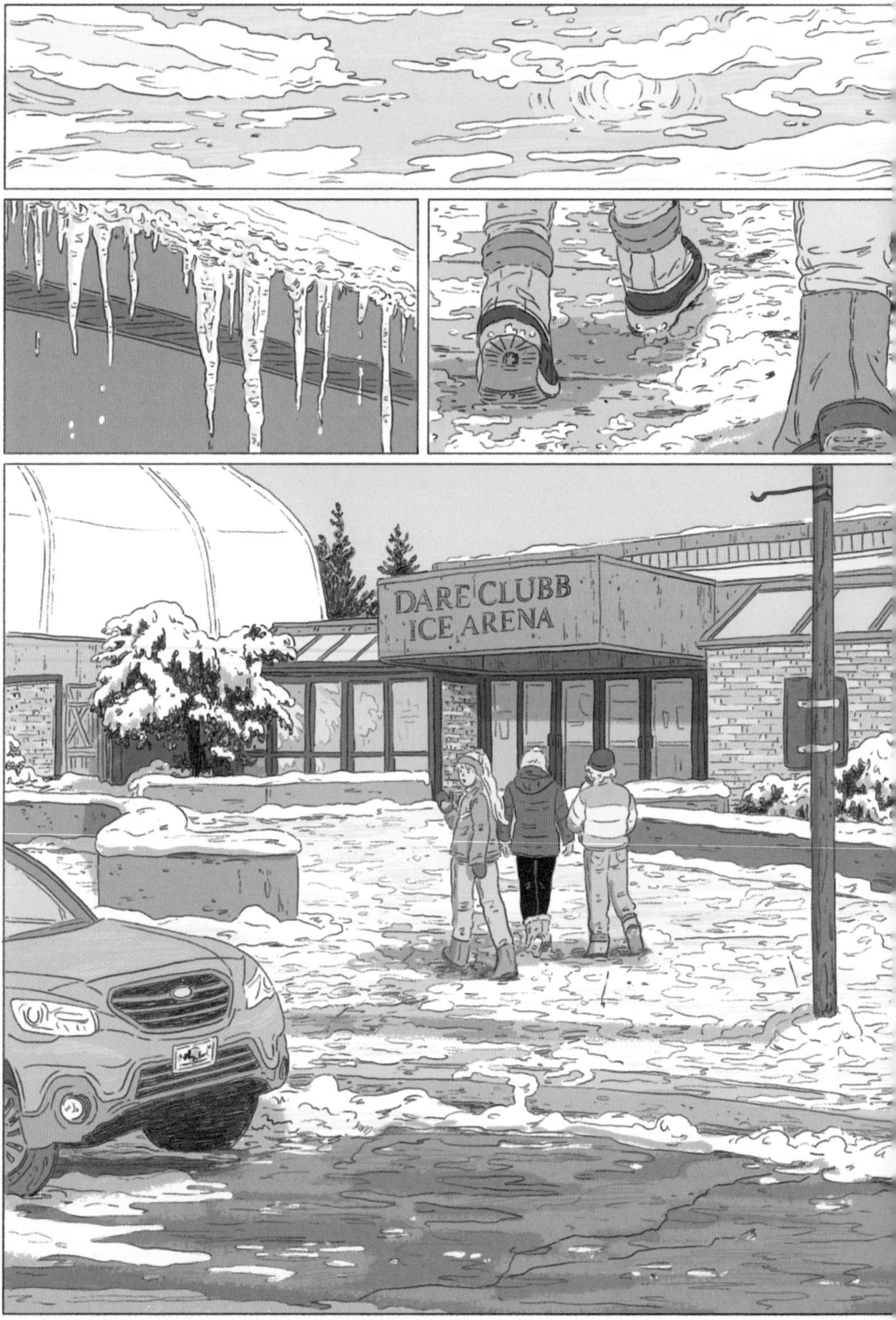
DARE CLUBB
ICE ARENA

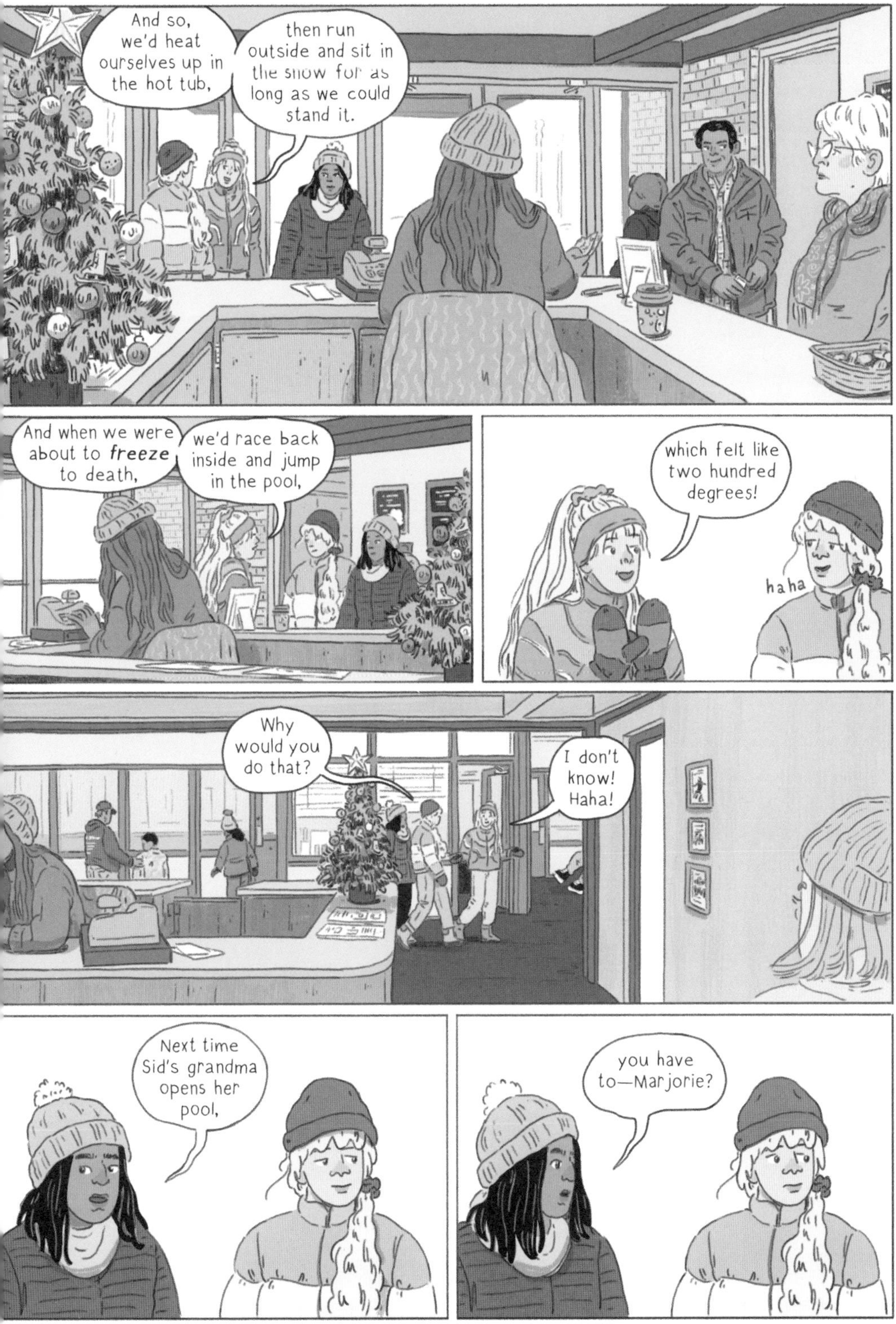
And so, we'd heat ourselves up in the hot tub,
then run outside and sit in the snow for as long as we could stand it.
And when we were about to **freeze** to death,
we'd race back inside and jump in the pool,
which felt like two hundred degrees!
haha
Why would you do that?
I don't know! Haha!
Next time Sid's grandma opens her pool,
you have to—Marjorie?

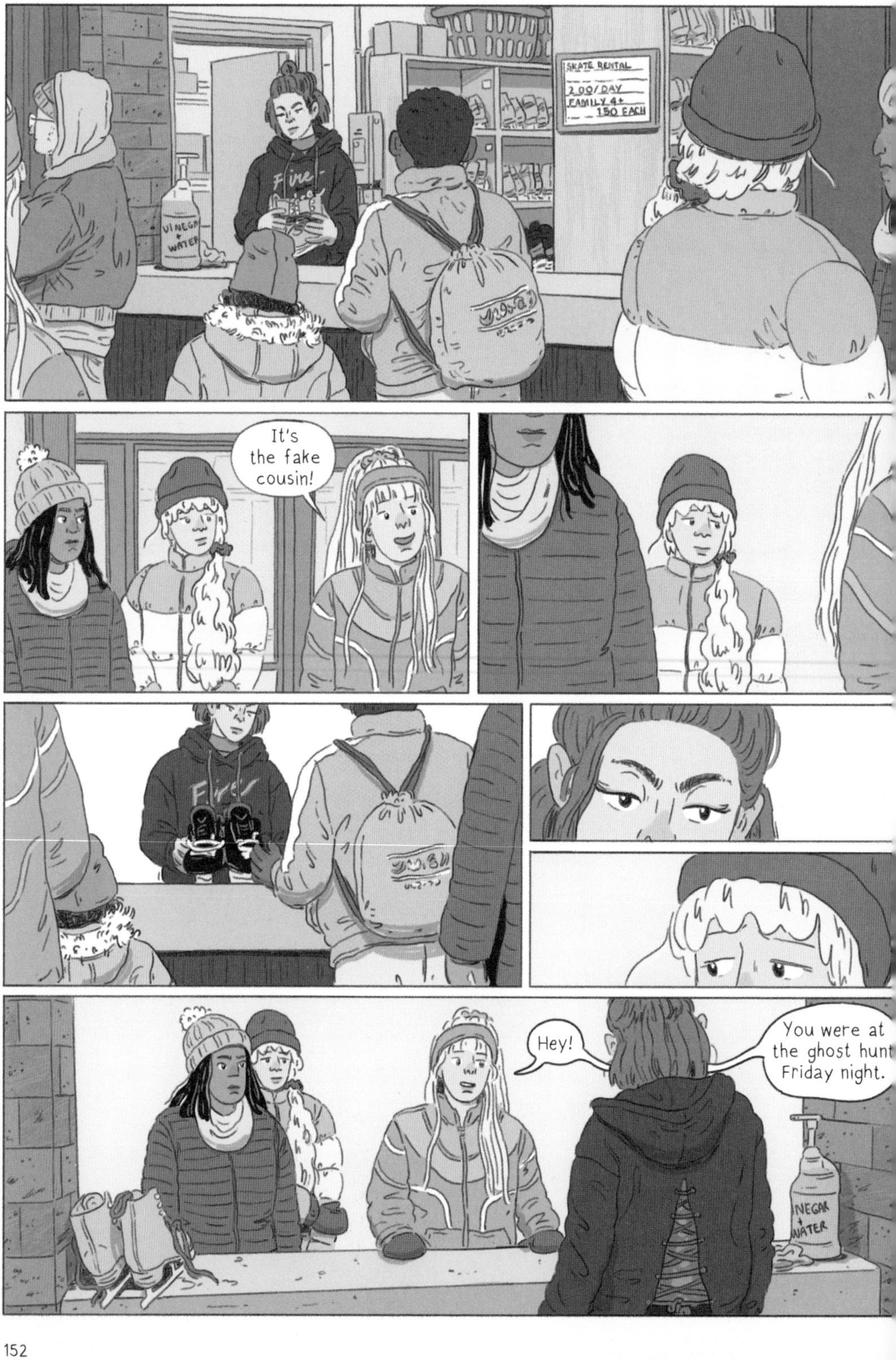
SKATE RENTAL
2.00/DAY
FAMILY 4+
150 EACH
It's the fake cousin!
Hey!
You were at the ghost hunt Friday night.

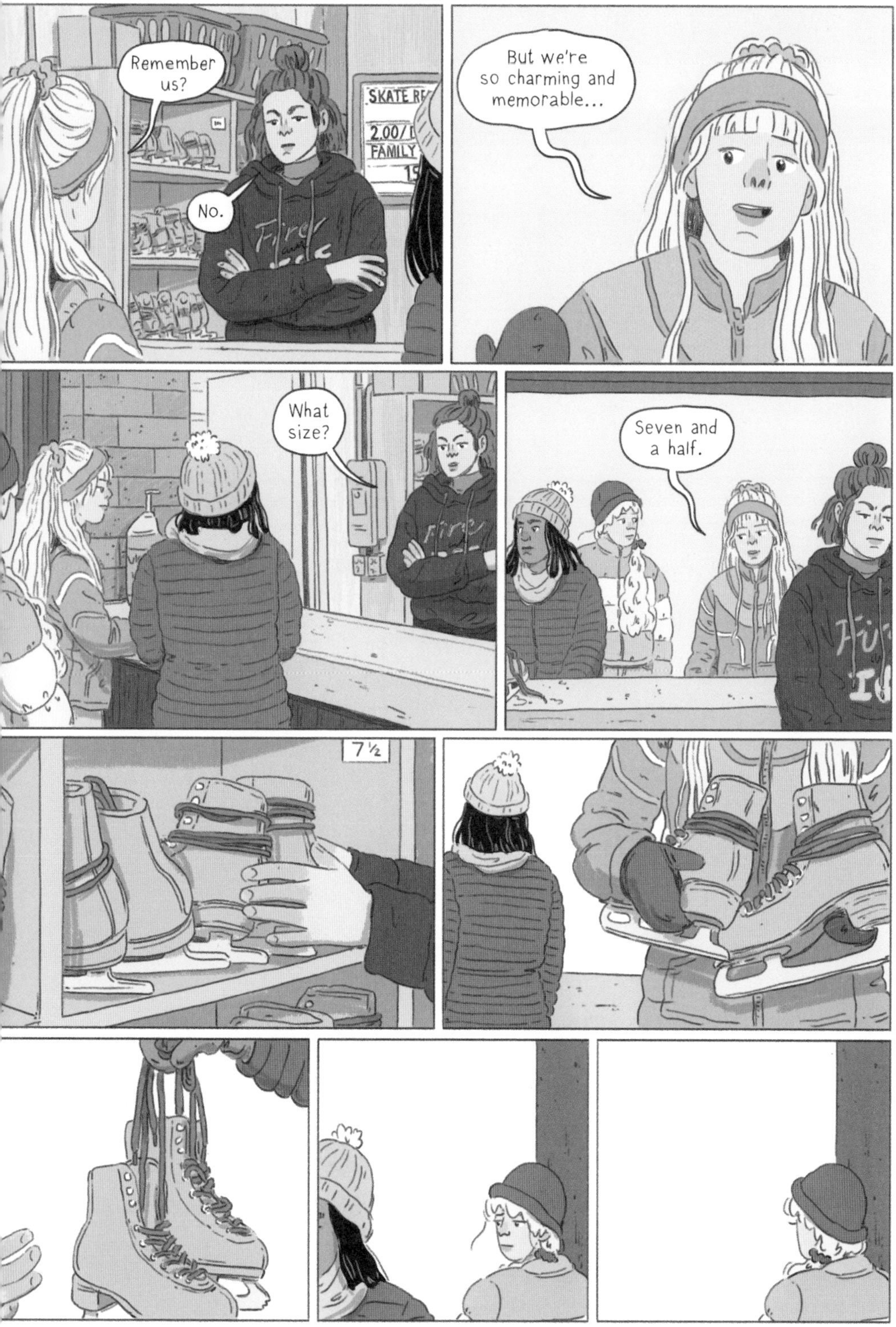
Remember us?
No.
SKATE RE
2.00/
FAMILY
15
But we're so charming and memorable...
What size?
Seven and a half.
7½

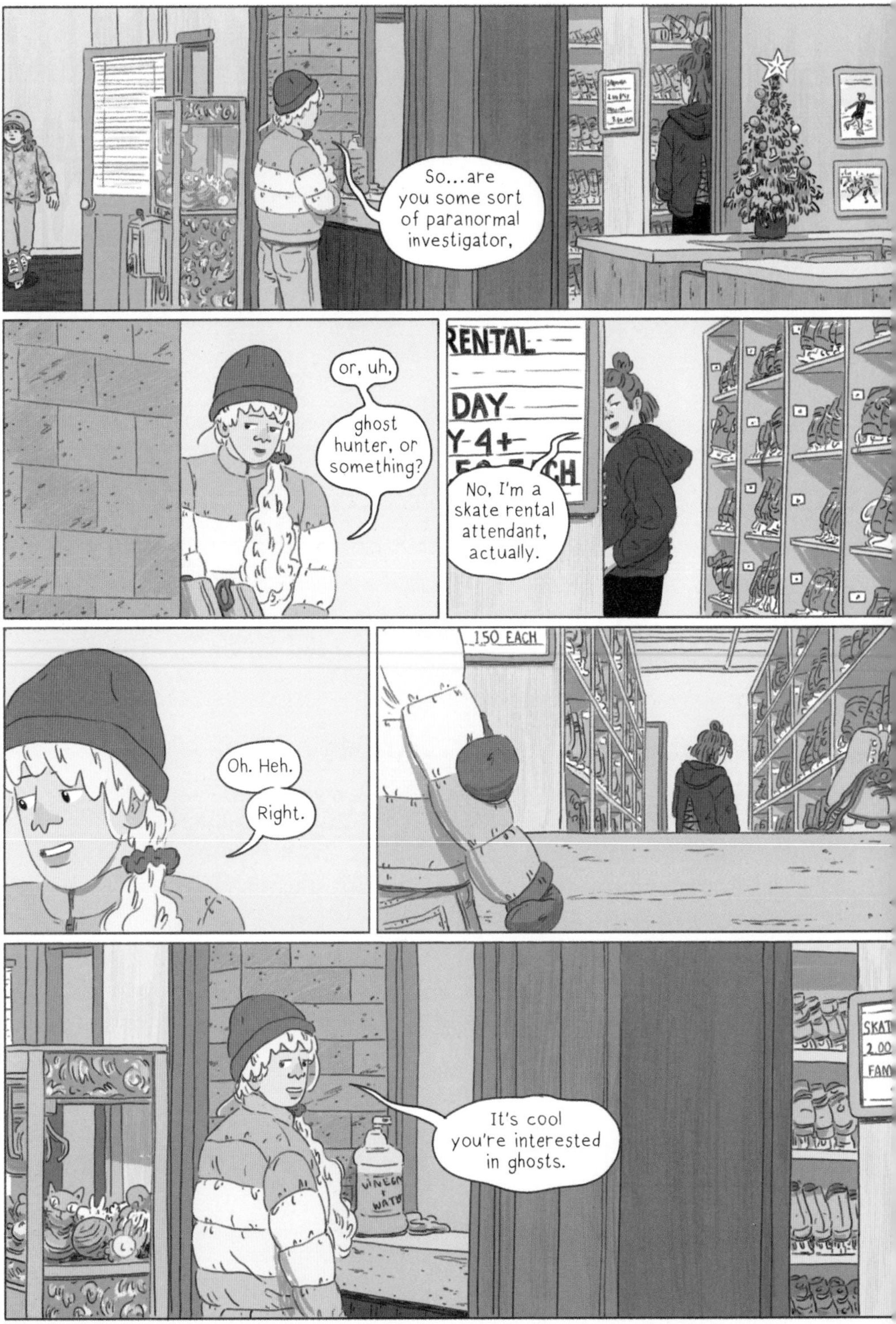
So...are you some sort of paranormal investigator,
or, uh,
ghost hunter, or something?
RENTAL
DAY
No, I'm a skate rental attendant, actually.
Oh. Heh.
Right.
150 EACH
It's cool you're interested in ghosts.

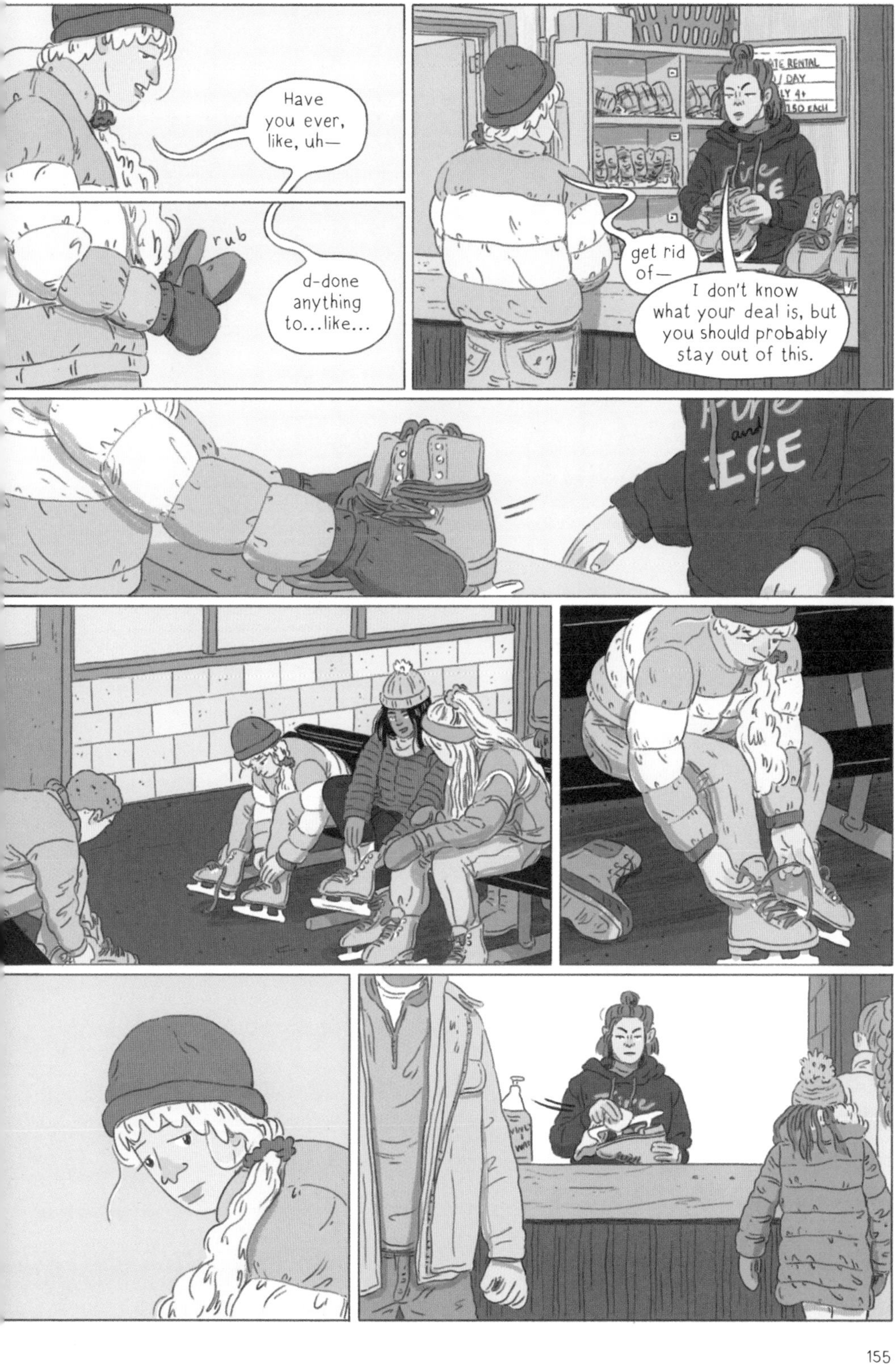
Have you ever, like, uh—
rub
d-done anything to...like...
get rid of—
I don't know what your deal is, but you should probably stay out of this.

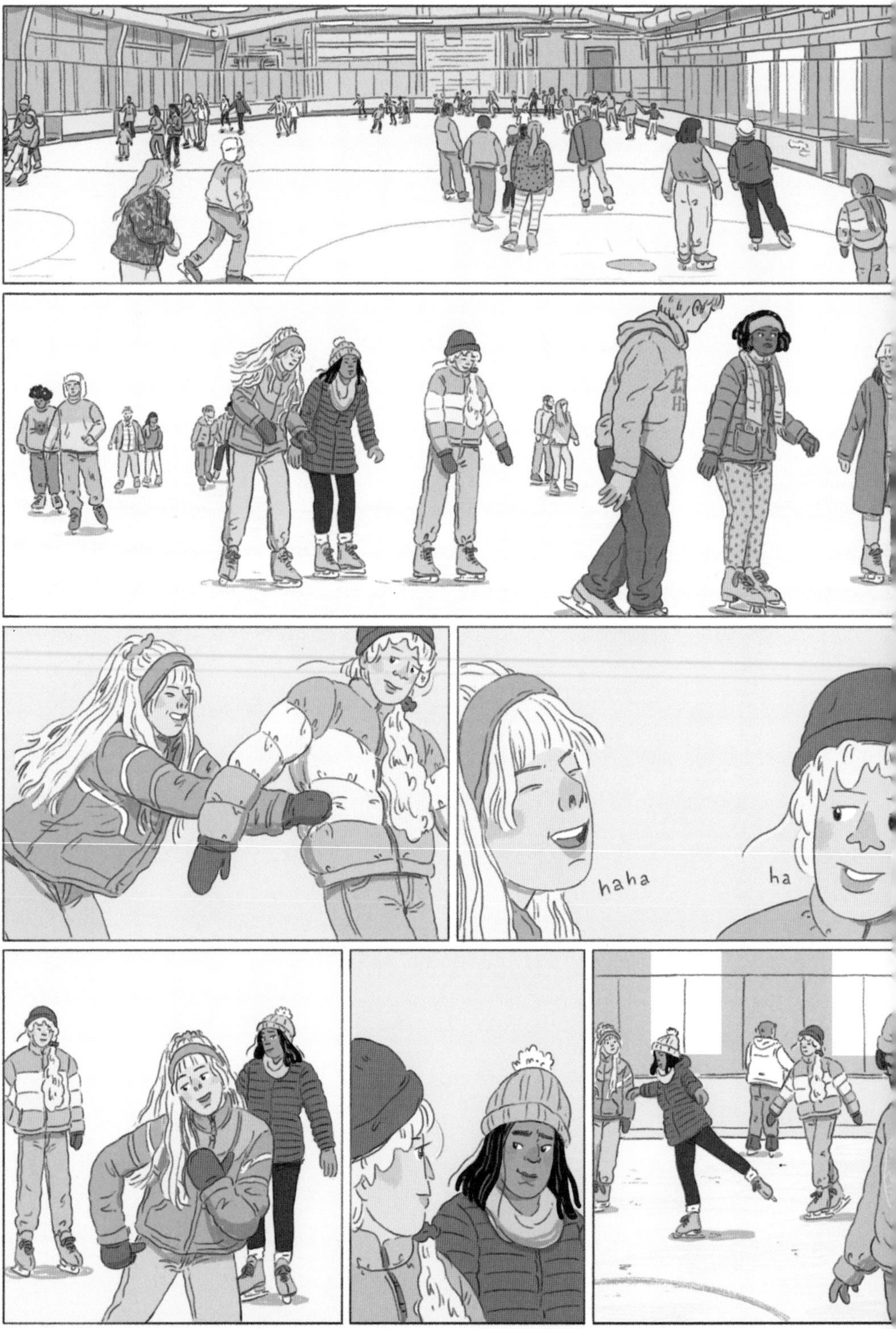
haha
ha

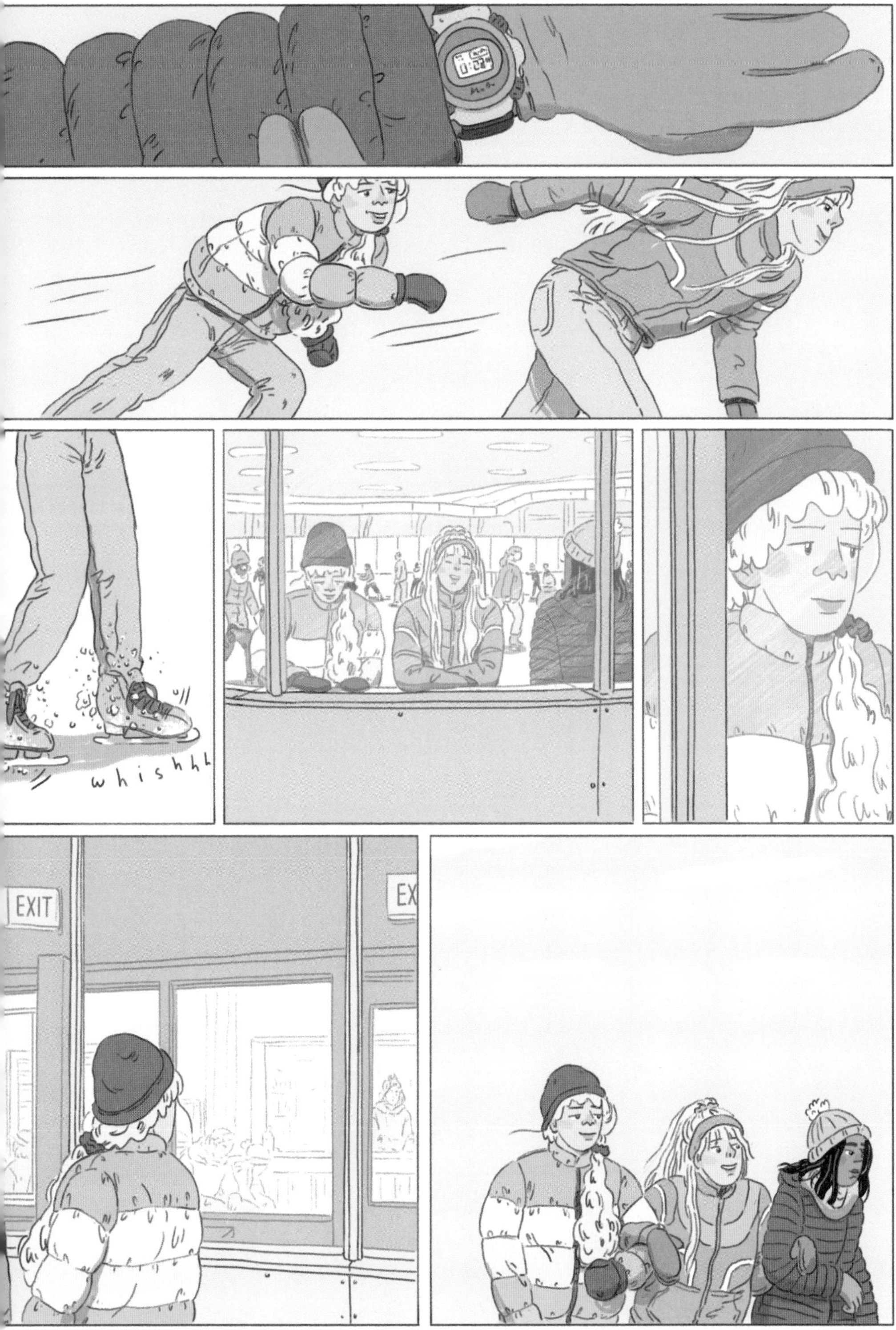
whishhh
EXIT
EX

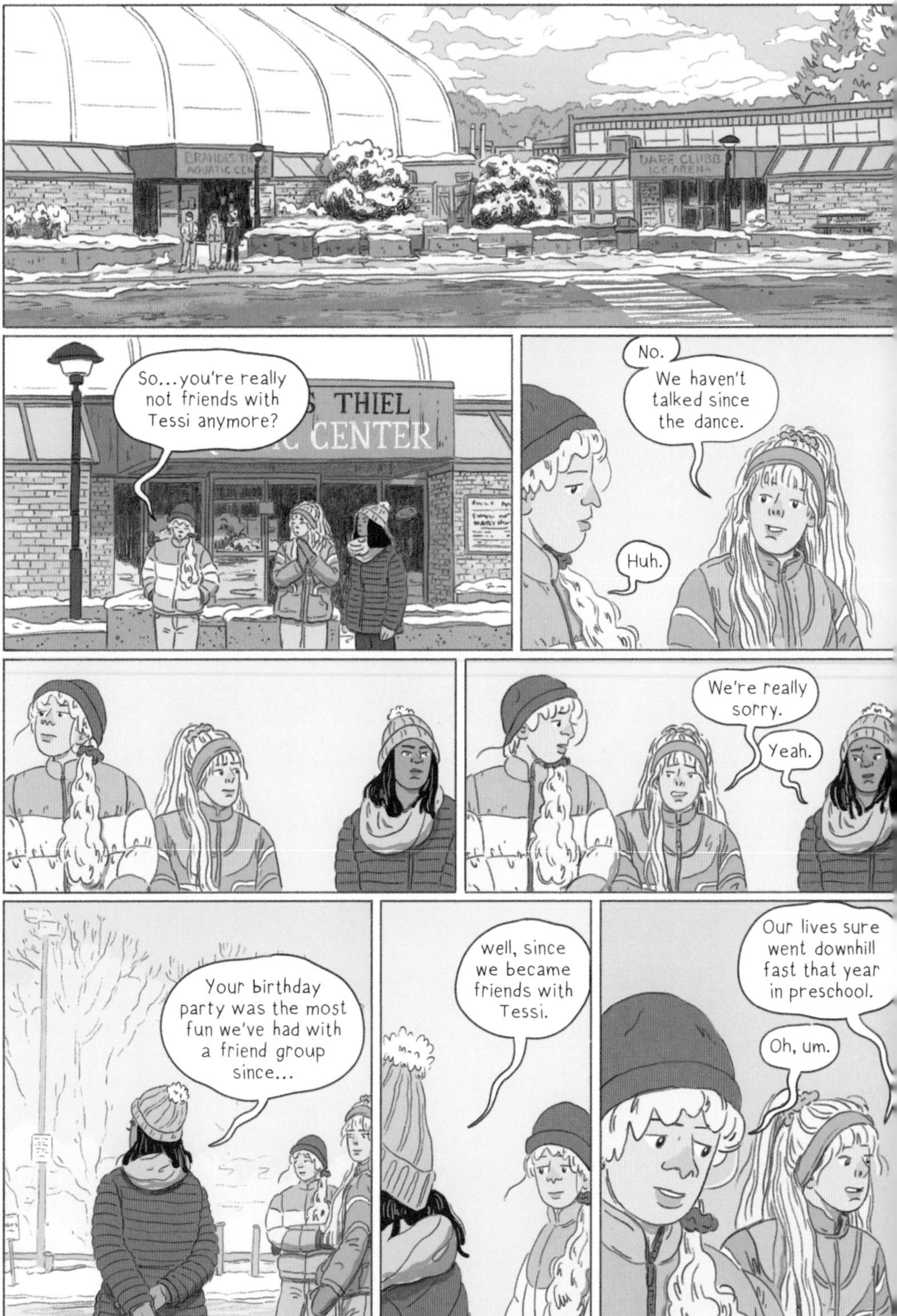
BRANDES THIEL AQUATIC CENTER
DARE CLUBB ICE ARENA
So...you're really not friends with Tessi anymore?
No.
We haven't talked since the dance.
Huh.
We're really sorry.
Yeah.
Your birthday party was the most fun we've had with a friend group since...
well, since we became friends with Tessi.
Our lives sure went downhill fast that year in preschool.
Oh, um.

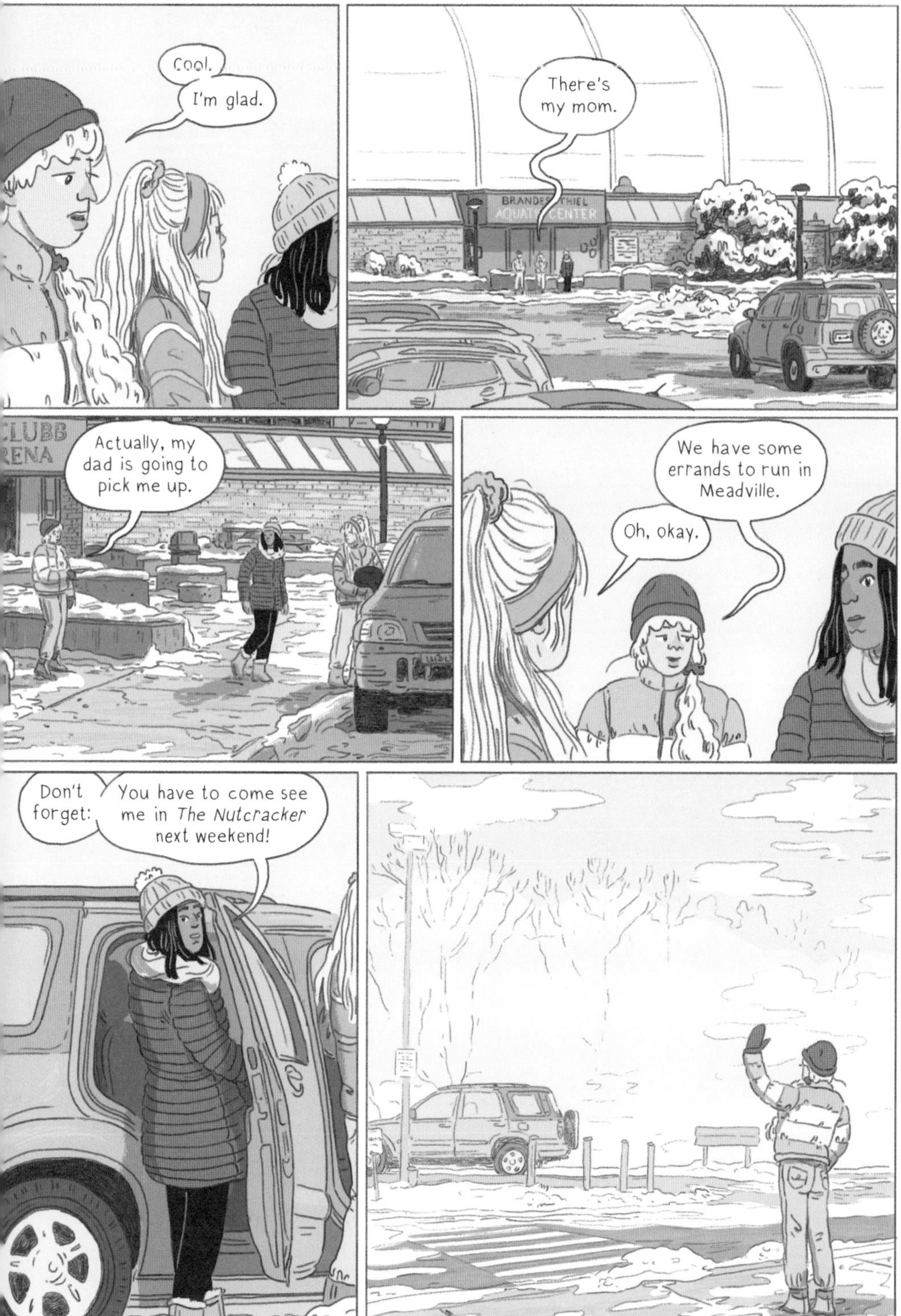
Cool.
I'm glad.
There's my mom.
Actually, my dad is going to pick me up.
We have some errands to run in Meadville.
Oh, okay.
Don't forget:
You have to come see me in *The Nutcracker* next weekend!

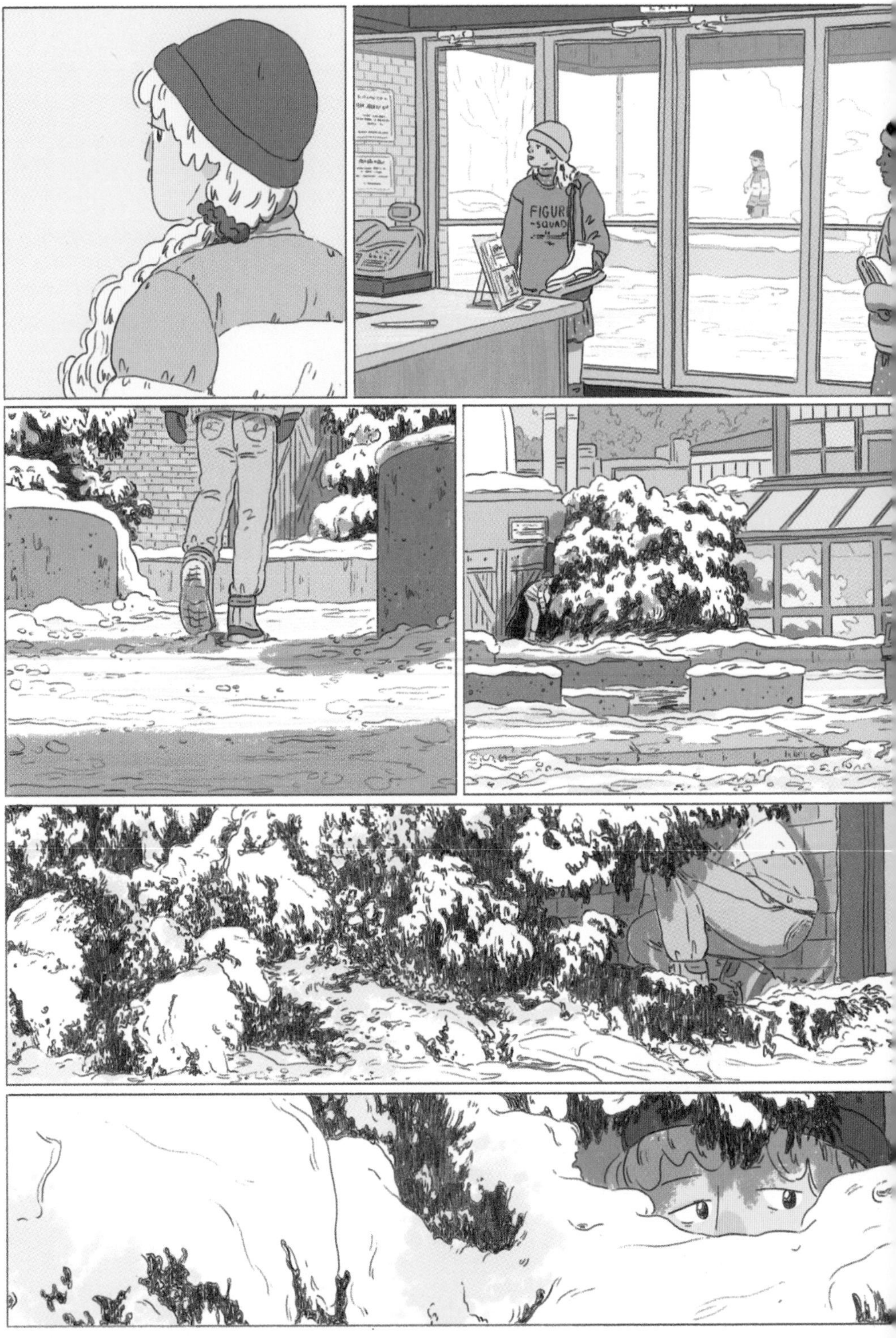
FIGURE
SQUAD

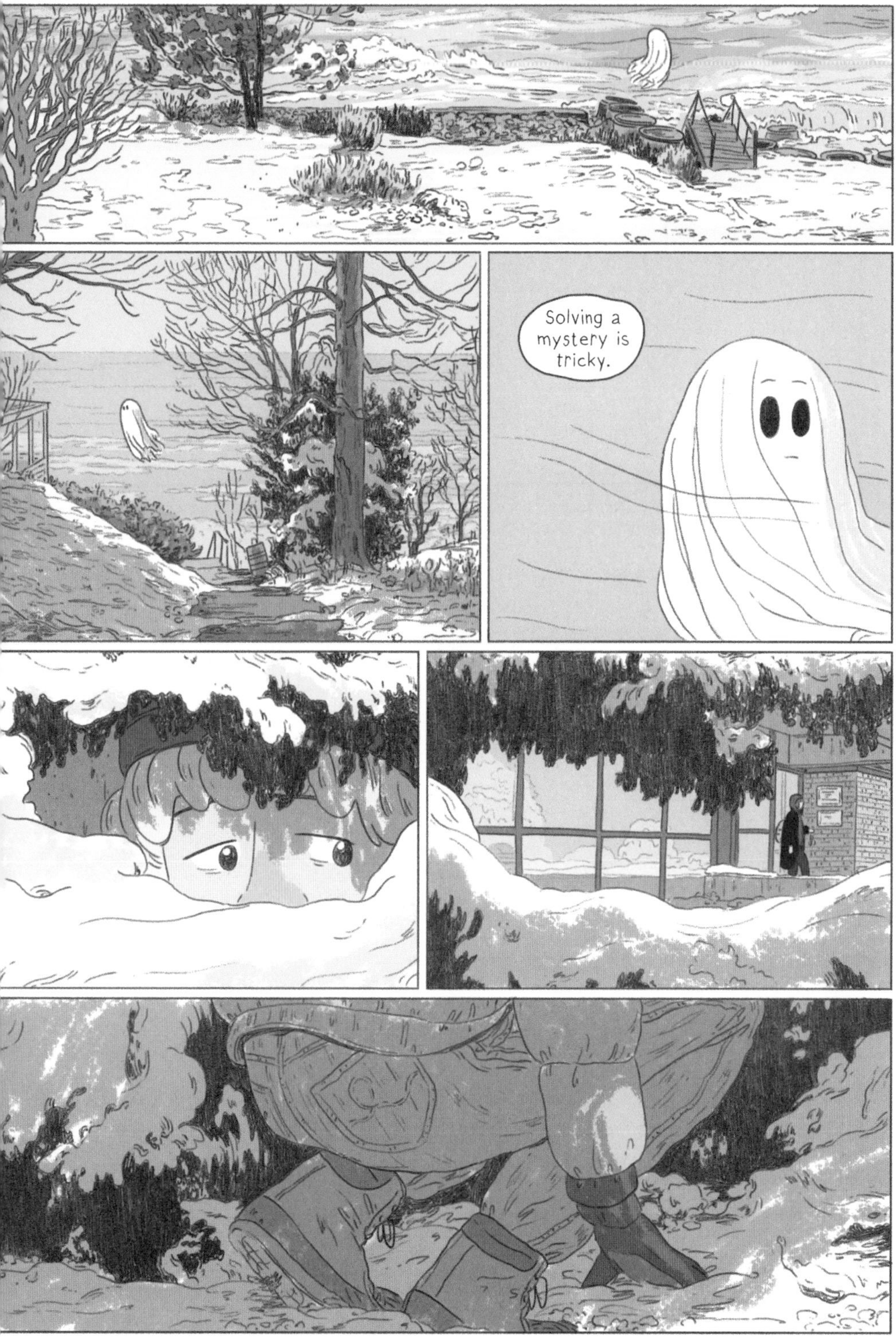
Solving a mystery is tricky.

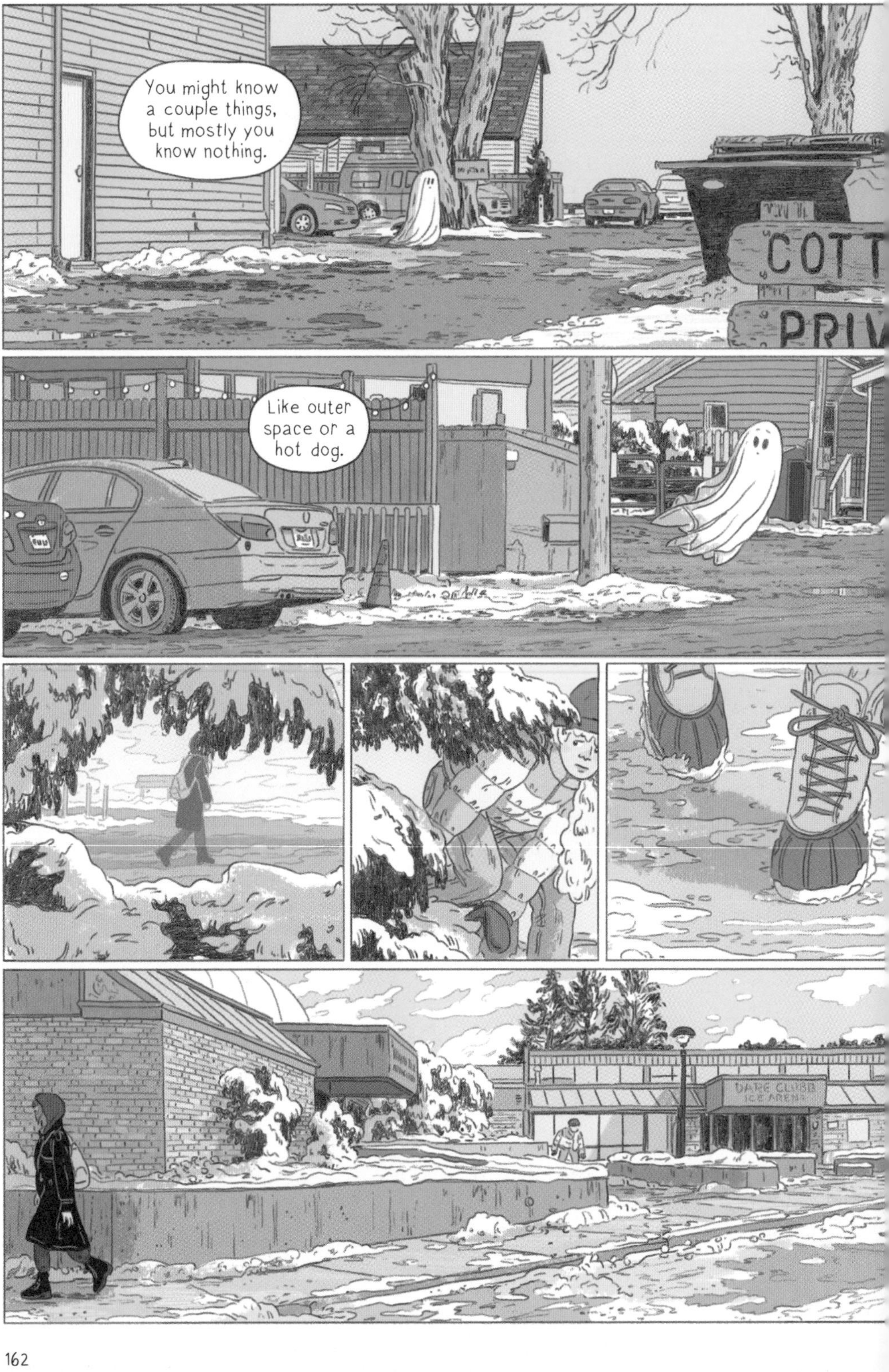
You might know a couple things, but mostly you know nothing.
Like outer space or a hot dog.
DARE CLUBB
ICE ARENA

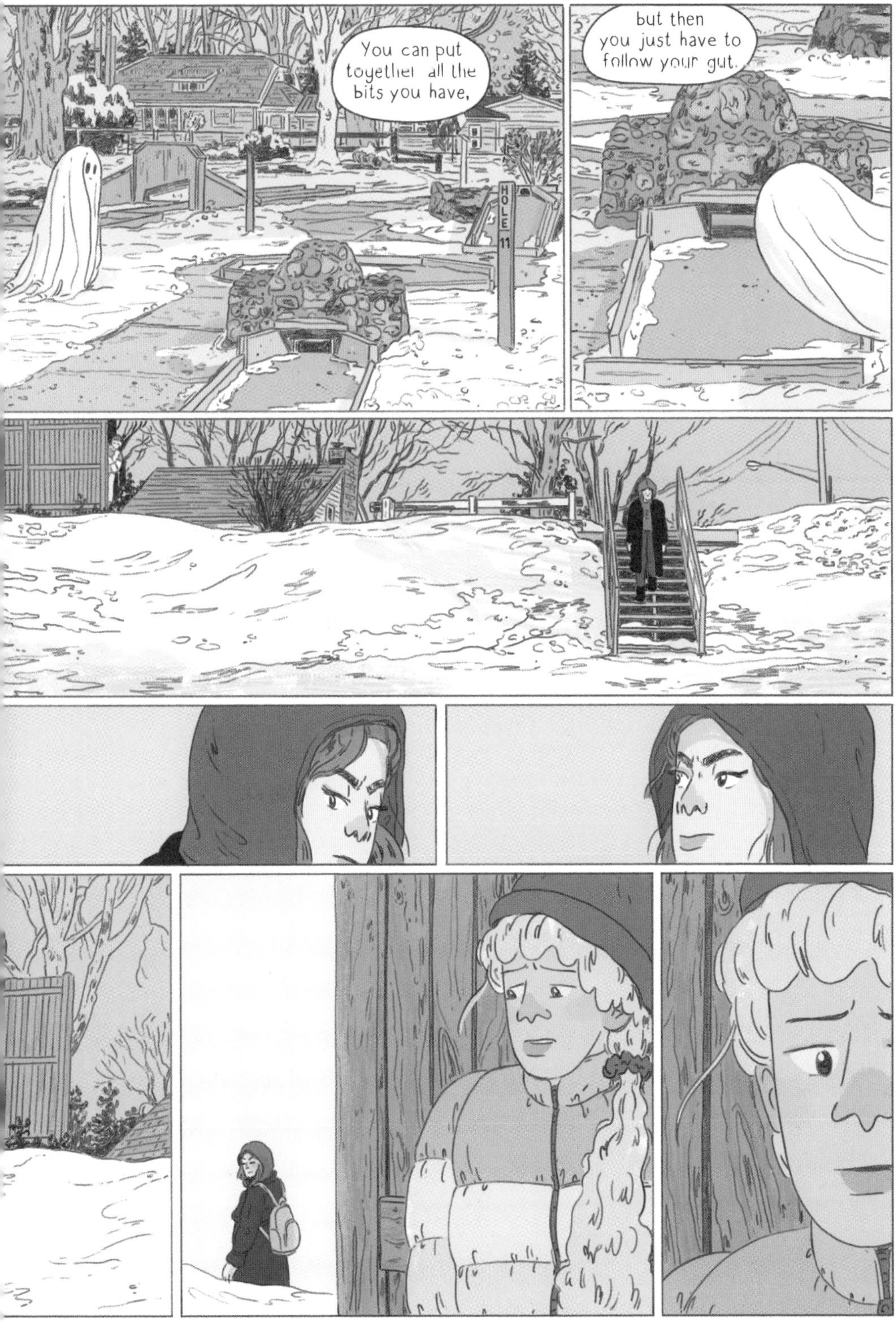
You can put together all the bits you have,
HOLE 11
but then you just have to follow your gut.

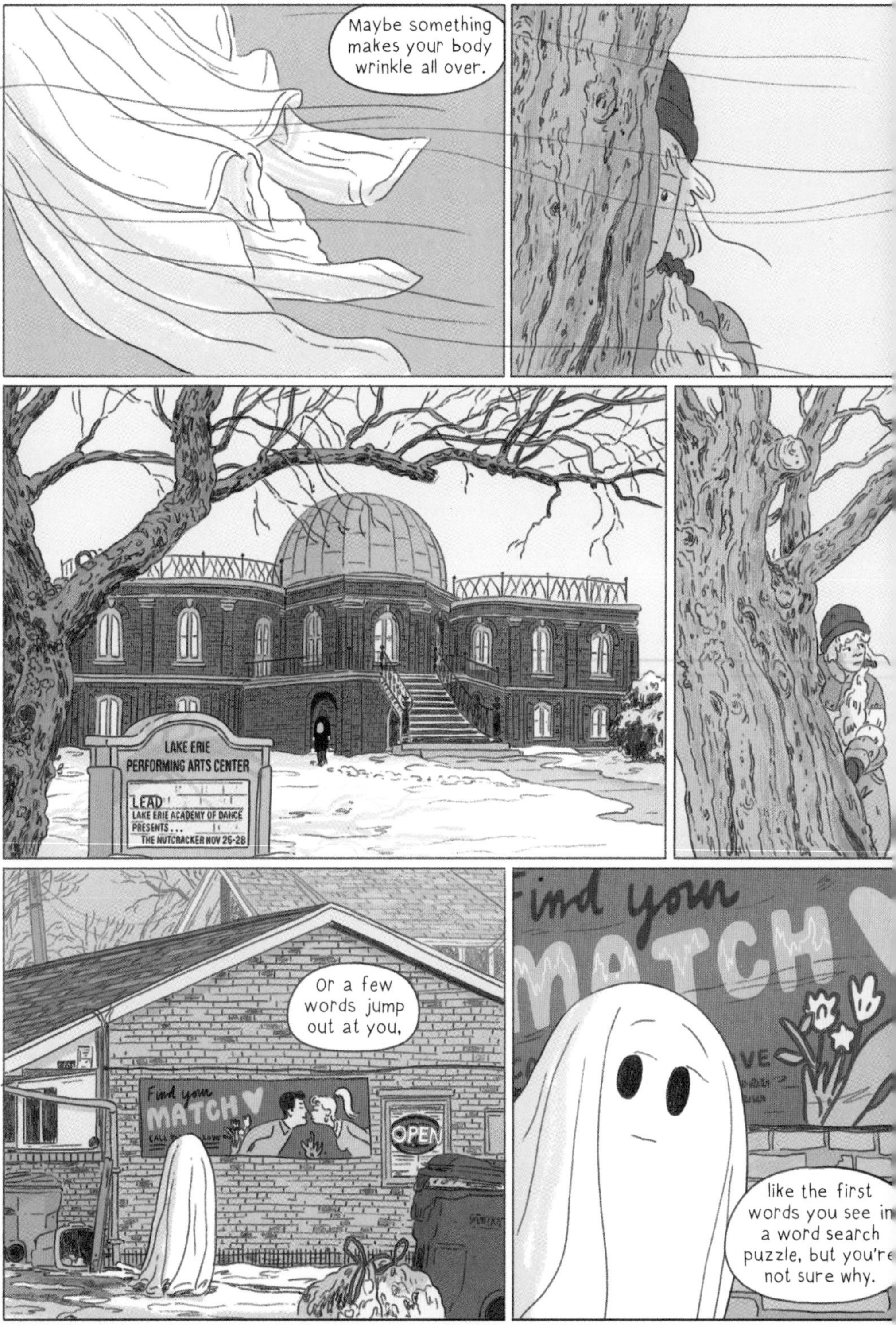
Maybe something makes your body wrinkle all over.
LAKE ERIE PERFORMING ARTS CENTER
LEAD
LAKE ERIE ACADEMY OF DANCE
PRESENTS...
THE NUTCRACKER NOV 26-28
Find you MATCH
OPEN
Or a few words jump out at you,
Find you MATCH
like the first words you see in a word search puzzle, but you're not sure why.

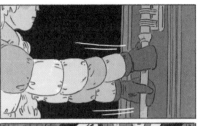

Maybe it doesn't mean anything, but it's all you've got.

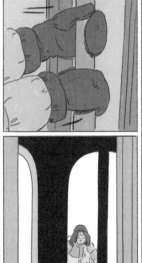

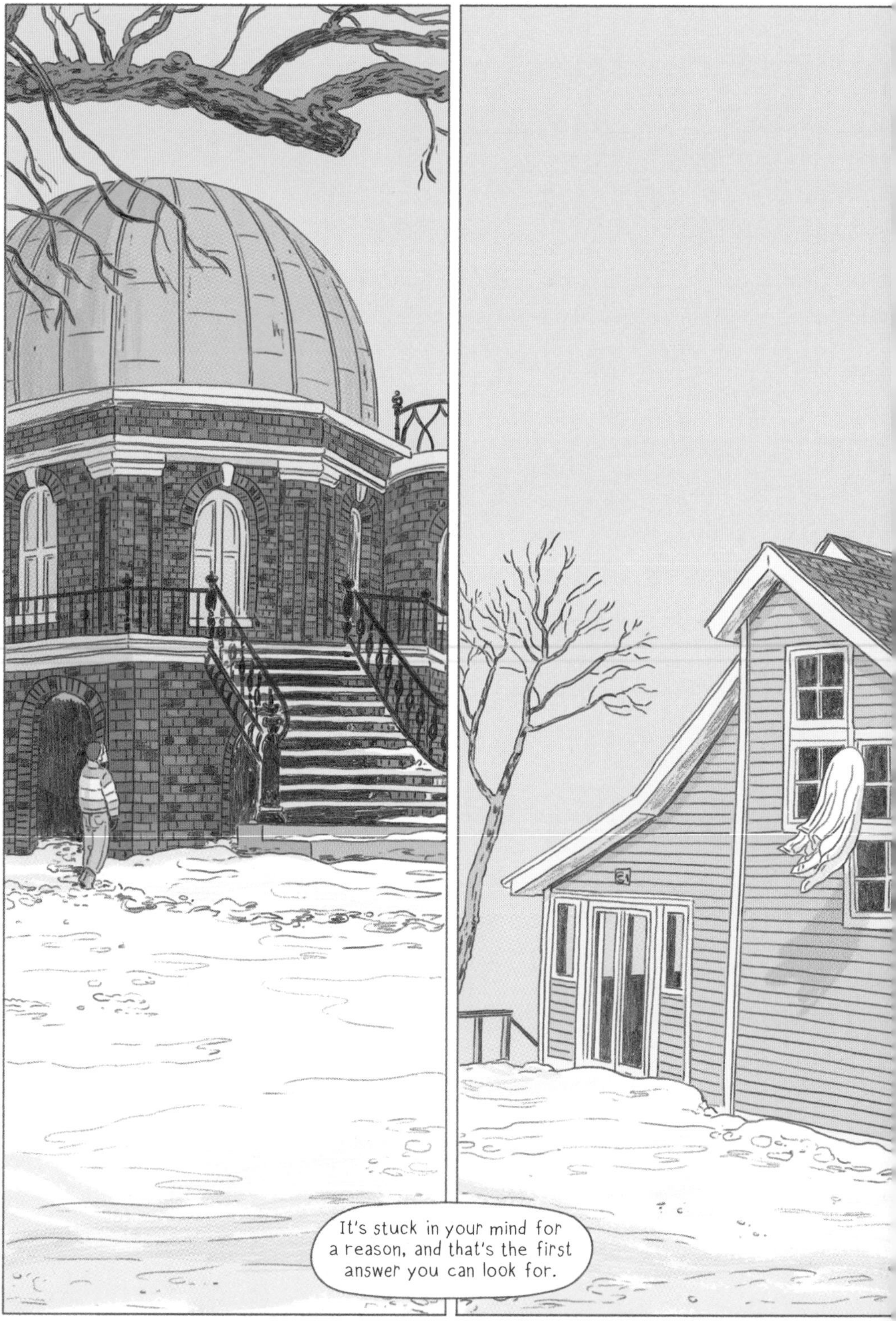
It's stuck in your mind for a reason, and that's the first answer you can look for.

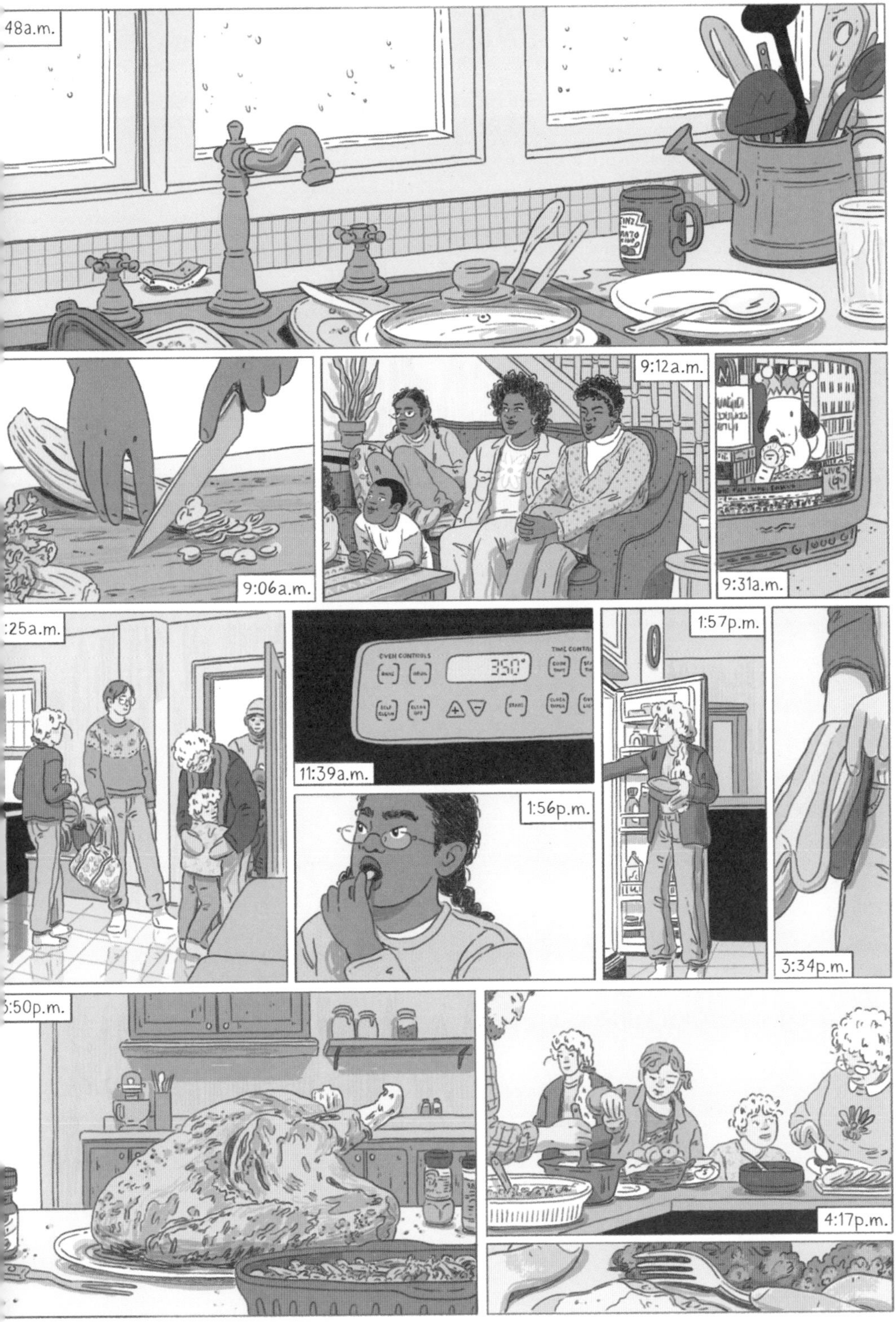
48a.m.
9:06a.m.
9:12a.m.
9:31a.m.
:25a.m.
350°
11:39a.m.
1:56p.m.
1:57p.m.
3:34p.m.
:50p.m.
4:17p.m.

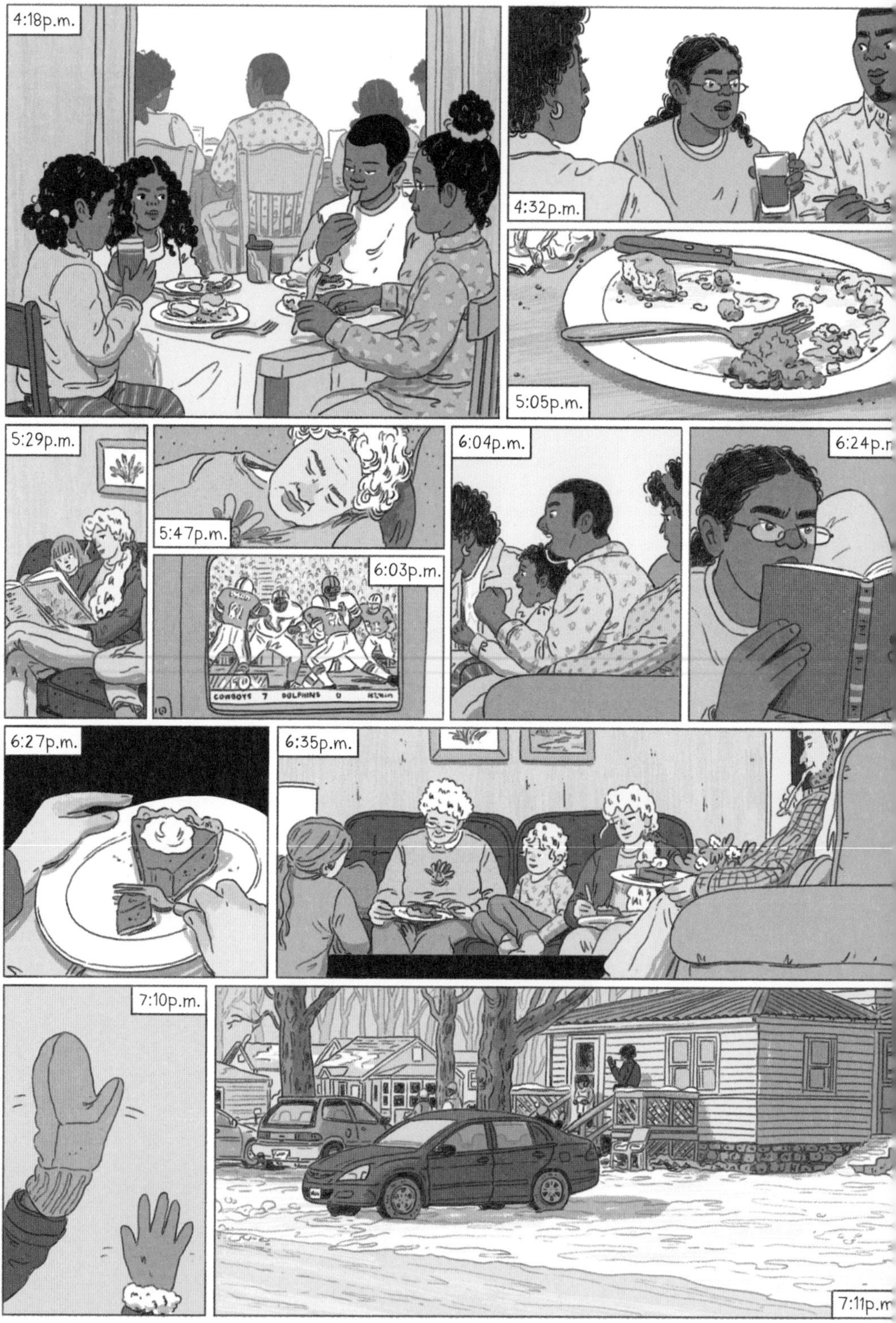

4:18p.m.
4:32p.m.
5:05p.m.
5:29p.m.
5:47p.m.
6:03p.m.
COWBOYS 7 DOLPHINS 0
6:04p.m.
6:24p.m.
6:27p.m.
6:35p.m.
7:10p.m.
7:11p.m.

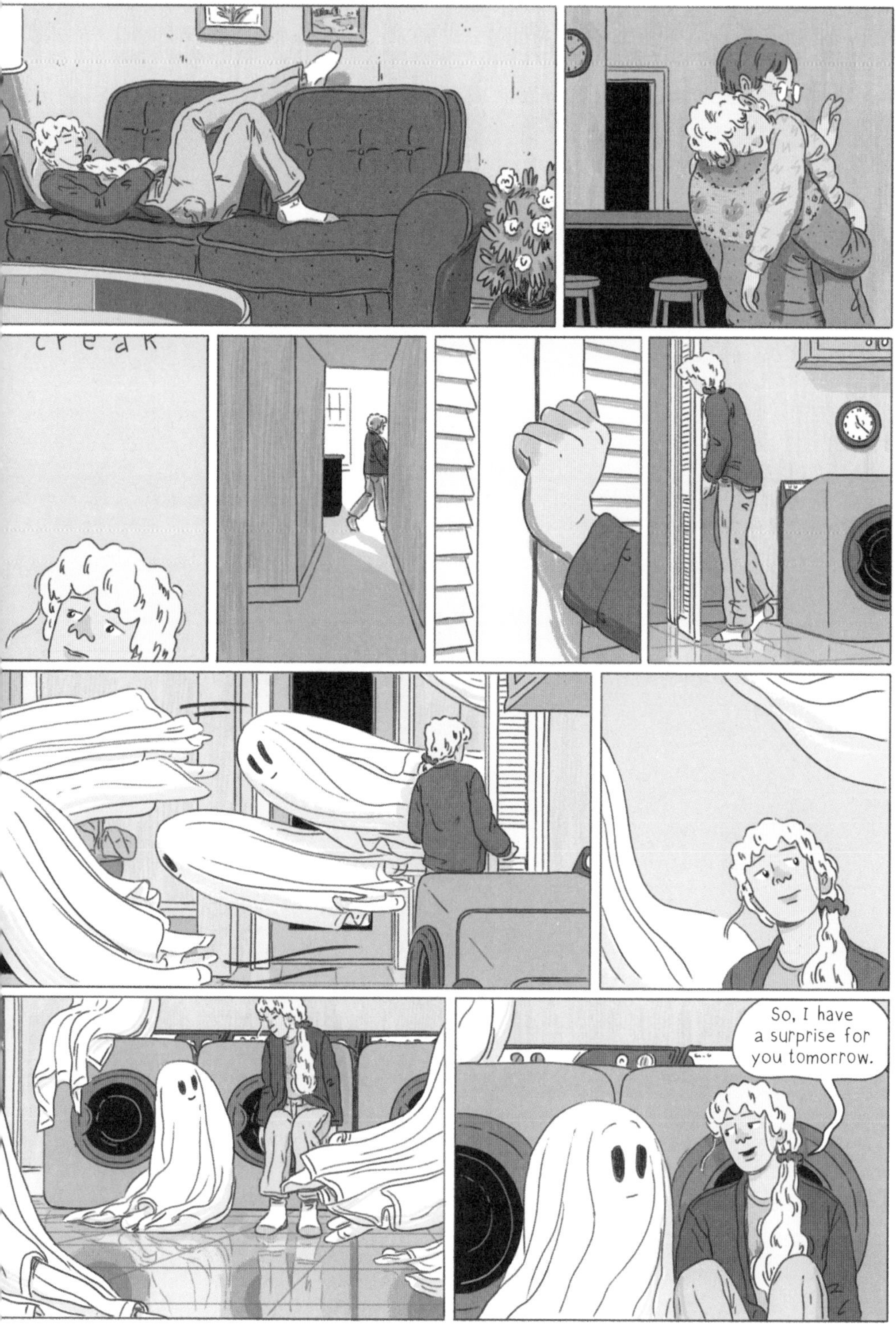
creak
So, I have a surprise for you tomorrow.

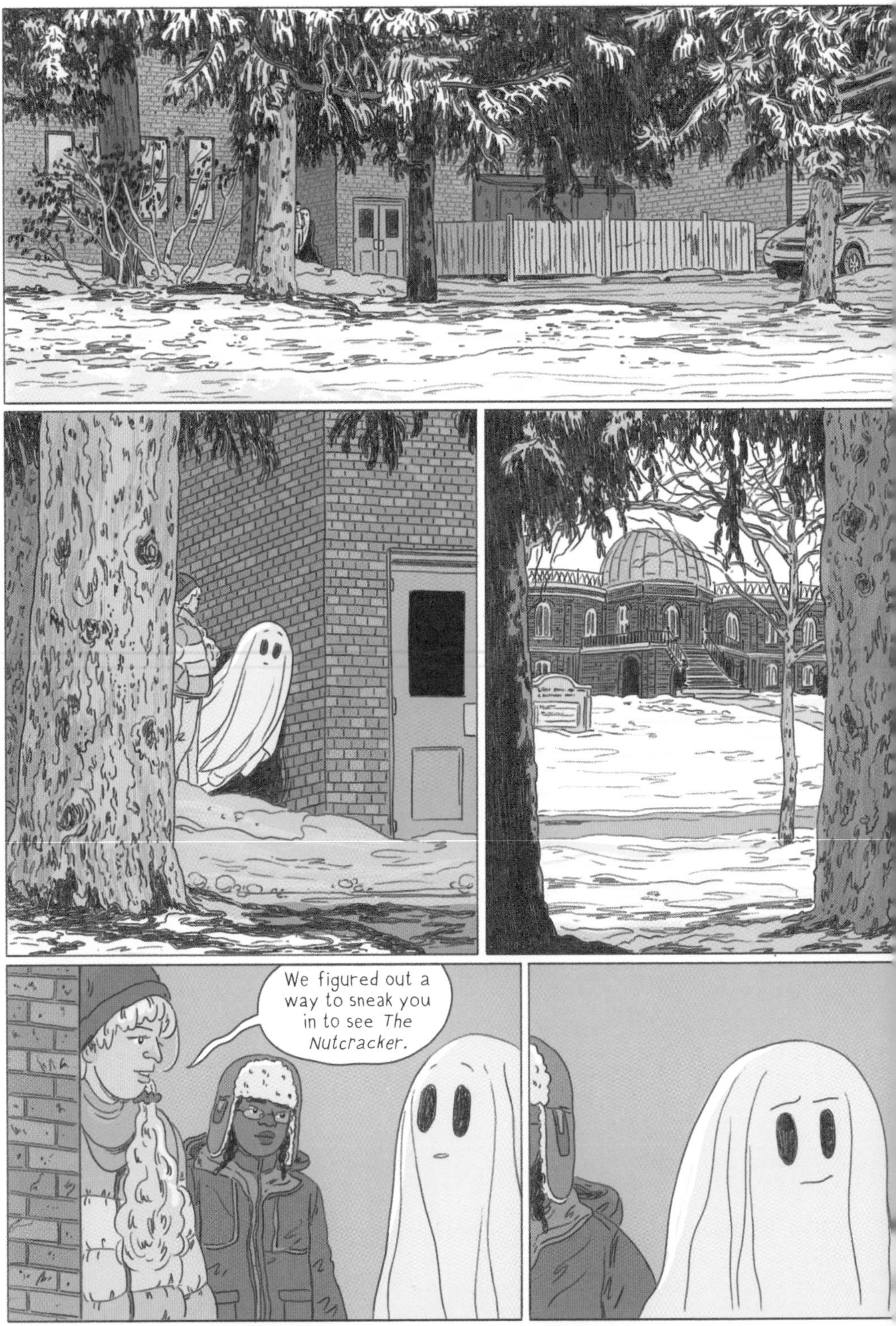
We figured out a way to sneak you in to see *The Nutcracker*.

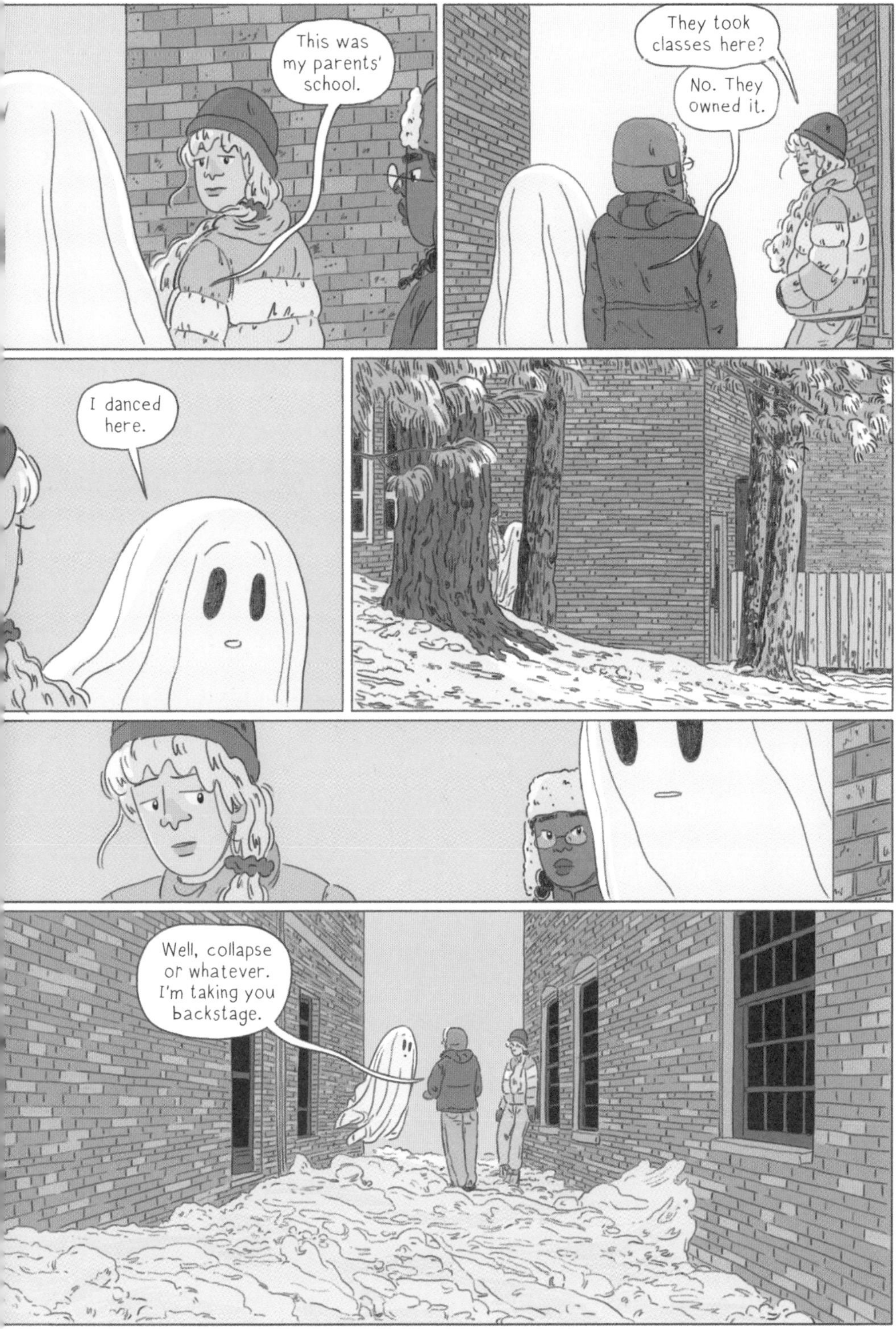
This was my parents' school.
They took classes here?
No. They owned it.
I danced here.
Well, collapse or whatever. I'm taking you backstage.

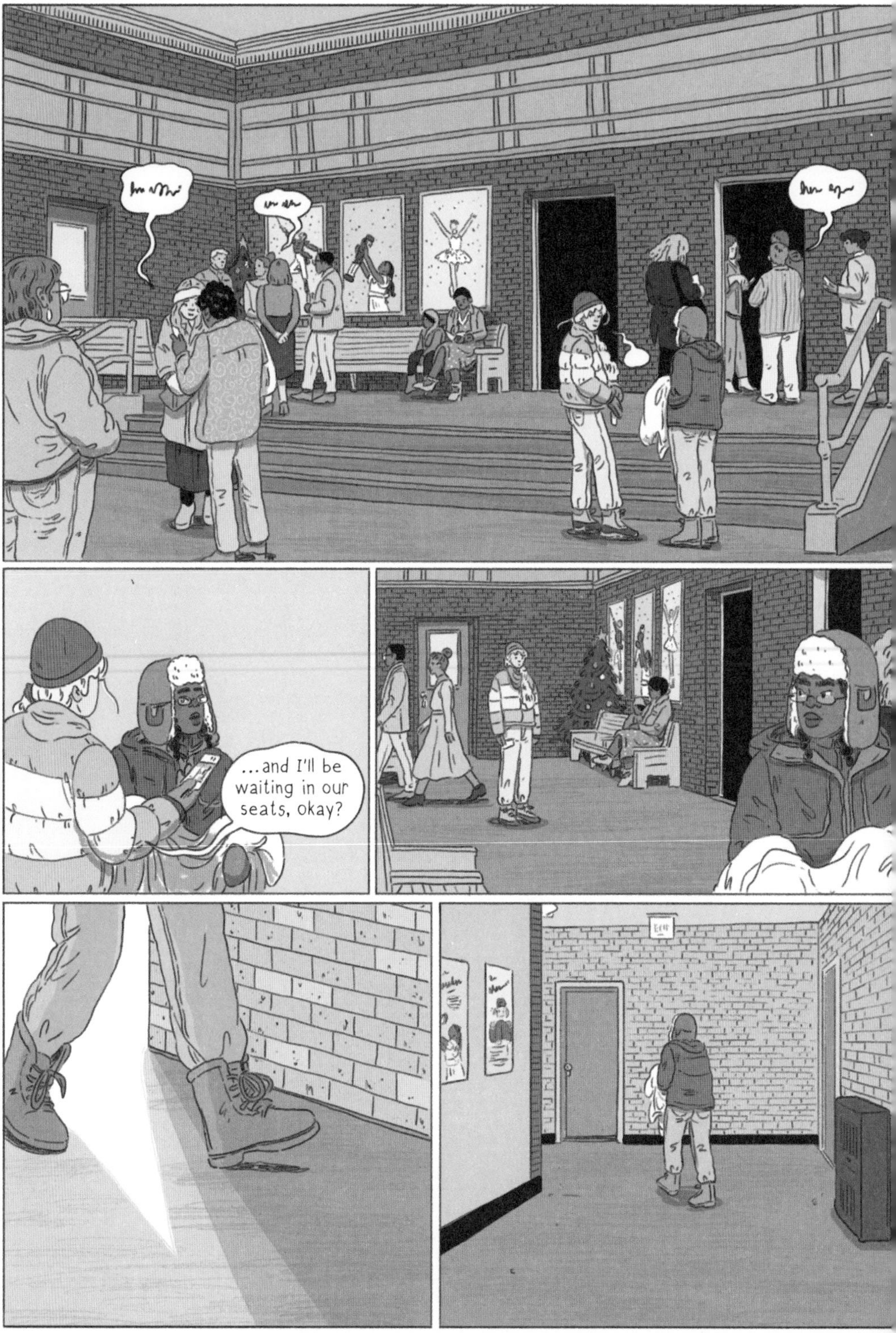
...and I'll be waiting in our seats, okay?

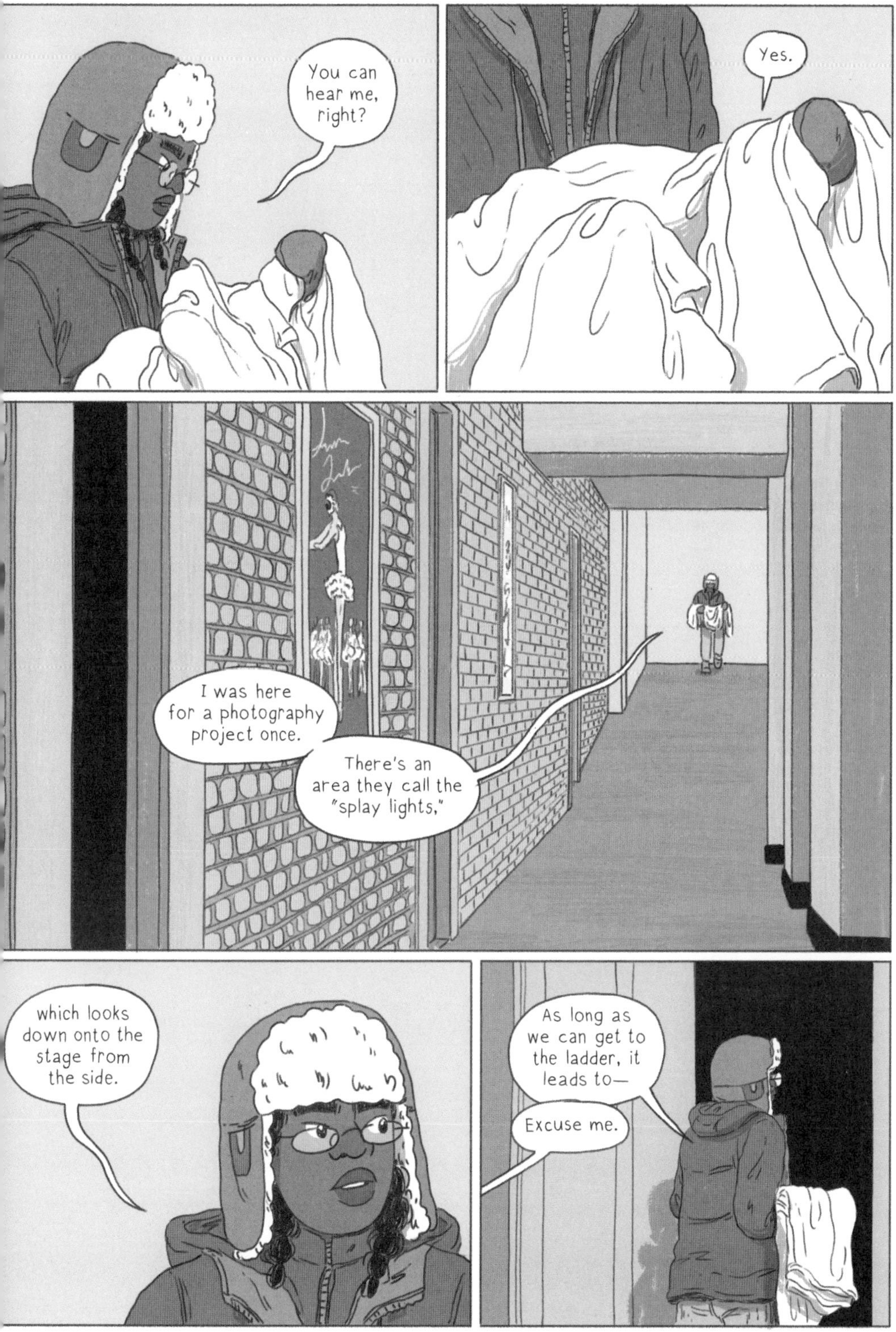
You can hear me, right?
Yes.
I was here for a photography project once.
There's an area they call the "splay lights,"
which looks down onto the stage from the side.
As long as we can get to the ladder, it leads to—
Excuse me.

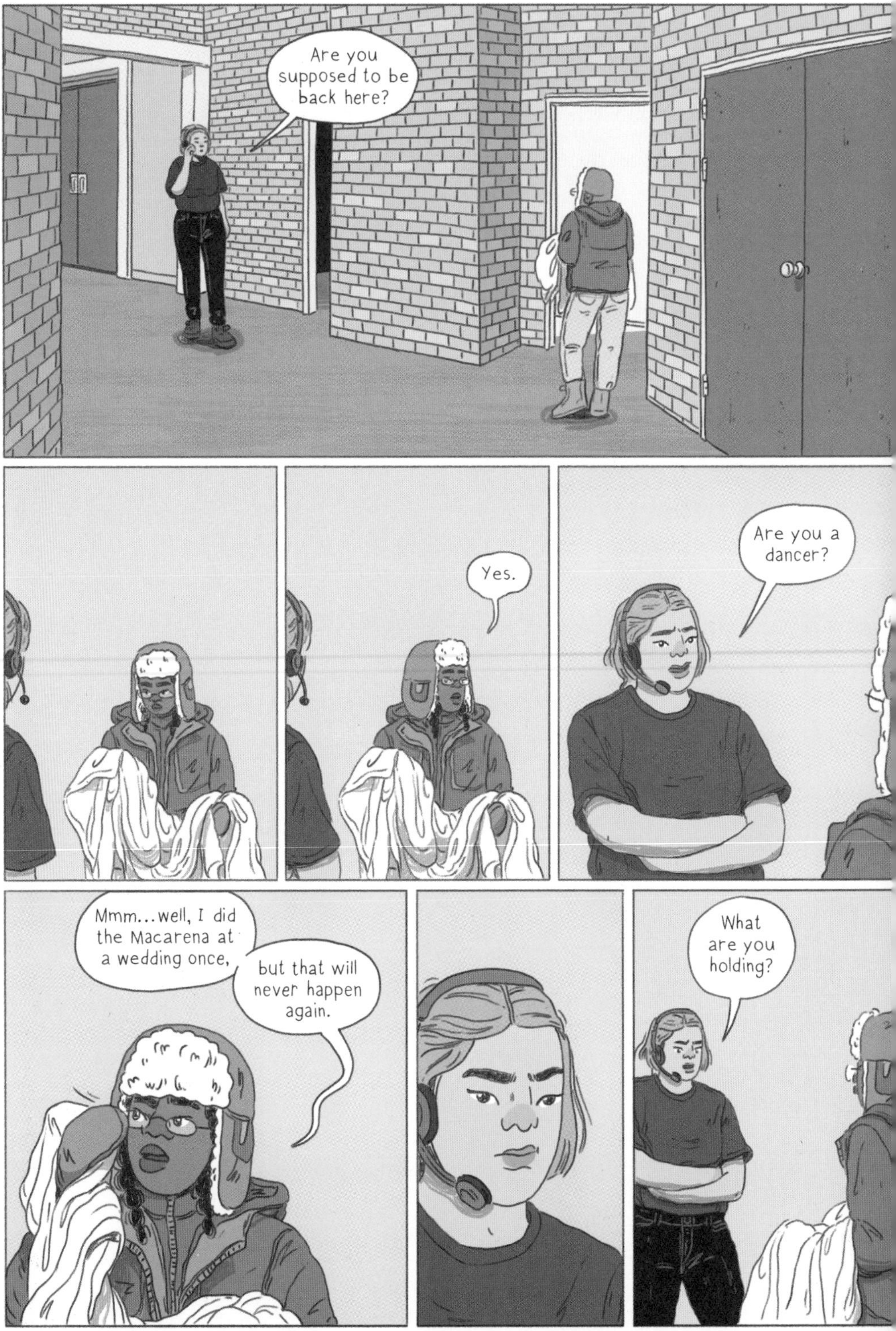
Are you supposed to be back here?
Yes.
Are you a dancer?
Mmm...well, I did the Macarena at a wedding once,
but that will never happen again.
What are you holding?

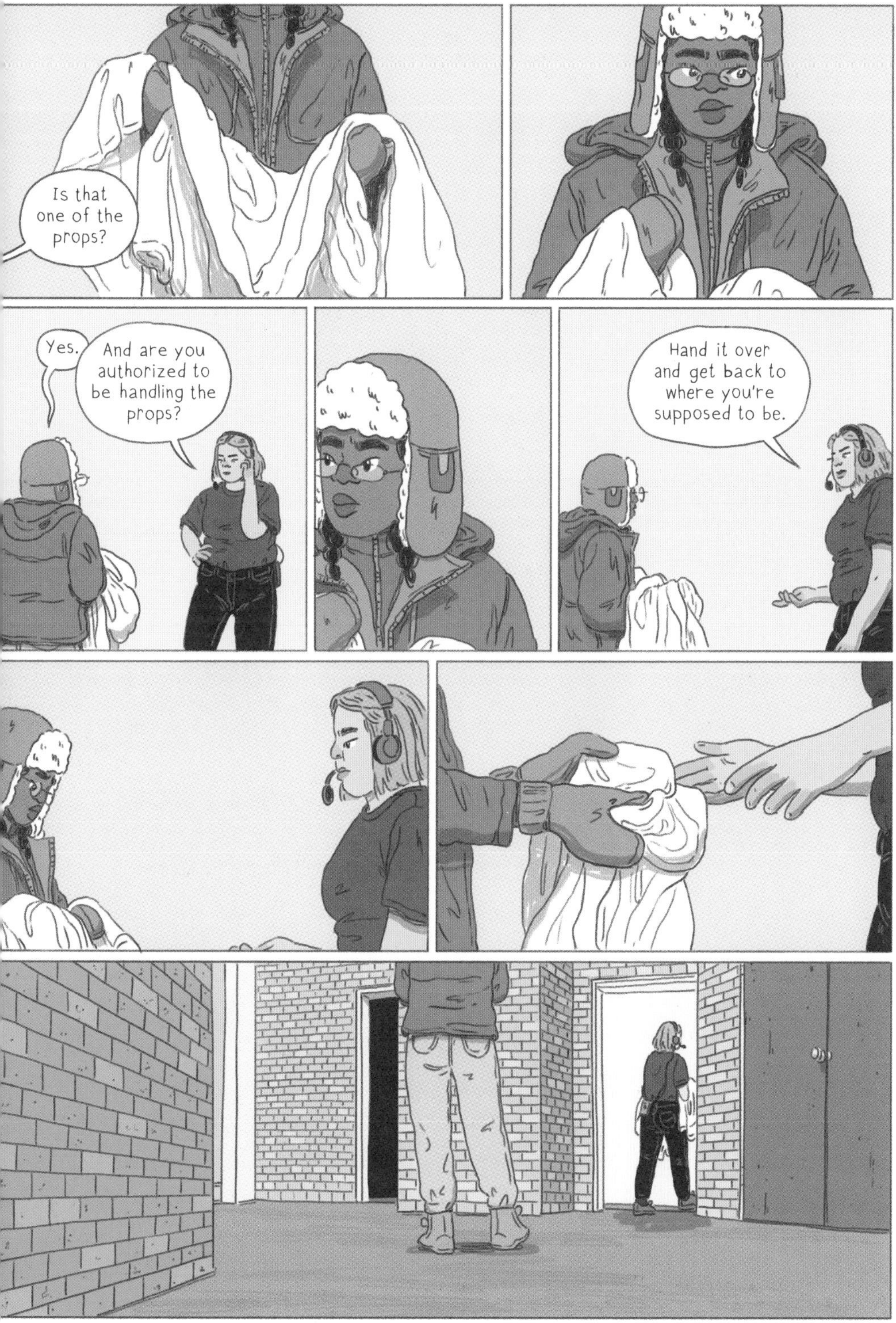
Is that one of the props?
Yes.
And are you authorized to be handling the props?
Hand it over and get back to where you're supposed to be.

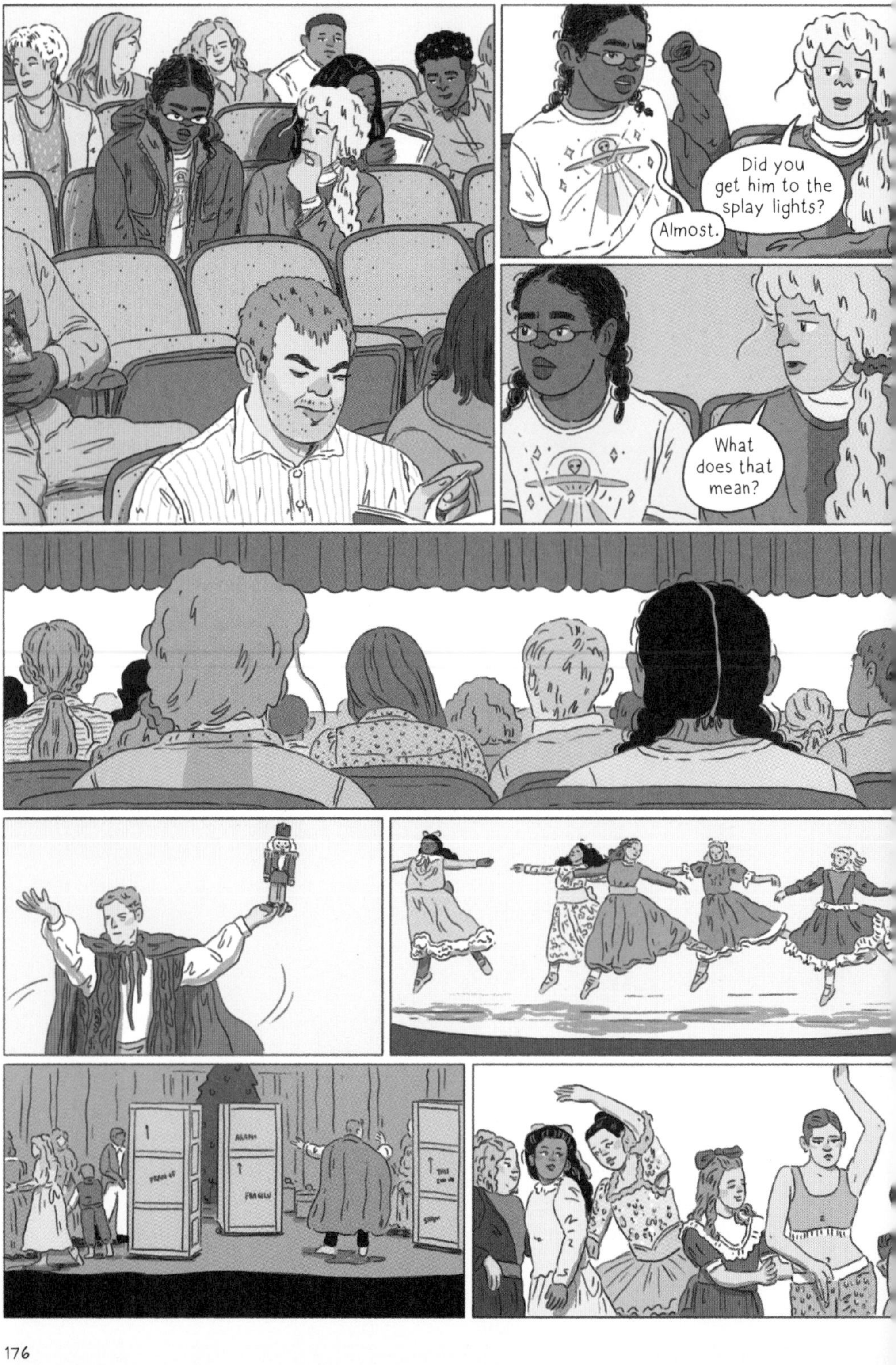
Did you get him to the splay lights?
Almost.
What does that mean?

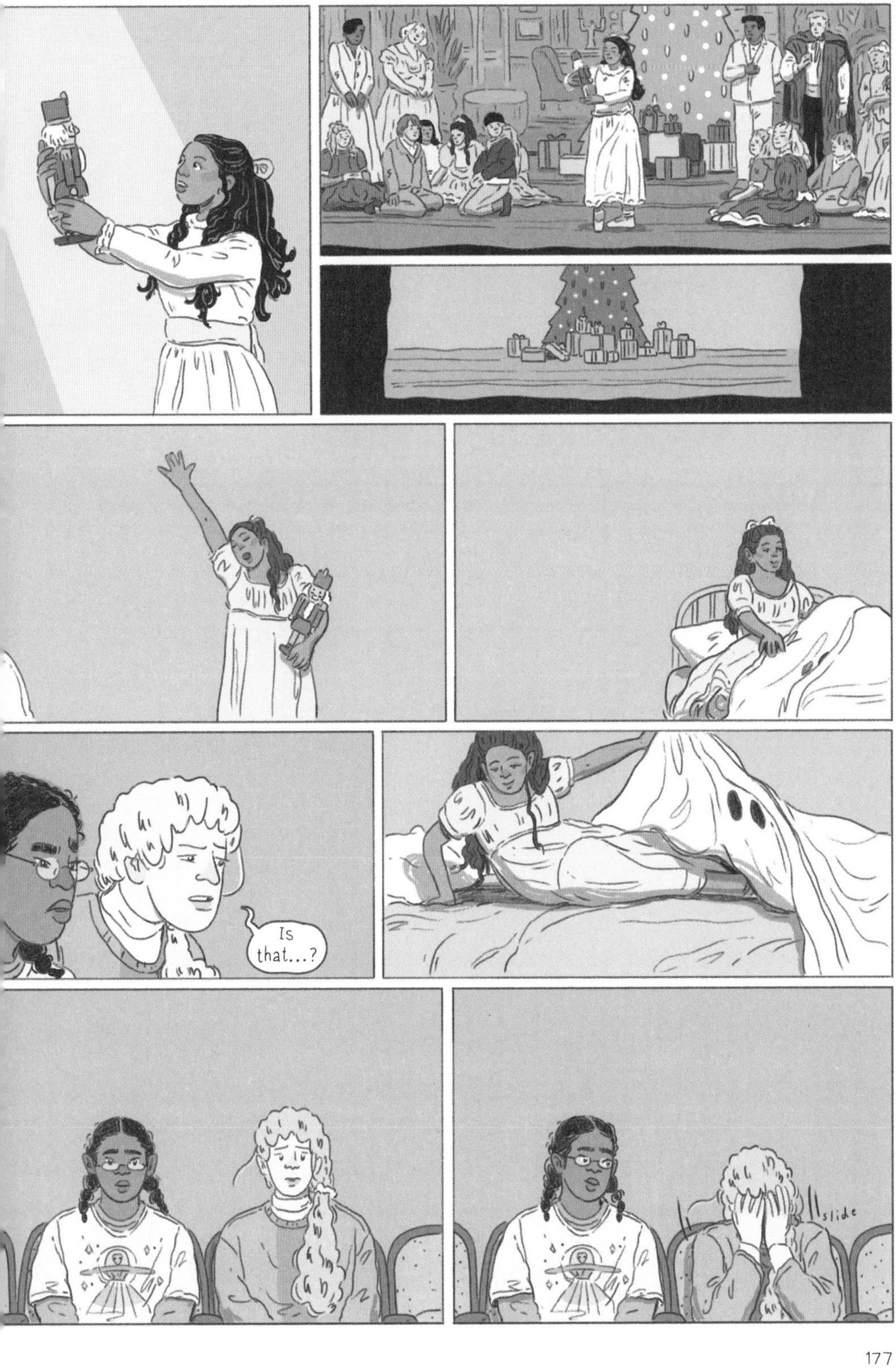
Is that...?
slide

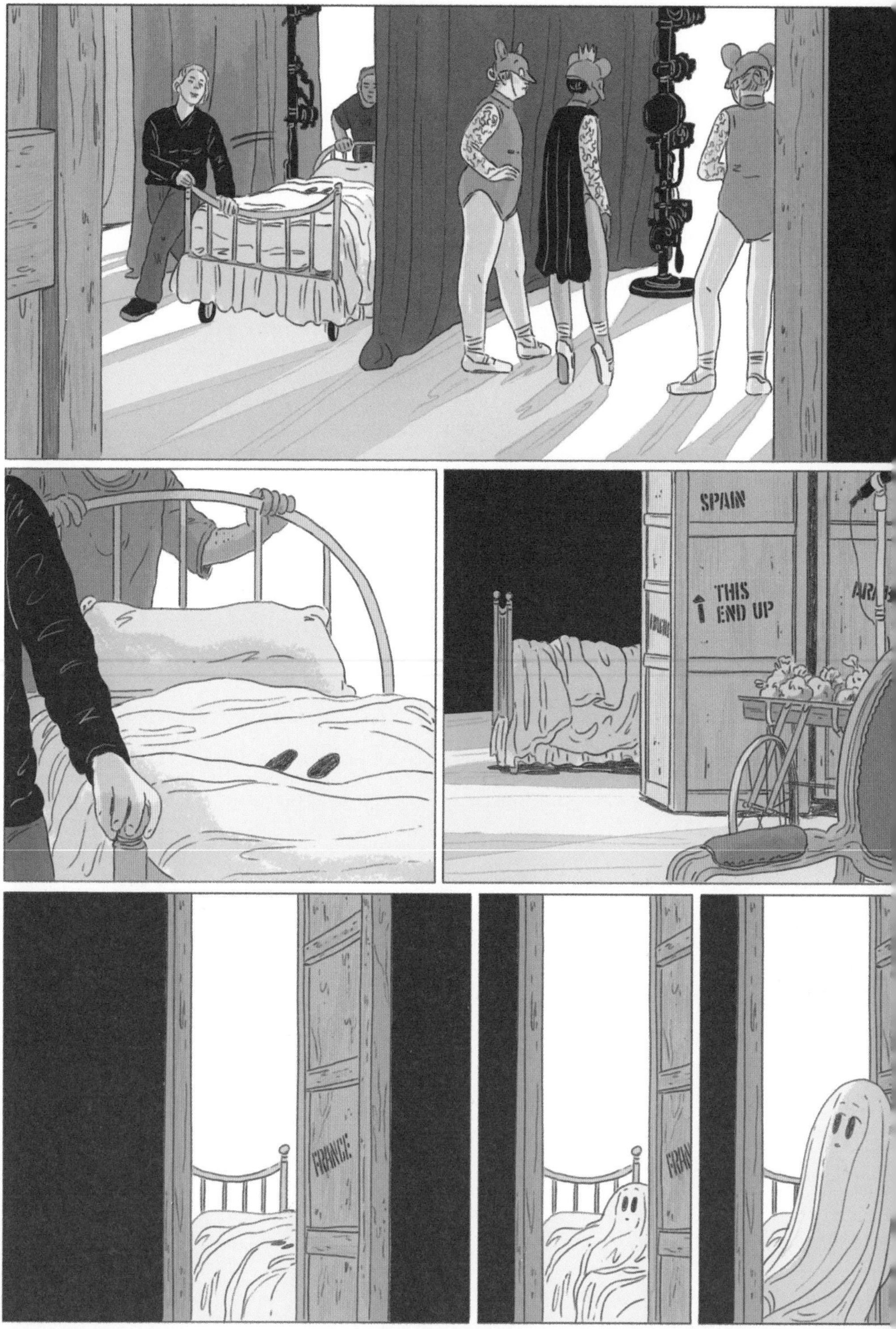
SPAIN
THIS END UP
FRANCE

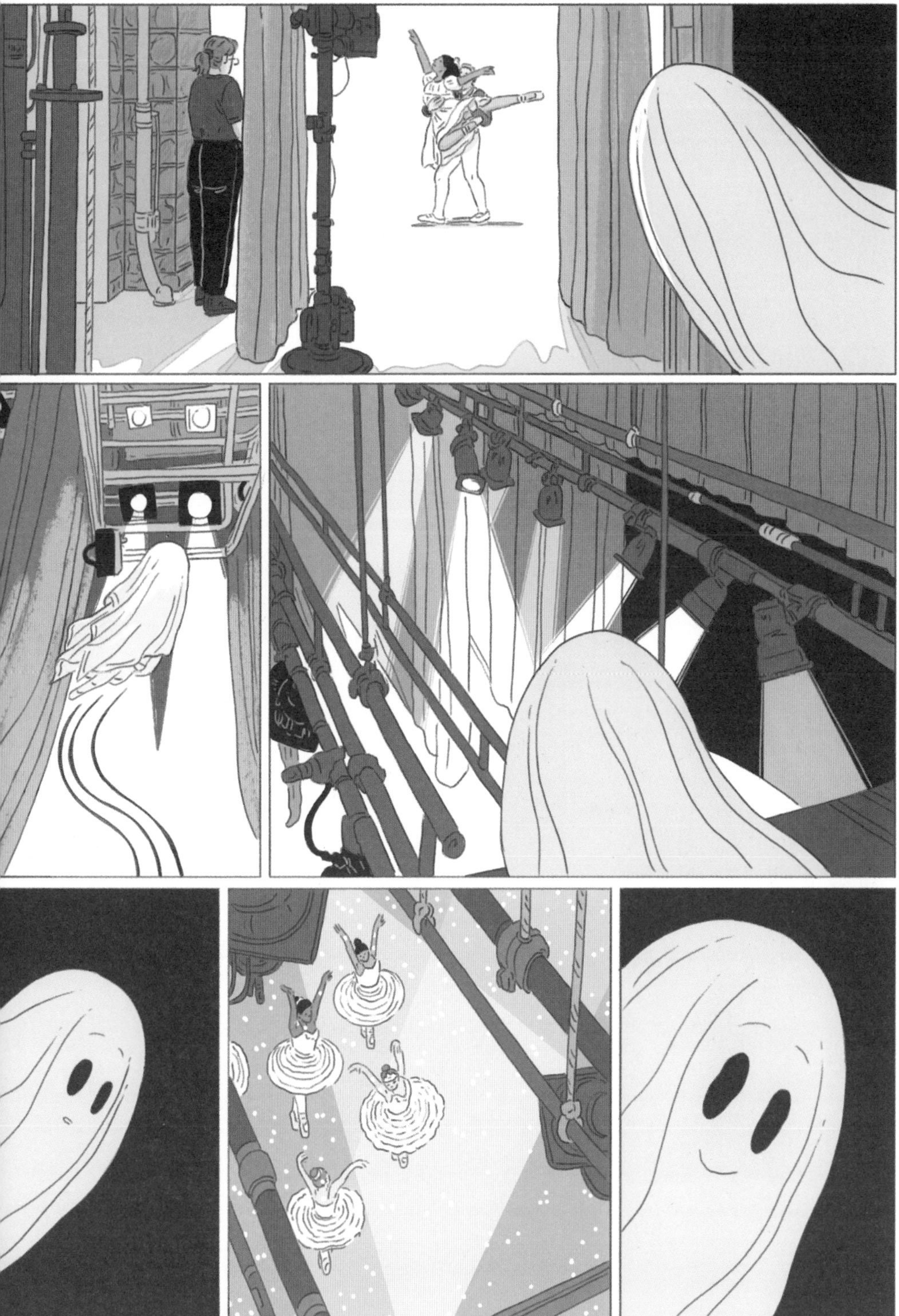

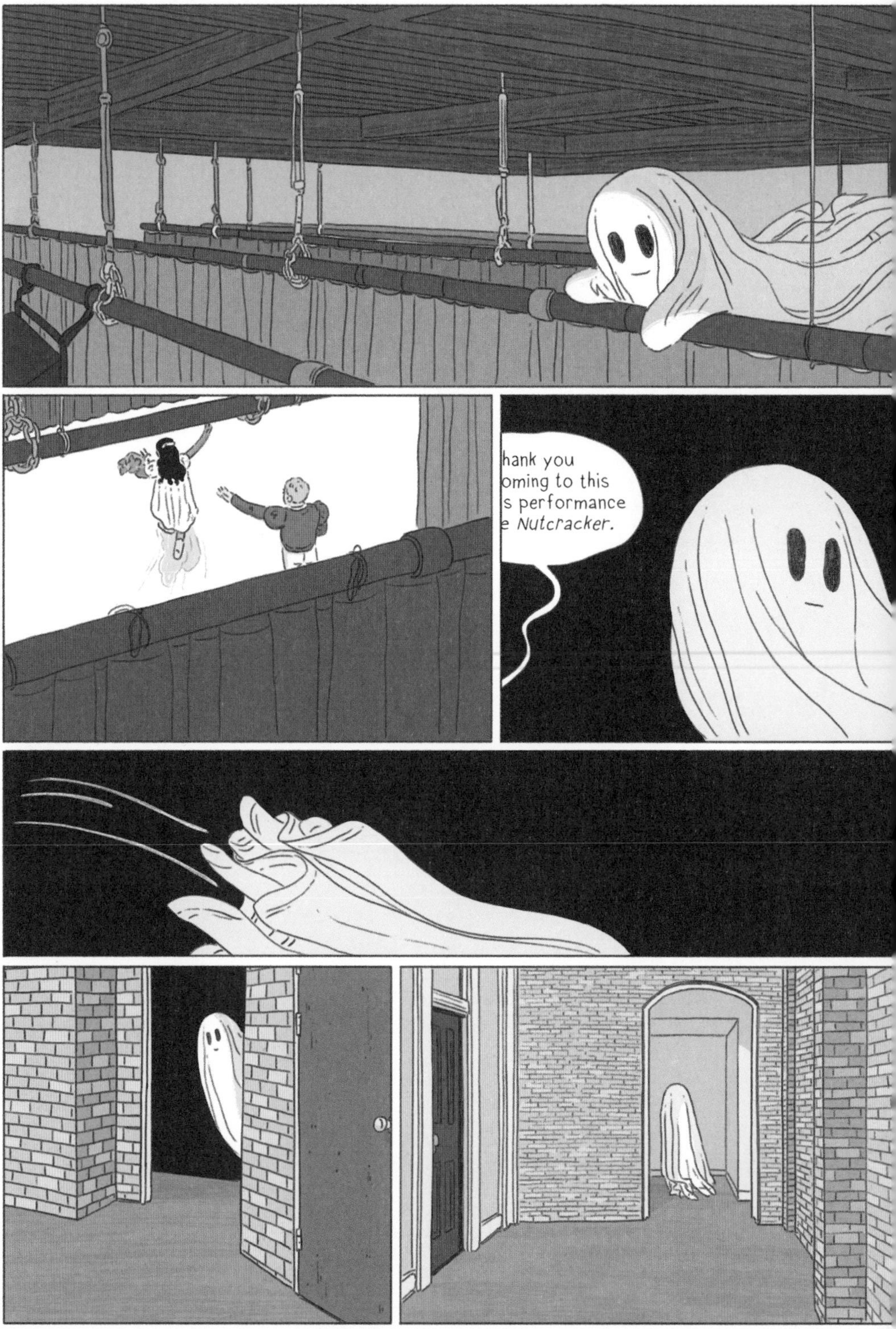
hank you
oming to this
s performance
e *Nutcracker.*

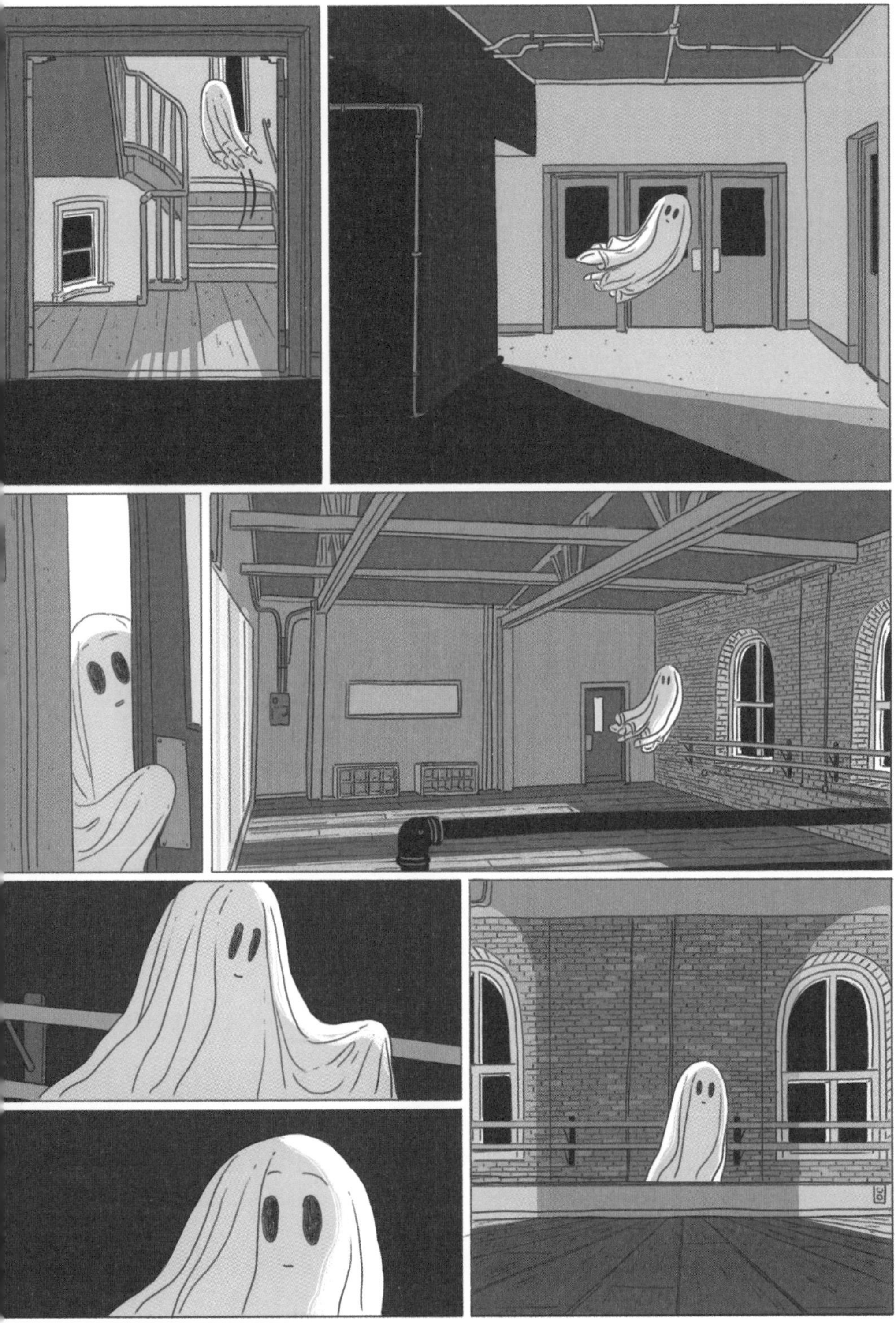

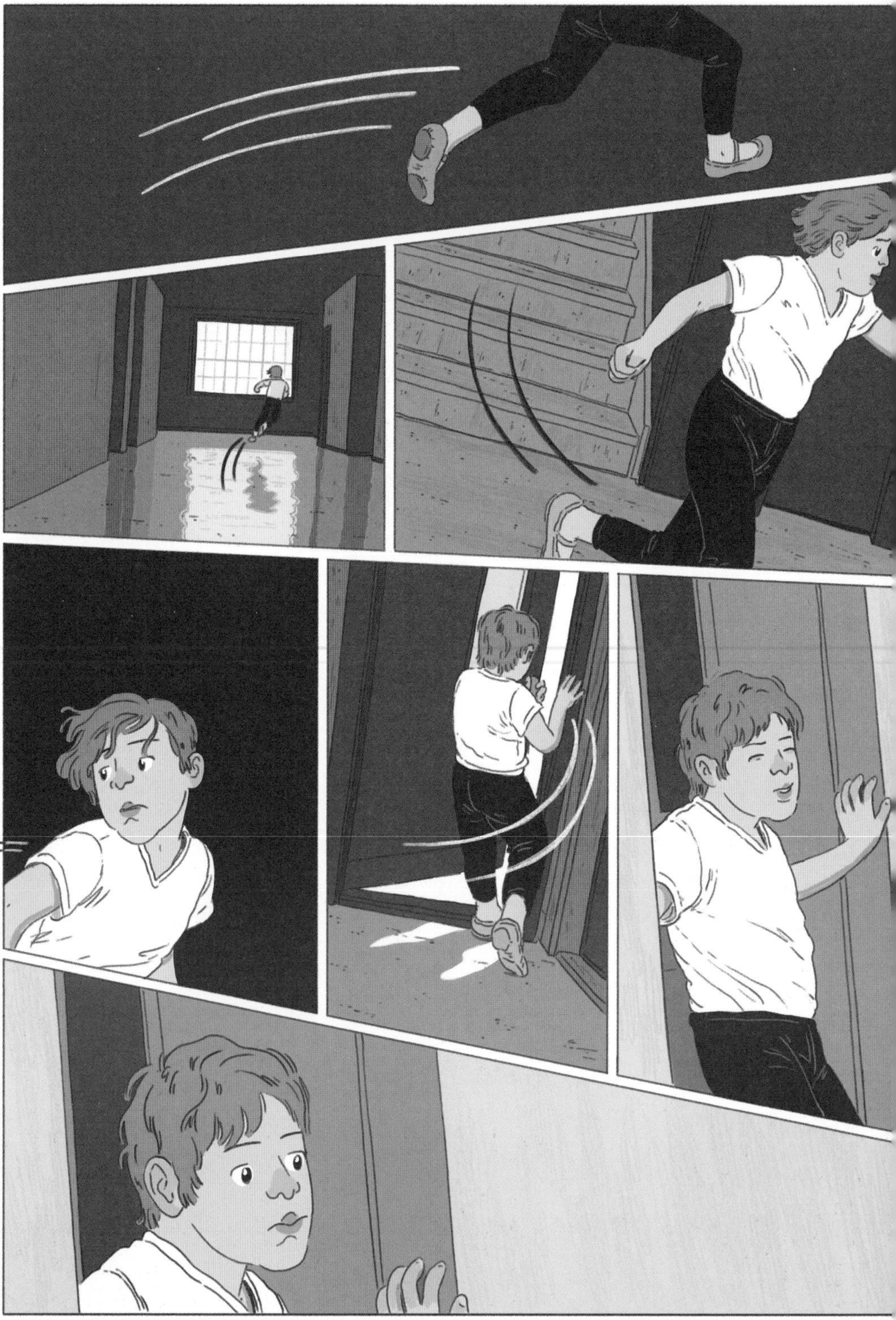

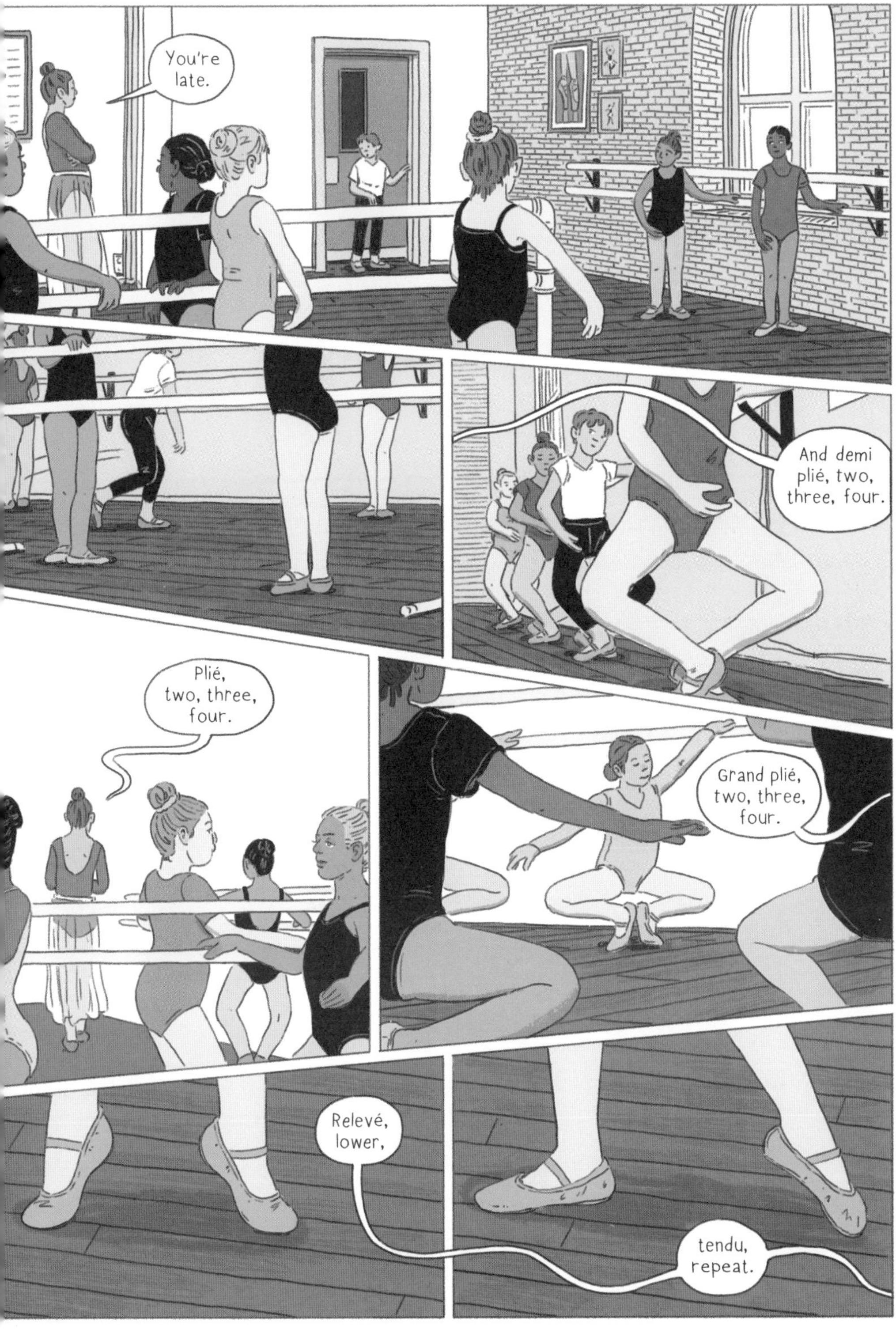
You're late.
And demi plié, two, three, four.
Plié, two, three, four.
Grand plié, two, three, four.
Relevé, lower,
tendu, repeat.

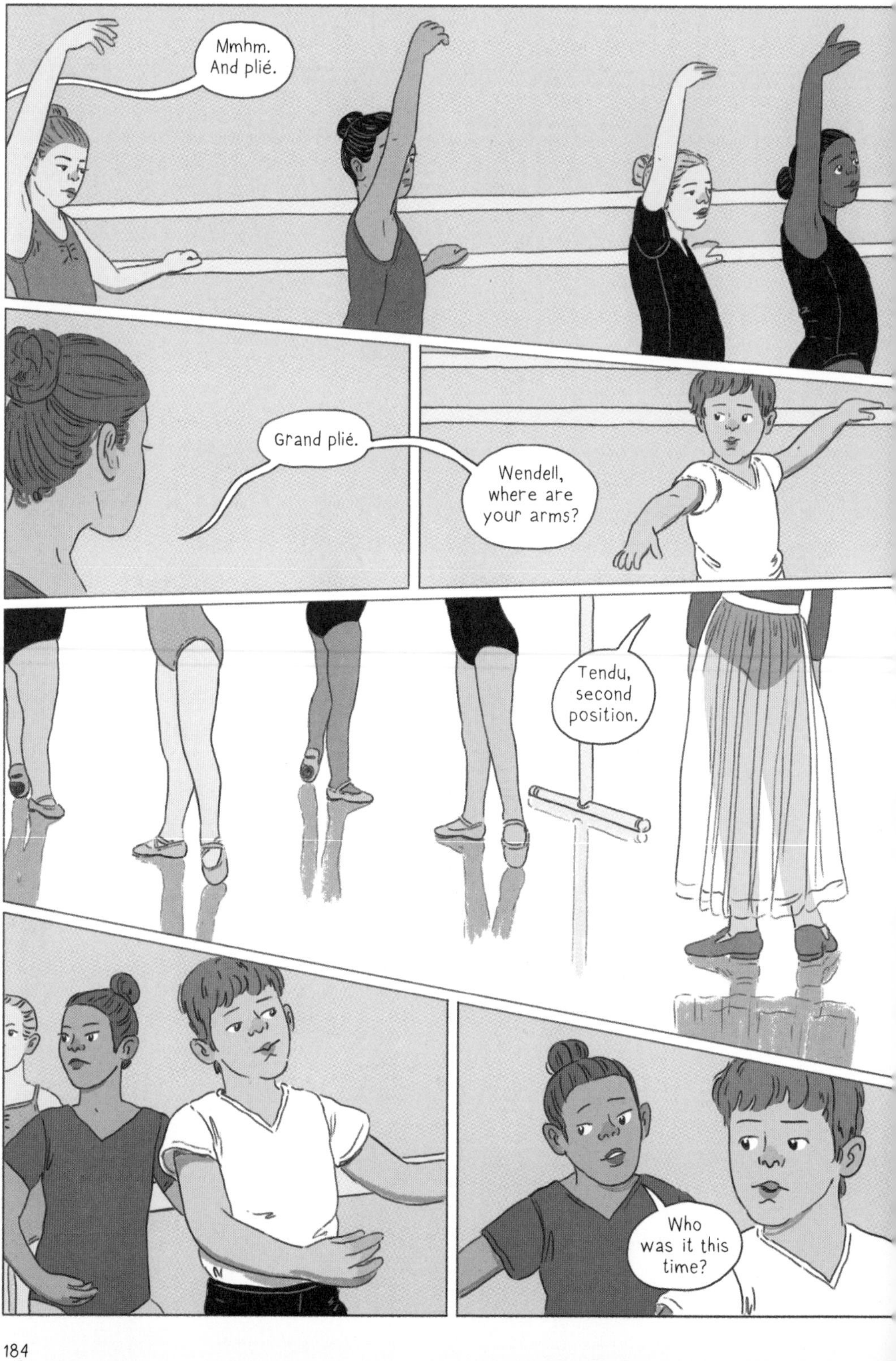
Mmhm.
And plié.
Grand plié.
Wendell, where are your arms?
Tendu, second position.
Who was it this time?

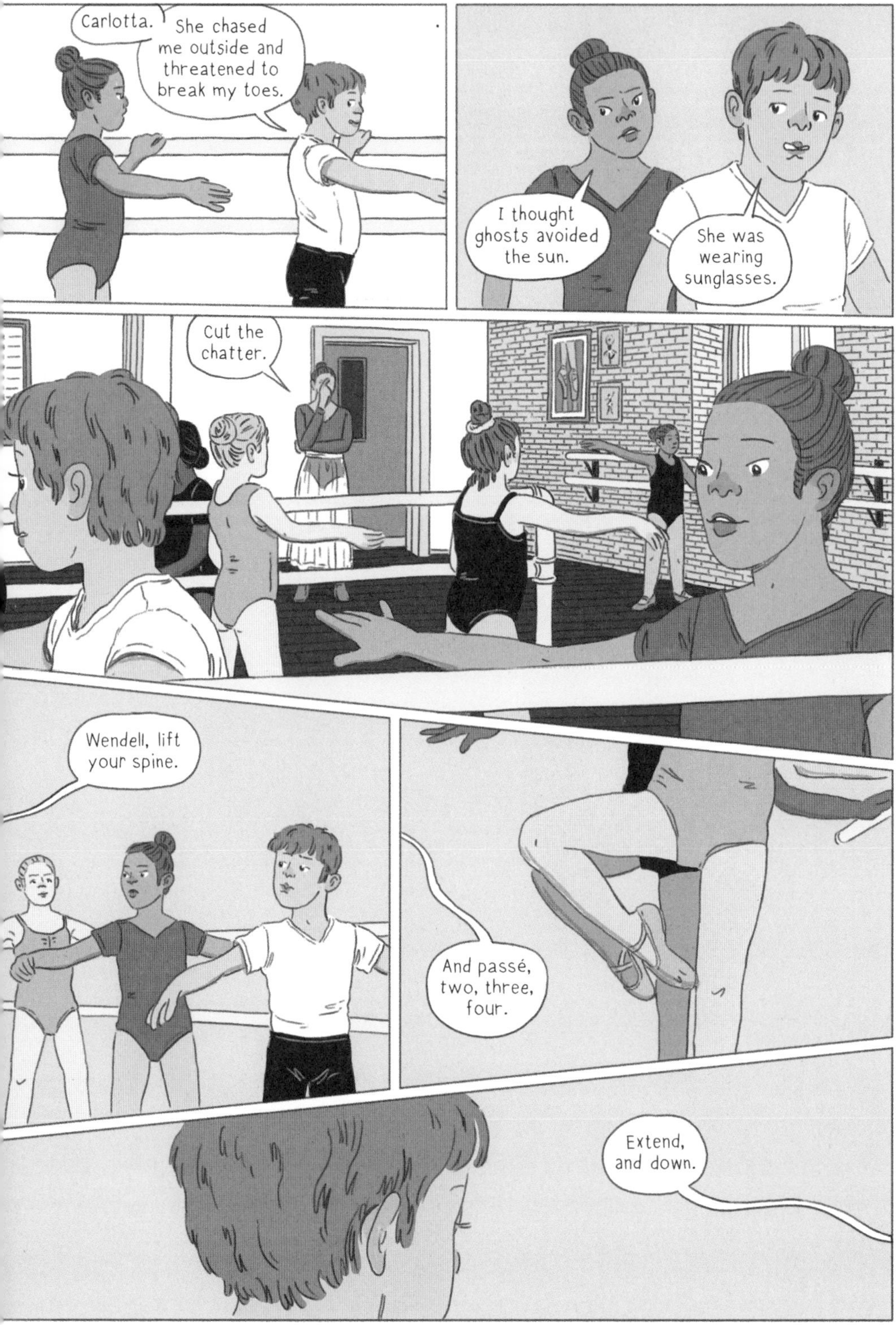
Carlotta.
She chased me outside and threatened to break my toes.
I thought ghosts avoided the sun.
She was wearing sunglasses.
Cut the chatter.
Wendell, lift your spine.
And passé, two, three, four.
Extend, and down.

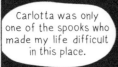
Carlotta was only one of the spooks who made my life difficult in this place.

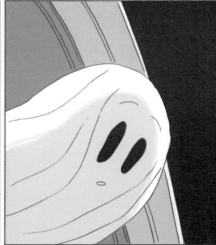

The Sea Witch made sure of it.

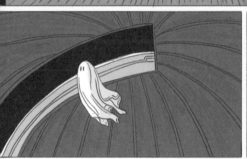

The Sea Witch followed me everywhere I went, and introduced me to all her spook friends.

And once you're on a first-name basis with a spook, they won't leave you alone.

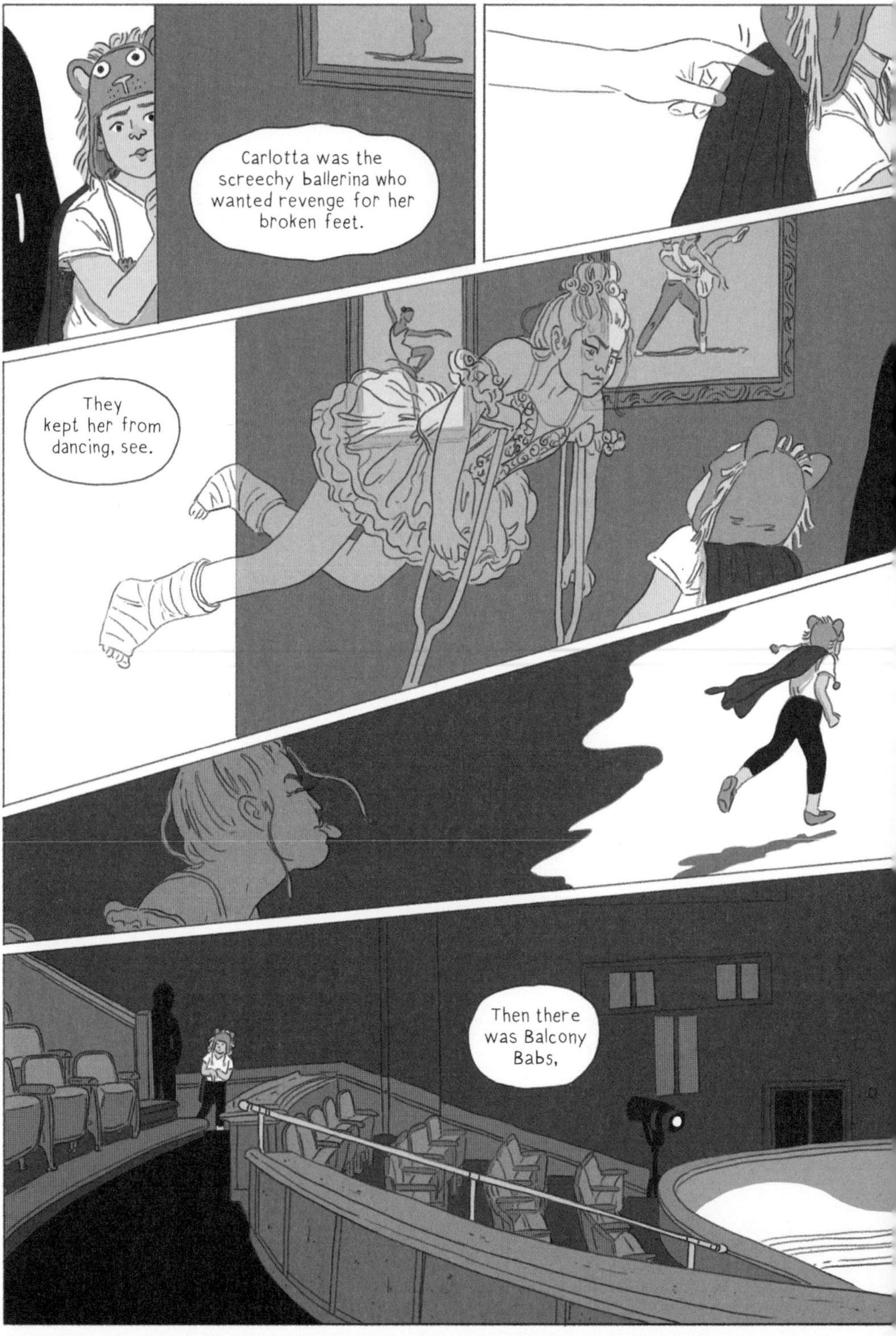
Carlotta was the screechy ballerina who wanted revenge for her broken feet.
They kept her from dancing, see.
Then there was Balcony Babs,

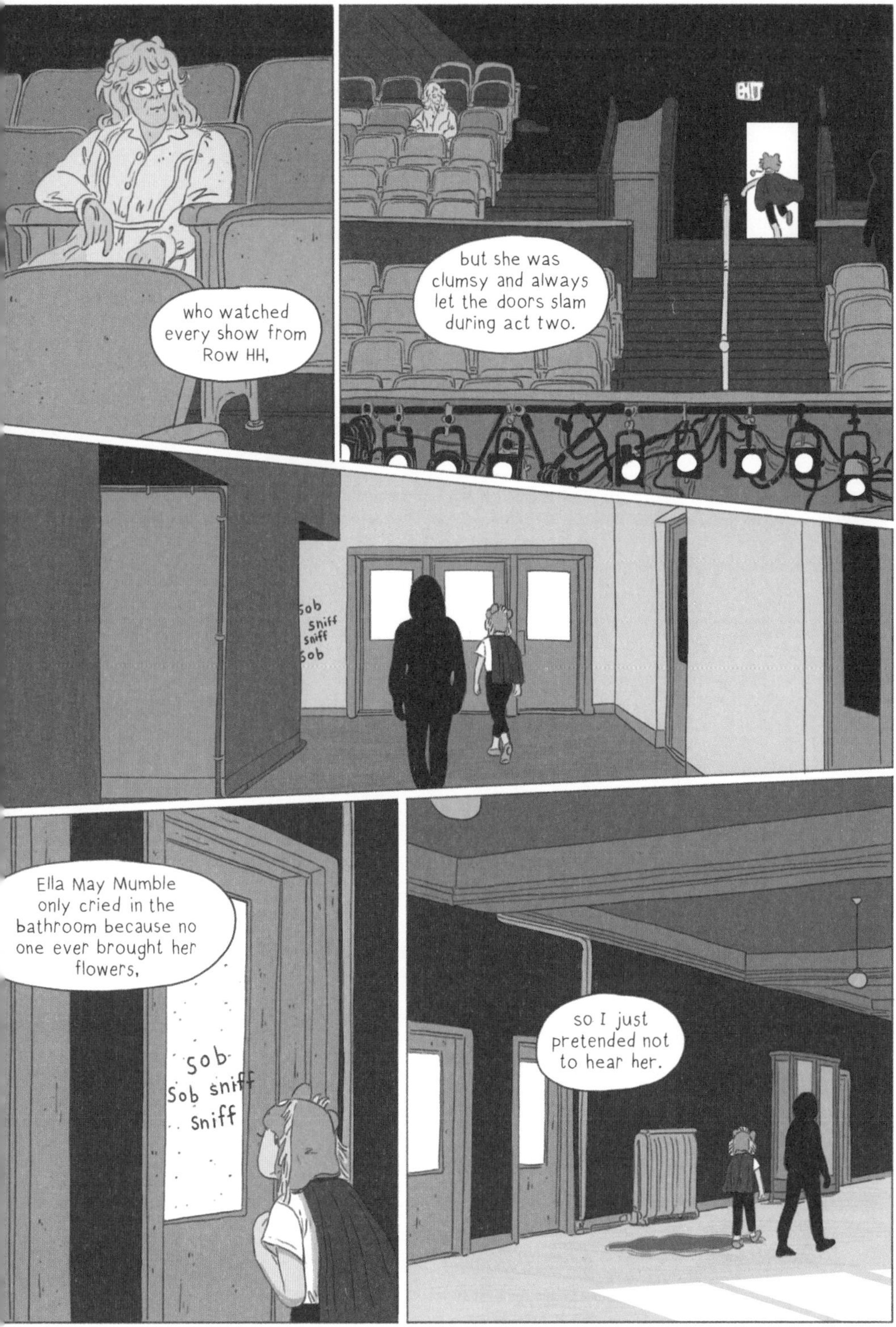
who watched every show from Row HH,
but she was clumsy and always let the doors slam during act two.
EXIT
sob sniff sniff sob
Ella May Mumble only cried in the bathroom because no one ever brought her flowers,
sob Sob sniff sniff
so I just pretended not to hear her.

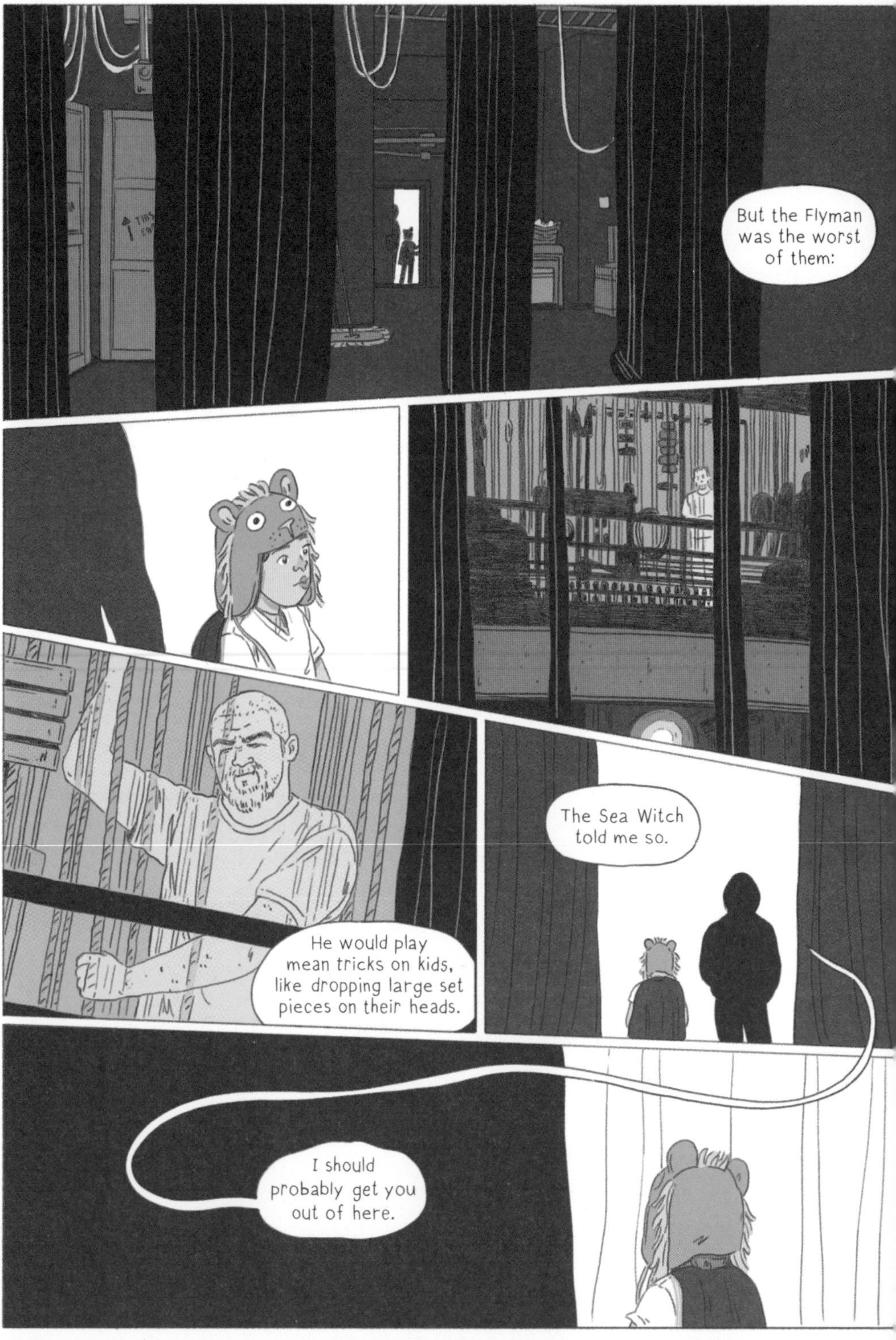
But the Flyman was the worst of them:
He would play mean tricks on kids, like dropping large set pieces on their heads.
The Sea Witch told me so.
I should probably get you out of here.

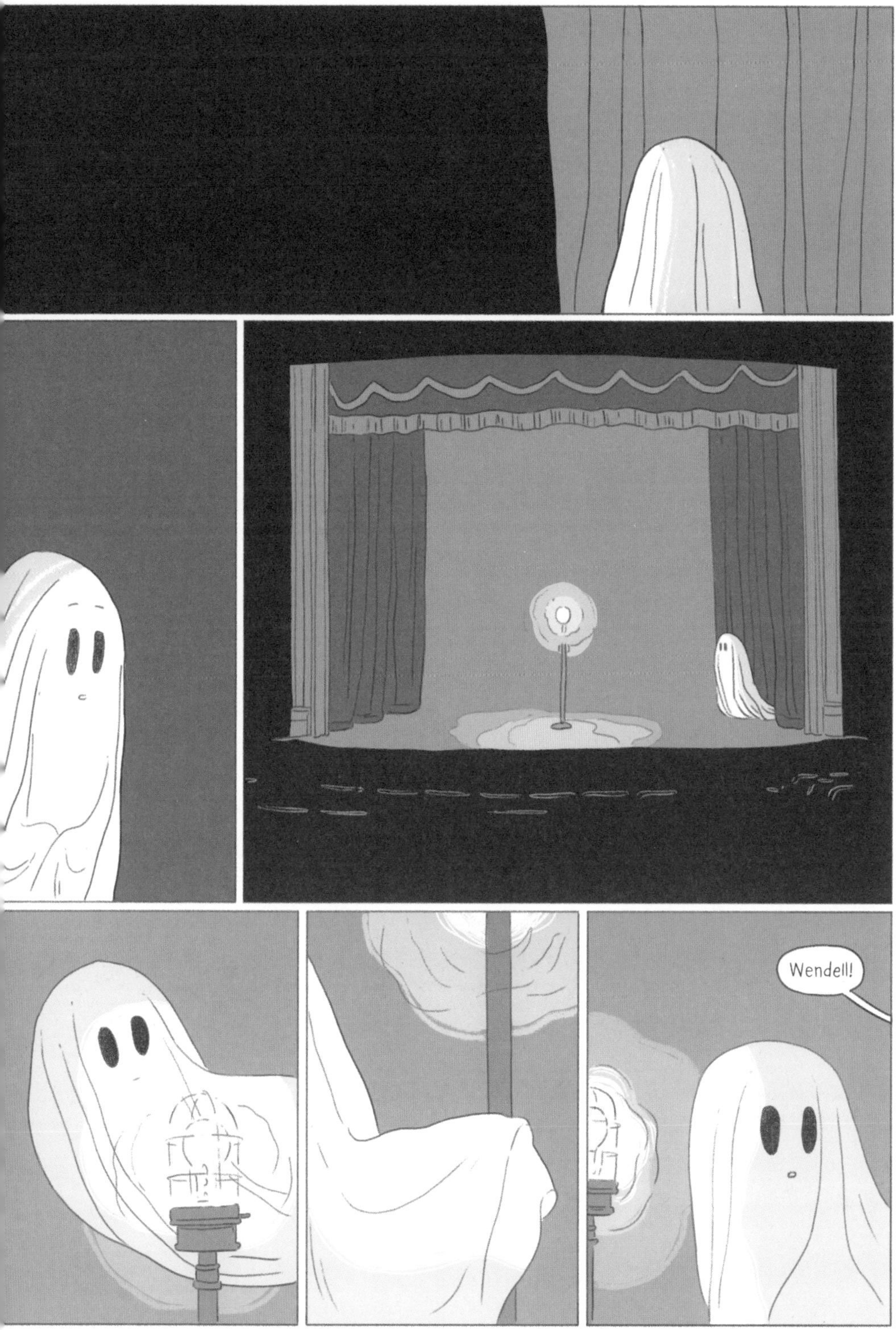
Wendell!

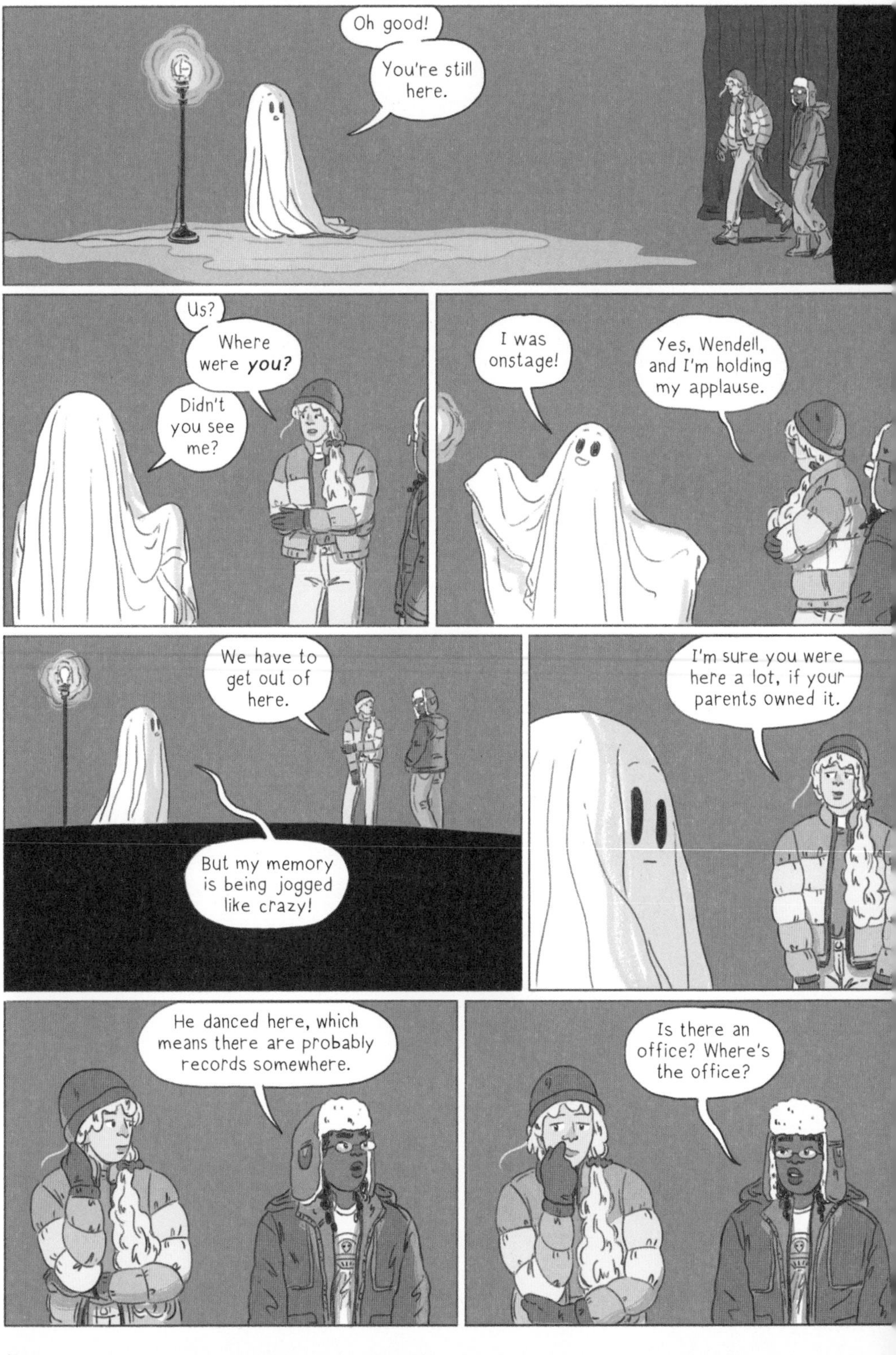
Oh good!
You're still here.
Us?
Where were *you?*
Didn't you see me?
I was onstage!
Yes, Wendell, and I'm holding my applause.
We have to get out of here.
But my memory is being jogged like crazy!
I'm sure you were here a lot, if your parents owned it.
He danced here, which means there are probably records somewhere.
Is there an office? Where's the office?

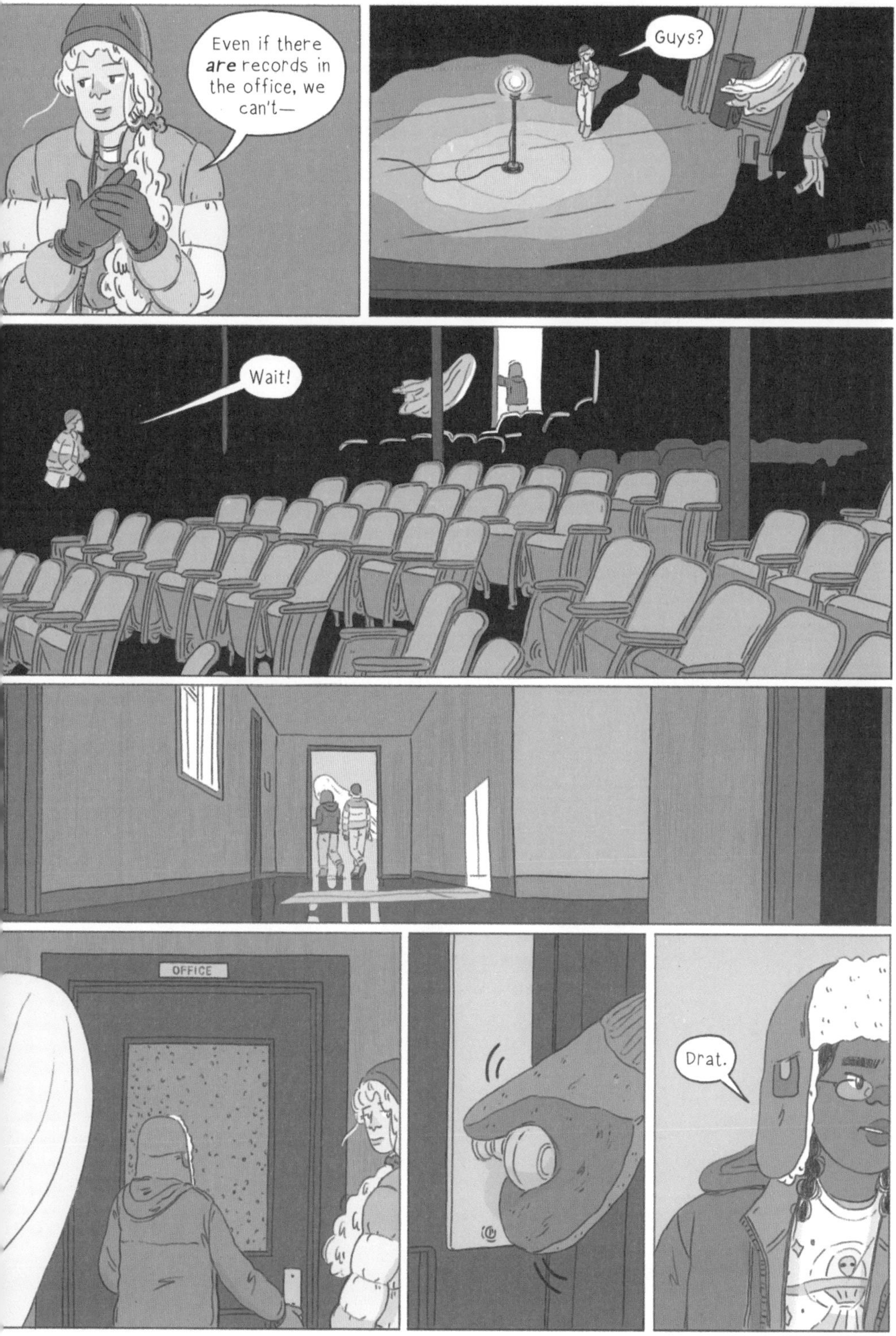
Even if there **are** records in the office, we can't—
Guys?
Wait!
OFFICE
Drat.

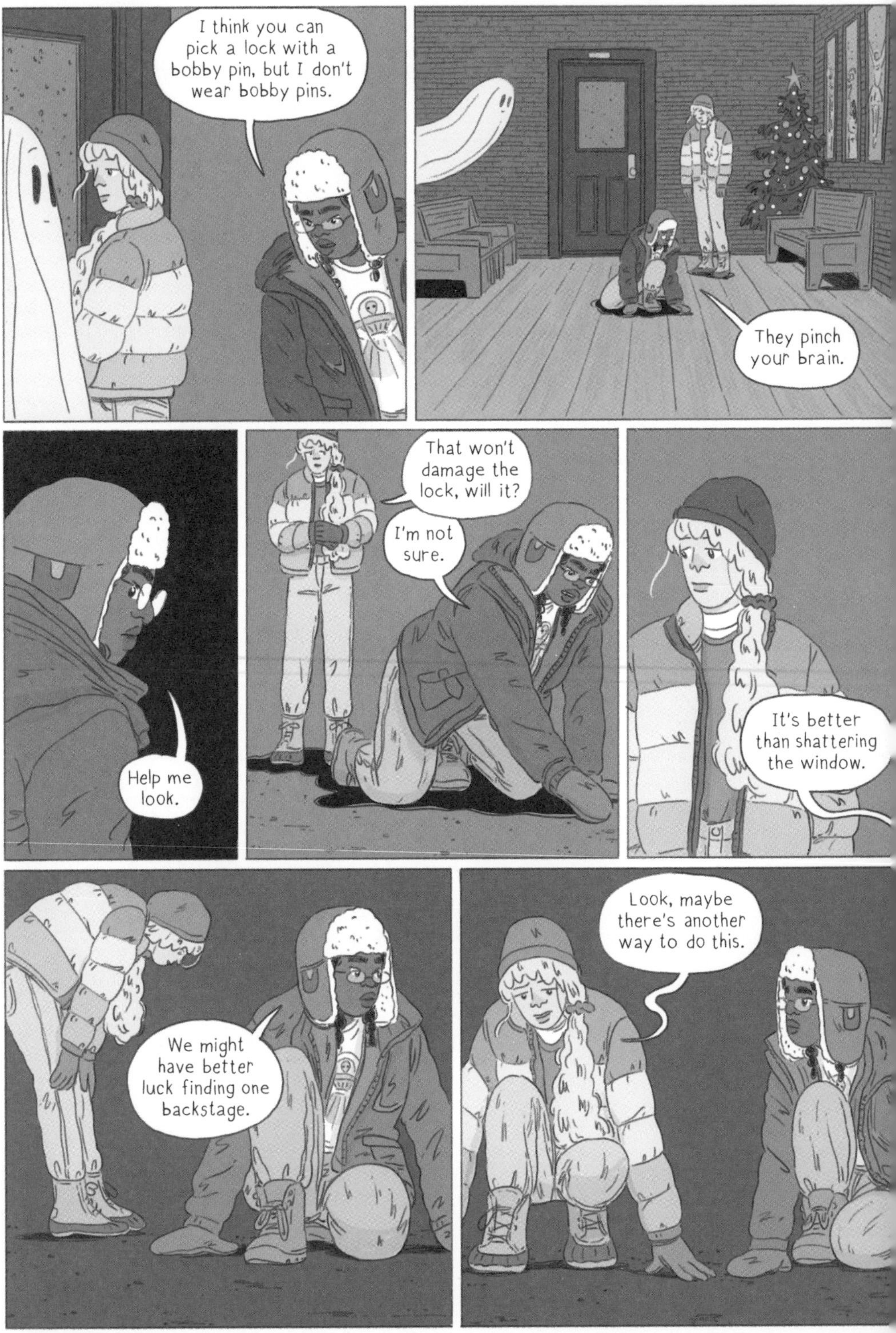
I think you can pick a lock with a bobby pin, but I don't wear bobby pins.
They pinch your brain.
Help me look.
That won't damage the lock, will it?
I'm not sure.
It's better than shattering the window.
We might have better luck finding one backstage.
Look, maybe there's another way to do this.

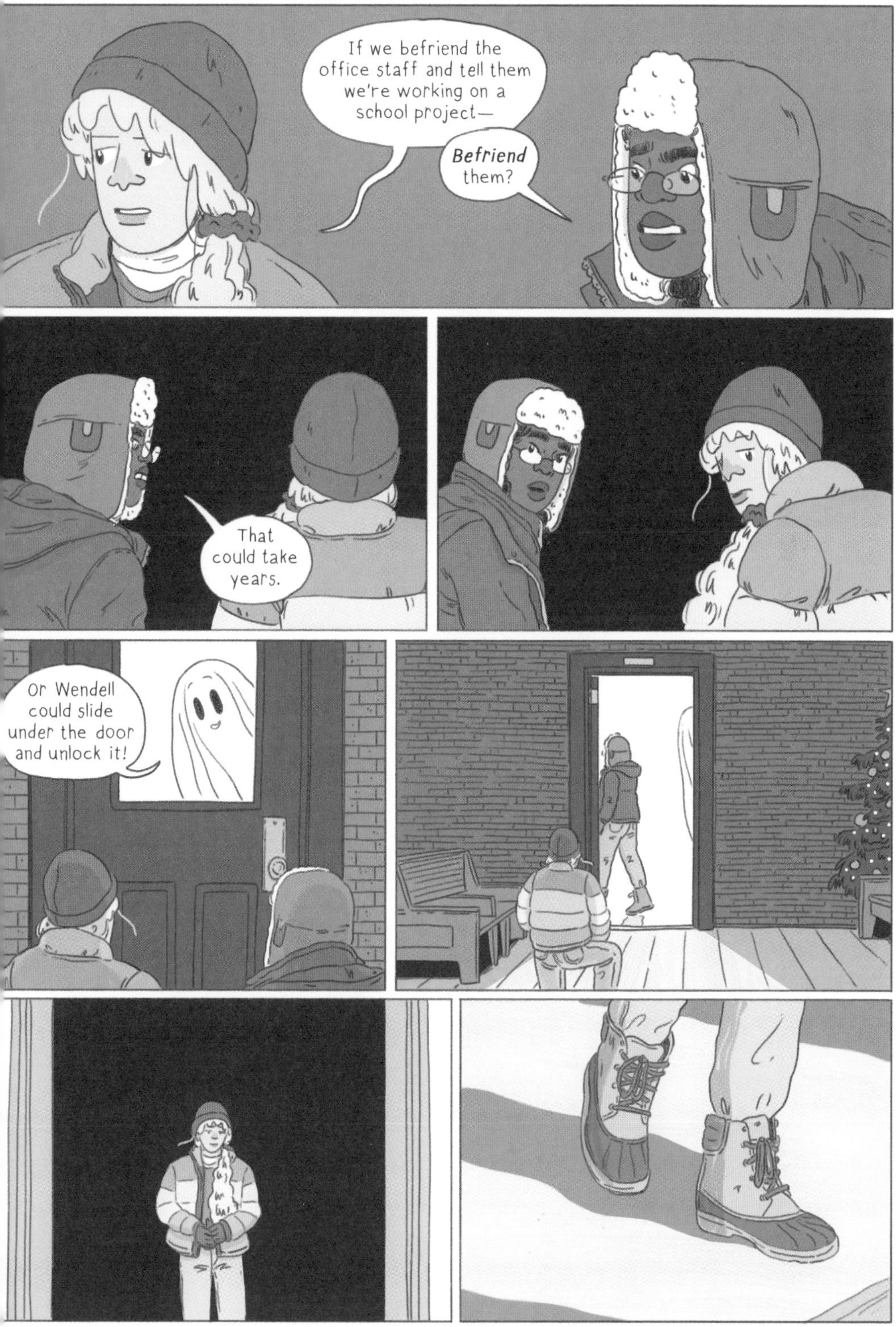

If we befriend the office staff and tell them we're working on a school project—
Befriend them?
That could take years.
Or Wendell could slide under the door and unlock it!

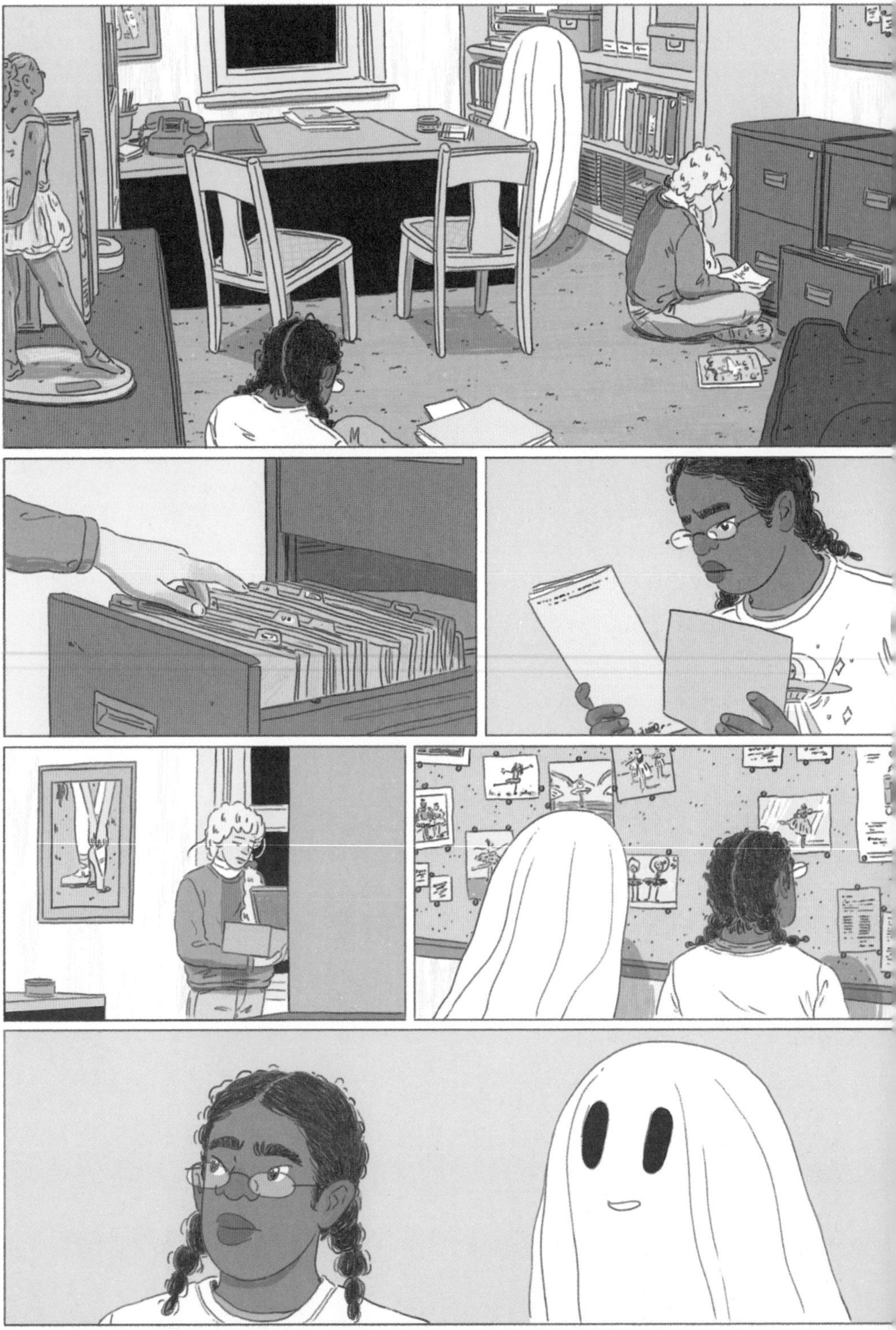

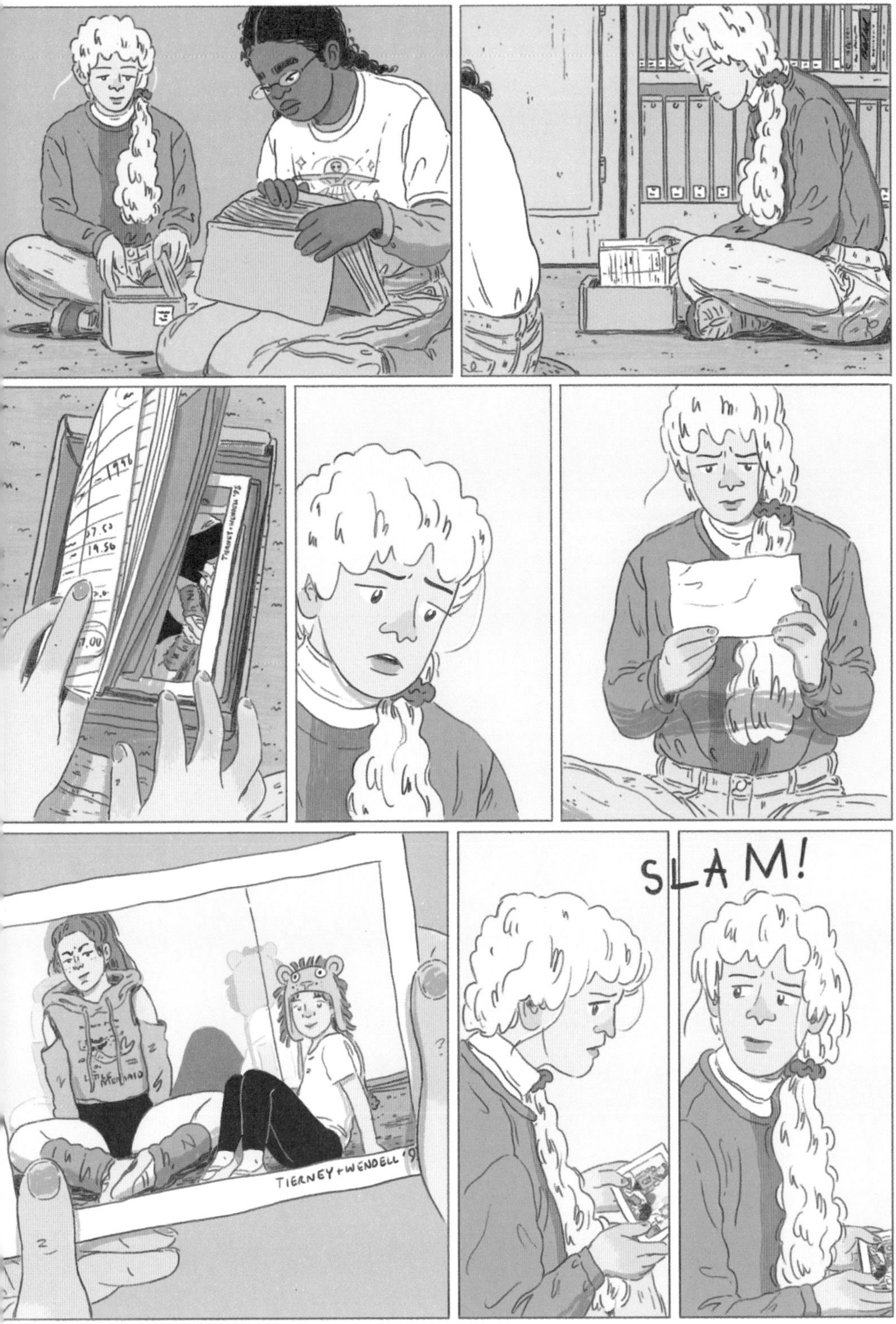
TIERNEY + WENDELL '9
SLAM!

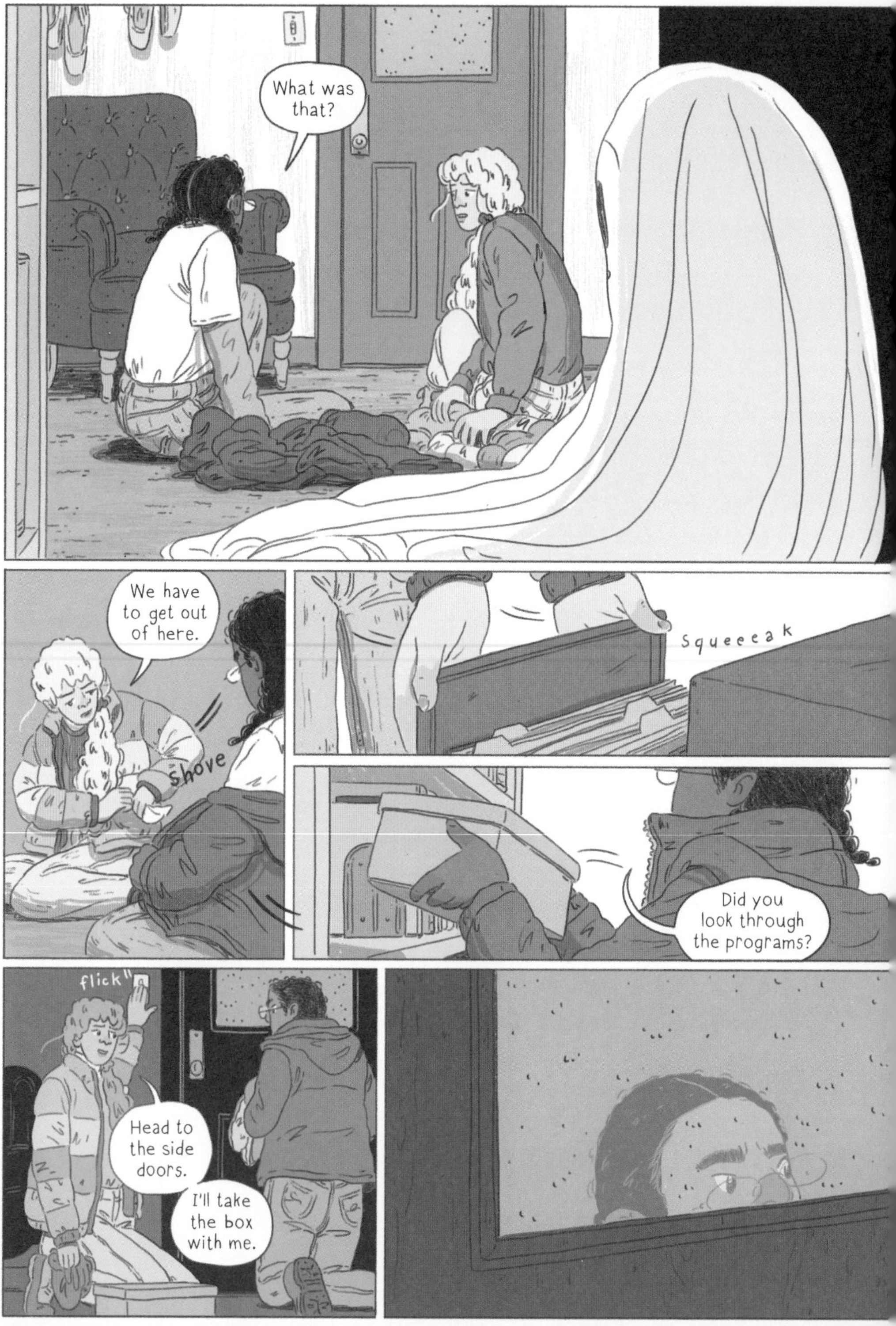
What was that?
We have to get out of here.
Shove
Squeeeak
Did you look through the programs?
flick
Head to the side doors.
I'll take the box with me.

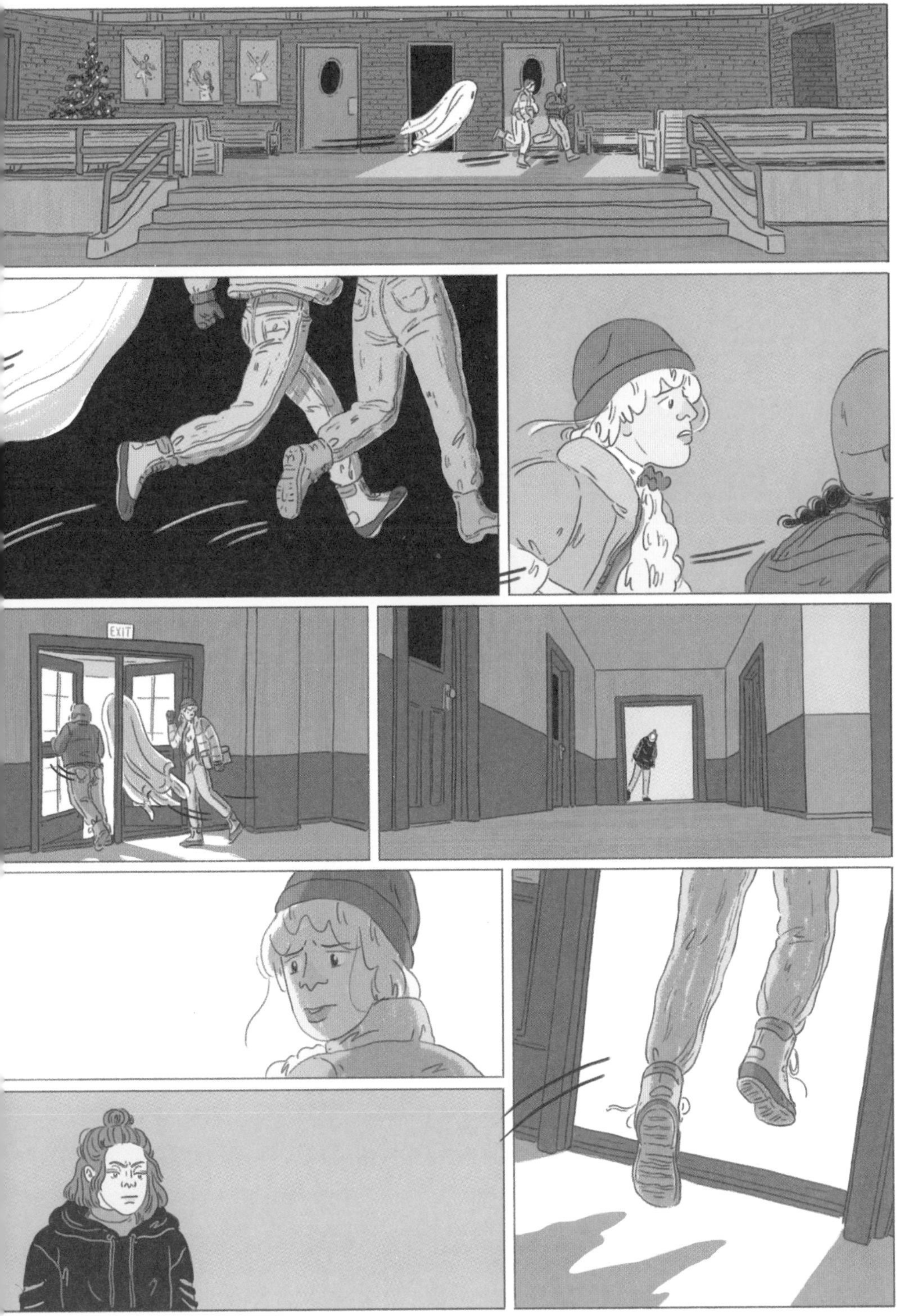
EXIT

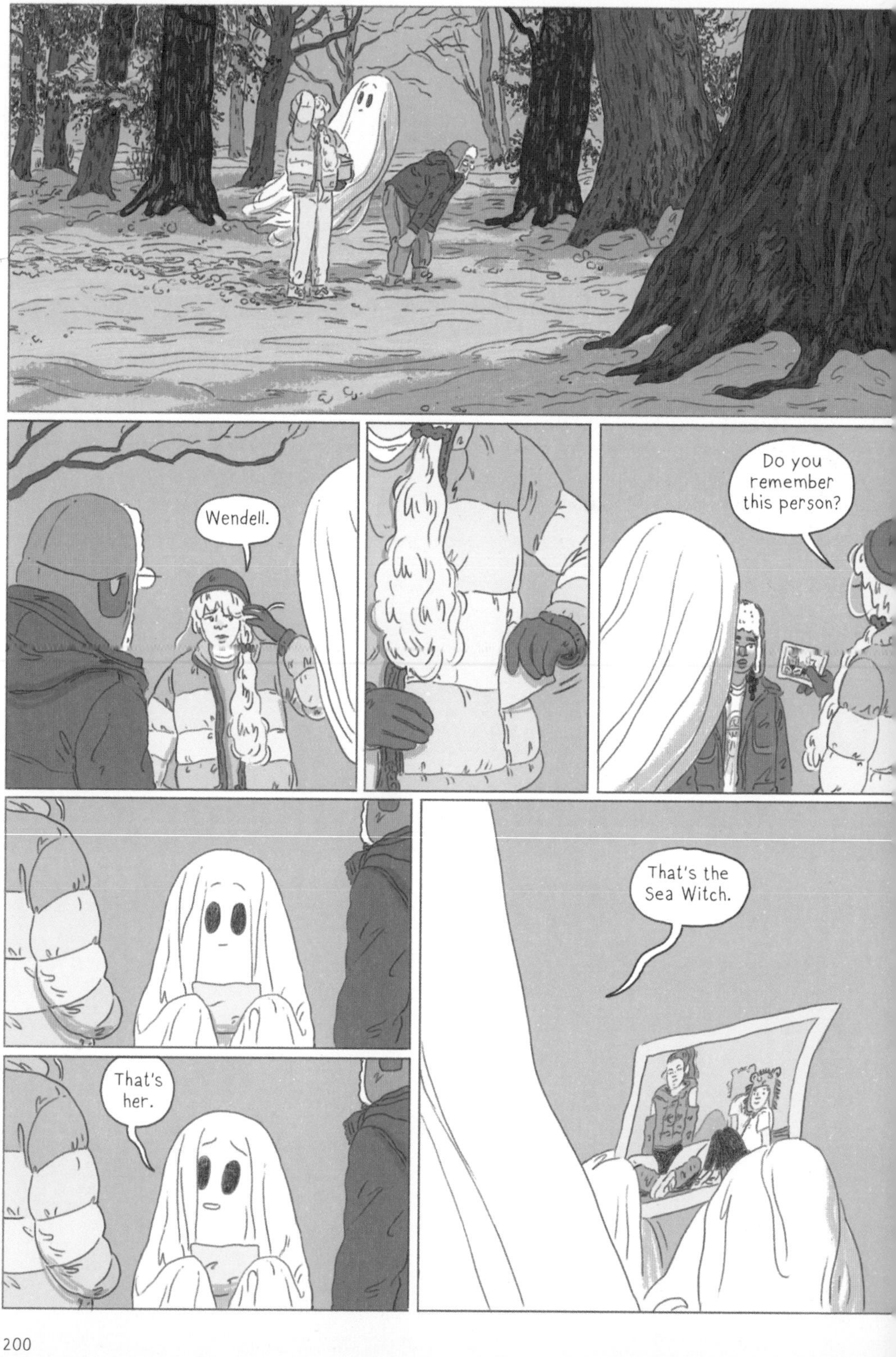
Wendell.
Do you remember this person?
That's her.
That's the Sea Witch.

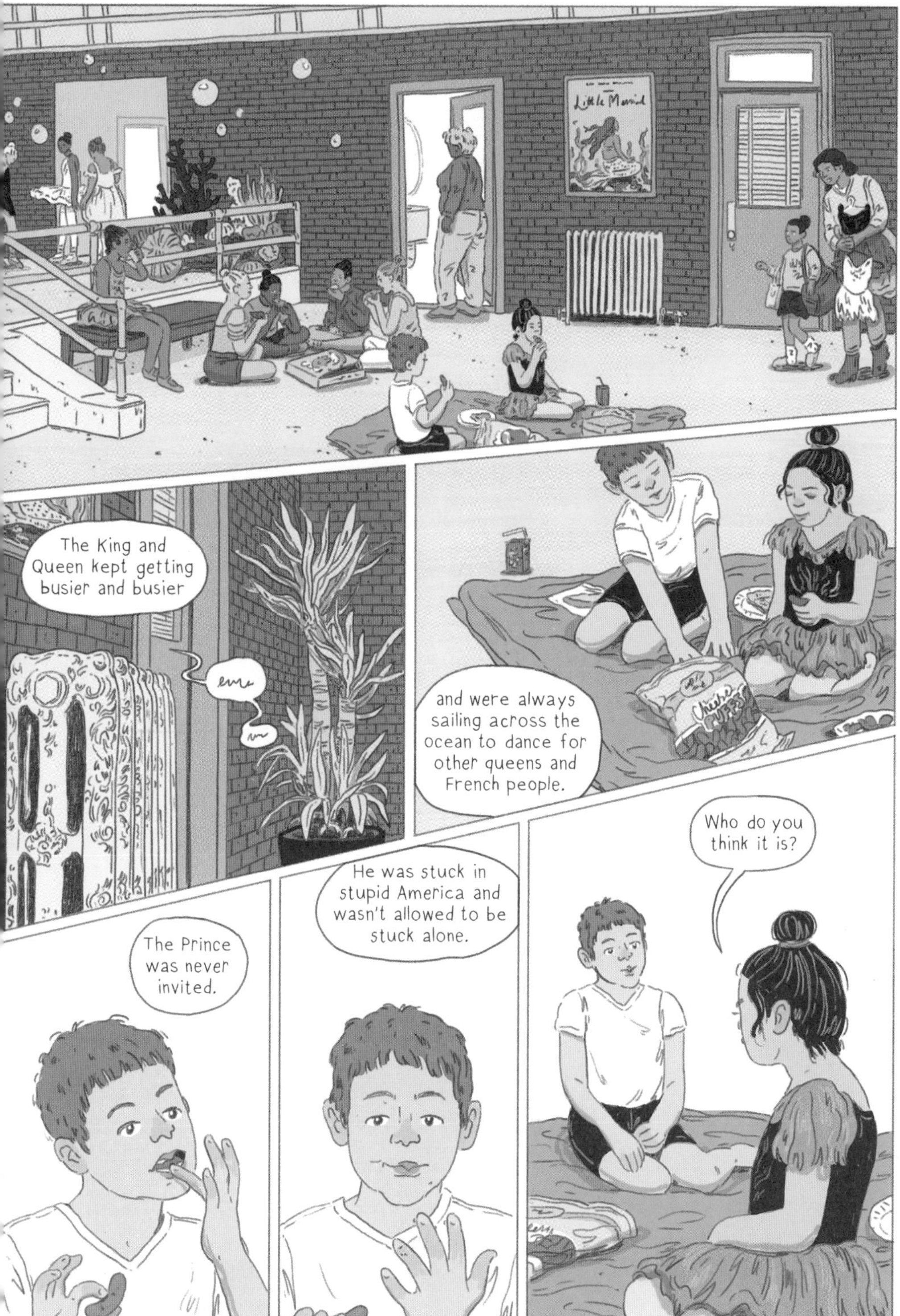
Little Mermaid
The King and Queen kept getting busier and busier
and were always sailing across the ocean to dance for other queens and French people.
Cheese Puffs
The Prince was never invited.
He was stuck in stupid America and wasn't allowed to be stuck alone.
Who do you think it is?

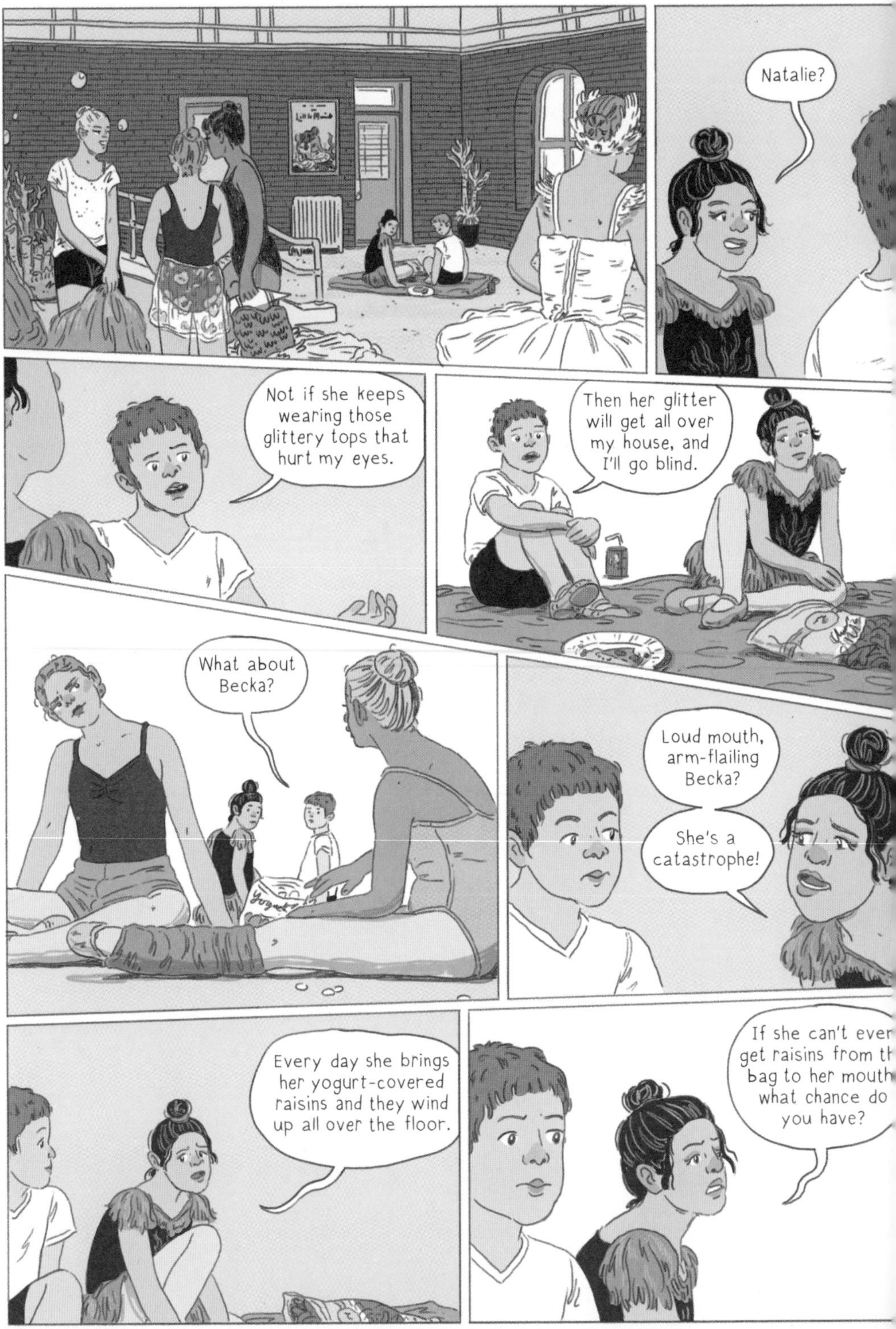
Natalie?
Not if she keeps wearing those glittery tops that hurt my eyes.
Then her glitter will get all over my house, and I'll go blind.
What about Becka?
Loud mouth, arm-flailing Becka?
She's a catastrophe!
Every day she brings her yogurt-covered raisins and they wind up all over the floor.
If she can't ever get raisins from th bag to her mouth what chance do you have?

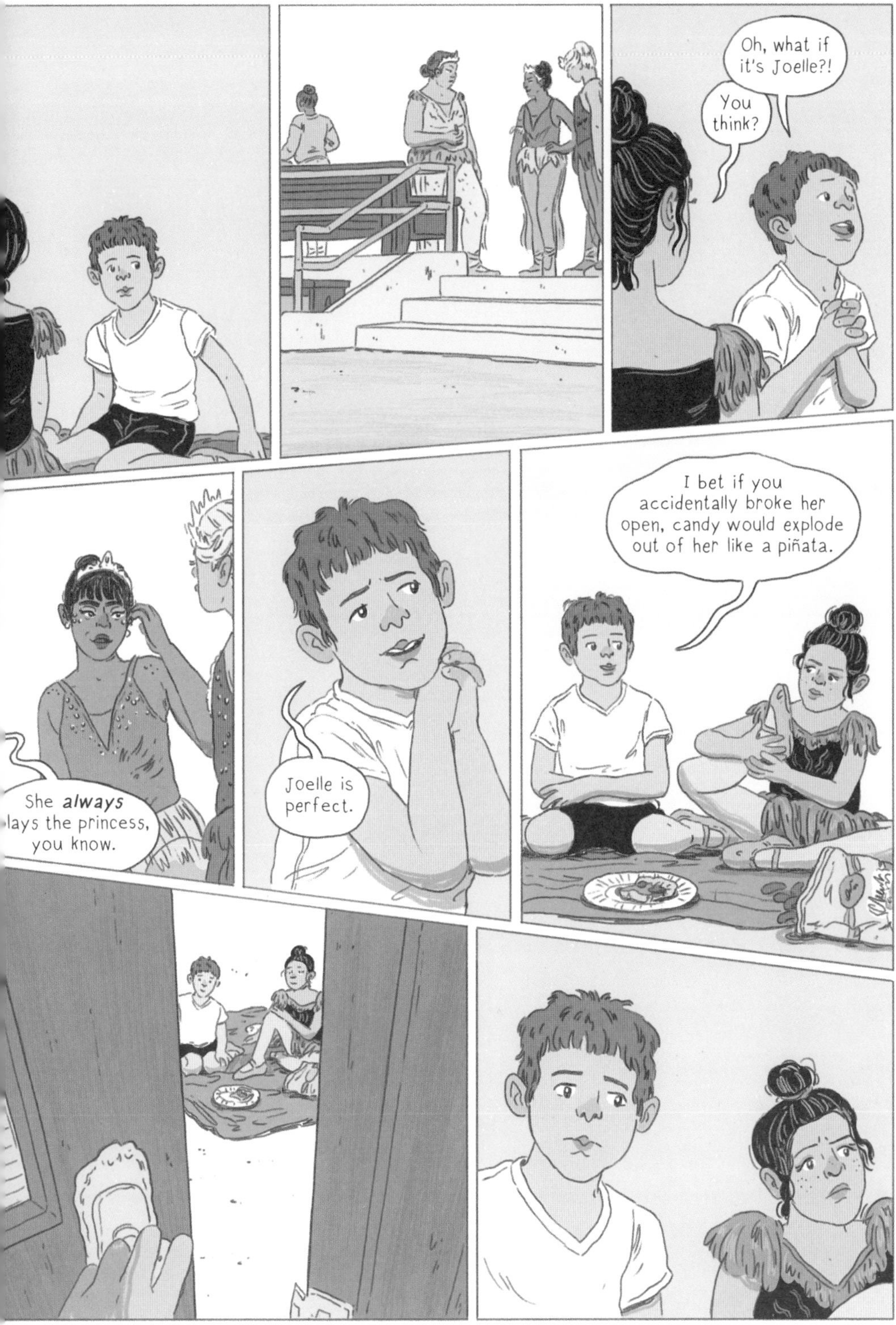
Oh, what if it's Joelle?!
You think?
She always lays the princess, you know.
Joelle is perfect.
I bet if you accidentally broke her open, candy would explode out of her like a piñata.

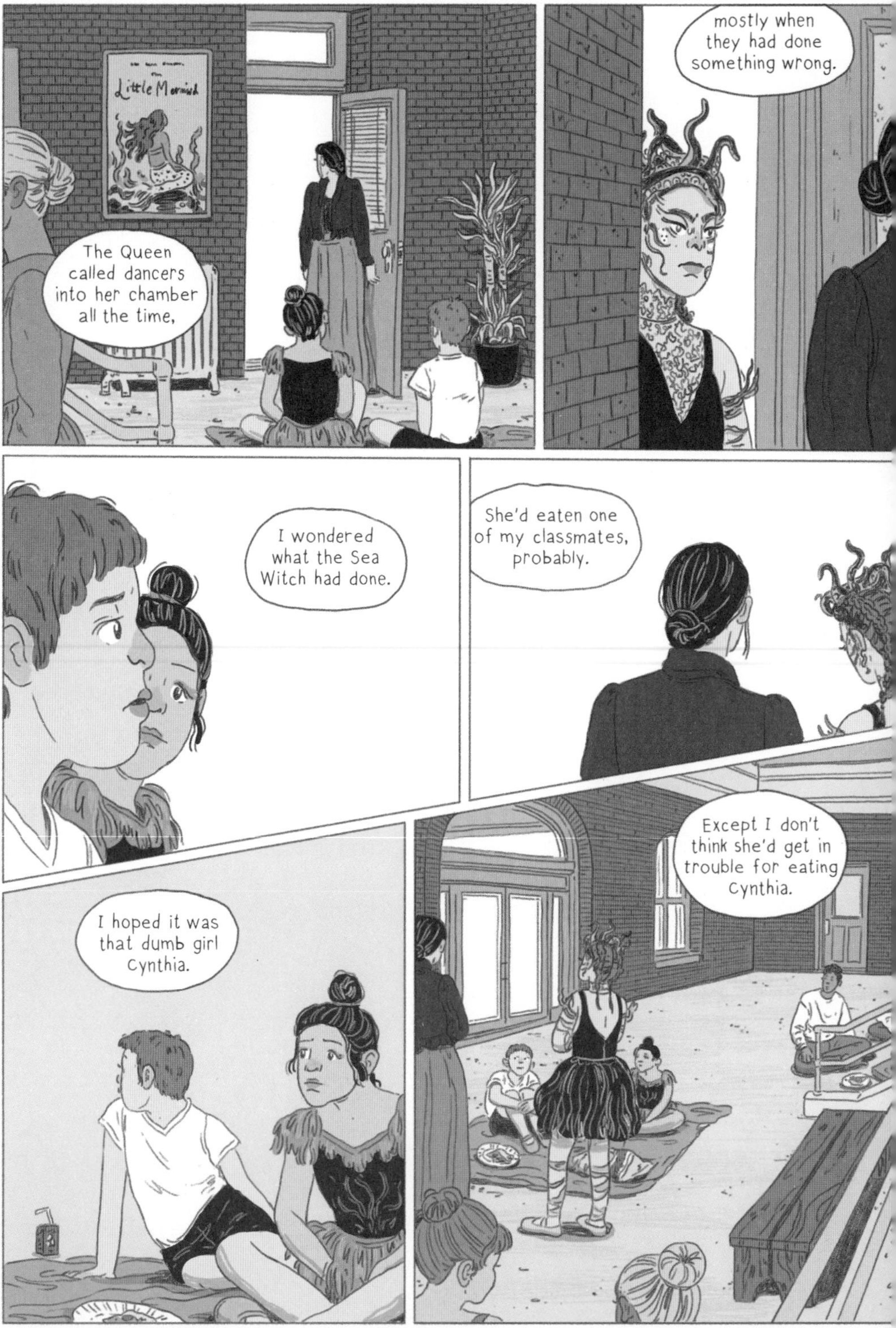
Little Mermaid
The Queen called dancers into her chamber all the time,
mostly when they had done something wrong.
I wondered what the Sea Witch had done.
She'd eaten one of my classmates, probably.
I hoped it was that dumb girl Cynthia.
Except I don't think she'd get in trouble for eating Cynthia.

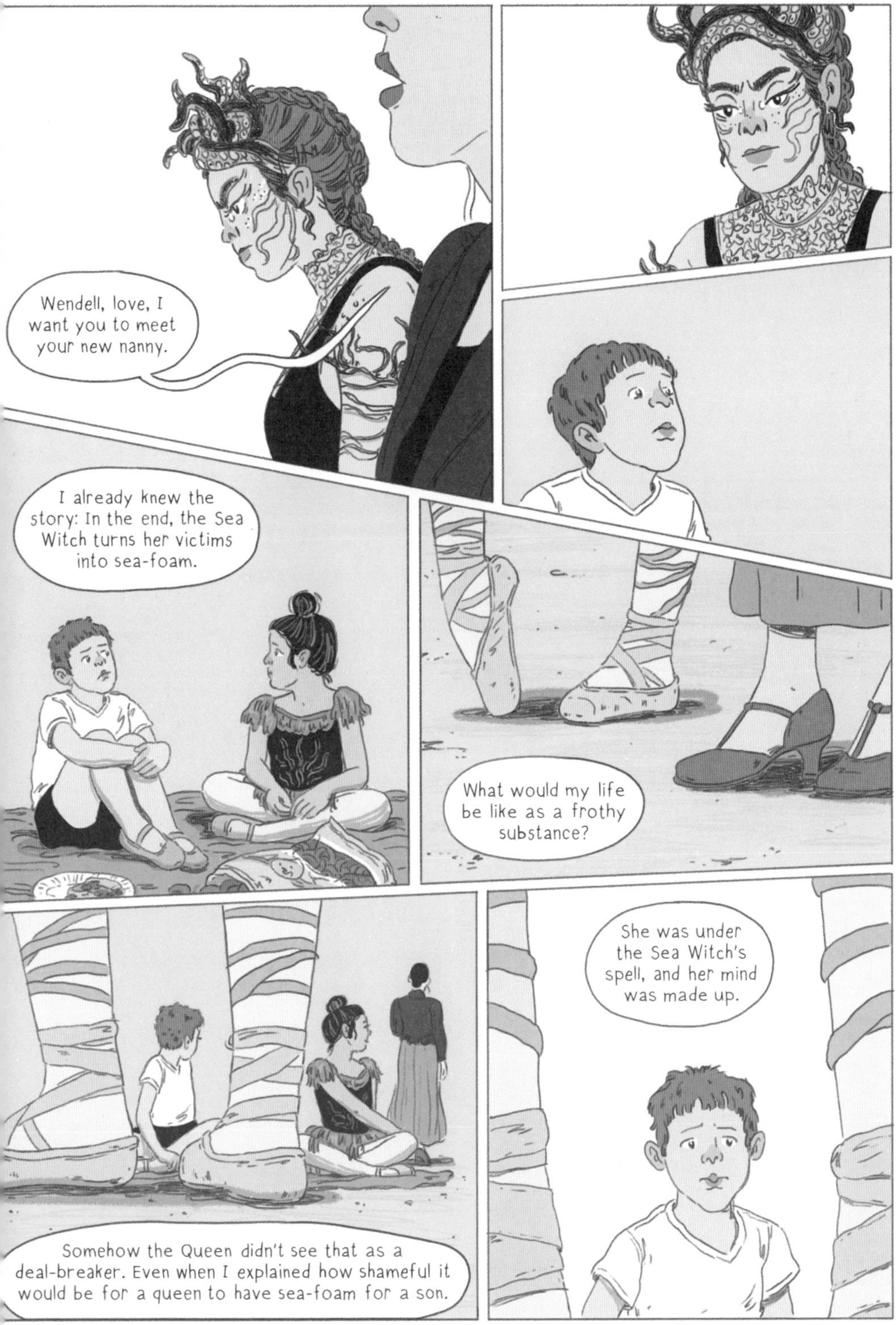
Wendell, love, I want you to meet your new nanny.
I already knew the story: In the end, the Sea Witch turns her victims into sea-foam.
What would my life be like as a frothy substance?
Somehow the Queen didn't see that as a deal-breaker. Even when I explained how shameful it would be for a queen to have sea-foam for a son.
She was under the Sea Witch's spell, and her mind was made up.

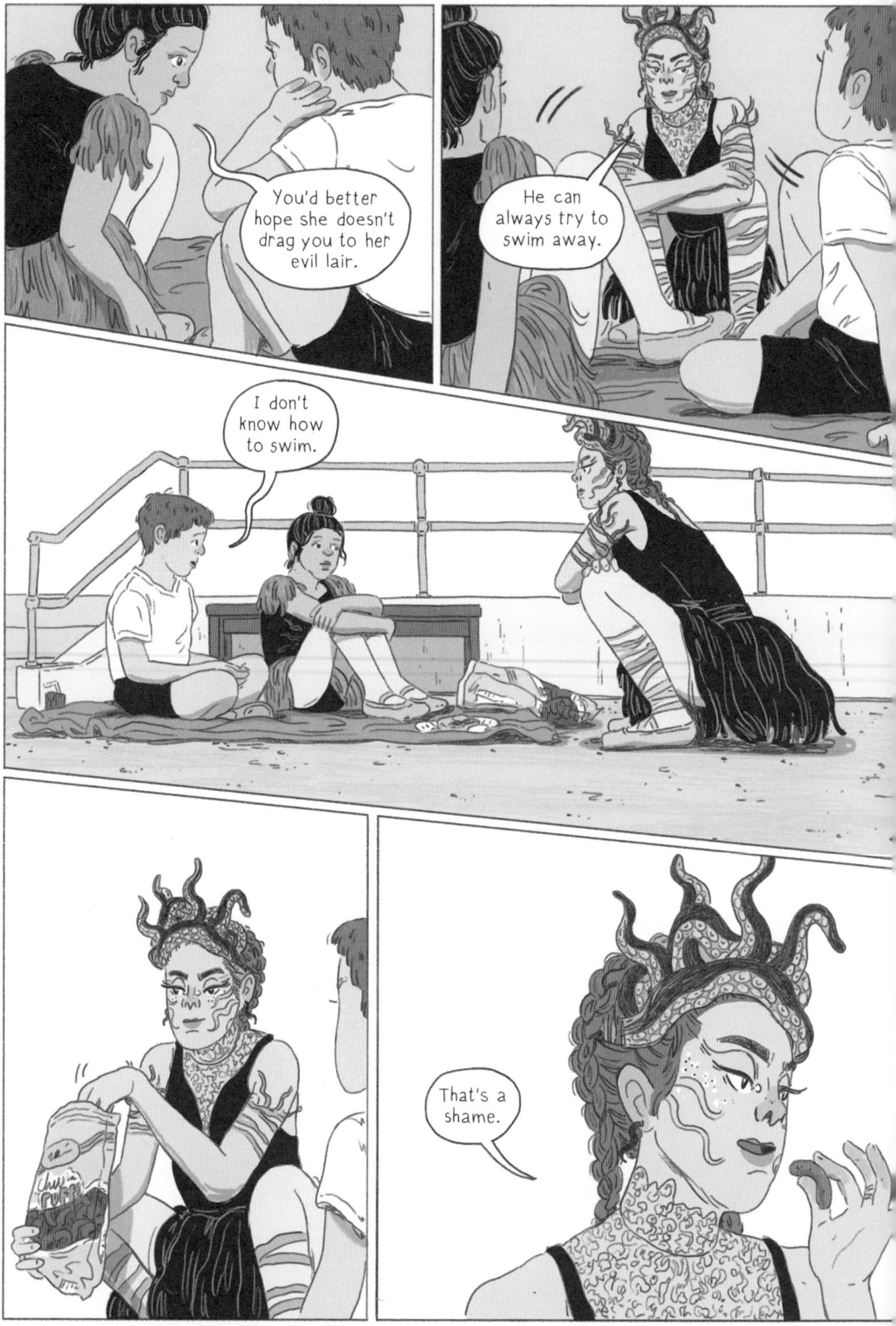
You'd better hope she doesn't drag you to her evil lair.
He can always try to swim away.
I don't know how to swim.
That's a shame.

...I think she watched me from then on, whenever my parents couldn't.

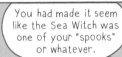

You had made it seem like the Sea Witch was one of your "spooks" or whatever.

The memories are all fuzzy.

I didn't know.

That she was your nanny?

Do you see what's going on here?! The ghost equipment **works.**

She must have known Wendell was here.

And for some reason, she's trying to get rid of him specifically.

I mean, why else would she be alone at the theater this late?

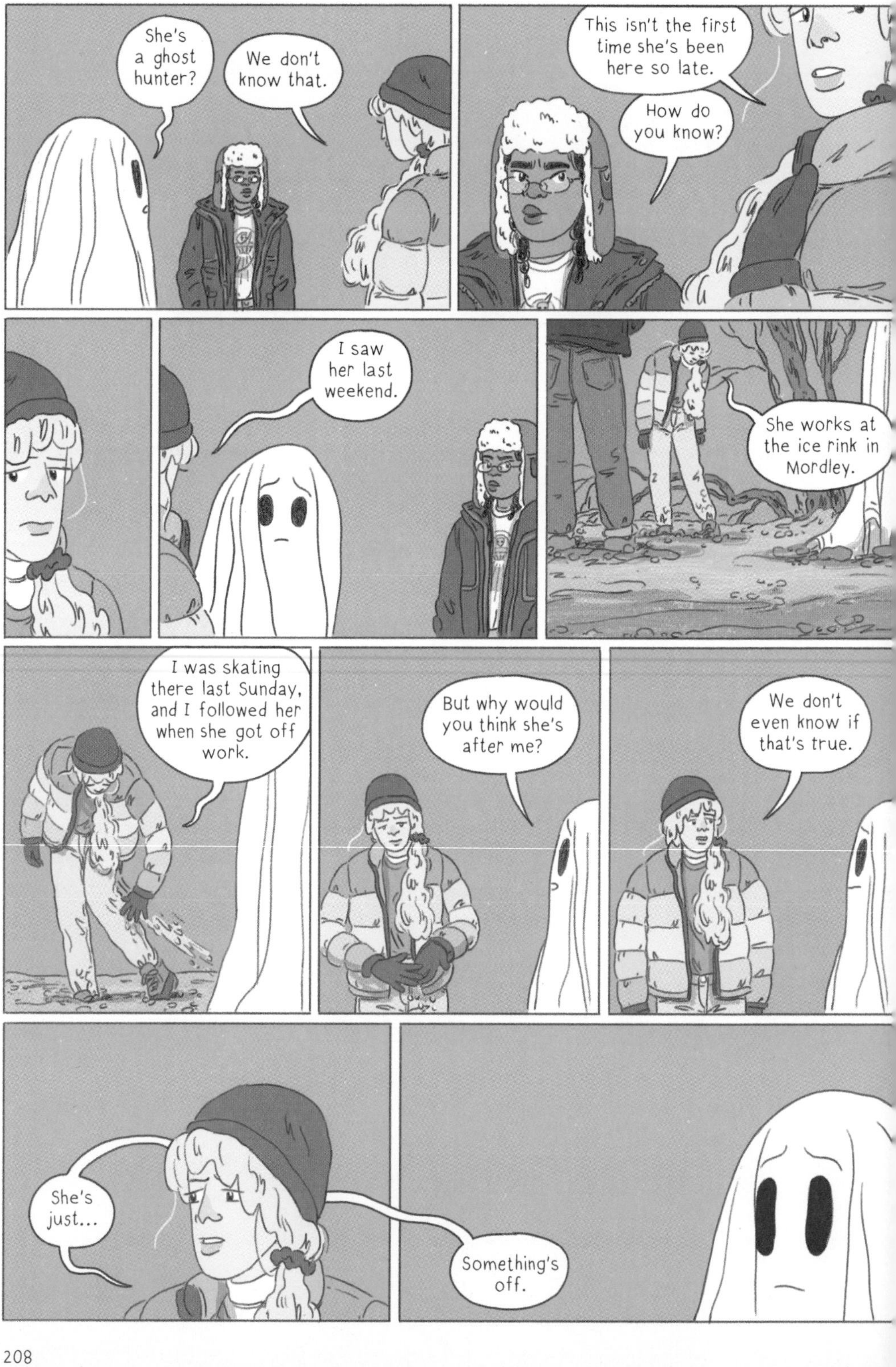
She's a ghost hunter?
We don't know that.
This isn't the first time she's been here so late.
How do you know?
I saw her last weekend.
She works at the ice rink in Mordley.
I was skating there last Sunday, and I followed her when she got off work.
But why would you think she's after me?
We don't even know if that's true.
She's just...
Something's off.

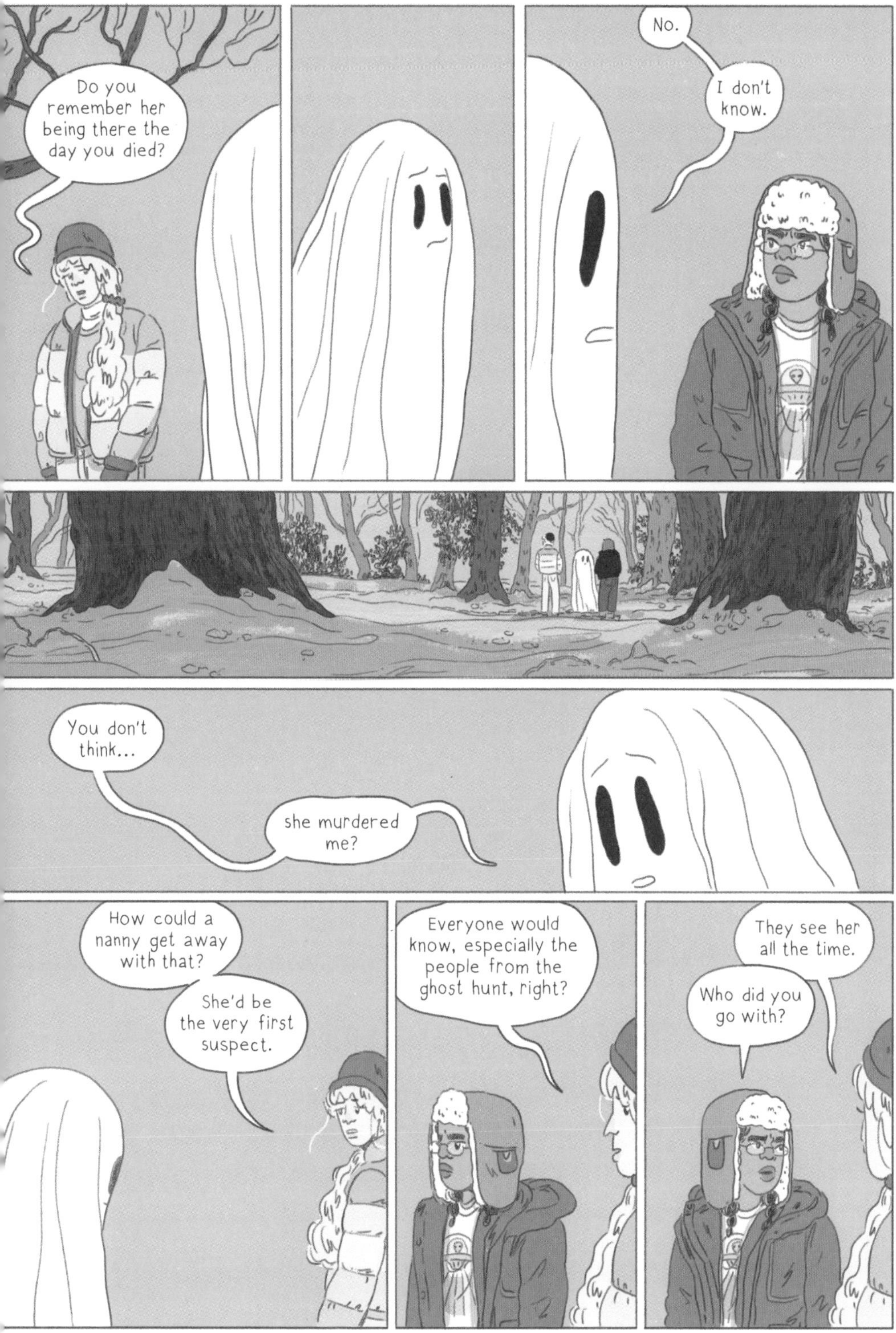
Do you remember her being there the day you died?
No.
I don't know.
You don't think...
she murdered me?
How could a nanny get away with that?
She'd be the very first suspect.
Everyone would know, especially the people from the ghost hunt, right?
They see her all the time.
Who did you go with?

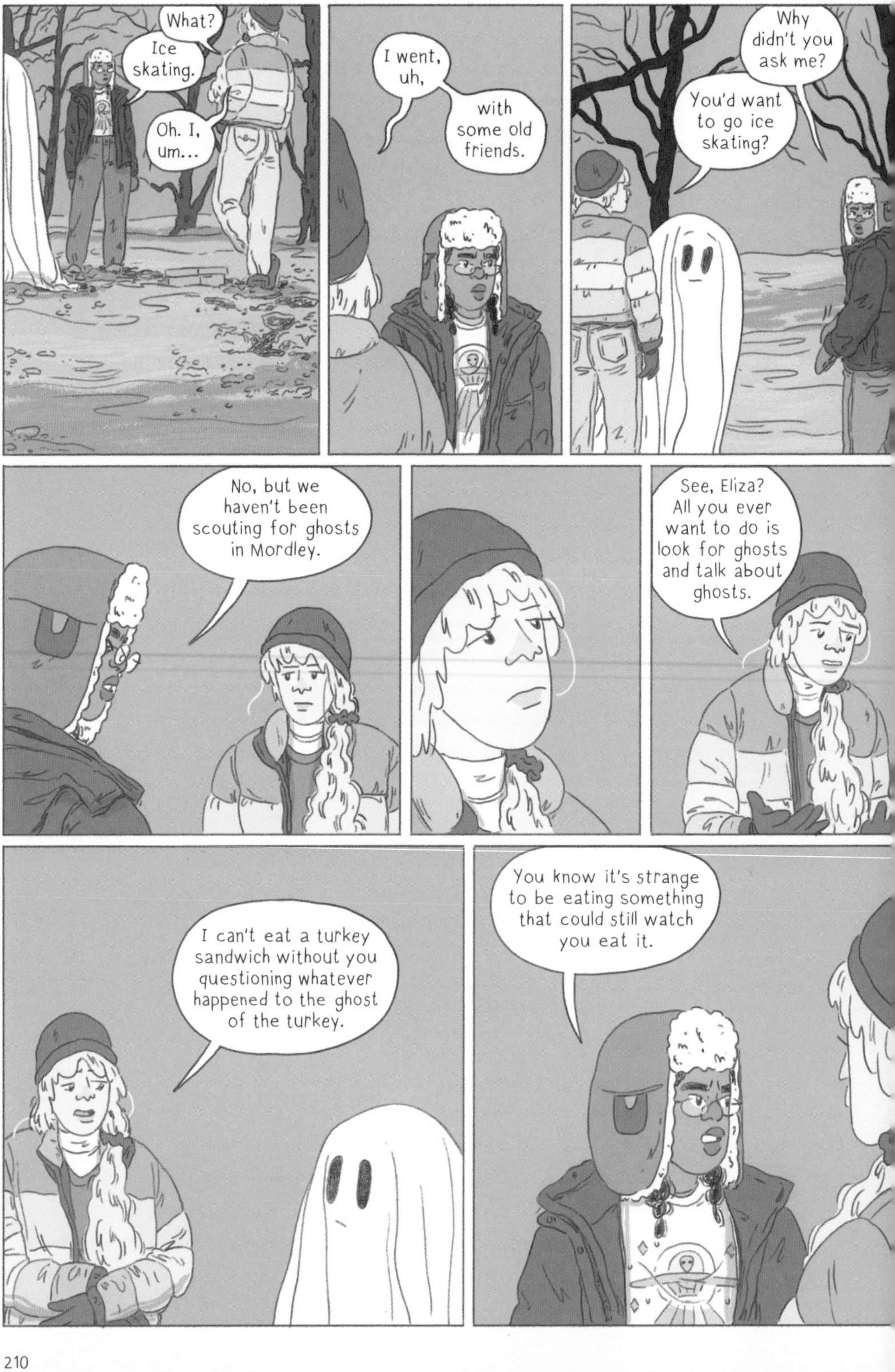
What?
Ice skating.
Oh. I, um...
I went, uh,
with some old friends.
Why didn't you ask me?
You'd want to go ice skating?
No, but we haven't been scouting for ghosts in Mordley.
See, Eliza? All you ever want to do is look for ghosts and talk about ghosts.
I can't eat a turkey sandwich without you questioning whatever happened to the ghost of the turkey.
You know it's strange to be eating something that could still watch you eat it.

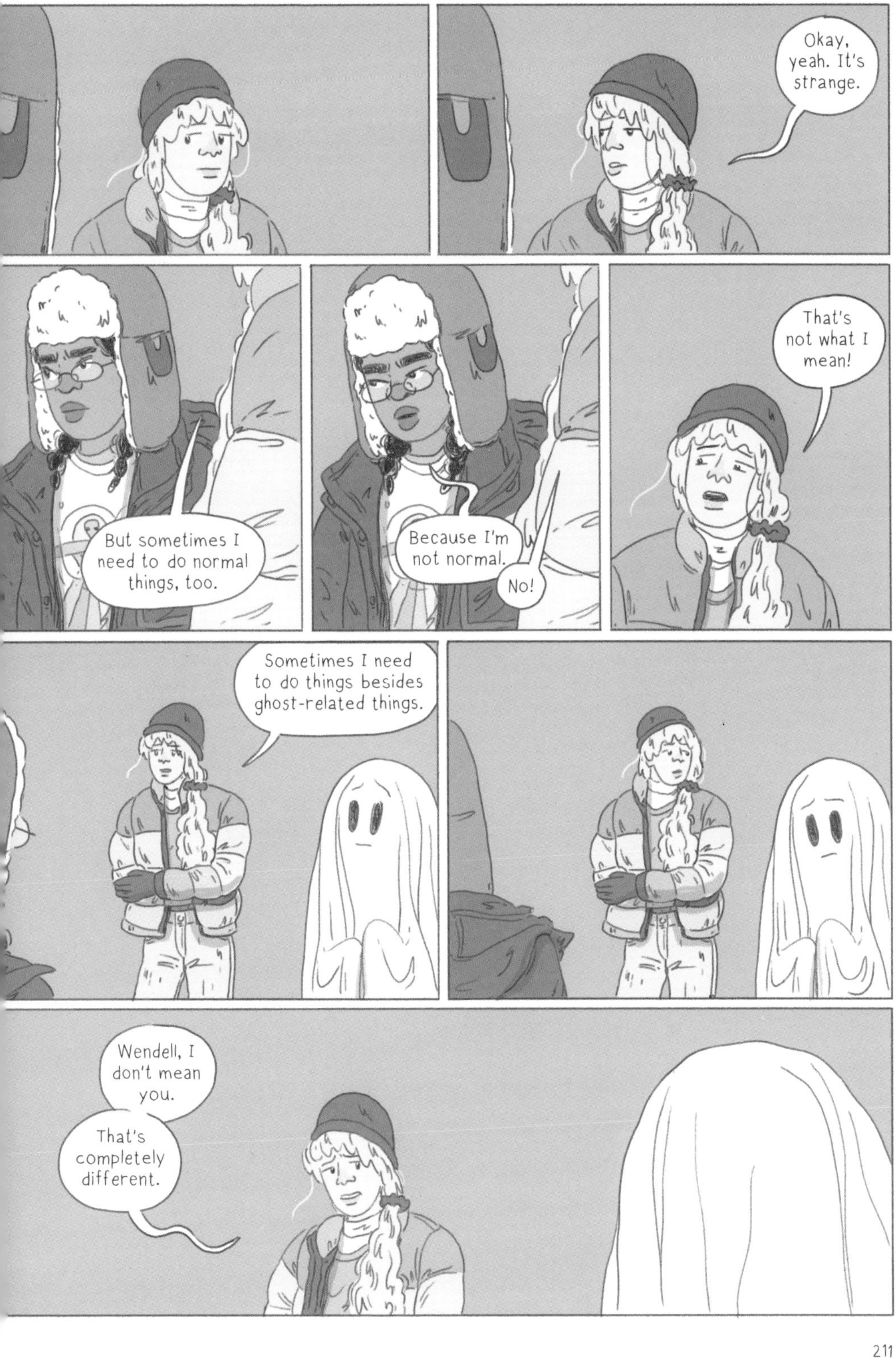

Okay, yeah. It's strange.
But sometimes I need to do normal things, too.
Because I'm not normal.
No!
That's not what I mean!
Sometimes I need to do things besides ghost-related things.
Wendell, I don't mean you.
That's completely different.

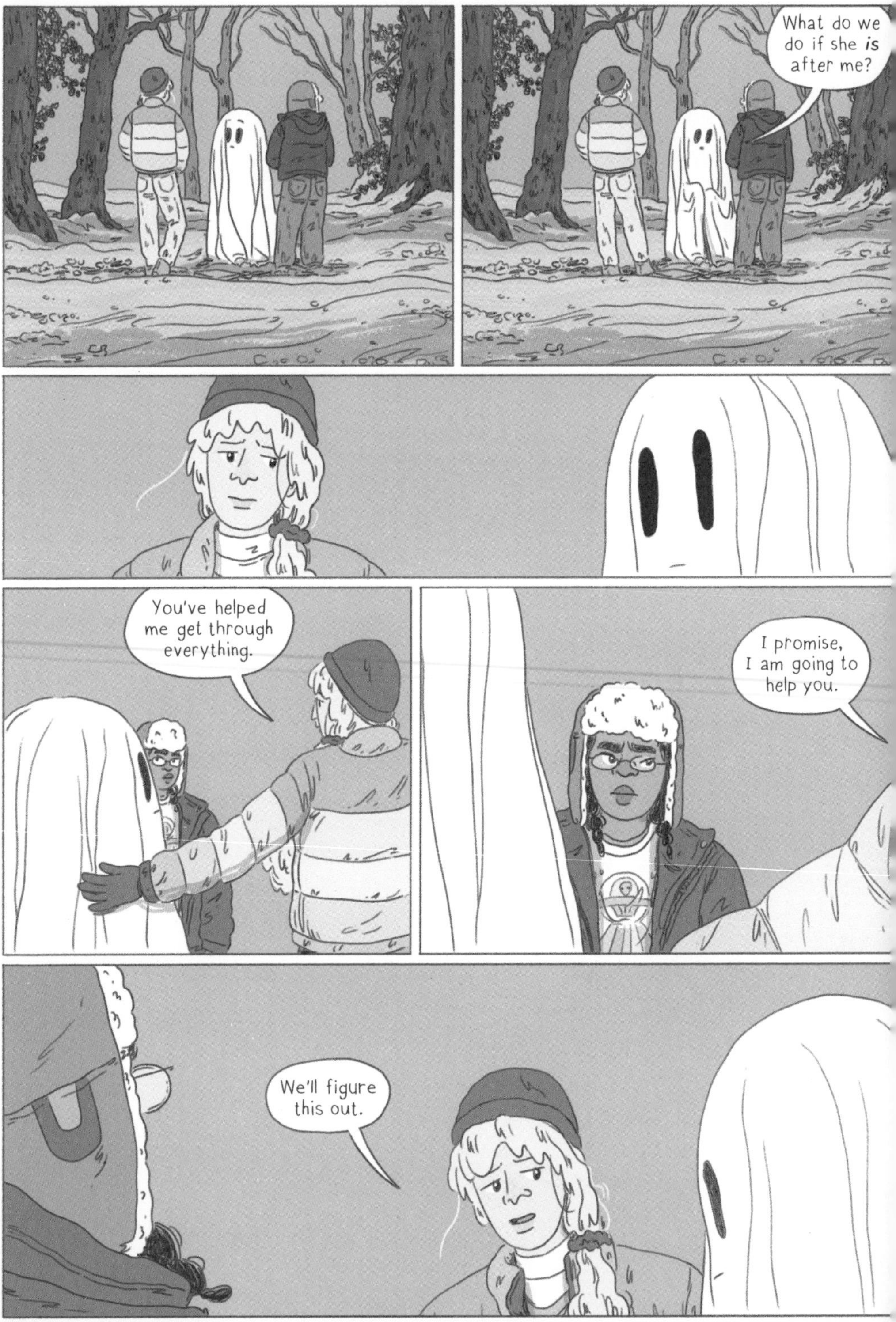
What do we do if she *is* after me?
You've helped me get through everything.
I promise, I am going to help you.
We'll figure this out.

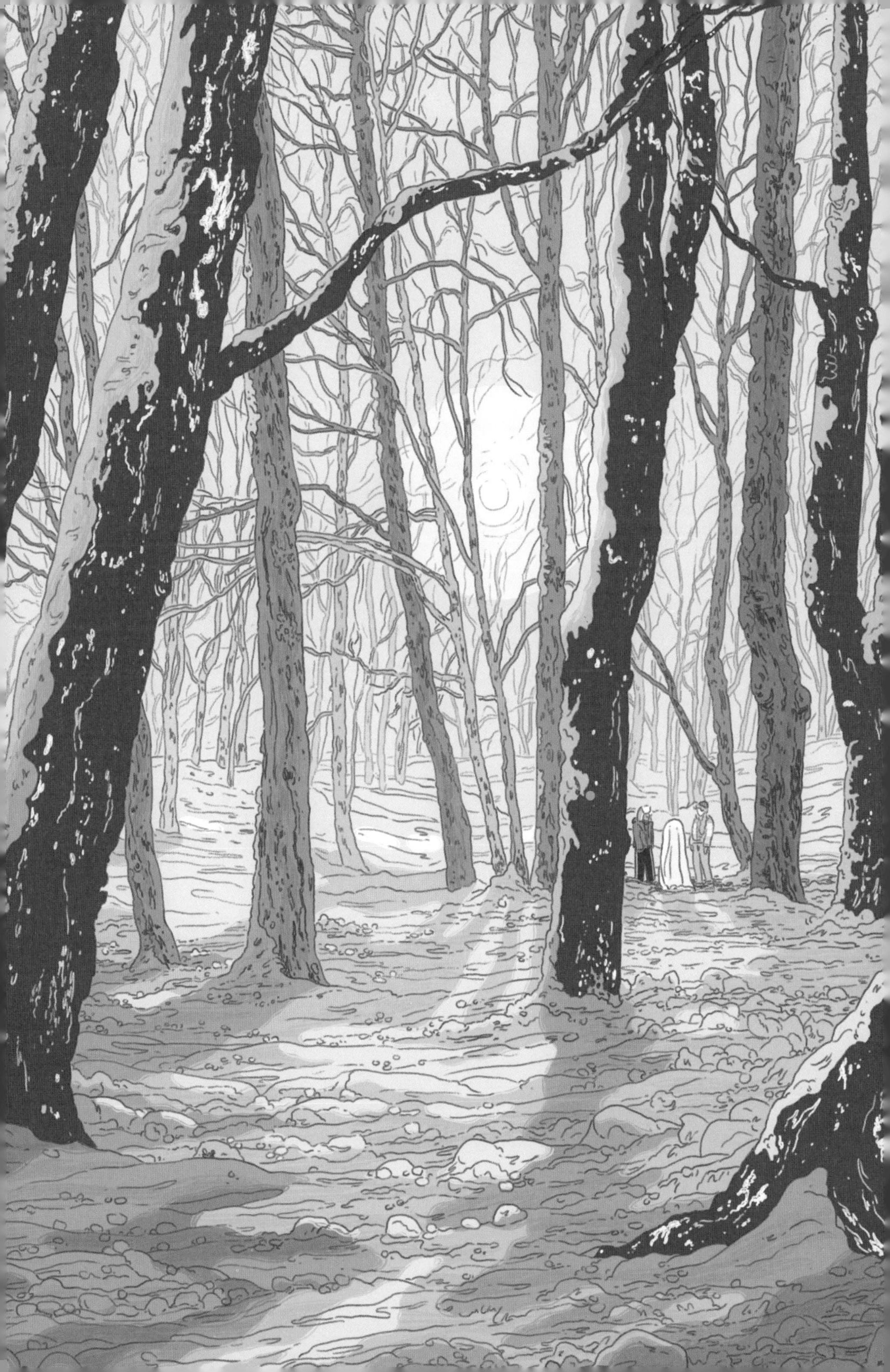

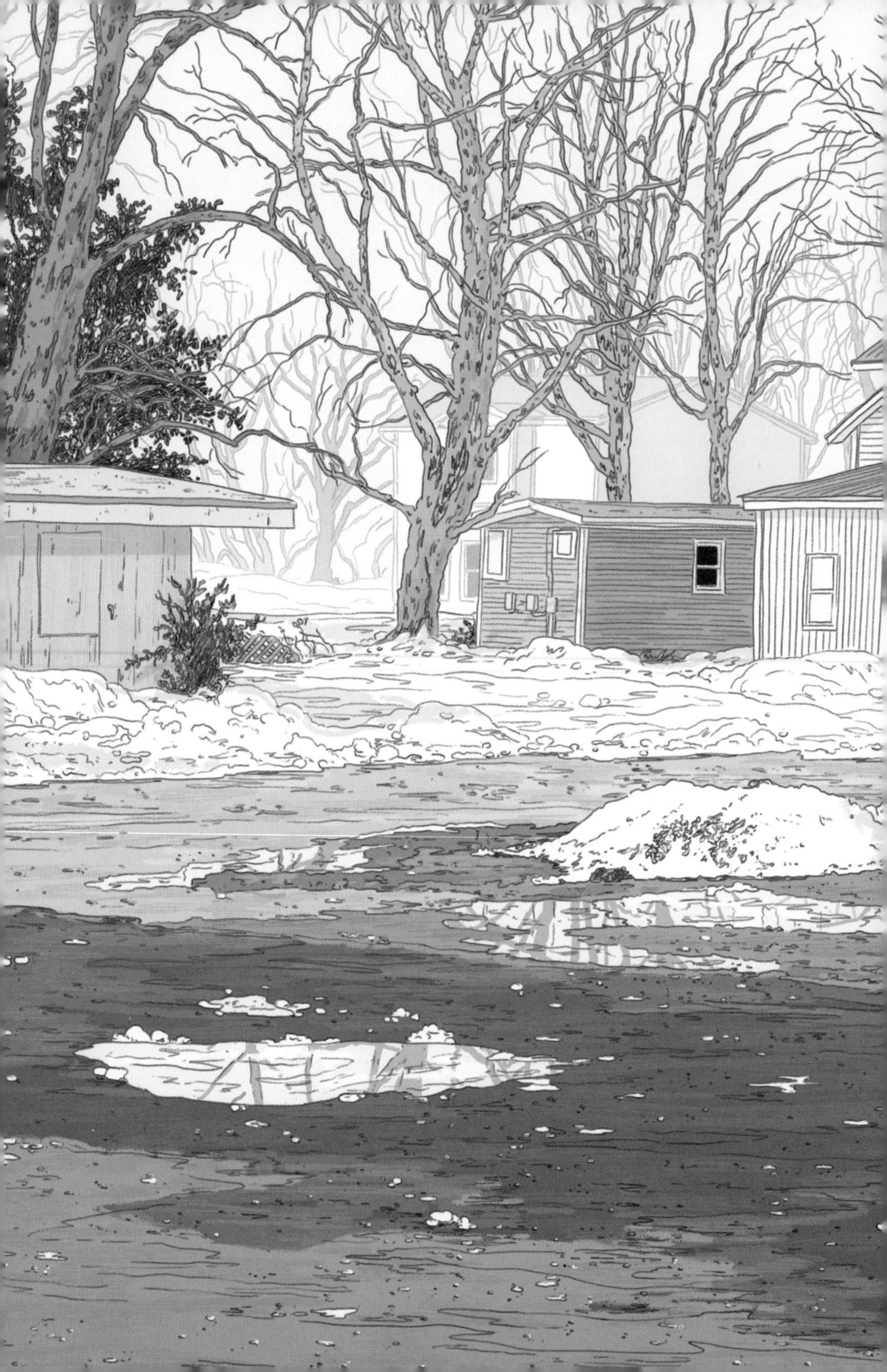

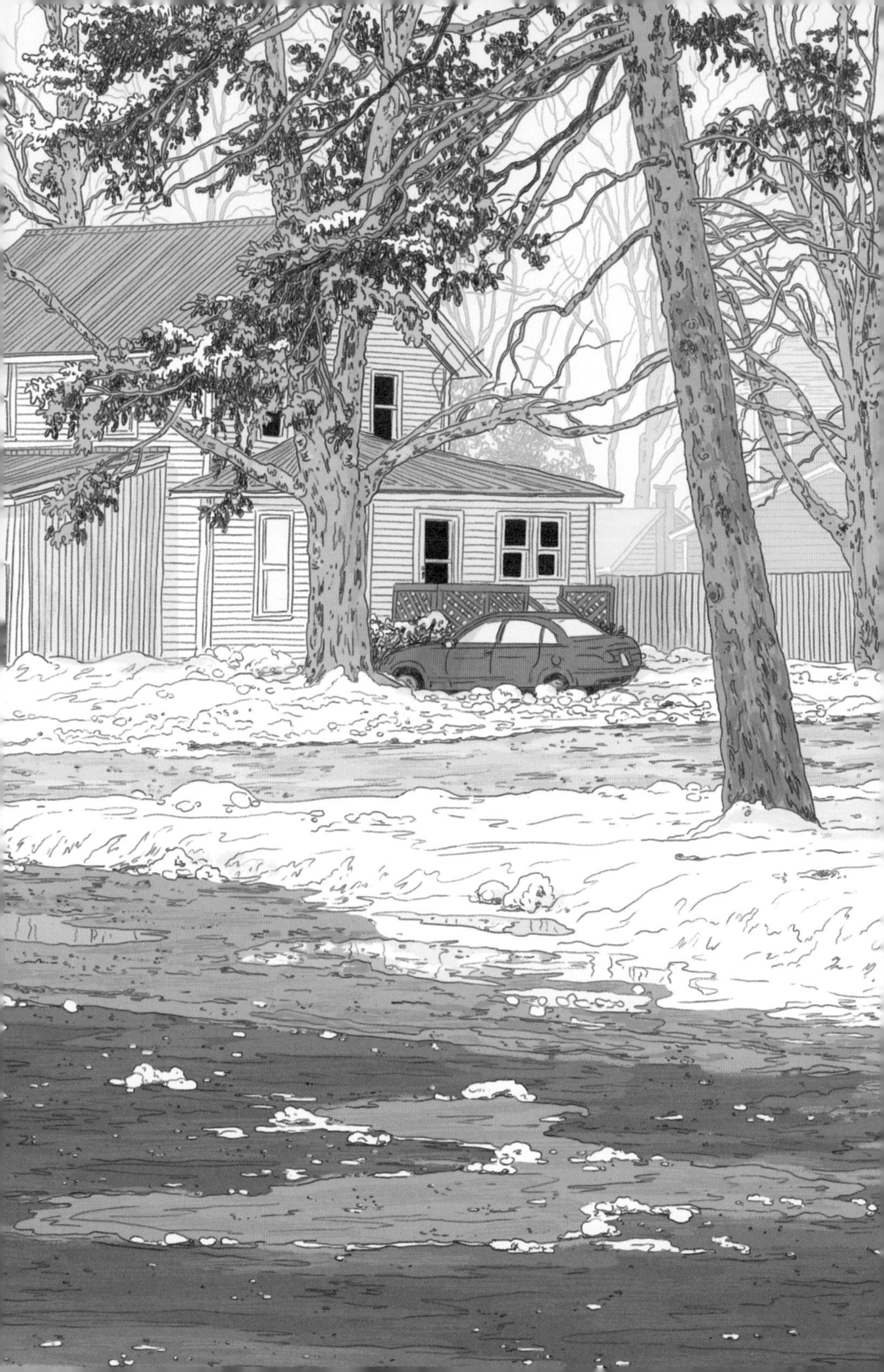

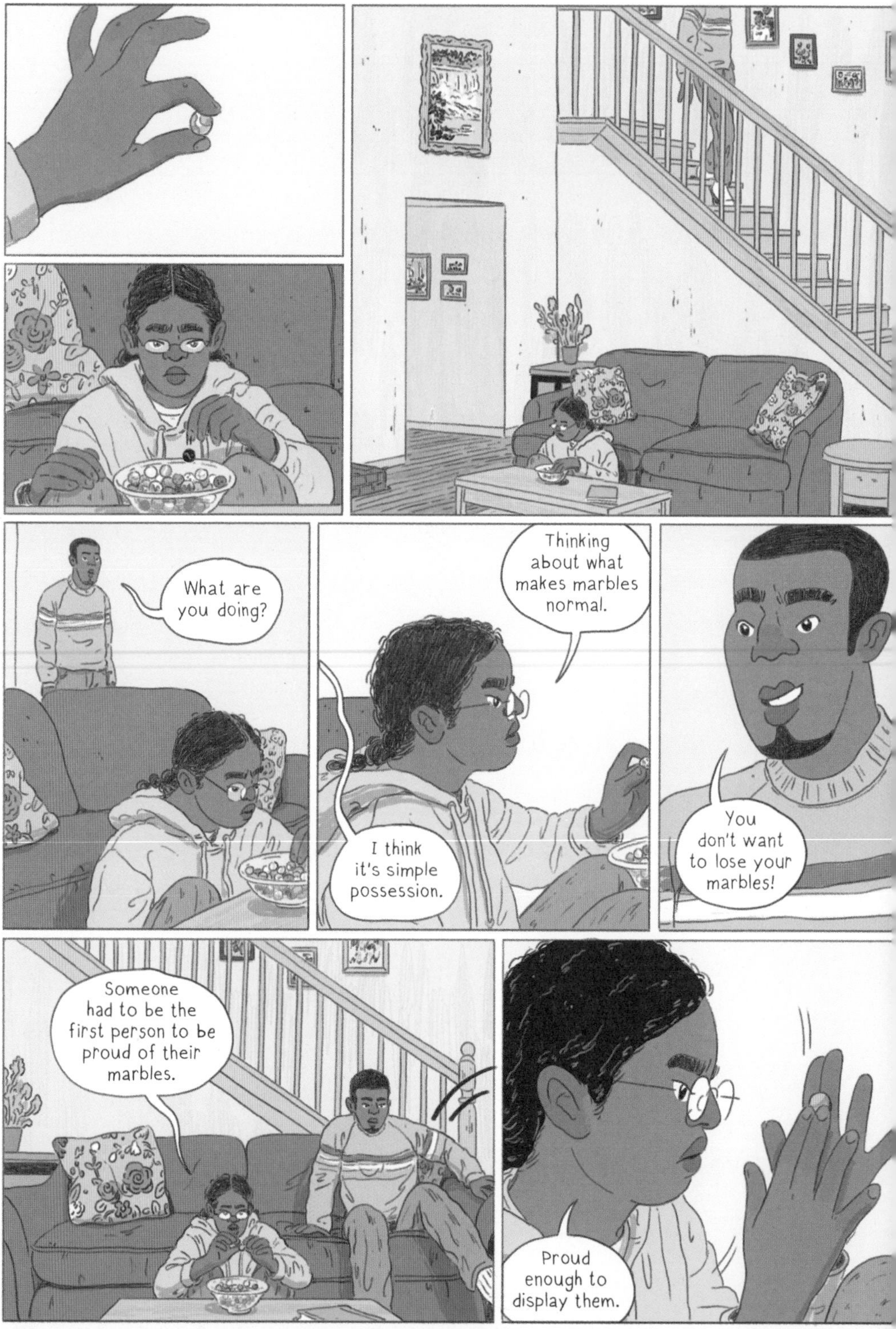
What are you doing?
Thinking about what makes marbles normal.
I think it's simple possession.
You don't want to lose your marbles!
Someone had to be the first person to be proud of their marbles.
Proud enough to display them.

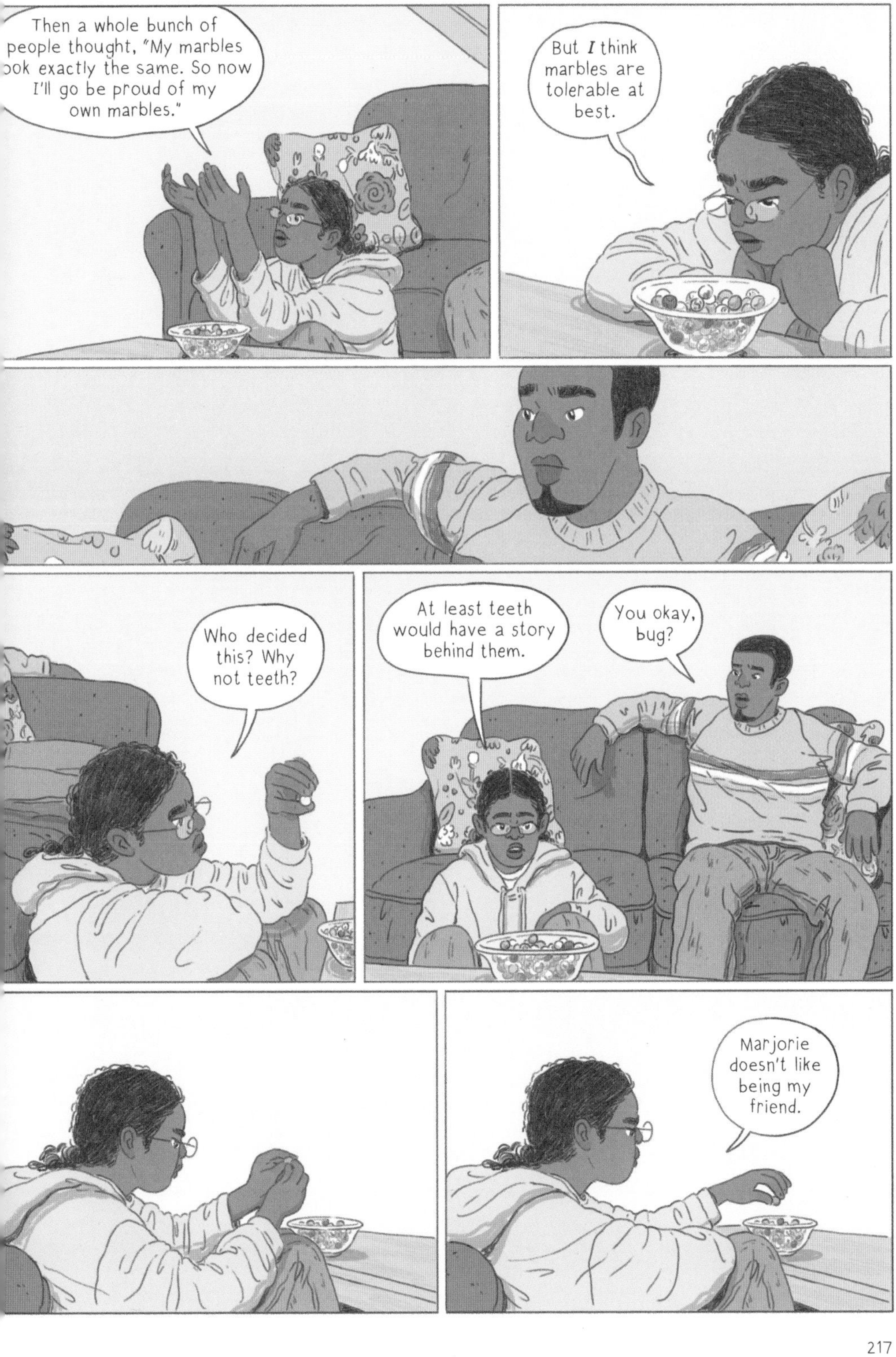
Then a whole bunch of people thought, "My marbles ook exactly the same. So now I'll go be proud of my own marbles."
But *I* think marbles are tolerable at best.
Who decided this? Why not teeth?
At least teeth would have a story behind them.
You okay, bug?
Marjorie doesn't like being my friend.

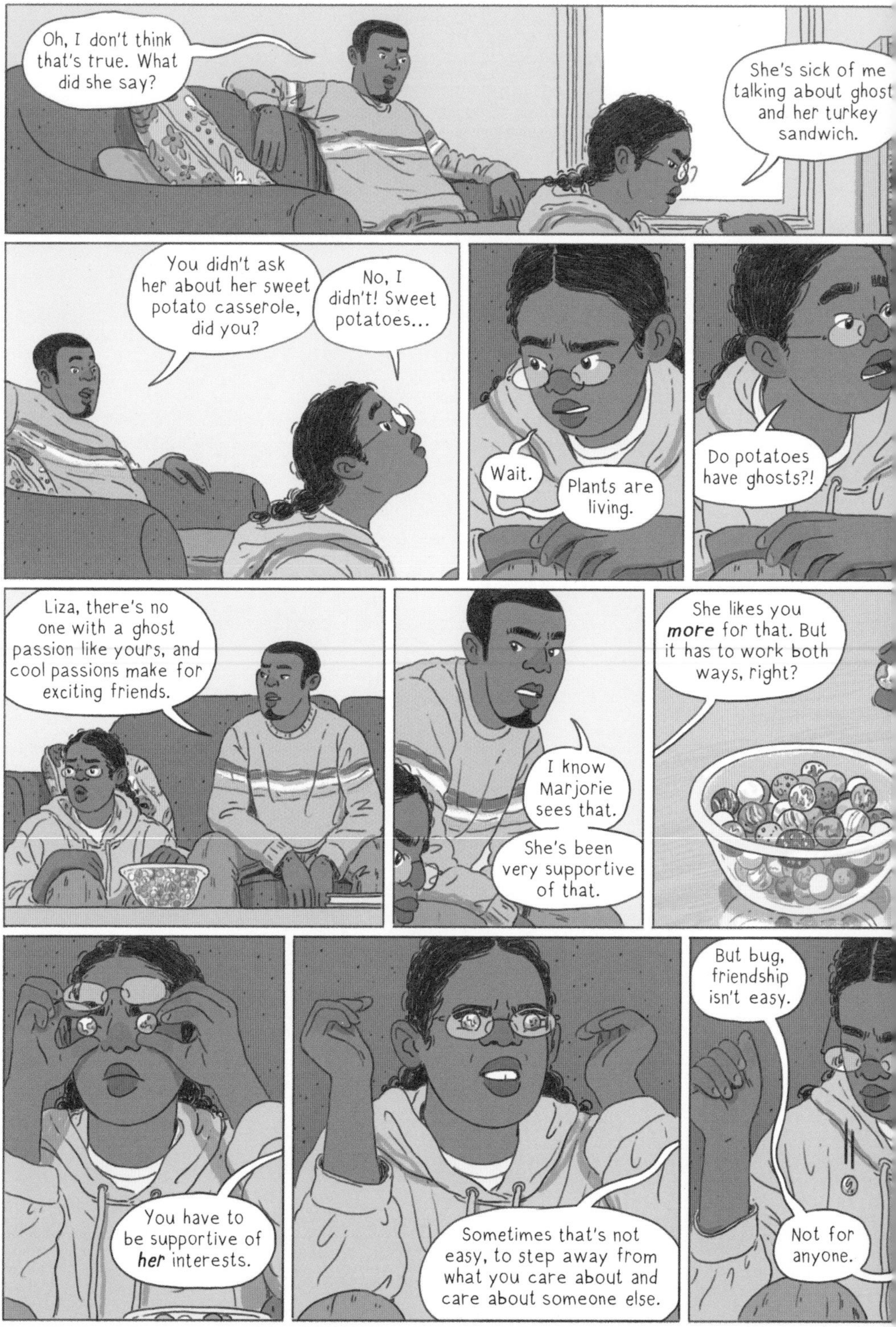
Oh, I don't think that's true. What did she say?
She's sick of me talking about ghost and her turkey sandwich.
You didn't ask her about her sweet potato casserole, did you?
No, I didn't! Sweet potatoes...
Wait.
Plants are living.
Do potatoes have ghosts?!
Liza, there's no one with a ghost passion like yours, and cool passions make for exciting friends.
I know Marjorie sees that.
She's been very supportive of that.
She likes you **more** for that. But it has to work both ways, right?
You have to be supportive of ***her*** interests.
Sometimes that's not easy, to step away from what you care about and care about someone else.
But bug, friendship isn't easy.
Not for anyone.

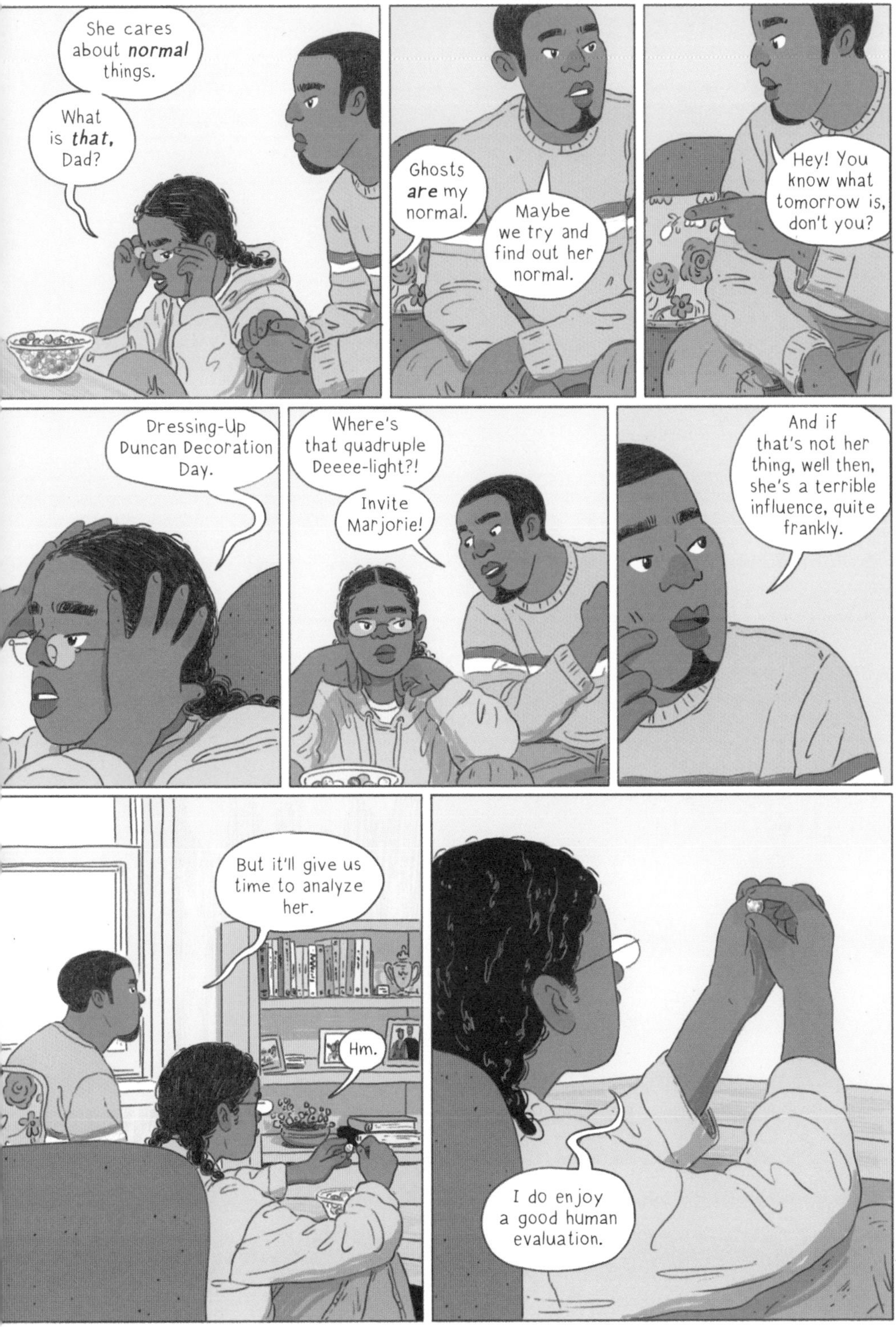
She cares about **normal** things.
What is ***that,*** Dad?
Ghosts **are** my normal.
Maybe we try and find out her normal.
Hey! You know what tomorrow is, don't you?
Dressing-Up Duncan Decoration Day.
Where's that quadruple Deeee-light?!
Invite Marjorie!
And if that's not her thing, well then, she's a terrible influence, quite frankly.
But it'll give us time to analyze her.
Hm.
I do enjoy a good human evaluation.

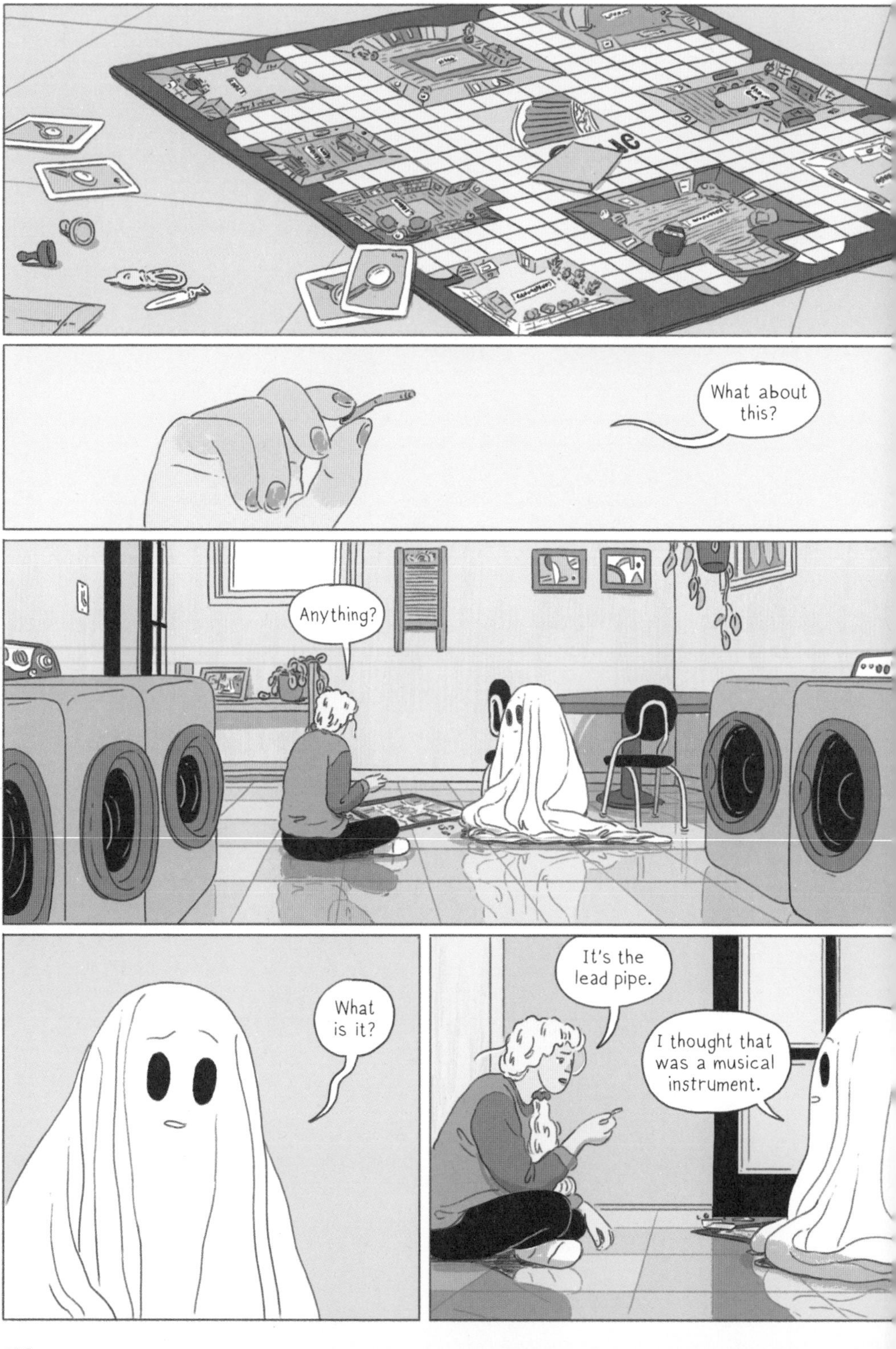
What about this?
Anything?
What is it?
It's the lead pipe.
I thought that was a musical instrument.

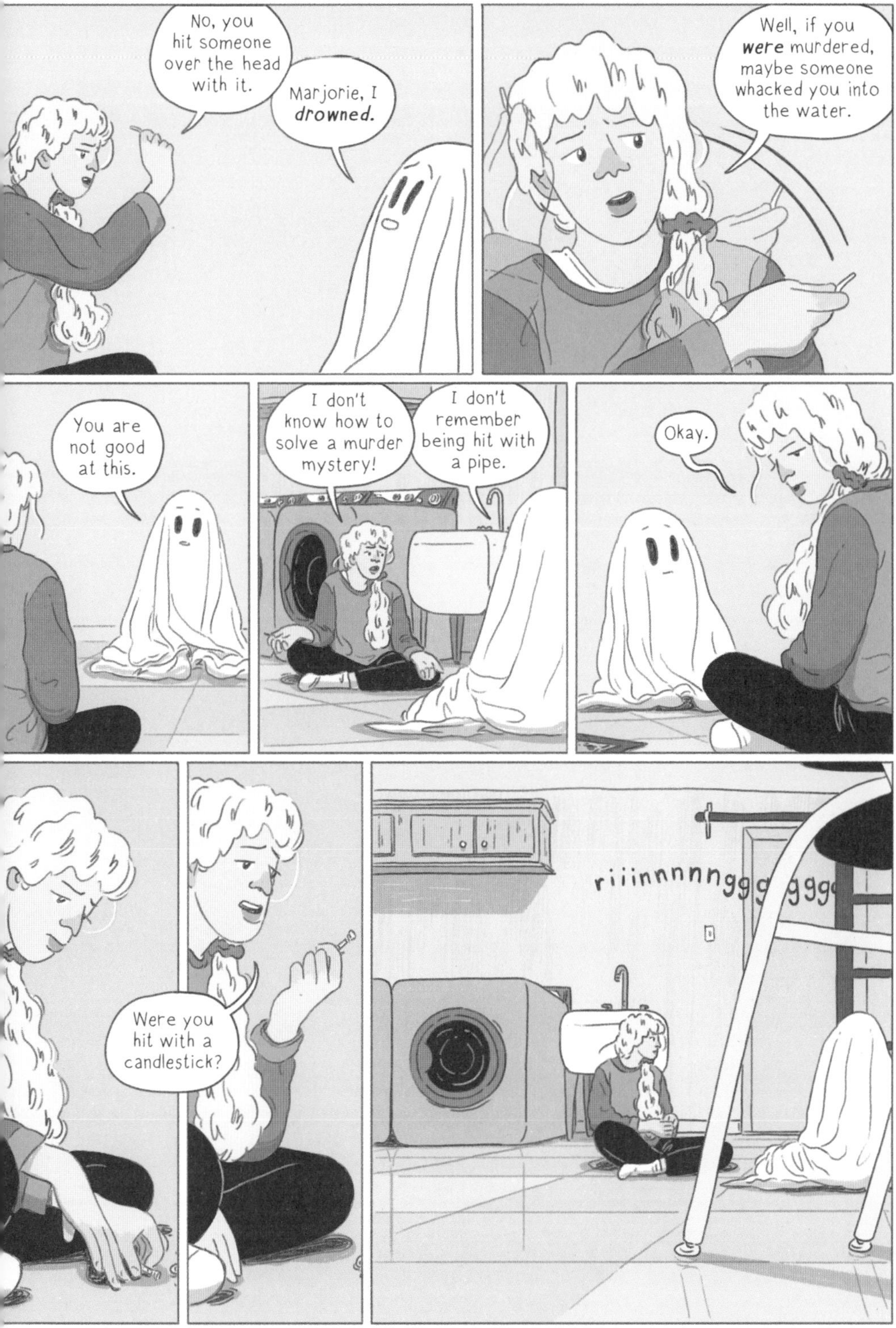
No, you hit someone over the head with it.
Marjorie, I **drowned.**
Well, if you ***were*** murdered, maybe someone whacked you into the water.
You are not good at this.
I don't know how to solve a murder mystery!
I don't remember being hit with a pipe.
Okay.
Were you hit with a candlestick?
riiinnnnnggggggg

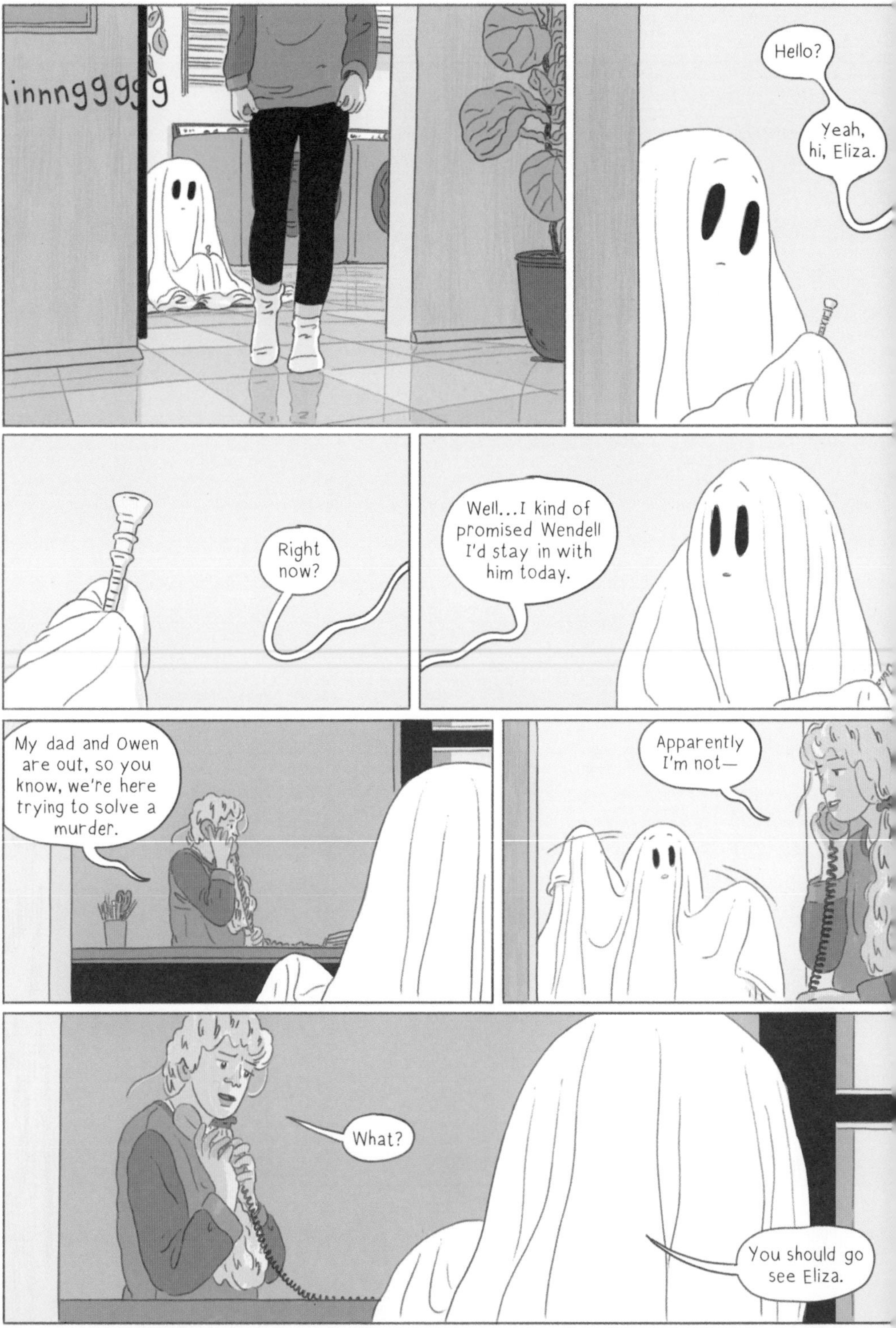

innngggg
Hello?
Yeah, hi, Eliza.
Right now?
Well...I kind of promised Wendell I'd stay in with him today.
My dad and Owen are out, so you know, we're here trying to solve a murder.
Apparently I'm not—
What?
You should go see Eliza.

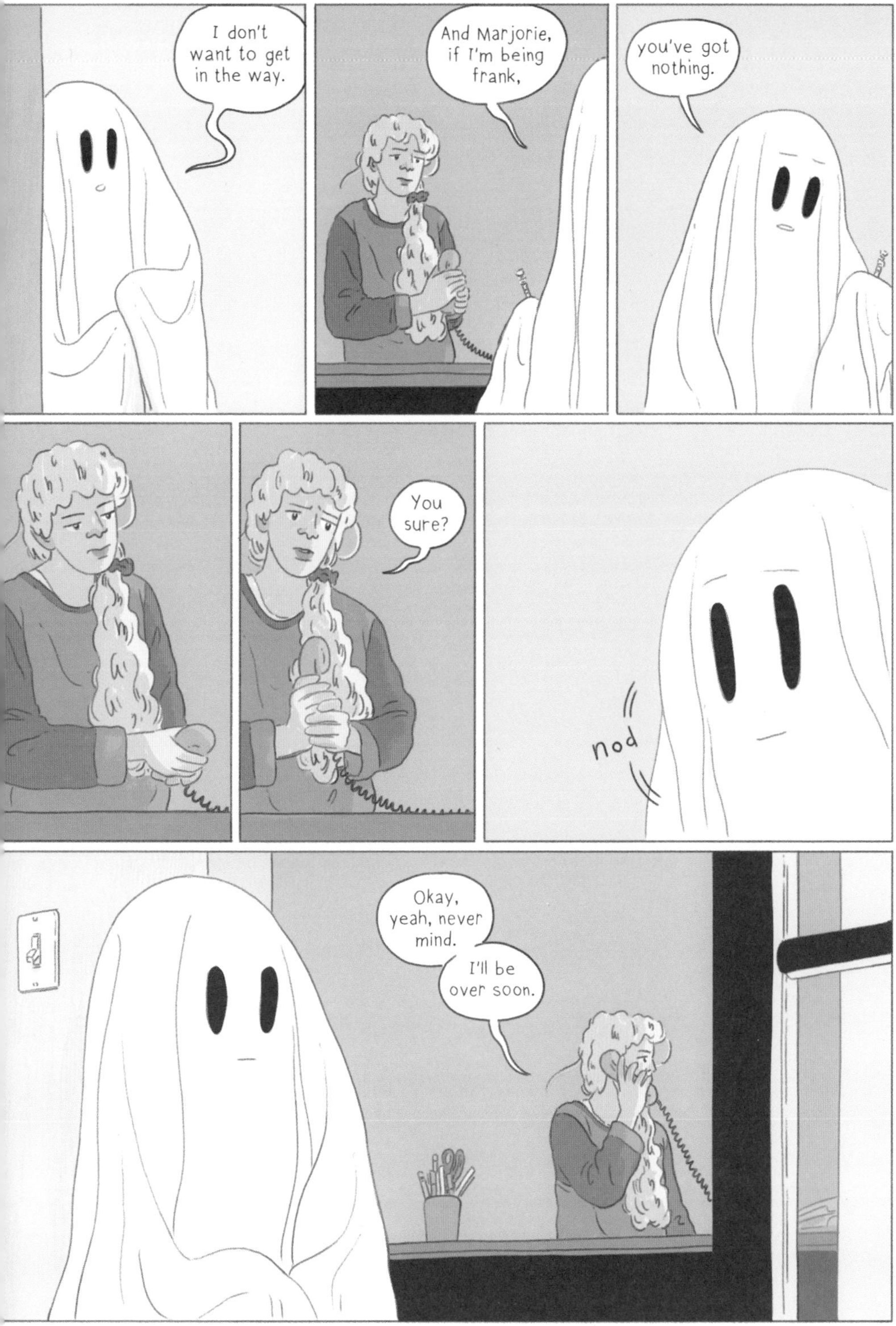
I don't want to get in the way.
And Marjorie, if I'm being frank,
you've got nothing.
You sure?
nod
Okay, yeah, never mind.
I'll be over soon.

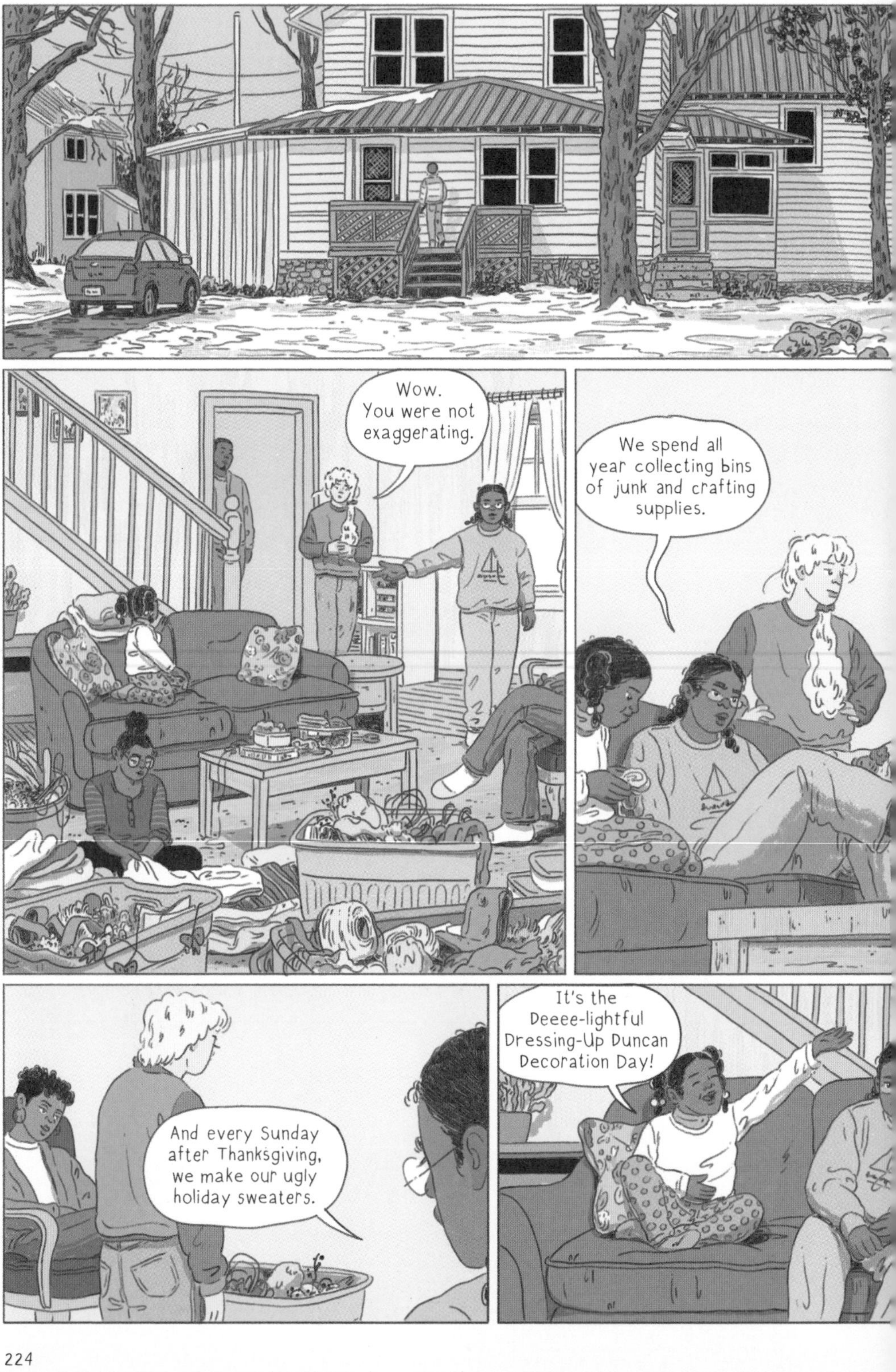
Wow.
You were not exaggerating.
We spend all year collecting bins of junk and crafting supplies.
And every Sunday after Thanksgiving, we make our ugly holiday sweaters.
It's the Deeee-lightful Dressing-Up Duncan Decoration Day!

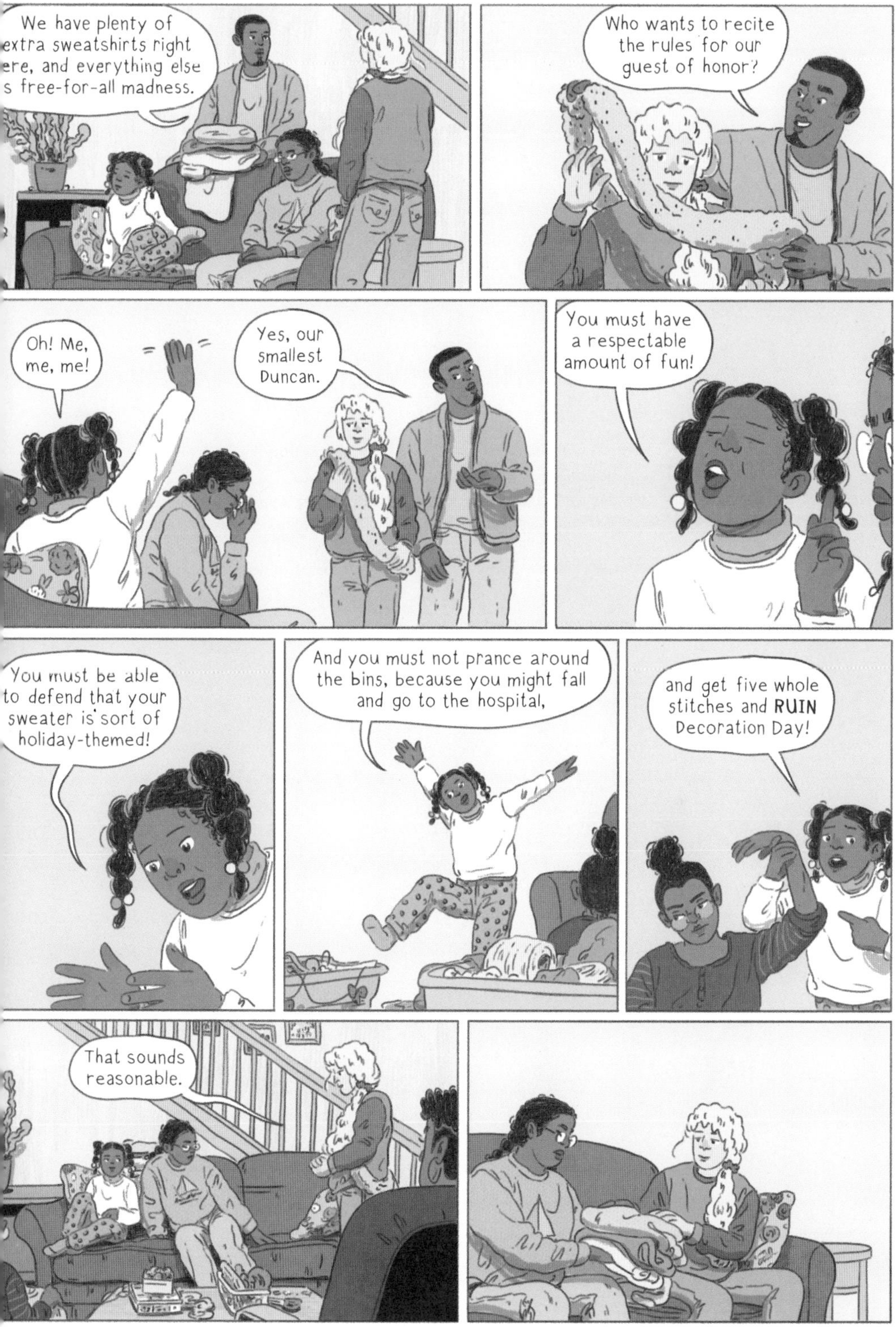
We have plenty of extra sweatshirts right ere, and everything else s free-for-all madness.
Who wants to recite the rules for our guest of honor?
Oh! Me, me, me!
Yes, our smallest Duncan.
You must have a respectable amount of fun!
You must be able to defend that your sweater is sort of holiday-themed!
And you must not prance around the bins, because you might fall and go to the hospital,
and get five whole stitches and RUIN Decoration Day!
That sounds reasonable.

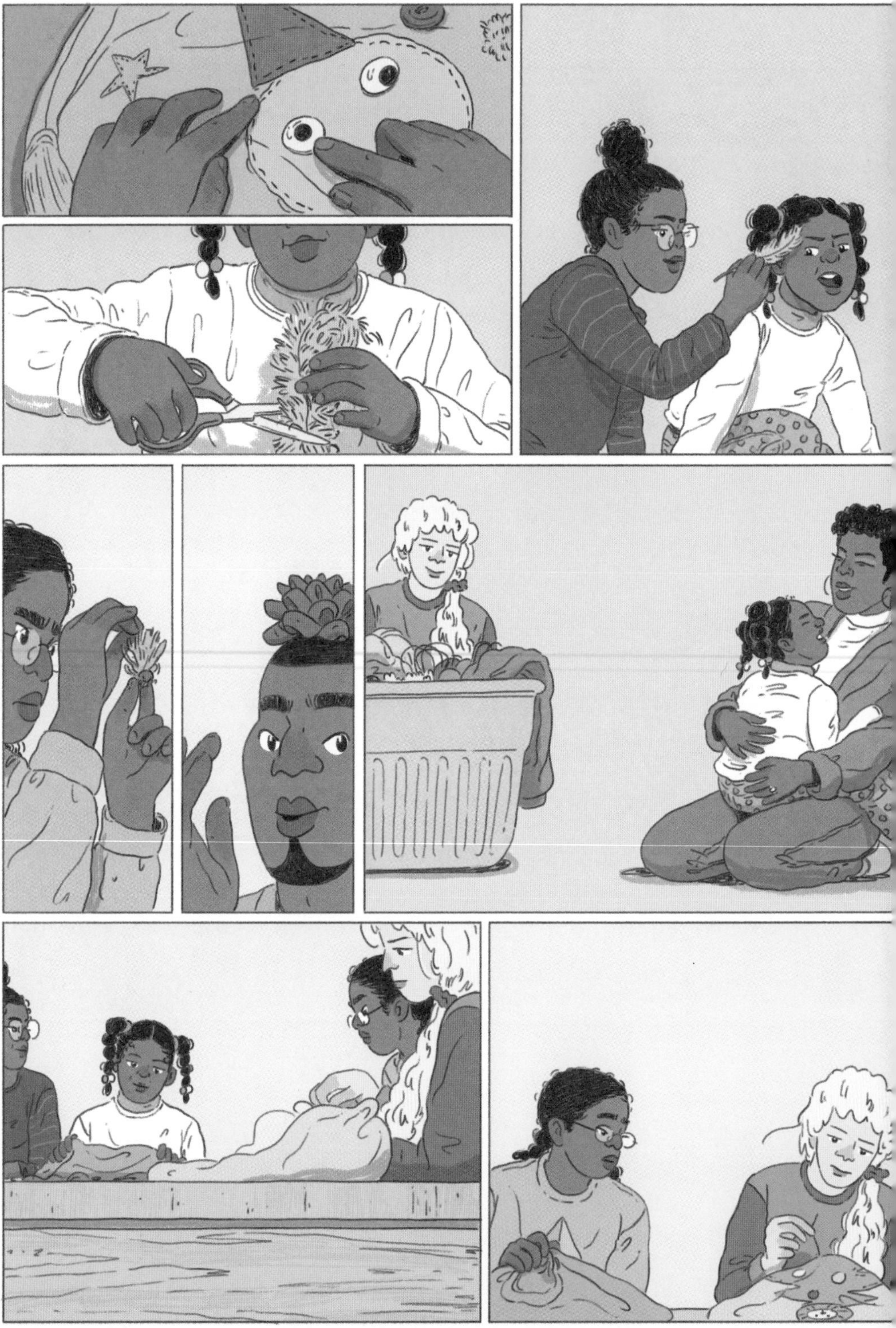

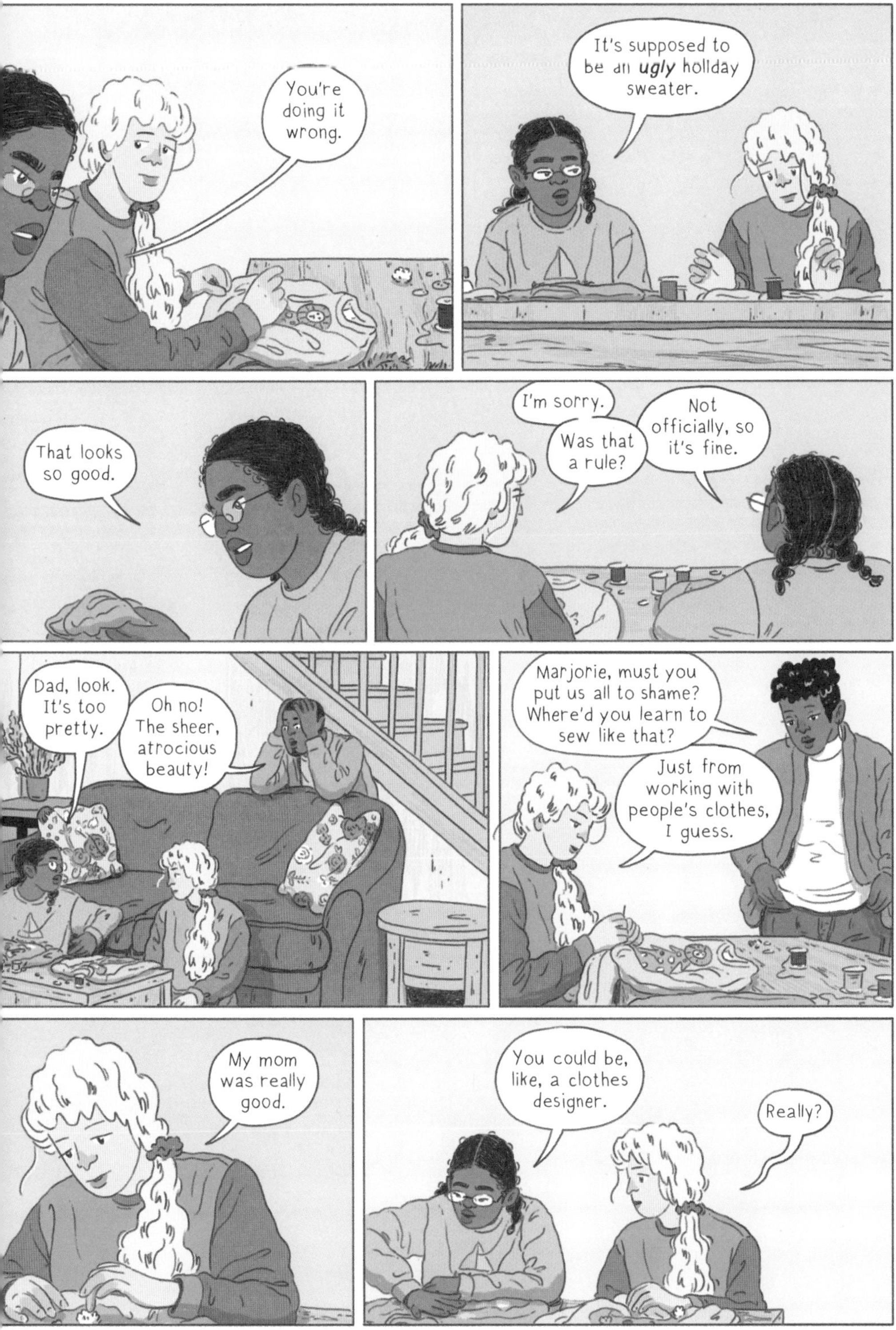

You're doing it wrong.
It's supposed to be an **ugly** holiday sweater.
That looks so good.
I'm sorry.
Was that a rule?
Not officially, so it's fine.
Dad, look. It's too pretty.
Oh no! The sheer, atrocious beauty!
Marjorie, must you put us all to shame? Where'd you learn to sew like that?
Just from working with people's clothes, I guess.
My mom was really good.
You could be, like, a clothes designer.
Really?

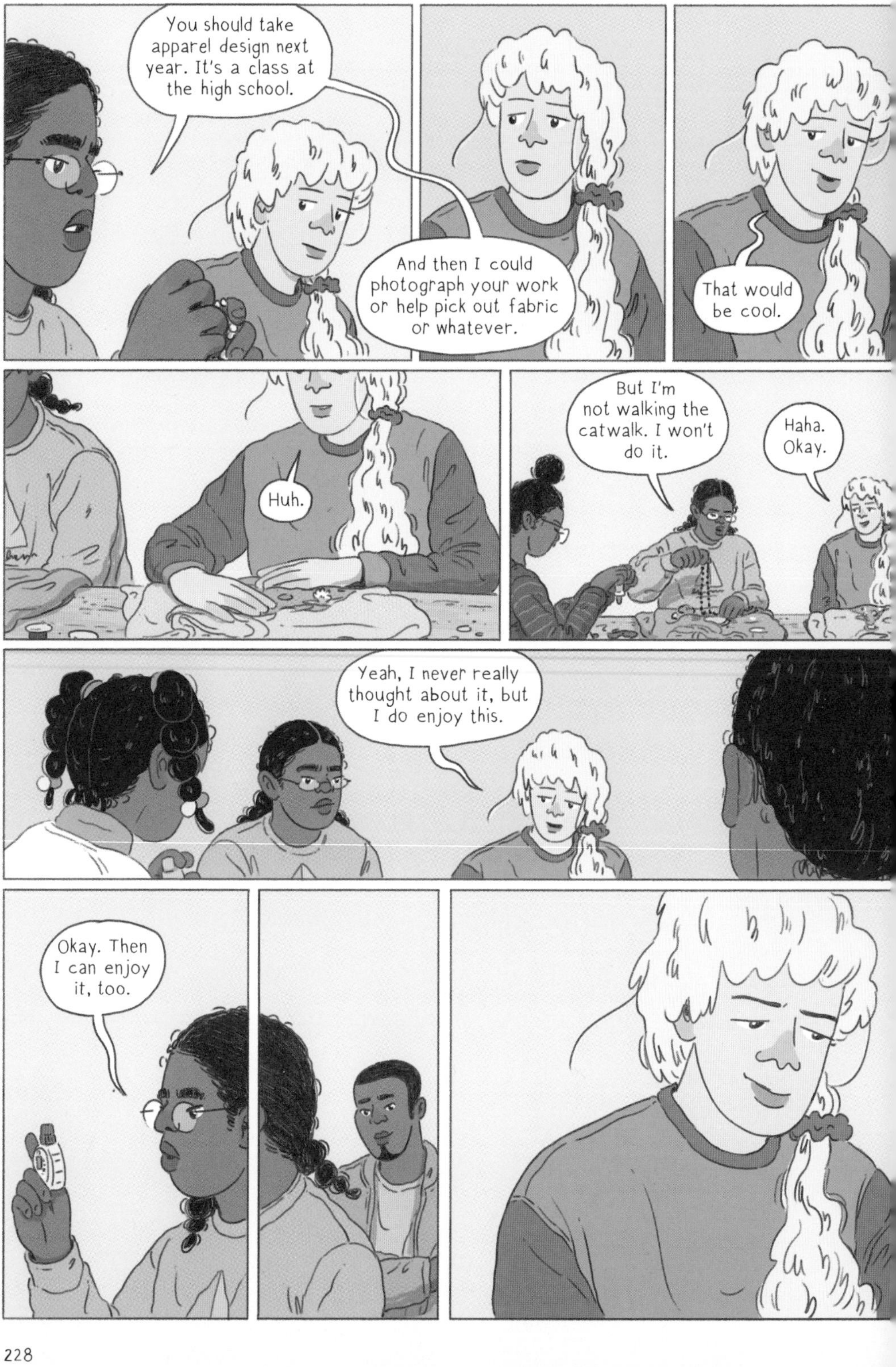
You should take apparel design next year. It's a class at the high school.
And then I could photograph your work or help pick out fabric or whatever.
That would be cool.
Huh.
But I'm not walking the catwalk. I won't do it.
Haha. Okay.
Yeah, I never really thought about it, but I do enjoy this.
Okay. Then I can enjoy it, too.

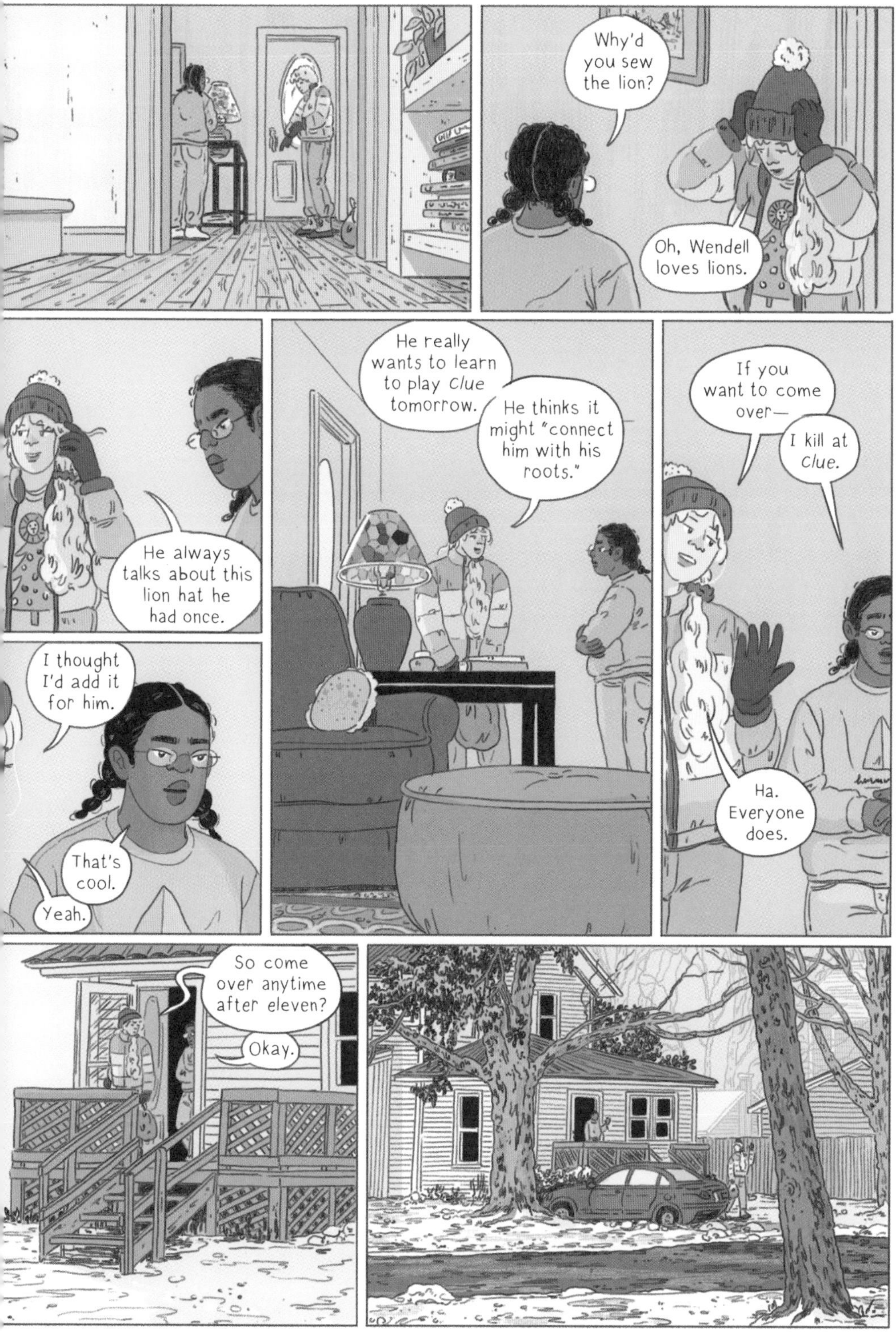
Why'd you sew the lion?
Oh, Wendell loves lions.
He always talks about this lion hat he had once.
I thought I'd add it for him.
That's cool.
Yeah.
He really wants to learn to play *Clue* tomorrow.
He thinks it might "connect him with his roots."
If you want to come over—
I kill at *Clue*.
Ha. Everyone does.
So come over anytime after eleven?
Okay.

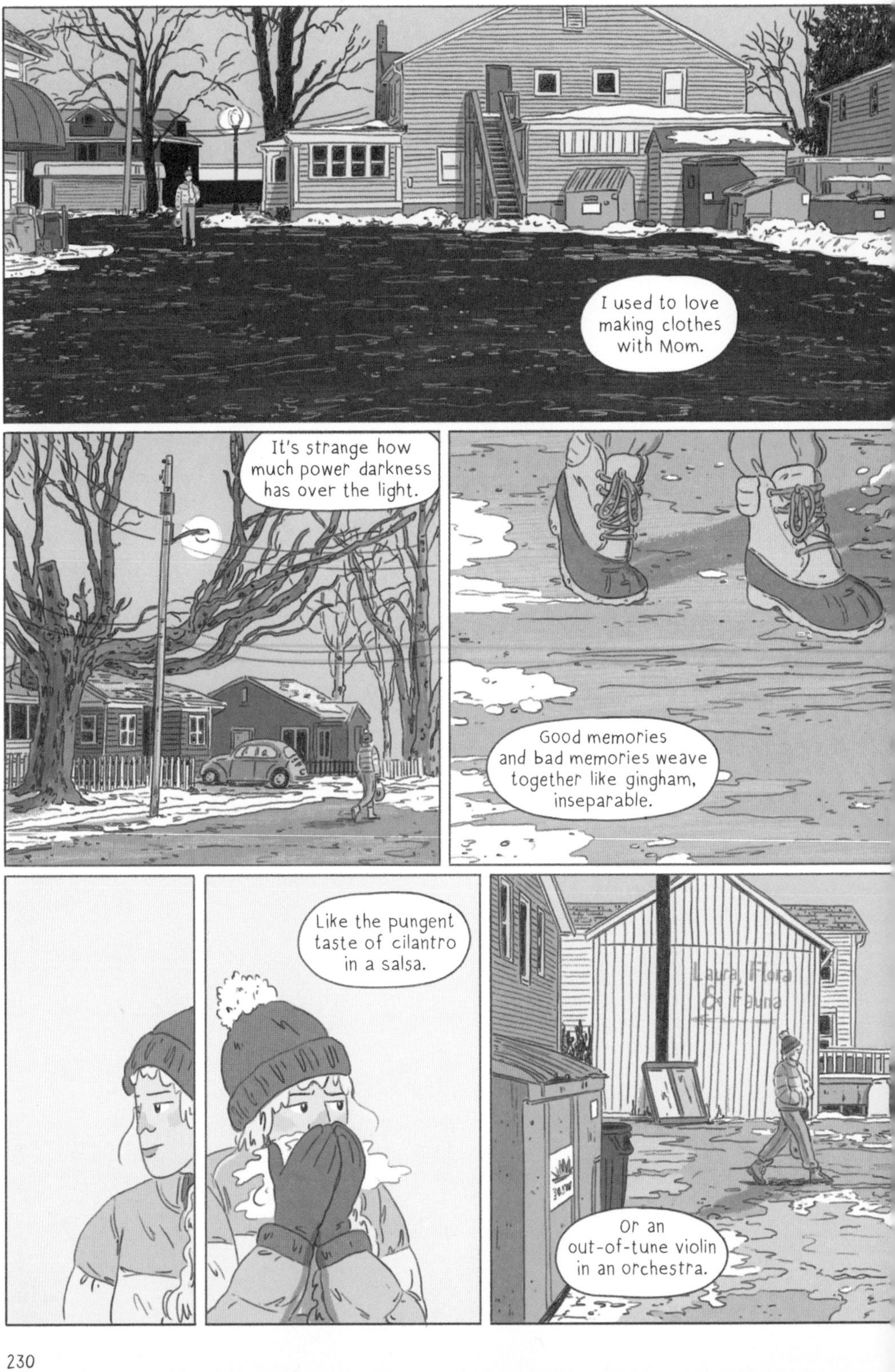
I used to love making clothes with Mom.
It's strange how much power darkness has over the light.
Good memories and bad memories weave together like gingham, inseparable.
Like the pungent taste of cilantro in a salsa.
Laura, Flora & Fauna
Or an out-of-tune violin in an orchestra.

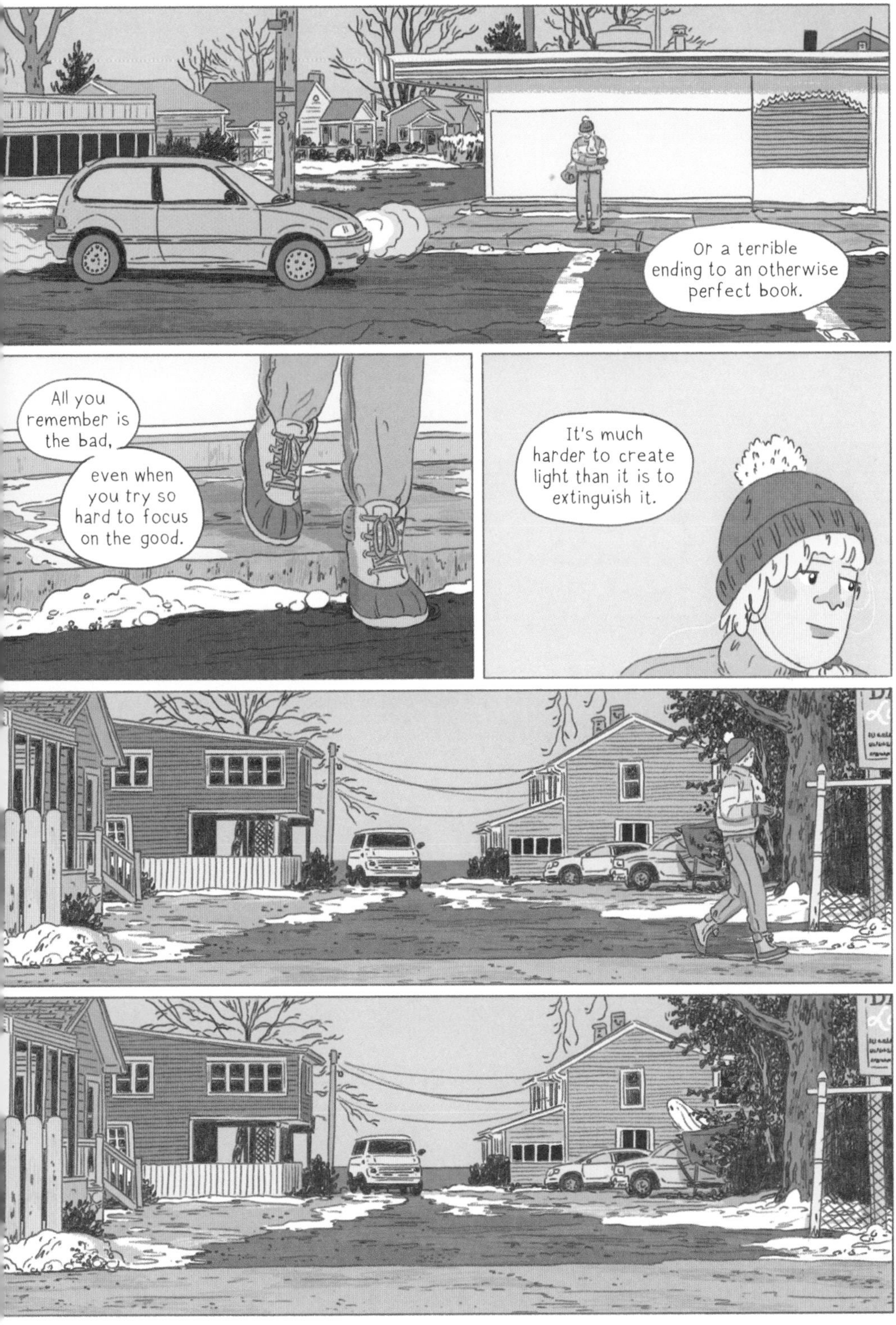
Or a terrible ending to an otherwise perfect book.
All you remember is the bad,
even when you try so hard to focus on the good.
It's much harder to create light than it is to extinguish it.

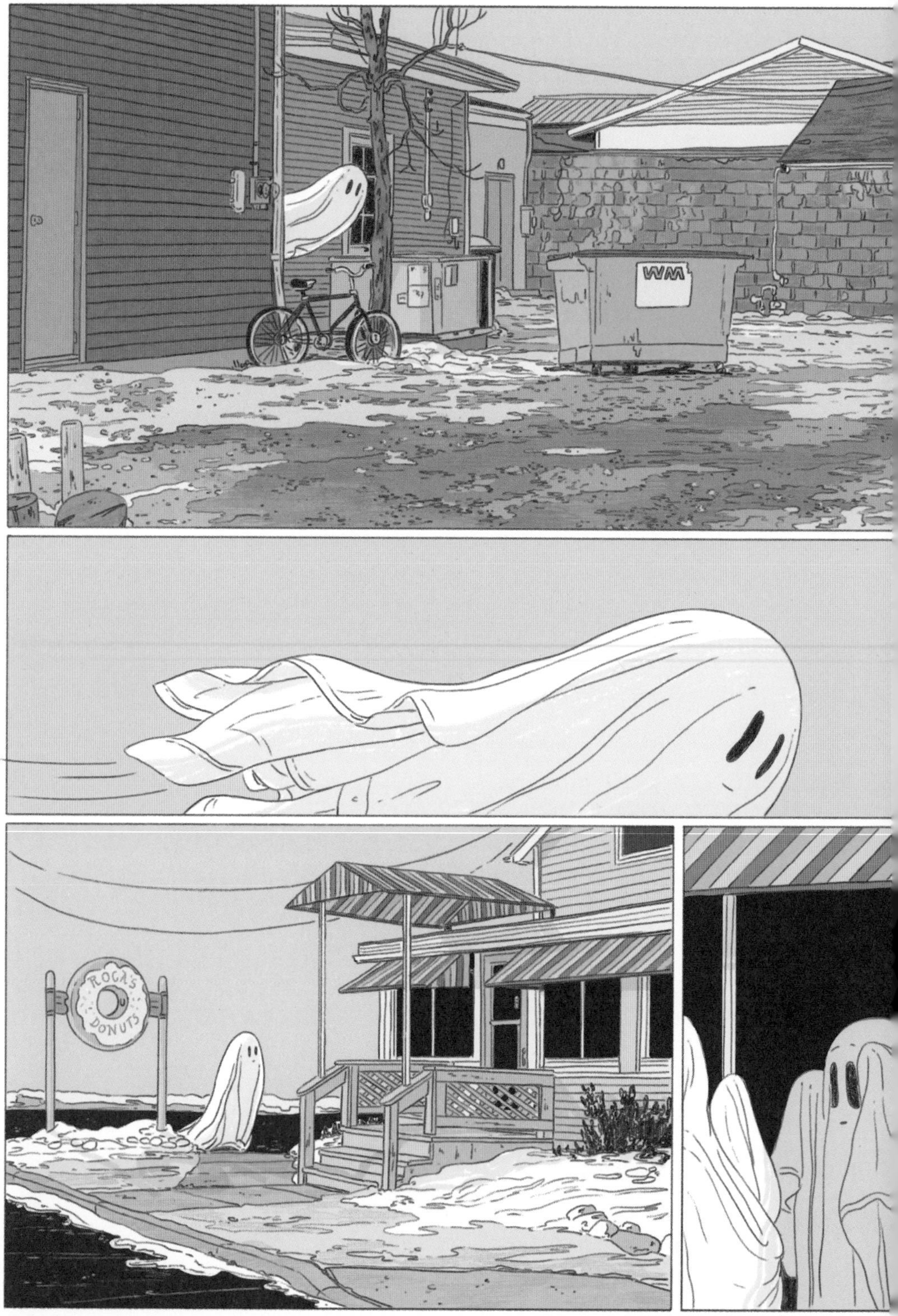
WM
ROGA'S
DONUTS

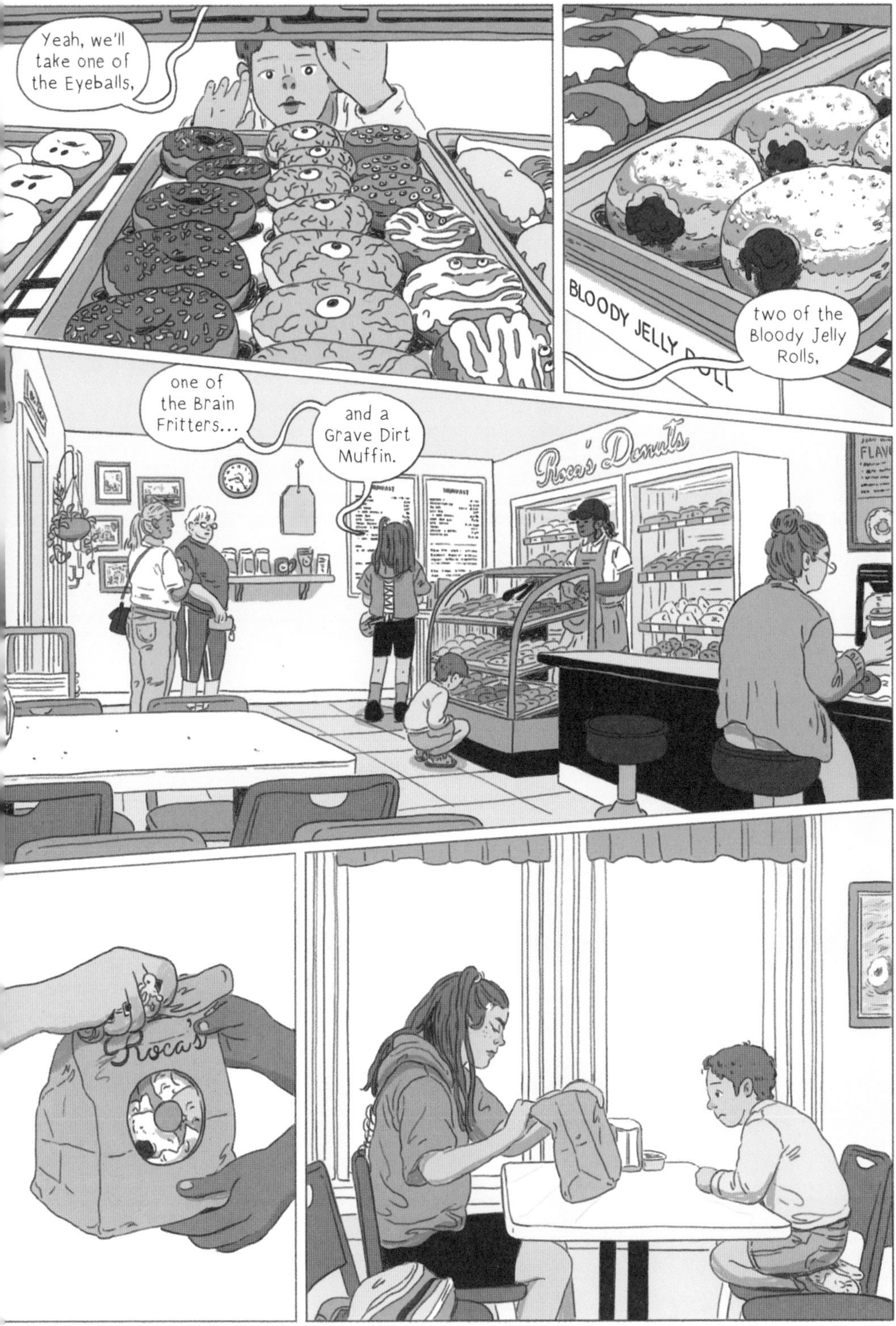
Yeah, we'll take one of the Eyeballs,
BLOODY JELLY ROLL
two of the Bloody Jelly Rolls,
one of the Brain Fritters...
and a Grave Dirt Muffin.
Roca's Donuts
FLAV
Roca's

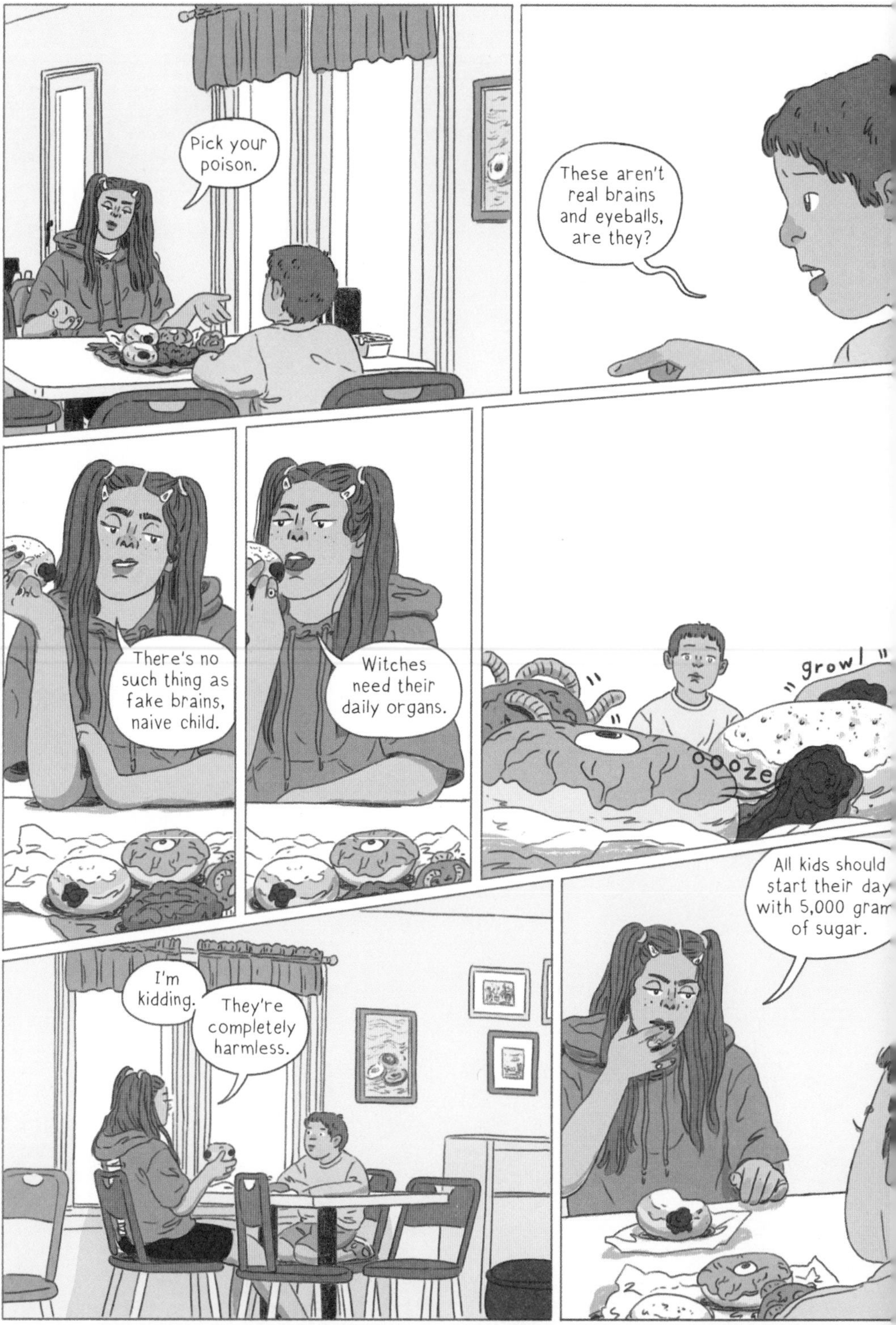
Pick your poison.
These aren't real brains and eyeballs, are they?
There's no such thing as fake brains, naive child.
Witches need their daily organs.
growl
oooze
All kids should start their day with 5,000 gram of sugar.
I'm kidding.
They're completely harmless.

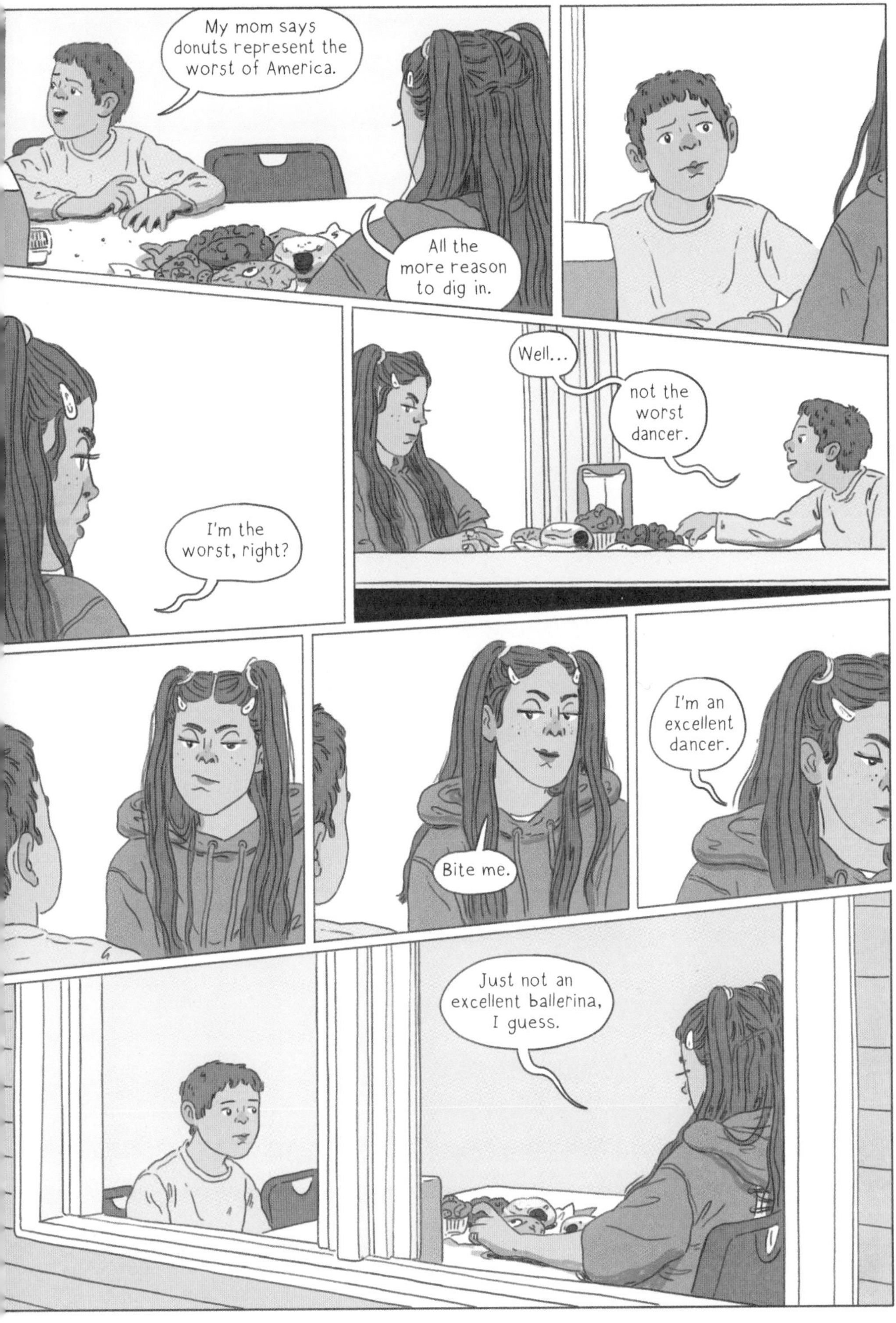
My mom says donuts represent the worst of America.
All the more reason to dig in.
I'm the worst, right?
Well...
not the worst dancer.
Bite me.
I'm an excellent dancer.
Just not an excellent ballerina, I guess.

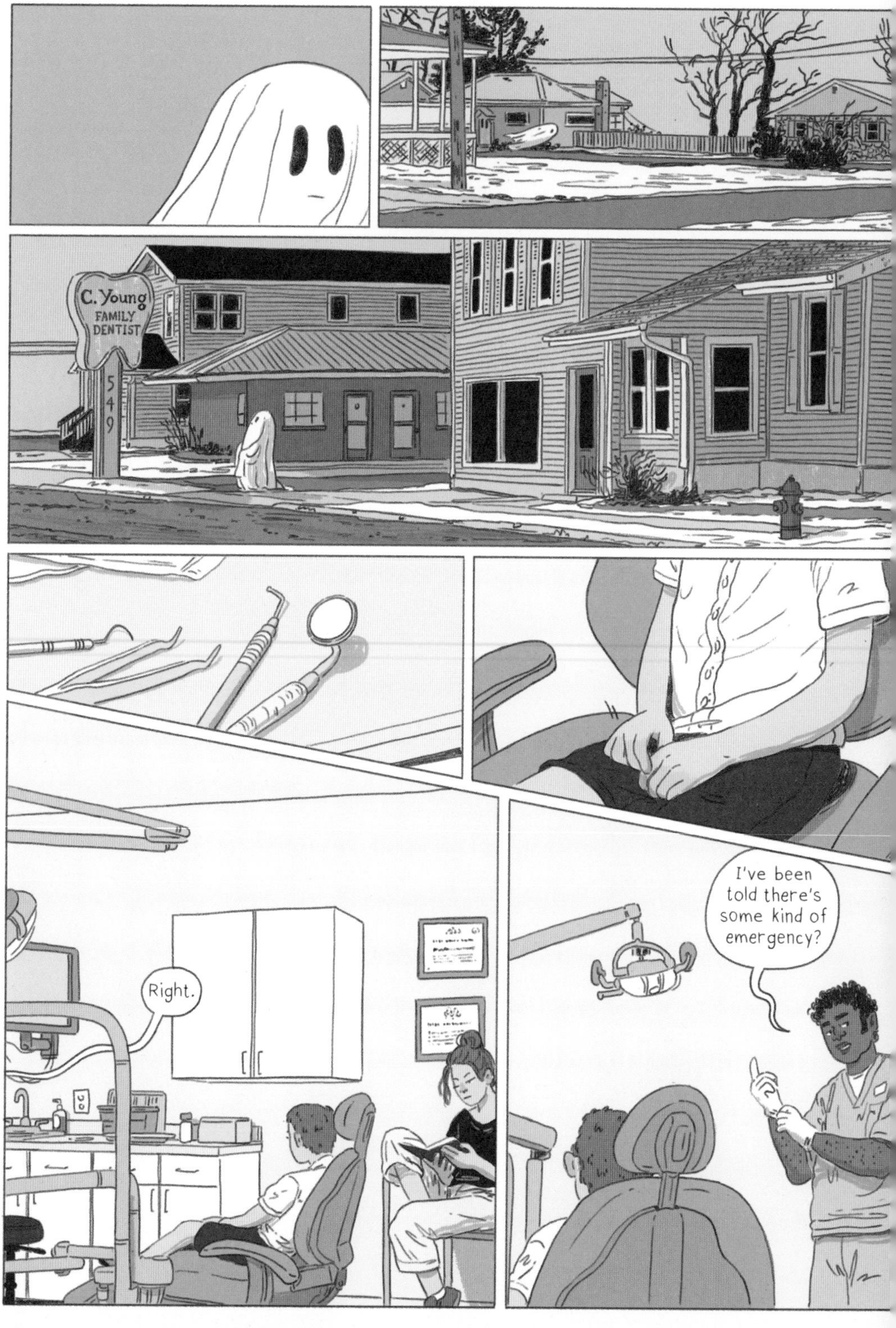
C. Young
FAMILY
DENTIST
549
Right.
I've been told there's some kind of emergency?

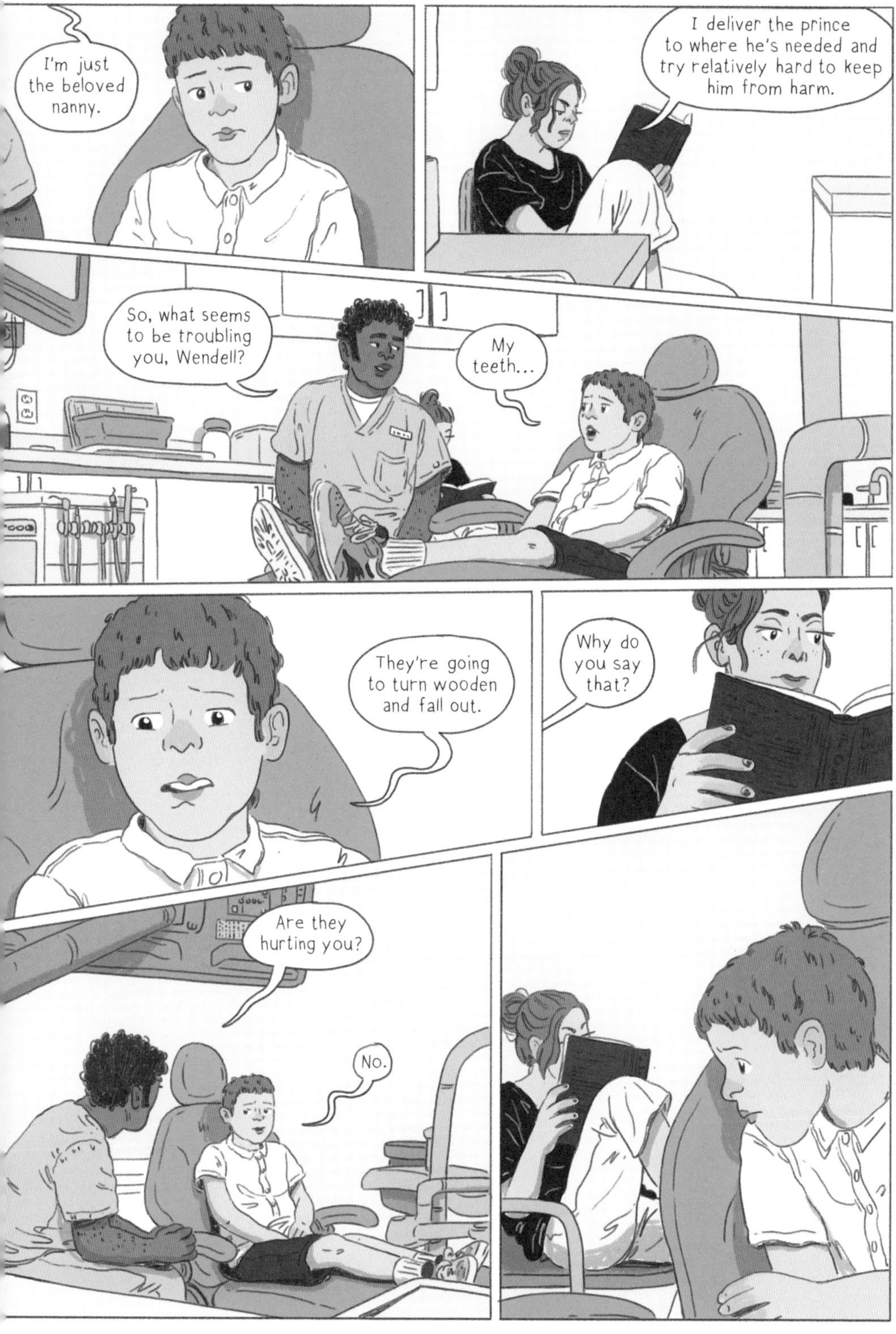
I'm just the beloved nanny.
I deliver the prince to where he's needed and try relatively hard to keep him from harm.
So, what seems to be troubling you, Wendell?
My teeth...
They're going to turn wooden and fall out.
Why do you say that?
Are they hurting you?
No.

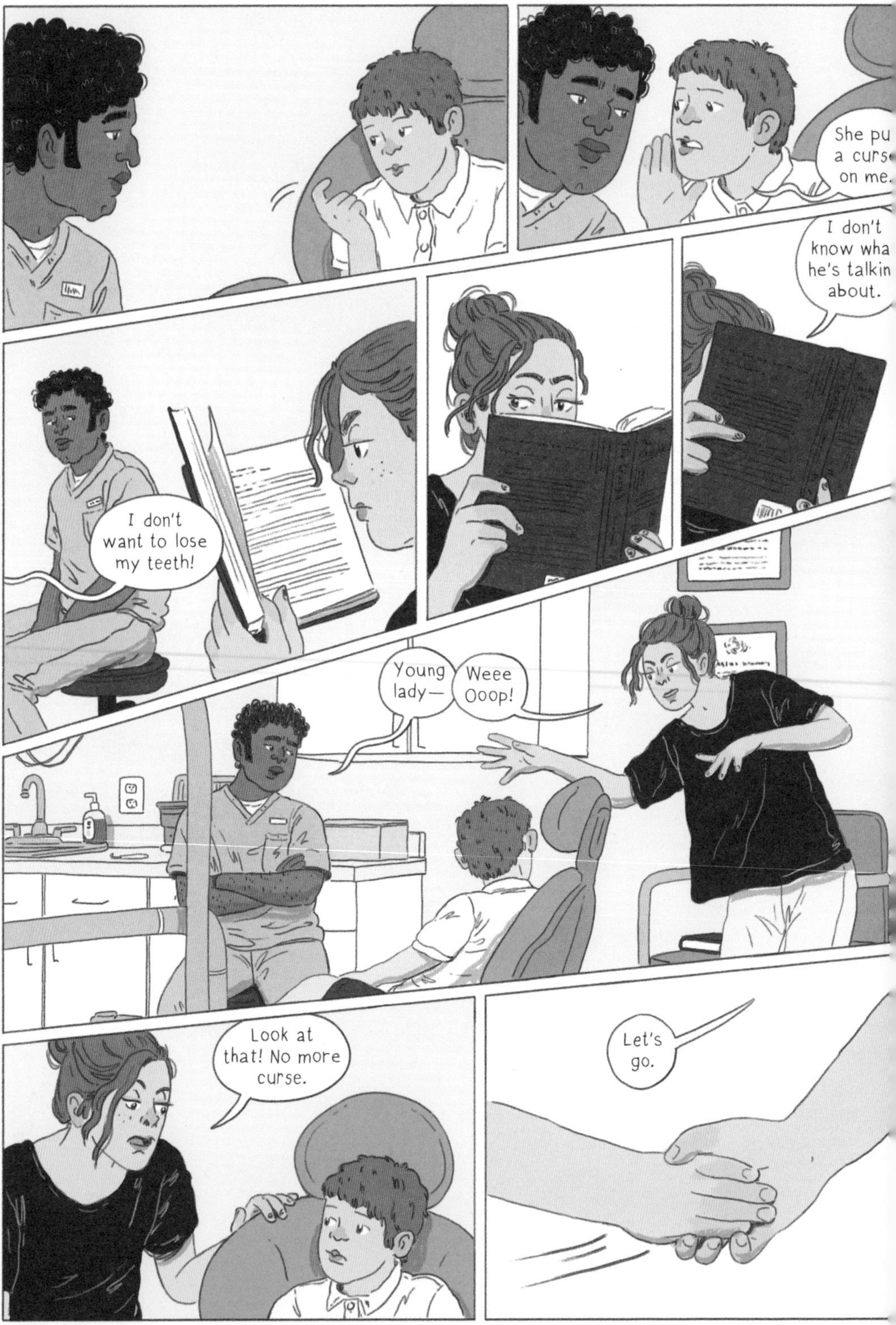
She pu
a curs
on me.
I don't
know wha
he's talkin
about.
I don't
want to lose
my teeth!
Young
lady—
Weee
Ooop!
Look at
that! No more
curse.
Let's
go.

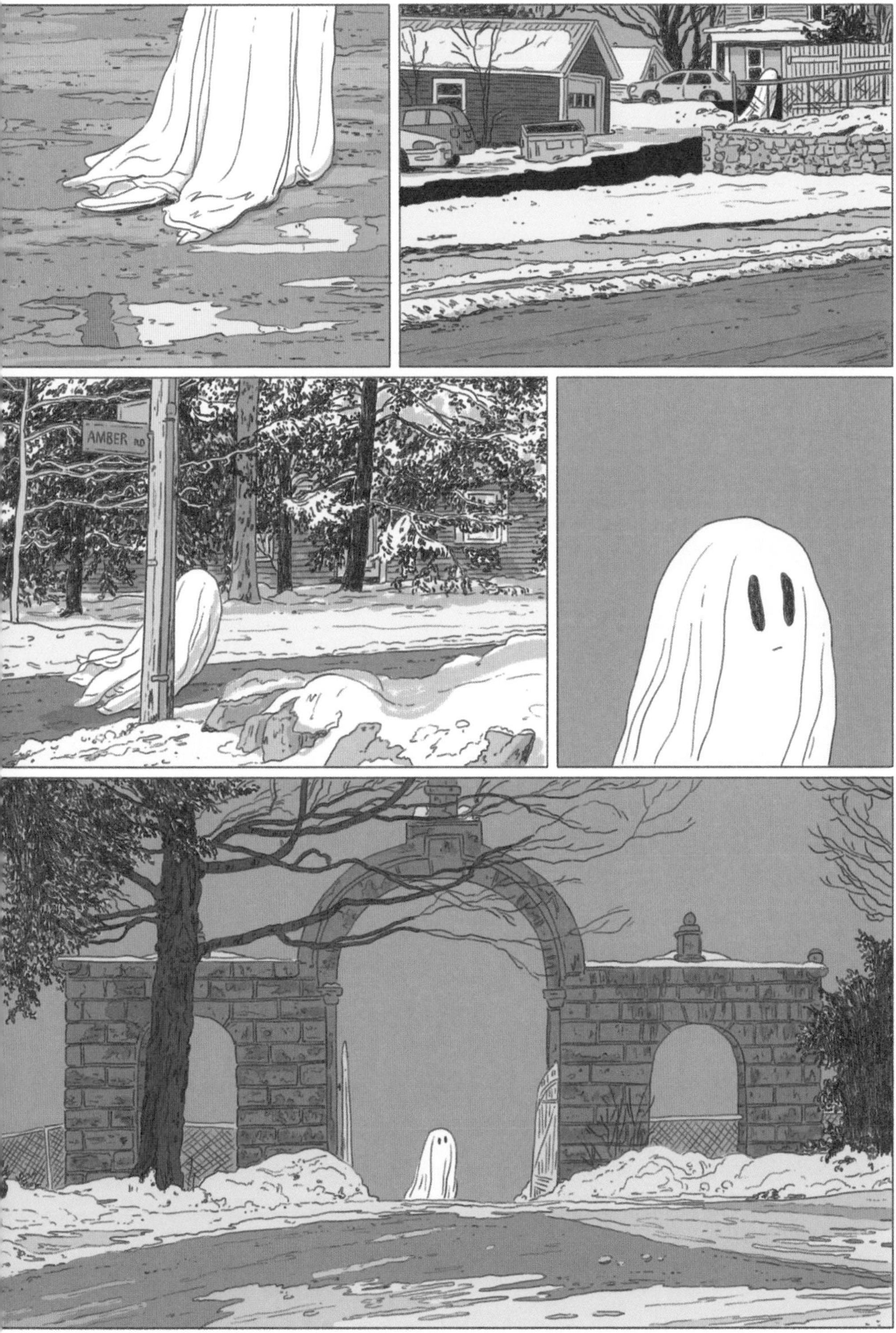
AMBER RD

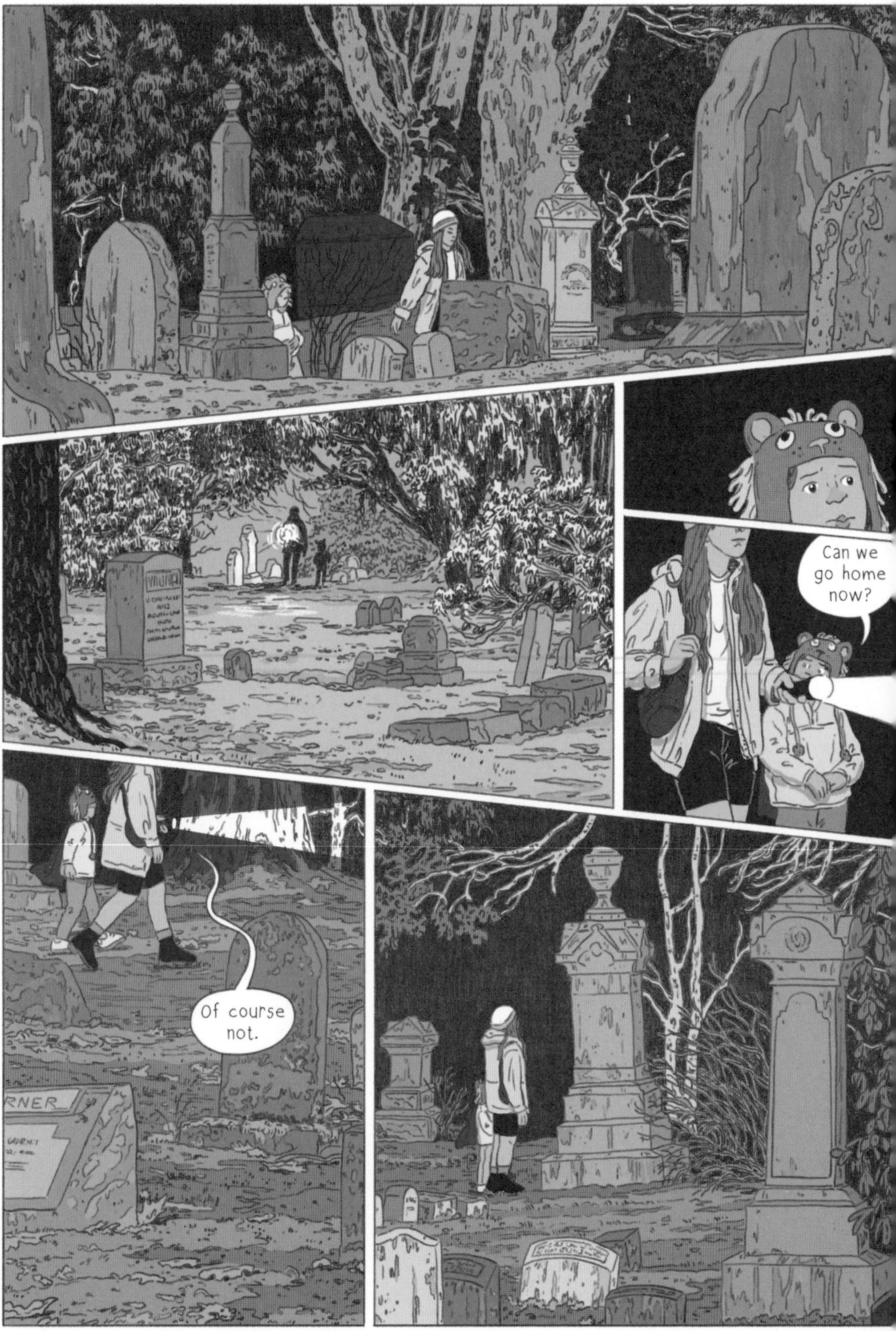
Can we go home now?
Of course not.
RNER

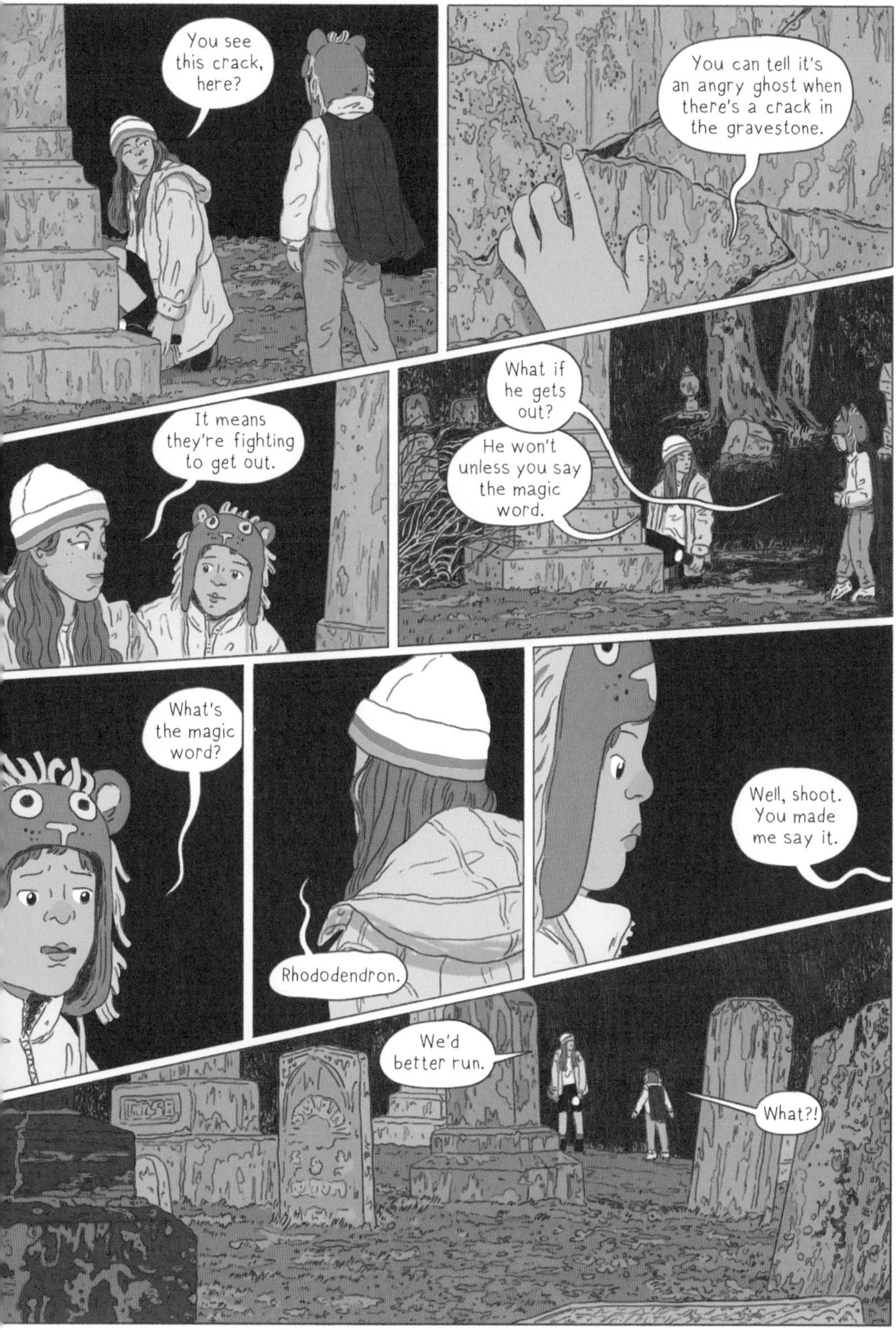
You see this crack, here?
You can tell it's an angry ghost when there's a crack in the gravestone.
It means they're fighting to get out.
What if he gets out?
He won't unless you say the magic word.
What's the magic word?
Rhododendron.
Well, shoot. You made me say it.
We'd better run.
What?!

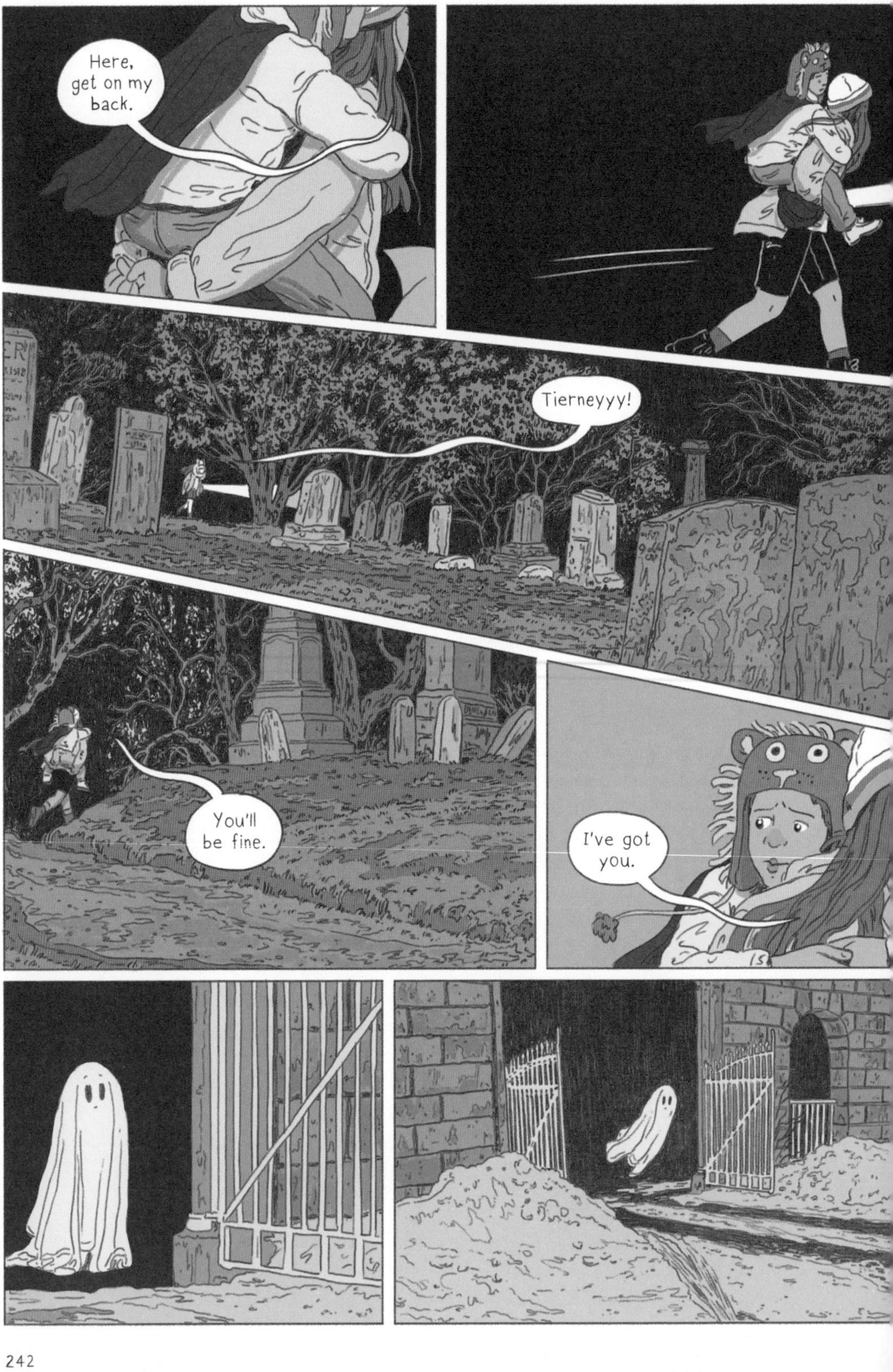
Here, get on my back.
Tierneyyy!
You'll be fine.
I've got you.

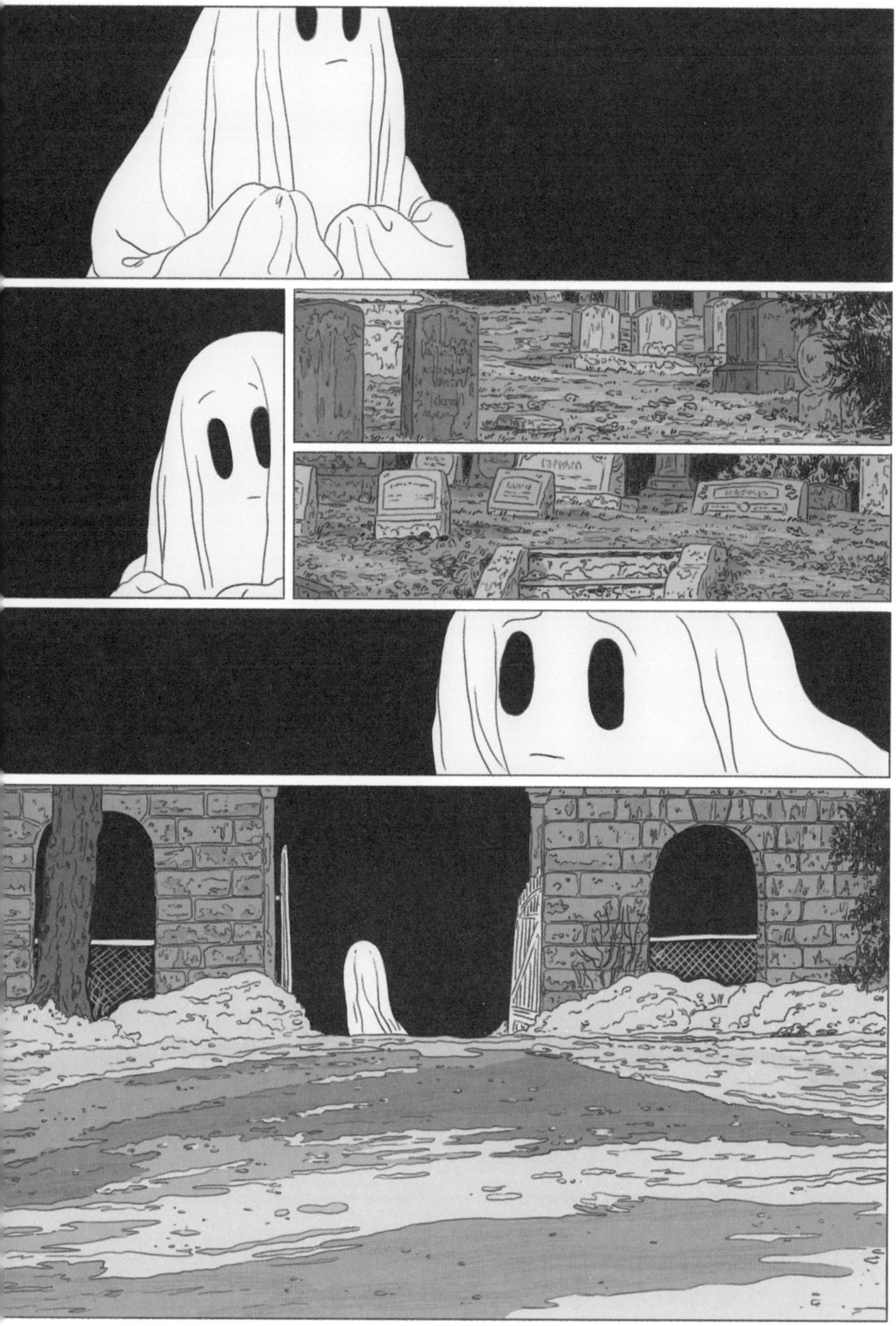

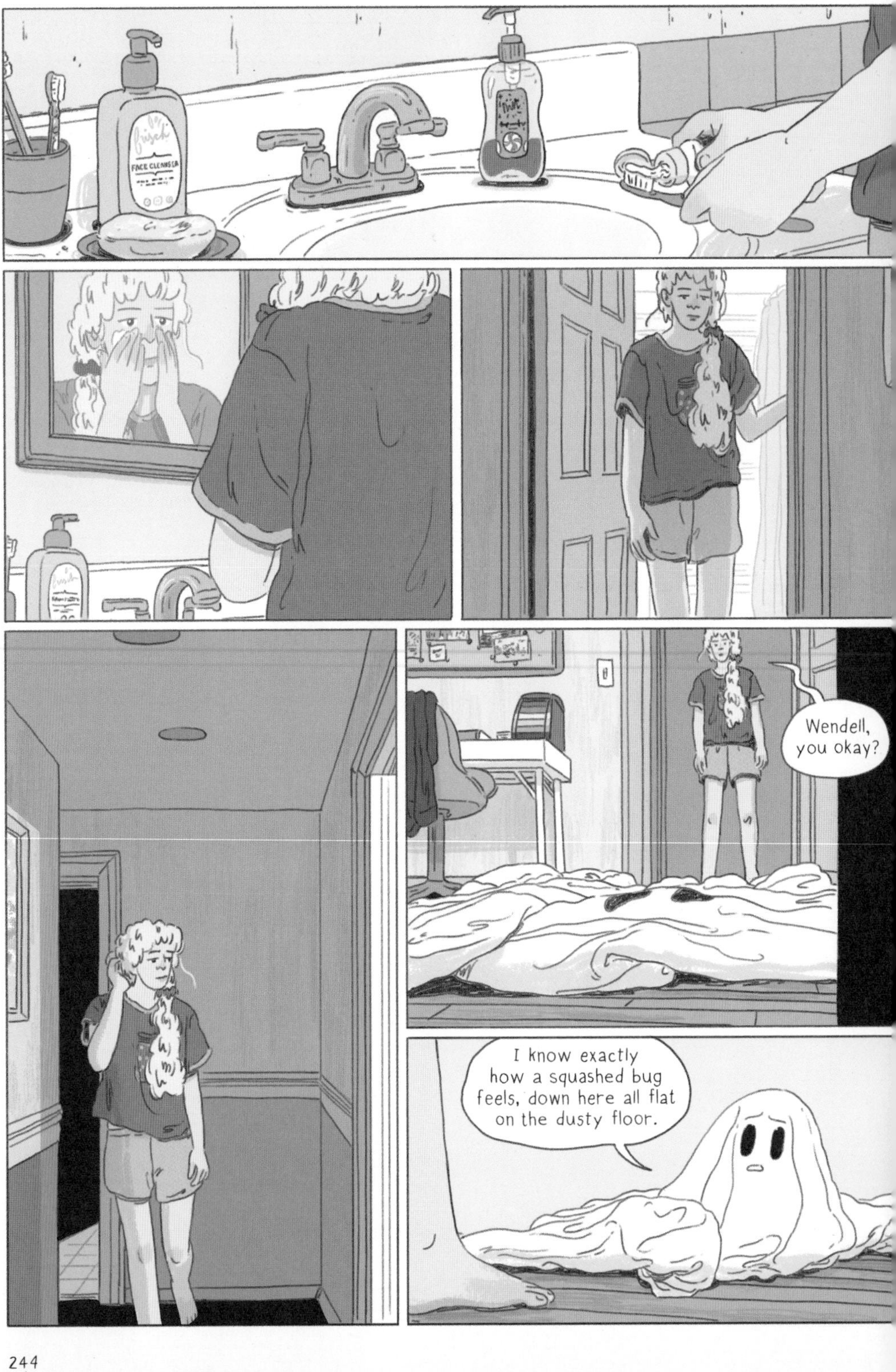
Wendell,
you okay?
I know exactly how a squashed bug feels, down here all flat on the dusty floor.

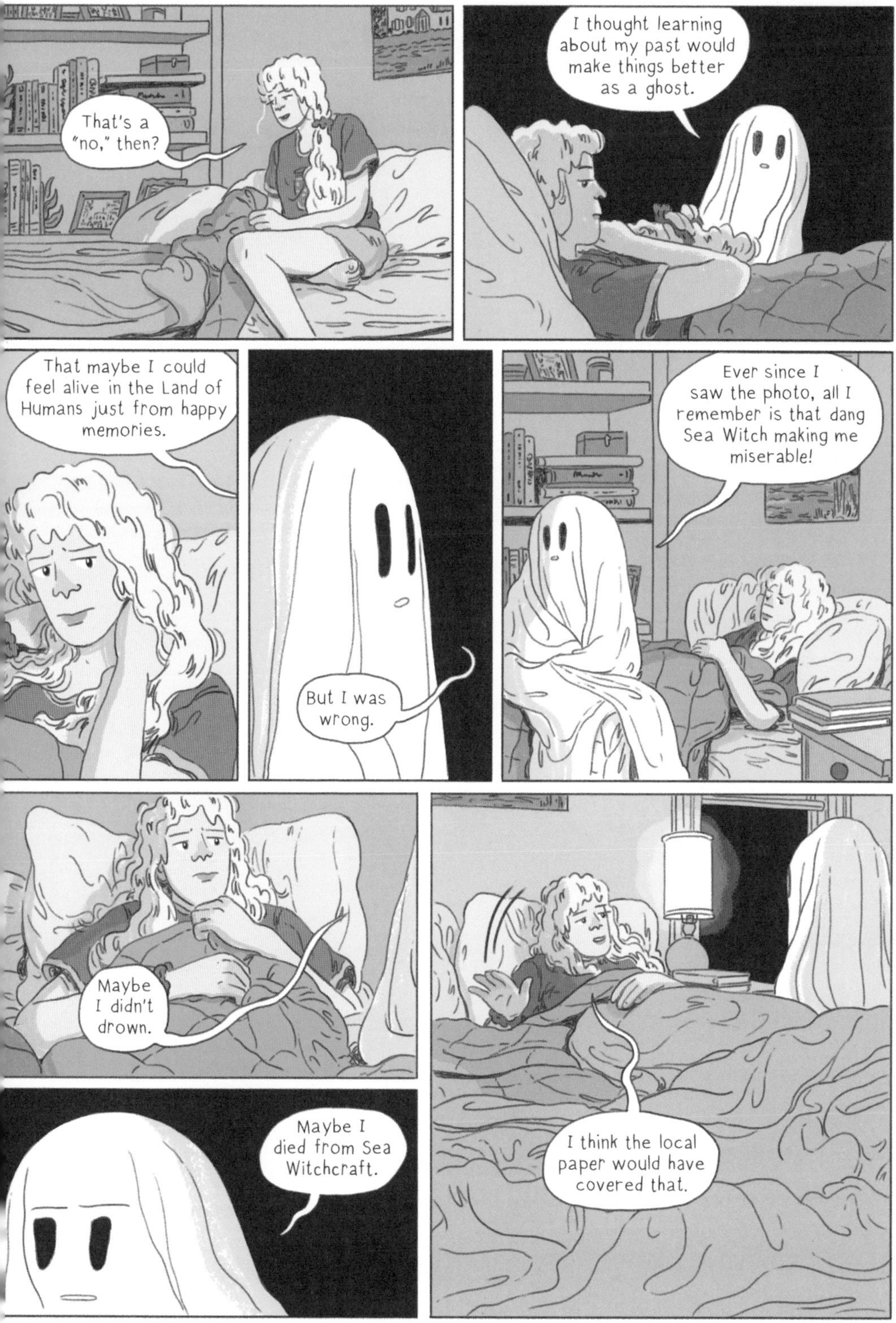

That's a "no," then?
I thought learning about my past would make things better as a ghost.
That maybe I could feel alive in the Land of Humans just from happy memories.
But I was wrong.
Ever since I saw the photo, all I remember is that dang Sea Witch making me miserable!
Maybe I didn't drown.
Maybe I died from Sea Witchcraft.
I think the local paper would have covered that.

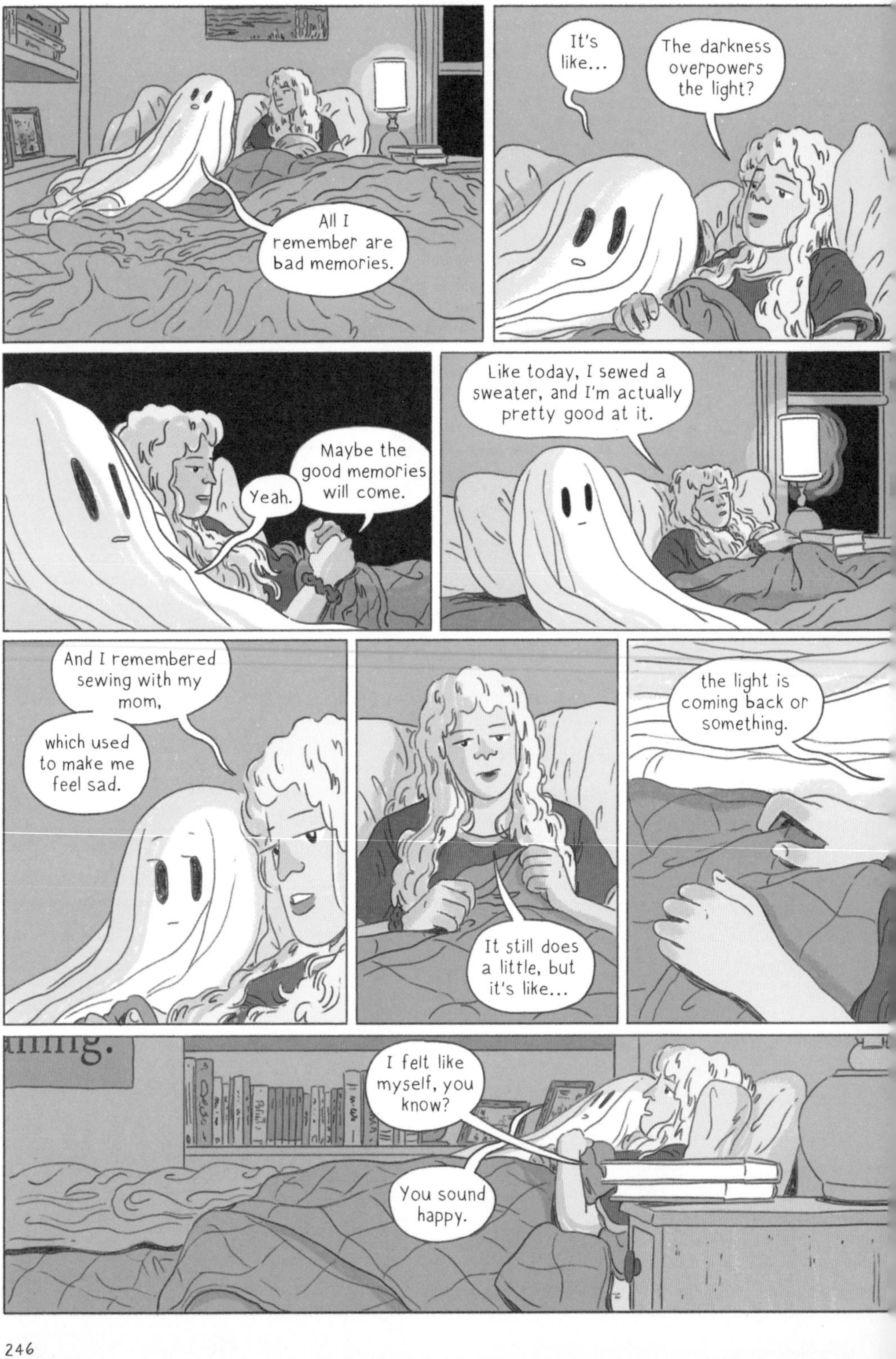
All I remember are bad memories.
It's like...
The darkness overpowers the light?
Yeah.
Maybe the good memories will come.
Like today, I sewed a sweater, and I'm actually pretty good at it.
And I remembered sewing with my mom,
which used to make me feel sad.
It still does a little, but it's like...
the light is coming back or something.
I felt like myself, you know?
You sound happy.

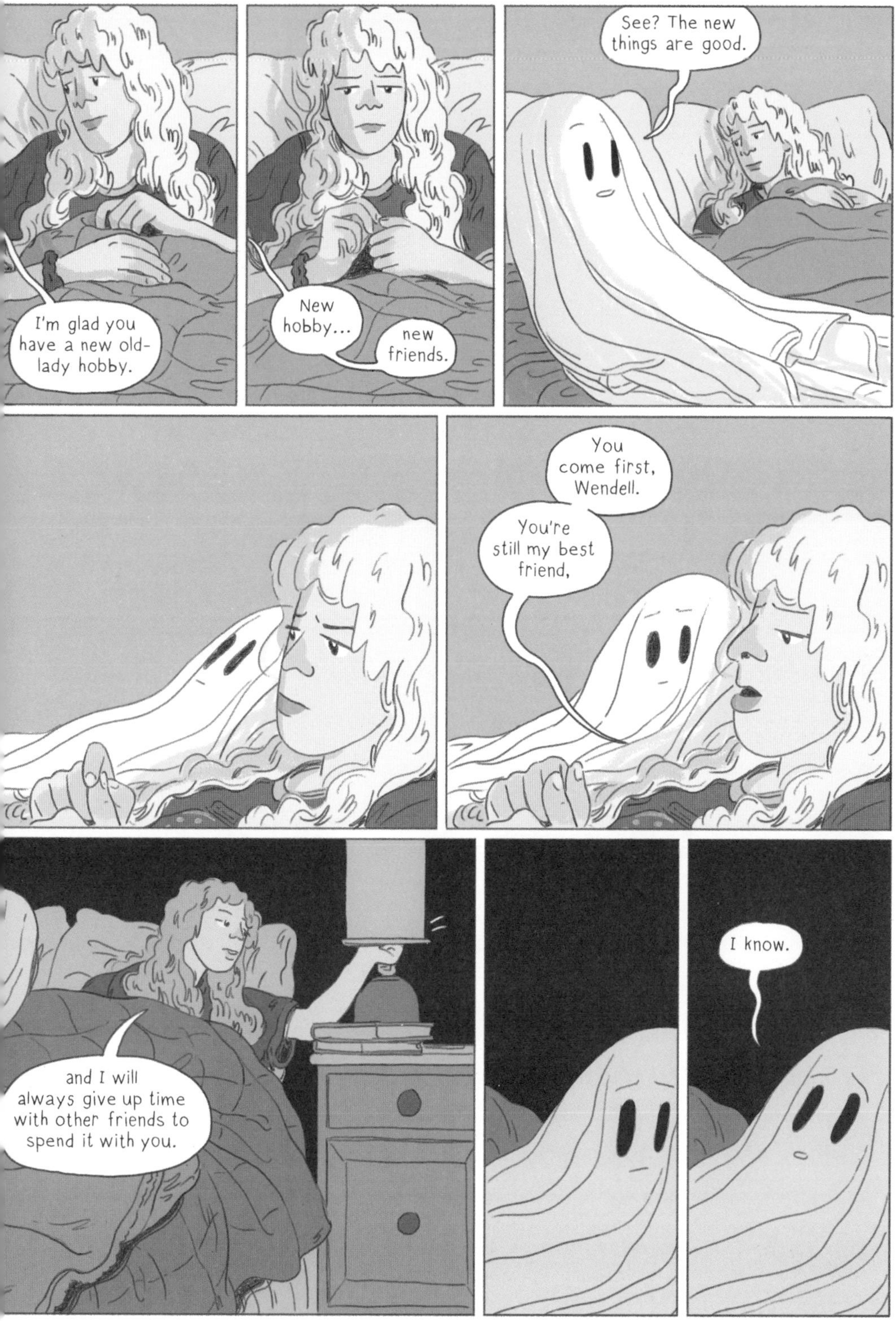
I'm glad you have a new old-lady hobby.
New hobby...
new friends.
See? The new things are good.
You come first, Wendell.
You're still my best friend,
and I will always give up time with other friends to spend it with you.
I know.

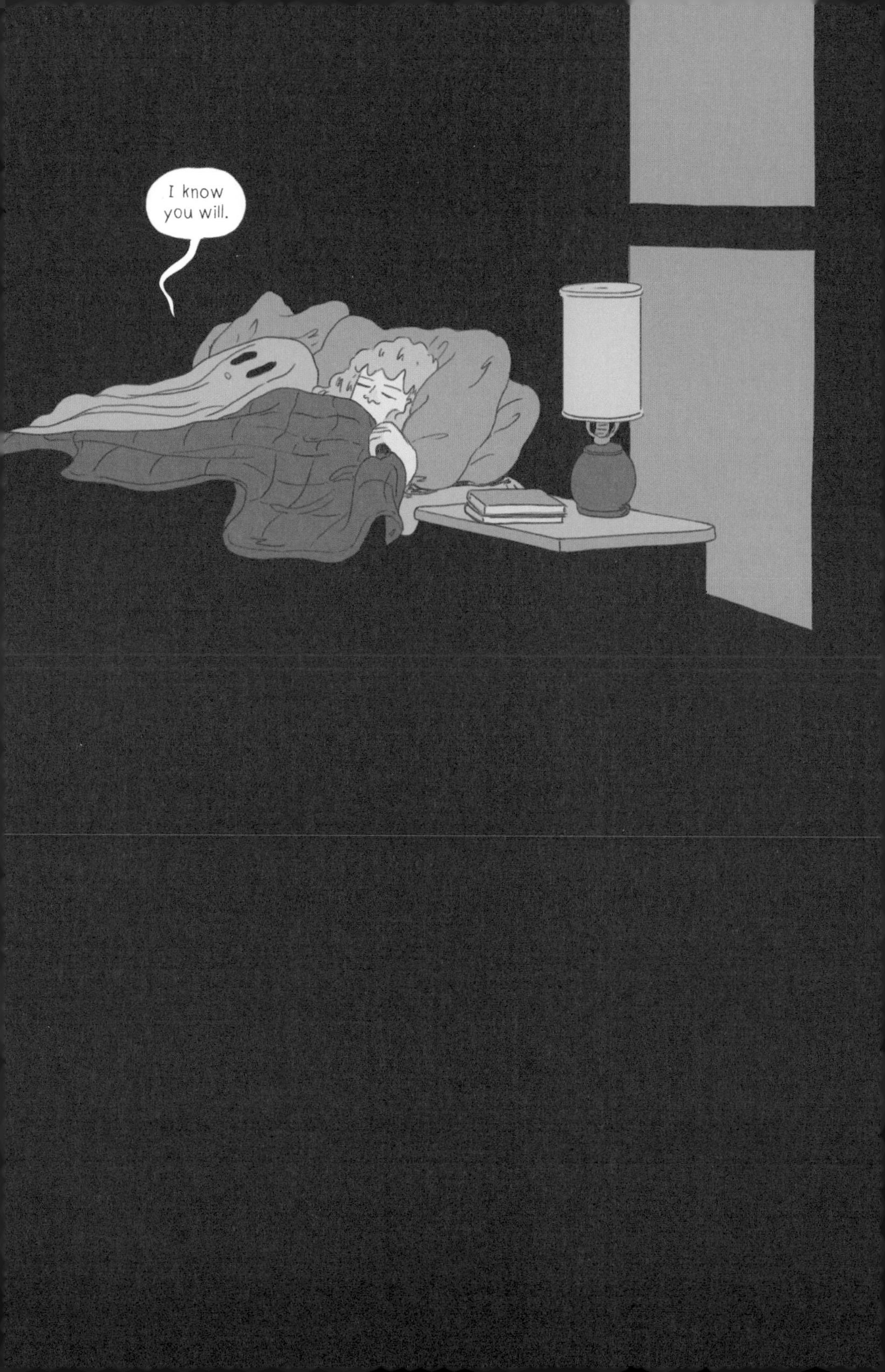
I know you will.

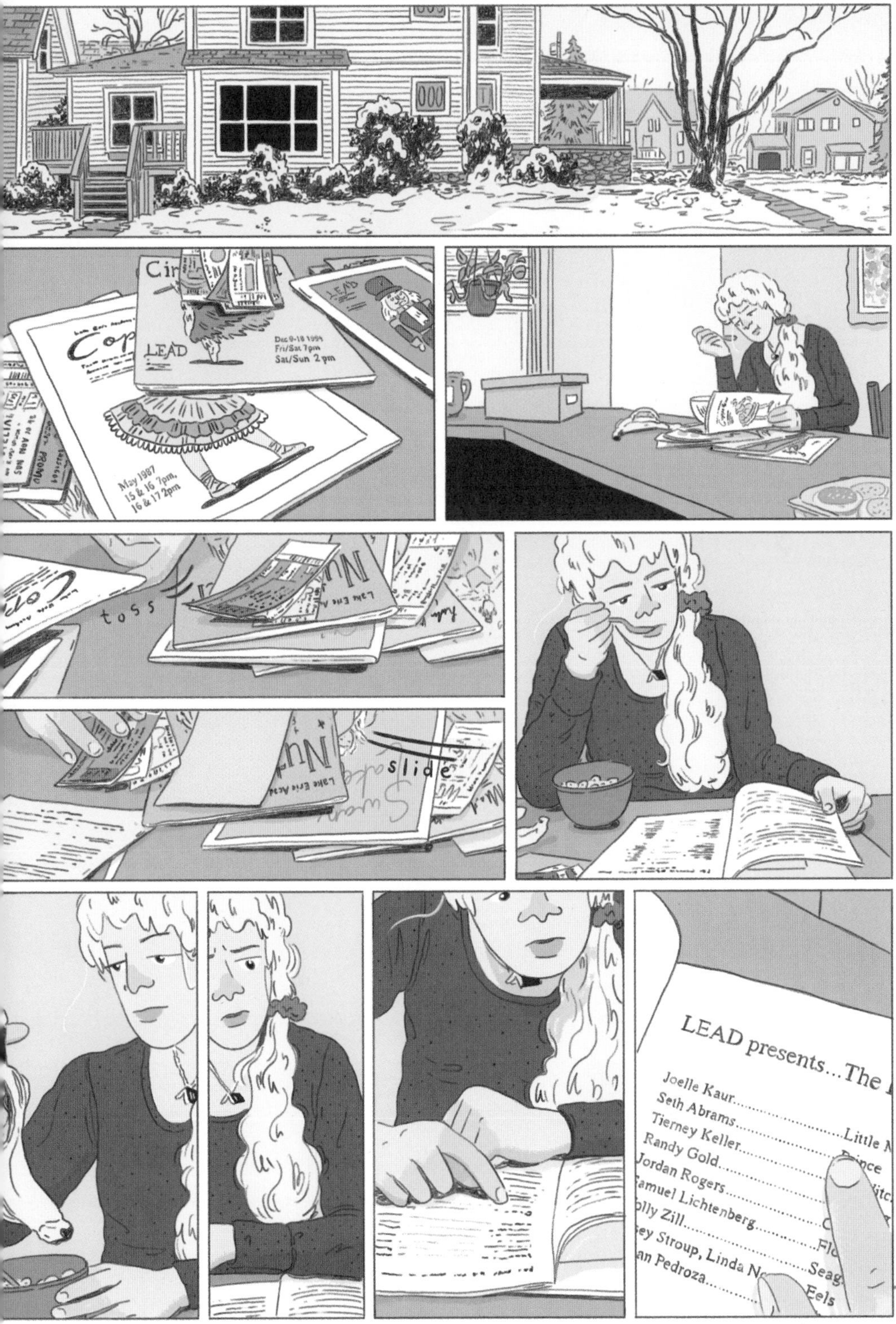
LEAD
Dec 9-18 1994
Fri/Sat 7pm
Sat/Sun 2pm
May 1987
15 & 16 7pm,
16 & 17 2pm
toss
slide
LEAD presents...The
Joelle Kaur
Seth Abrams.....Little
Tierney Keller
Randy Gold
Jordan Rogers
amuel Lichtenberg
lly Zill
ey Stroup, Linda N
an Pedroza.....Eels

Mrs. Kaur? It's Marjorie,
Can I talk to Sasha, please?
Hi!
Hey, you said your sister is in town, right?
I had some questions about high school stuff,
and I thought maybe I could ask her.
Joelle Kaur
Seth Abrams
Tierney Keller
Randy Gold
Jorden Rogers
Samuel Lichtenberg
Holly Zill
Casey Stroup, Linda Nix
Eels
Morgan Pedroza
Chef
Mersisters: Bethany Abbot, Kylie Anderson, Wanda Ellis, Emily Karson, Anne Patrick, Jenna Yan
Sailors: Mary Dalco, Megan Hutchins, Sara Johnson, Lin Liev, Teresa Nicholson, Dina Nuen, Shari Parker, Harriet Pond, Lisa Rogers, Marissa Stevens, Eva Tyler, Becca Underhill, Nina Walter

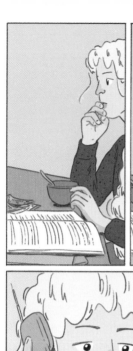

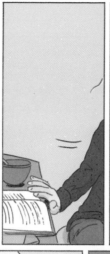

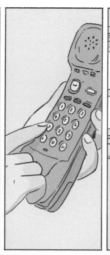

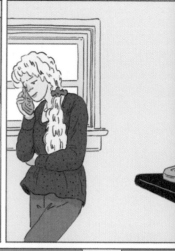

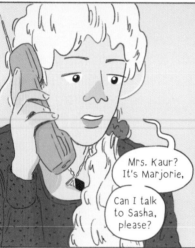

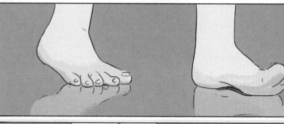

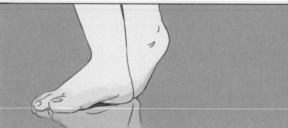

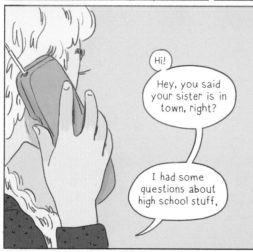

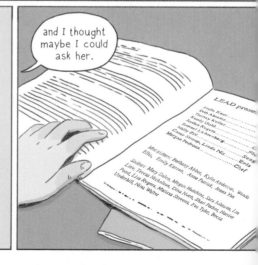

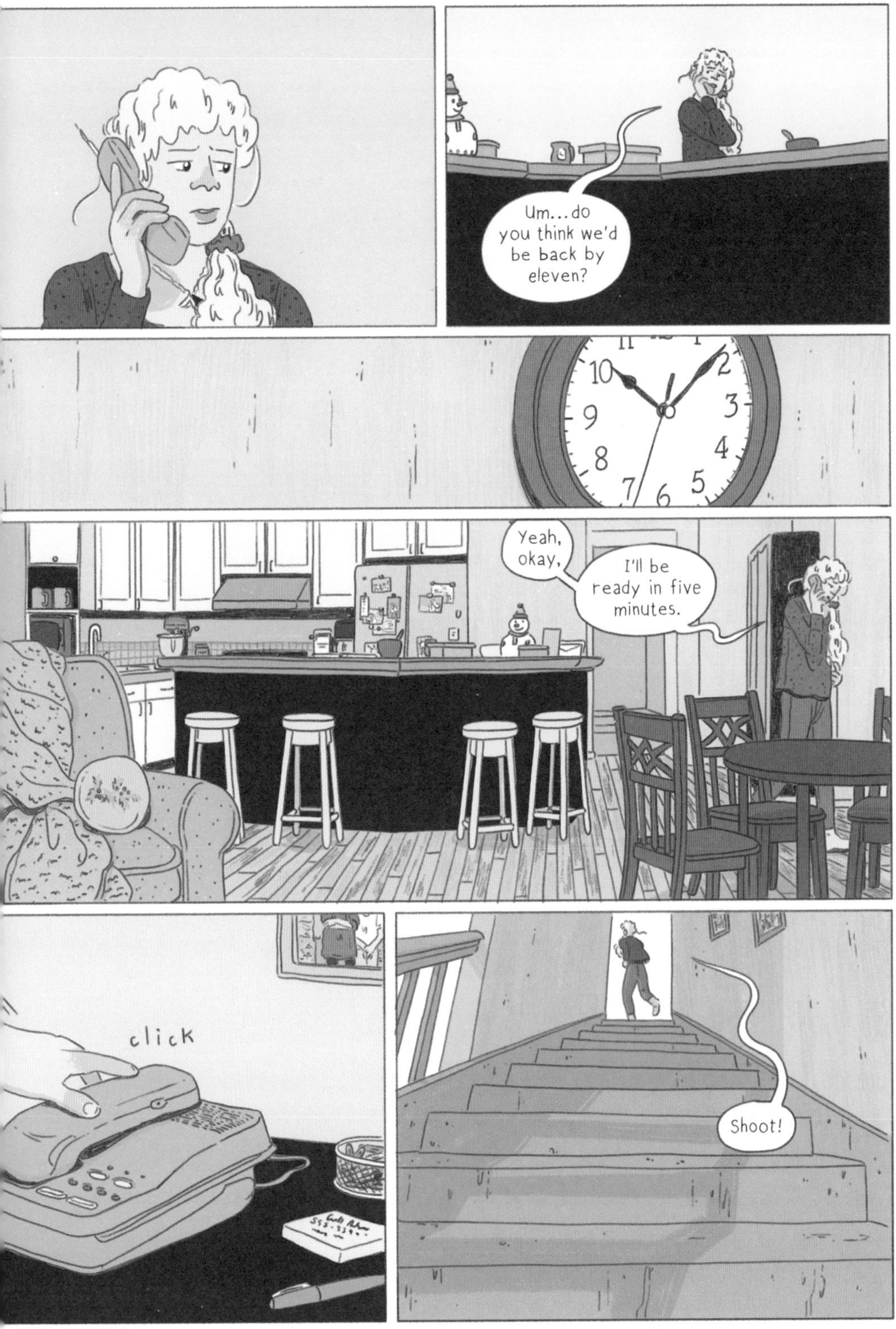
Um...do you think we'd be back by eleven?
Yeah, okay,
I'll be ready in five minutes.
click
Shoot!

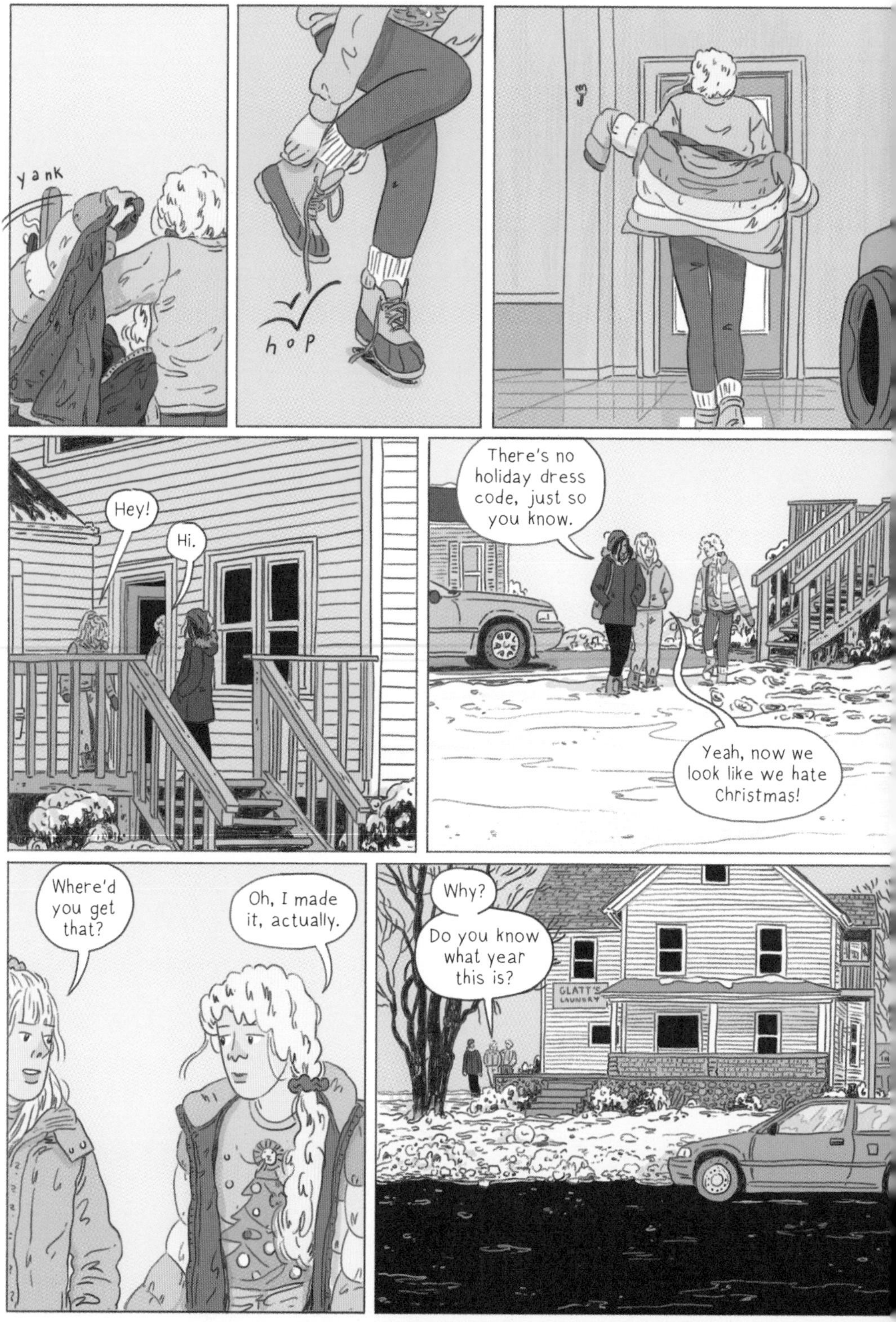
yank
hop
Hey!
Hi.
There's no holiday dress code, just so you know.
Yeah, now we look like we hate Christmas!
Where'd you get that?
Oh, I made it, actually.
Why?
Do you know what year this is?
GLATT'S LAUNDRY

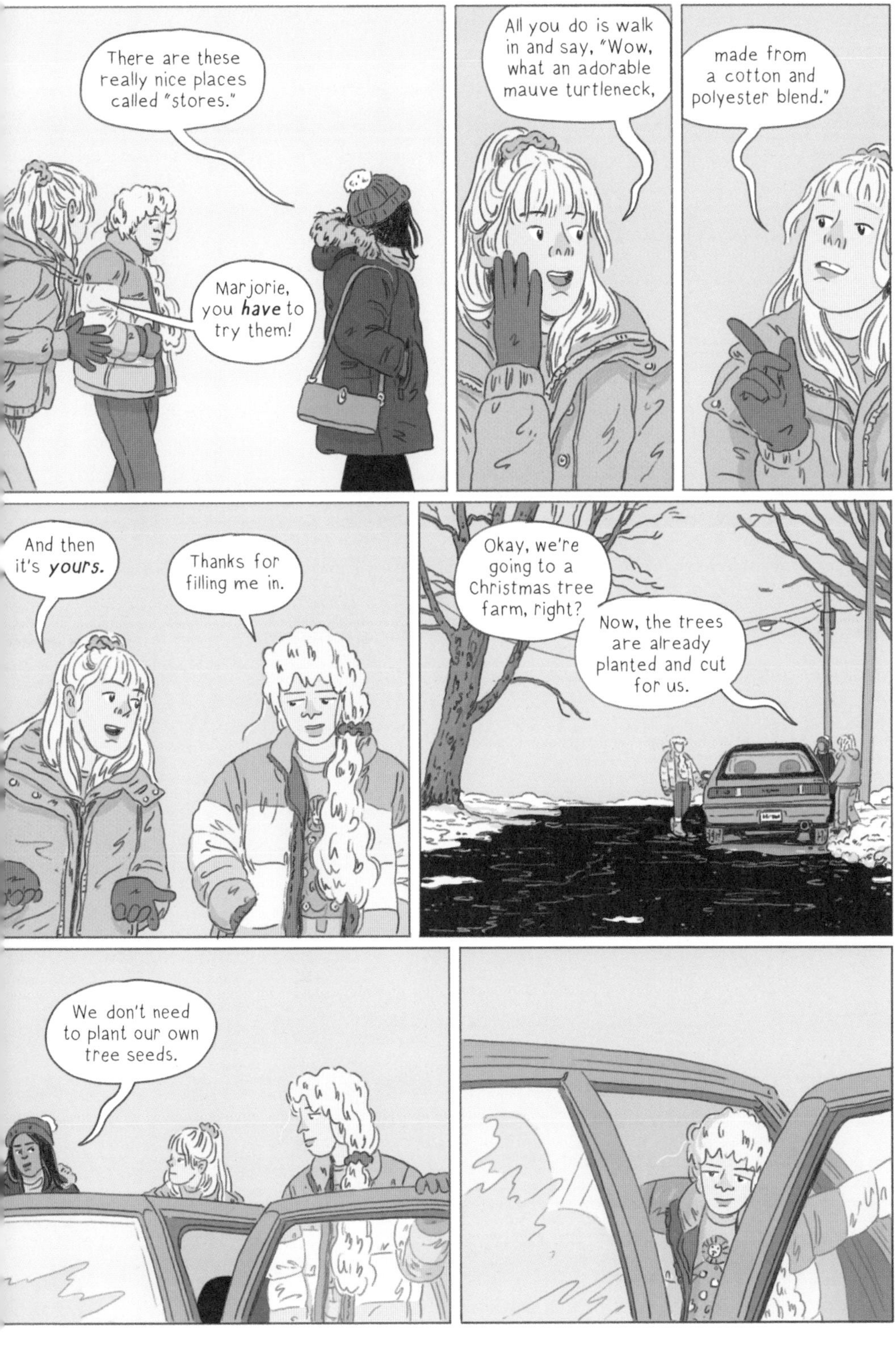
There are these really nice places called "stores."
Marjorie, you *have* to try them!
All you do is walk in and say, "Wow, what an adorable mauve turtleneck,
made from a cotton and polyester blend."
And then it's *yours.*
Thanks for filling me in.
Okay, we're going to a Christmas tree farm, right?
Now, the trees are already planted and cut for us.
We don't need to plant our own tree seeds.

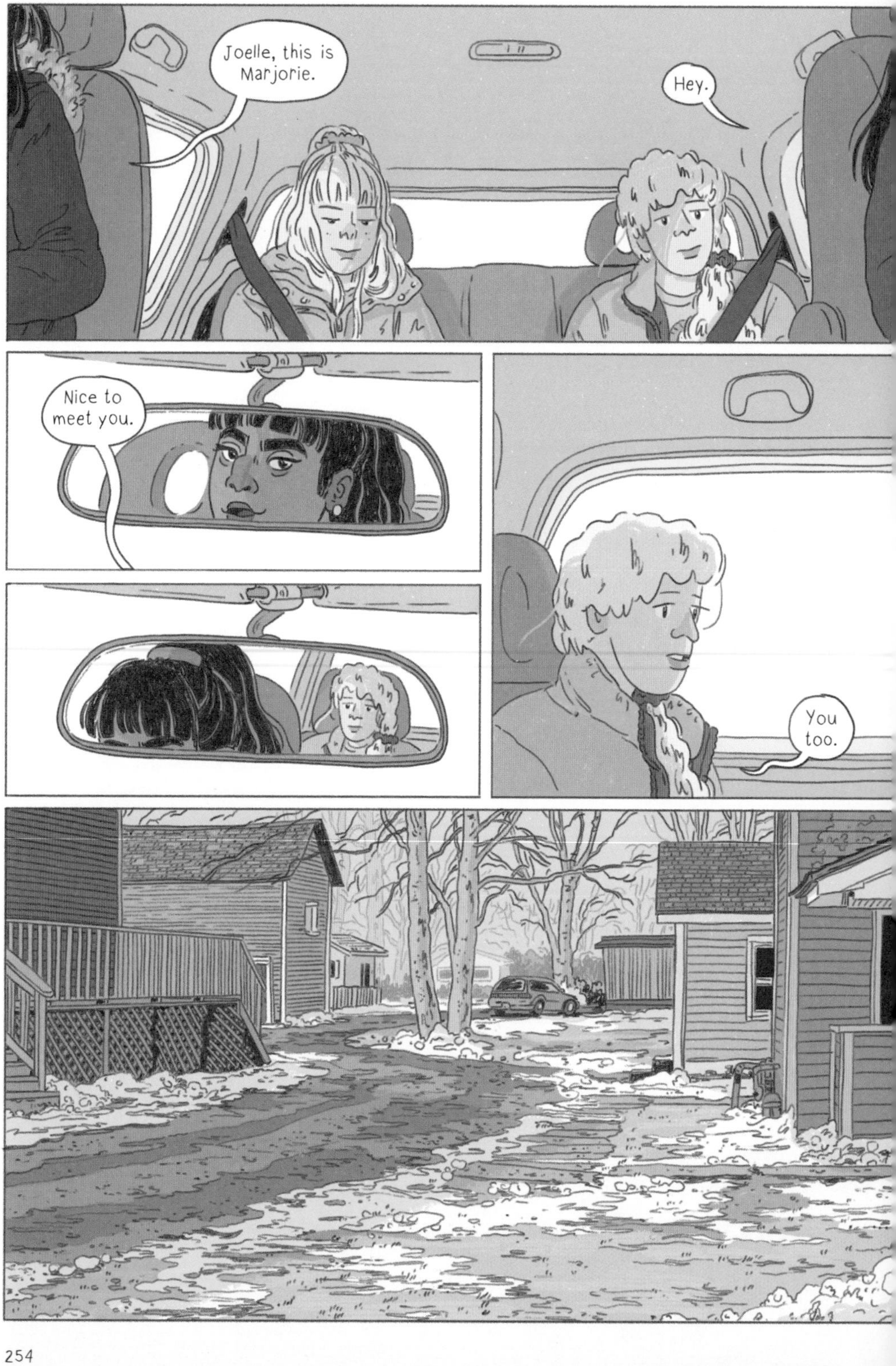
Joelle, this is Marjorie.
Hey.
Nice to meet you.
You too.

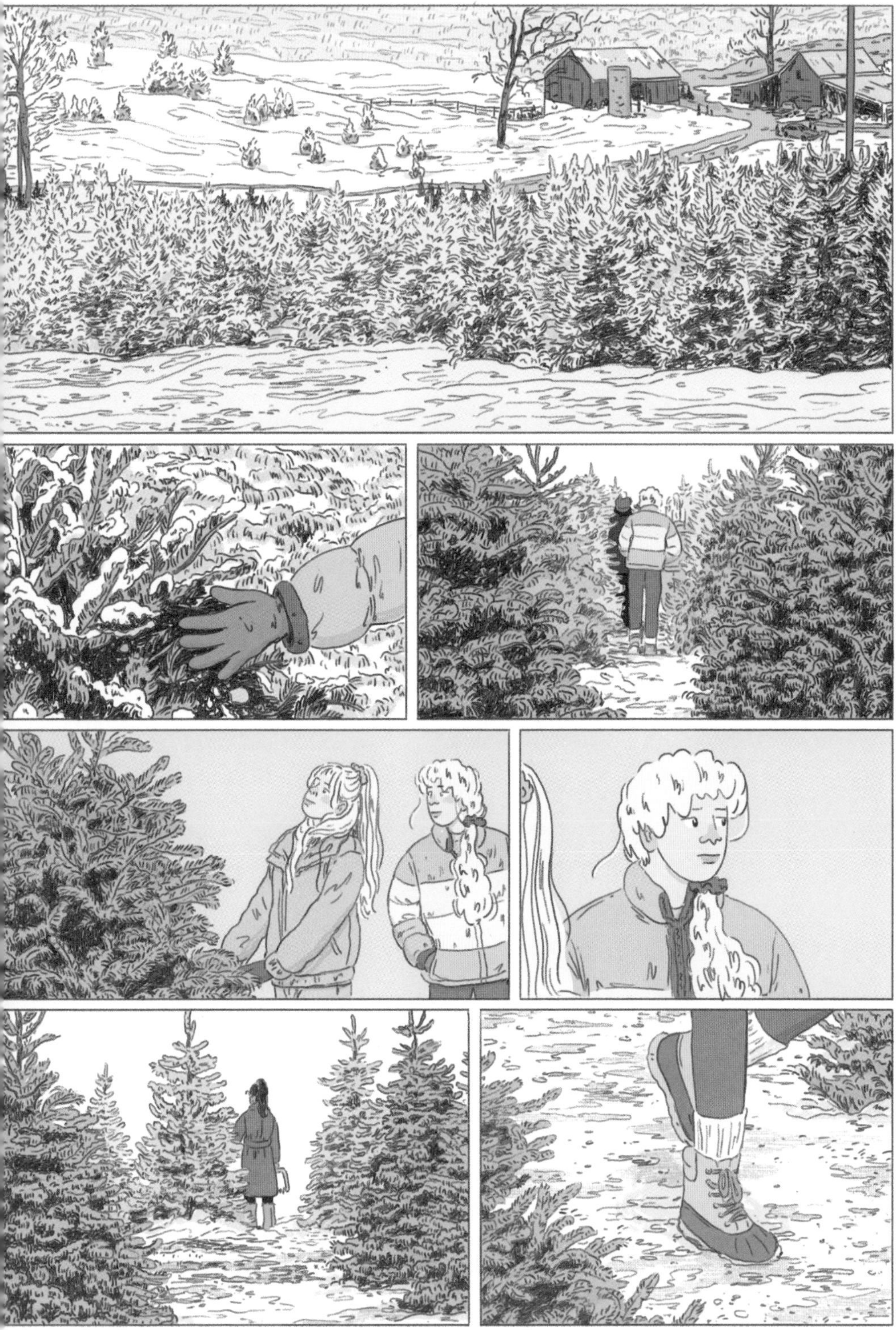

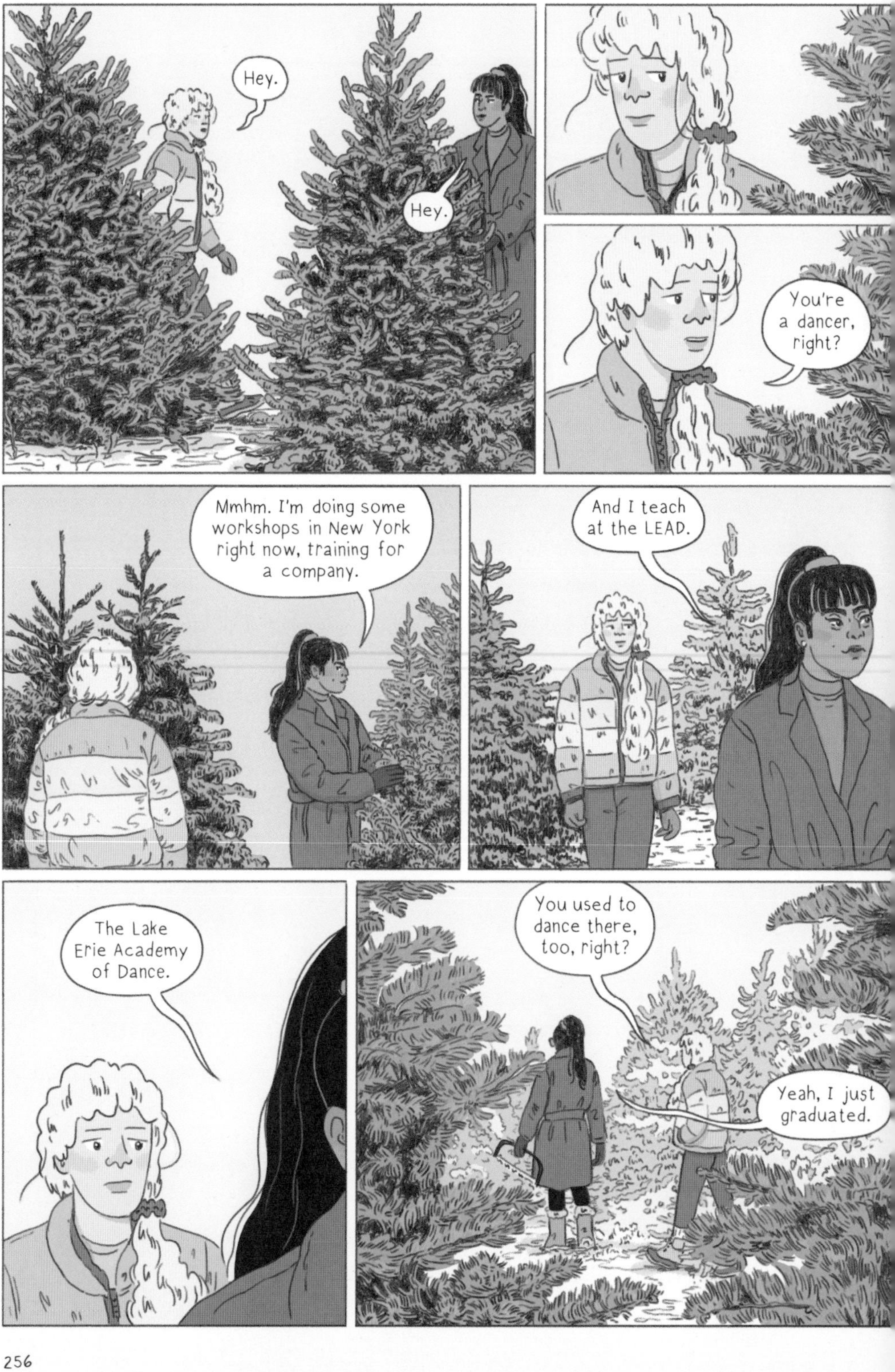
Hey.
Hey.
You're a dancer, right?
Mmhm. I'm doing some workshops in New York right now, training for a company.
And I teach at the LEAD.
The Lake Erie Academy of Dance.
You used to dance there, too, right?
Yeah, I just graduated.

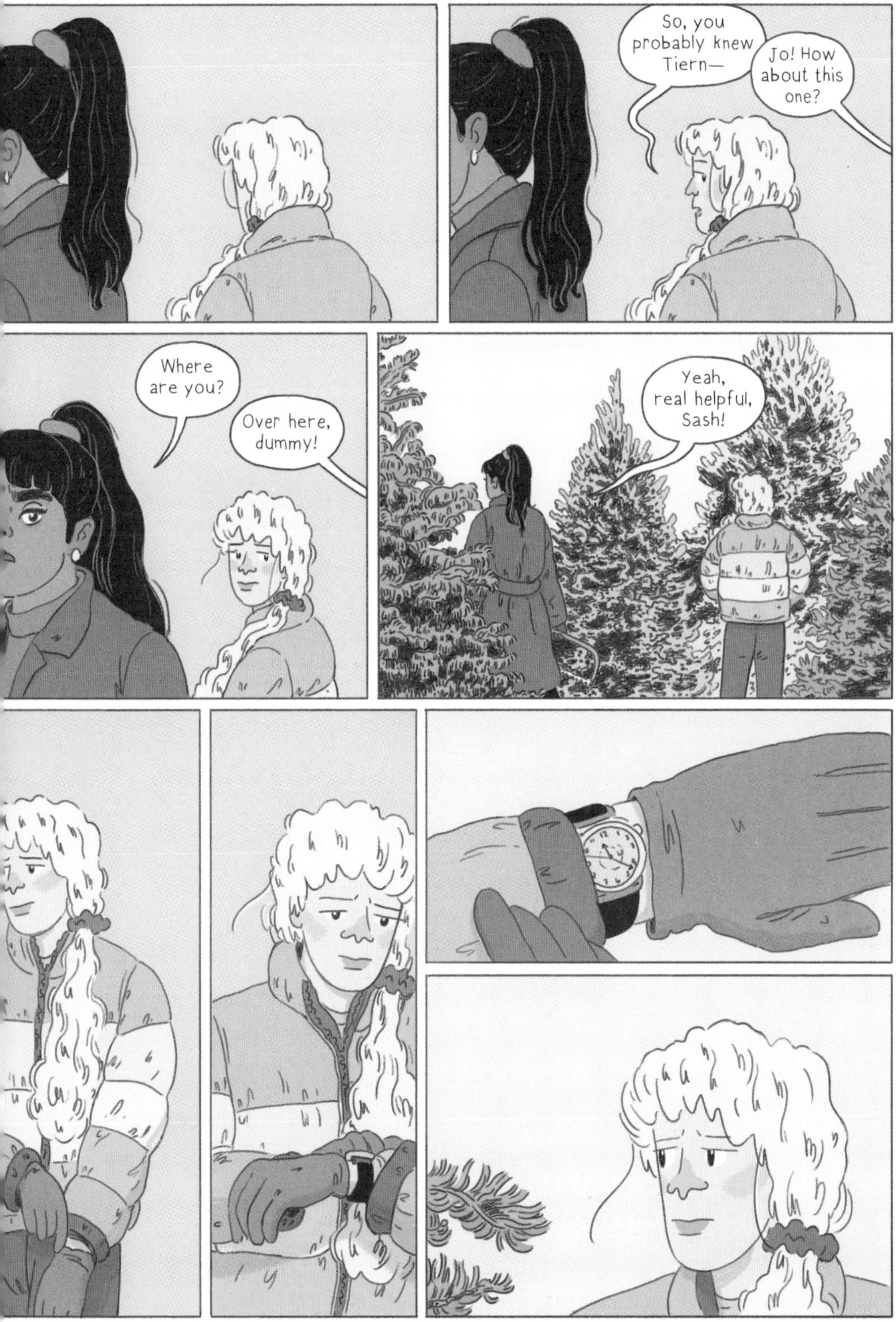

So, you probably knew Tiern—
Jo! How about this one?
Where are you?
Over here, dummy!
Yeah, real helpful, Sash!

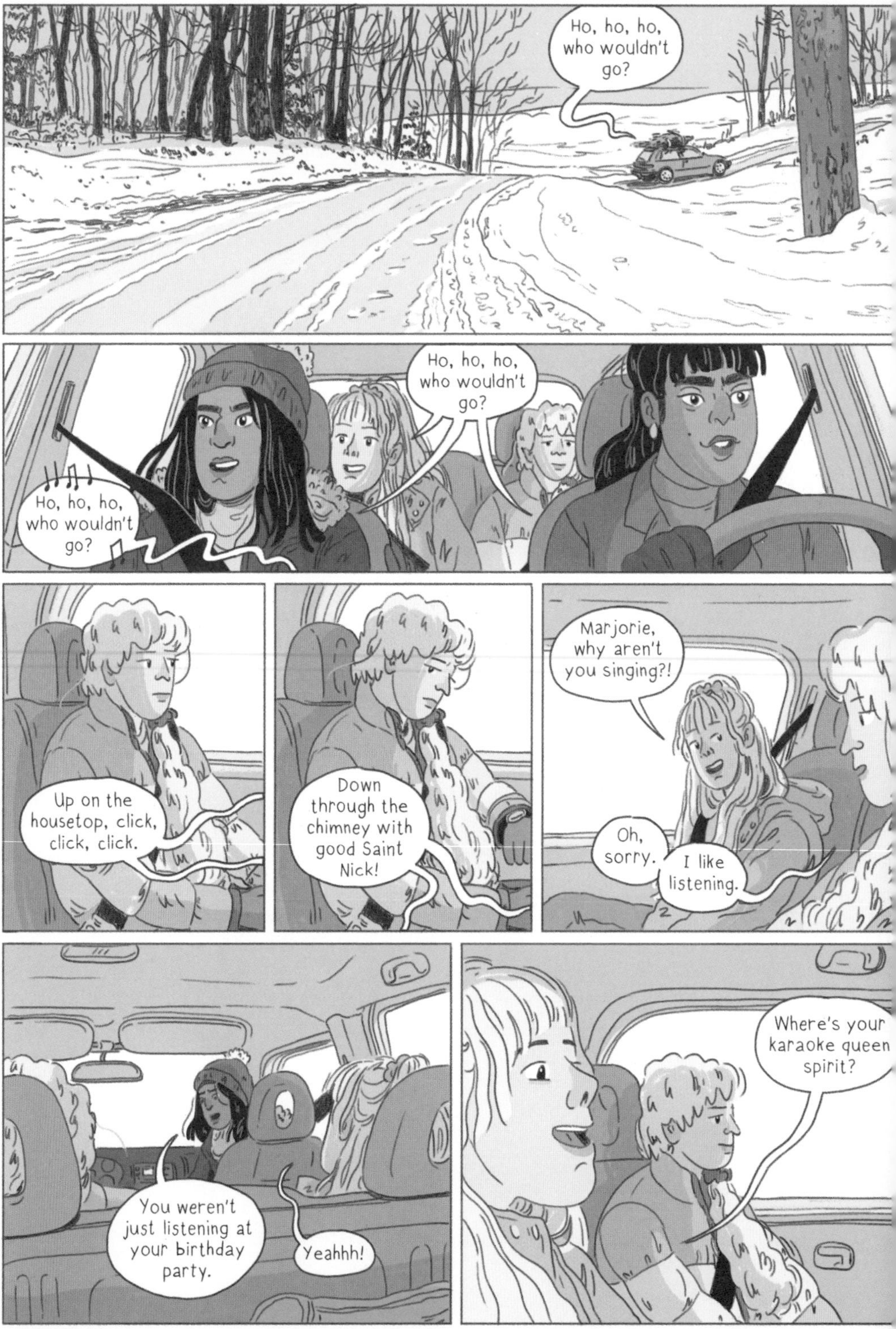
Ho, ho, ho, who wouldn't go?
Ho, ho, ho, who wouldn't go?
Ho, ho, ho, who wouldn't go?
Up on the housetop, click, click, click.
Down through the chimney with good Saint Nick!
Marjorie, why aren't you singing?!
Oh, sorry.
I like listening.
You weren't just listening at your birthday party.
Yeahhh!
Where's your karaoke queen spirit?

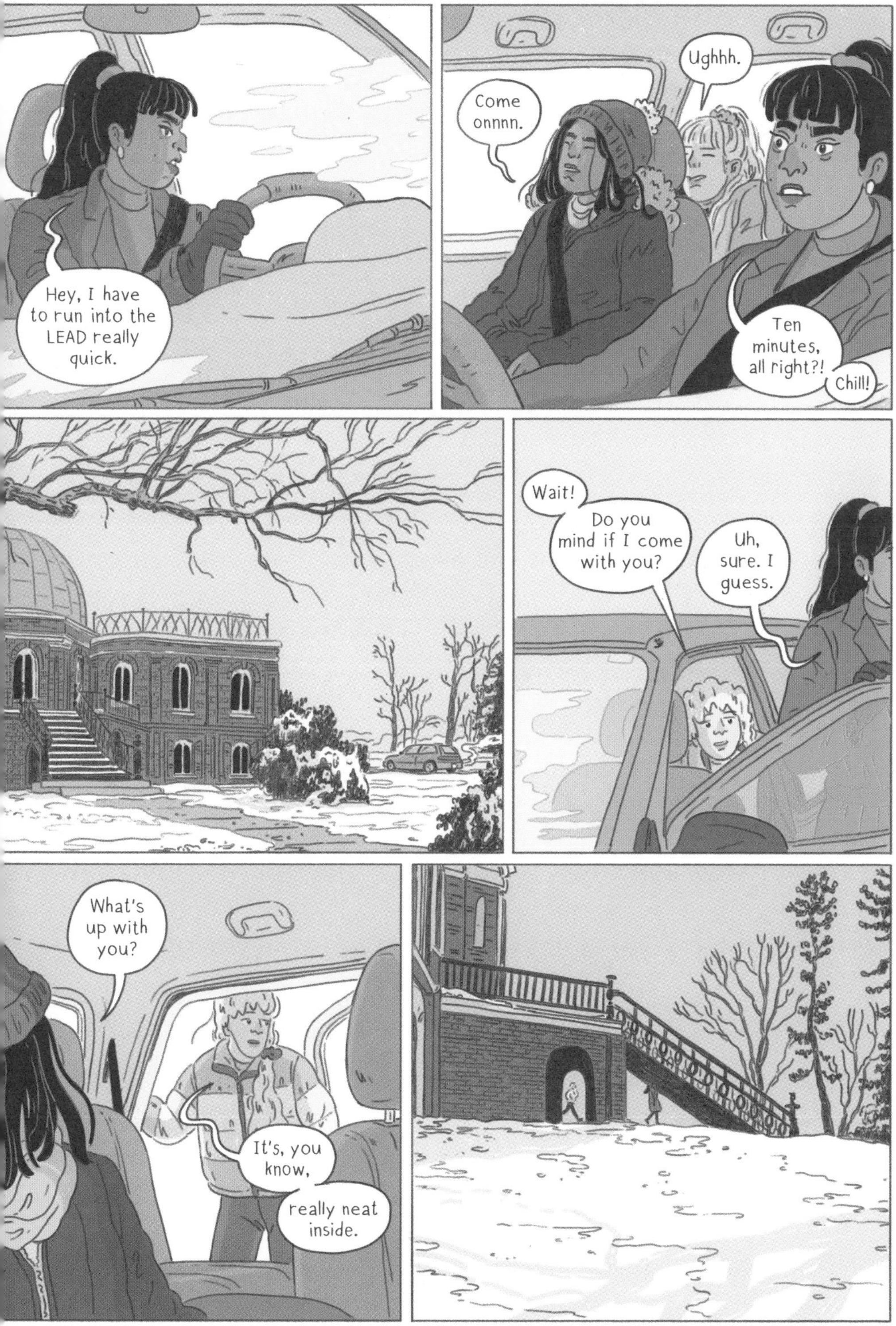
Hey, I have to run into the LEAD really quick.
Come onnnn.
Ughhh.
Ten minutes, all right?!
Chill!
Wait!
Do you mind if I come with you?
Uh, sure. I guess.
What's up with you?
It's, you know,
really neat inside.

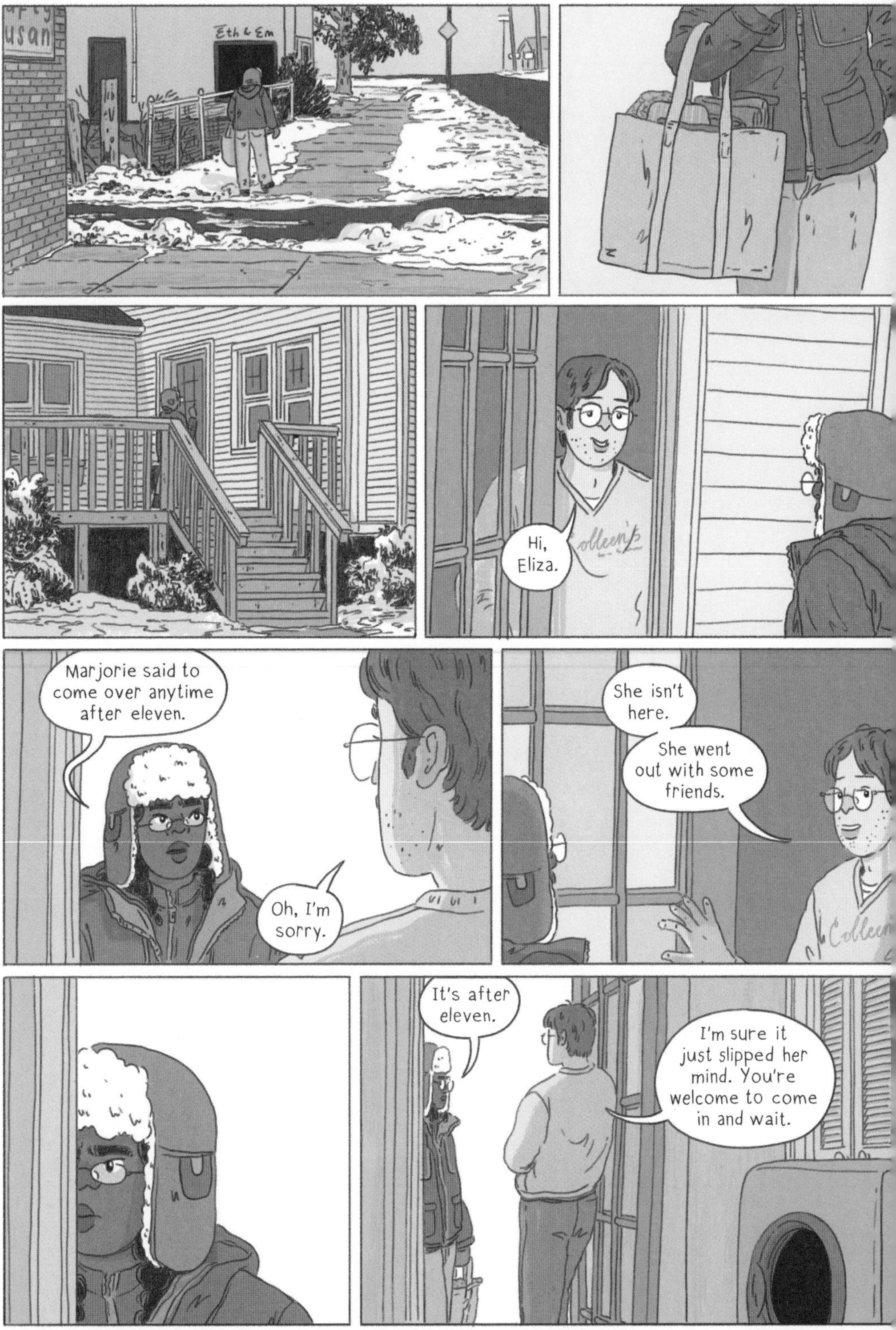

Eth & Em
Hi, Eliza.
Colleen's
Marjorie said to come over anytime after eleven.
Oh, I'm sorry.
She isn't here.
She went out with some friends.
It's after eleven.
I'm sure it just slipped her mind. You're welcome to come in and wait.

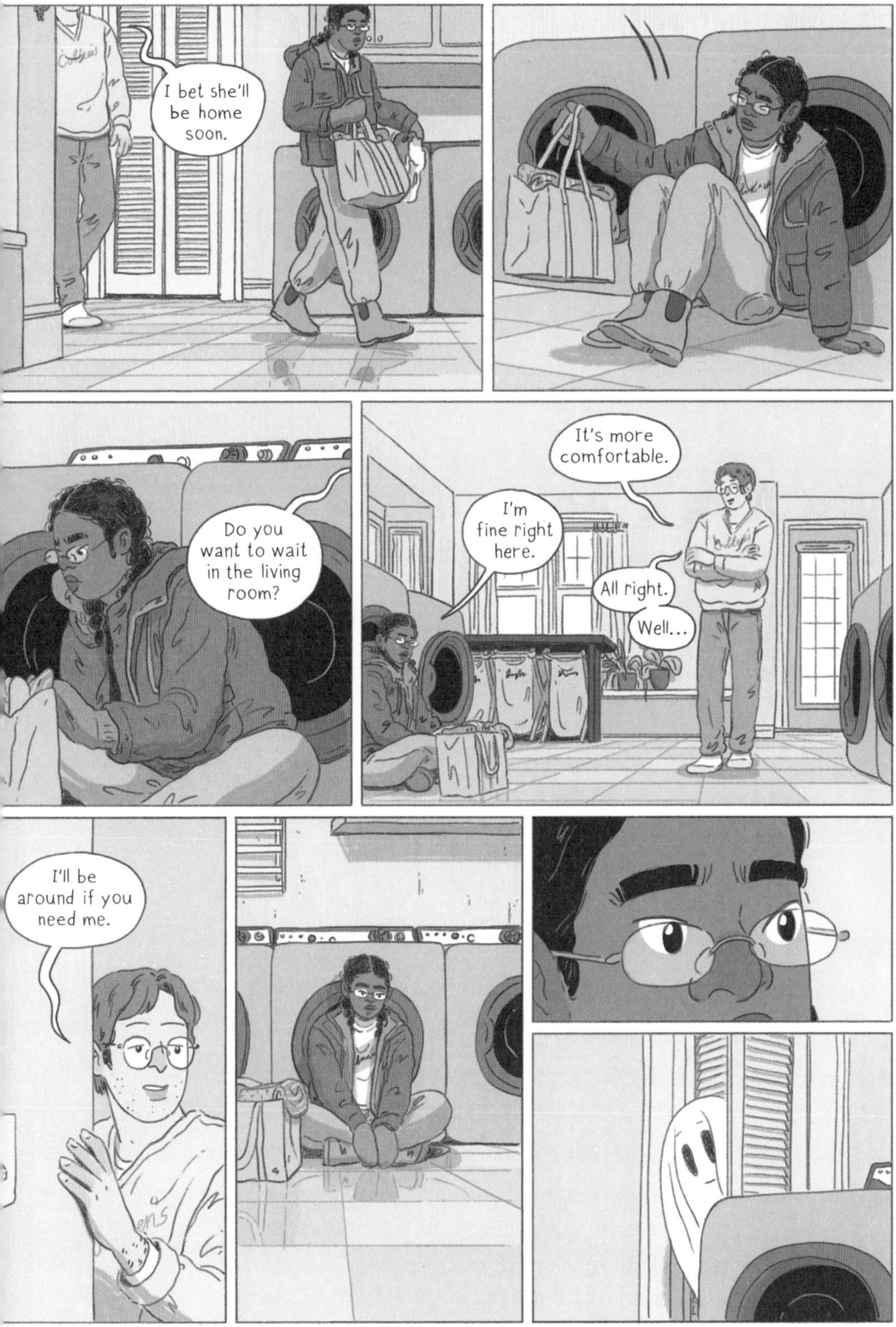
I bet she'll be home soon.
Do you want to wait in the living room?
It's more comfortable.
I'm fine right here.
All right.
Well...
I'll be around if you need me.

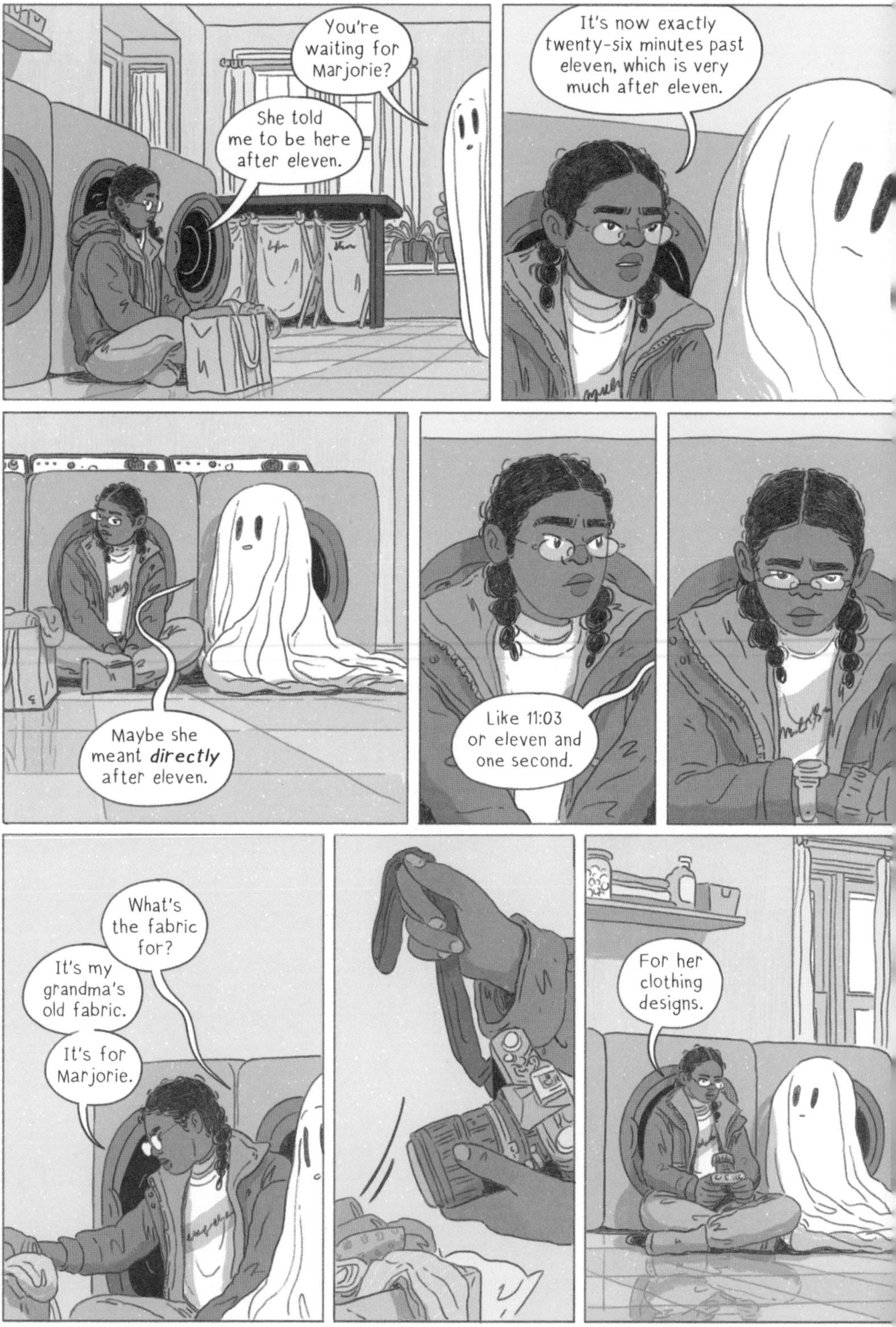
You're waiting for Marjorie?
She told me to be here after eleven.
It's now exactly twenty-six minutes past eleven, which is very much after eleven.
Maybe she meant **directly** after eleven.
Like 11:03 or eleven and one second.
What's the fabric for?
It's my grandma's old fabric.
It's for Marjorie.
For her clothing designs.

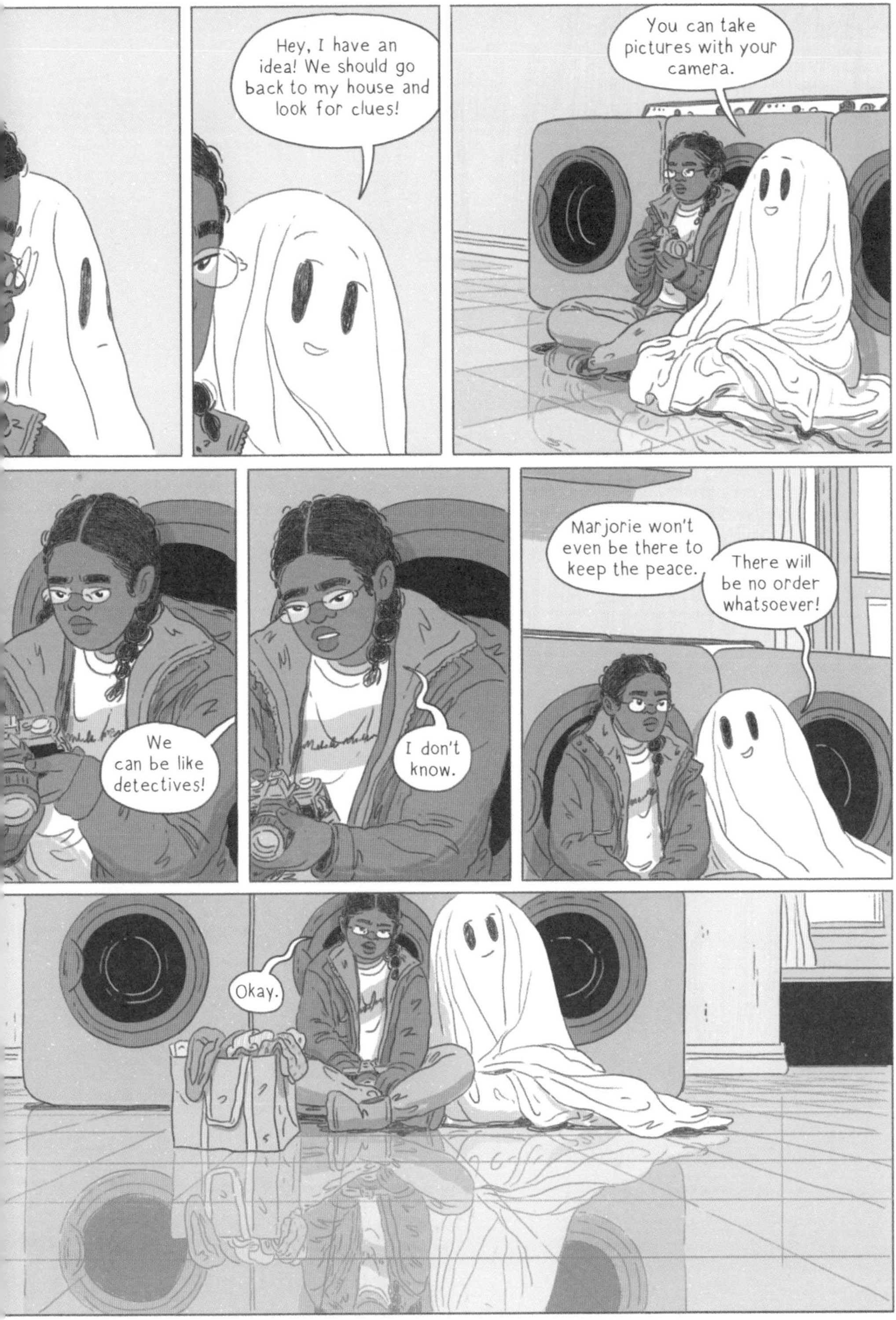
Hey, I have an idea! We should go back to my house and look for clues!
You can take pictures with your camera.
We can be like detectives!
I don't know.
Marjorie won't even be there to keep the peace.
There will be no order whatsoever!
Okay.

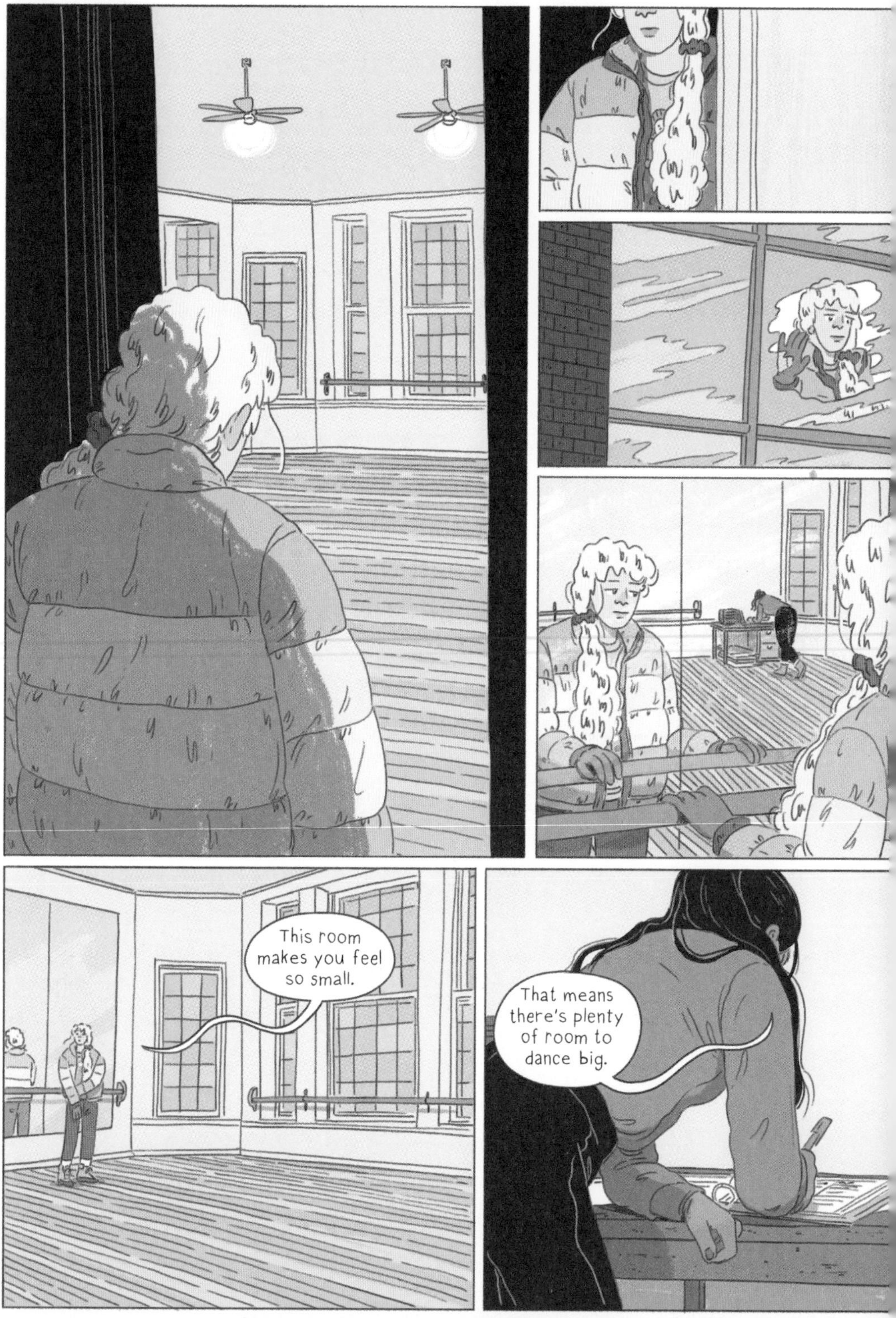
This room makes you feel so small.
That means there's plenty of room to dance big.

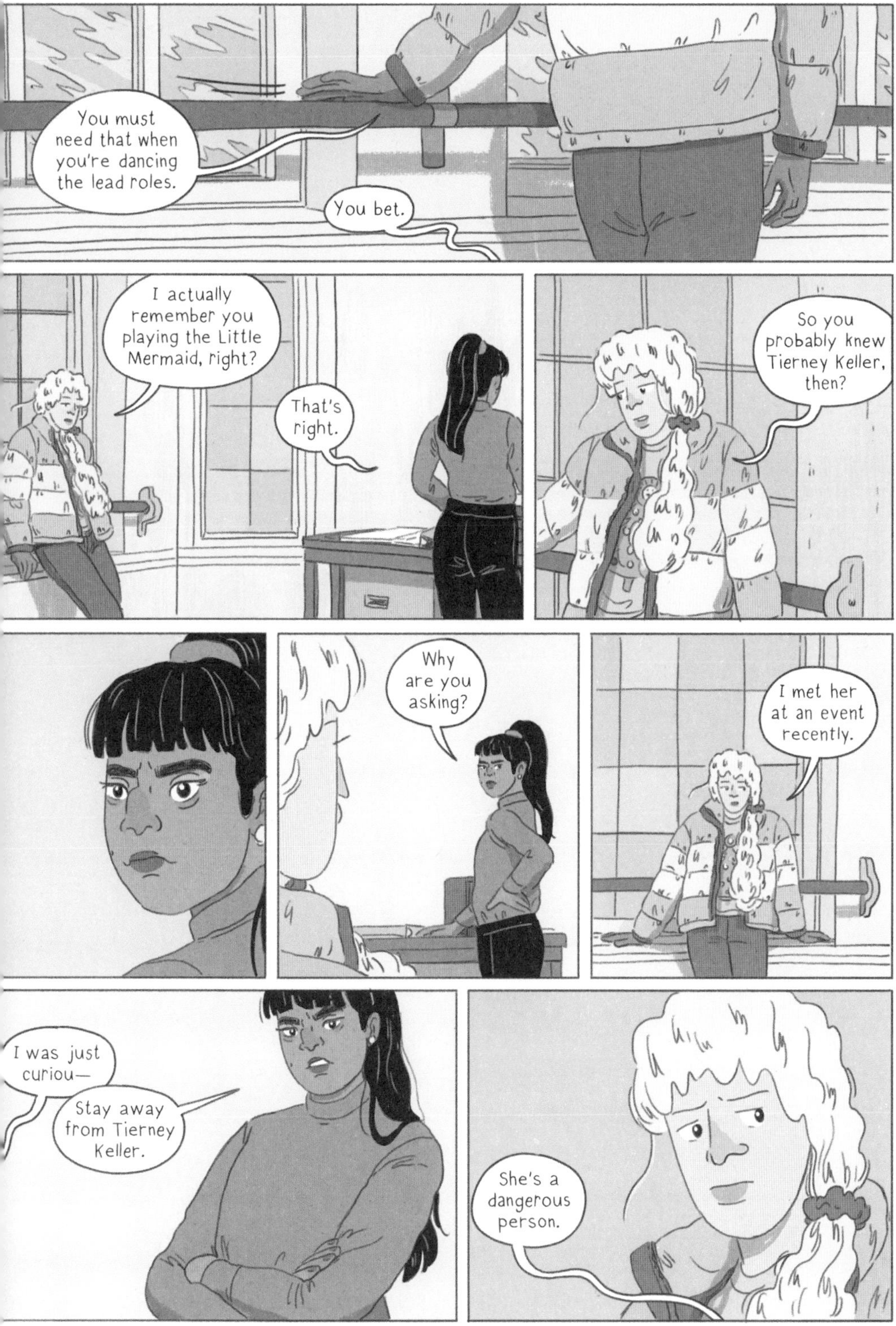
You must need that when you're dancing the lead roles.
You bet.
I actually remember you playing the Little Mermaid, right?
That's right.
So you probably knew Tierney Keller, then?
Why are you asking?
I met her at an event recently.
I was just curiou—
Stay away from Tierney Keller.
She's a dangerous person.

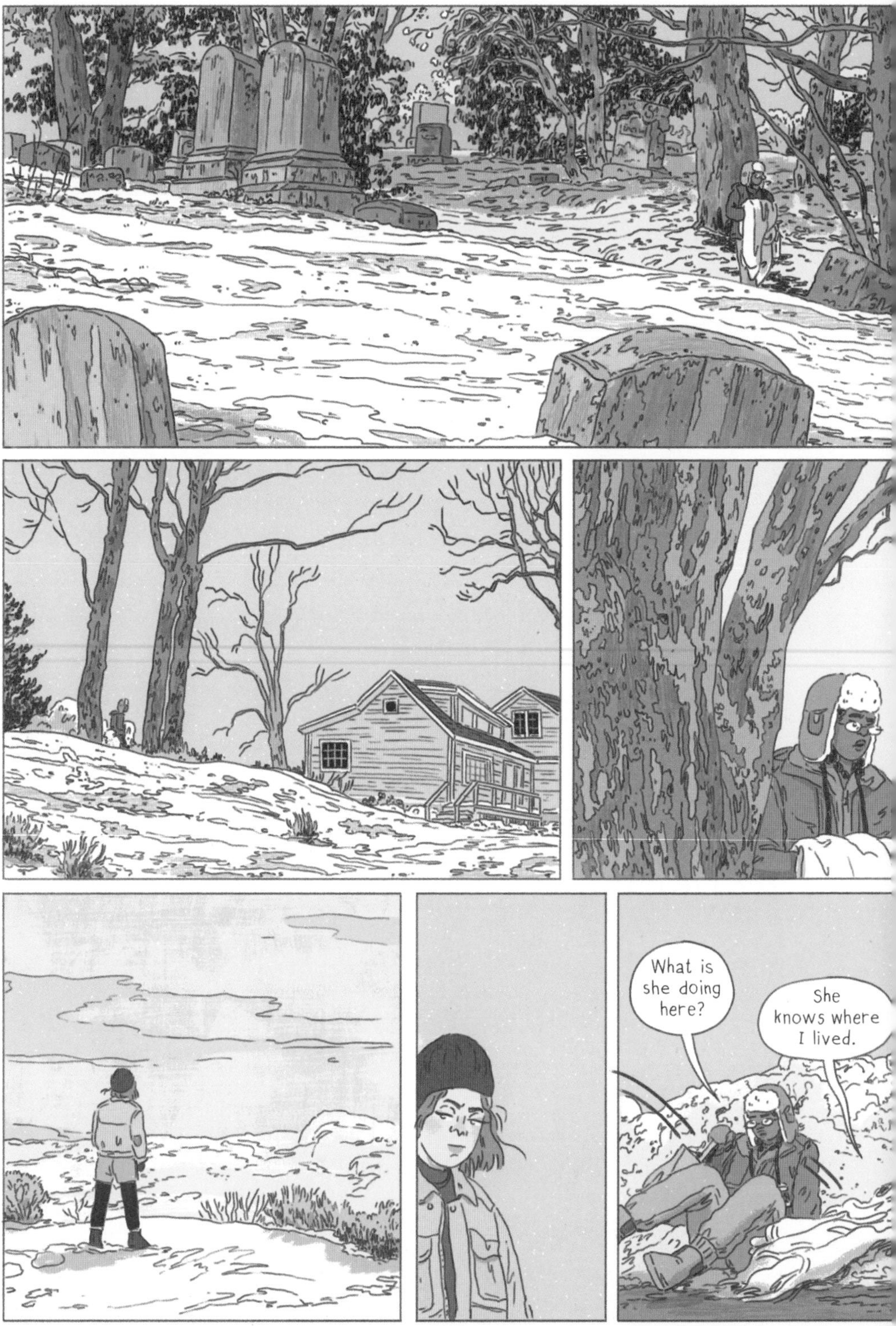
What is she doing here?
She knows where I lived.

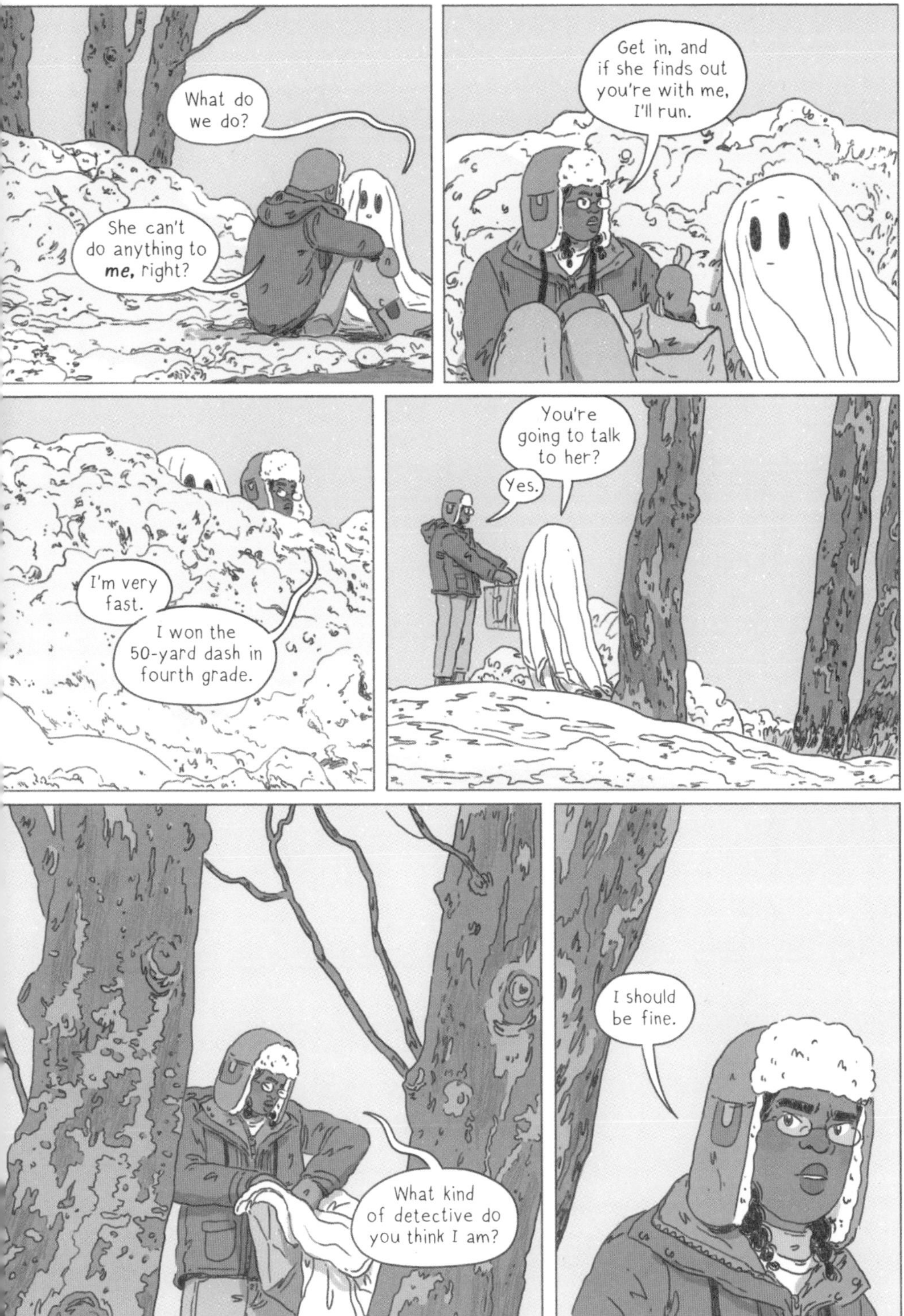
What do we do?
She can't do anything to **me,** right?
Get in, and if she finds out you're with me, I'll run.
I'm very fast.
I won the 50-yard dash in fourth grade.
You're going to talk to her?
Yes.
What kind of detective do you think I am?
I should be fine.

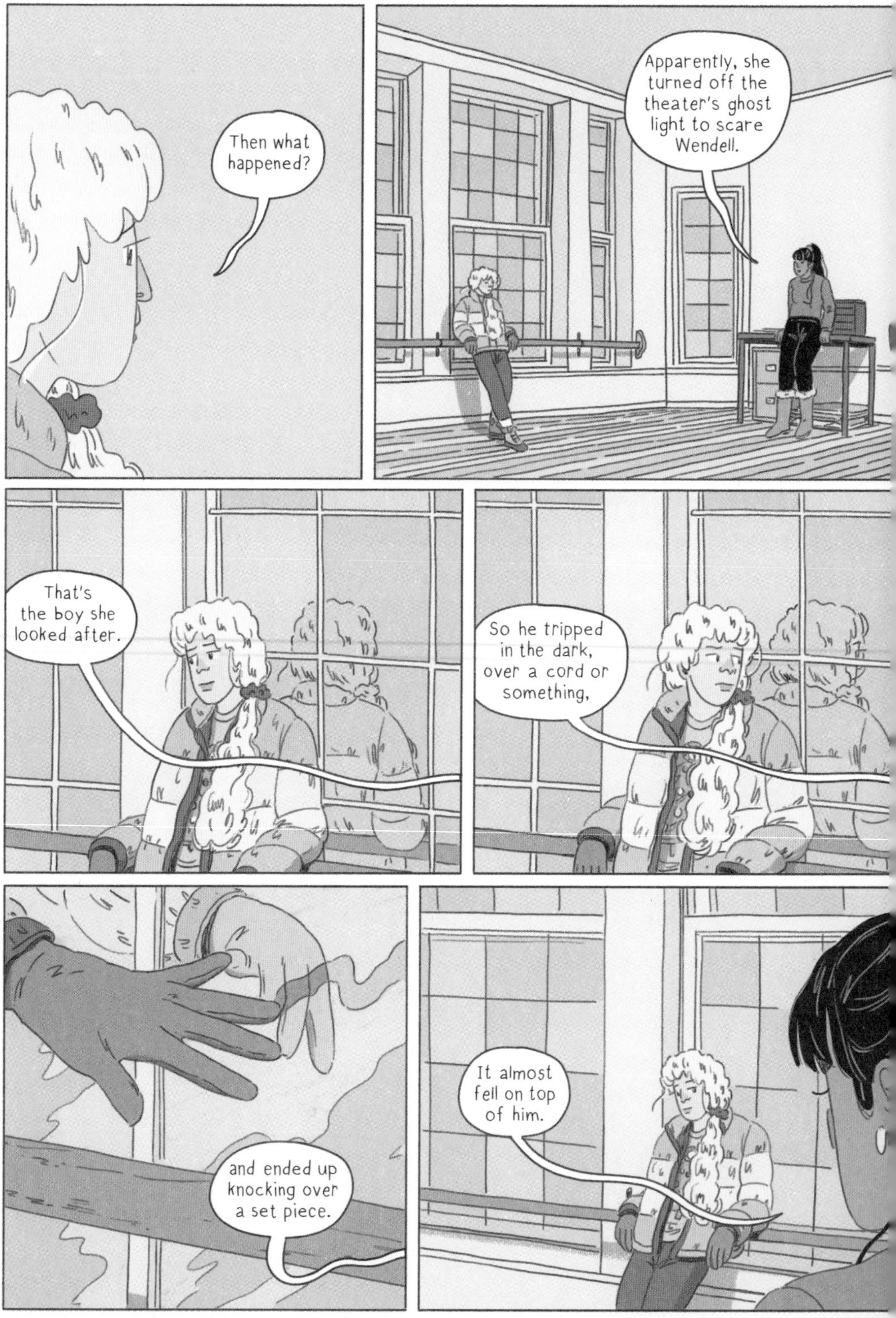

Then what happened?
Apparently, she turned off the theater's ghost light to scare Wendell.
That's the boy she looked after.
So he tripped in the dark, over a cord or something,
and ended up knocking over a set piece.
It almost fell on top of him.

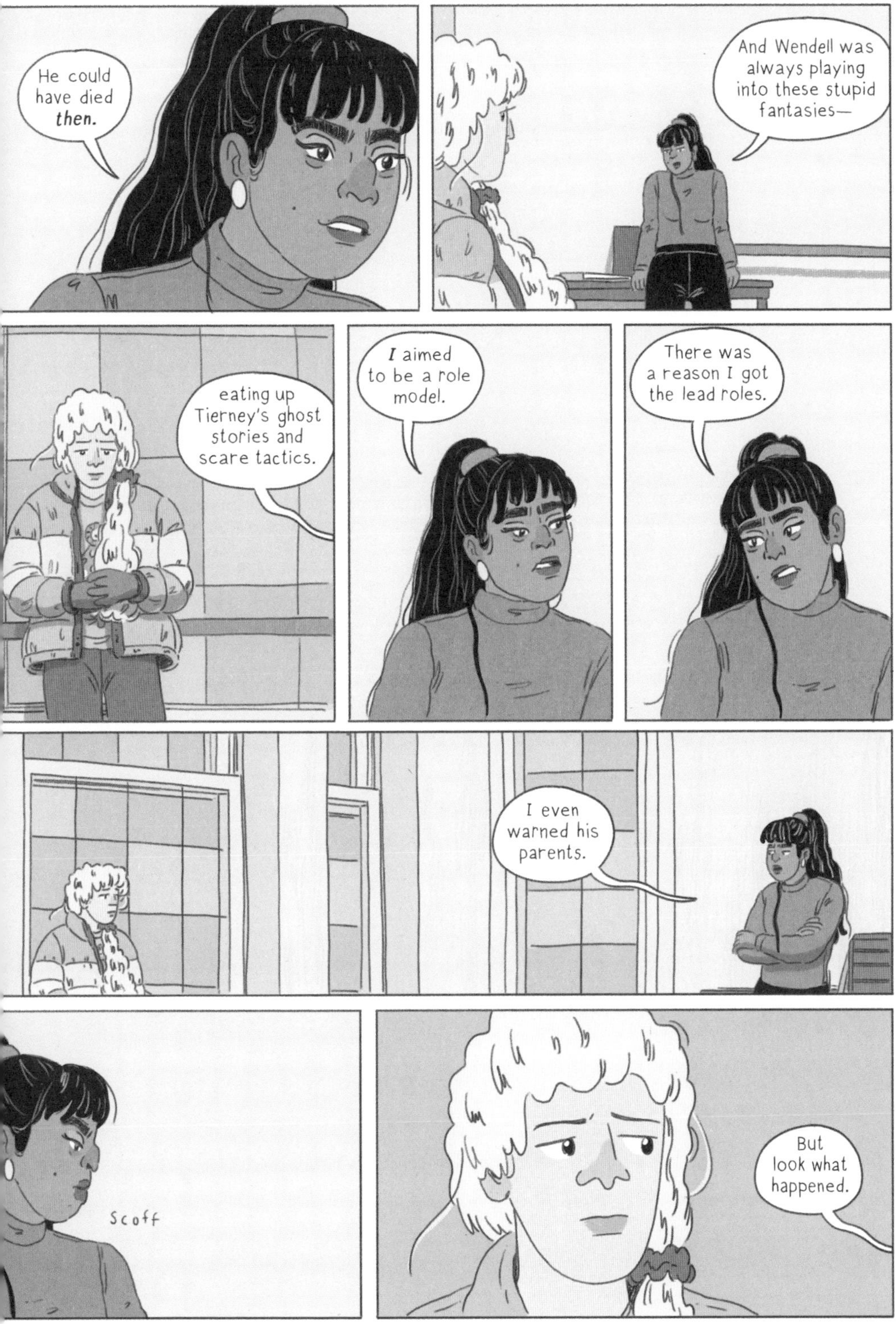
He could have died *then.*
And Wendell was always playing into these stupid fantasies—
eating up Tierney's ghost stories and scare tactics.
I aimed to be a role model.
There was a reason I got the lead roles.
I even warned his parents.
Scoff
But look what happened.

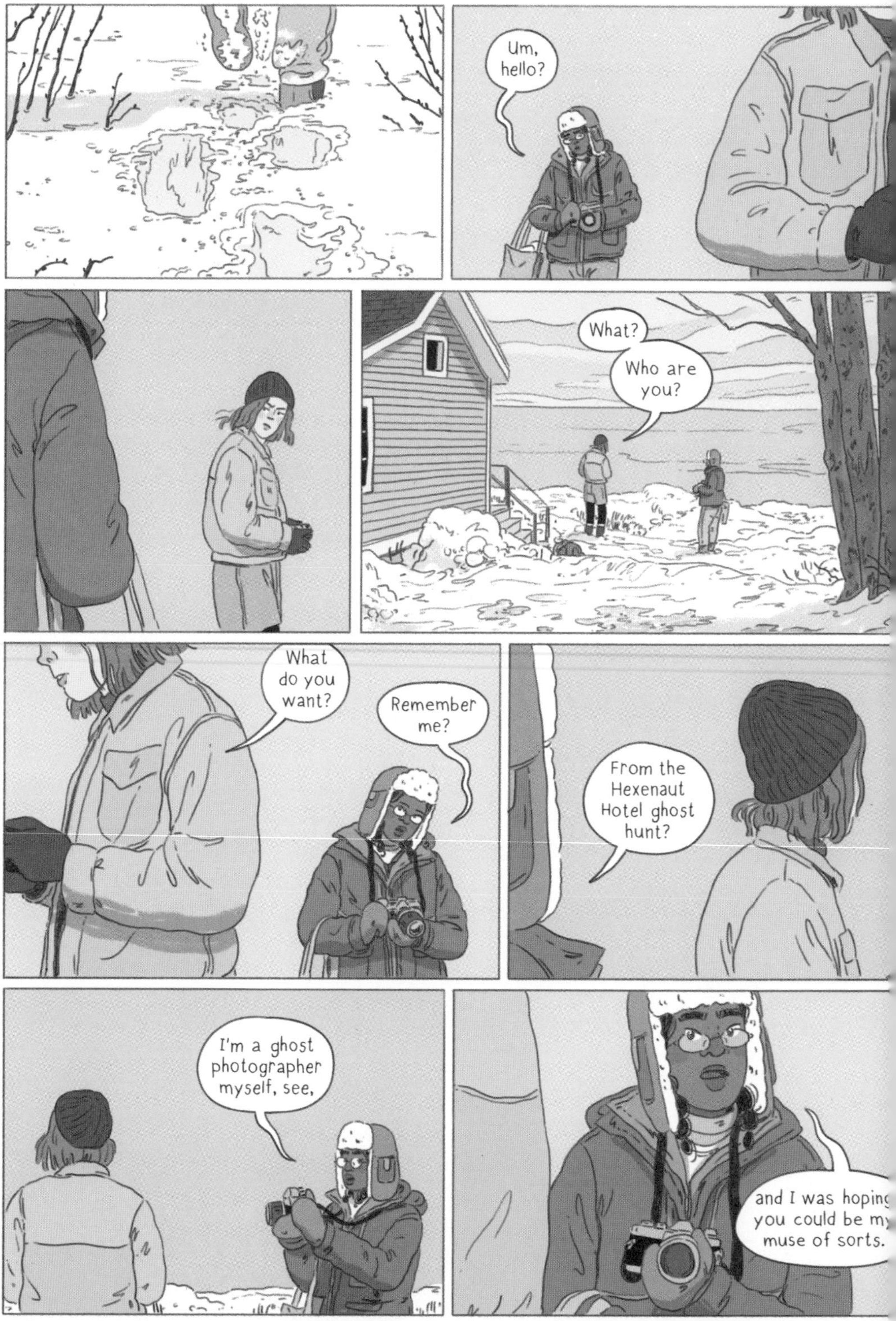
Um, hello?
What?
Who are you?
What do you want?
Remember me?
From the Hexenaut Hotel ghost hunt?
I'm a ghost photographer myself, see,
and I was hoping you could be my muse of sorts.

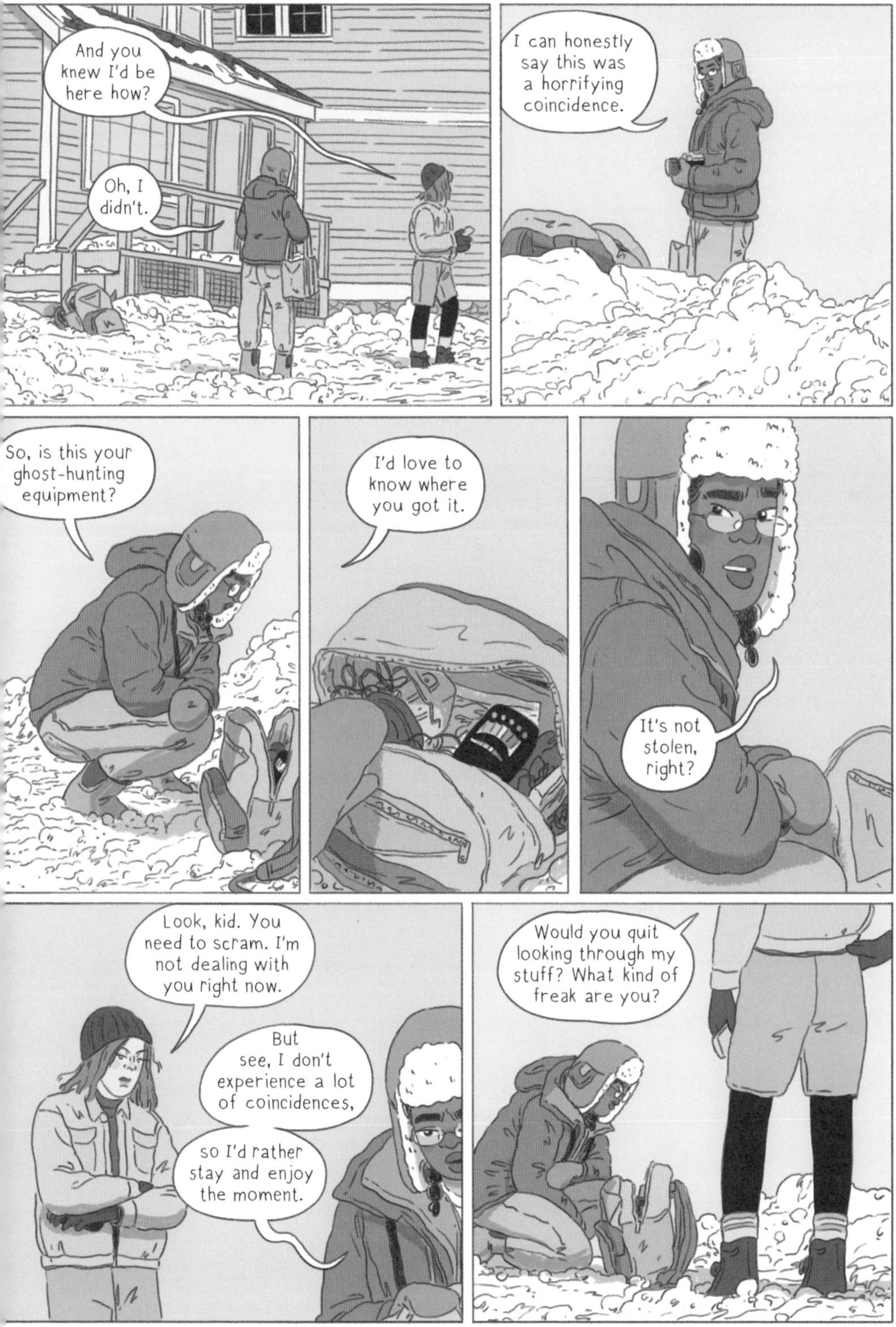
And you knew I'd be here how?
Oh, I didn't.
I can honestly say this was a horrifying coincidence.
So, is this your ghost-hunting equipment?
I'd love to know where you got it.
It's not stolen, right?
Look, kid. You need to scram. I'm not dealing with you right now.
But see, I don't experience a lot of coincidences,
so I'd rather stay and enjoy the moment.
Would you quit looking through my stuff? What kind of freak are you?

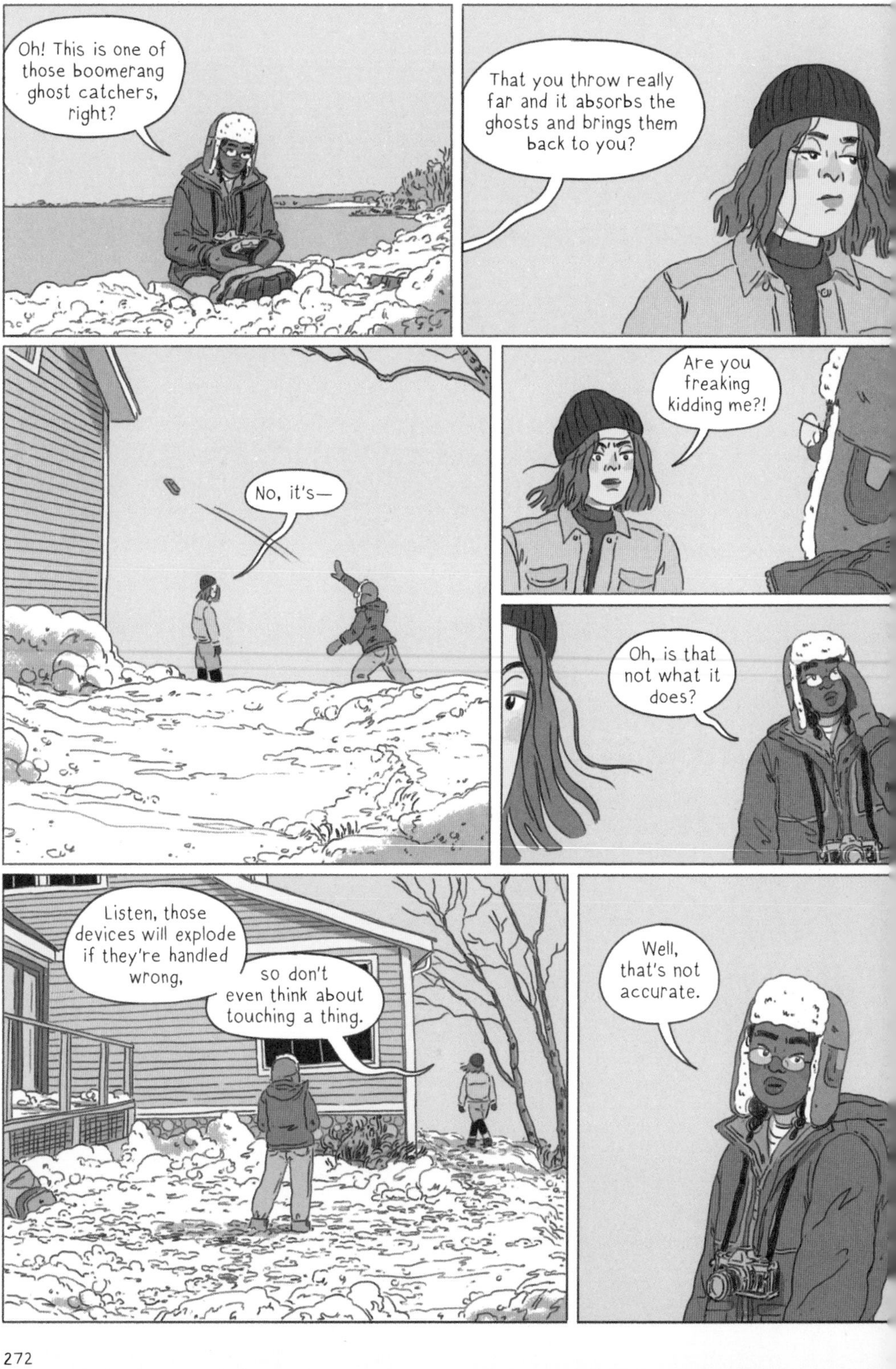
Oh! This is one of those boomerang ghost catchers, right?
That you throw really far and it absorbs the ghosts and brings them back to you?
No, it's—
Are you freaking kidding me?!
Oh, is that not what it does?
Listen, those devices will explode if they're handled wrong,
so don't even think about touching a thing.
Well, that's not accurate.

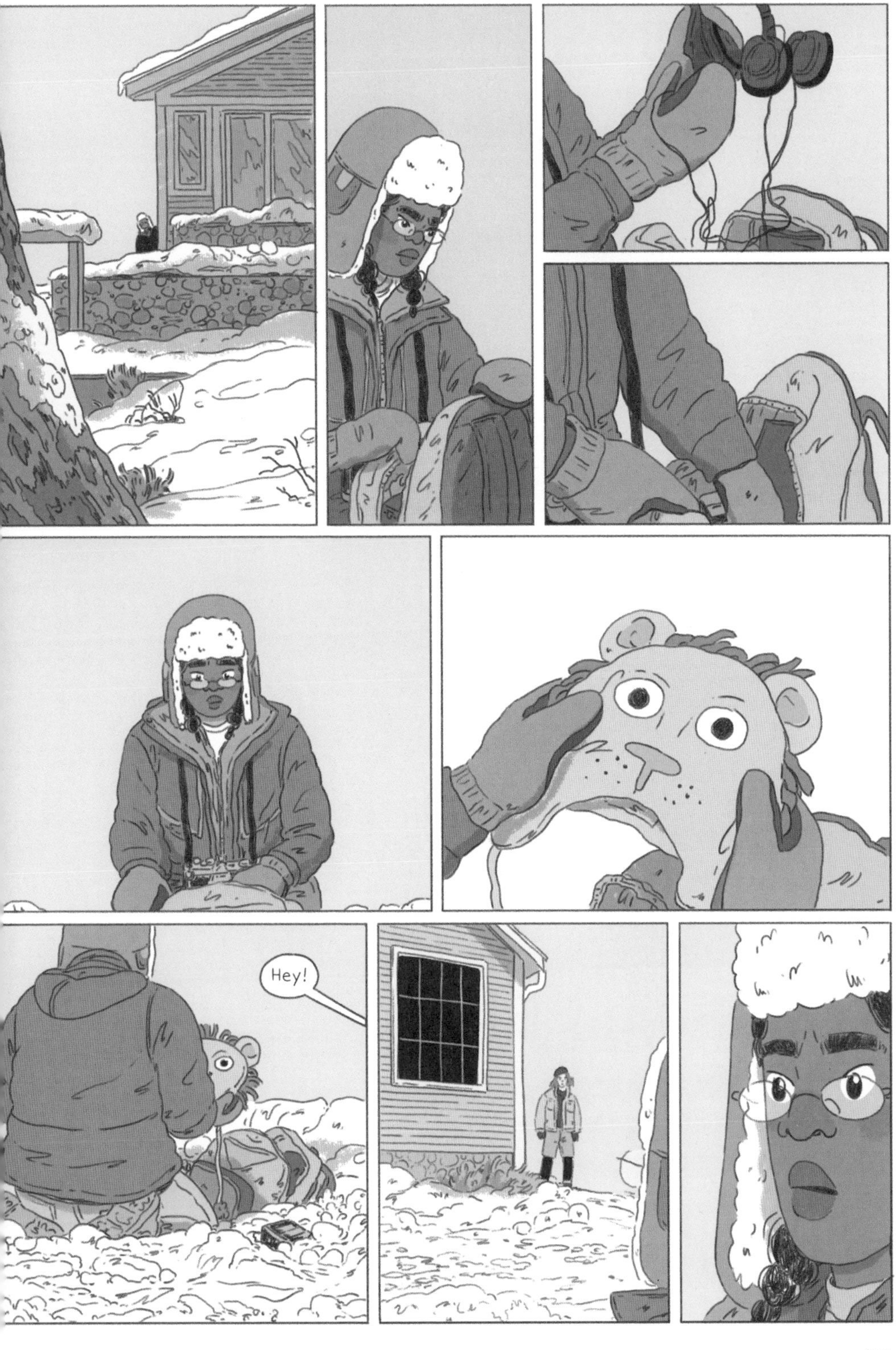
Hey!

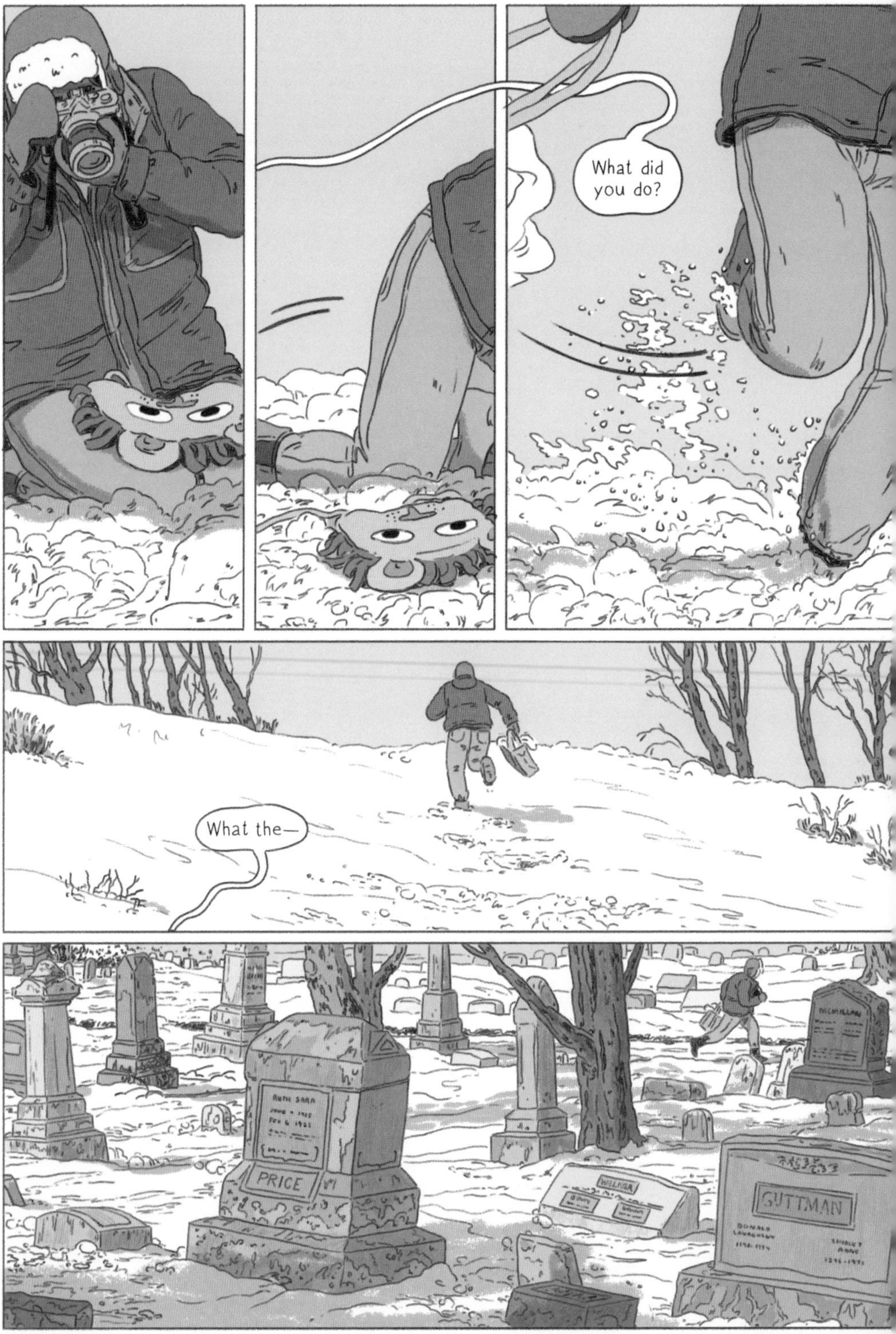
What did you do?
What the—
RUTH SARA
PRICE
WALKER
MCMILLAN
GUTTMAN

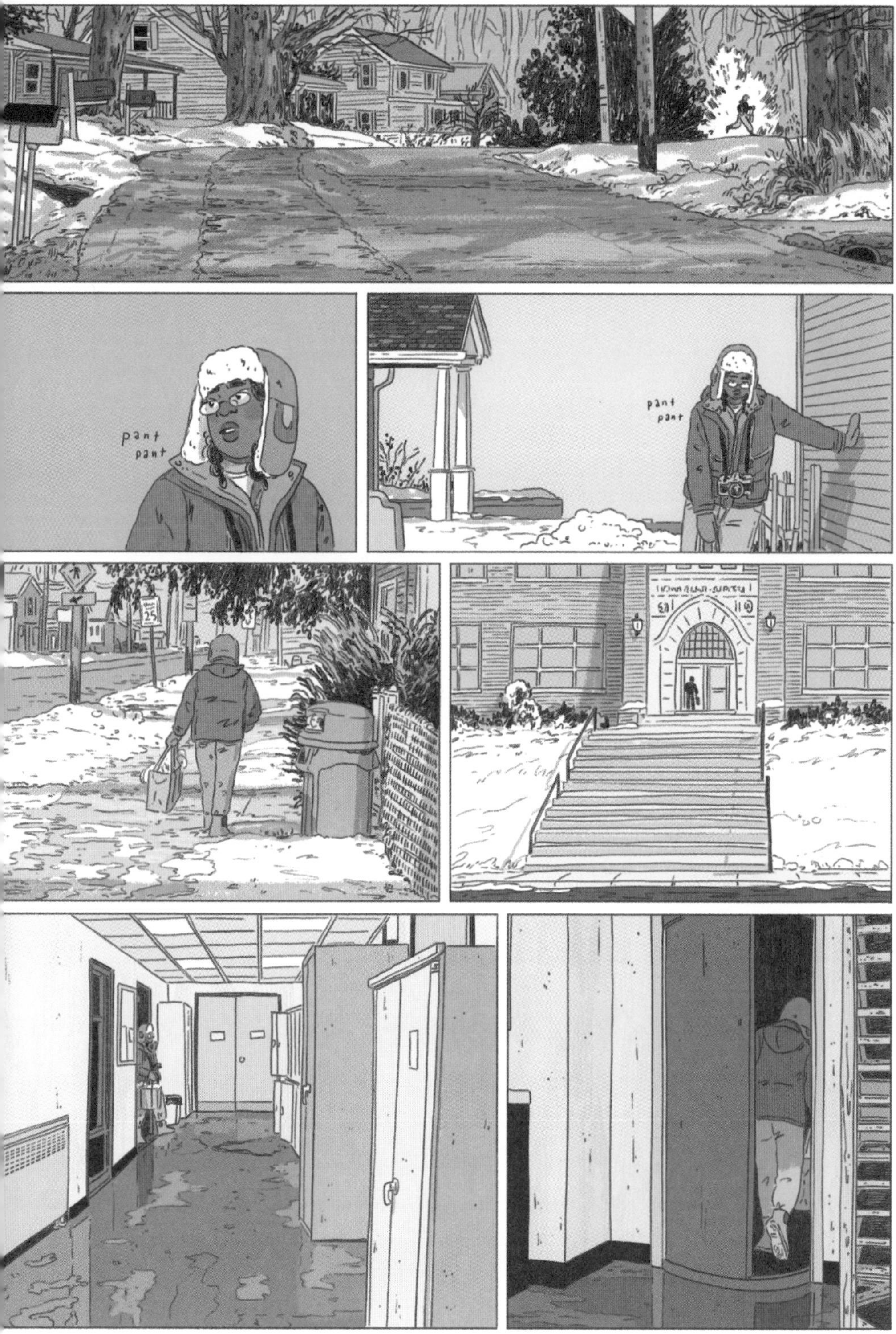
pant
pant
pant
pant
25

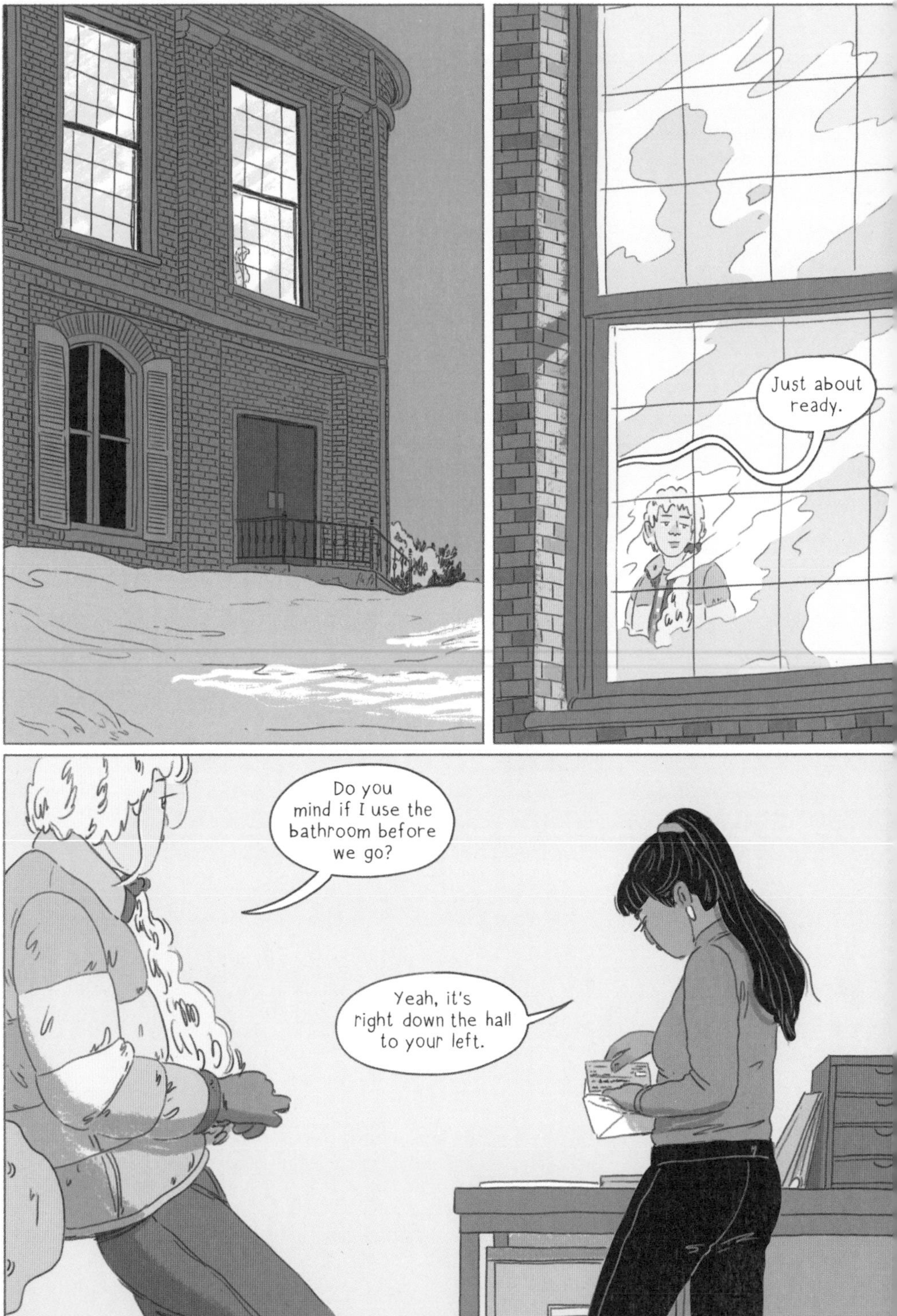
Just about ready.
Do you mind if I use the bathroom before we go?
Yeah, it's right down the hall to your left.

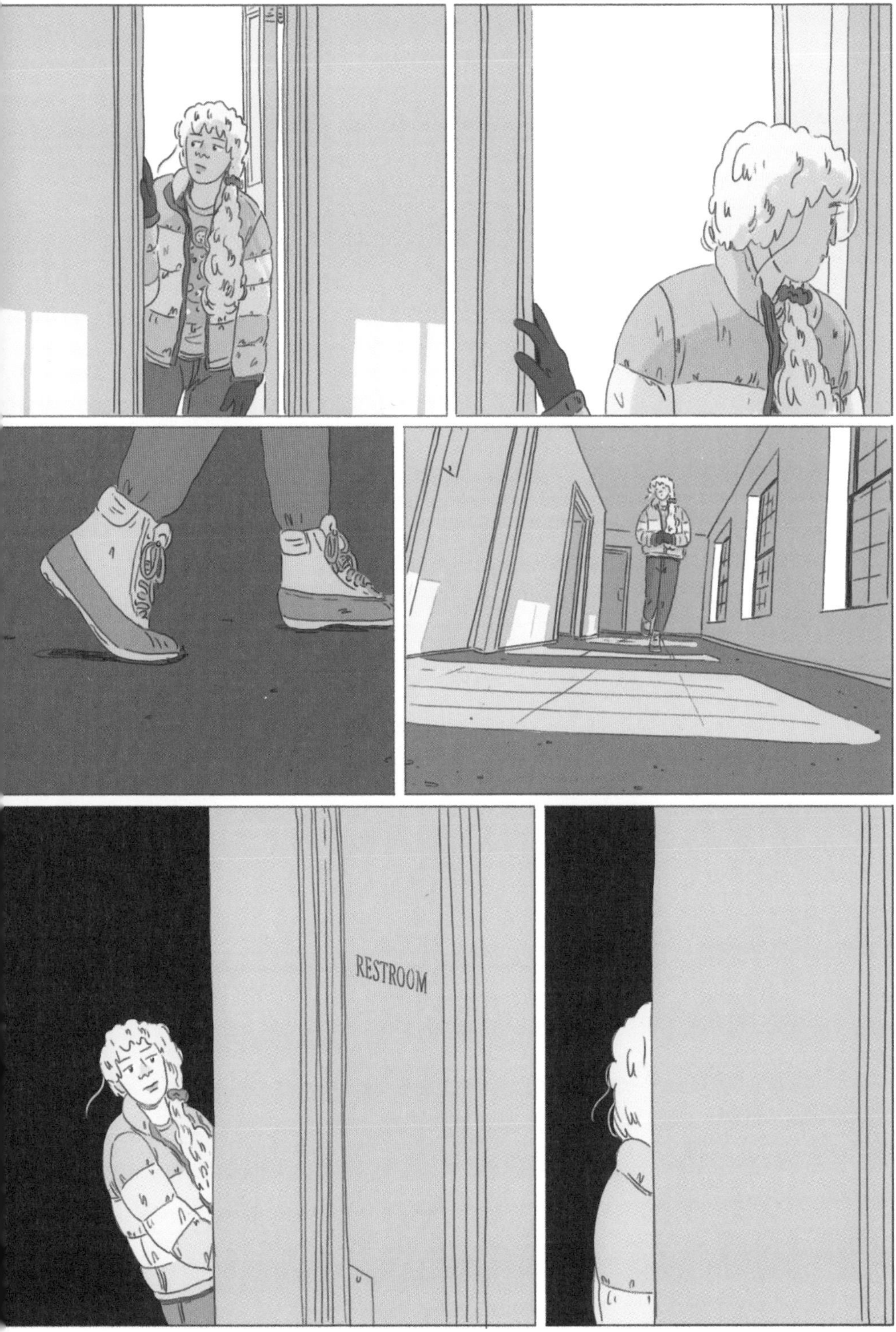
RESTROOM

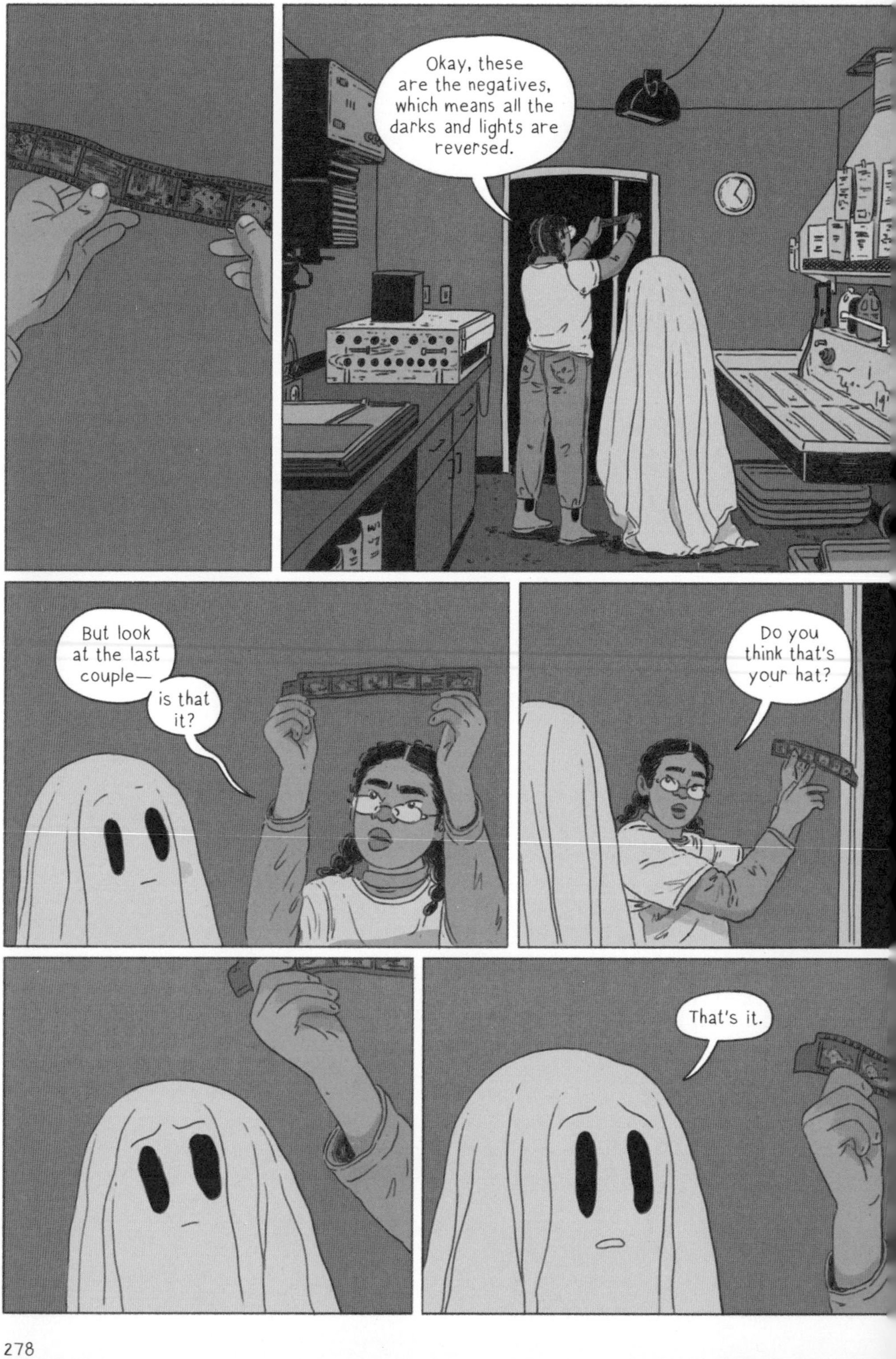
Okay, these are the negatives, which means all the darks and lights are reversed.
But look at the last couple—
is that it?
Do you think that's your hat?
That's it.

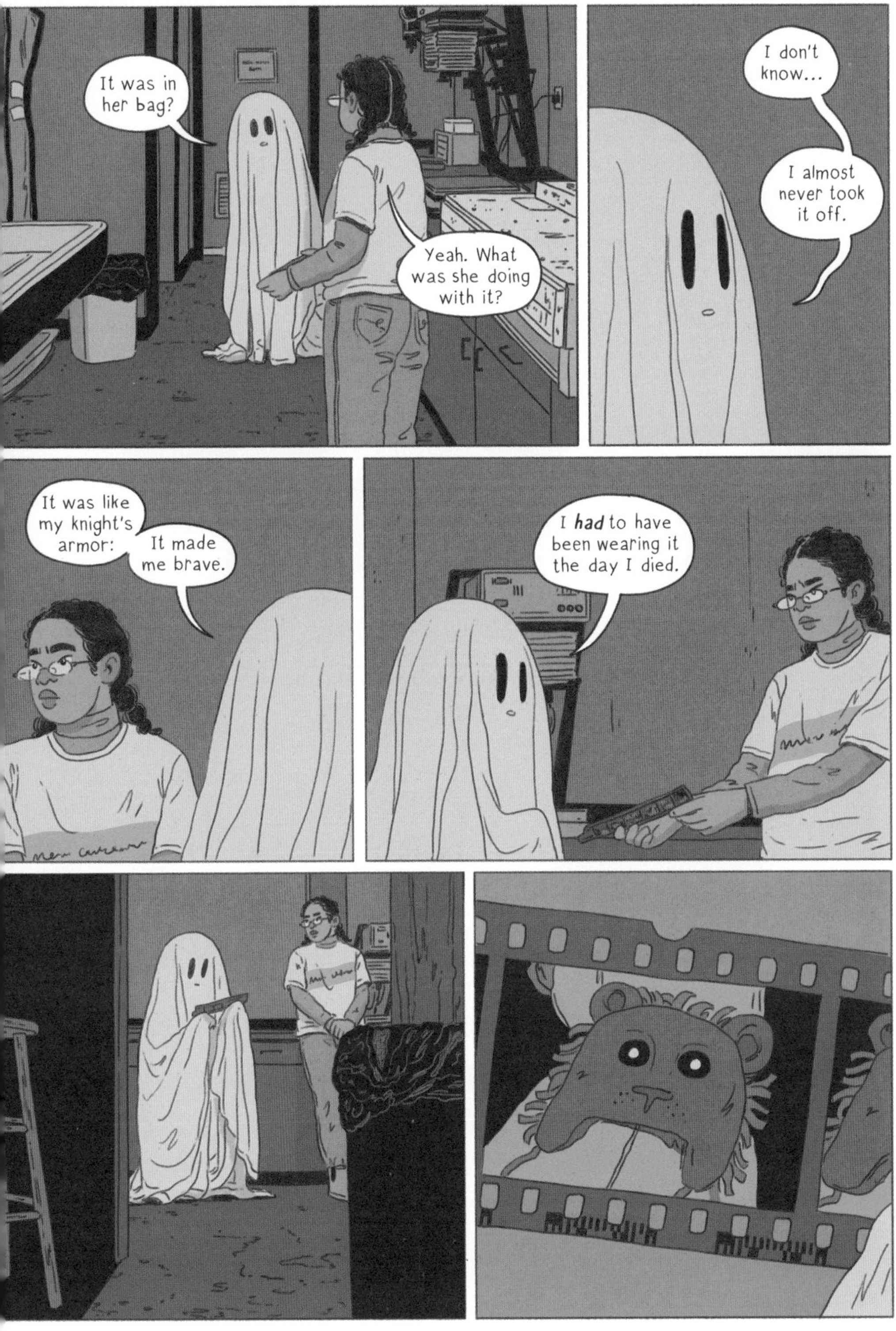
It was in her bag?
Yeah. What was she doing with it?
I don't know...
I almost never took it off.
It was like my knight's armor:
It made me brave.
I **had** to have been wearing it the day I died.

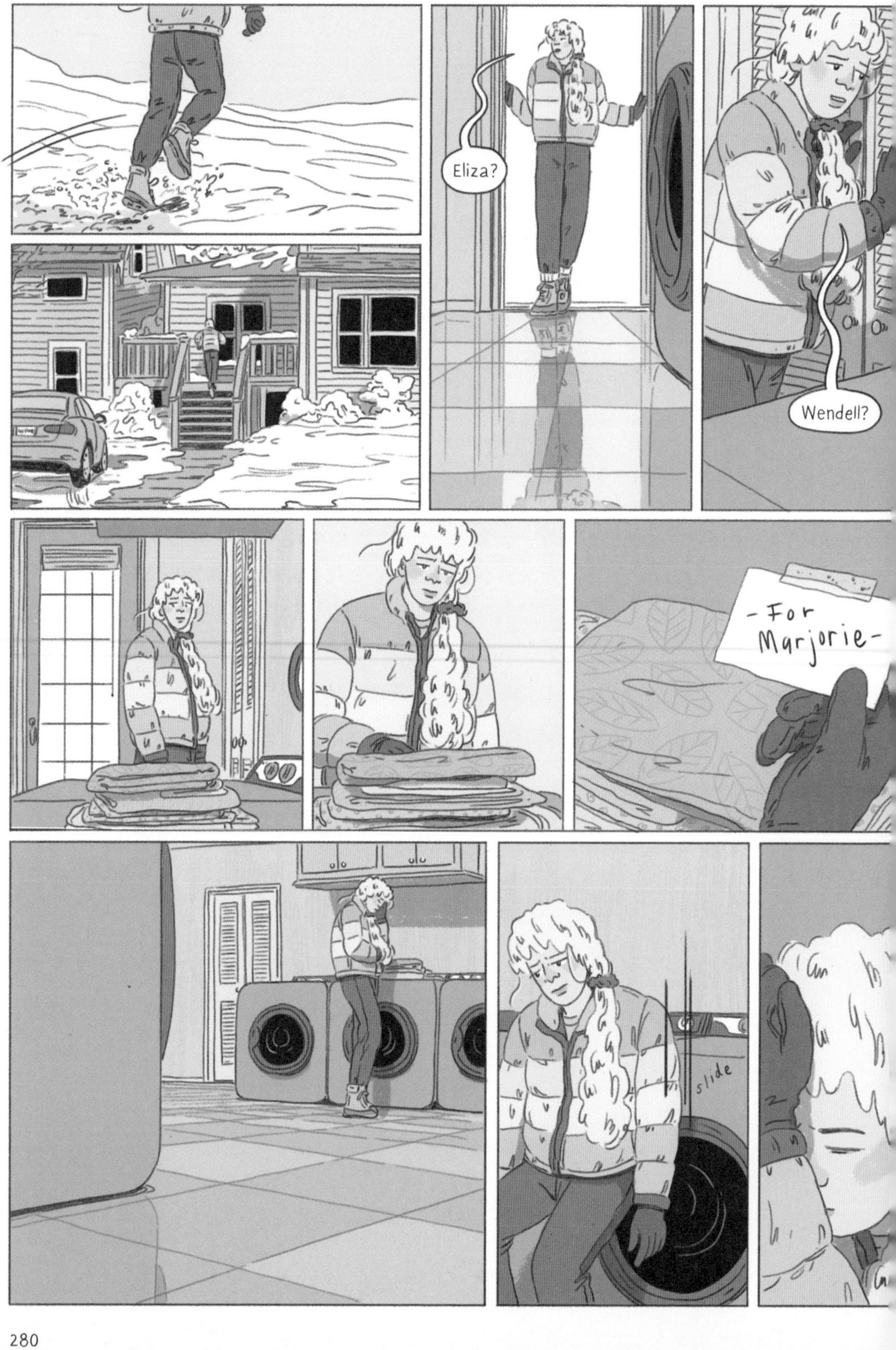

Eliza?
Wendell?
-For Marjorie-
slide

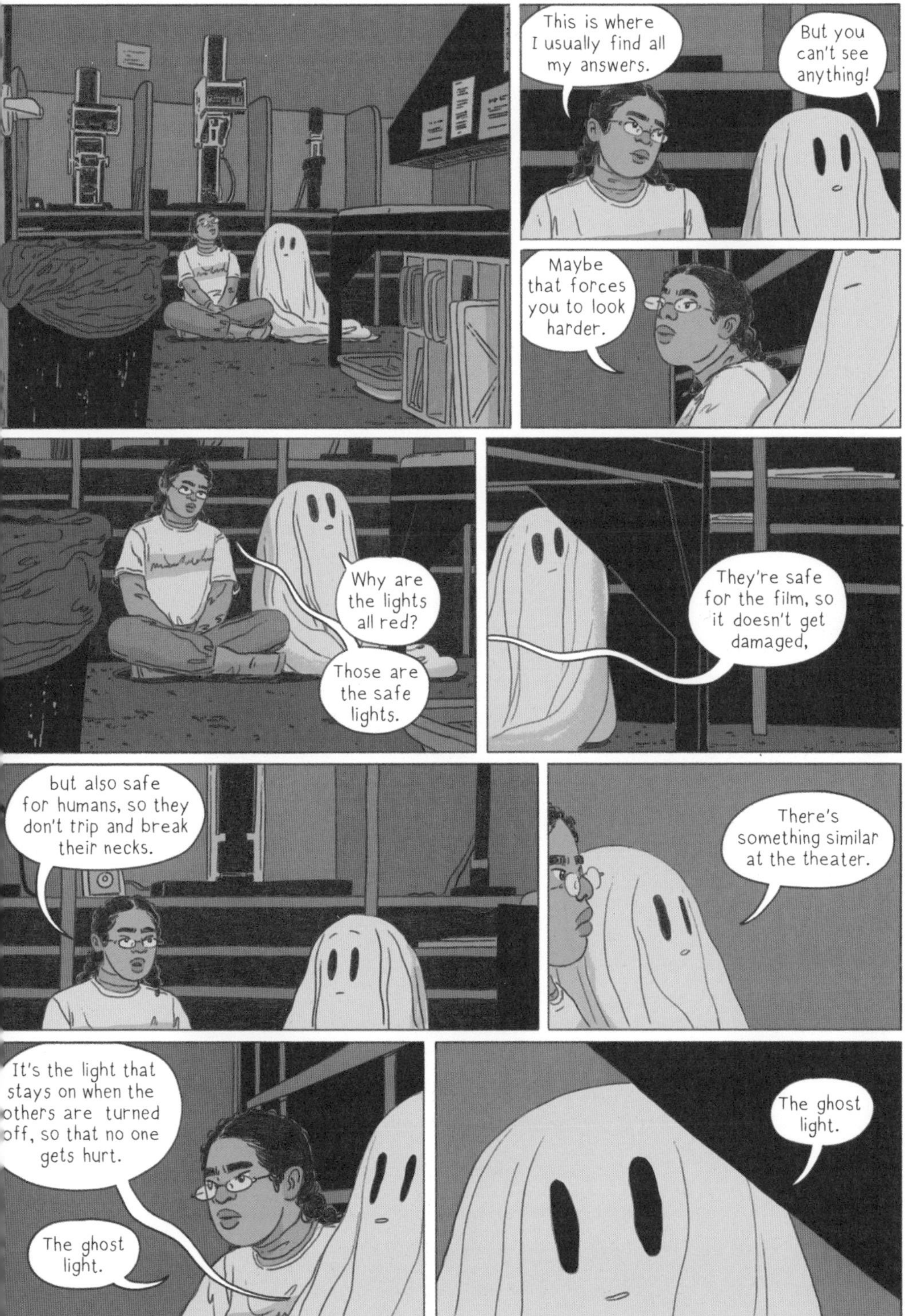
This is where I usually find all my answers.
But you can't see anything!
Maybe that forces you to look harder.
Why are the lights all red?
Those are the safe lights.
They're safe for the film, so it doesn't get damaged,
but also safe for humans, so they don't trip and break their necks.
There's something similar at the theater.
It's the light that stays on when the others are turned off, so that no one gets hurt.
The ghost light.
The ghost light.

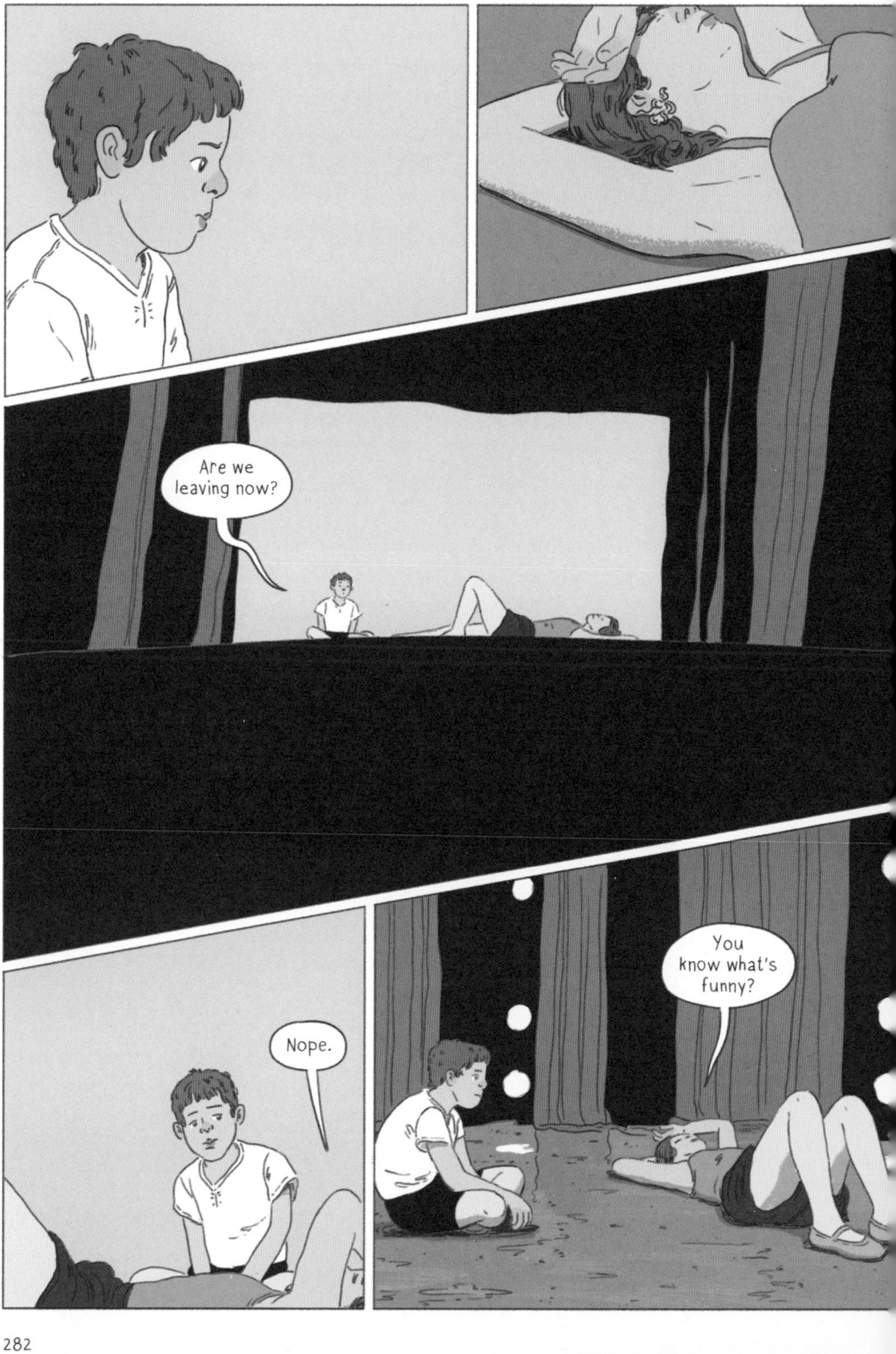
Are we leaving now?
Nope.
You know what's funny?

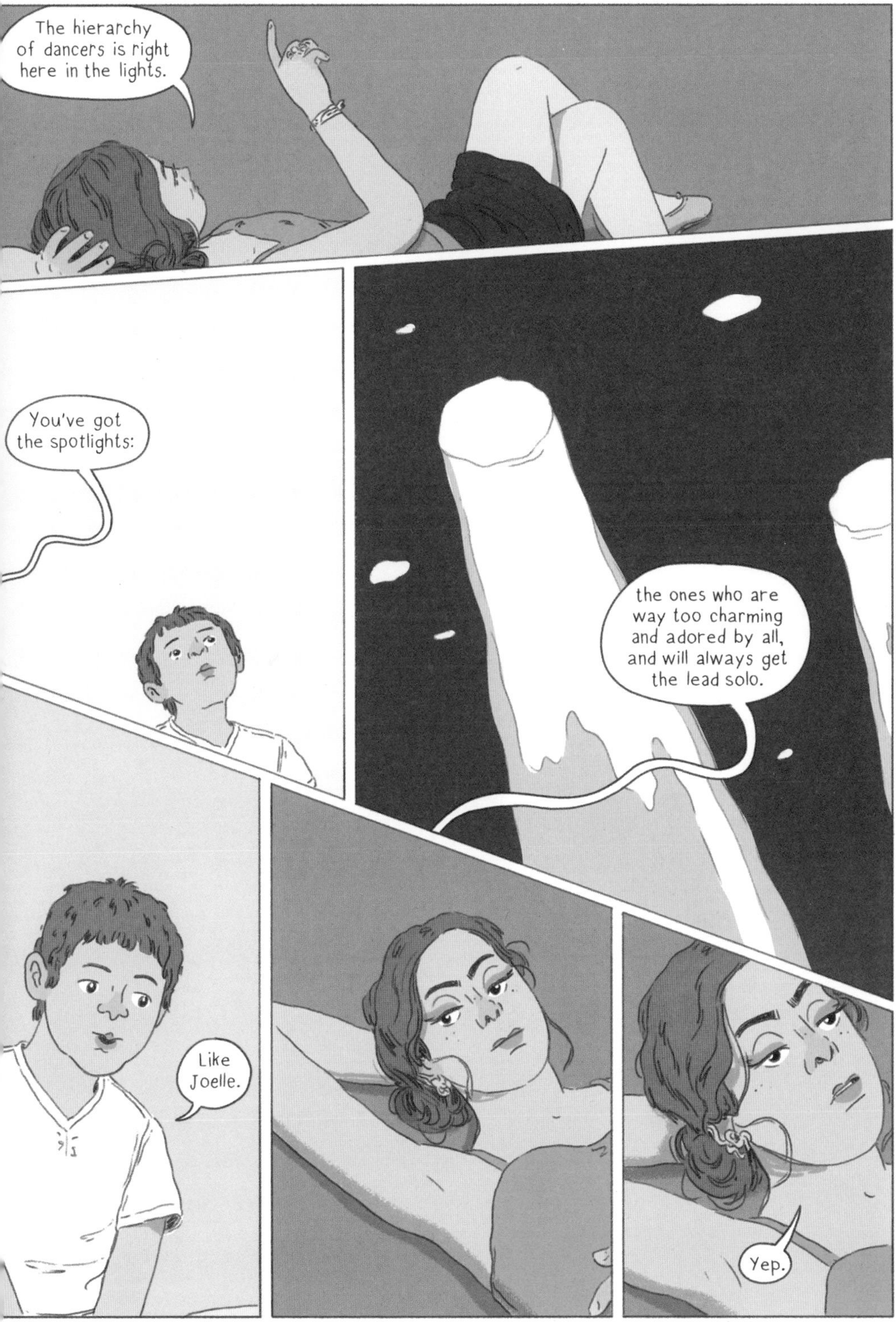
The hierarchy of dancers is right here in the lights.
You've got the spotlights:
the ones who are way too charming and adored by all, and will always get the lead solo.
Like Joelle.
Yep.

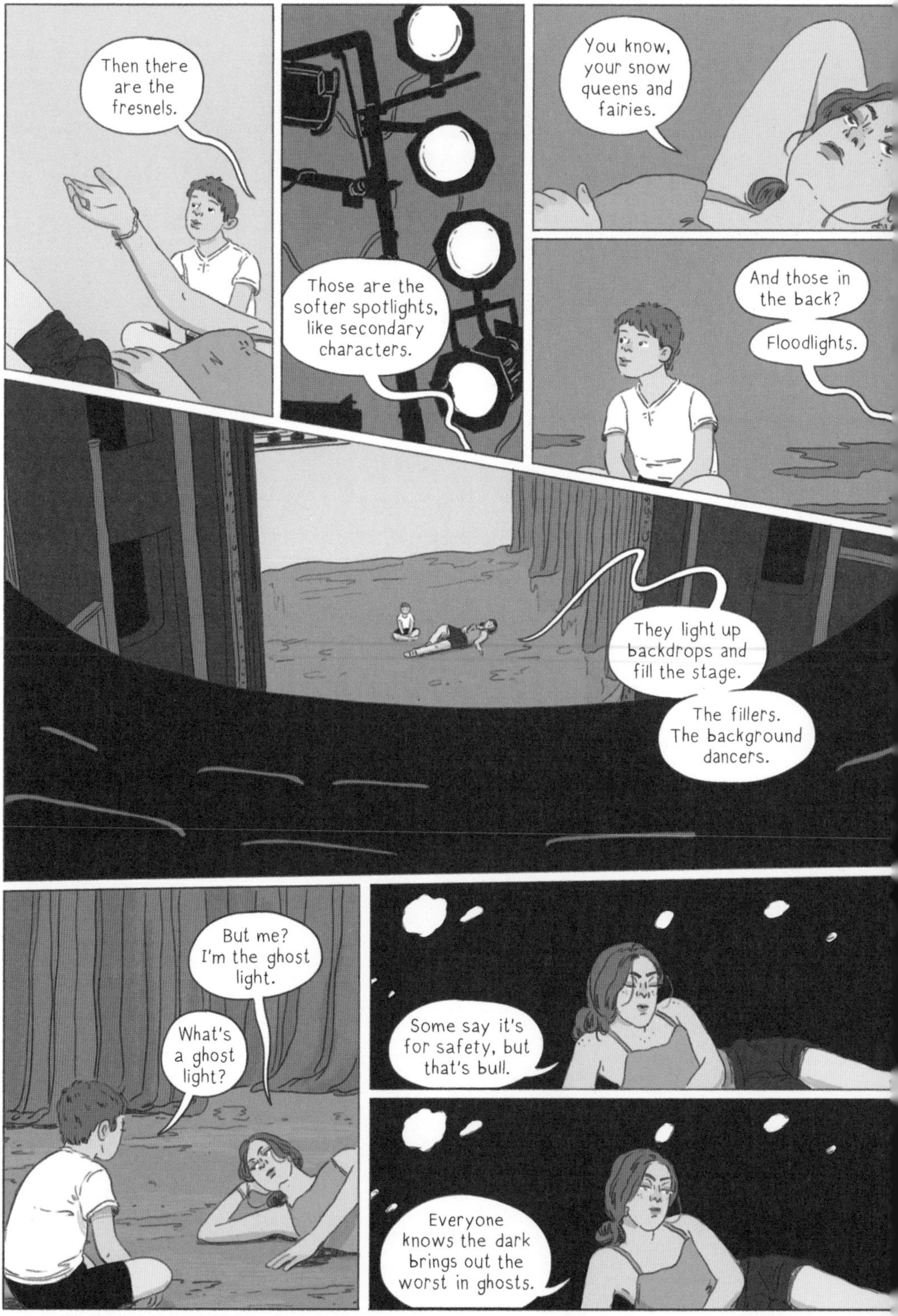
Then there are the fresnels.
Those are the softer spotlights, like secondary characters.
You know, your snow queens and fairies.
And those in the back?
Floodlights.
They light up backdrops and fill the stage.
The fillers. The background dancers.
But me? I'm the ghost light.
What's a ghost light?
Some say it's for safety, but that's bull.
Everyone knows the dark brings out the worst in ghosts.

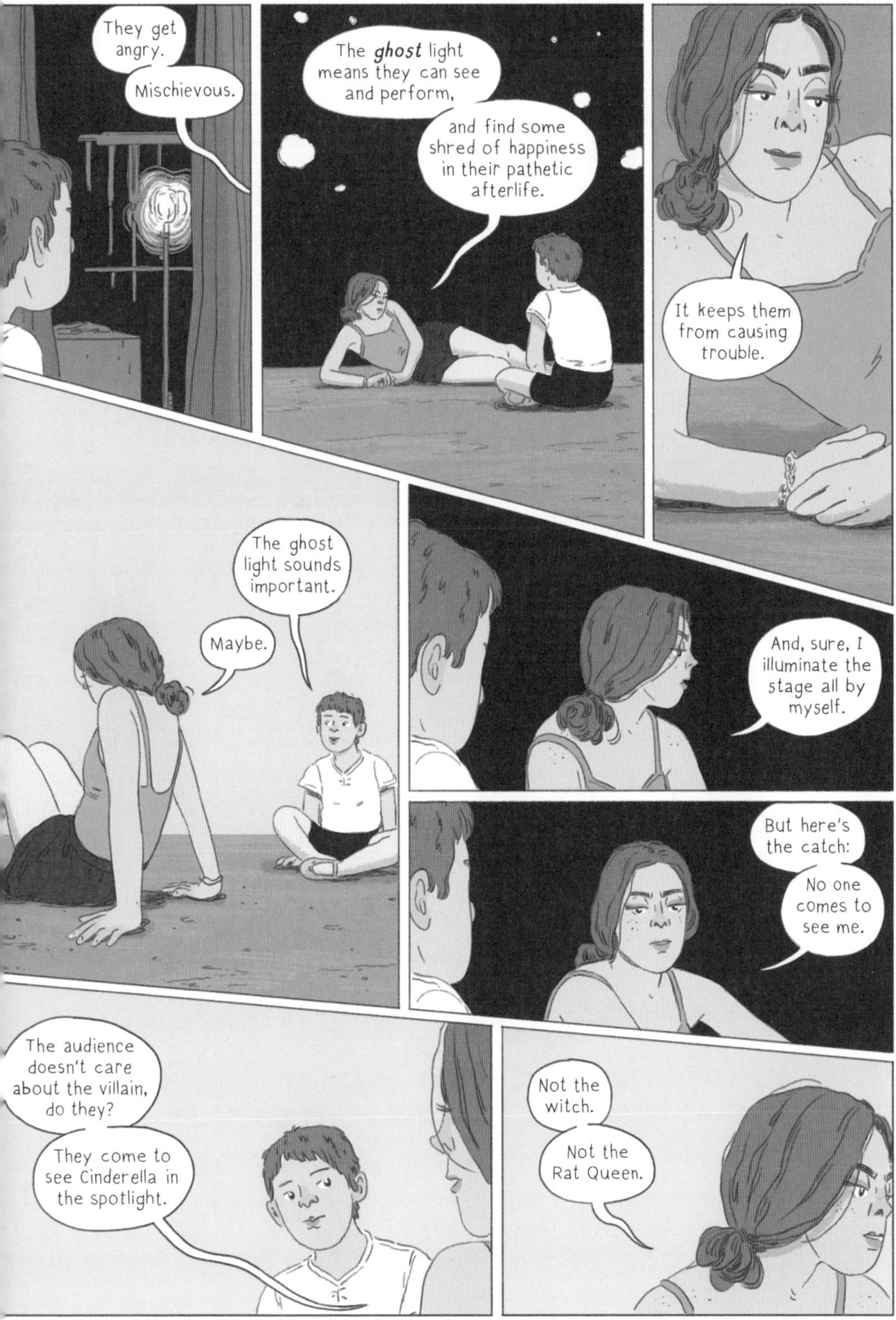
They get angry.
Mischievous.
The ghost light means they can see and perform,
and find some shred of happiness in their pathetic afterlife.
It keeps them from causing trouble.
The ghost light sounds important.
Maybe.
And, sure, I illuminate the stage all by myself.
But here's the catch:
No one comes to see me.
The audience doesn't care about the villain, do they?
They come to see Cinderella in the spotlight.
Not the witch.
Not the Rat Queen.

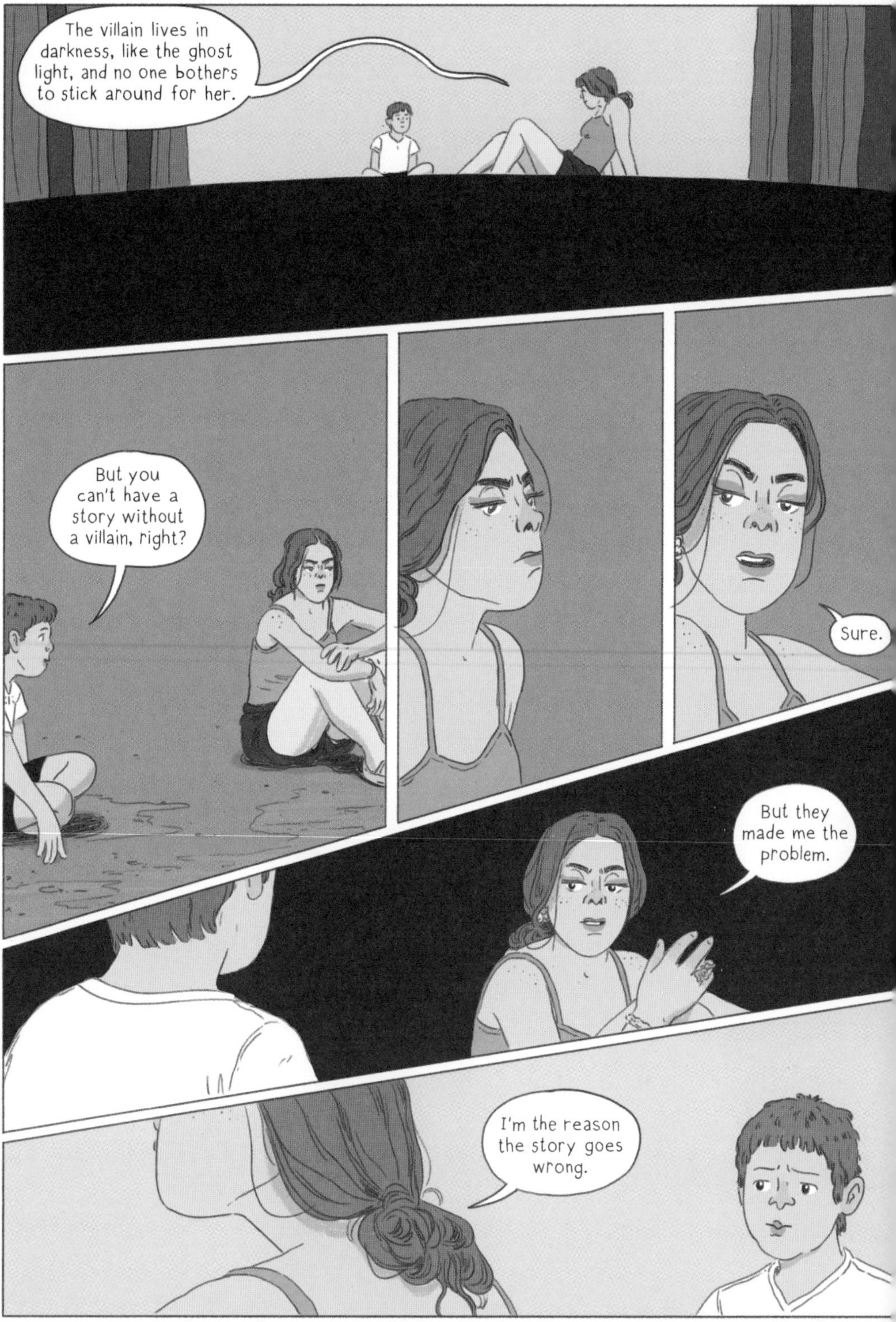
The villain lives in darkness, like the ghost light, and no one bothers to stick around for her.
But you can't have a story without a villain, right?
Sure.
But they made me the problem.
I'm the reason the story goes wrong.

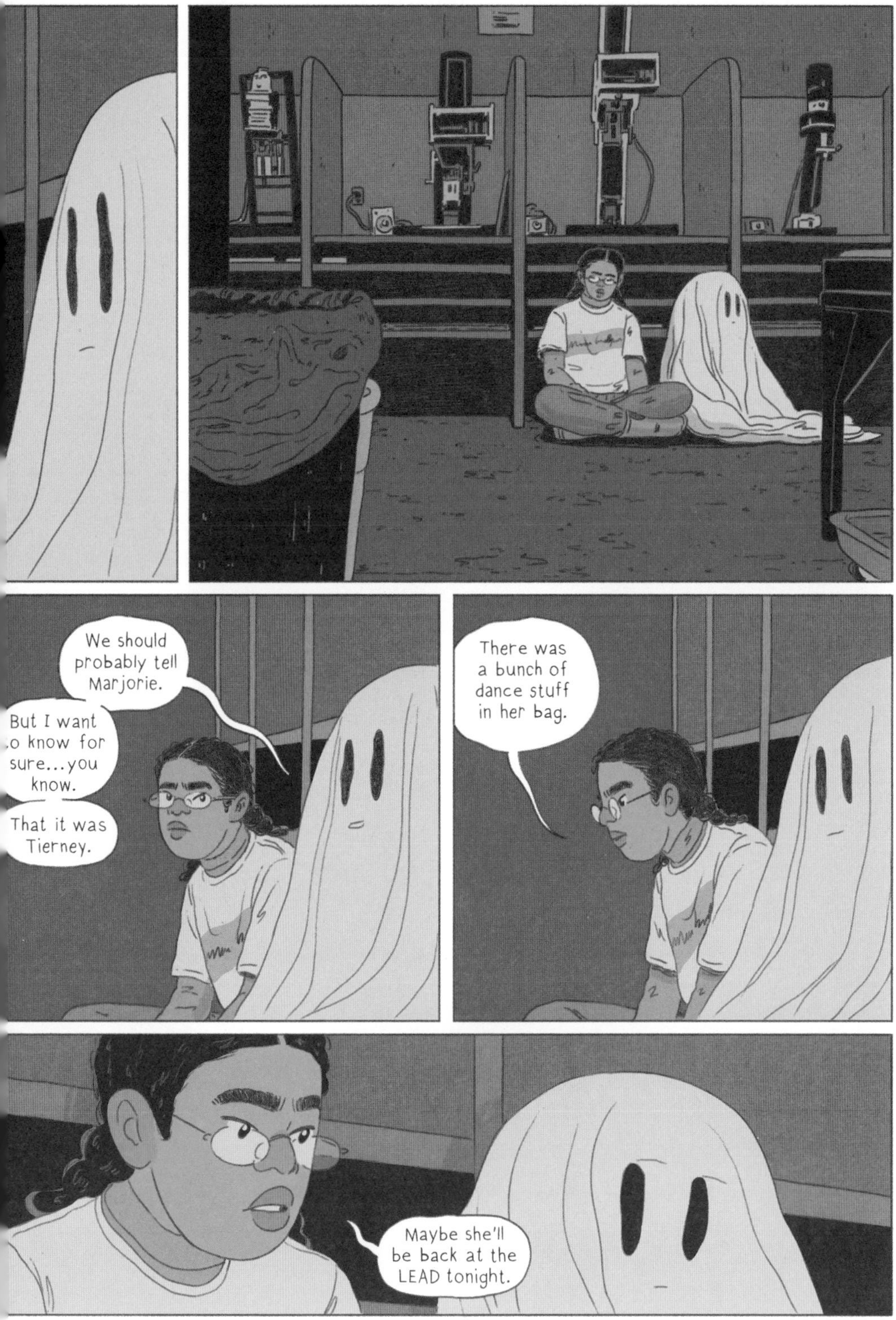
We should probably tell Marjorie.
But I want to know for sure...you know.
That it was Tierney.
There was a bunch of dance stuff in her bag.
Maybe she'll be back at the LEAD tonight.

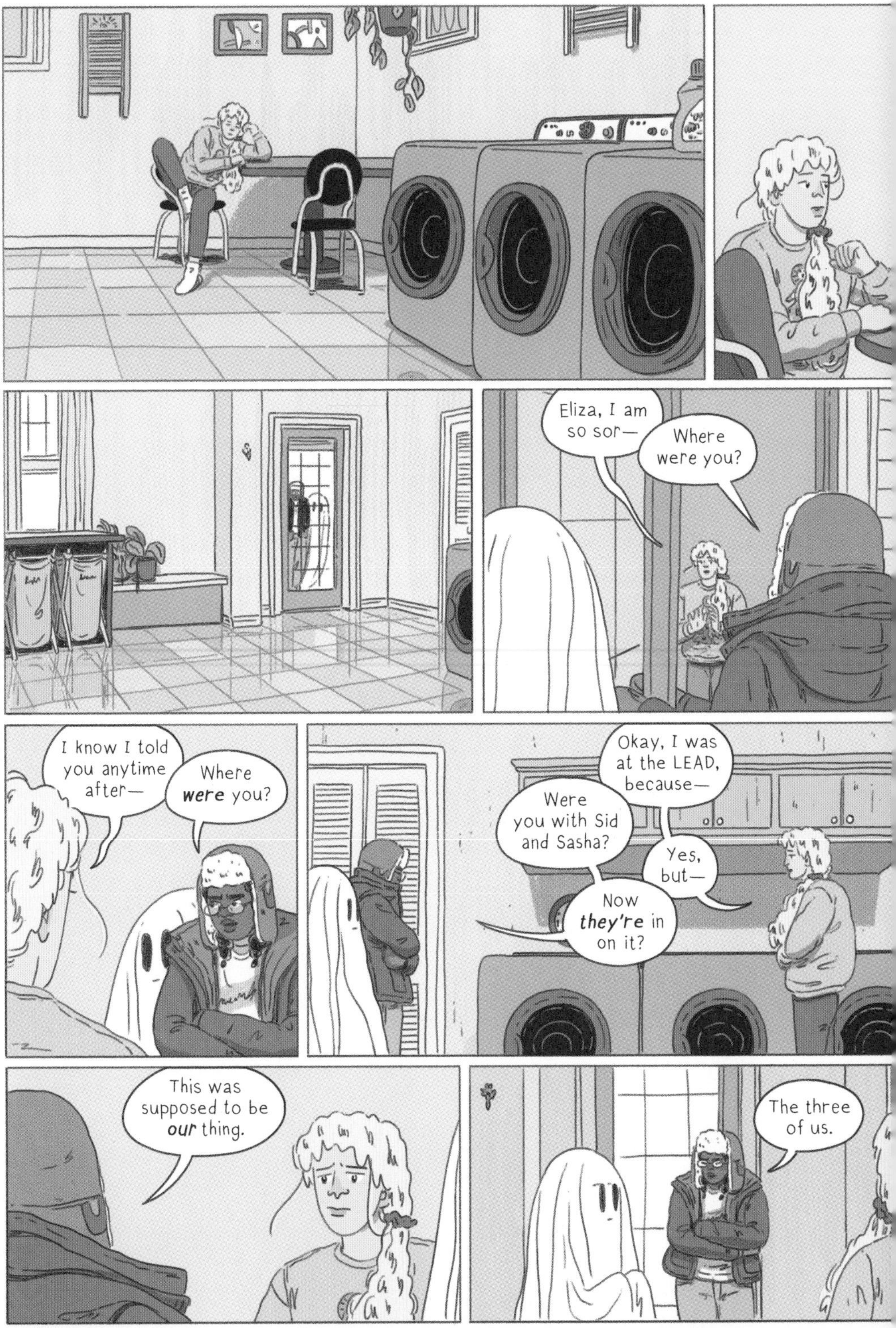
Eliza, I am so sor—
Where were you?
I know I told you anytime after—
Where *were* you?
Okay, I was at the LEAD, because—
Were you with Sid and Sasha?
Yes, but—
Now *they're* in on it?
This was supposed to be *our* thing.
The three of us.

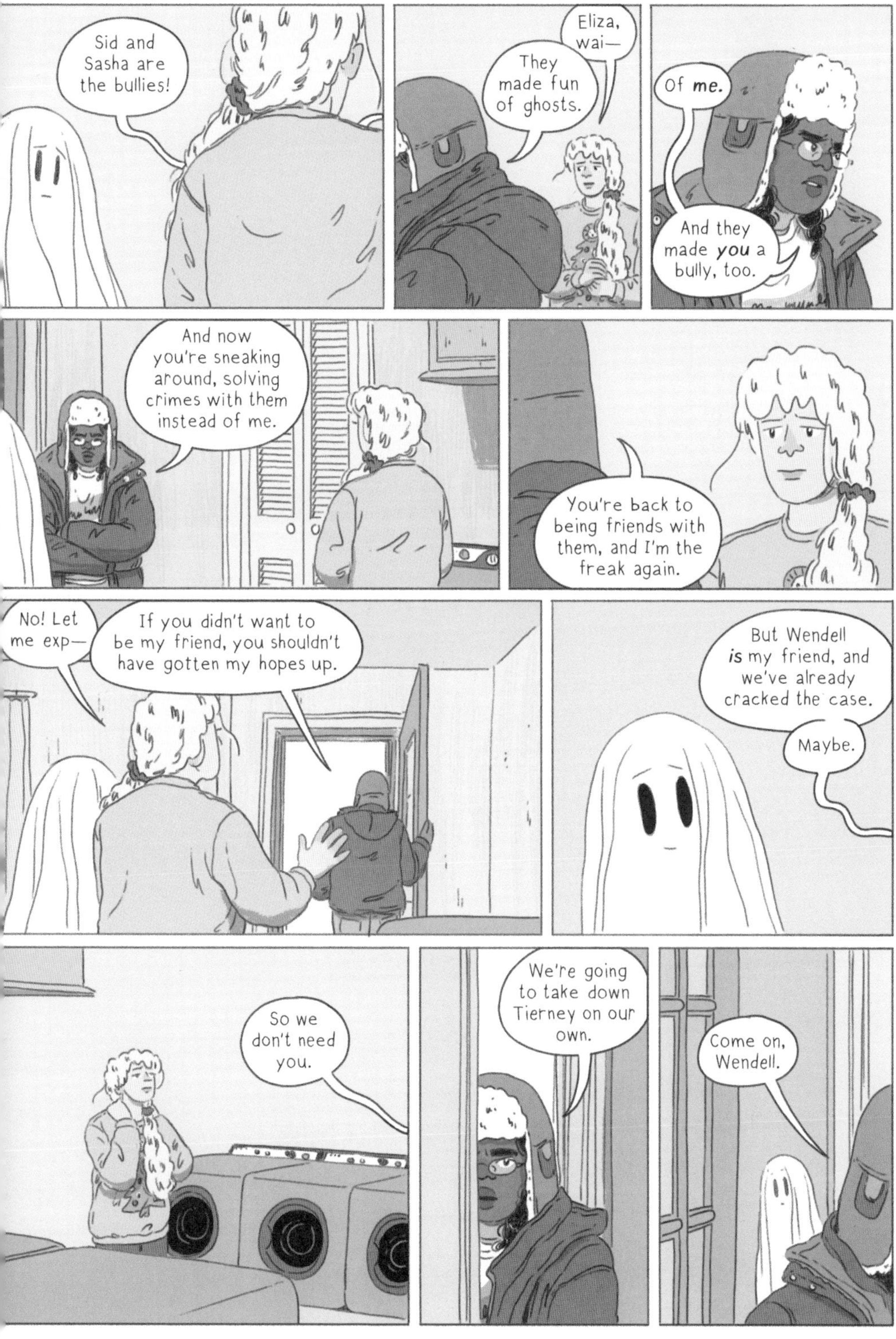
Sid and Sasha are the bullies!
Eliza, wai—
They made fun of ghosts.
Of me.
And they made you a bully, too.
And now you're sneaking around, solving crimes with them instead of me.
You're back to being friends with them, and I'm the freak again.
No! Let me exp—
If you didn't want to be my friend, you shouldn't have gotten my hopes up.
But Wendell is my friend, and we've already cracked the case.
Maybe.
So we don't need you.
We're going to take down Tierney on our own.
Come on, Wendell.

What does she mean, cracked the case?

Tierney has my lion hat. That probably means she murdered me.

What?

Wait—

So I guess we have our *lead.* Ha.

If only I could enjoy how funny I am.

Wendell...

Wait, are you going to the LEAD?

Wendell!

I wish you would have been there.

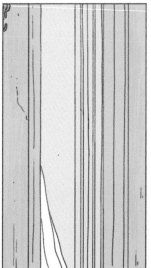

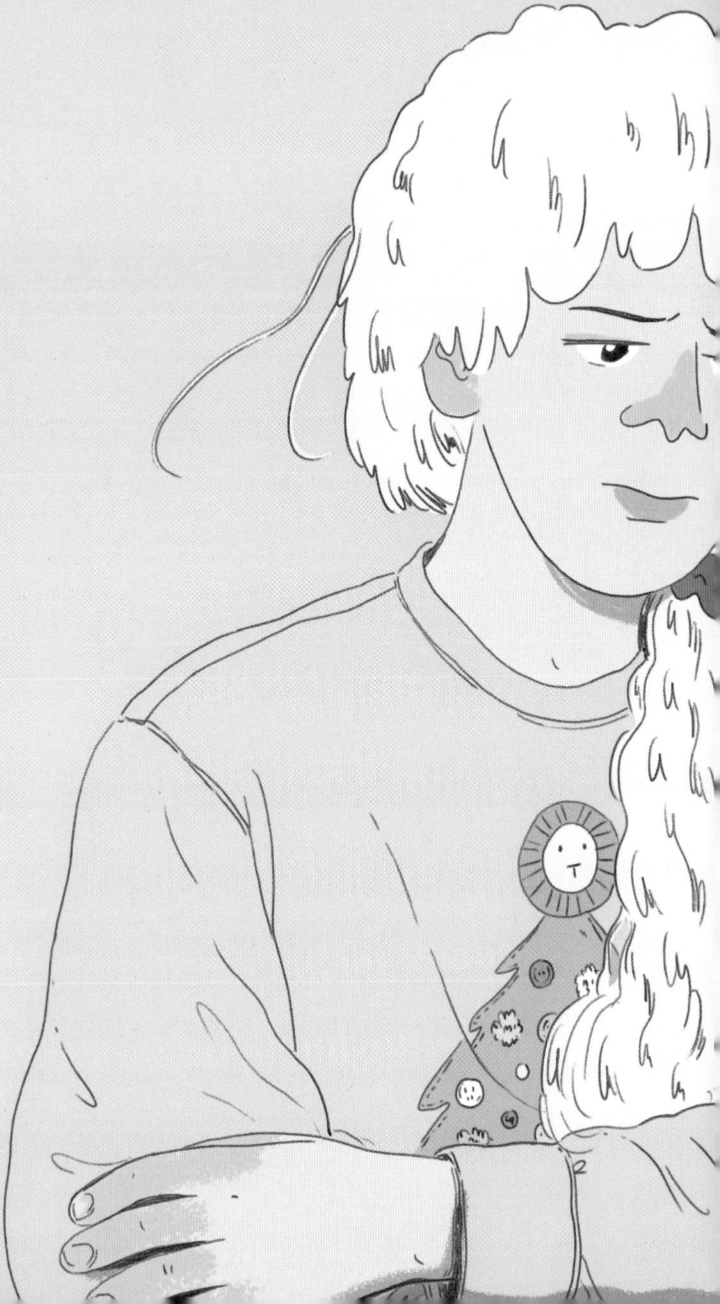

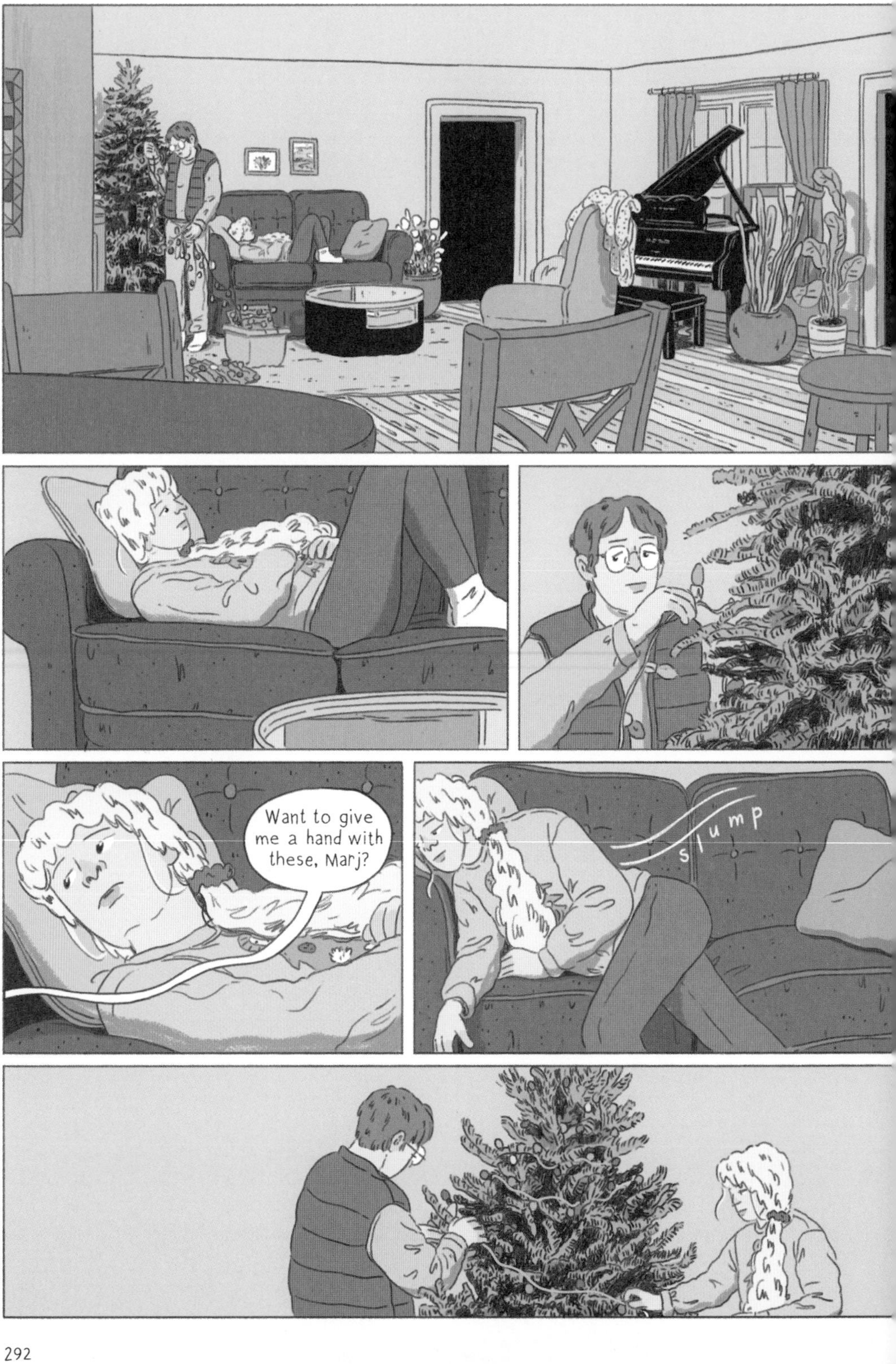
Want to give me a hand with these, Marj?
slump

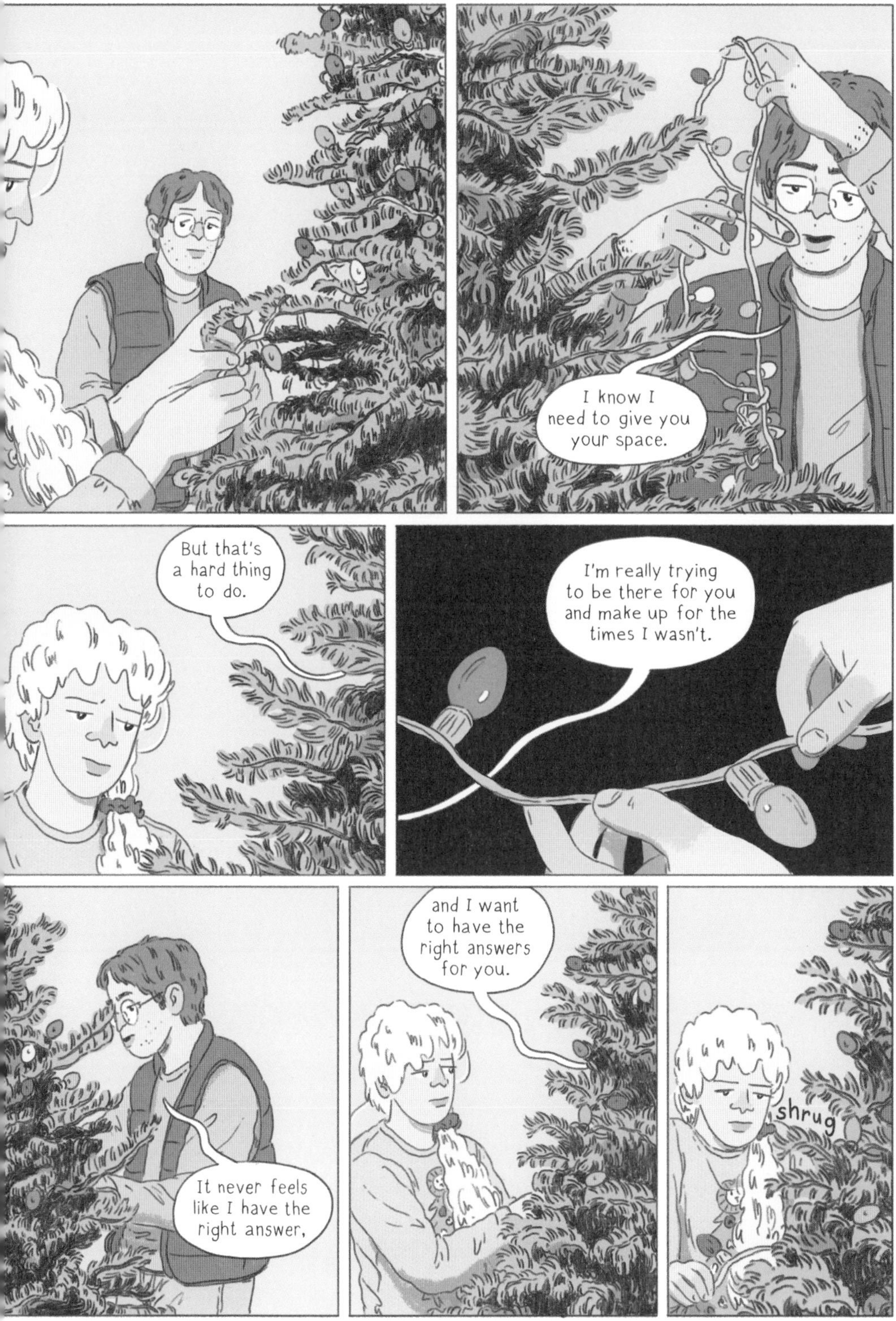
I know I need to give you your space.
But that's a hard thing to do.
I'm really trying to be there for you and make up for the times I wasn't.
It never feels like I have the right answer,
and I want to have the right answers for you.
shrug

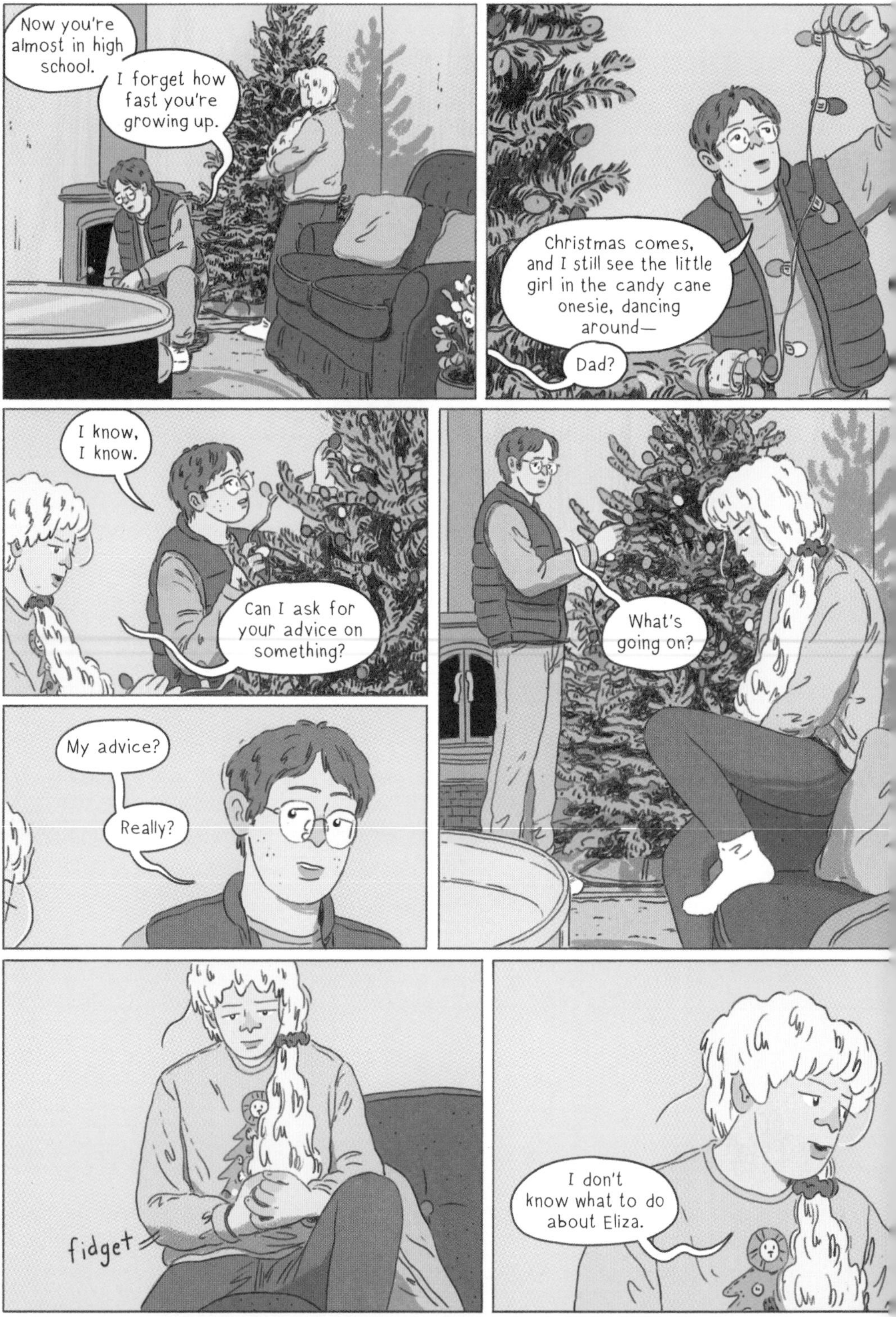
Now you're almost in high school.
I forget how fast you're growing up.
Christmas comes, and I still see the little girl in the candy cane onesie, dancing around—
Dad?
I know, I know.
Can I ask for your advice on something?
What's going on?
My advice?
Really?
fidget
I don't know what to do about Eliza.

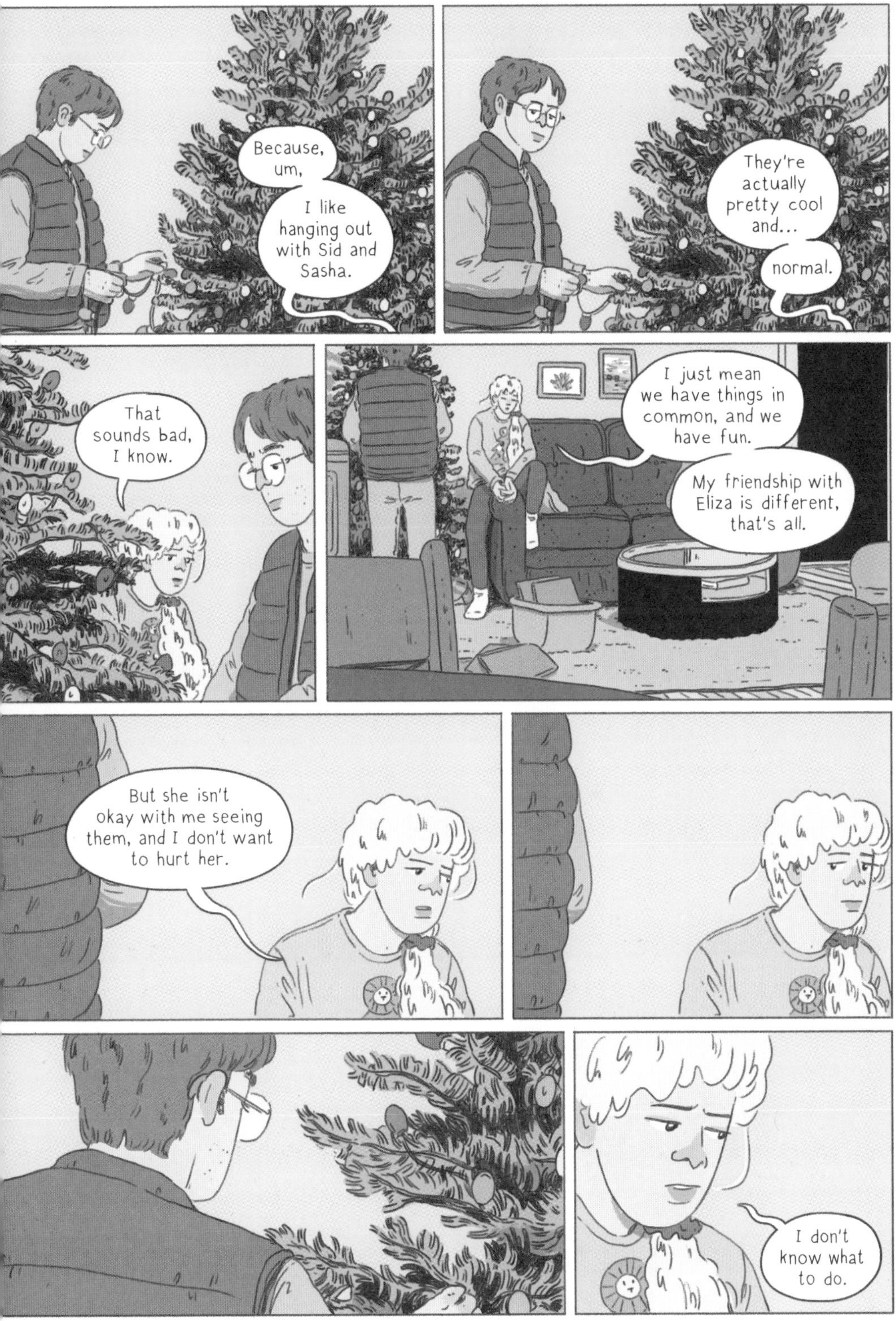
Because, um,
I like hanging out with Sid and Sasha.
They're actually pretty cool and...
normal.
That sounds bad, I know.
I just mean we have things in common, and we have fun.
My friendship with Eliza is different, that's all.
But she isn't okay with me seeing them, and I don't want to hurt her.
I don't know what to do.

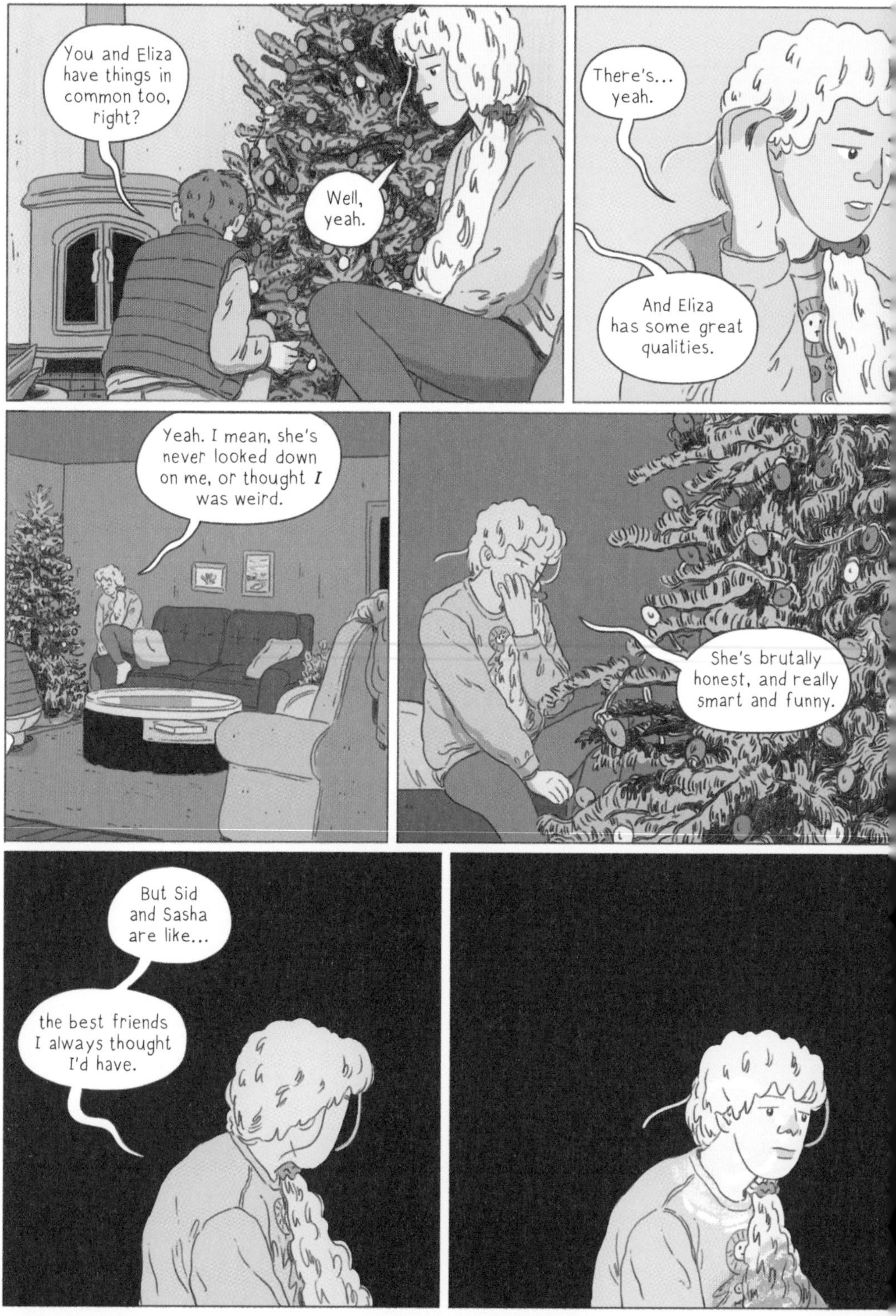
You and Eliza have things in common too, right?
Well, yeah.
There's... yeah.
And Eliza has some great qualities.
Yeah. I mean, she's never looked down on me, or thought *I* was weird.
She's brutally honest, and really smart and funny.
But Sid and Sasha are like...
the best friends I always thought I'd have.

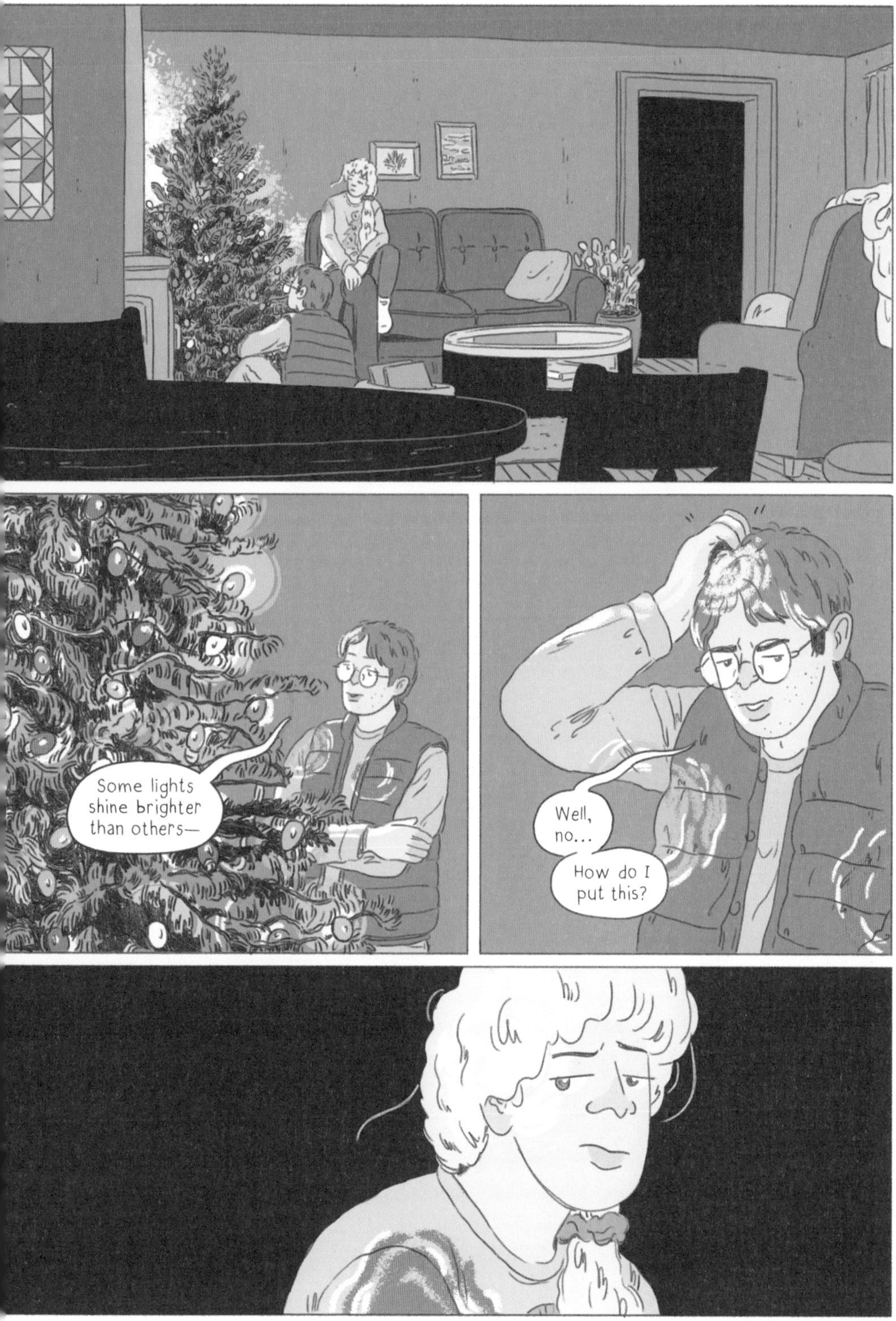
Some lights shine brighter than others—
Well, no...
How do I put this?

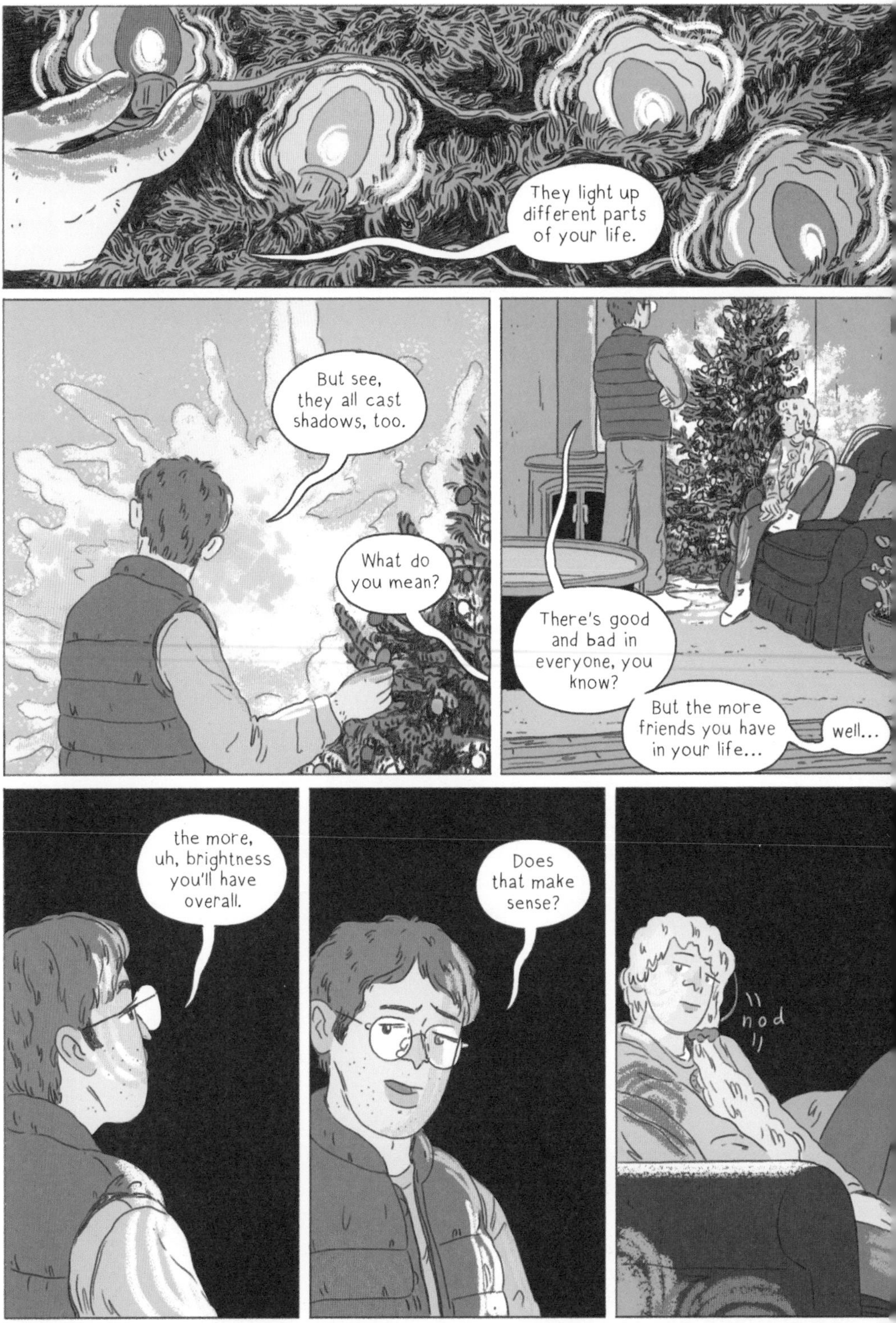
They light up different parts of your life.
But see, they all cast shadows, too.
What do you mean?
There's good and bad in everyone, you know?
But the more friends you have in your life...
well...
the more, uh, brightness you'll have overall.
Does that make sense?
nod

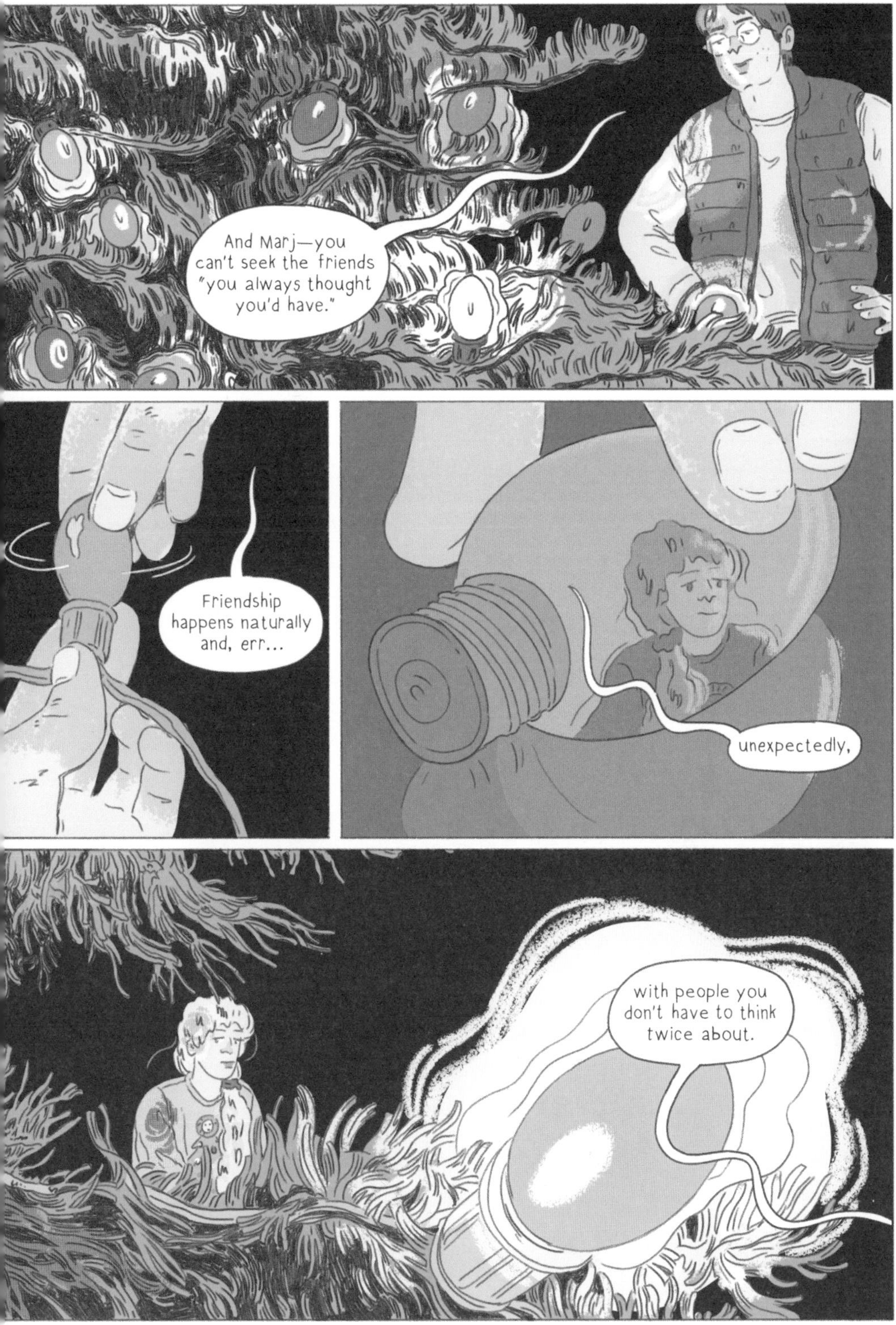
And Marj—you can't seek the friends "you always thought you'd have."
Friendship happens naturally and, err...
unexpectedly,
with people you don't have to think twice about.

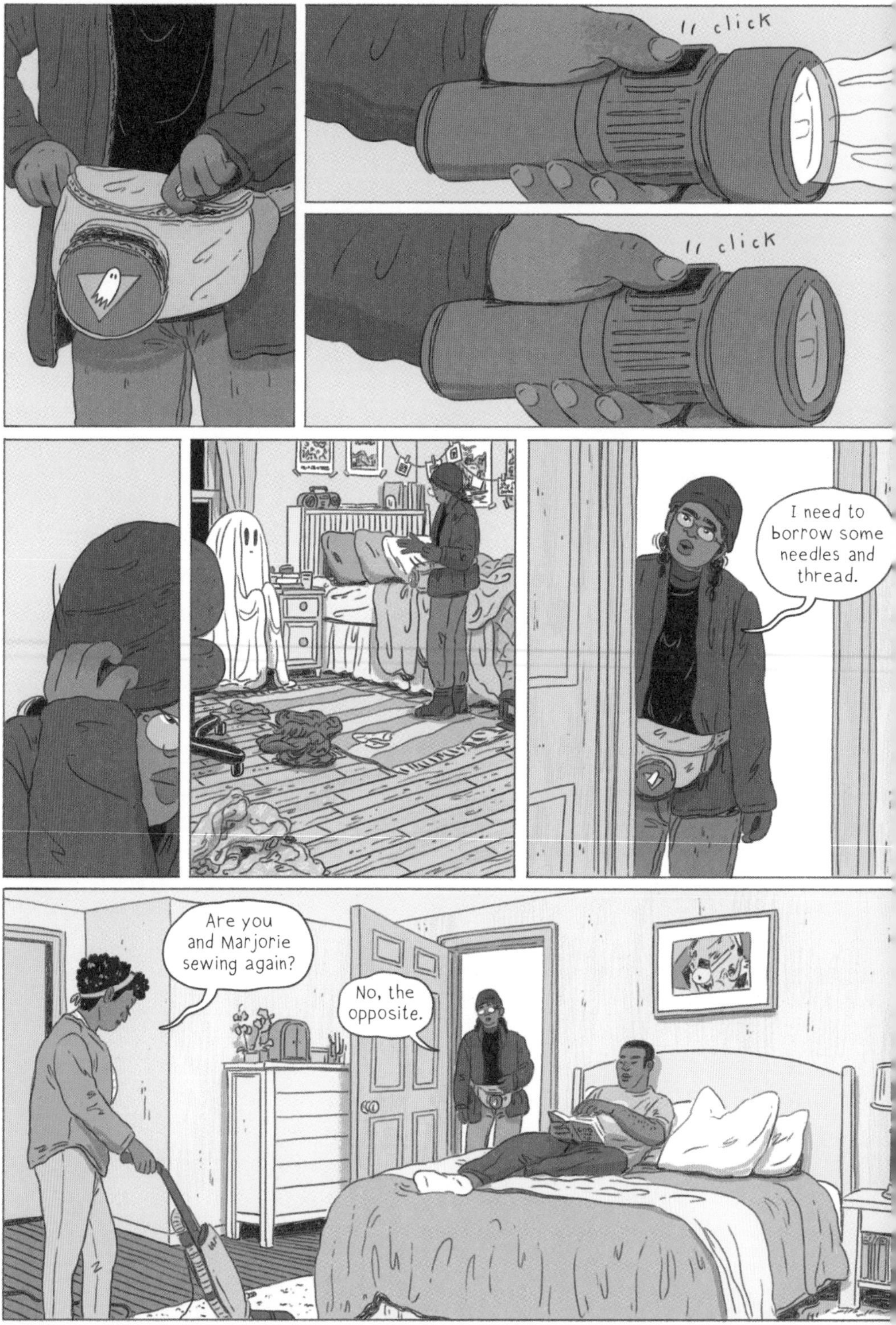
click
click
I need to borrow some needles and thread.
Are you and Marjorie sewing again?
No, the opposite.

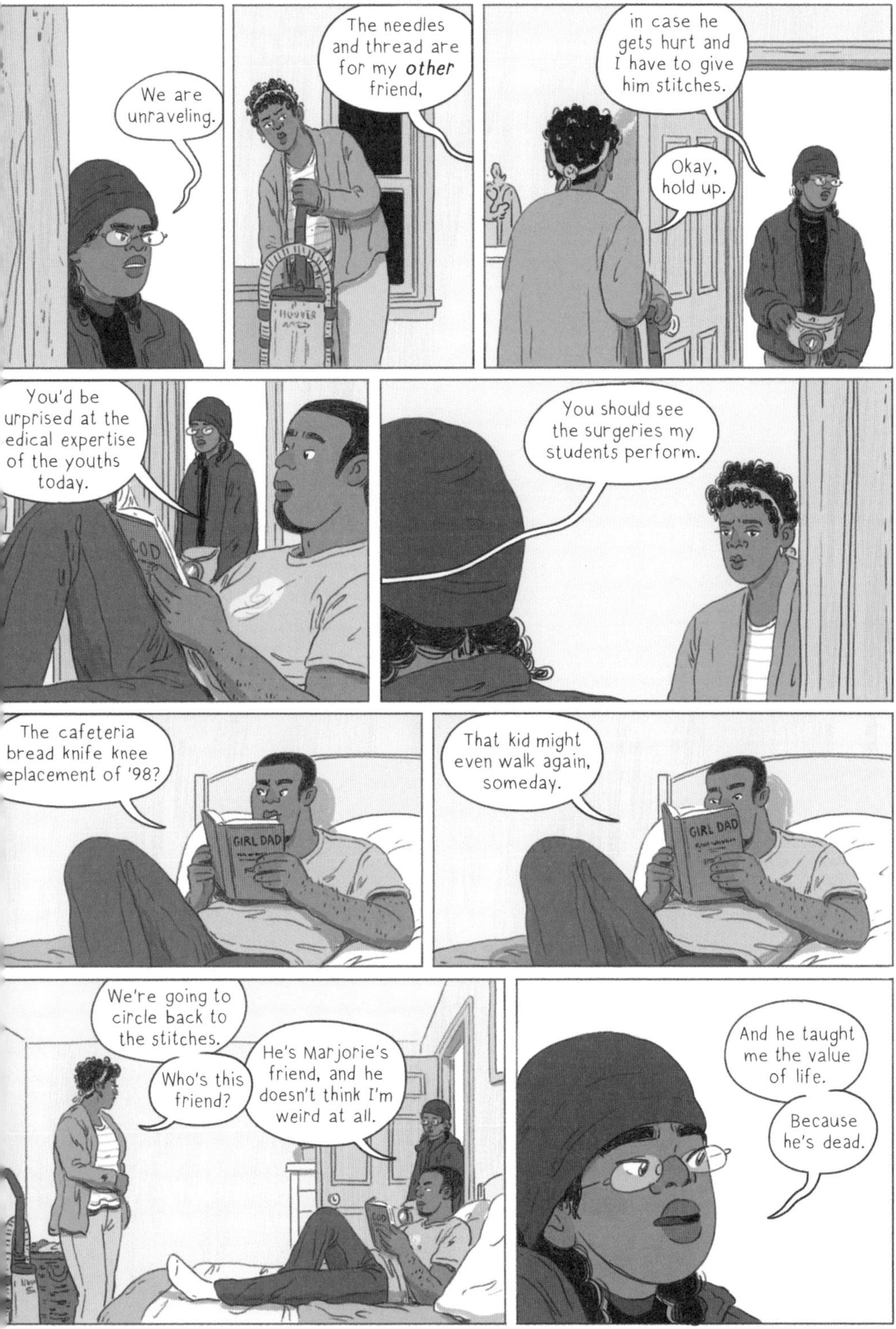
We are unraveling.
The needles and thread are for my *other* friend,
in case he gets hurt and I have to give him stitches.
Okay, hold up.
You'd be urprised at the edical expertise of the youths today.
You should see the surgeries my students perform.
The cafeteria bread knife knee eplacement of '98?
GIRL DAD
That kid might even walk again, someday.
GIRL DAD
We're going to circle back to the stitches.
Who's this friend?
He's Marjorie's friend, and he doesn't think I'm weird at all.
And he taught me the value of life.
Because he's dead.

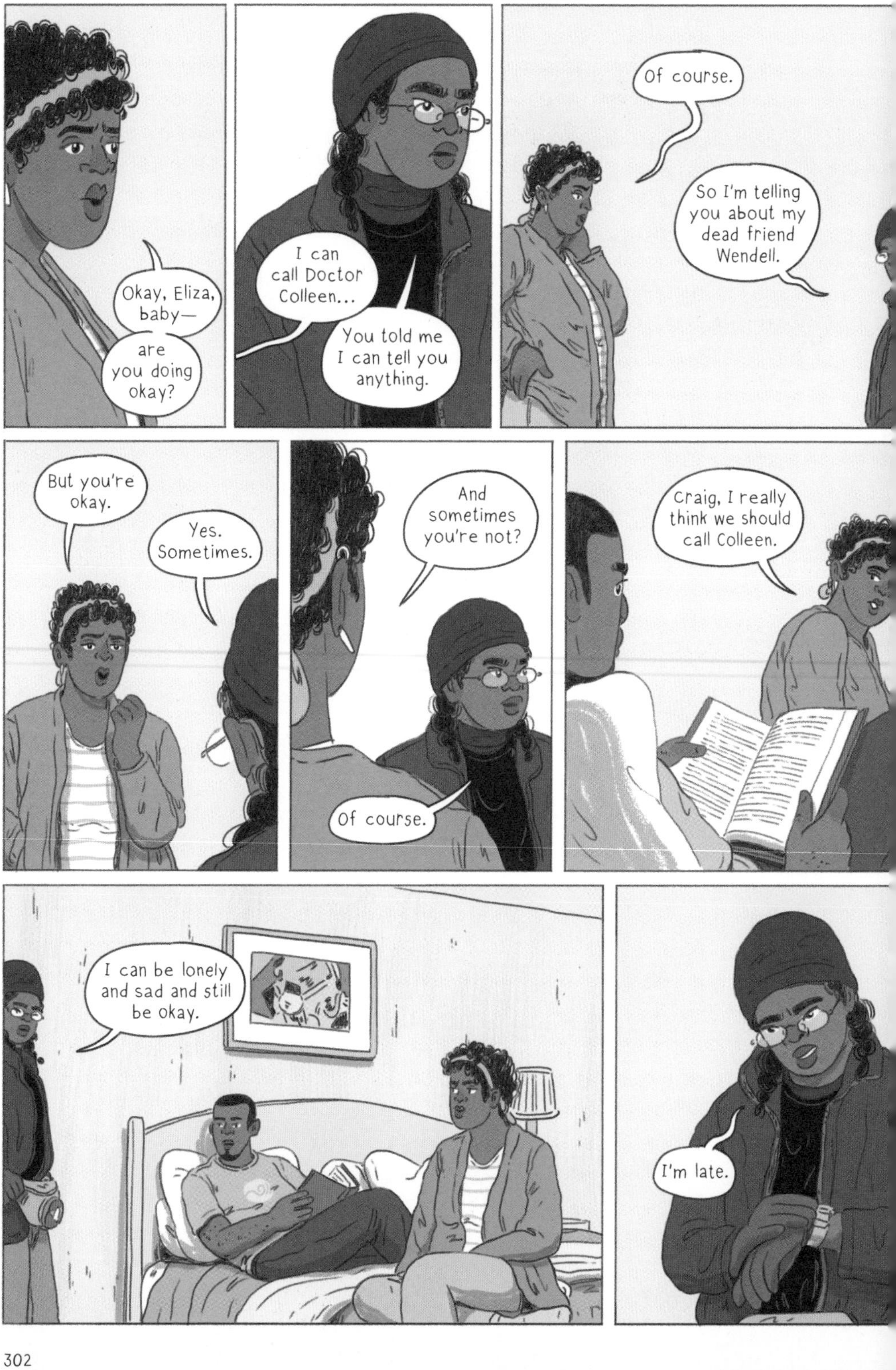
Okay, Eliza, baby—
are you doing okay?
I can call Doctor Colleen...
You told me I can tell you anything.
Of course.
So I'm telling you about my dead friend Wendell.
But you're okay.
Yes. Sometimes.
And sometimes you're not?
Of course.
Craig, I really think we should call Colleen.
I can be lonely and sad and still be okay.
I'm late.

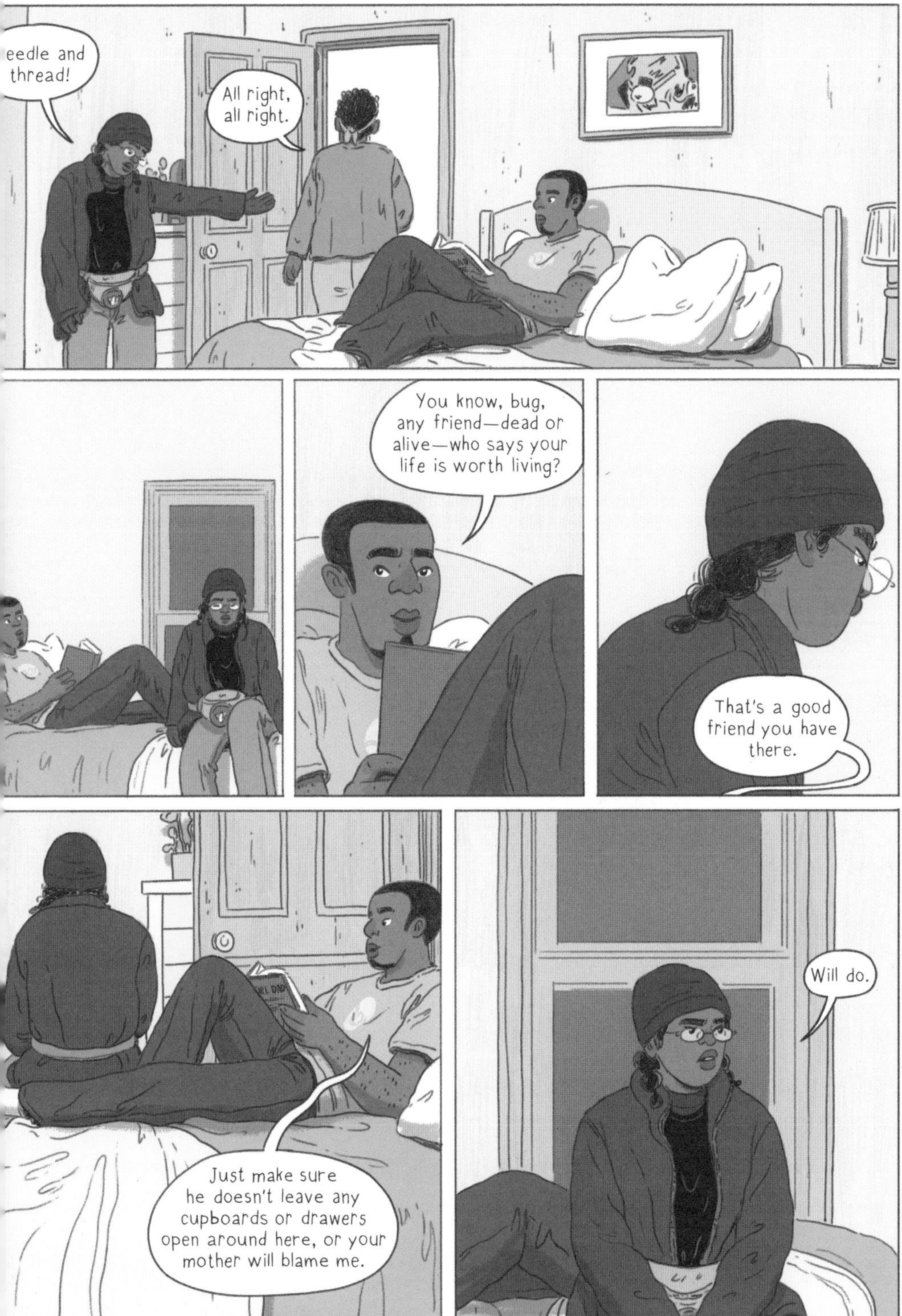

eedle and thread!
All right, all right.
You know, bug, any friend—dead or alive—who says your life is worth living?
That's a good friend you have there.
Just make sure he doesn't leave any cupboards or drawers open around here, or your mother will blame me.
Will do.

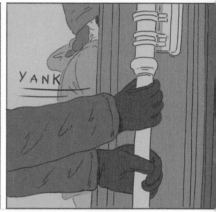

YANK

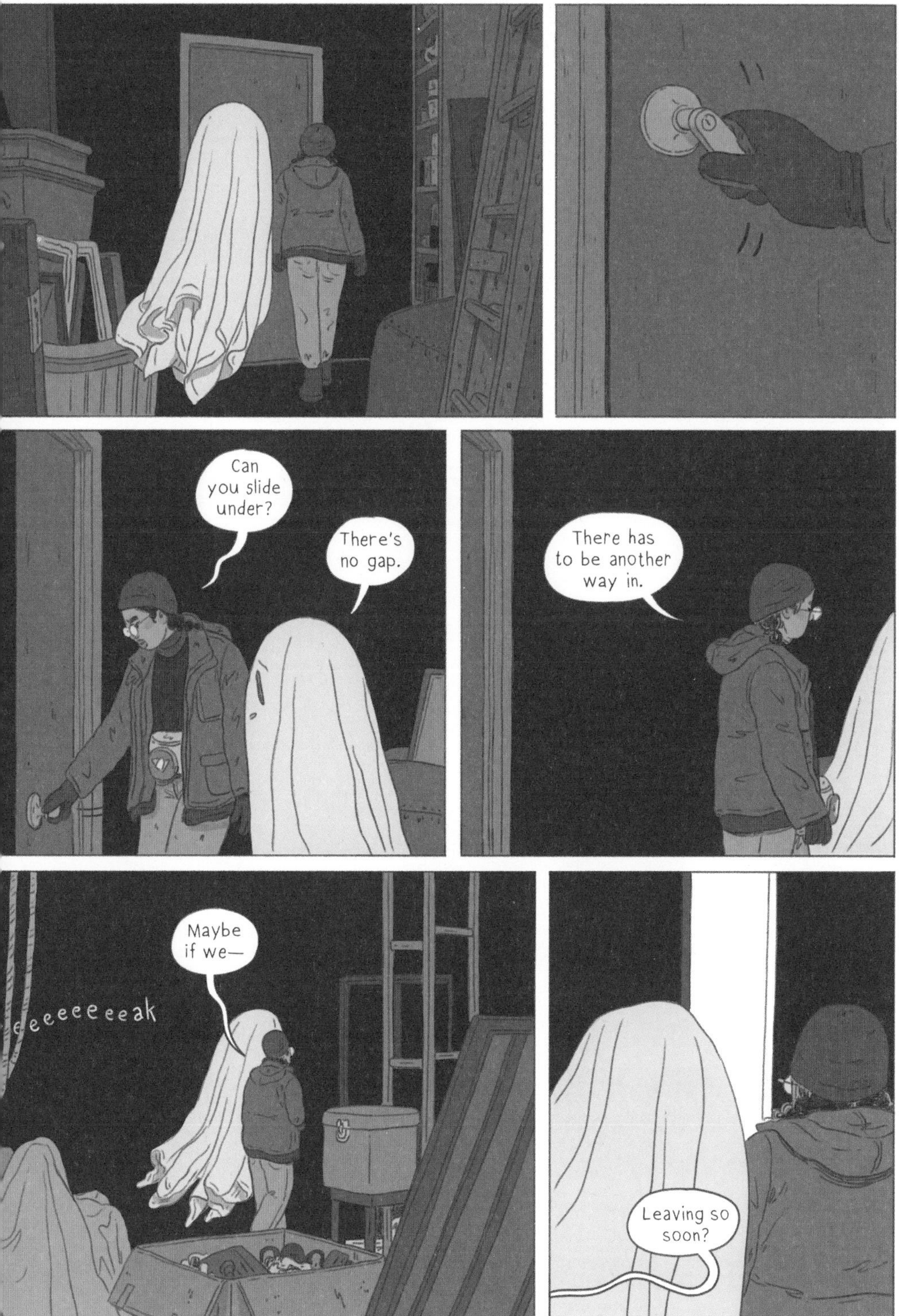
Can you slide under?
There's no gap.
There has to be another way in.
Maybe if we—
eeeeeeeeak
Leaving so soon?

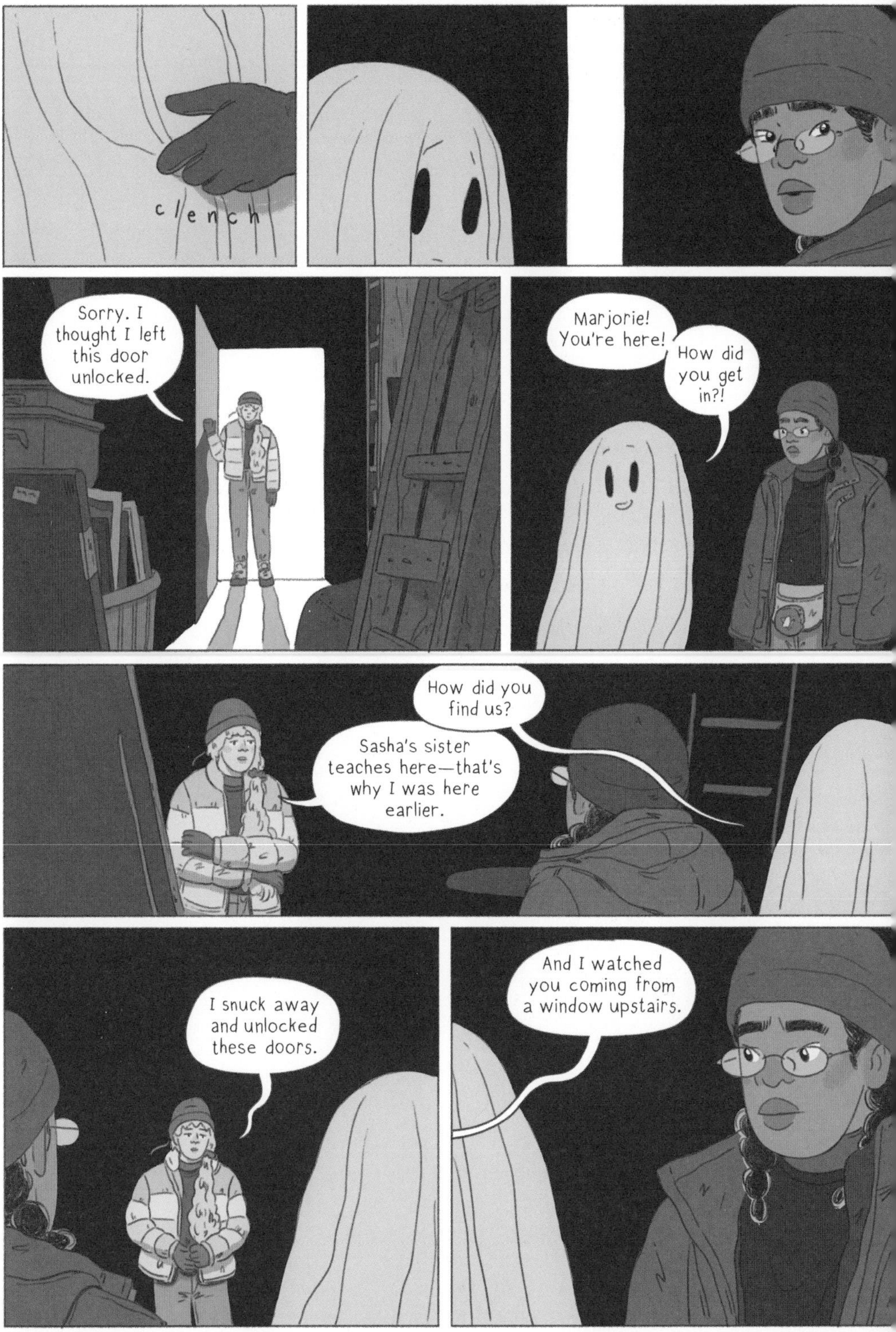
clench
Sorry. I thought I left this door unlocked.
Marjorie! You're here!
How did you get in?!
How did you find us?
Sasha's sister teaches here—that's why I was here earlier.
I snuck away and unlocked these doors.
And I watched you coming from a window upstairs.

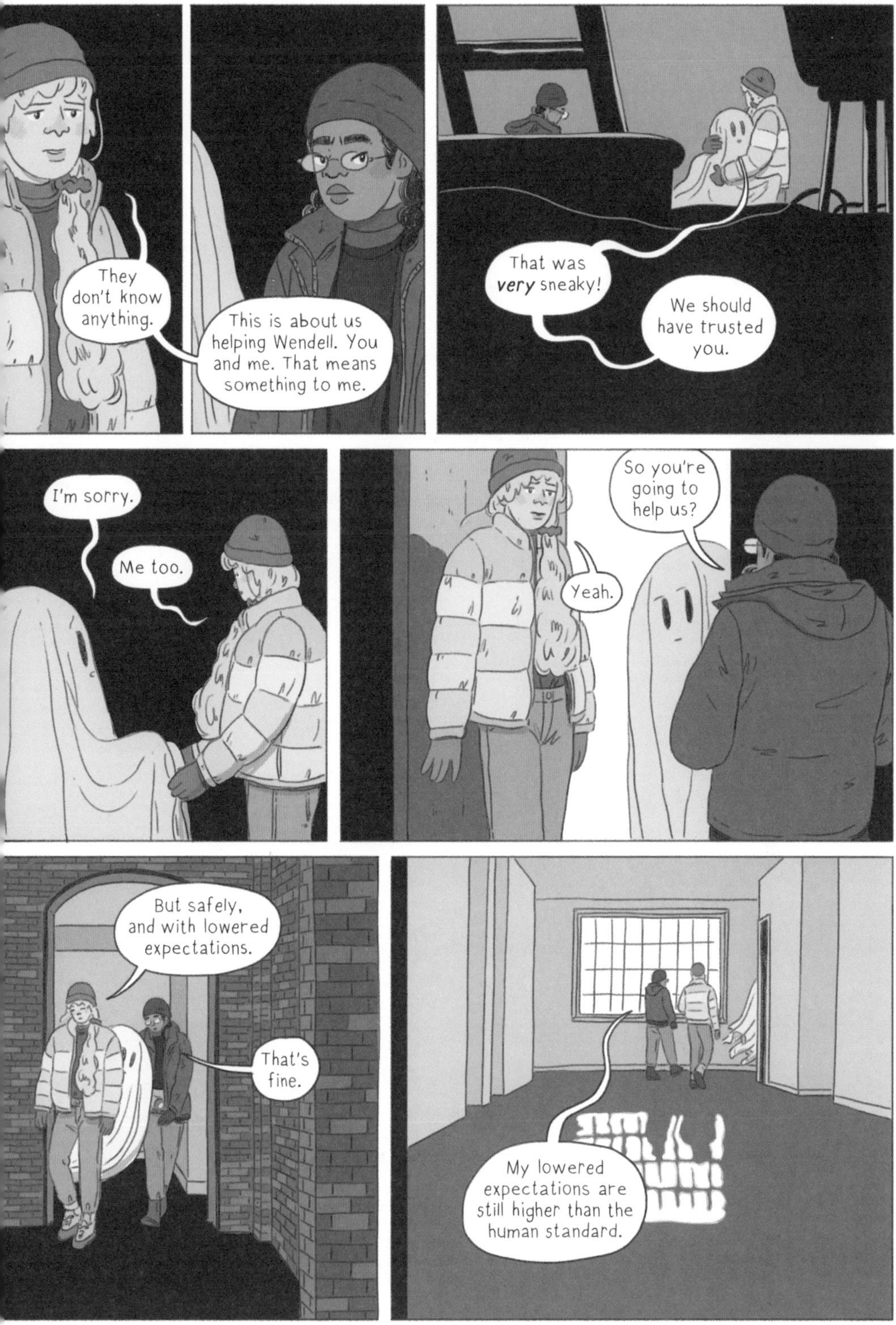
They don't know anything.
This is about us helping Wendell. You and me. That means something to me.
That was *very* sneaky!
We should have trusted you.
I'm sorry.
Me too.
So you're going to help us?
Yeah.
But safely, and with lowered expectations.
That's fine.
My lowered expectations are still higher than the human standard.

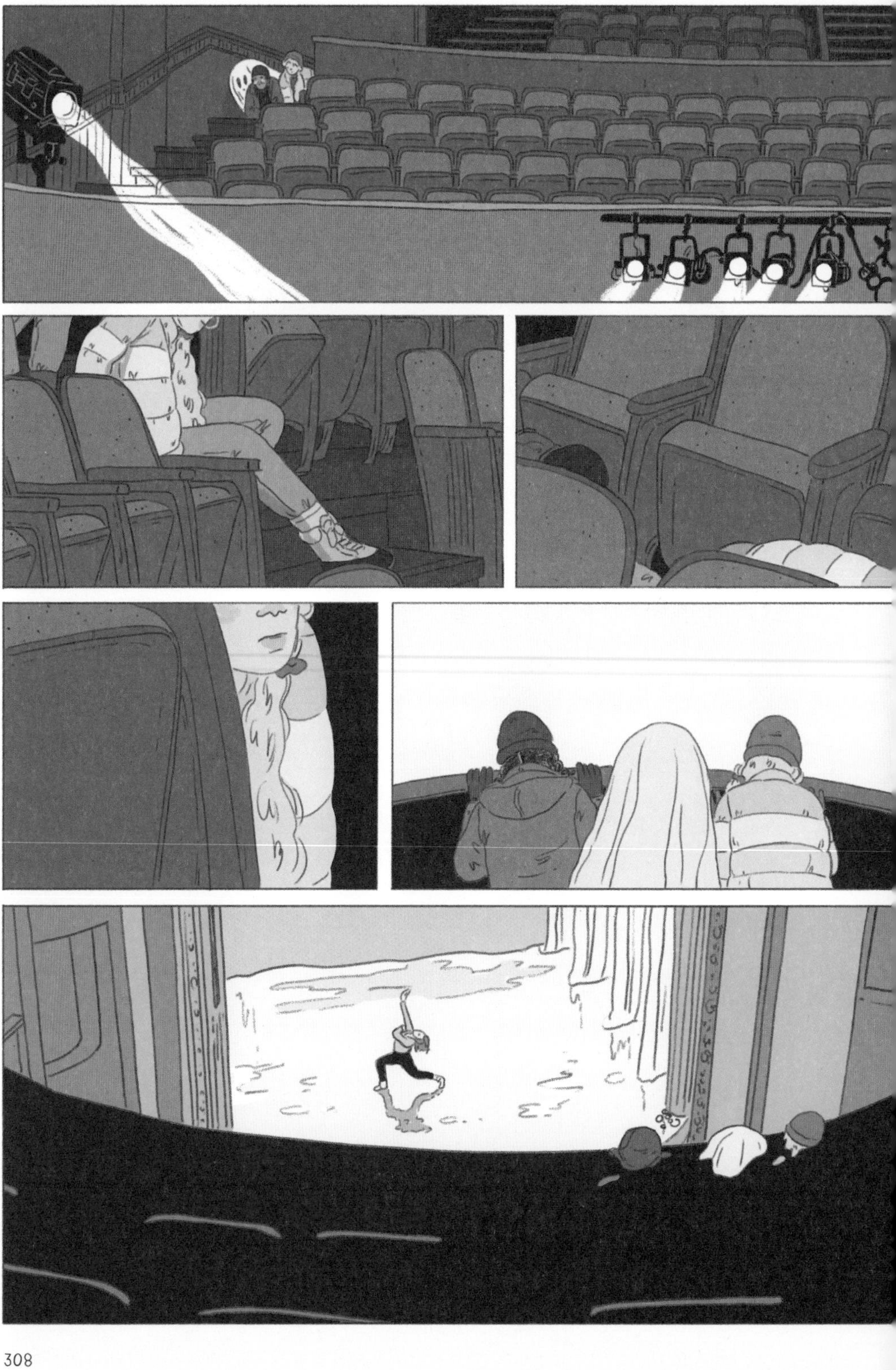

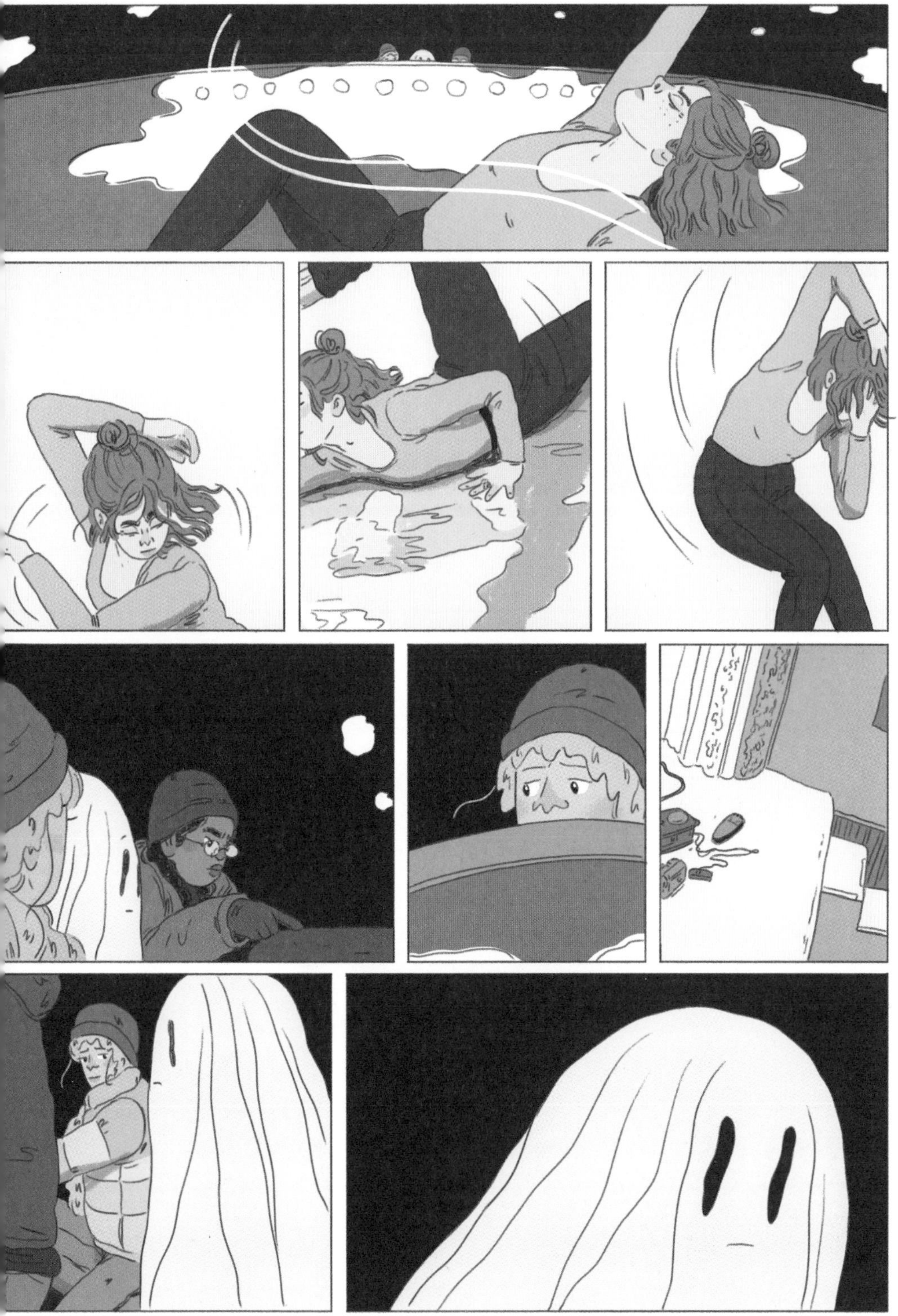

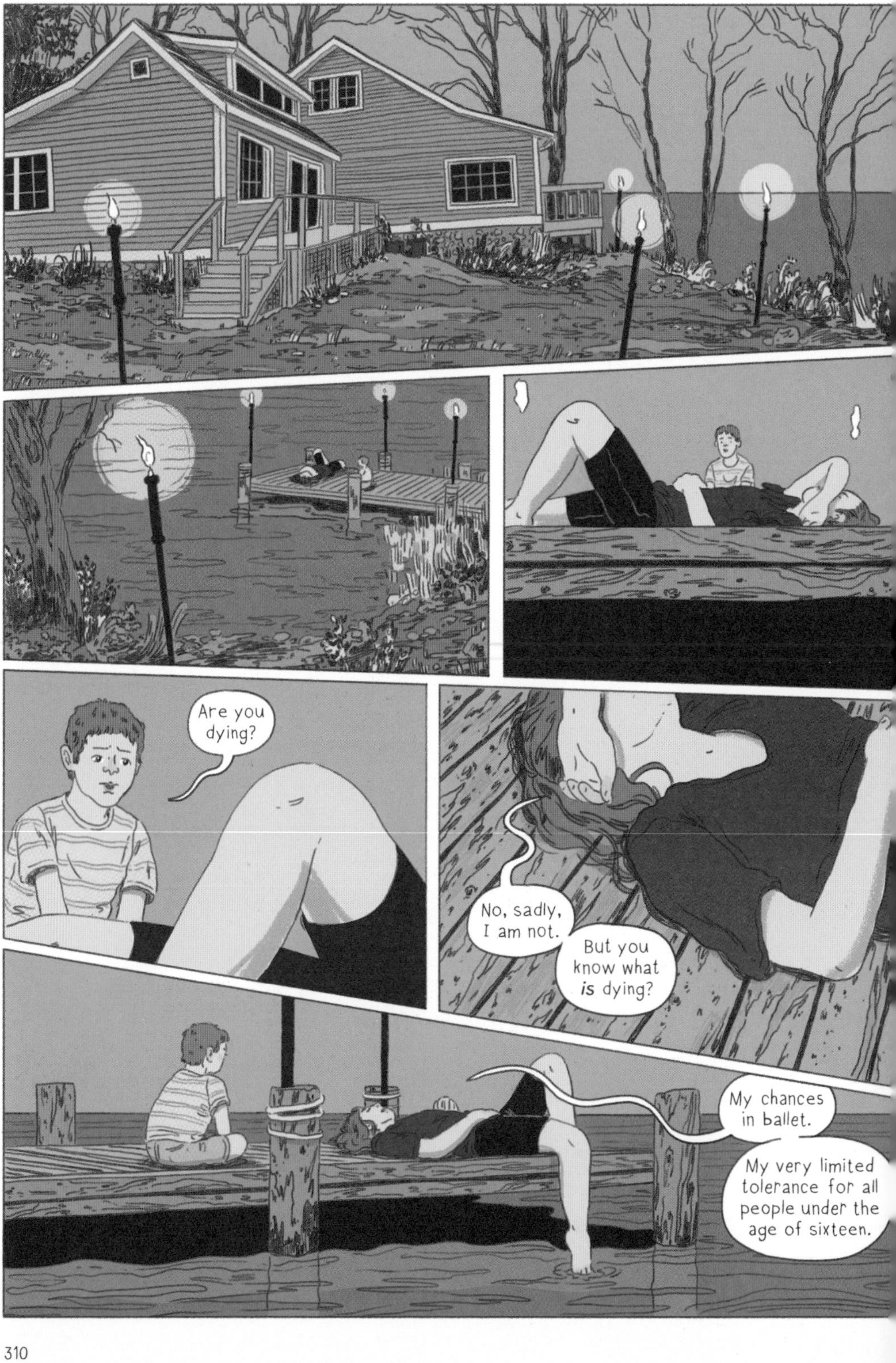
Are you dying?
No, sadly, I am not.
But you know what *is* dying?
My chances in ballet.
My very limited tolerance for all people under the age of sixteen.

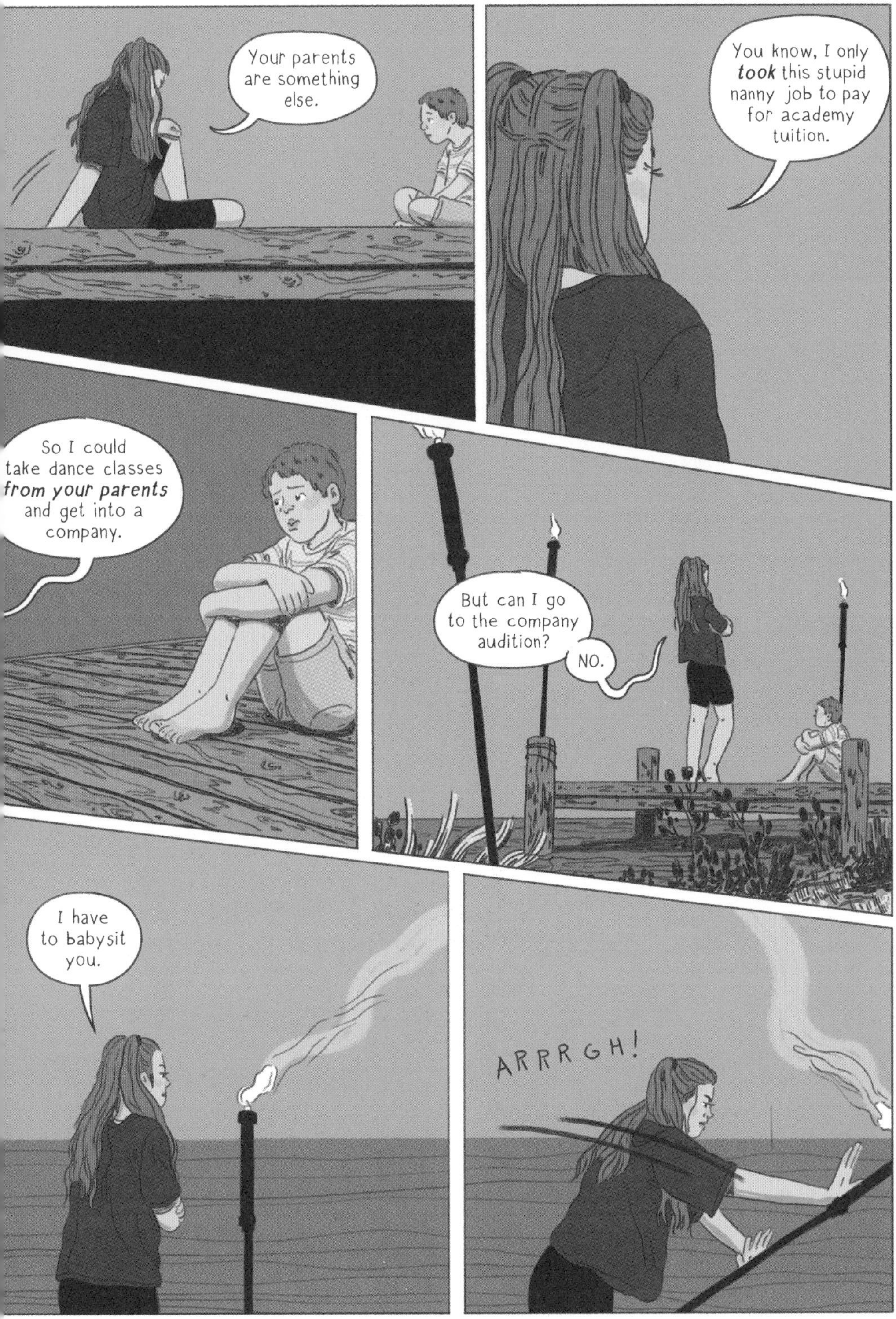
Your parents are something else.
You know, I only **took** this stupid nanny job to pay for academy tuition.
So I could take dance classes **from your parents** and get into a company.
But can I go to the company audition?
NO.
I have to babysit you.
ARRRGH!

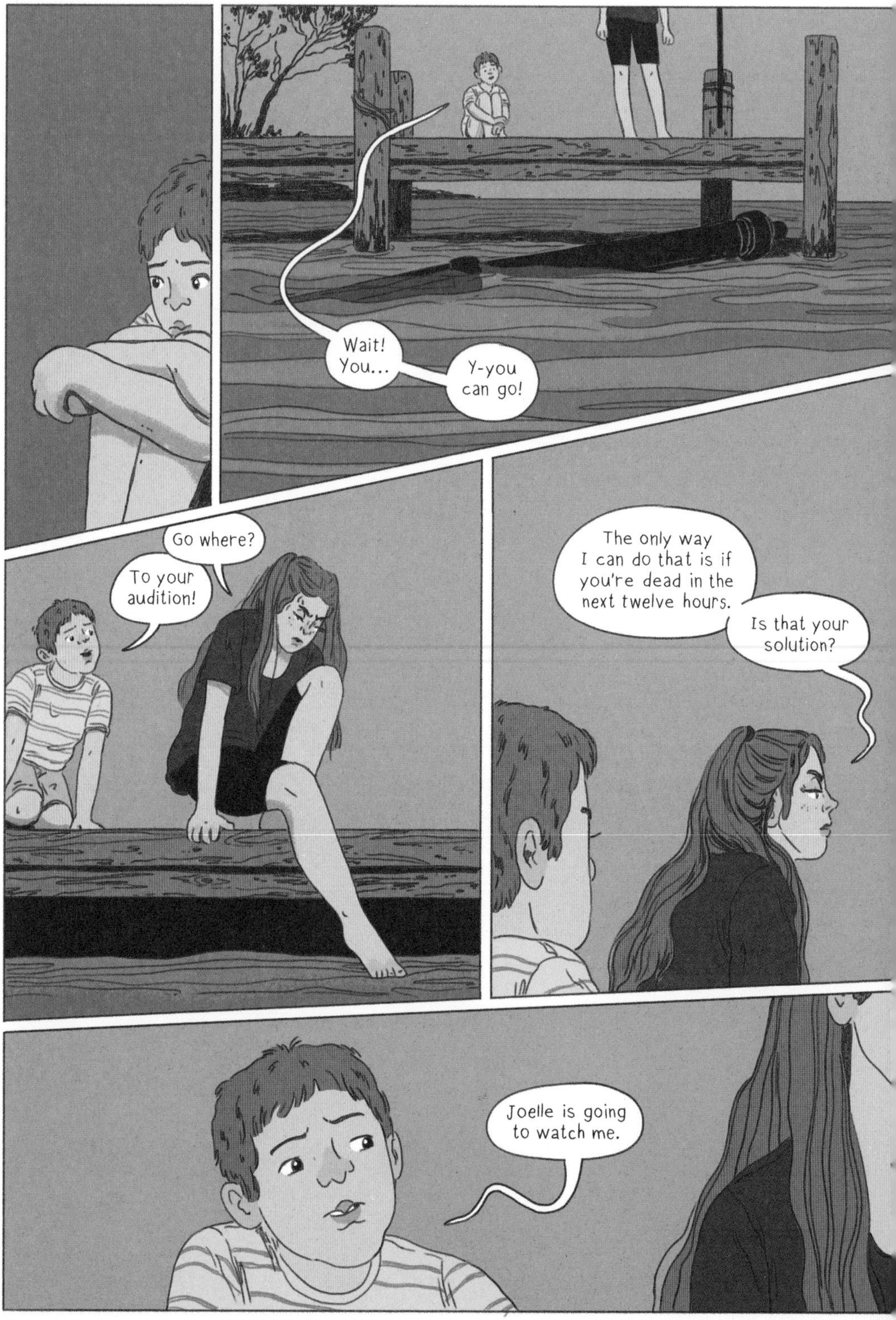
Wait! You...
Y-you can go!
Go where?
To your audition!
The only way I can do that is if you're dead in the next twelve hours.
Is that your solution?
Joelle is going to watch me.

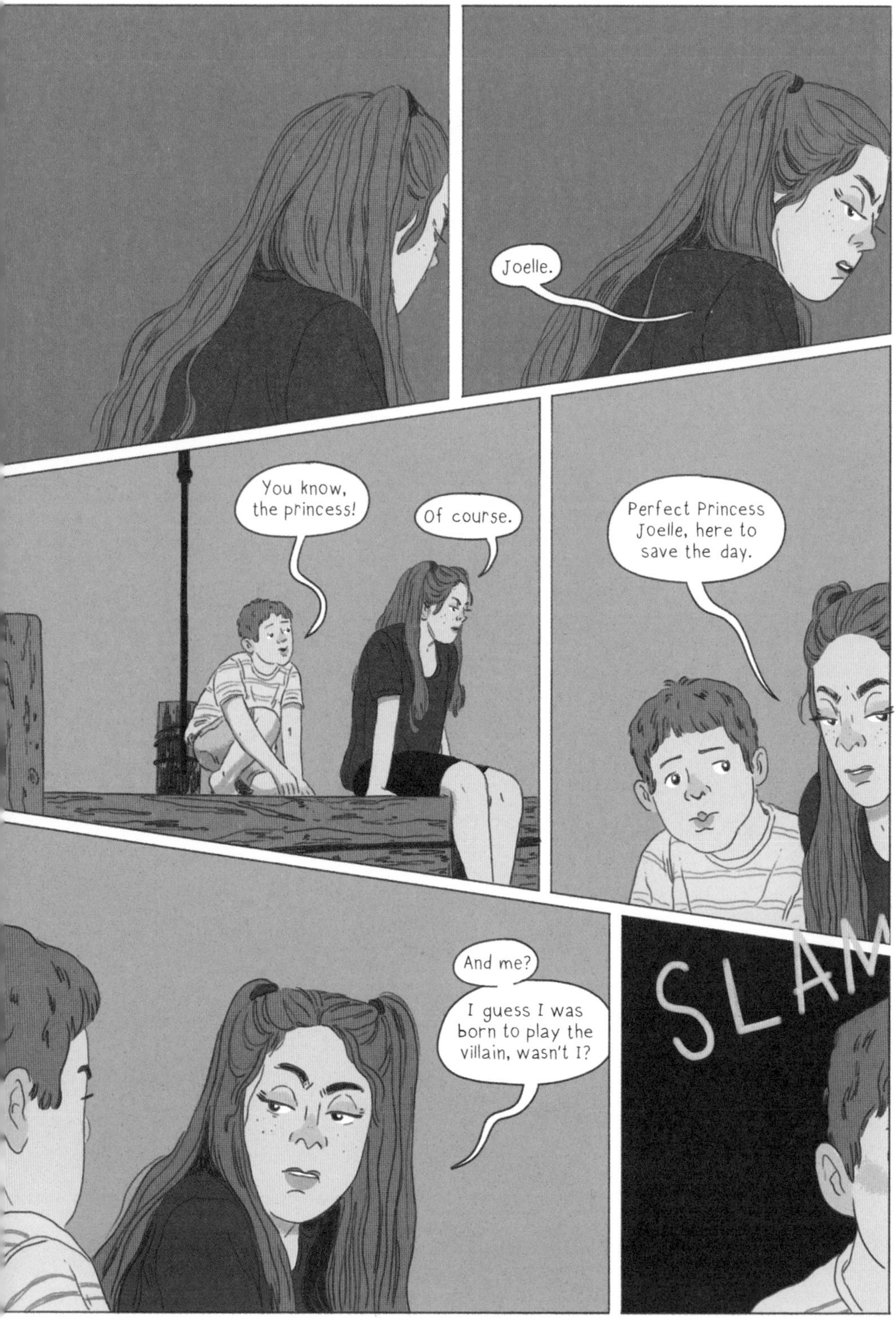
Joelle.
You know, the princess!
Of course.
Perfect Princess Joelle, here to save the day.
And me?
I guess I was born to play the villain, wasn't I?
SLAM

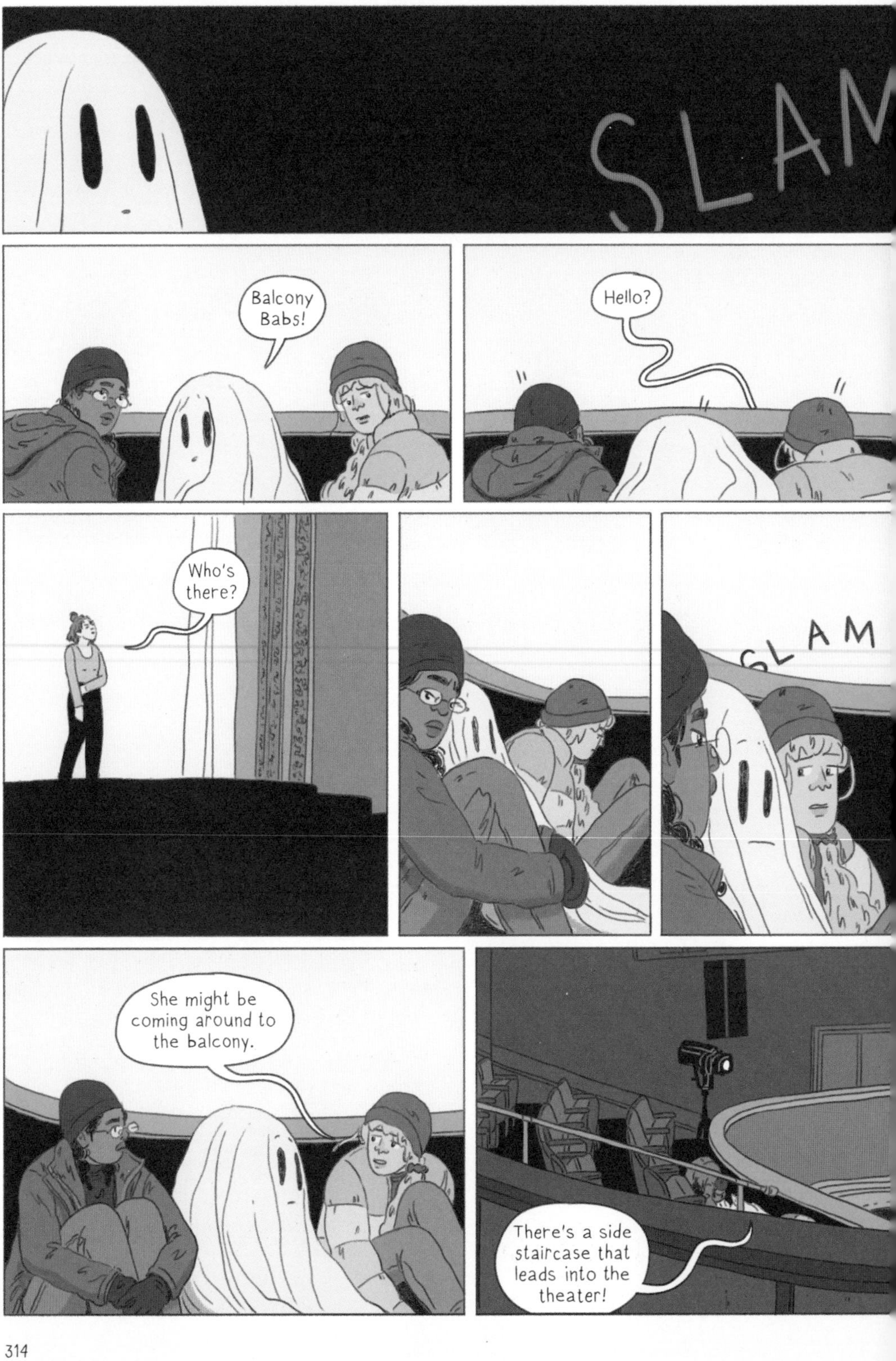
SLAM
Balcony Babs!
Hello?
Who's there?
SLAM
She might be coming around to the balcony.
There's a side staircase that leads into the theater!

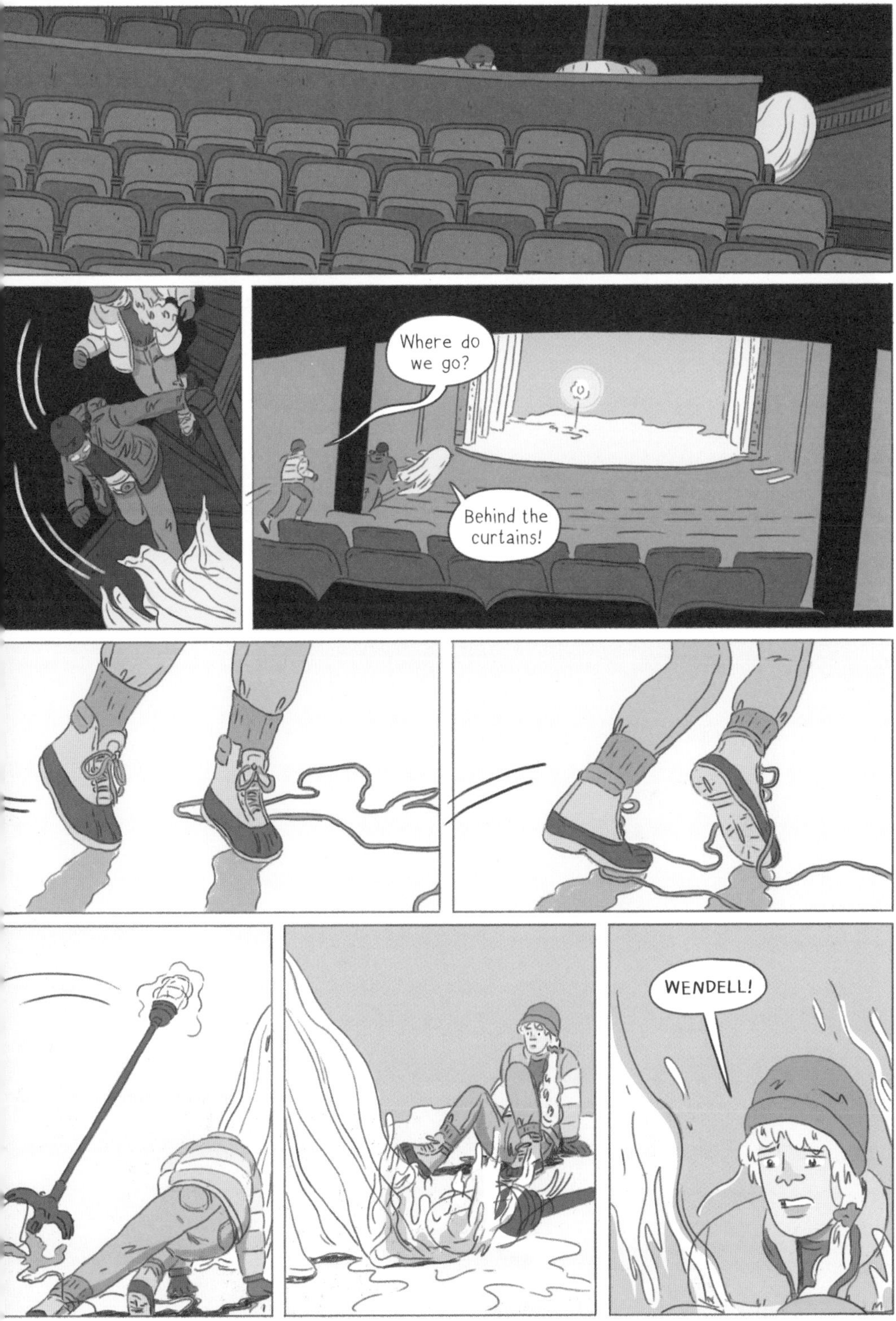

Where do we go?
Behind the curtains!
WENDELL!

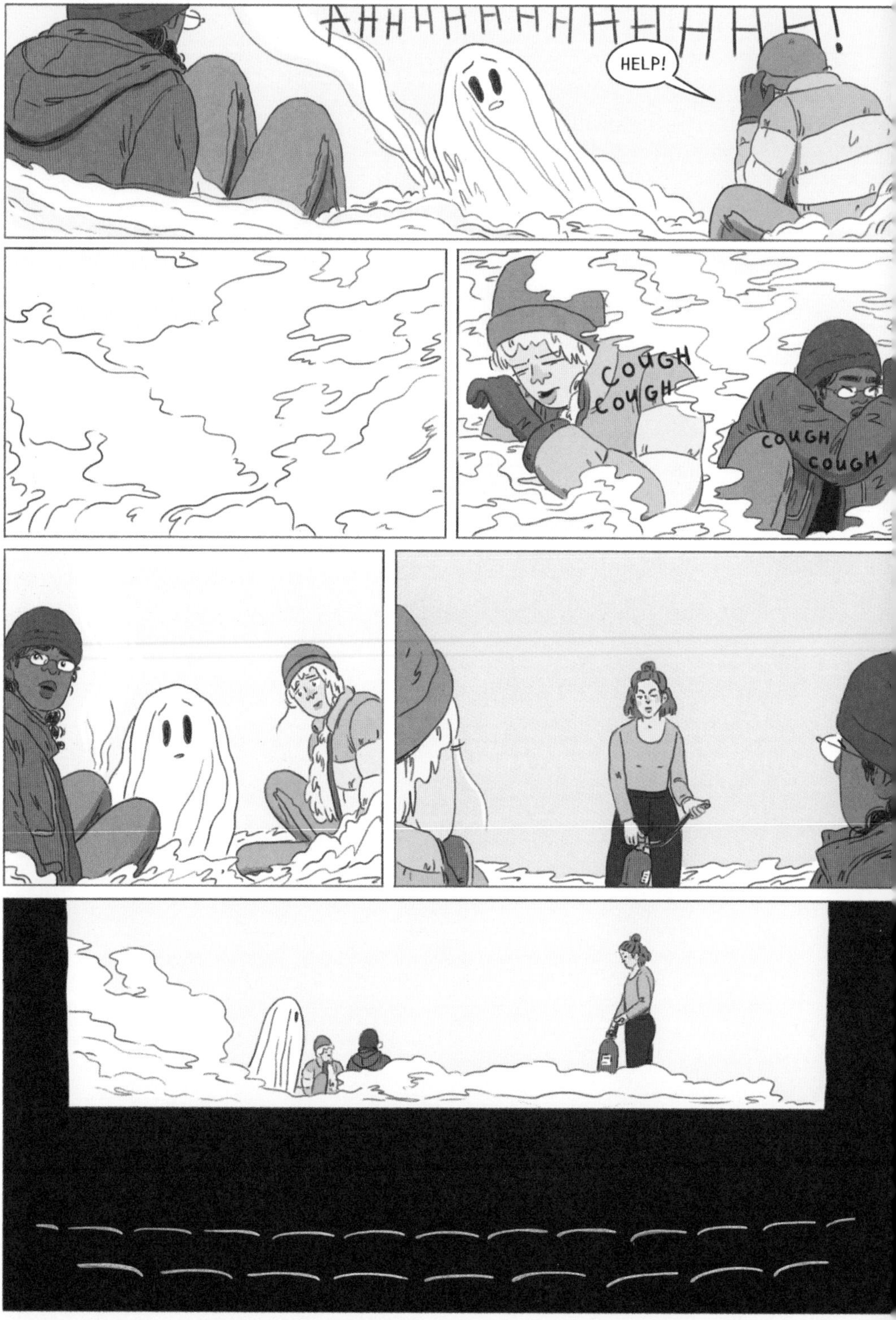
AHHHHHHHHHHHHHH!
HELP!
COUGH COUGH
COUGH COUGH

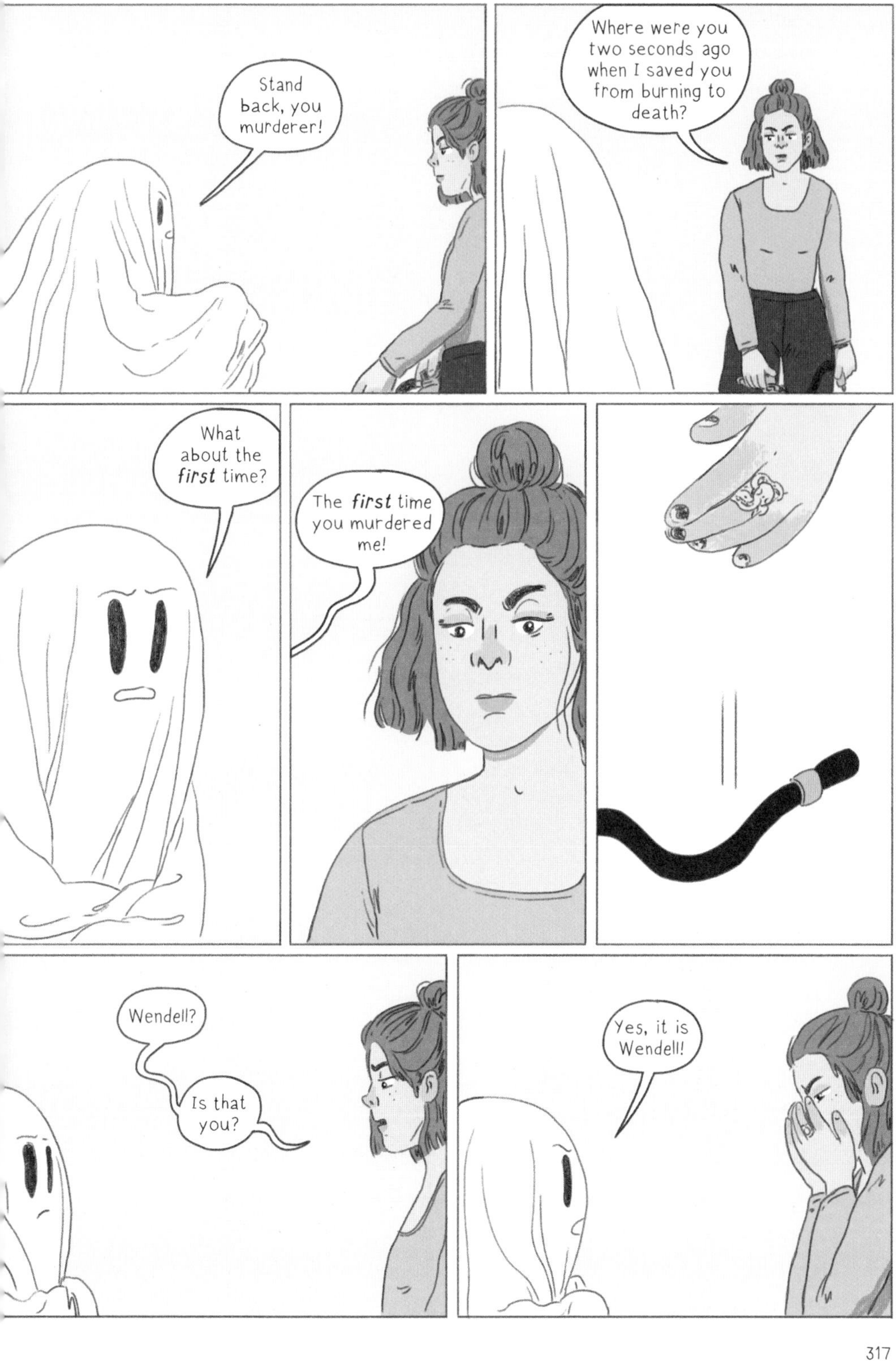
Stand back, you murderer!
Where were you two seconds ago when I saved you from burning to death?
What about the *first* time?
The *first* time you murdered me!
Wendell?
Is that you?
Yes, it is Wendell!

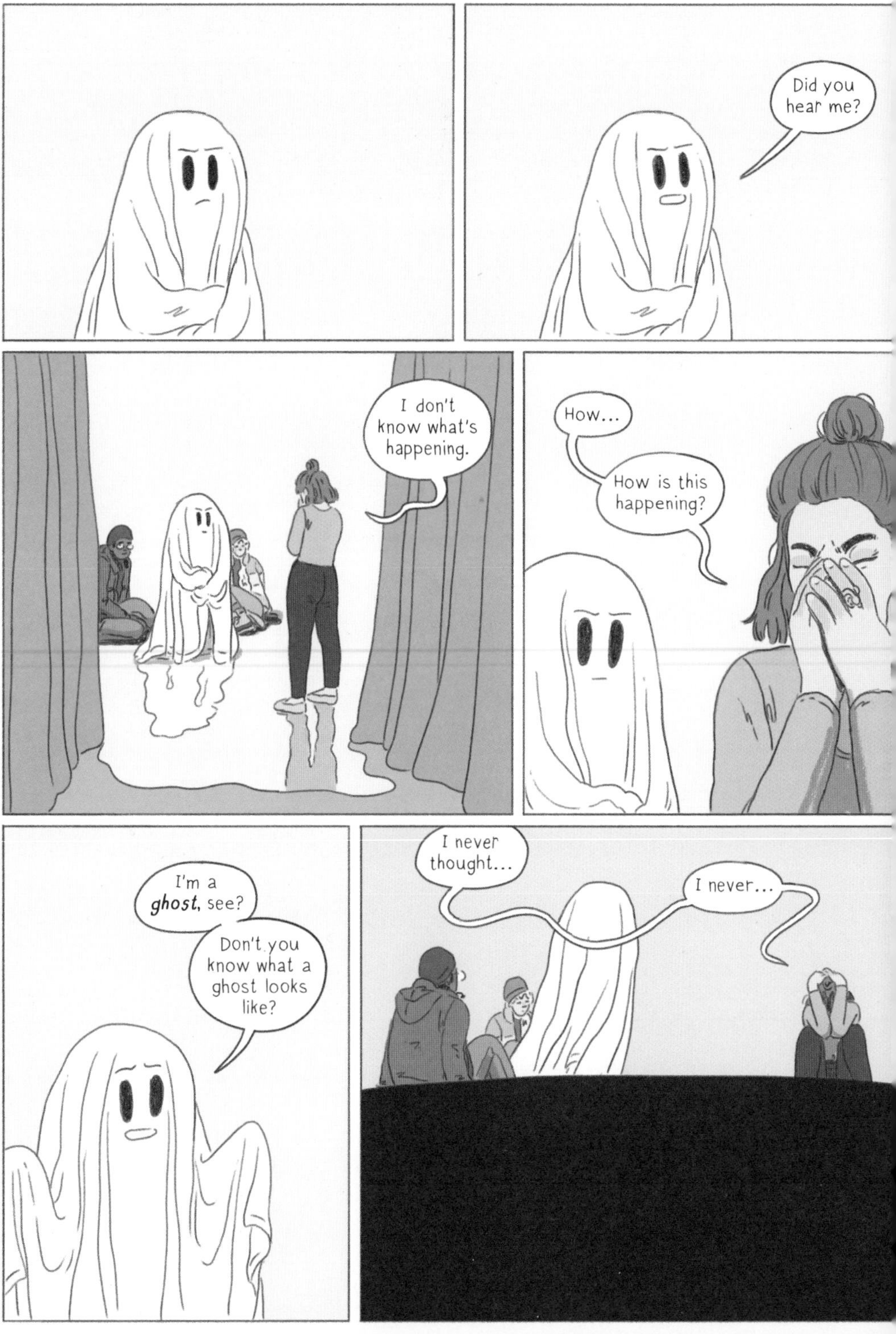
Did you hear me?
I don't know what's happening.
How...
How is this happening?
I'm a *ghost*, see?
Don't you know what a ghost looks like?
I never thought...
I never...

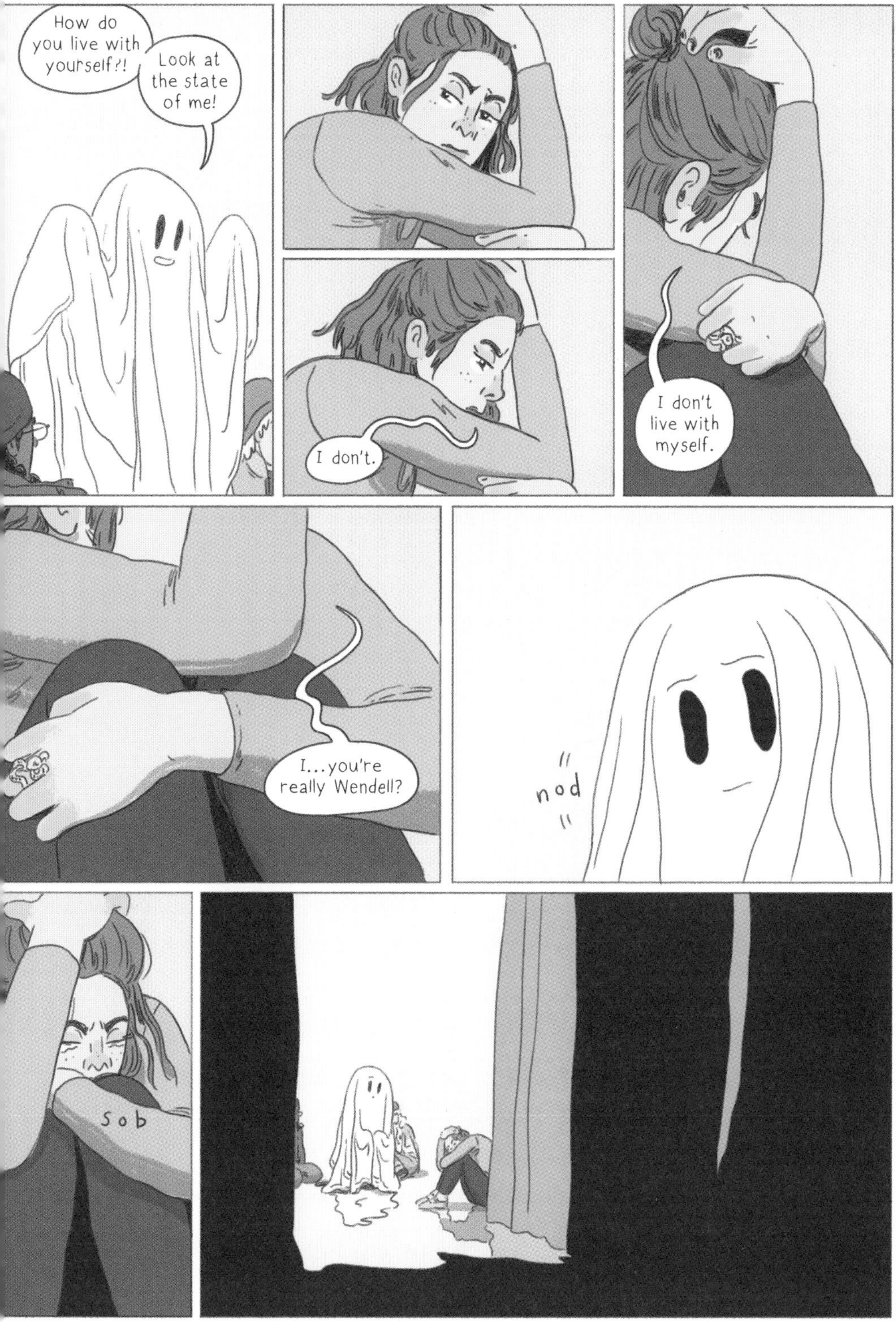
How do you live with yourself?!
Look at the state of me!
I don't.
I don't live with myself.
I...you're really Wendell?
nod
sob

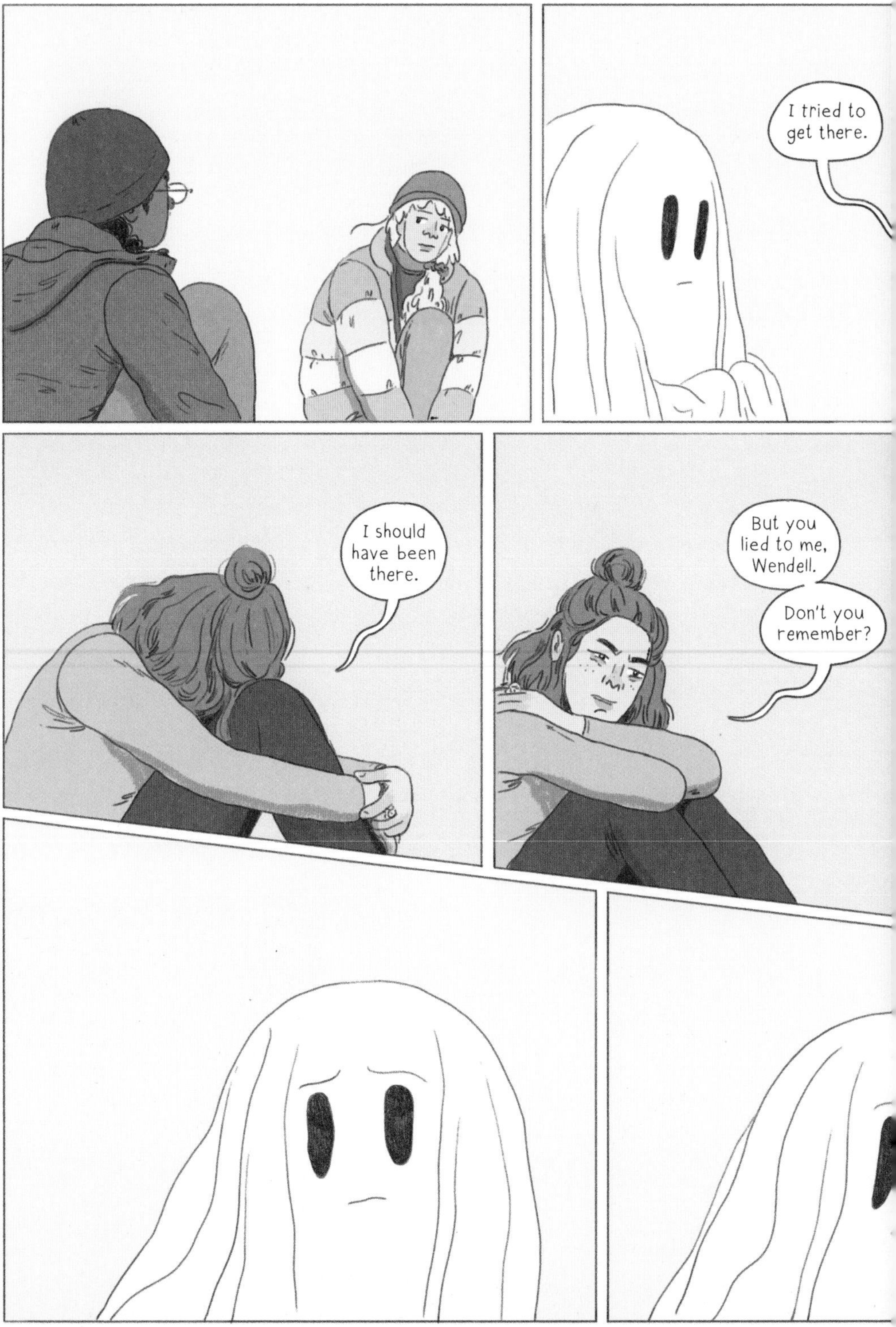
I tried to get there.
I should have been there.
But you lied to me, Wendell.
Don't you remember?

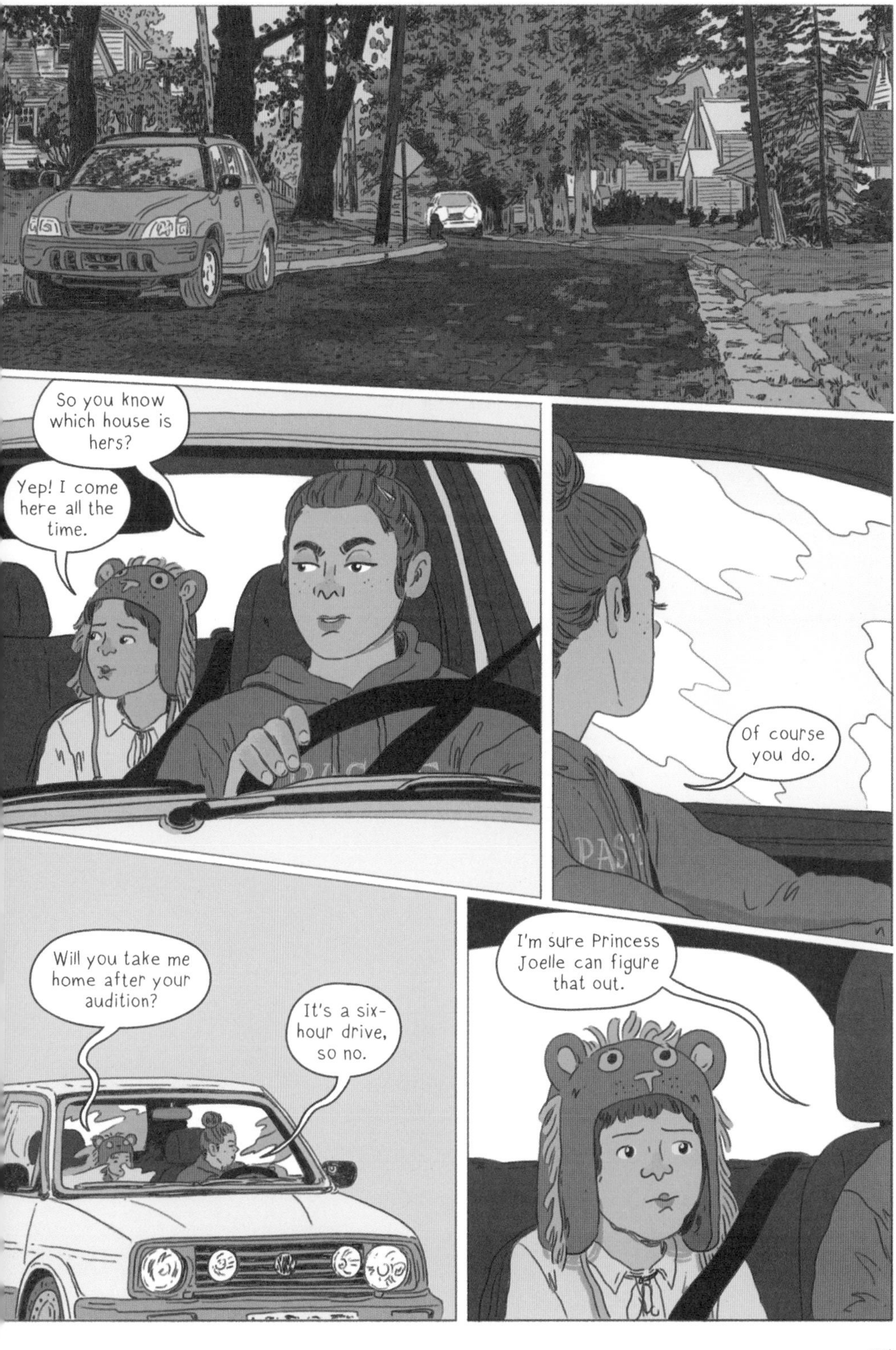
So you know which house is hers?
Yep! I come here all the time.
Of course you do.
Will you take me home after your audition?
It's a six-hour drive, so no.
I'm sure Princess Joelle can figure that out.

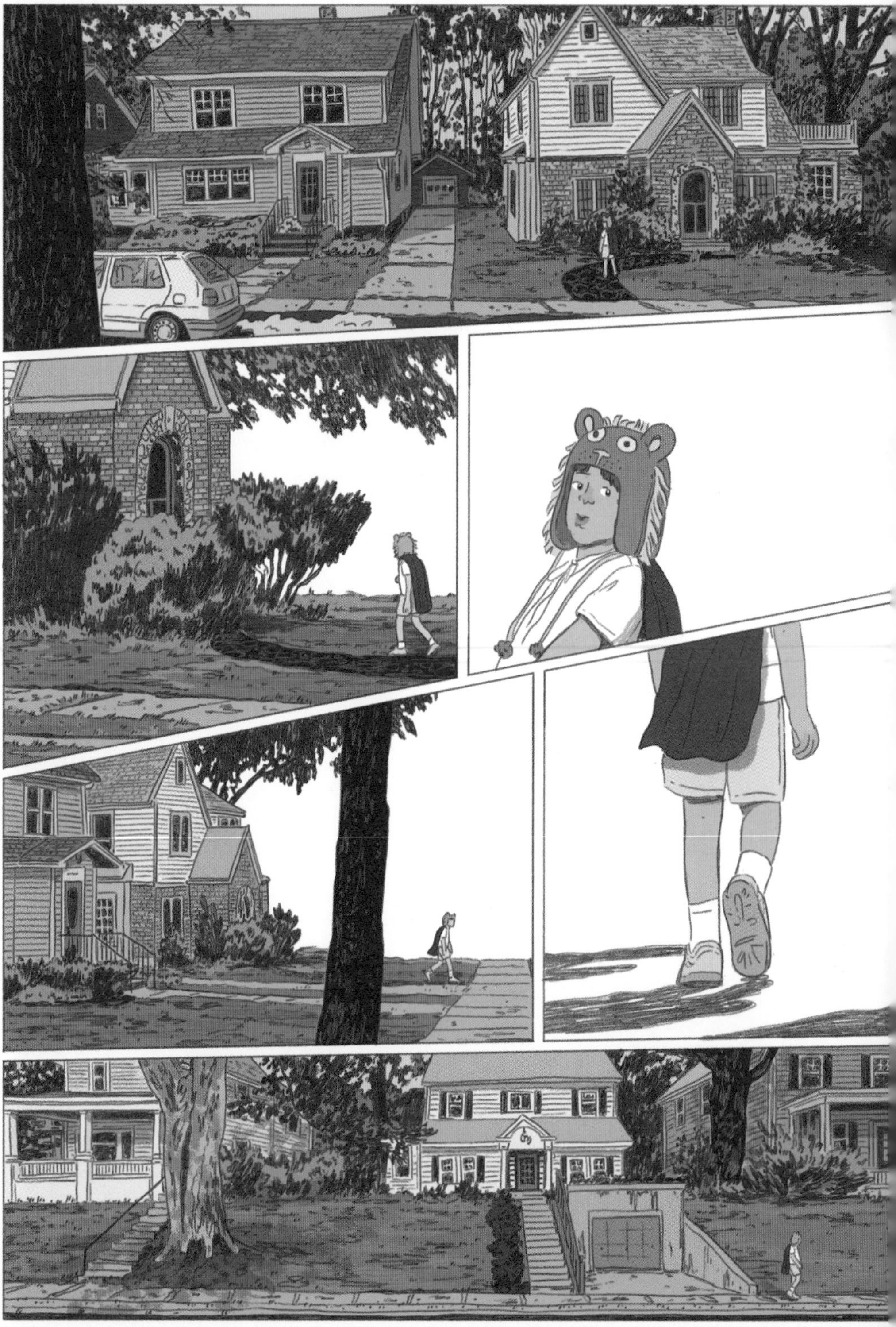

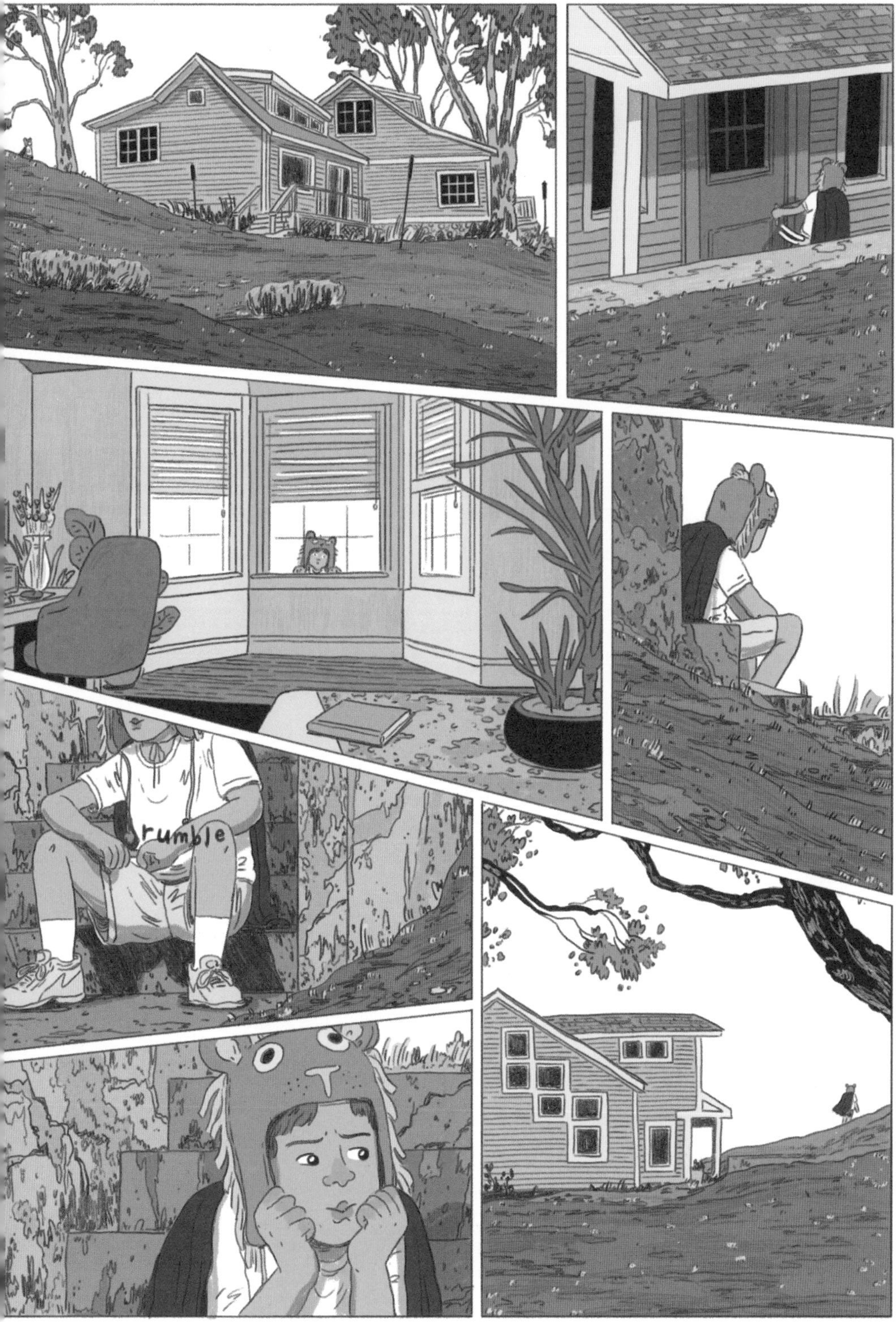
rumble

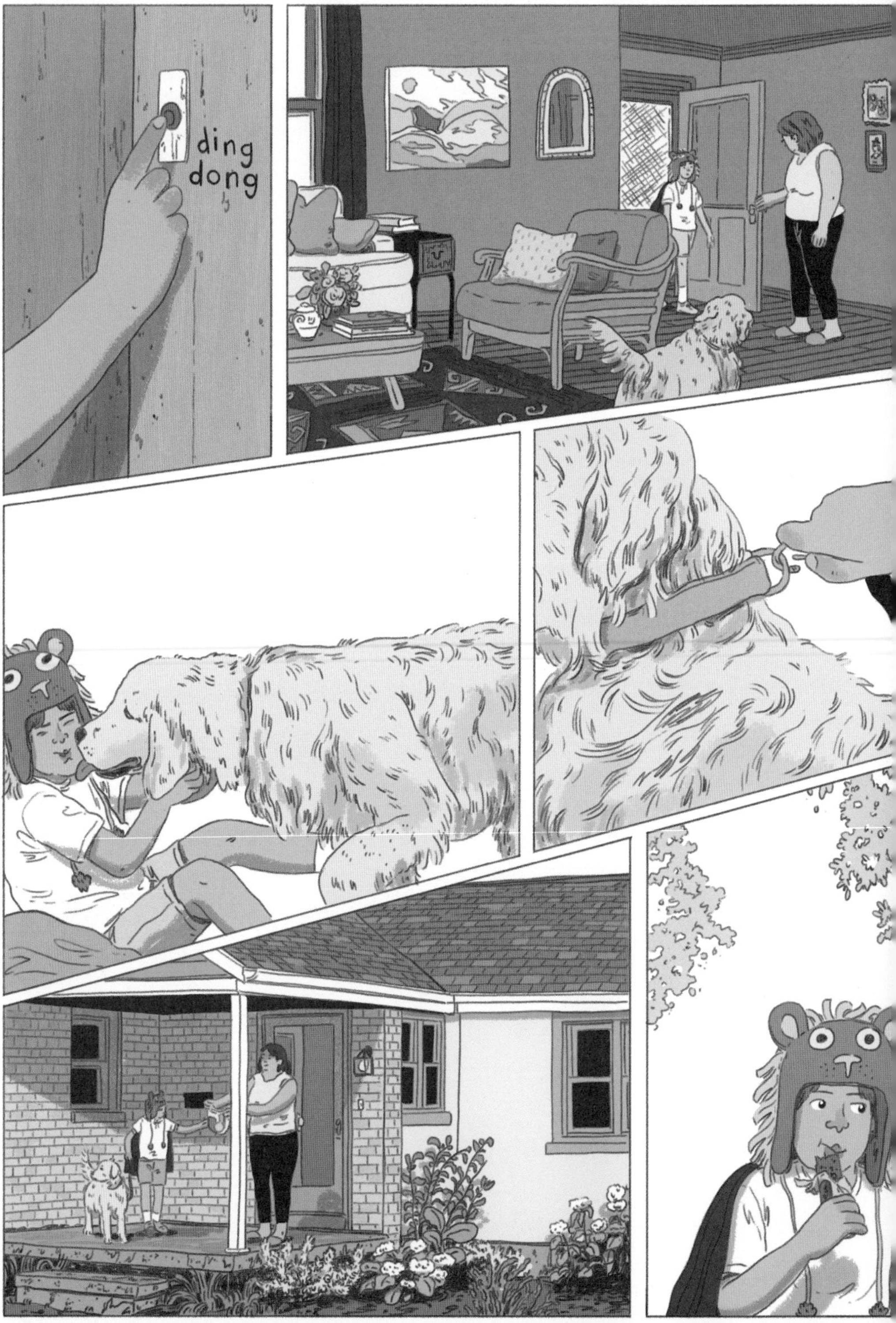
ding dong

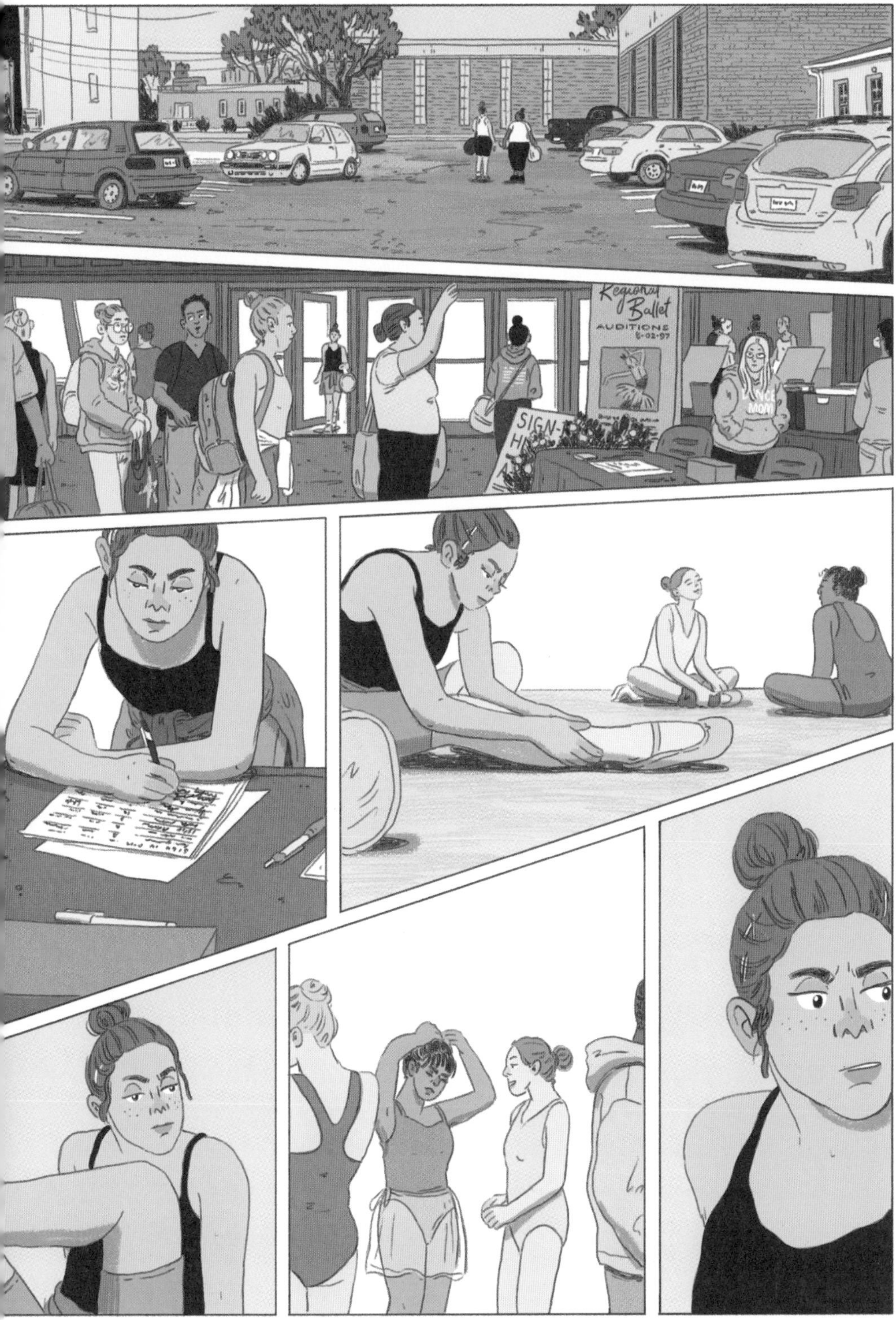
Regional Ballet
AUDITIONS
8-02-97
SIGN-
MOM

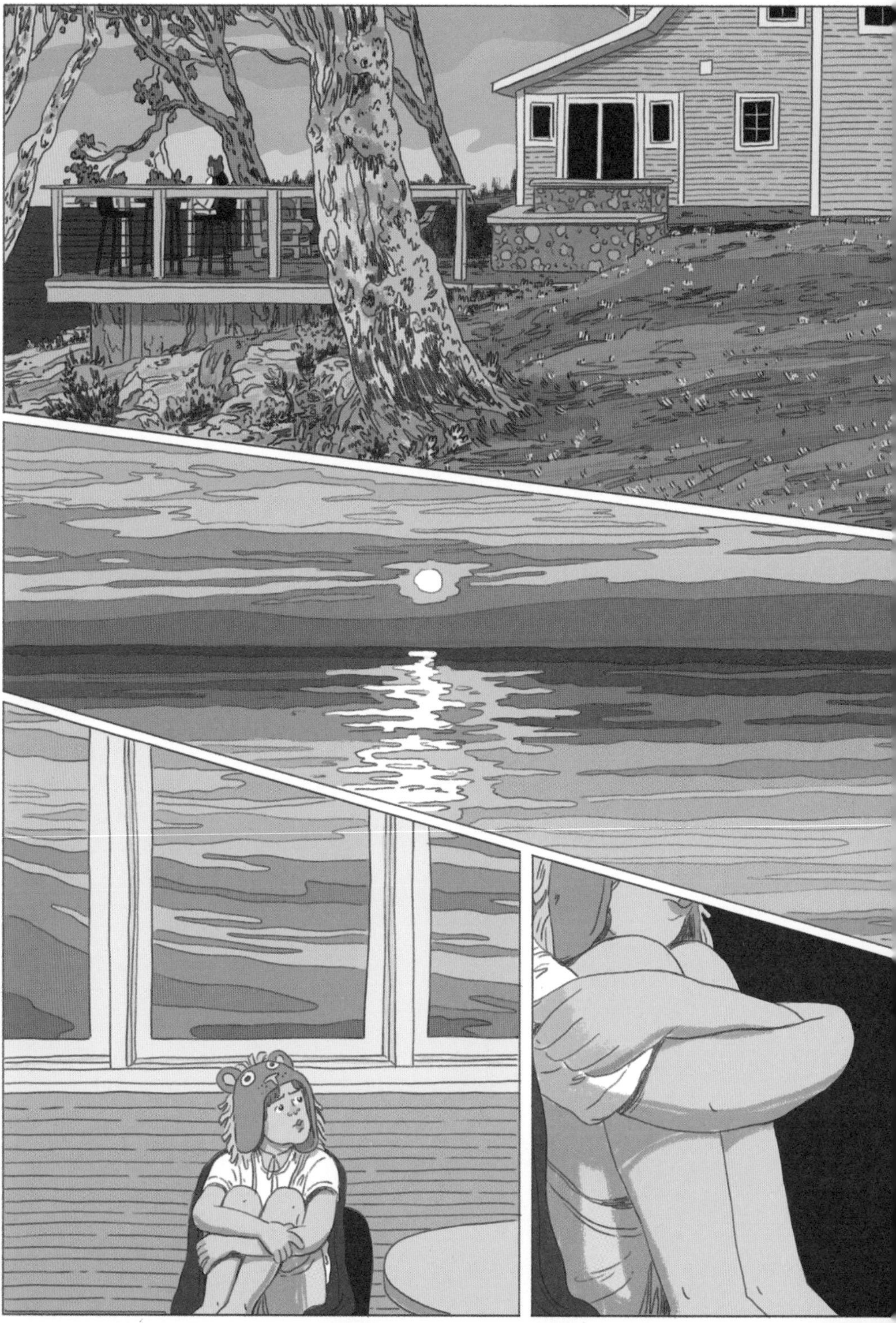

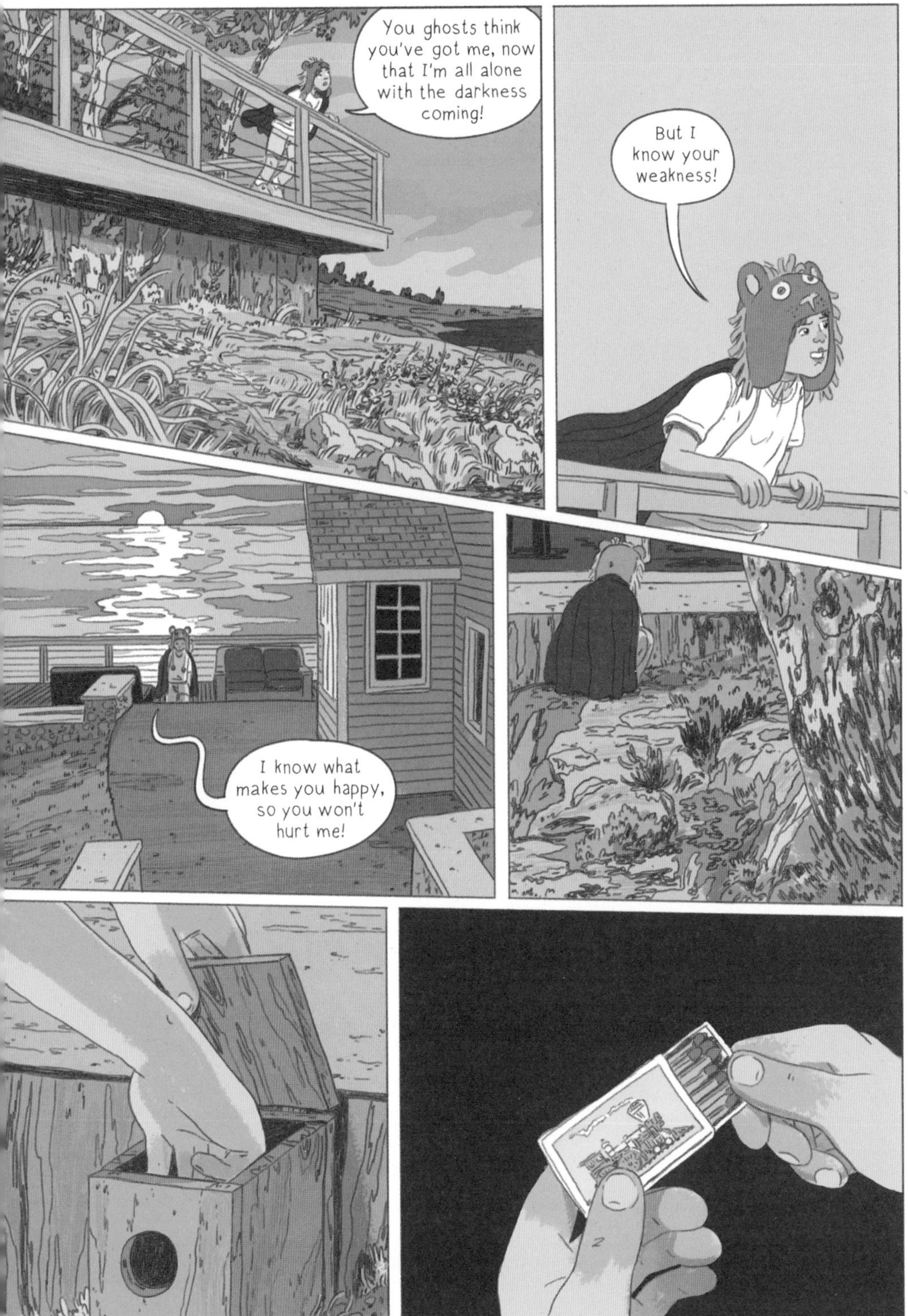
You ghosts think you've got me, now that I'm all alone with the darkness coming!
But I know your weakness!
I know what makes you happy, so you won't hurt me!

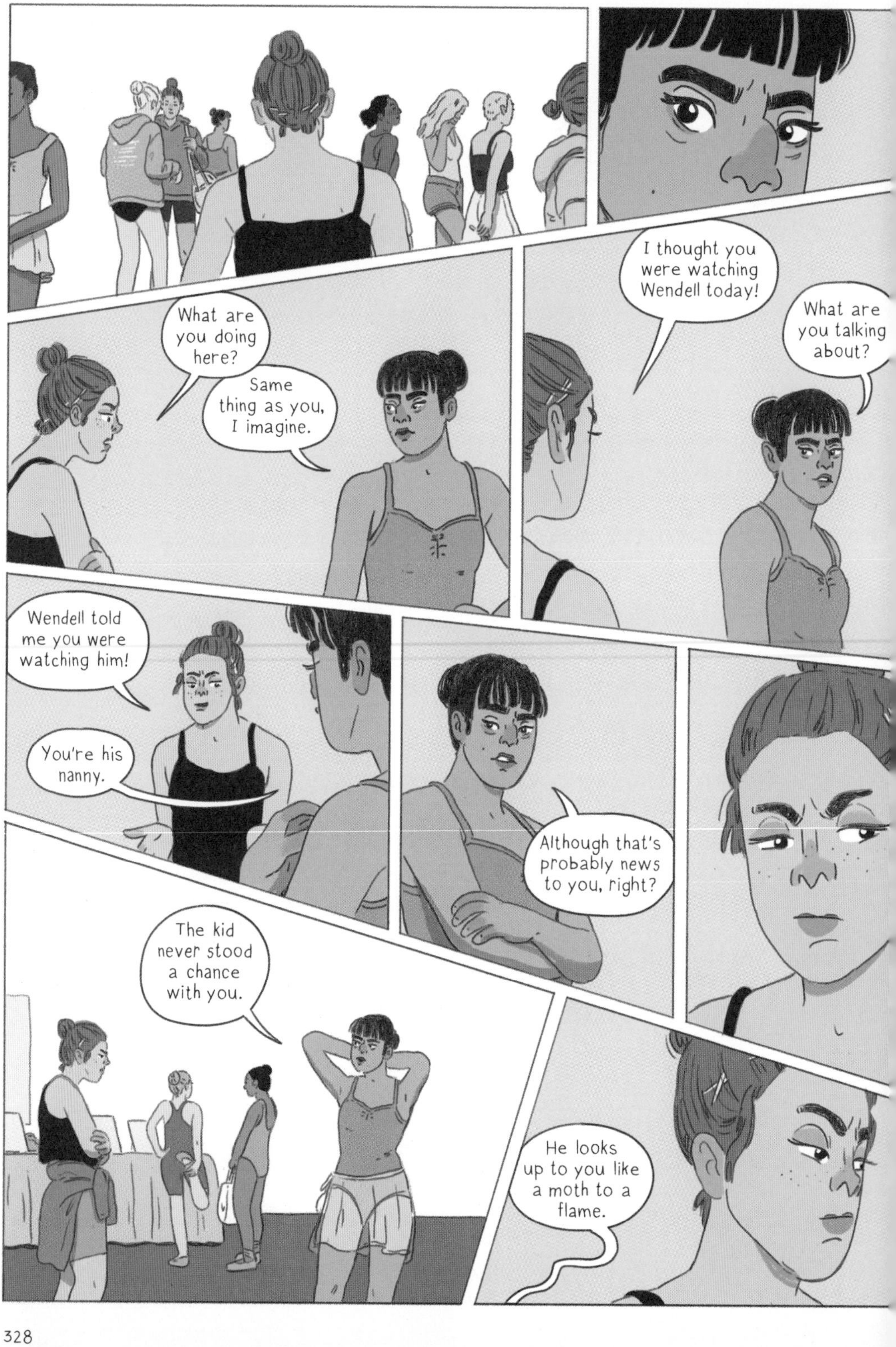
What are you doing here?
Same thing as you, I imagine.
I thought you were watching Wendell today!
What are you talking about?
Wendell told me you were watching him!
You're his nanny.
Although that's probably news to you, right?
The kid never stood a chance with you.
He looks up to you like a moth to a flame.

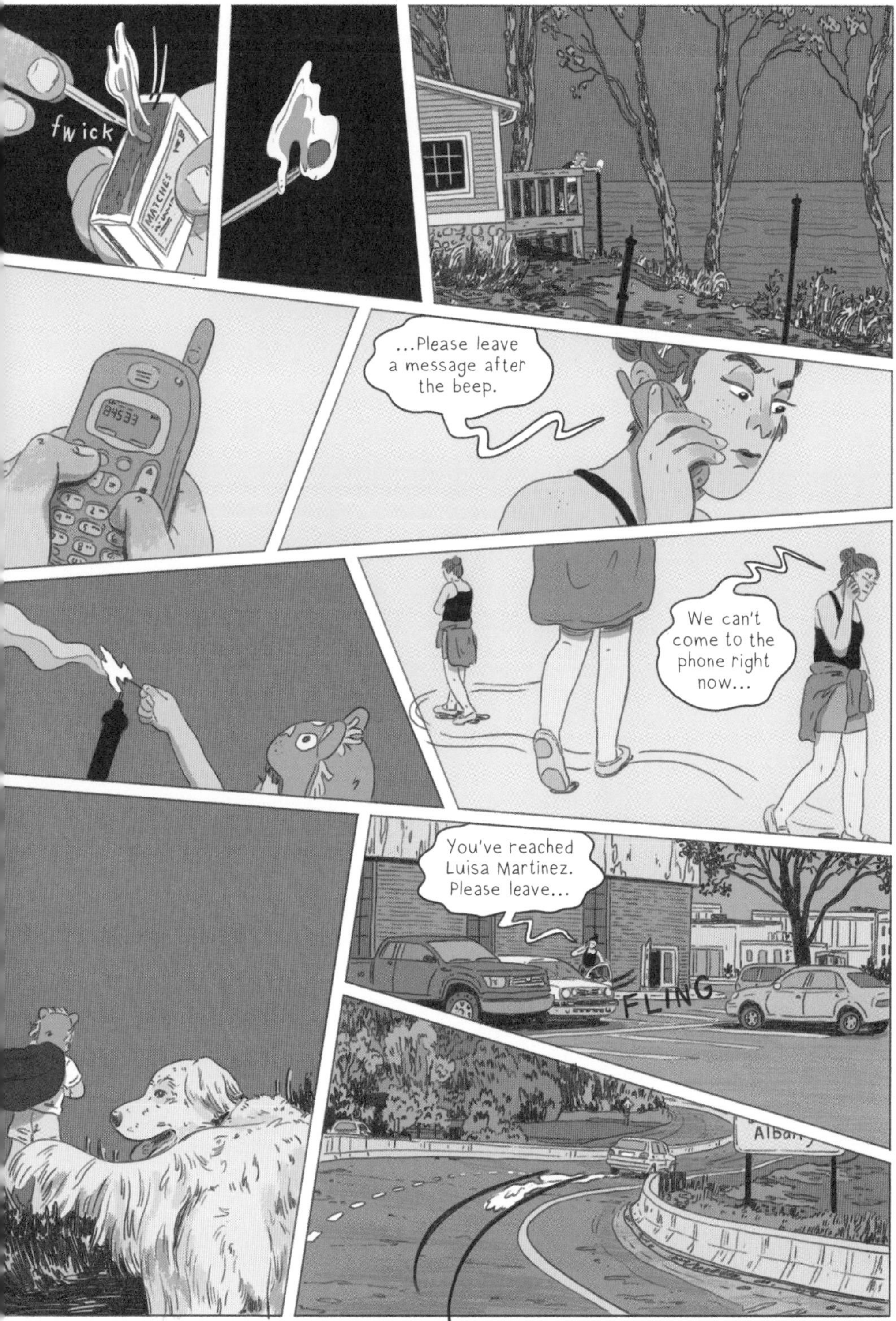
fwick
MATCHES
84533
...Please leave a message after the beep.
We can't come to the phone right now...
You've reached Luisa Martinez. Please leave...
FLING

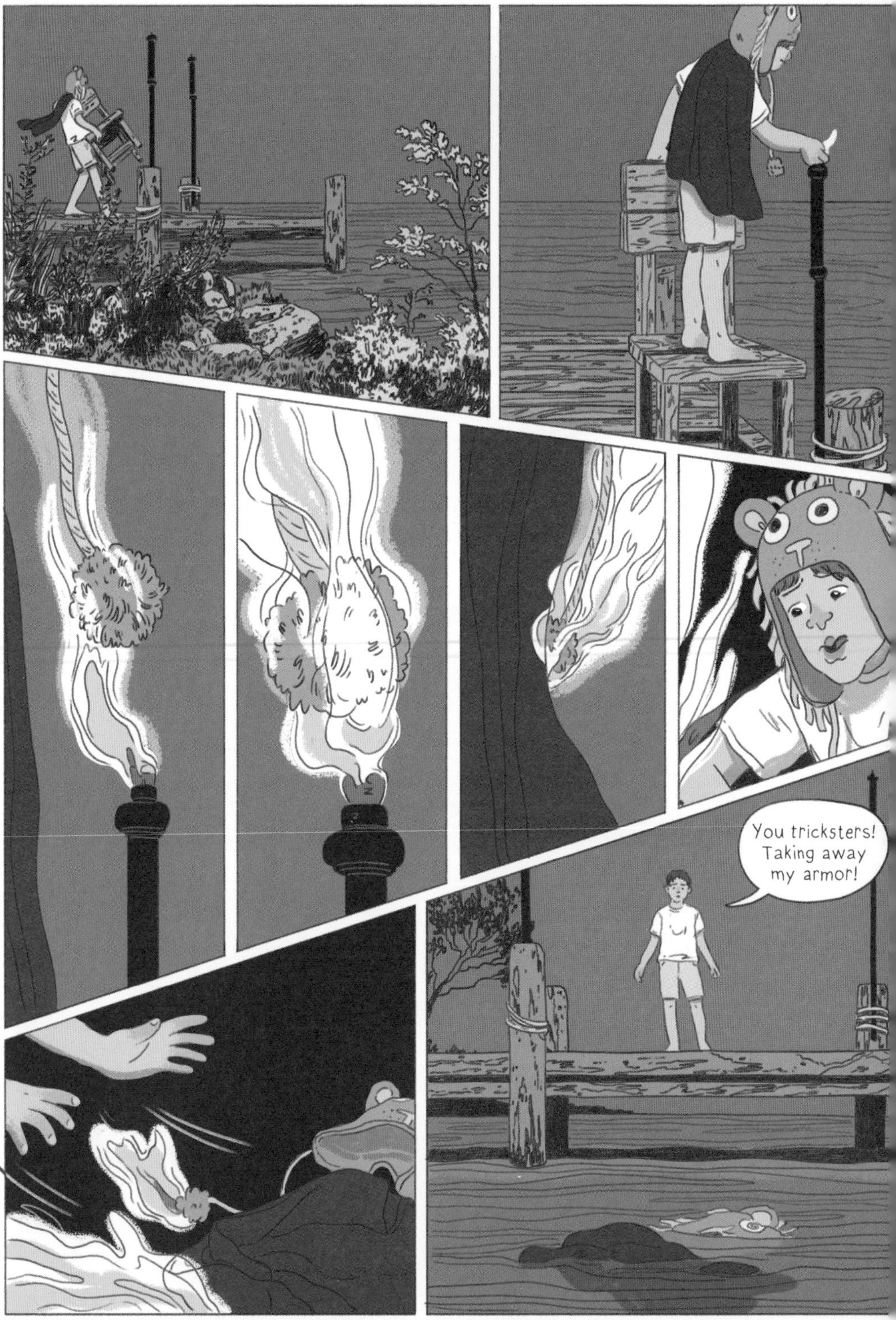
You tricksters! Taking away my armor!

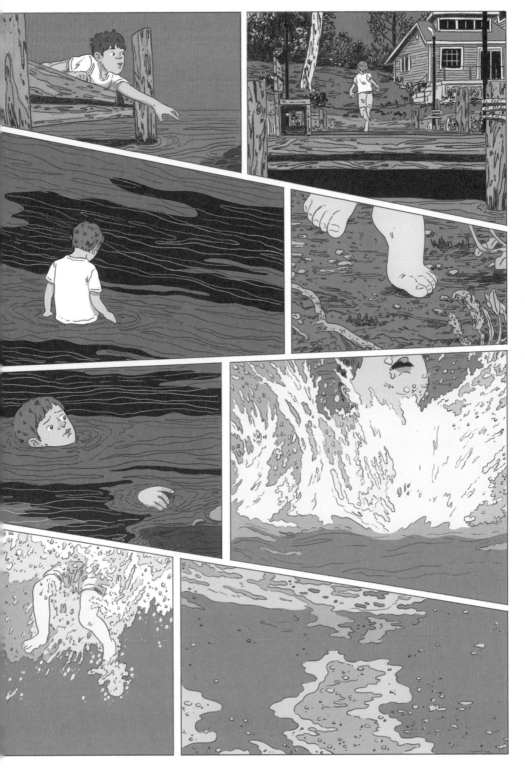

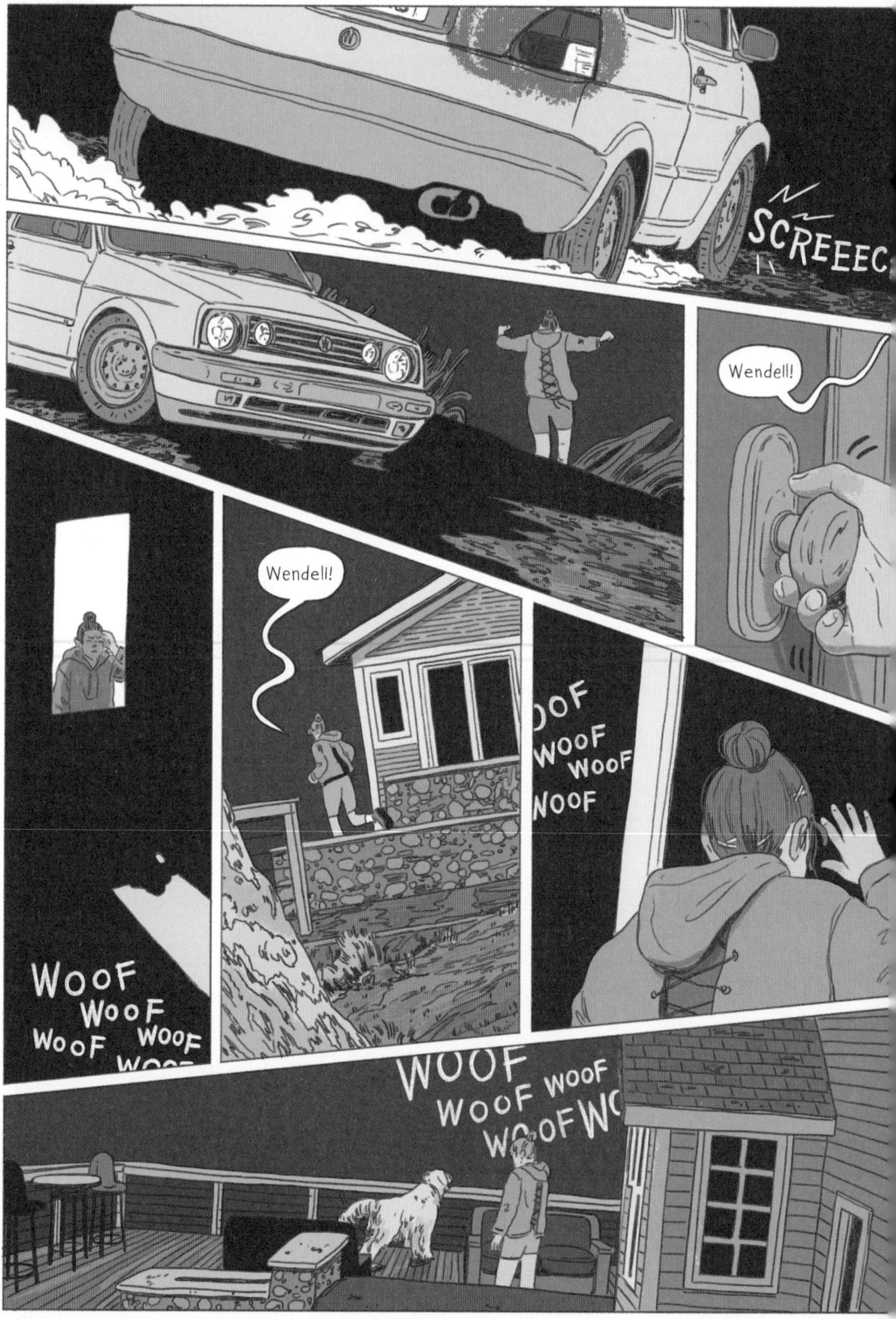
SCREEEC
Wendell!
Wendell!
WOOF
WOOF
WOOF WOOF
WOOF
WOOF
WOOF
WOOF
WOOF
WOOF
WOOF WOOF
WOOF

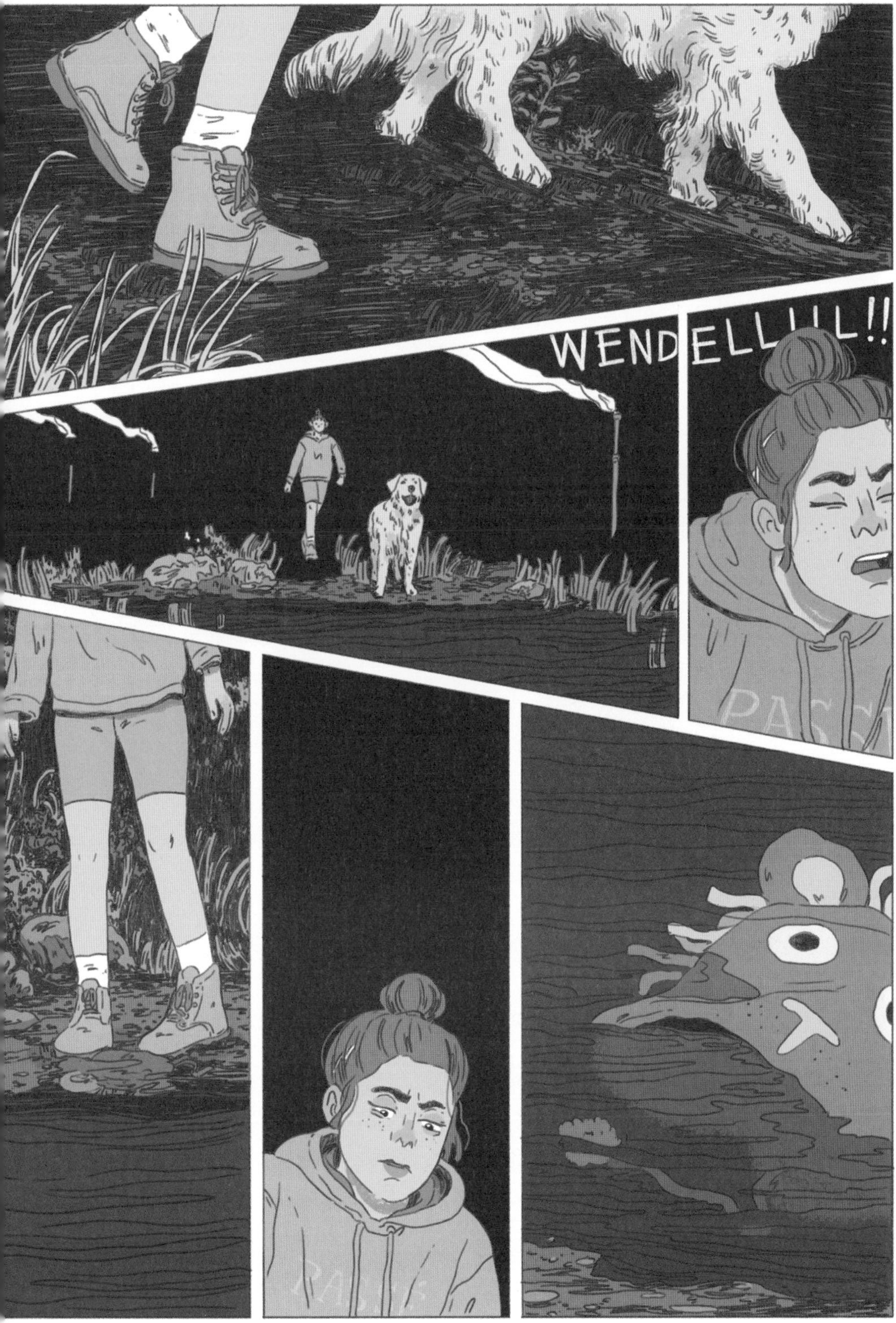
WENDELLLLL!!

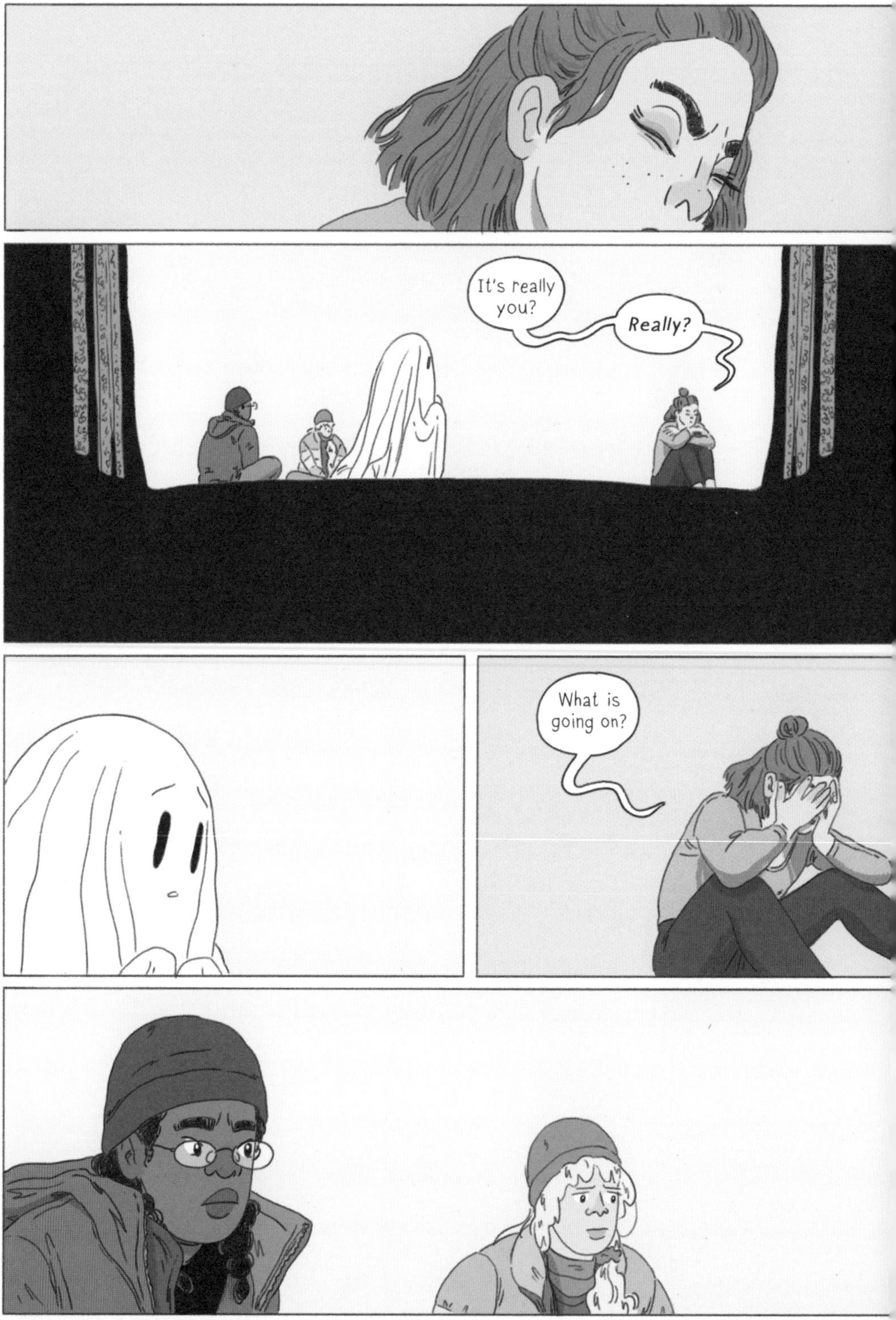
It's really you?
Really?
What is going on?

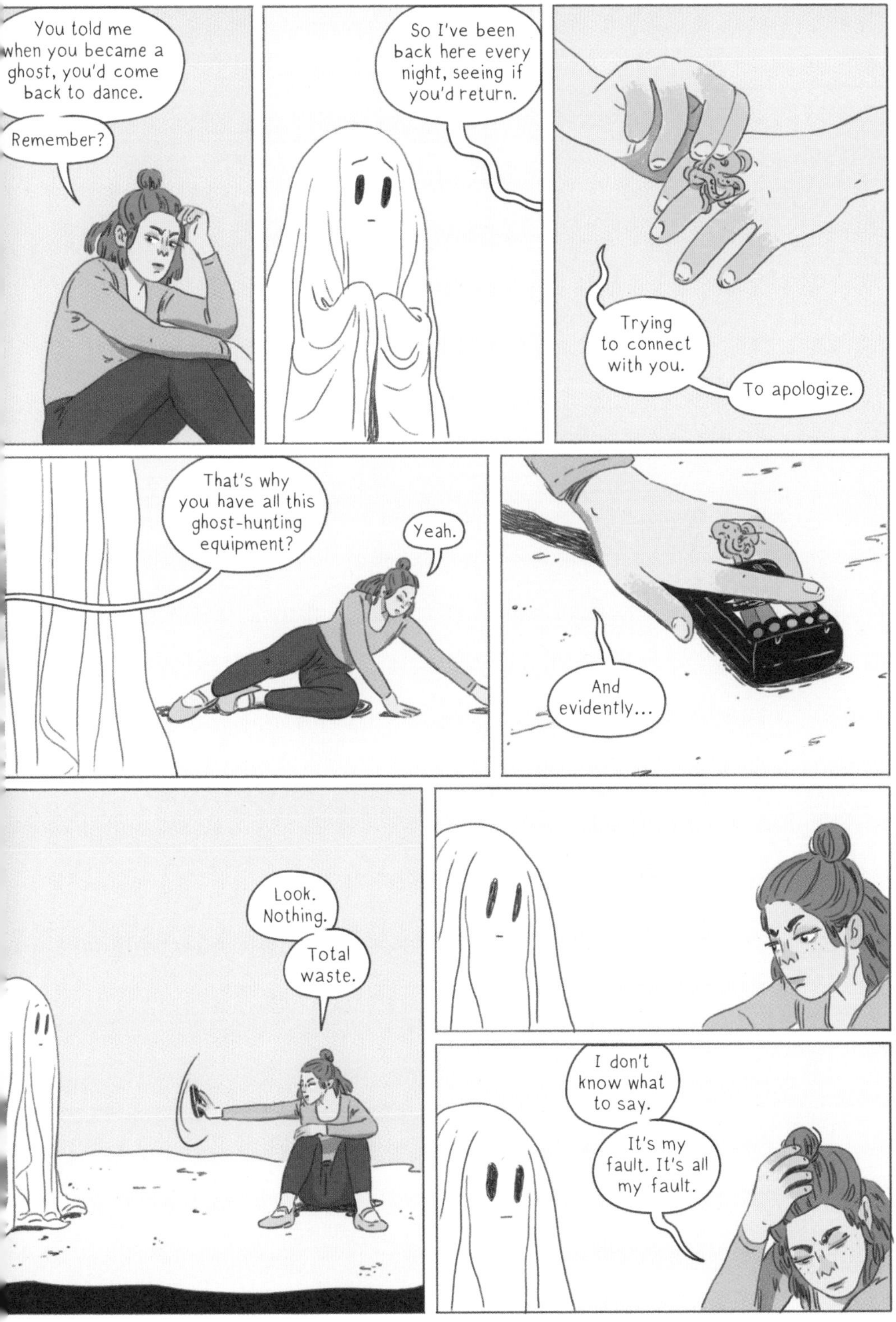
You told me when you became a ghost, you'd come back to dance.
Remember?
So I've been back here every night, seeing if you'd return.
Trying to connect with you.
To apologize.
That's why you have all this ghost-hunting equipment?
Yeah.
And evidently...
Look. Nothing.
Total waste.
I don't know what to say.
It's my fault. It's all my fault.

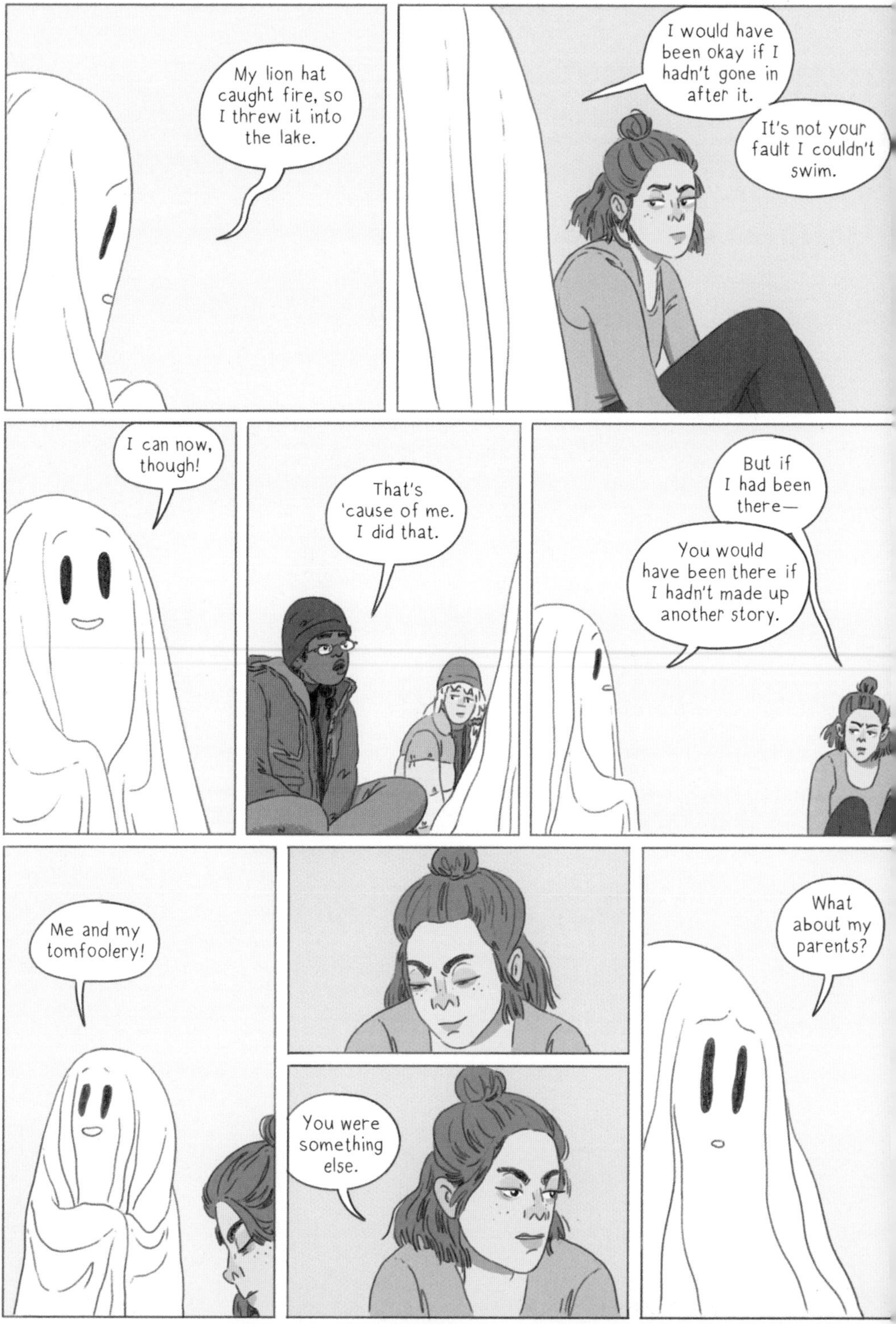
My lion hat caught fire, so I threw it into the lake.
I would have been okay if I hadn't gone in after it.
It's not your fault I couldn't swim.
I can now, though!
That's 'cause of me. I did that.
But if I had been there—
You would have been there if I hadn't made up another story.
Me and my tomfoolery!
You were something else.
What about my parents?

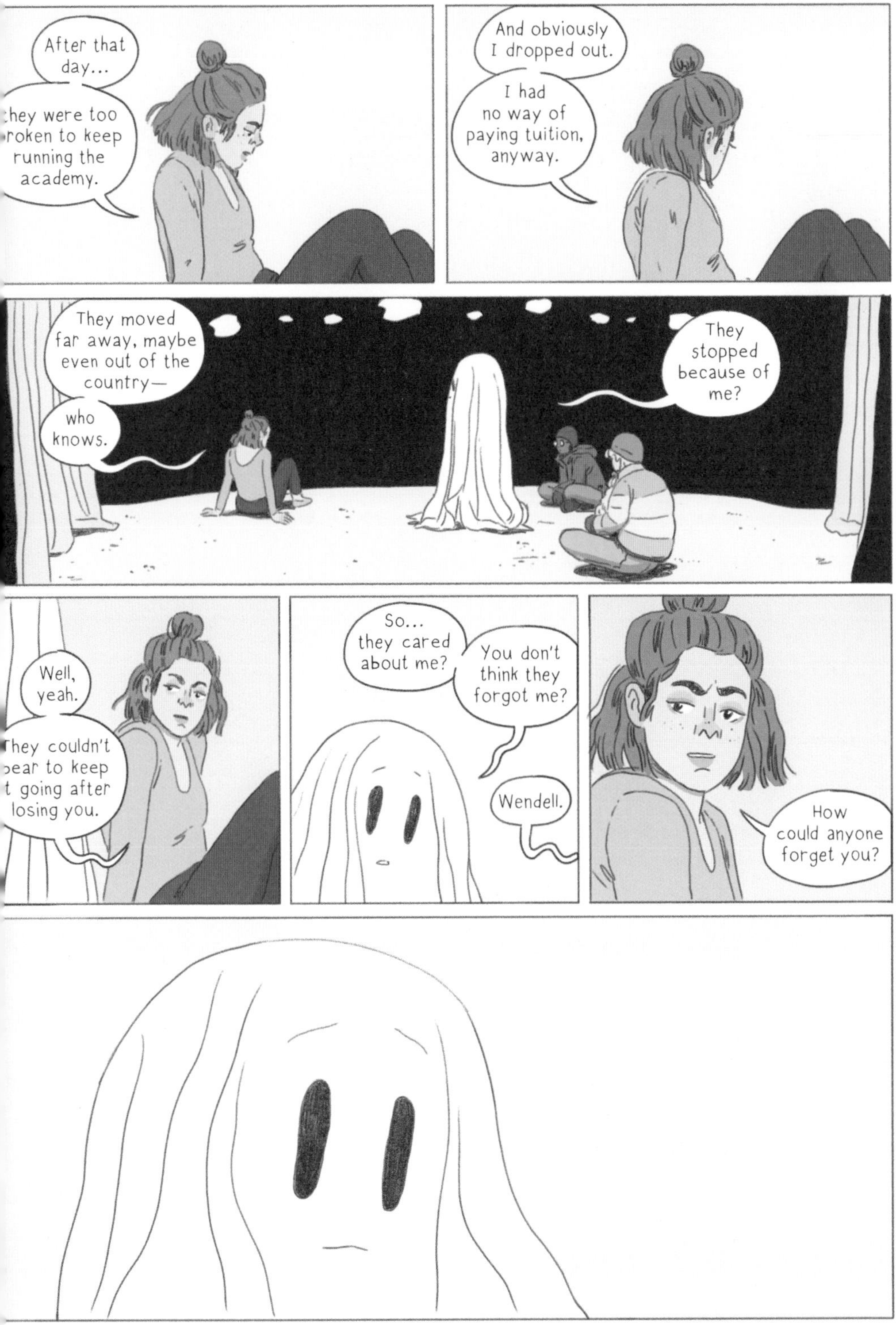
After that day...
:hey were too roken to keep running the academy.
And obviously I dropped out.
I had no way of paying tuition, anyway.
They moved far away, maybe even out of the country—
who knows.
They stopped because of me?
Well, yeah.
They couldn't bear to keep t going after losing you.
So... they cared about me?
You don't think they forgot me?
Wendell.
How could anyone forget you?

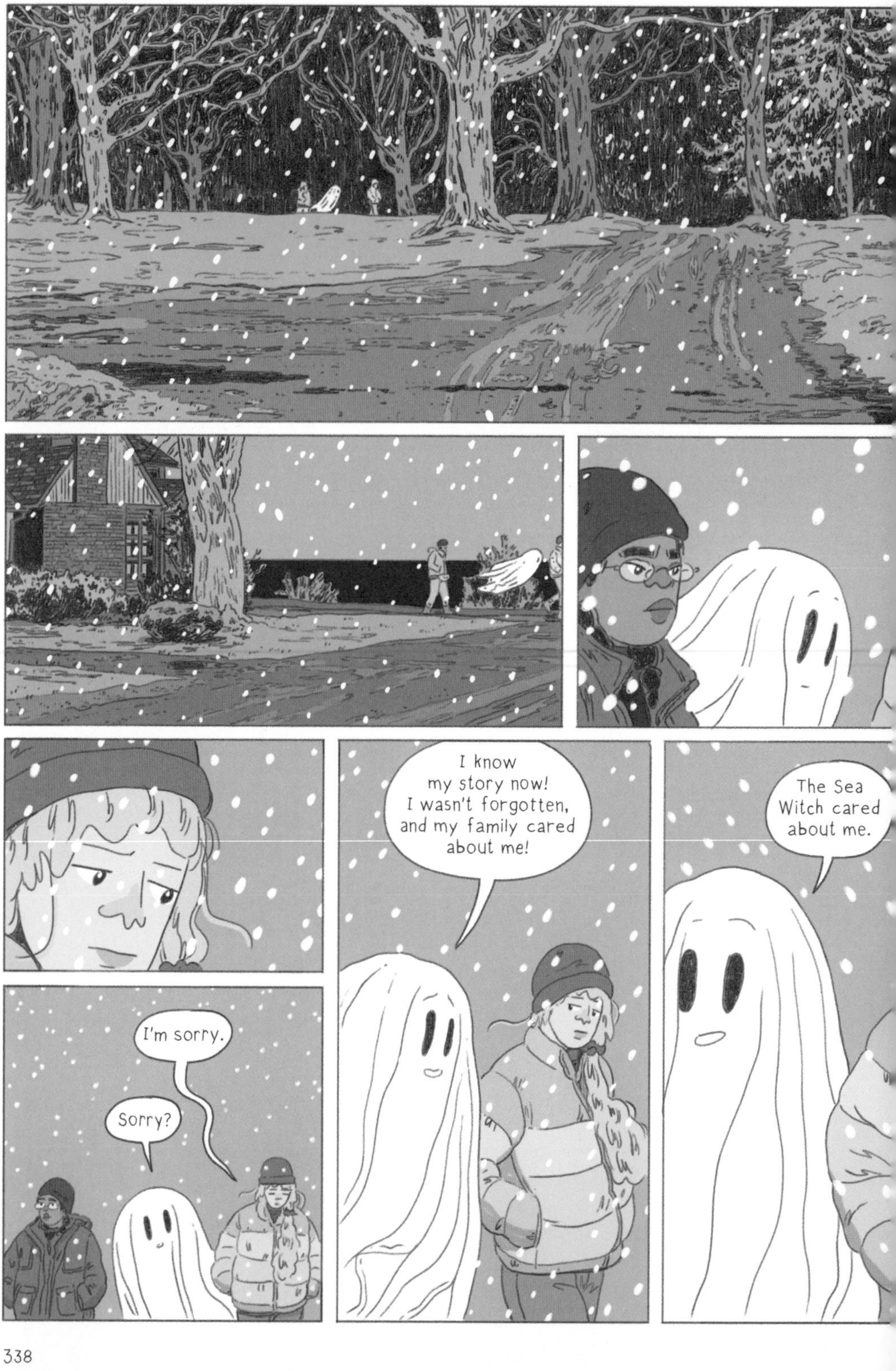
I know my story now! I wasn't forgotten, and my family cared about me!
The Sea Witch cared about me.
I'm sorry.
Sorry?

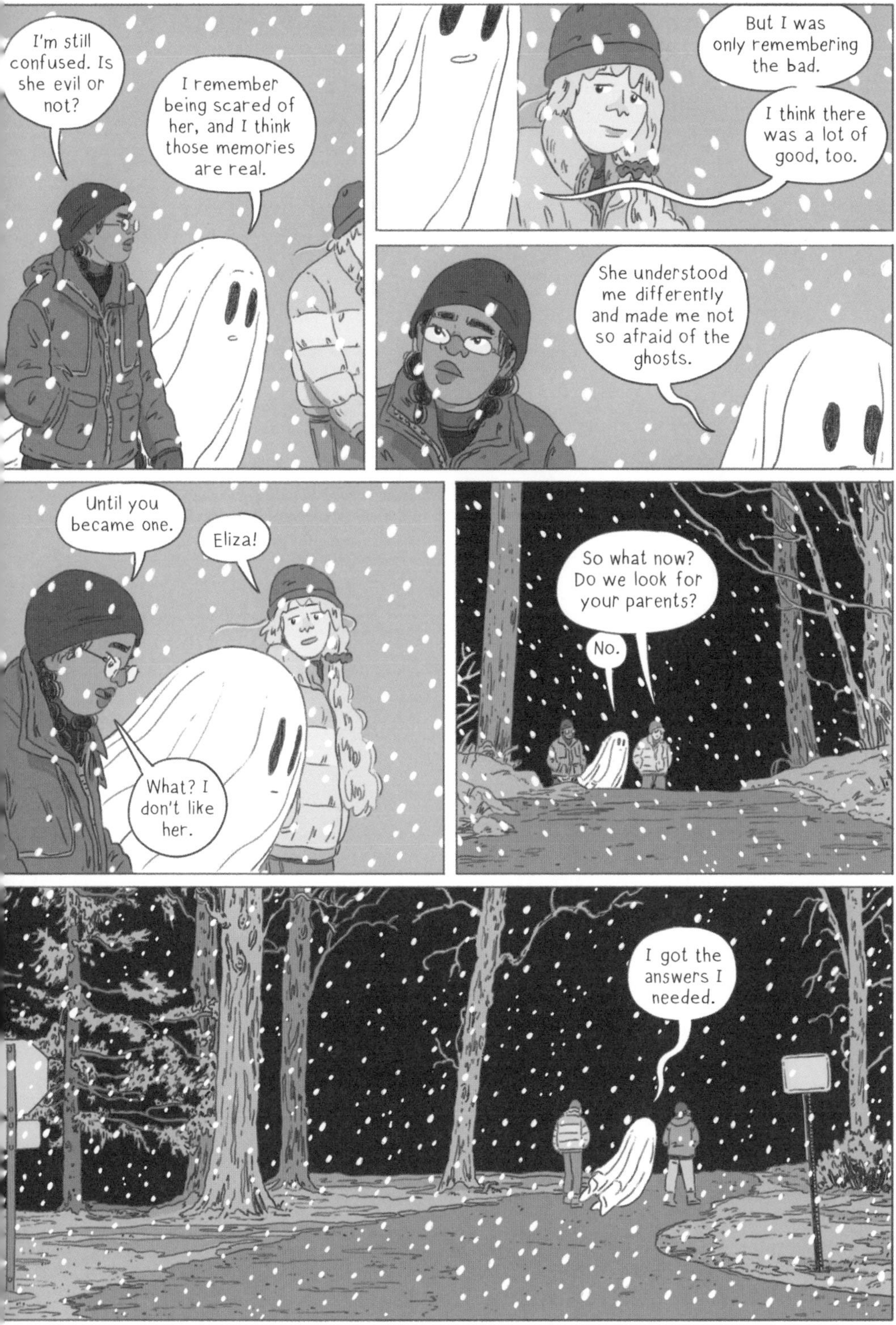
I'm still confused. Is she evil or not?
I remember being scared of her, and I think those memories are real.
But I was only remembering the bad.
I think there was a lot of good, too.
She understood me differently and made me not so afraid of the ghosts.
Until you became one.
Eliza!
What? I don't like her.
So what now? Do we look for your parents?
No.
I got the answers I needed.

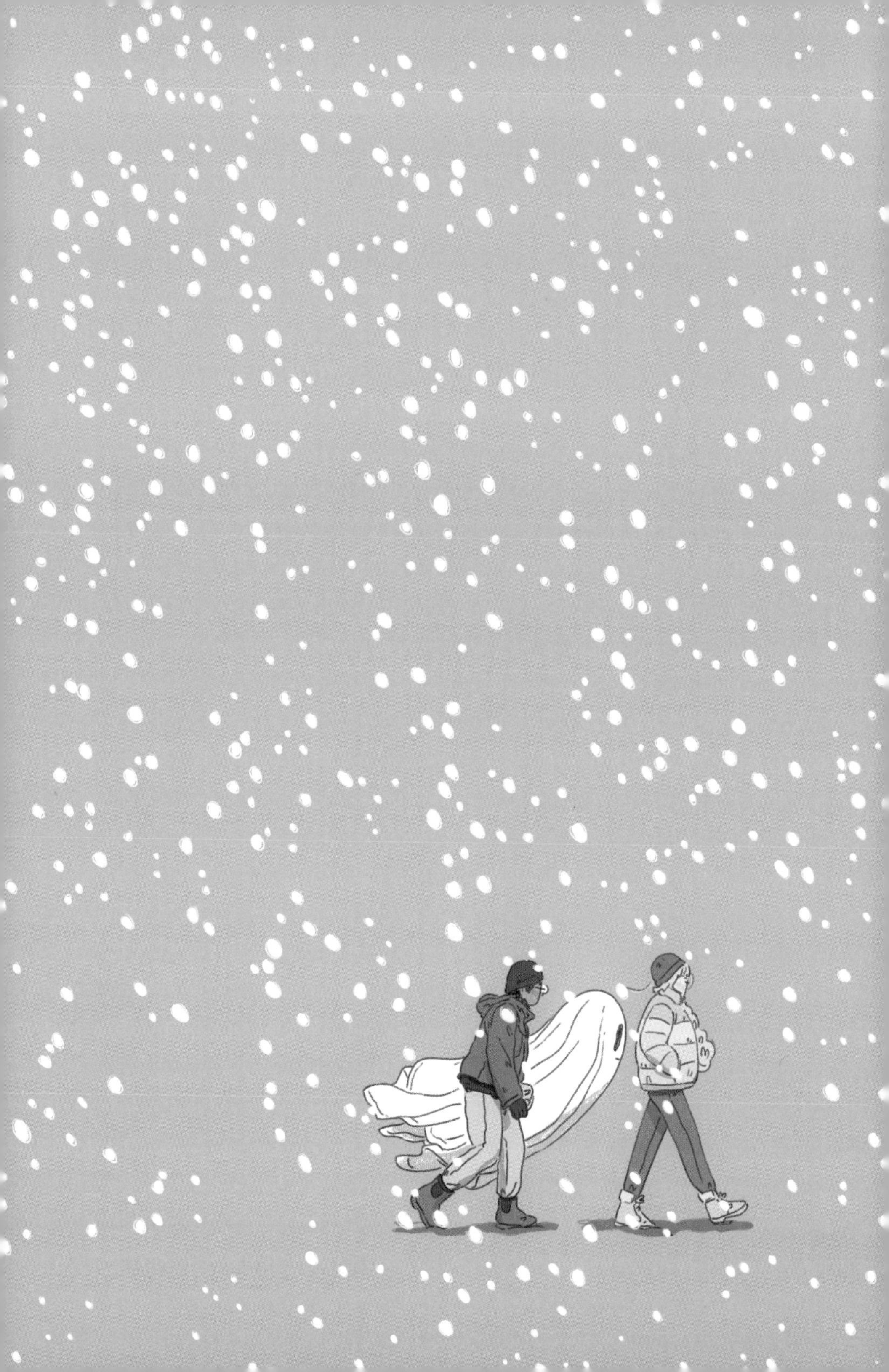

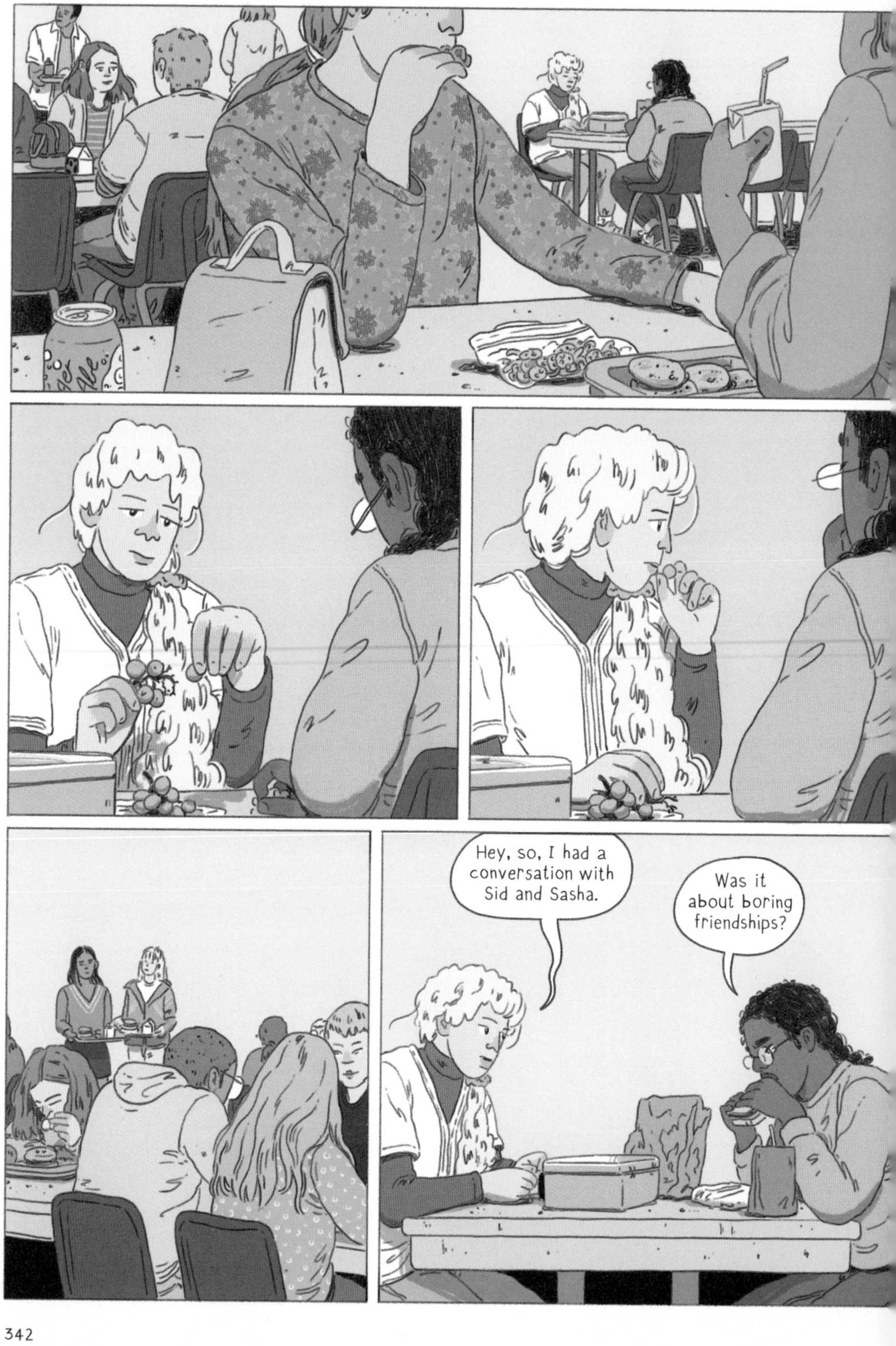
Hey, so, I had a conversation with Sid and Sasha.
Was it about boring friendships?

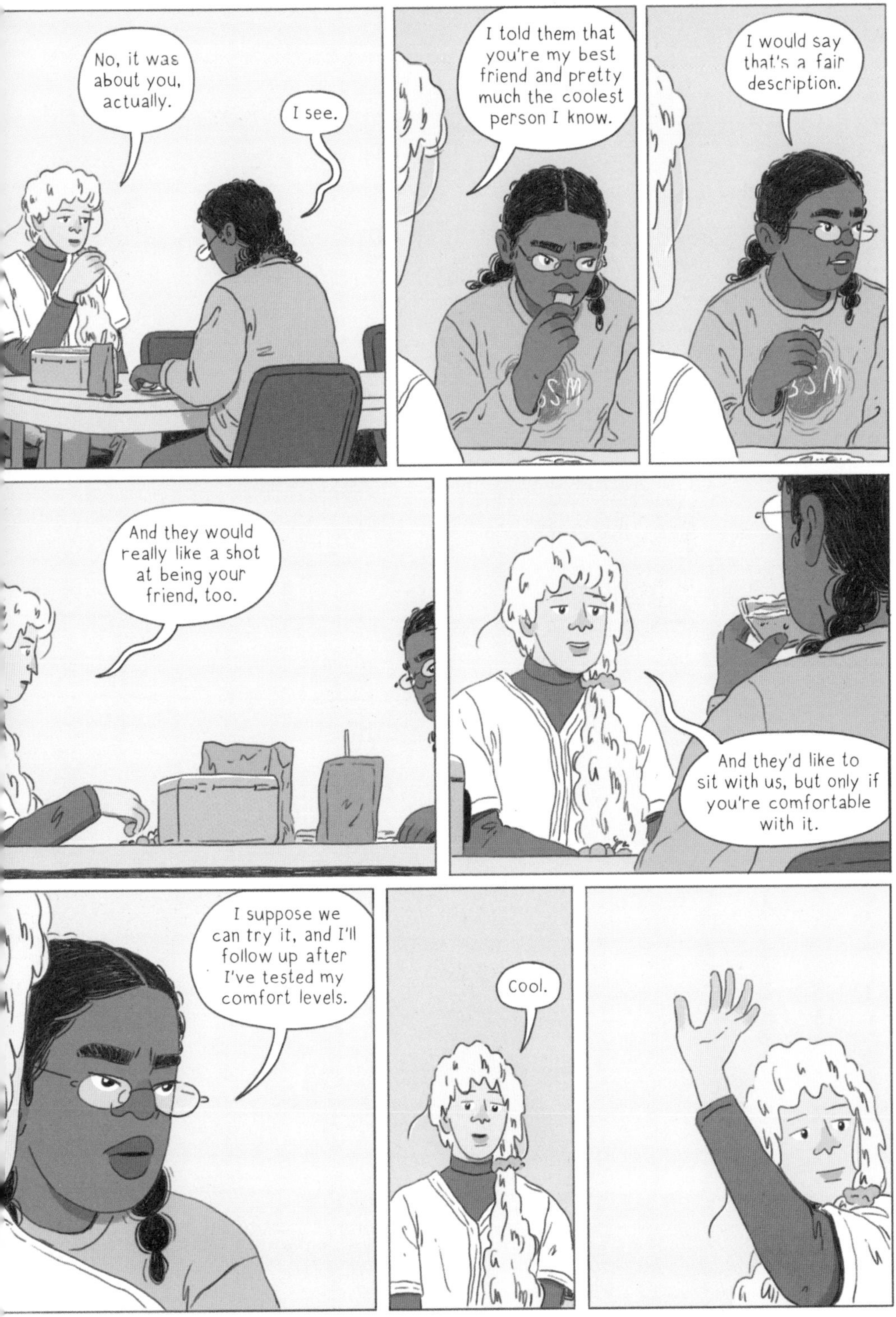

No, it was about you, actually.
I see.
I told them that you're my best friend and pretty much the coolest person I know.
I would say that's a fair description.
And they would really like a shot at being your friend, too.
And they'd like to sit with us, but only if you're comfortable with it.
I suppose we can try it, and I'll follow up after I've tested my comfort levels.
Cool.

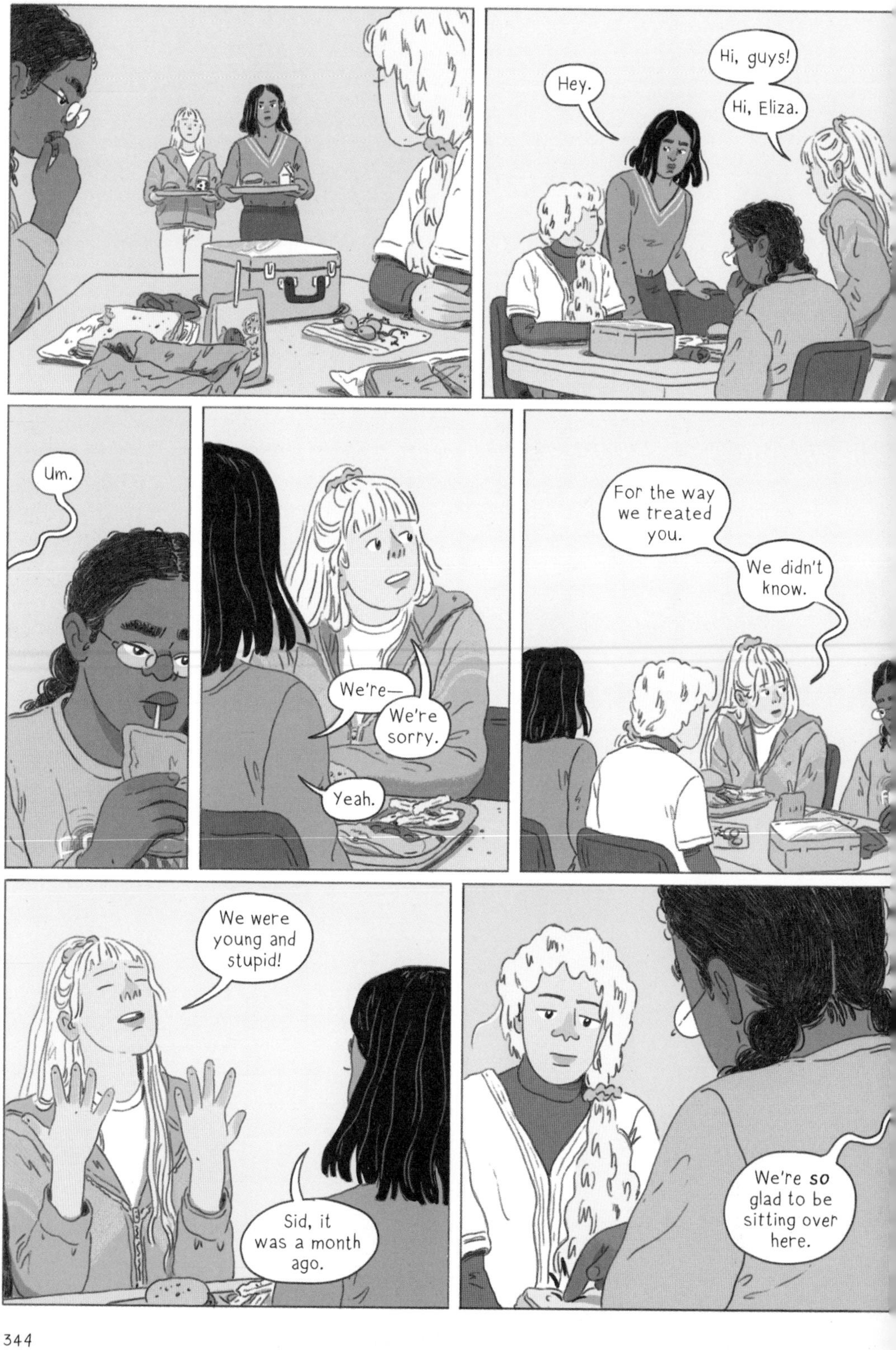
Hey.
Hi, guys!
Hi, Eliza.
Um.
We're—
We're sorry.
Yeah.
For the way we treated you.
We didn't know.
We were young and stupid!
Sid, it was a month ago.
We're **so** glad to be sitting over here.

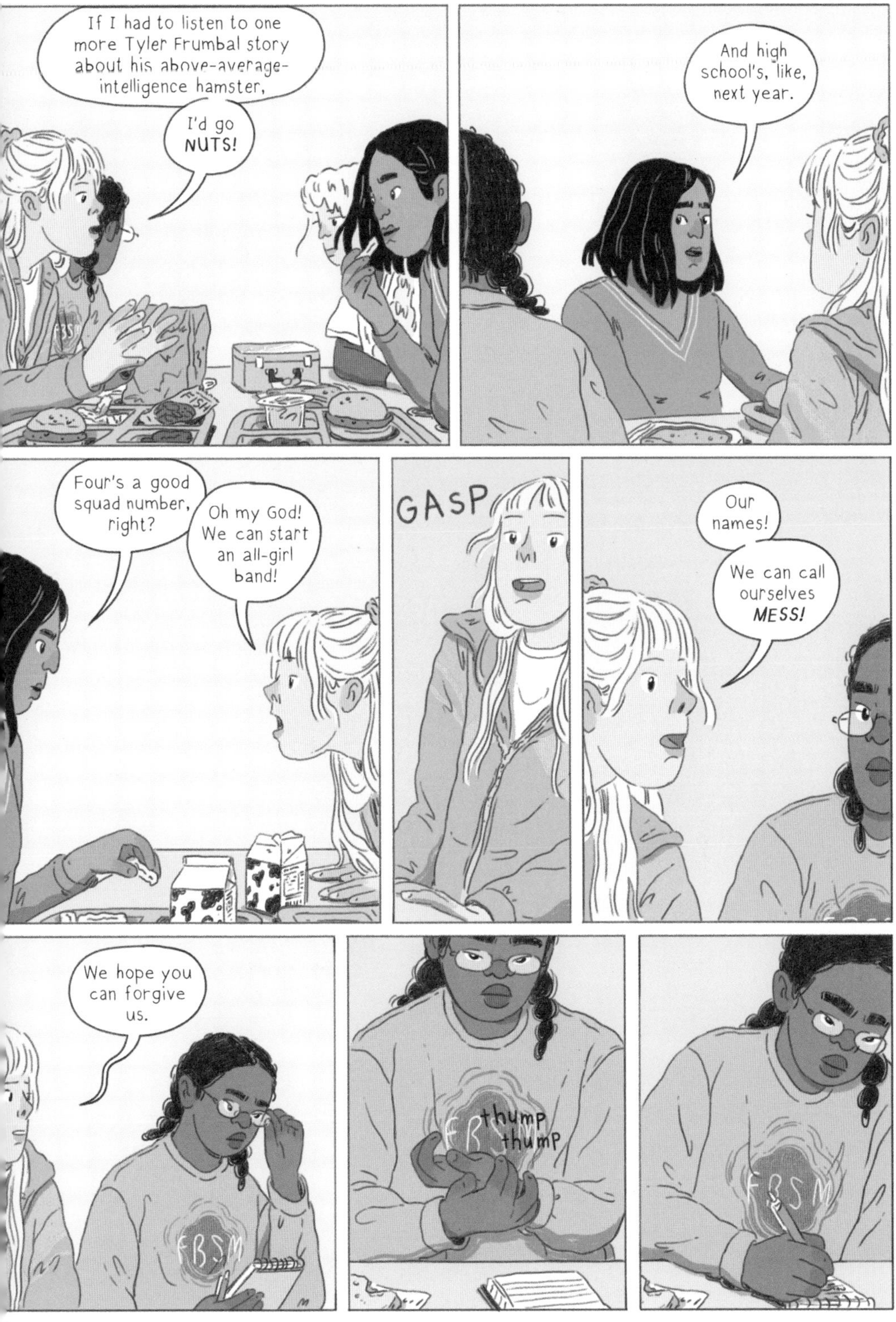
If I had to listen to one more Tyler Frumbal story about his above-average-intelligence hamster,
I'd go NUTS!
FISH
And high school's, like, next year.
Four's a good squad number, right?
Oh my God! We can start an all-girl band!
GASP
Our names!
We can call ourselves MESS!
We hope you can forgive us.
FBSM
thump thump
FBSM

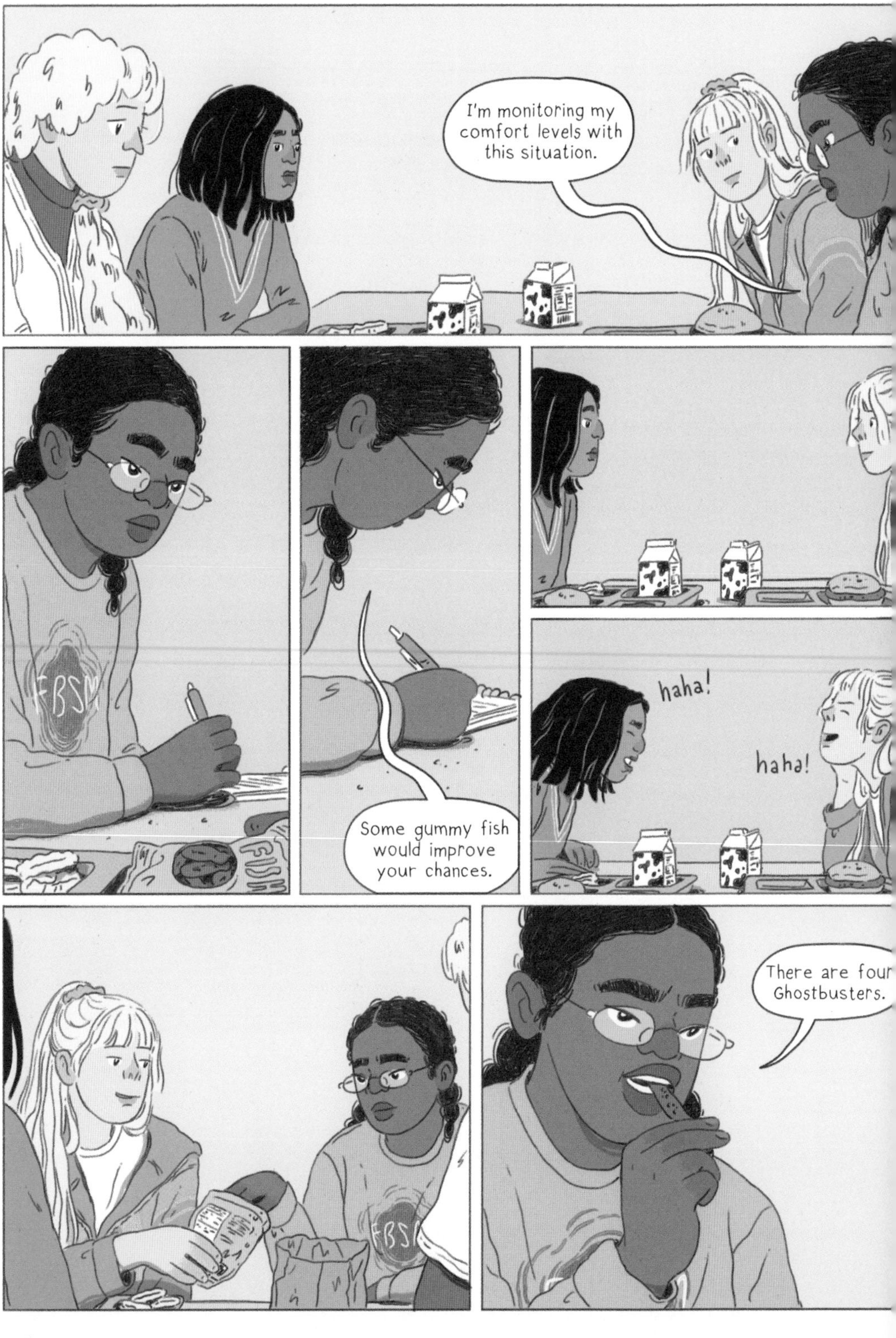
I'm monitoring my comfort levels with this situation.
Some gummy fish would improve your chances.
haha!
haha!
There are four Ghostbusters.

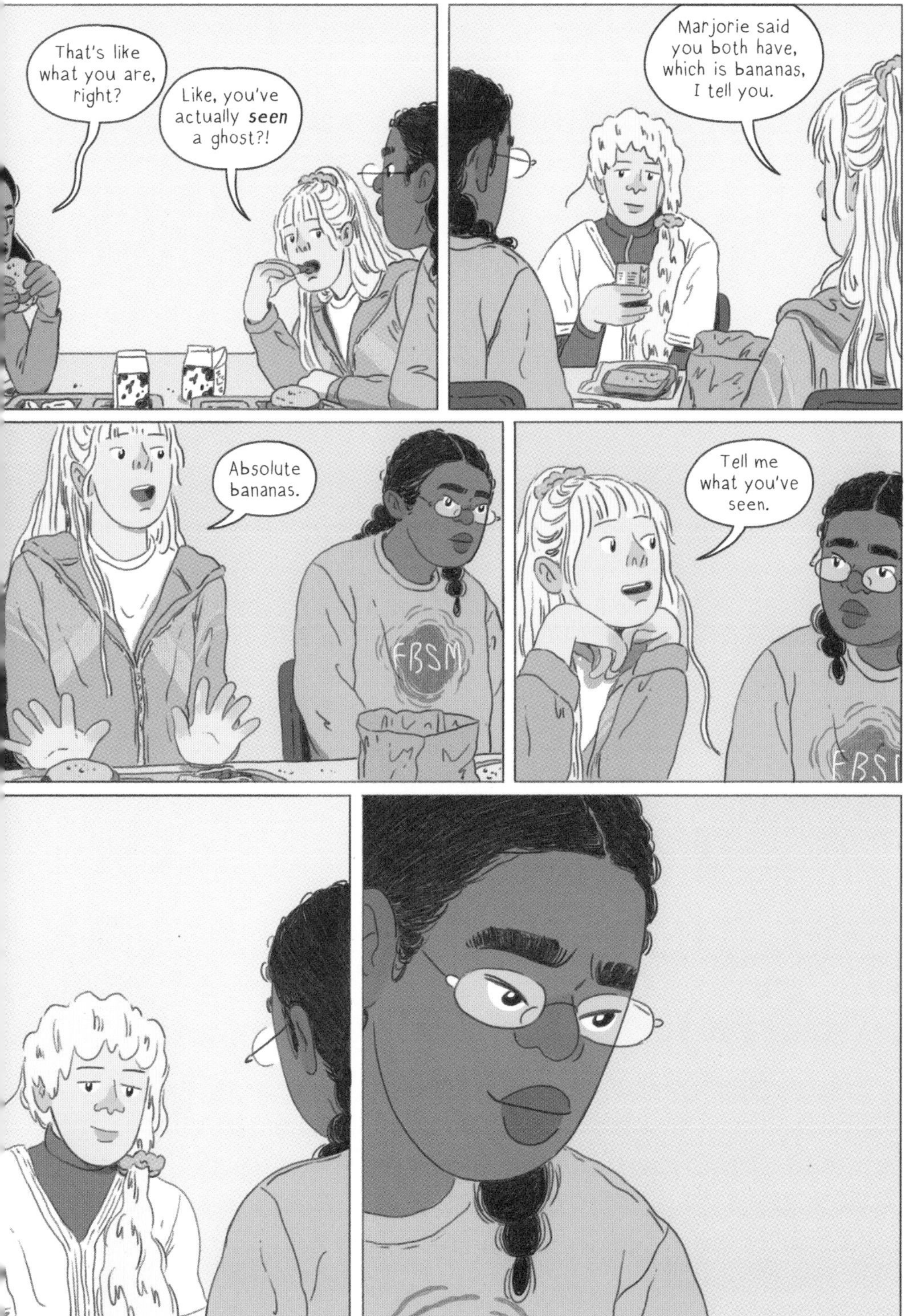
That's like what you are, right?
Like, you've actually **seen** a ghost?!
Marjorie said you both have, which is bananas, I tell you.
Absolute bananas.
FBSM
Tell me what you've seen.

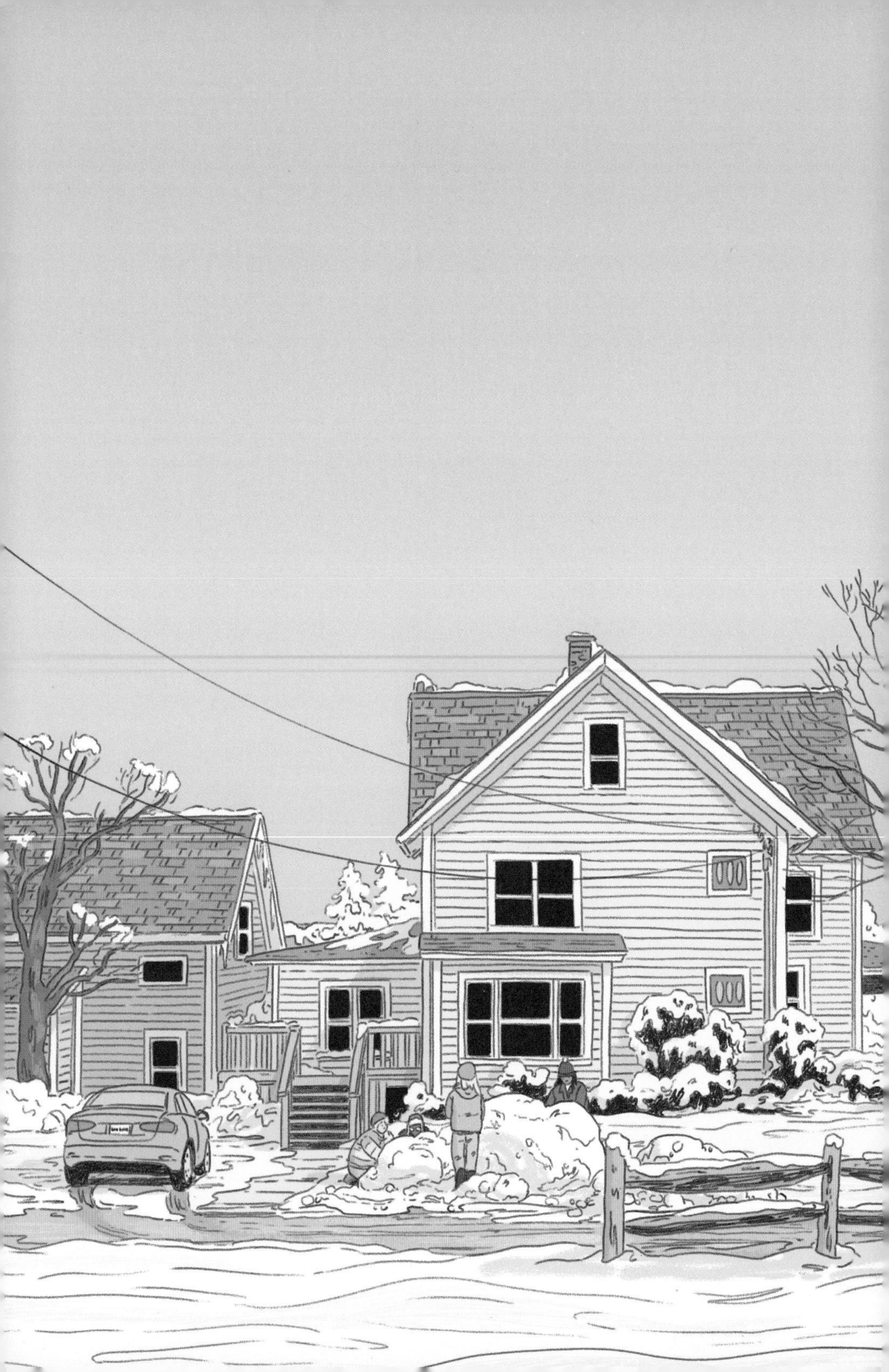

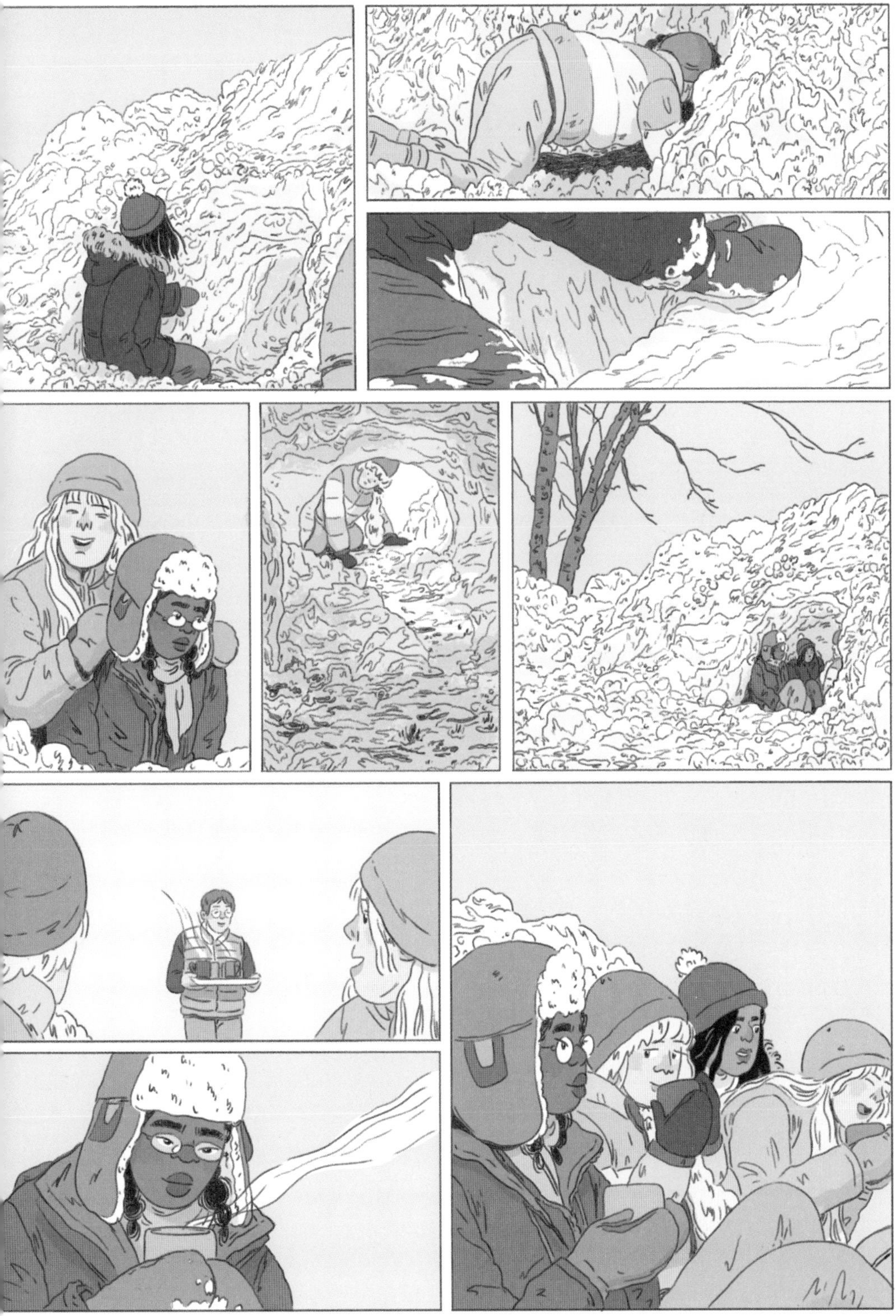

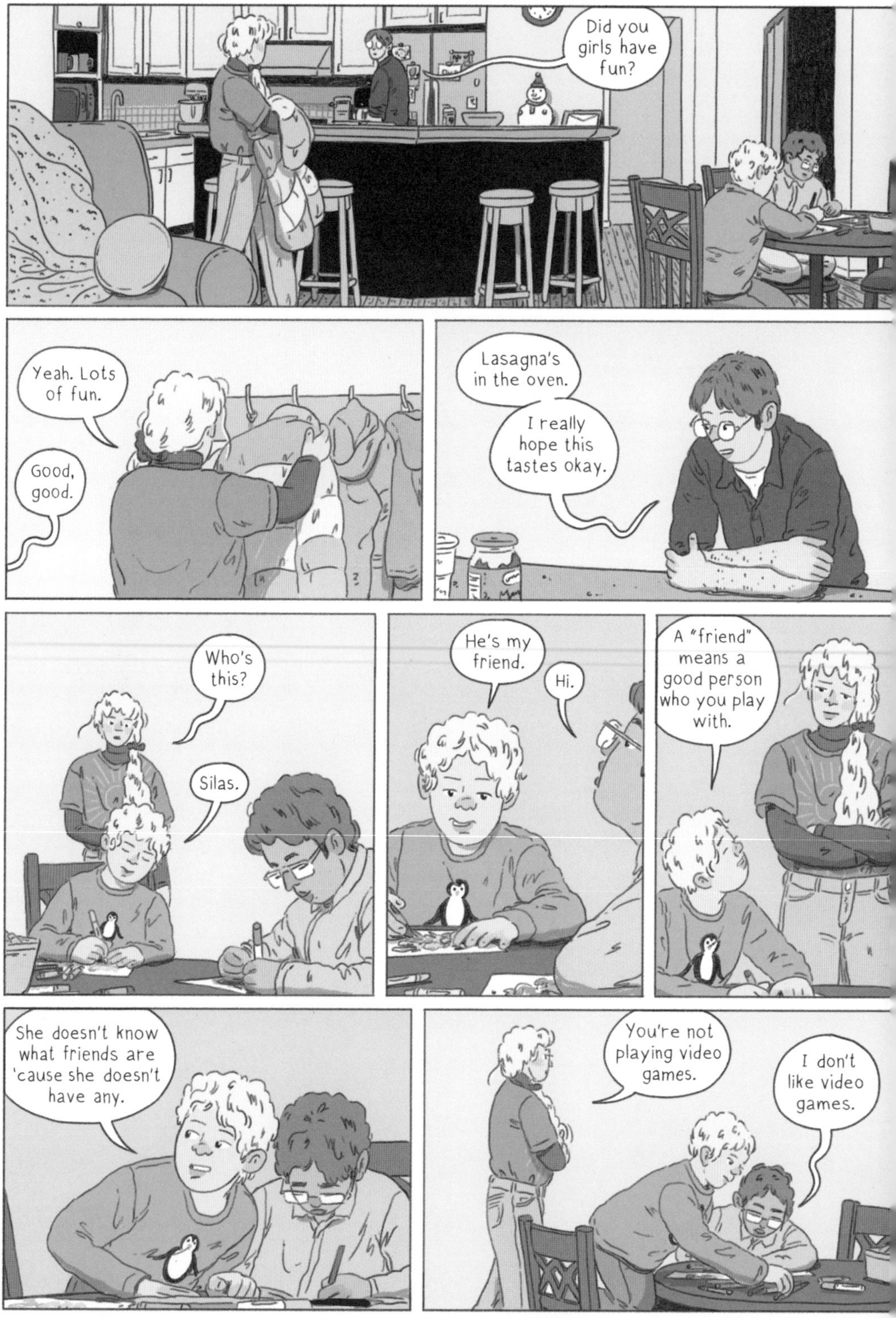
Did you girls have fun?
Yeah. Lots of fun.
Good, good.
Lasagna's in the oven.
I really hope this tastes okay.
Who's this?
Silas.
He's my friend.
Hi.
A "friend" means a good person who you play with.
She doesn't know what friends are 'cause she doesn't have any.
You're not playing video games.
I don't like video games.

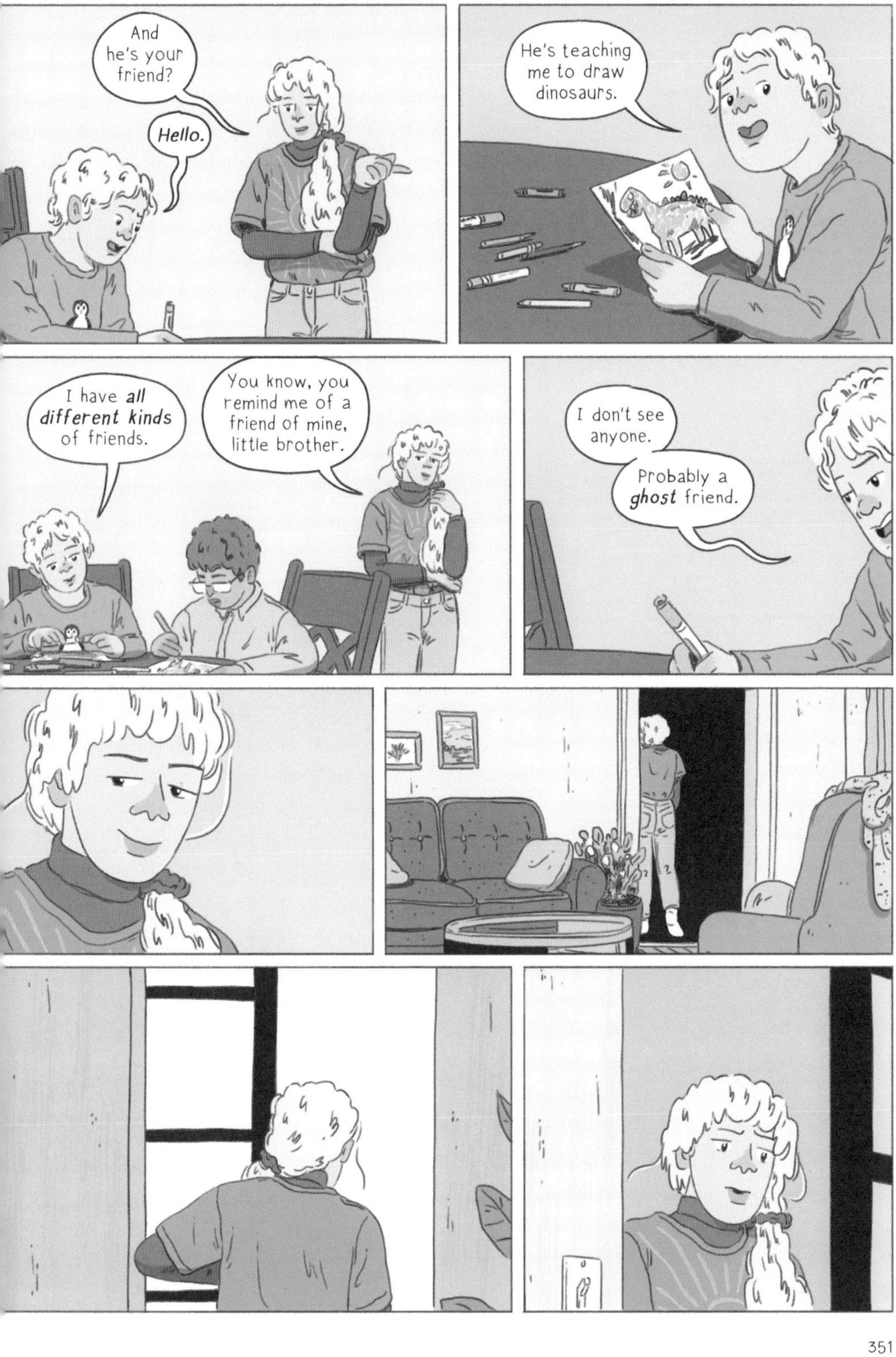

And he's your friend?
Hello.
He's teaching me to draw dinosaurs.
I have **all different kinds** of friends.
You know, you remind me of a friend of mine, little brother.
I don't see anyone.
Probably a *ghost* friend.

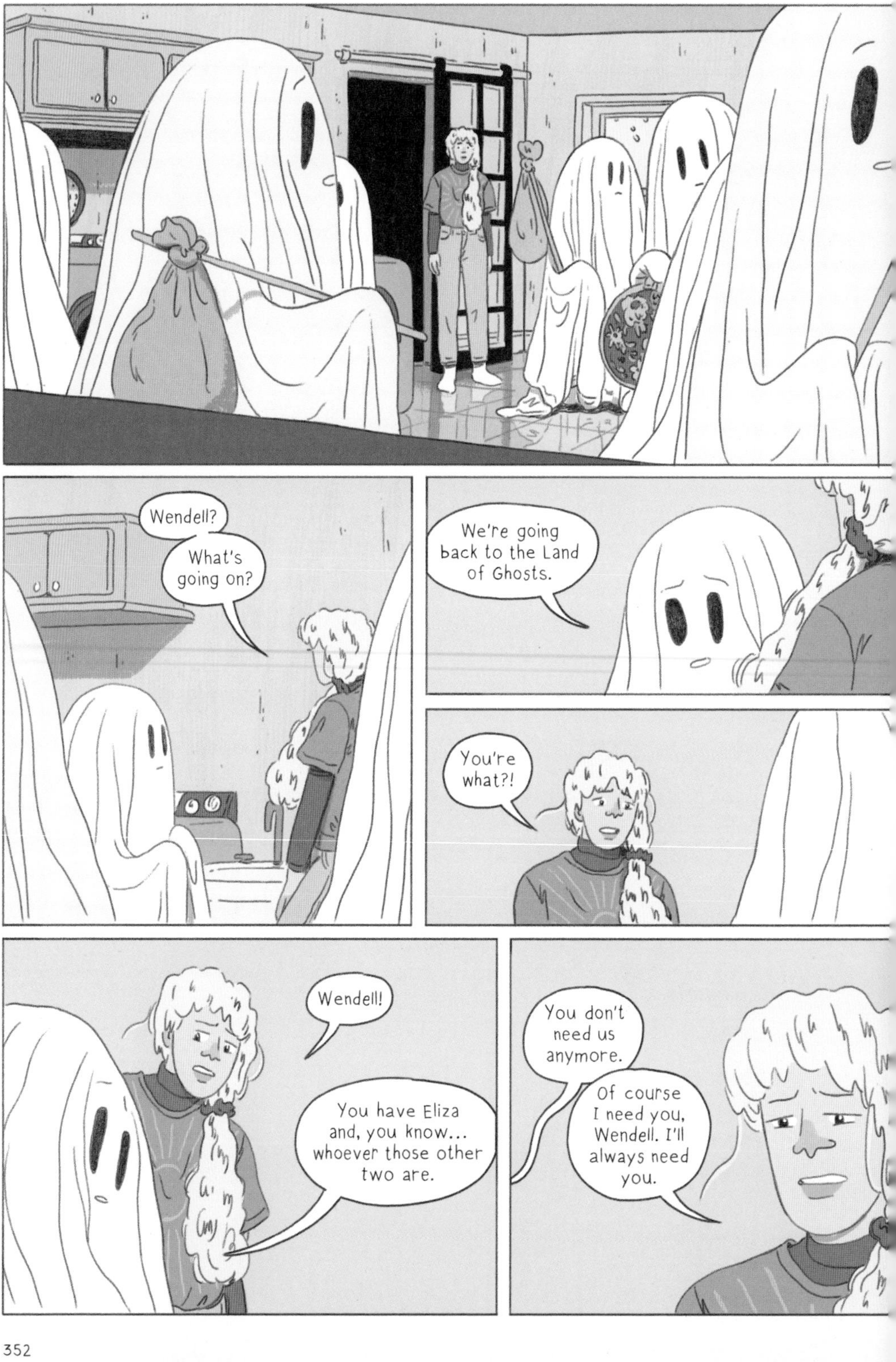

Wendell?
What's going on?
We're going back to the Land of Ghosts.
You're what?!
Wendell!
You have Eliza and, you know... whoever those other two are.
You don't need us anymore.
Of course I need you, Wendell. I'll always need you.

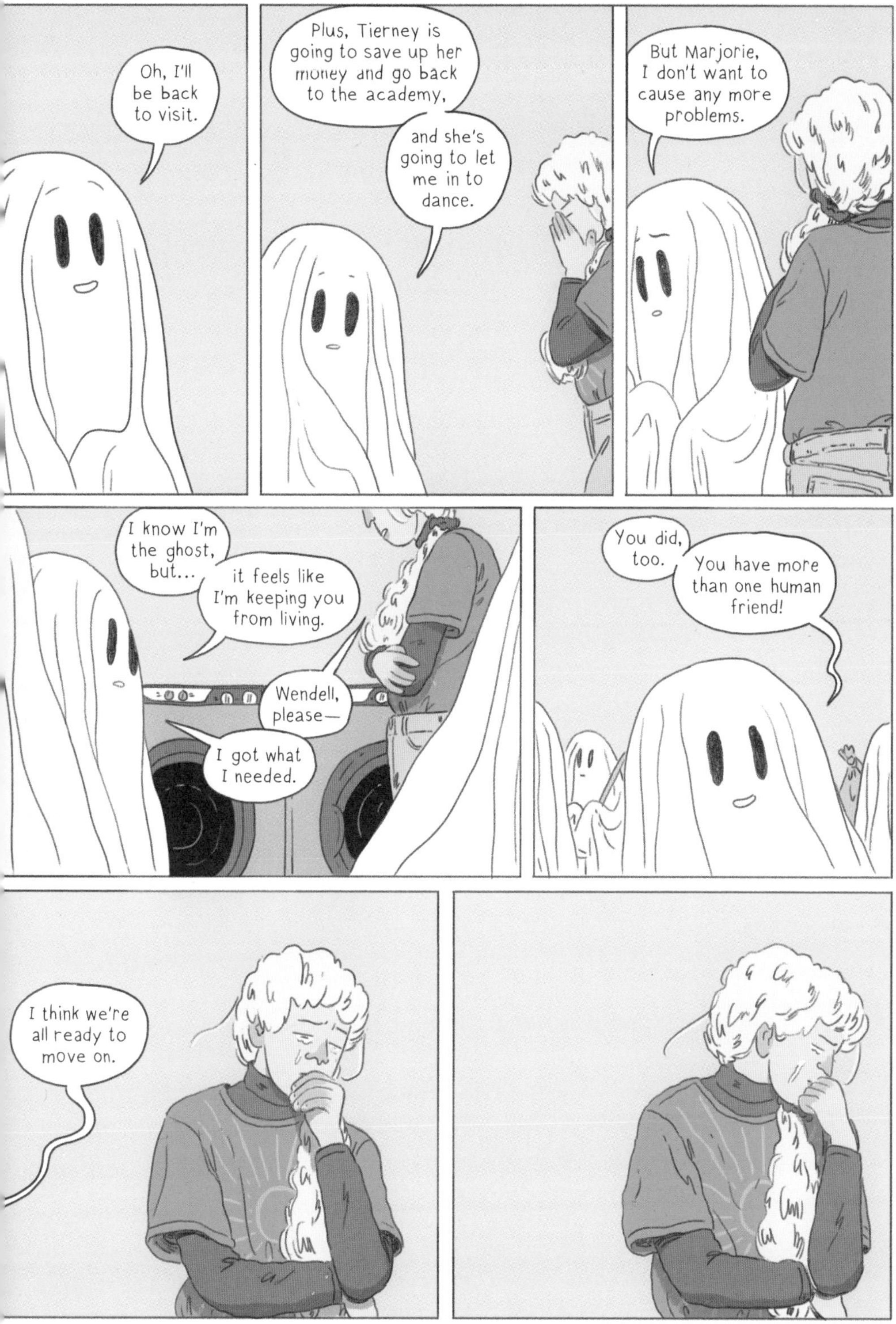
Oh, I'll be back to visit.
Plus, Tierney is going to save up her money and go back to the academy,
and she's going to let me in to dance.
But Marjorie, I don't want to cause any more problems.
I know I'm the ghost, but...
it feels like I'm keeping you from living.
Wendell, please—
I got what I needed.
You did, too.
You have more than one human friend!
I think we're all ready to move on.

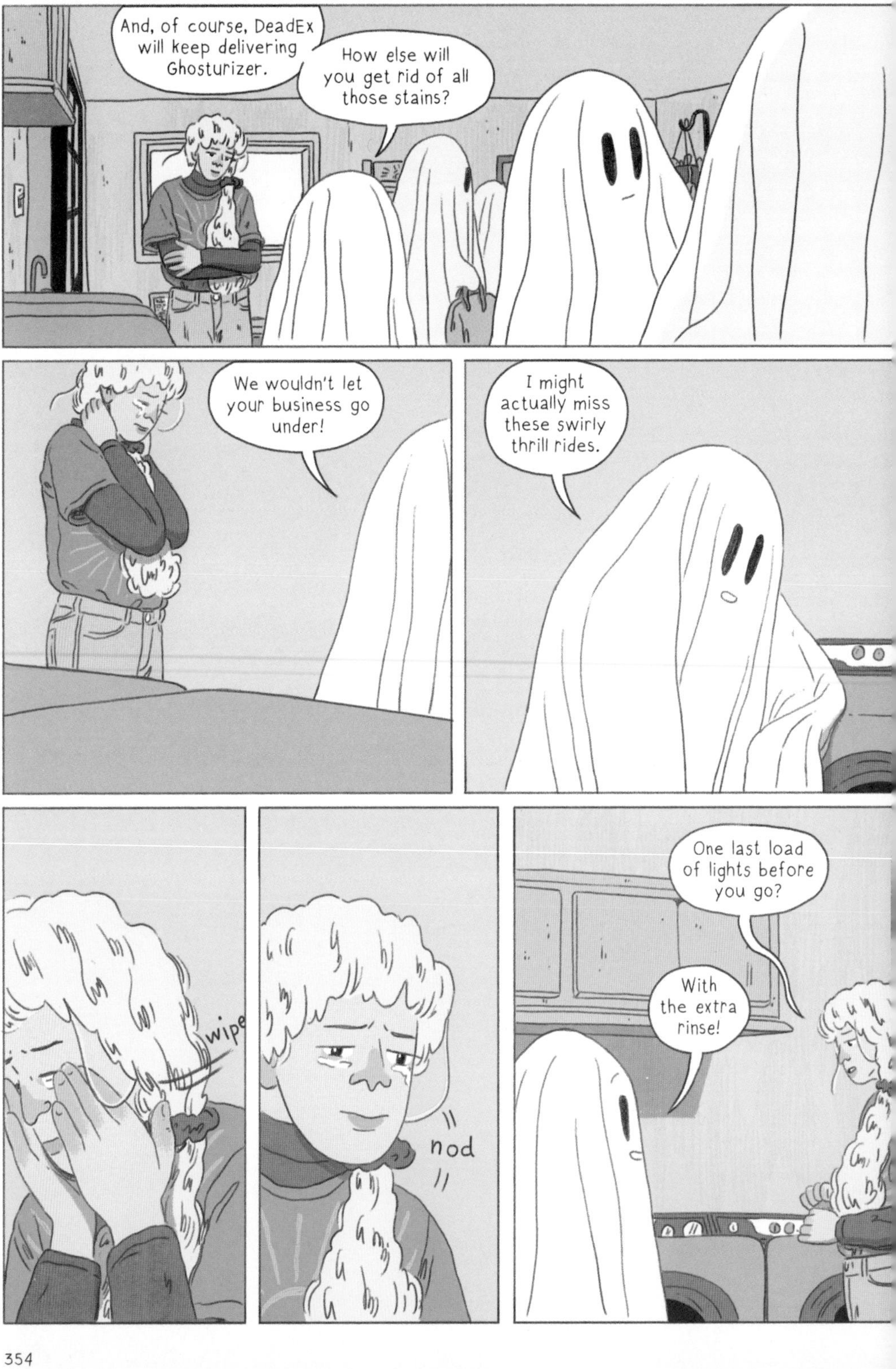
And, of course, DeadEx will keep delivering Ghosturizer.
How else will you get rid of all those stains?
We wouldn't let your business go under!
I might actually miss these swirly thrill rides.
wipe
nod
One last load of lights before you go?
With the extra rinse!

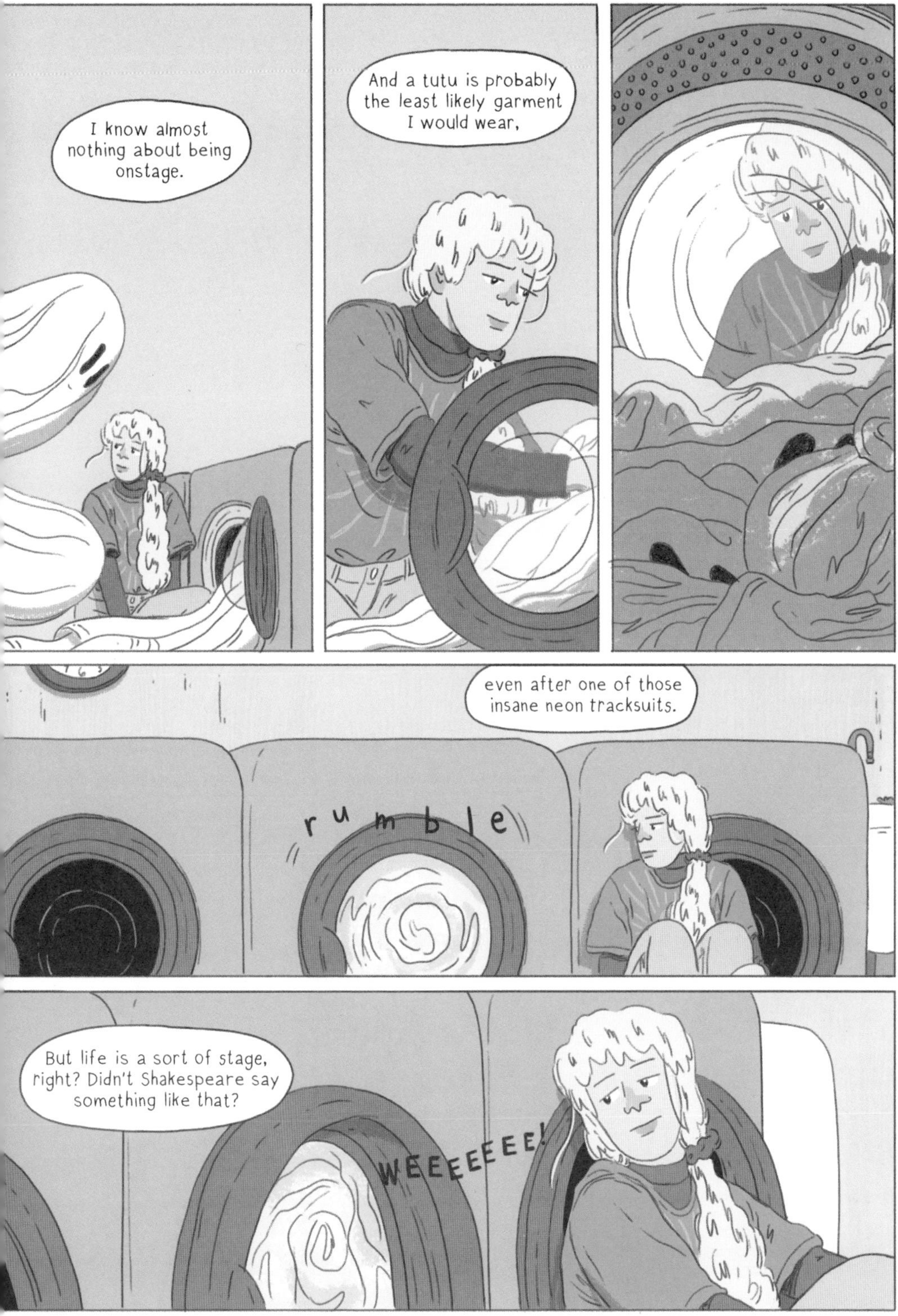
I know almost nothing about being onstage.
And a tutu is probably the least likely garment I would wear,
even after one of those insane neon tracksuits.
rumble
But life is a sort of stage, right? Didn't Shakespeare say something like that?
WEEEEEEE!

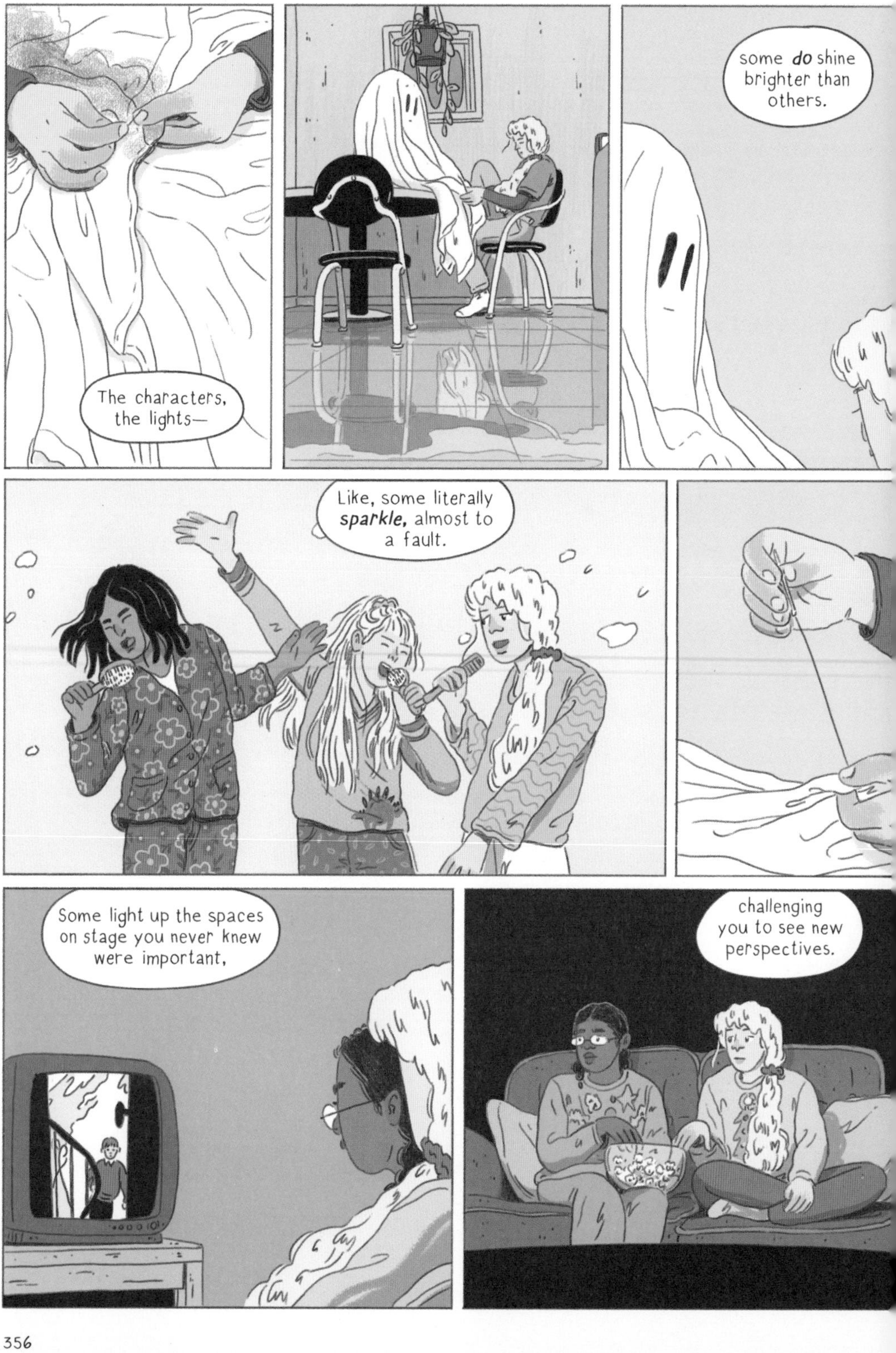
The characters, the lights—
some *do* shine brighter than others.
Like, some literally ***sparkle,*** almost to a fault.
Some light up the spaces on stage you never knew were important,
challenging you to see new perspectives.

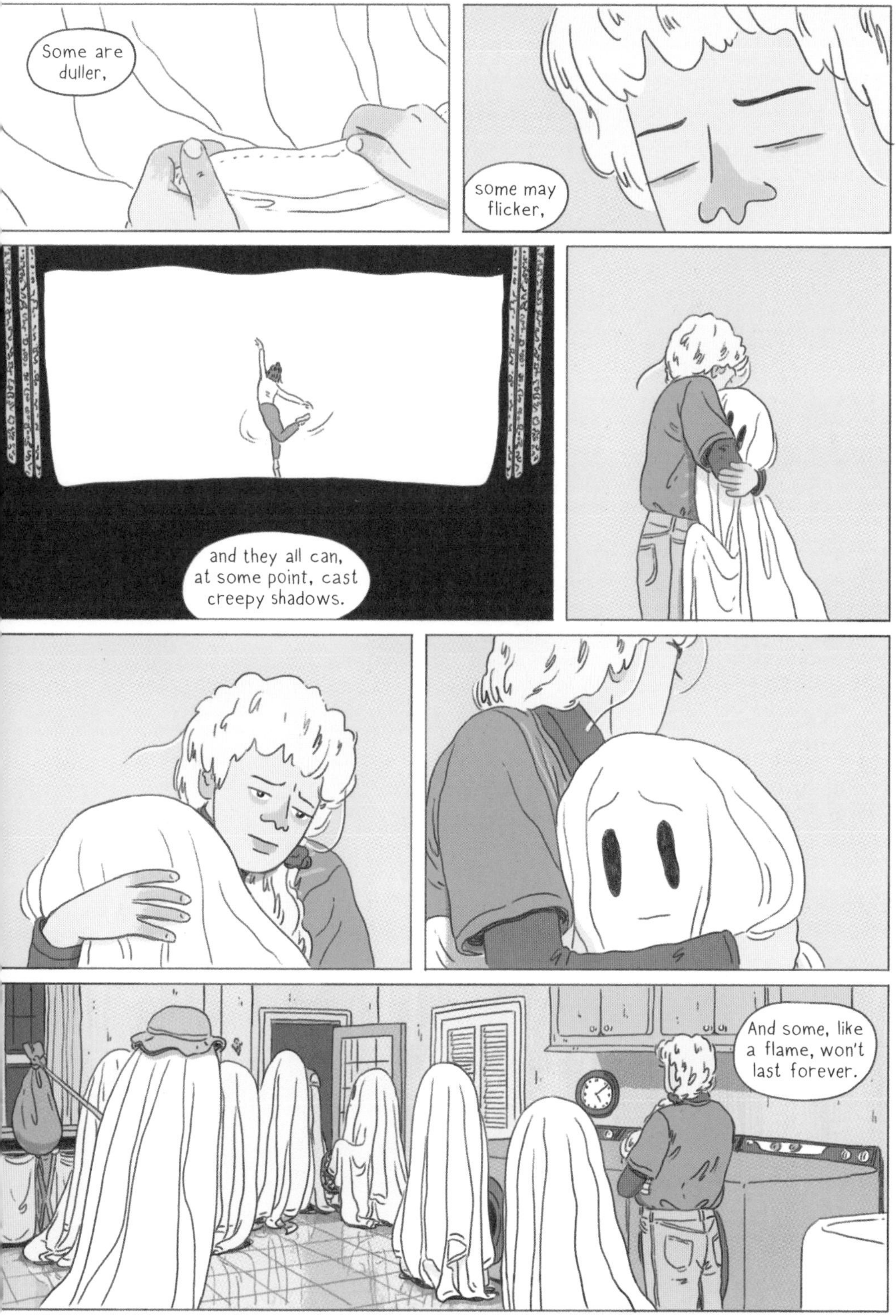
Some are duller,
some may flicker,
and they all can, at some point, cast creepy shadows.
And some, like a flame, won't last forever.

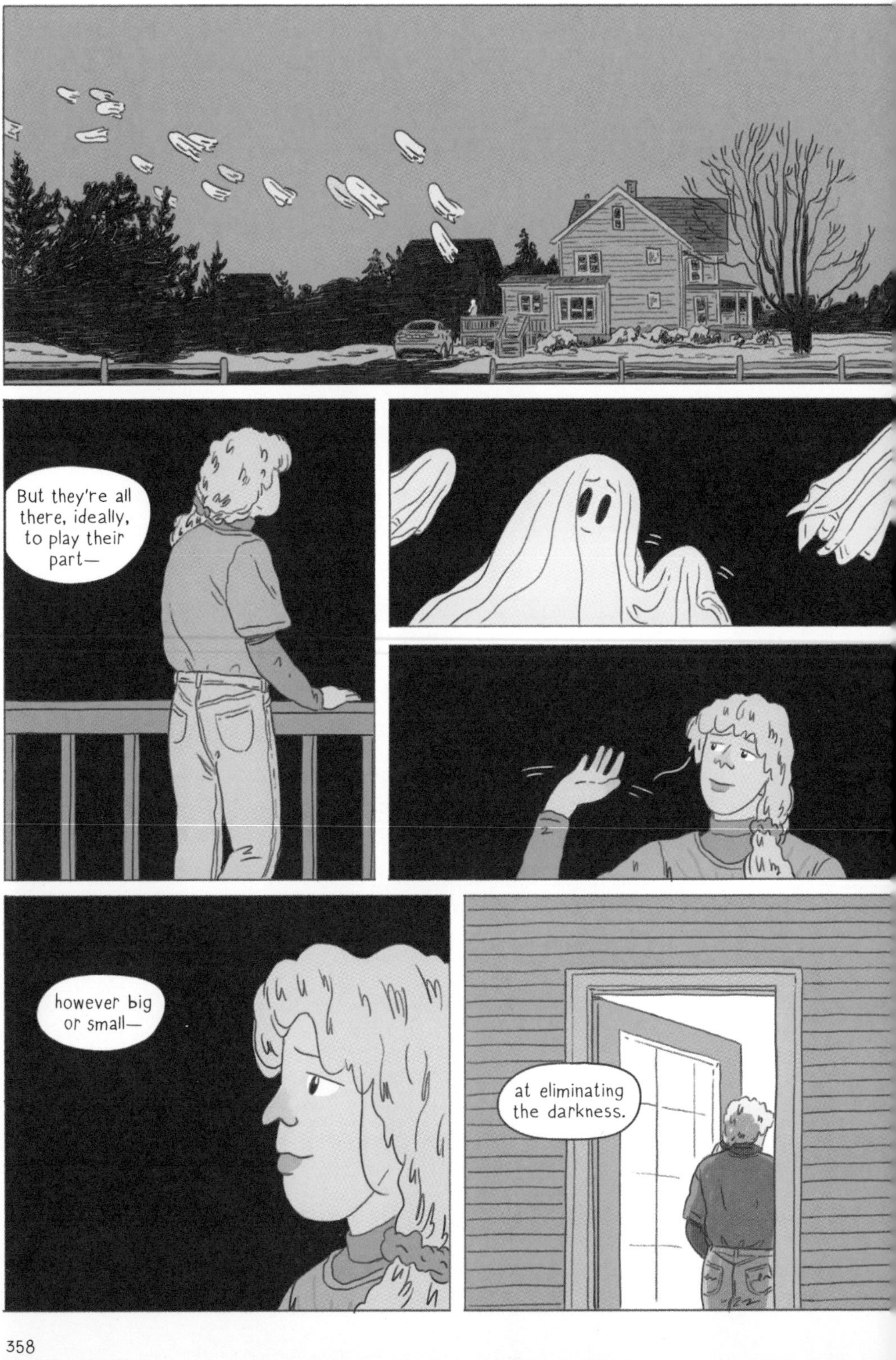
But they're all there, ideally, to play their part—
however big or small—
at eliminating the darkness.

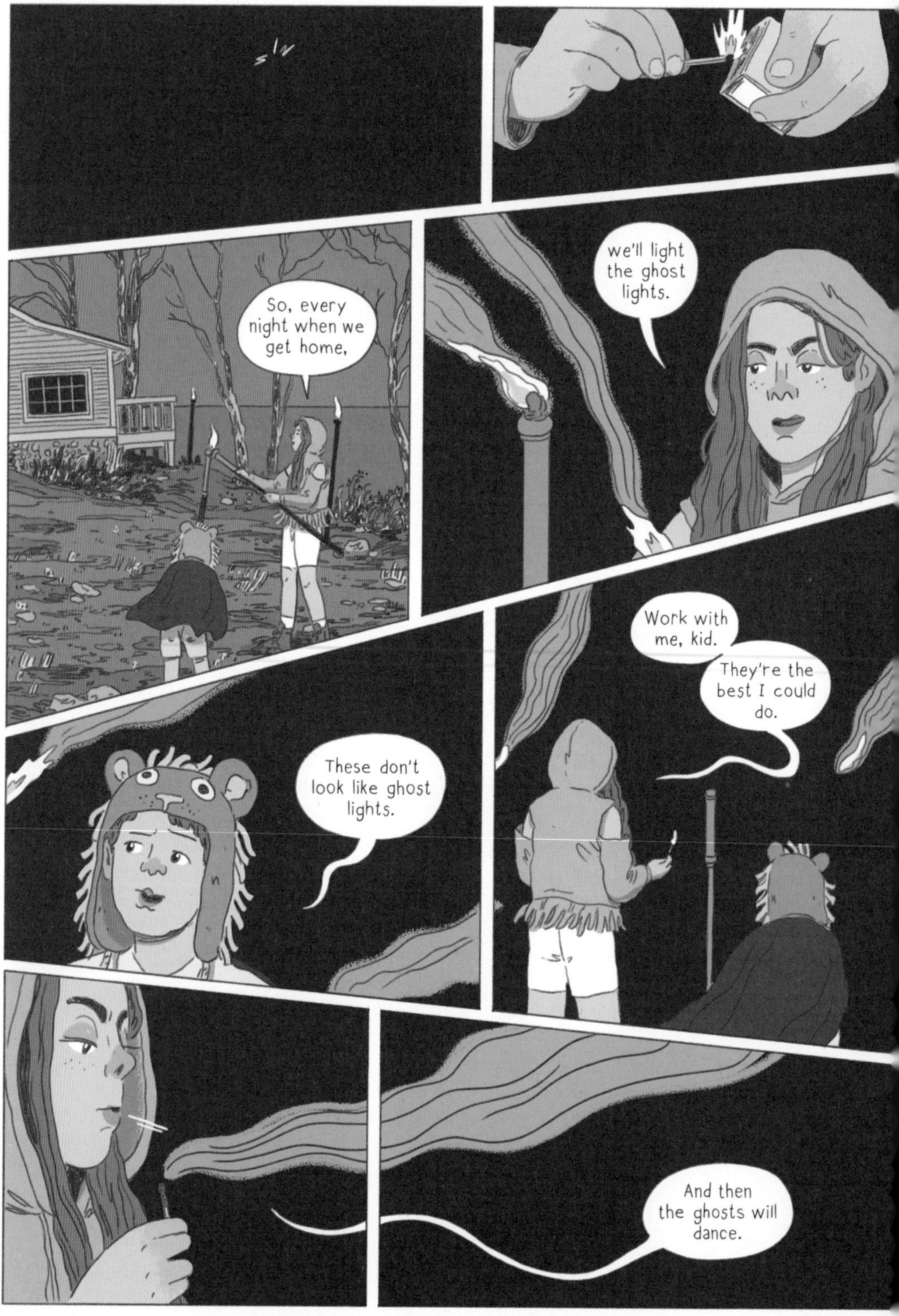
s!n
So, every night when we get home,
we'll light the ghost lights.
These don't look like ghost lights.
Work with me, kid.
They're the best I could do.
And then the ghosts will dance.

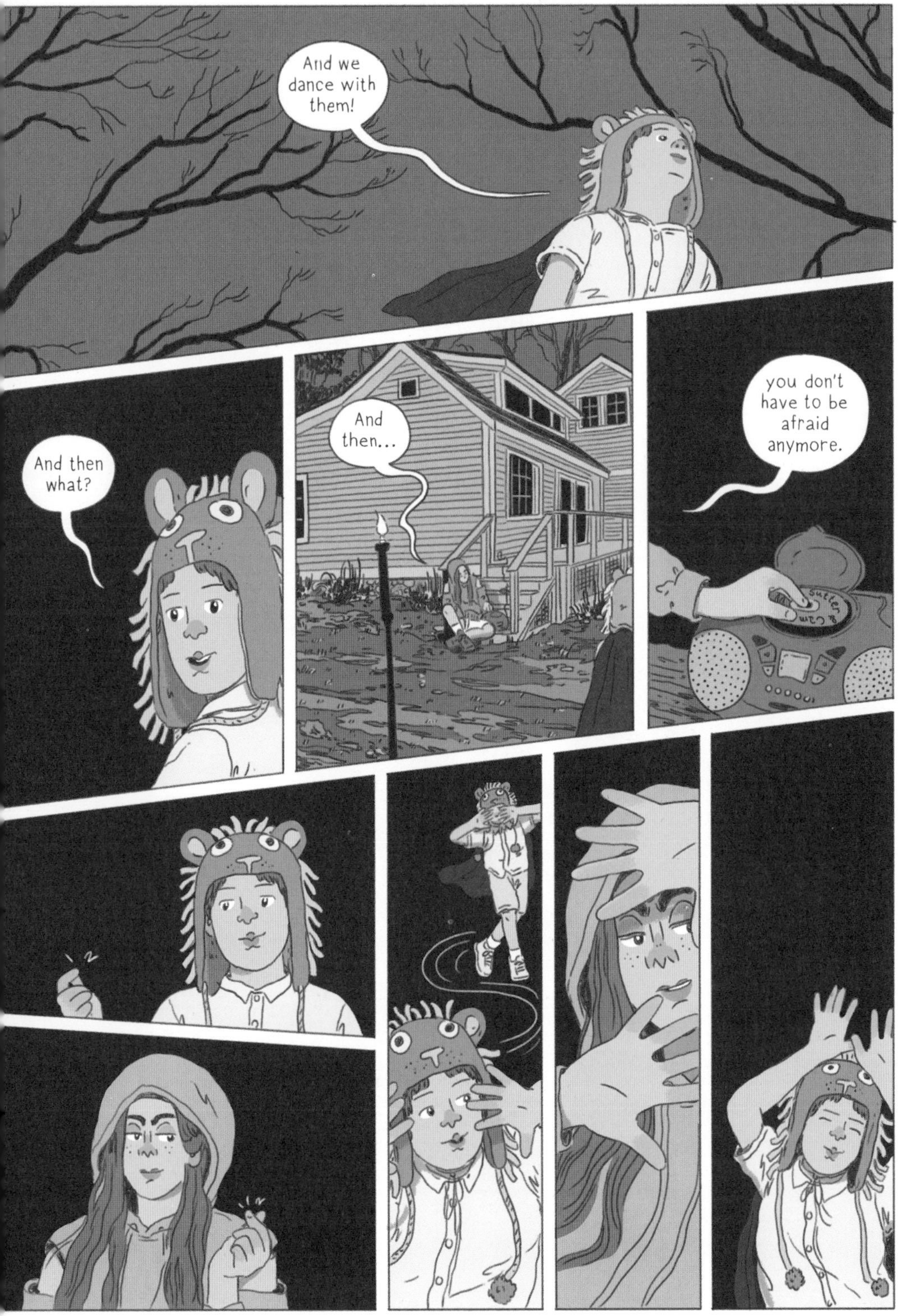

And we dance with them!
And then what?
And then...
you don't have to be afraid anymore.

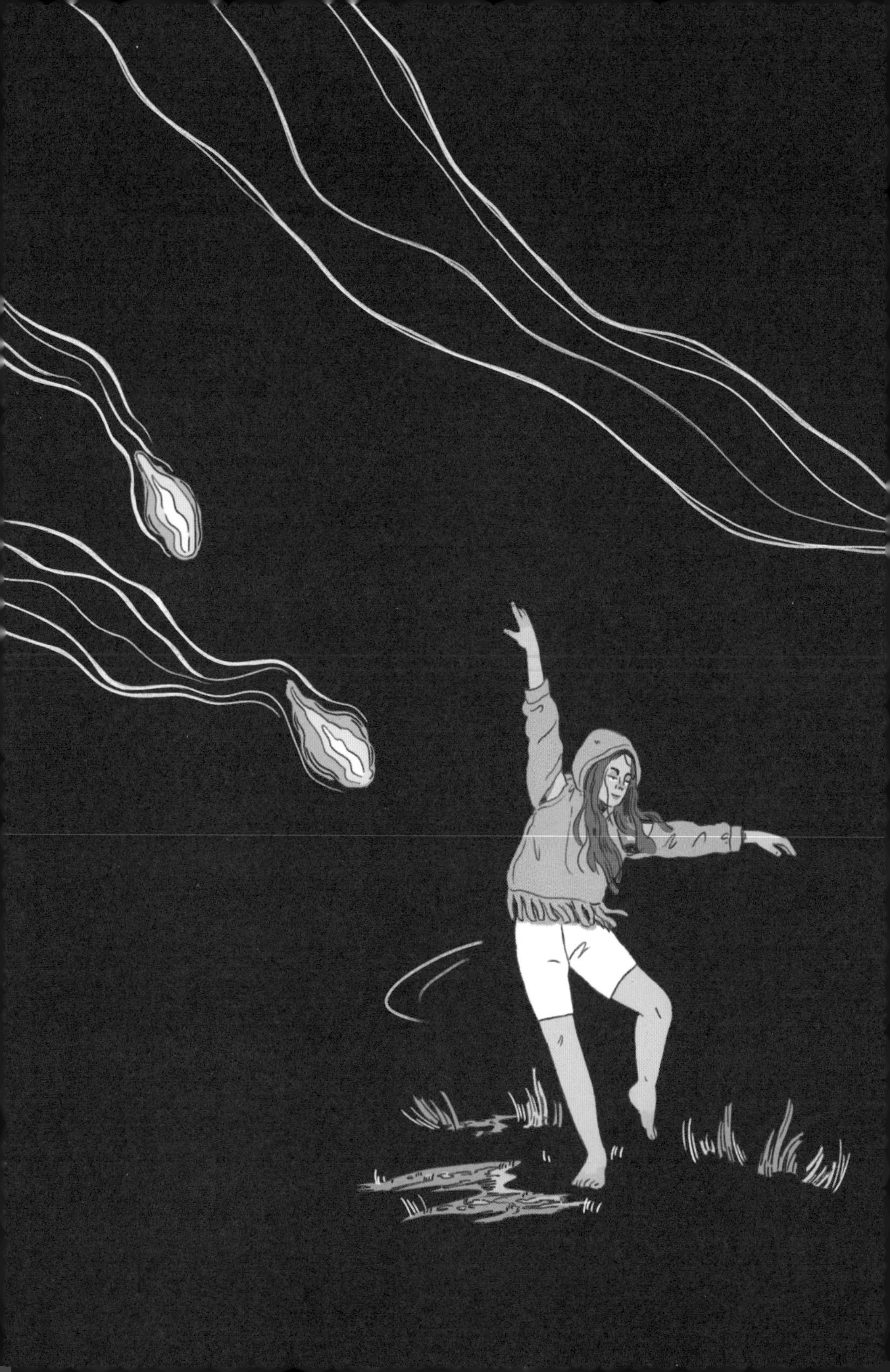

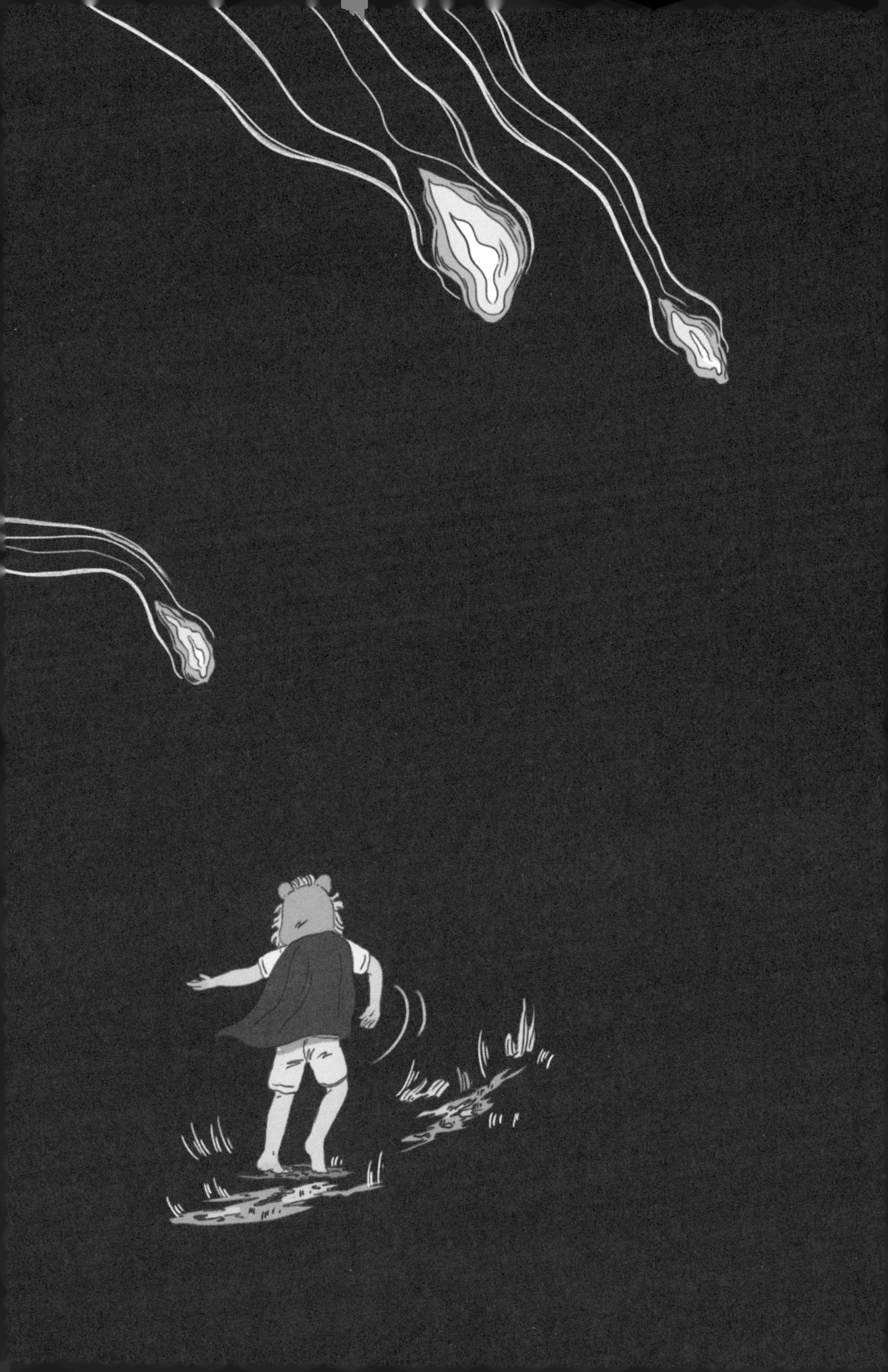

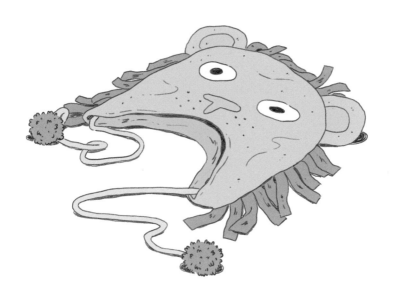

READ THE WHOLE GHOSTLY SERIES!

SHEETS

The story begins in *Sheets*! Marjorie and Wendell are both a bit different. Marjorie Glatt is trying to survive middle school and run her family's laundromat when Wendell arrives in the Land of Humans and decides to the use the laundromat as his own ghost playground, which jeopardizes the family business.

SHEETS
Brenna Thummler

DELICATES

The story continues in *Delicates*! When Marjorie starts to befriend the bullies at school, Wendell begins to feel even more invisible than he already is. Eliza Duncan, a ghost photography enthusiast, feels invisible, too. Always labeled as different, Eliza starts to feel like a ghost herself.

The Sequel to Sheets
DELICATES
Brenna Thummler

ONI PRESS

ACKNOWLEDGMENTS

My editor, Grace Scheipeter, for her attentiveness,
patience, and friendship, especially in handling ghosts
and delicate situations.

Andrea Colvin, who laid the groundwork for a lifelong
adventure, and who inspires me every day.

The entire Oni Press team for their diligence
and endless support.

Hannah Mann, the most wonderful agent,
who has helped me keep my sanity.

My friends from Lion Forge and Andrews McMeel, who
continue to boost my confidence.

Gretchen Myers, for raising me in the world of dance.

My friends, family, and cat, for their constant love
and encouragement.

And finally, everyone who has read, shared,
and supported the Sheets trilogy since its inception.
I'm so fortunate to have gone on this haunted
adventure with you all.

Created by **Brenna Thummler**
Designed by **Sarah Rockwell**
Edited by **Grace Scheipeter**

PUBLISHED BY ONI-LION FORGE PUBLISHING GROUP, LLC.

Hunter Gorinson, president & publisher • Sierra Hahn, editor in chief • Troy Look, vp of publishing services • Katie Sainz, director of marketing • Angie Knowles, director of design & production • Michael Torma, senior sales manager • Desiree Rodriguez, digital marketing manager • Sarah Rockwell, senior graphic designer • Carey Soucy, senior graphic designer • Matt Harding, digital prepress technician • Chris Cerasi, managing editor • Bess Pallares, senior editor • Grace Scheipeter, senior editor Gabriel Granillo, editor • Zack Soto, editor • Sara Harding, executive assistant Jung Hu Lee, logistics coordinator & editorial assistant • Kuian Kellum, warehouse assistant

Joe Nozemack, publisher emeritus

onipress.com /onipress
brennathummler.com /brennathummler

First Edition: September 2023

ISBN: 978-1-63715-231-7
eISBN: 978-1-63715-254-6

Printed in China.

Library of Congress Control Number: 2023932049
1 2 3 4 5 6 7 8 9 10